Books by J. Lloyd Morgan

Bring Down the Rain

Wall of Faith

The Mirror of the Soul
(Written in conjunction with Chris de Burgh)

The Night the Port-A-Potty Burned Down and Other Stories

The Bariwon Chronicles:
The Hidden Sun
The Waxing Moon
The Zealous Star

THE BARIWON CHRONICLES

J. Lloyd Morgan

Pendr Publishing

To Mom, who always encouraged me to ask, "What if?"

INTRODUCTION

I was once asked, "Now that you know what you know, would you go back and change anything in *The Hidden Sun?*" My answer? "No, I don't think I would. The book represents a time of my life and there is a certain innocence in its writing."

So, as you are holding a new and updated version of not only *The Hidden Sun,* but also *The Waxing Moon* and *The Zealous Star,* you are certainly justified in asking, "What gives?"

Once I realized that there would be more books after *The Hidden Sun* in the series, I vowed that each book would be able to stand on its own. In other words, I wanted each book to be a complete story. I believe I accomplished that.

Yet, as I finished *The Zealous Star,* I recognized there were a lot of threads that ran through the series as a whole. The idea of combining the three books into one epic story appealed to me. As I considered it, I figured I could add certain scenes I had cut originally, not because they were bad, but because they detracted the book from standing on its own. In putting these three books together, I could include these deleted scenes as well as a few new scenes.

In the end, the changes in this book were additions, not revisions. I even went as far as to include secrets behind the books as well as a list of all the characters and who they are.

The Bariwon Chronicles is more than just three books thrown together. It's an epic story told in three acts in a way I couldn't accomplish before.

TABLE OF CONTENTS

Part 1

THE HIDDEN SUN

CHAPTER 1

"The sun's playing hide-and-seek," Princess Eliana said.

Anemone looked up from her reading to see the seven-year-old girl sitting at her desk and peering out the window. "What's that, dear?"

"I see a sunbeam, but it's still raining. It's like the sun is playing hide-and-seek with the rain. But how can that be? I thought sun and rain were opposites."

Anemone smiled to herself at the young girl's comment. She stood and walked to the window, passing the tapestries that hung on the wall, and looked through the third-story glass window. Over the town and the farms that surrounded the castle, she could see the rain steadily falling, although a section of clouds had parted and bright beams of sunshine fell on the kingdom of Bariwon.

"Well," Anemone said, turning back to the princess, "sometimes things seem to be opposite but are not."

After putting her book down on the desk, Eliana folded her arms and stuck out her lower lip. "I don't like the rain. I want it to be sunny all the time."

Normally, the princess would be studying with one of the several savants, but court was being held today and her teachers were involved with the proceedings, leaving Anemone in charge of Eliana's schooling for the afternoon.

Sensing a greater teaching opportunity, Anemone said, "But without the rain, nothing would grow."

"When I become queen, I'll change that." Eliana sounded determined.

"You'll change what?" asked a deep voice from the other side of the room.

Both Anemone and Eliana turned in reaction.

"Father!" Eliana exclaimed, jumping out of her chair and running to the tall man standing just inside the doorframe. King Kenrik was dressed in the regal attire he wore when presiding over court. A golden crown studded with sapphires sat prominently on his head, while a long, blue cape trimmed in gold draped his shoulders.

When Eliana reached her father, she hugged him tightly around the waist.

"Your daughter would like to command the weather when she becomes queen, Your Majesty," Anemone said with a touch of humor.

The king smoothed Eliana's long, blonde hair. "Oh, is that so?"

"Yes! When I'm queen, I'll make it sunny all the time." Eliana smiled up at her father, her big blue eyes twinkling.

He lowered himself to his daughter's level and cupped her face in his hands. "Eliana, the way you can make the kingdom sunny is to be a good leader. Keep studying the Tome of Laws. As queen, you will need to know what the laws are so you can follow and enforce them."

Eliana stepped back and rolled her eyes. "But Father, it's so boring!"

Kenrik looked past his daughter to Anemone. "Has she been reading today?"

"Oh, yes, Your Majesty. It was a perfect day for it, with the rain," Anemone said, motioning to the window.

He turned his attention back to his daughter. "Ah, and what have you been reading about today, sweetheart?"

"I'll show you." She took her father by the hand and walked over to where a book lay open on the desk.

Kenrik looked at the text and pointed to several passages that had been circled, with drawings of little flowers and hearts next to them. "Sweetheart, have you been drawing in this book?

The princess nodded. "Uh-huh. It needed some pictures."

Anemone's eyes widened and she walked over, sighing when she saw what Eliana had done.

"Books are far too valuable to draw in Eliana, especially this one," Kenrik explained. "Promise me you won't do that anymore."

Clearly crestfallen at having disappointed her father, Eliana said, "I'm sorry. I promise."

"Enough on that." Kenrik changed his voice to a lighter tone. "Show me what you've been reading."

"I'm here on chapter eleven." Eliana pointed to the page. "It says that I get to be queen when I'm twenty-one. But that is so far away."

The king grinned. He stroked his daughter's hair. "I'm sure it will be here before we know it."

He turned at the sound of someone clearing his throat and saw his father, Councilor Philip, who was dressed in similar fashion to the king, but not as ornately.

Philip wore a crown of a simpler design with only one gem set in the middle. "Son, court is waiting."

This also caught Eliana's attention. "Grandfather!" she called out, waving to him.

"Hello, Princess." The elderly man smiled. "You look very beautiful today. Each time I see you, you look more and more like your mother, rest her soul. Is that a new dress?"

"It is!" Eliana did a twirl. "Vashti made it for me. Isn't it pretty?"

Stepping to where he could see Anemone, Philip nodded to her. "Nursemaid, when you see the seamstress, please tell her she's made another fine creation."

Anemone curtsied. "I will."

"Again, we must be off. There is much to do this afternoon," Councilor Philip said, his voice losing the pleasant tone it had before.

King Kenrik embraced his daughter once more. "I know I've been busy lately, sweetheart, but after the upcoming Mortentaun, we'll spend more time together, I promise."

Eliana sighed as she watched her father and grandfather walk off.

"All right, back to your studies, Princess," Anemone said. "Becoming queen takes preparation and hard work."

Sighing again, Eliana walked back to her desk and looked down at the large leather-bound book in front of her. Outside, the sun was again hidden by clouds, and it started raining harder than before.

⚜

Rinan stood next to his father, transfixed upon the battle in front of him. Two men, dressed in chain mail, were standing near the center of a large field. One wore a tunic of red and silver. The other was clad in blue, trimmed with yellow. Each held a sword which they used to attack and counterattack each other—sometimes with compact, quick blows; other times with broad, sweeping strokes.

A crowd of thousands stood and watched the combatants. The cool spring air helped offset the heat generated by so many bodies packed in closely. Before the battle had begun, Rinan could smell roasted apples, freshly baked bread, and other scents he had yet to experience. Now, during the combat, Rinan thought he could almost smell something else: excitement.

The man in red feigned a high blow, then followed with a low slash. The man in the blue tunic was deceived by the trick, and took the sword fully against his left shin. He nearly fell down, causing a collective gasp from the crowd, but was able to regain his balance in time.

If the swords had been metal, and not wood, Rinan imagined the damage would have been worse. With the man in blue still smarting from the last blow, his opponent pressed the attack. To Rinan, it seemed like the man in blue didn't have a chance. He was smaller, didn't have as long of a reach, and wasn't nearly as strong. Yet, when the next attack came, the blue combatant jumped back and out of the way. He did the same with the next several blows, avoiding them instead of trying to block or counterattack.

"What is the man from Lebu doing?" Rinan asked his father.

Kelvin rested his hand on his ten-year-old's shoulder. "Changing the dynamic of the battle. Using what skills he has to make up for where he is weak."

"But how can he win if he isn't fighting?"

"There are more ways to win than to knock down your opponent. See? Watch."

The area where the men were fighting was a large circle. White powder made from crushed rocks outlined the boarders. Both men were next to the edge now. The people standing close to the fighting backed up, and just in time. The man in red made an exaggerated lunge, trying to make contact with his quicker opponent. Instead of dodging to the left or right, the man in blue ducked below the lunge, allowing the larger man to overextend himself and fall forward, tripping. This placed the man in red outside of the circle.

The crowd cheered, though Rinan wasn't sure why. A third man rushed into the circle, yelling loudly, "The contestant from Lebu has defeated the contestant from Erd!"

"I don't understand, Father," Rinan said.

"The men fighting in the Mortentaun win if they can knock their opponent down, get him to yield, or get him out of the circle," Kelvin said. "Remember that. If you aren't successful trying one tactic, try another. Even when things seem desperate, there is always hope."

"I'm going to fight in the Mortentaun one day," Rinan vowed. "And I'm going to win."

"Are you now?" Kelvin asked. "Do you understand what that means?"

"Yeah. I want to be a guardian. I want to serve the kingdom."

Kelvin once again clasped a hand on his son's shoulder. "Then I'll make sure you get the training you need."

CHAPTER 2

Thirteen Years Later

Rinan's hands were still stinging from fending off the last attack when Eadward lunged again. Moving fluidly, Rinan batted away his opponent's sword, getting some satisfaction in that Eadward's hair and underarms were soaking wet while he remained dry.

"At least be man enough to sweat!" Eadward exclaimed, obviously noticing the same thing.

Rinan grinned. "Maybe if you didn't fight like my grandmother, rest her soul, I would."

The taunt had the desired effect as Eadward went to strike again, this time keeping his blade low at first, but then swinging it upward. Rinan parried, pushing both swords up and over their heads. Giving another roguish grin Rinan knew the older man hated, he quickly pivoted his hips, brought up his right leg bent at the knee, and kicked as hard as he could into Eadward's stomach. With the heavy, two-handed wooden broadsword still over his head, Eadward lost his balance and landed squarely on his rear.

"You kicked me!" Eadward gasped.

The castle's main hall filled with laughter from those attending the weekly sparring contest. Nobles stood by servants. Guardians intermingled with villagers. Savants and clergy laughed side by side, all enjoying the display of skill from the two men.

Rinan lowered his sword and offered his hand to his fallen opponent. "I couldn't help it. You left yourself wide open."

"That's a trick I'd expect of someone from Lebu," Eadward grumbled, massaging his backside.

"Yes, and there are plenty more where that came from," Rinan said lightly.

He turned toward the eastern end of the hall, noticing with satisfaction that Eadward did the same, meaning he wasn't going to contest the action. Rinan pointed his sword straight up in salute and awaited the king's decision. Standing in front of his throne that sat prominently on a raised dais, King Kenrik said, "Well, this has certainly been one of the more interesting sparring contests we've had in a while."

Rinan knew he should be completely focused on his king, but he quickly glanced over at Princess Eliana. At twenty years old, the golden-haired beauty was only a few years younger than Rinan. She sat next to her grandfather, Councilor Phillip, her hands folded politely in her lap as she watched her father speak. "But I've come to expect surprising things from you, Guardian Rinan," the king continued.

Hearing his name, Rinan quickly looked back at the king. If King Kenrik noticed this lapse of attention, he didn't let it show.

"While the kick was…unusual, it wasn't technically against the rules. I proclaim Royal Guardian Rinan the winner," the king said.

Rinan bowed his head in acknowledgement while the crowd cheered. When he looked up, his gaze fell once again on Princess Eliana. She acknowledged him looking at her and responded with a warm smile.

"Guardian Rinan," King Kenrik said, "as victor of this week's sparring contest, you will of course join us for dinner as our guest. I do hope, however, that you will not be kicking any of our servers."

"I shall try to restrain myself, Your Majesty." Rinan smiled and bowed.

The crowd was still laughing when the king announced, "The sparring contest is complete!"

The crowd slowly started to exit the main hall, though Rinan remained in place. He watched Eliana as she chatted and laughed with several people on their way out. Her countenance darkened slightly when Eadward approached, motioning for her to exit through the door that led to the royal chambers. As her personal guardian, Eadward was charged to protect the princess, though Rinan thought the man took his duties too literally.

Rinan inclined his head when Eadward looked back at him. Rather than nod in return, Eadward glared.

At that moment, Rinan felt a hand slap him on the shoulder. He turned and saw Wayte, captain of the royal guardians. The man was a bit shorter than he, with dark, curly hair. Rinan smiled.

"Eadward has never liked you, and you are not helping things by making a fool of him in public," Wayte chided gently.

"It's good to see you, Captain." Rinan saluted. "When did you get back?"

Wayte returned the salute. "Just in time to see that fancy move of yours."

"The kick? Well, the object *is* to knock your opponent off his feet. At the time, it seemed the best way."

Wayte grinned and shook his head. "Just remember—the most immediate solution is not always the best one. I do not suppose your show there had anything to do with trying to impress the king, now would it?"

Rinan feigned innocence. "And why would I want to impress the king?"

His captain playfully punched Rinan in the shoulder. "You know as well as I do, although I am not sure I would wish being the princess's next personal guardian on my worst enemy."

"Why would you say that?" Rinan asked. "Princess Eliana has been nothing but kind to me."

Wayte waved a hand dismissively. "Oh, no, not her. She would not be the problem."

"What are you not telling me?" Rinan knew that being so inquisitive with his superior could be taken as disrespectful, but his captain had him curious.

Wayte didn't appear offended by the question. "I discovered something rather…unpleasant on my trip." Leaning in closer, he said in a subdued tone, "Among the places I visited was the district of Erd. Governor Abrecan announced that a large vein of silver was recently discovered on his land. He will no doubt use that in the Shoginoc. It could give him quite the advantage in winning the right to marry his son Daimh to Princess Eliana."

Dread swept over Rinan. "Oh, no, not that oaf." Rinan had met Daimh on a few occasions and had taken an instant dislike to the man, which was significant because Rinan had always prided himself on being able to get along with anyone. There was just *something* about the way Daimh carried himself that Rinan found disagreeable. Wayte was right—whoever became Eliana's personal guardian would also have to deal with Daimh, provided Erd was victorious at the Shoginoc.

"And it gets worse," Wayte continued. "While I could not find any blatant violations of the laws, the people of Erd are miserable. Governor Abrecan has raised taxes as high as he can, his wife has not been seen in public for months, and anyone who has a disagreement with him seems to disappear."

"Surely the Hierarchy of Magistrates won't let Abrecan get away with what you are implying," Rinan asked almost hopefully.

Wayte sighed. "That is the problem. No one I spoke with is willing to come forth against the governor, most likely out of fear. I tried to convince them, but the people of Erd can be difficult."

Rinan nodded knowingly, thinking of someone else he knew from that district.

"Speaking of such people," Wayte said, "you had better try to make amends with Eadward before dinner. He was not happy losing to you—again."

⇥✦⇤

This wasn't the first royal meal Rinan had been invited to attend as a guest; he had won several sparring contests in the past. However, it was the first time he had been seated so close to the head table. The banquet hall was of a decent size, with a long table down the center that ran perpendicular to the head table.

King Kenrik sat in the center of this table with an empty chair to his right out of respect for his late wife. Princess Eliana sat to his left, followed by Councilor Phillip. To the councilor's left was yet another empty chair—this for Phillip's wife, who had passed away the previous year.

Rinan had been placed right up against the head table, which put him directly in front of the princess. The close proximity to Eliana made Rinan feel very self-conscious during the meal. At one point, Seanan, the head of the Hierarchy of Magistrates, was telling a story and Rinan, trying to stay focused on the magistrate and not on Eliana, missed a chunk of meat and ended up putting a forkful of nothing in his mouth. While embarrassing enough, it was even worse when Eliana made it clear she had seen his mistake. She held her fork with food on the end of it, and the smile on her face read, "See? This is how it is done." Rinan smiled sheepishly in return, then impaled his previous target with conviction, which brought a nod of approval from the princess.

At the end of the meal, King Kenrik stood, bringing silence to the room. "Today's participants in the sparring contest were not chosen at random," he began.

Motioning toward Eadward, who was just a bit further down the table from Rinan, King Kenrik said, "Royal Guardian Eadward, you have served faithfully for almost fifteen years, the last three as my daughter's personal guardian. You have kept her safe, and for that, I am grateful."

Eadward stood and bowed as those in attendance clapped. The king waited for the applause to finish before continuing.

"After the Mortentaun next month, Eadward is retiring, which means, of course, that my daughter will need a new personal guardian. I felt it prudent to choose one sooner, rather than later, so the newly selected guardian can be properly trained."

The banquet hall was quiet now. Rinan realized he wasn't breathing and forced himself to slowly exhale. He looked quickly at Eliana, but she was once again watching her father and not giving anything away.

"I've chosen a replacement," Kenrik said, "and even though he has been with us just a short time, it is my pleasure to announce that I have selected Royal Guardian Rinan."

Despite the initial excitement from the proclamation, Rinan suddenly felt a weight press down on him. Perhaps it was due to what Wayte had told him earlier, or maybe he suddenly realized the importance of the charge. Regardless, he put on a gracious smile in response to the applause and cheers.

Kenrik held up a hand, and the hall quieted. Turning his attention back to Eadward, the king said, "Eadward, your final duty is to train Rinan."

Eadward nodded, though he looked as if he had just eaten something vile.

"Good," the king said, either ignoring or not noticing Eadward's reaction. "Royal Guardian Rinan, I want your training to start immediately. Please go with Eadward to escort my daughter back to her chambers."

"Of course, Your Majesty." Rinan began to stand.

Touching her father's arm, Eliana said, "I'm certain this is a task Rinan can do without Eadward's help. After all, he has more than proven he can protect me."

The king looked down at his daughter, and after pausing a moment, said, "Yes, of course. You're quite right, dear. Eadward, you may remain. Rinan, you may escort the princess."

Eliana stood, and the rest of the room followed. Rinan walked over to her, bowed, and motioned for her to lead on. Smiling, she nodded to him. As they walked out of the hall, they passed Eadward, who was once again glaring, his face a most unpleasant shade of red.

Rinan took his position slightly behind and to the side of Eliana, as was customary. While walking down the well-lit hallway that led from the banquet hall to the princess's chambers, he tried to think of something to say, but everything he came up with sounded weak.

Eliana strode on confidently, not rushing, but not going slowly, either. Arriving at the large stairway that led to the upper levels, she put one hand almost daintily on the banister and started to ascend. Rinan followed a respectful distance behind.

At the top of the stairs hung a large tapestry. While most of the tapestries in the castle depicted various landscapes or former members of royalty, this one was unique. In addition to being the largest by a good margin, it was the only one that depicted more than one person. It showed five men standing around a table, on which sat a thick, leather-bound book. A large plaque below the tapestry read, "The authors of the Tome of Laws." Rinan often wondered why, in a castle built for kings and queens, the most honorific display was given to magistrates.

When she arrived at the top of the stairs, Eliana continued on toward her chambers, with Rinan close behind.

"I was hoping it would be you," she said, startling Rinan, not only in breaking the silence, but at what she had said.

"Oh? And why is that, Princess?" Rinan asked, for lack of a better response.

Eliana stopped, faced him, and appeared to consider him a moment before speaking. "From my point of view," she said, "everyone here is so serious. It's all about duty and following protocols. It's about doing what we are expected to do. People forget there is more to life than that."

The statement confused Rinan. "I'm not sure how that pertains to me, Princess. I've always tried to fulfill my duties to the best of my ability."

"Oh, I am sure you have, or my father wouldn't have selected you. It's more than that. I've seen you admire the tapestries when you thought no one was watching. I've heard from the savants that you've done well in your studies and have not only learned how to read, but have requested books to read on your own time. I've watched you in the sparring contests, and you seem to enjoy yourself, while others treat it as life or death. I wanted my next personal guardian to be someone who actually takes time to enjoy life."

Rinan couldn't think of a proper reply, but fortunately Eliana spared him the embarrassment of standing there like a fool and continued down the hallway.

A thrill tickled the back of Rinan's neck. So, the princess had been watching and noticing him. For the briefest of moments, he entertained the idea of him and Eliana…but no. She was to be married to someone else in a few months. Rinan was to be her personal guardian—nothing else.

Eliana stopped again, this time to face one of the hanging tapestries. "This is one of my favorites," she said. The scene displayed a large tree perched majestically on a slightly sloping hill. In the background were the castle and the surrounding town. The flowers and green grass indicated it to be spring or summer, and although the sunshine was quite pronounced, dark storm clouds lingered on the horizon. The plaque read, "Rain and Sunshine."

"It's so peaceful," Rinan commented.

Folding her arms, Eliana said, "It is, isn't it? I've always wondered if the rain was about to arrive or if it was just leaving."

"Funny you should say that. I've wondered the same thing as well."

Arching an eyebrow, Eliana said, "Is that so? Well, perhaps it was crafted to beg such a question. I actually found this tree when I was younger. It's not far from the castle. Growing up, I would always beg Anemone to take me there for picnics. I miss being able to do things like that."

Turning suddenly toward Rinan, she poked him in the chest. "Just promise me you won't be as stuffy as Eadward. That man is so dull. All he wants to talk about is the Shoginoc, or how I will rule Bariwon when I become queen. You must promise to let me have some fun once in a while."

Looking into her sparkling blue eyes, Rinan doubted he could deny her anything. "I promise," was all he could say.

-->‡<--

Priest Sherwyn adjusted the light blue mantle draped over his golden-colored robe before standing to address the court. Captain Wayte of the royal guardians had just completed reporting on his most recent inspection. Several of the districts had been visited, and it didn't surprise Sherwyn in the least that the report concerning Erd was less than favorable.

"I believe this to be a serious problem," he said, coming to his feet.

King Kenrik, sitting upon his throne, frowned at the statement. "Would you care to elaborate, Priest Sherwyn?"

Walking out from behind the table where he had been seated, Sherwyn moved to a position where he could address the king, the savants, and the

Hierarchy of Magistrates. Captain Wayte remained standing in the center of the hall, where he had just completed his report.

The hall was normally bright at this time of day, but overcast skies muted the light. Sherwyn noted that this was not unlike Abrecan's shady tactics, and as the castle priest, he felt he should shed some light of knowledge on the subject.

"For years we've heard of Governor Abrecan's questionable behavior, yet nothing has been done about it," Sherwyn said. "You just heard Captain Wayte say that not only are there continuing concerns in Erd, but that Governor Abrecan may have the key to being selected at the next Shoginoc. I fear for Bariwon's future if he is chosen."

Kenrik's eyebrows furrowed. "Magistrate Seanan, every concern about Abrecan has been investigated, yes?"

The head magistrate sat in the center of the table with the other four members of the hierarchy. Sherwyn had always liked and respected the man, though he feared time was taking its toll on the aged magistrate.

Seanan nodded, making the wisps of white hair on his head flutter. "Oh, yes, Your Majesty. While there have been some suspicious activities in recent years, the magistrate in Erd—Caldre is his name—assures me there have been no infractions to any of the rules found in the Tome of Laws."

Sherwyn felt his position slipping. "Captain Wayte, will you explain what you found concerning Lady Calla?"

Seeming to sense Sherwyn's urgency, Wayte said without preamble, "Governor Abrecan claims that his wife has been seriously ill and unable to make public appearances. Several people I spoke with told me her illness came on suddenly right after she had an argument with Abrecan at a social gathering."

Rubbing his hand over his bald head, Sherwyn asked, "And were you able to meet with Lady Calla to confirm what happened?"

"No. I asked to see her, but Abrecan would not allow it," Wayte replied. "He said his wife needed her rest and was not to be disturbed."

"That is a reasonable course of action, and not an infraction of the law," Magistrate Seanan interjected.

Sherwyn sighed. "There is an old saying, 'Clouds cannot hide the light of the sun forever.' I submit to you that it is cloudy in Erd, and Abrecan is the storm."

"That's very poetic, Priest Sherwyn," the king said. "But I am unclear on what action you think we should take."

Clearing his throat and standing as tall as he could, Sherwyn then said, "I believe Governor Abrecan should be excluded from the Shoginoc."

The hall exploded with both protest and support for the idea. The king rose and motioned the people to silence.

"Priest Sherwyn, the Shoginoc has helped keep the peace for generations. Unless there is proof of violations, we can't exclude anyone."

Sherwyn expected such a response. He didn't truly believe Abrecan would be excluded, but he made his point and believed his next request *would* be considered. Facing the Hierarchy of Magistrates, he said, "Then I would appeal to the magistrates to consider carefully at the Shoginoc. There will be other districts attempting to prove their worth. I'm sure Governor Abrecan will have quite the showing, but I would beg of you to consider the other contestants seriously."

※

"I wish you the best of luck …" Eliana said to the young man before her.

"Cameron," he said, his eyes not meeting hers.

Eliana nodded. "Then, Cameron, I shall be watching for your number and color on the leader board."

Rinan noticed that the young man continued to keep his eyes down, but there was something about his expression that led Rinan to believe his lowered gaze was less out of respect for the princess, and more out of his interest in the neckline of Eliana's dress.

Trumpets blared, indicating that the participants of the Mortentaun should gather at their assigned areas. It also meant the spectators needed to find a spot to watch the events.

Rinan escorted the princess to the platform reserved for the royalty. As the first group of men lined up for the preliminary event, a short dash to determine who was the fastest runner, Rinan was reminded that just a few short years ago, *he* was competing for the chance to become a guardian.

He looked over the field, where thousands upon thousands had gathered on wooden risers and sloping hills to watch young men from all over Bariwon compete. Banners representing the seven districts of the kingdom sat atop tall polls, fluttering in the warm spring breeze. Under each banner stood the competitors.

Surrounding the main field were tents of both visitors and merchants. Over the generations, the Mortentaun had grown to become the largest festival of the year, and it was something Rinan looked forward to each spring when he was growing up. His father and mother always made the trip from Lebu to attend. His mother would enter baking contests and was well known for her tarts. His father, on the other hand, always managed to find a card game, or other games of skill or chance, to occupy his time. When Rinan was old enough, he was allowed to go out by himself to watch the contestants spar in preparation, and like most boys his age, he dreamed of competing one day. Never in his wildest dreams did he think he would become the princess's personal guardian.

After watching the morning's events of the short dash, followed by a longer endurance run, Eliana once more went out among the crowd to visit with her future subjects. The crowd started to thin out some during the midday break, most people going to the merchants' shops that had been set up around the field.

The break prompted Eliana to retire to a tent that had been set up just for her. Finding the servants had a lunch already prepared, Eliana dismissed them. "You've done well. Please go and enjoy the festivities."

Rinan poured some water for Eliana, who had taken a seat next to a large gilded table set with bread, cheese, and sliced pears. There was also a tray covered with a large white cloth—a surprise Rinan had arranged for the princess.

"It's such a beautiful day, don't you think, Rinan?" Eliana asked.

Handing her the goblet of water, Rinan responded without thinking. "Not compared to you, Princess."

Eliana paused at Rinan's comment, then smiled at him. "Rinan, I do believe that is the sweetest thing I've heard you say."

Rinan felt his cheeks redden and wondered if he should apologize. Surely it wasn't appropriate for a guardian to say something like that to a member of the royalty. But the princess didn't seem to take offense—if anything, she seemed to have enjoyed it. Thank goodness Eadward was helping to judge the Mortentaun, or Rinan was sure he would have been rebuked by the older guardian.

"Speaking of sweet things," Rinan said, trying to change the subject, "I heard you liked these."

He lifted the cloth that covered the tray on the table, revealing a plate of strawberries.

"Oh!" Eliana exclaimed with delight. "Where did you get these? I thought it was too early in the year for strawberries."

"These are from Lebu, where I grew up," Rinan answered, offering her one. "My mother uses them in the tarts she makes for the baking contests. She brought extra as a gift for you, Princess."

"These are my favorite! Anemone would sometimes bring strawberries when we went on picnics when I was young." Eliana had taken a strawberry from Rinan, but stopped before she put it to her lips. Looking at Rinan mischievously, she said, "I have an idea."

"Oh?" Rinan answered, a bit uneasy.

"Remember the tree on the hill I told you about—the one on the tapestry by my chambers? It's not far from here. Let's go there."

Clasping his hands behind his back, Rinan asked, "Are you sure your father would approve?"

Eliana started to gather up the food. "Why not? I've spent all morning among the crowds. We can still be back in time for the afternoon events."

"Well, you are the princess." Rinan grabbed a blanket that was covering one of the chairs.

"Look at it this way—I'll have my personal guardian right beside me. How could anyone object to that?"

⊰⊱

"That one looks like a sunflower." Eliana pointed.

Rinan squinted and turned his head to one side. "Hmm. I guess."

"Well, what do you think it looks like?"

"To be honest, it just looks like a cloud to me."

Eliana flailed her arms in mock disgust. "Bah! You have no imagination."

Sitting on the blanket Rinan provided and leaning against the tree on the sloped hill, the princess was gazing at the sky, with Rinan standing guard over her. The light breeze kept the late spring day from getting too warm and had a calming effect, especially when relaxing after a filling meal.

Softly in the distance, Rinan could hear the Mortentaun starting up again. "We should probably head back, Princess." He offered a hand to help her up.

Eliana didn't take his hand. "Just a little while more. I'm really enjoying this moment. My life has been so busy lately, it's nice to take the chance to relax. Please sit down, Rinan."

He paused a moment, then nodded in acknowledgement of her wish. He sat down next to her on the blanket and looked up again at Eliana's sunflower cloud, and then beyond it, where dark clouds were forming on the horizon.

CHAPTER 3

"No, no, no!" Abrecan thundered, his voice echoing in the large room.

The man standing in front of the governor of Erd was visibly shaking, wringing his calloused hands nervously. "What would you have me do differently?" the metalworker asked, looking at the governor from under two bushy gray eyebrows.

Abrecan sat on a chair that could not quite be called a throne, but was of similar design. The room was patterned after the main hall of the castle, but instead of gold and royal blue, it was decorated in silver and crimson.

Sitting by Abrecan were two other men. On his left was Magistrate Caldre, bone-thin with a long, sharp nose and black hair pulled back into a ponytail. On Abrecan's right was his son, Daimh, who was tall and muscular. Daimh fidgeted in his chair, appearing disinterested.

There was an obvious resemblance between Daimh and Abrecan. Both were strikingly handsome, though the governor had a sharp look of intelligence in his eyes that the young man lacked.

Thrusting the silver chalice at the metalworker, Abrecan said, "It's too plain! It needs to impress any who see it. I want a new one right away— one worthy of a king. Now go!"

The metalworker all but ran from Abrecan, clutching the chalice to his chest. One of the guardians at the door gave the old man a swift kick in the rear as he left, bringing laughter from those in the room.

The only one who wasn't laughing was Daimh. His head was tilted back against his chair. He sighed dramatically. "Father, must I really be here for this?"

In a practiced voice of tolerance, Abrecan said, "Son, if we are boring you, why don't you go spar with one of the guardians?"

Daimh rose from his seat. "I suppose that would be more entertaining."

19

Walking over to the wall, he grabbed two large wooden swords from a weapons rack and ordered the nearest guardian, "Follow me."

The chosen guardian looked around like a cornered animal. Unable to escape, he bowed his head in resignation and followed Daimh out of the room. The other guardians avoided looking anywhere but straight ahead, clearly not wanting to get Daimh's attention.

Abrecan turned to Caldre. "It serves me right. His mother was beautiful when I met her, yet I've met rocks with more intelligence. I should have considered more than wealth and beauty when I married her."

Not hearing this for the first time, Caldre reminded Abrecan in a somewhat nasally voice, "But without her family's fortune, you wouldn't have had the means to become governor—or to promote me to magistrate."

"Bah!" Abrecan said. "I would have found a way. Speaking of my wife, what is the latest?"

"Lady Calla is still, let us say, afraid to leave the summer home," the magistrate said, a smirk playing across his face.

Abrecan nodded in approval. "Good. Just as long as she is away from here. She always demanded I take her places, or complain that I needed to spend more time with her. I swear I couldn't get anything done with her insipid behavior. I take it the guardians I assigned are keeping a close eye on her?"

"Oh, yes. She will not be bothering you or anyone."

"The way it should be." Abrecan smiled. "Now back to business. We must continue planning for the Shoginoc. It seems hard to believe we are only a few weeks away."

For the next several moments, Caldre outlined how the plans were proceeding.

Abrecan nodded, seeming pleased. Before the magistrate could complete his report, the door opened with a large *bang!* There stood Daimh, covered in sweat and still holding his wooden sword—though the blade was cracked and splintered.

"Father, we really need to get guardians who won't break so easily."

⊰⊹⊱

Eliana giggled when she saw Rinan's reaction. "I have to wear *that?*" he asked.

Seamstress Vashti nodded. "Yes, yes. Everyone at the party will be dressed up. I made this especially for you."

Rinan looked almost pleadingly at Eliana for help, but she didn't come to his rescue. "I think you'll look very dashing. Plus, Vashti spent a lot of time making the costumes, didn't you?"

The elderly seamstress nodded once again. "Yes, yes. Alana was very specific that she wanted a princess birthday party. It's a shame the only man we could get to attend was your personal guardian. I would like to have made more prince outfits."

Patting Rinan on the arm, Eliana said, "Oh, he doesn't mind. It will be fun."

She saw him once again eye the heavily embroidered tunic and almost shimmering leggings Vashti had laid out for him. After a moment, he let out a long breath.

-)‡‡(-

Checking herself one last time in the mirror, Eliana was satisfied that the princess costume she wore was proper. The irony wasn't lost on her that she, an actual princess, was dressing up as one for her niece's birthday party. The outfit wasn't that different from what she would wear to court, though as is the case with most costumes, the features on her dress were more exaggerated. The fluffy skirt was especially large, and she nearly tripped a couple of times when she wasn't paying attention.

After running a brush through her long, blonde hair again, she headed for the door. Exiting to the hallway, she found Rinan there, standing at attention. He looked adorable in his outfit. In addition to the fancy tunic and sleek leggings, Vashti had made him a rather flamboyant hat that all but hid his dark hair.

"Princess," he greeted somewhat stiffly.

"Rinan!" She smiled. "You look positively prince-like."

He shifted uncomfortably. "I feel like a fool."

"Ah, remember that this is for Alana. It's not every day you turn eight. Try to relax and have fun."

Rinan bowed his head in acknowledgement. "Shall we be off, then?"

Smiling again, Eliana said, "Yes, I think we shall."

-)‡‡(-

Rinan was the hit of the party. Eliana watched in delight as a dozen or so girls fawned over him. Ranging from age five to Eliana's twenty, each of them wore a dress created in similar princess fashion, though Alana's dress was even more elaborate, which was only fitting for the birthday girl.

The party started off with several games and activities, one of which was a pretend ball. Rinan had taken time to dance with every young lady, making sure each one felt important when it was her turn.

Once Rinan relaxed, Eliana was amazed at how charming and wonderful he was with the girls, perhaps because there were no other guardians in attendance. On their way to the party, Rinan had been teased mercilessly by any passing guardians, but here, he appeared to be more like himself. He laughed and smiled and even playfully teased the little princesses. Eliana tried to imagine her former personal guardian, Eadward, doing that, and had to laugh at the thought.

Throughout the course of the party, Eliana caught Rinan's gaze here and there, but once they exchanged smiles, he would quickly turn away.

One of the last activities of the party was a game called Choose or Lose. The rules were fairly simple. Each young lady would pull a slip of paper from a crystal bowl. On each slip was the name of either a district or a town in the kingdom. Once they had all selected, Rinan would draw a slip of paper from another bowl, which would match one of the slips of paper the girls had drawn. Rinan would then randomly choose three girls. If he guessed right and one of them matched him, he would be the victor. If he guessed wrong, things got a bit crazy. At that point, each of the girls would run around the room, trying to avoid being tagged by Rinan. Once he tapped a girl on the shoulder, she would be "out." The last princess remaining untouched would be the victor.

The first two times, Rinan had guessed correctly, and each of the girls in the hall wanted him to try again until he guessed wrong. On the third time, that is exactly what happened. Once he chose the third girl and was incorrect, each of the girls started running in different directions. Or at least, that was Eliana's intention. In reality, she spun around, promptly tripped on her fluffy dress, and fell down. Rinan rushed to her side, and reaching down, took her by the hand. He carefully helped her to her feet, his hand holding hers for longer than was needed. They held each other's gaze for one drawn-out moment. Eliana felt her cheeks flush, and there was an odd tingling in her chest. Rinan seemed to blush as well, then, quickly letting go of her hand, reached out and tapped her on the shoulder.

"Got you," he said softly.

A light knocking on the door took Priest Sherwyn's attention away from his reading. Looking up from the papers on his desk, he said, "Yes?"

The large wooden door creaked open. The guardian standing there with black hair and stark gray eyes was unmistakable.

"Oh, Royal Guardian Rinan. Please come in." The priest stood and motioned to a chair next to his own.

After closing the door behind him, Rinan walked in and sat down with his head slightly bowed.

"What can I do for the princess's personal guardian at this late hour?" Sherwyn asked, sitting down and folding his hands on the desk.

Rinan licked his lips, paused a moment, and then said, "I need to ask for your help."

"Oh?"

Rinan braced himself. "I'm not sure I'm the right person to be Princess Eliana's personal guardian."

"King Kenrik thinks differently."

Rinan sighed in frustration. "It isn't that I can't keep her safe. It's just…"

The priest didn't say anything, but let the young man continue when he was ready.

Opening his hands with his palms up, Rinan said, "Spending as much time as I am with the princess seems to be effecting me in ways I don't think are appropriate." He continued, "As her personal guardian, I'm supposed to protect her. I think my desire to keep her safe has developed into something more." He paused again. "I think I'm falling in love with her."

Sherwyn nodded in acknowledgment. "Rinan, you are not the first guardian to feel this way toward someone he is sworn to protect. Even though royal guardians are forbidden to marry until after retirement, they don't stop being human while they are in service."

Rinan sighed. "But she is to be married this summer. And as you said, I'm not allowed to marry. That's why I came to see you."

Leaning back in his chair, Sherwyn said, "What would you ask of me?"

"I think it would be best if I resigned as her personal guardian." Rinan folded his arms. "I would ask that you be the one to tell her."

Sherwyn stood, then took his chair with him and came around the desk to sit next to Rinan. He placed a hand on the young man's shoulder. "Each year, hundreds of young men compete for the chance to be guardians. It's a great honor, not only for them, but also for their family and district. Being selected as a royal guardian is even more prestigious. You need to think about this a little while more."

"I don't see my feelings for her changing," Rinan said. "If anything, I can only see them getting stronger the more I am around her. I don't believe I can perform my duties under these circumstances."

"The only way to resign as her personal guardian is to resign as a guardian altogether. Are you willing to do that?"

"I...I don't know. It's just that, I mean, she is so..." Rinan looked down, his face showing his anguish.

Patting Rinan's shoulder, Sherwyn said, "Wait until the Shoginoc. See who is chosen and how things unfold. You may find that your sense of duty will override these feelings."

⊰⊹⊱

"Oh, my. What happened to you?" Anemone asked.

Eliana turned from the window, her long, blonde hair glistening in the summer sunlight. She was dressed in a white gown with gold and blue embroidery running the length of the sleeves, with more around the waist.

"Happened?"

Anemone walked to the princess and took her hands in her own. "When did that little girl I knew grow up? It's amazing how much you look like your mother, rest her soul."

Eliana glanced back out the window at the large, gathering crowd, and sighed. "I may look the part, but I don't feel it."

Rubbing her hand along Eliana's cheek, Anemone said, "What's this all about?"

"Look out there." The princess motioned toward the courtyard. "They are all here to see the Shoginoc. Today I'm going to meet the man I'm to marry, and instead of being excited, I feel almost sick."

"But you've been preparing for this day ever since you were a little girl," Anemone said.

Eliana moved away from the window and sat on the edge of her bed. "I know, but for some reason, it never seemed real until today. When I was younger, it seemed romantic, in a way, to meet my future husband at the Shoginoc. But lately, I've found myself dreading this whole experience."

"And why do you think that is?"

Eliana had given that question a lot of thought recently, and it had kept her up many a night. She knew that having her spouse chosen for her at the Shoginoc was inevitable. In the stories she was told growing up, each

Shoginoc was an almost magical experience, where two people who were destined to be together would meet, fall in love on the spot, and then live together in happiness for the rest of their lives. But lately she couldn't imagine how she could fall in love with a complete stranger. What if the man she was to marry was like Eadward?

A knock on the door prevented any other thought or conversation.

"Yes?" Eliana asked.

Rinan opened the door, dressed in his finest uniform. Standing at attention, he stiffly announced, "It is time to make your entrance, Princess."

⬦

Fanfare from the trumpets quieted the large crowd that had gathered in the main hall. All eyes turned to the wide doors at the end of the hall as they slowly opened. The fanfare increased in tempo when King Kenrik, Princess Eliana, and Councilor Philip entered.

The hall was decorated as Eliana had never seen it before. Flowers were hung from the rafters and chandeliers. The banners that hung from long, wooden staffs had all been replaced with newly sewn standards. The crowd was dressed mainly in gold and royal blue to show respect for the king, with the exception of the representatives of the seven districts, four of whom stood prominently in the center of the hall.

Dressed in deep blue and white was the governor of Donigi with his entourage. The district of Lewyol's group was outfitted in canary yellow and brown, which was a stark contrast to the representatives of Grenoa, in black and orange.

However, it was the district of Erd's party that caught Eliana's attention. Their armor was highly polished to show off the silver plating, and their crimson tunics were further embellished with silver-threaded embroidery. While all the groups were very well dressed, it was obvious those from Erd had put the most effort into their appearance.

Next to the thrones on the dais was a long table where the five members of the hierarchy sat—each of them now standing in respect for the royalty. Standing at the front and center of the dais was Priest Sherwyn. It was the responsibility of the castle priest to be the master of ceremonies for the Shoginoc.

The king, princess, and councilor were escorted to their thrones by their personal guardians. The crowd waited for the royalty to be seated, and then followed suit. Rinan took his position to the side and a bit behind the princess's throne.

Priest Sherwyn waited for the crowd to quiet before he spoke. "Welcome, one and all, to this most important event in our kingdom."

A round of applause broke out from the crowd. The priest waited for a moment before he continued with the ceremony. "It has been twenty-two years since our dearly departed Queen Lareyna was chosen from the district of Tevoil as the victor in the Shoginoc. Her marriage to King Kenrik followed soon afterward. From that union came our own Princess Eliana."

Another round of cheers broke out. Priest Sherwyn waited a moment and then continued, "Next month, Princess Eliana will turn twenty-one years of age. Magistrate Seanan will now explain more about the significance of that age, and why we are here today."

Turning to the magistrates, Priest Sherwyn nodded. Magistrate Seanan referenced the Tome of Laws and quoted from memory, "When the firstborn child of the king and queen reaches the age of twenty-one, he or she shall become the new king or queen. The former king and queen will become councilors to the newly crowned leader of Bariwon. An arranged marriage will be selected by a Shoginoc. In the spirit of the competition that is part of the history of the kingdom, each district will have the chance to participate. Whoever brings to the kingdom the most worth, as decided by the Hierarchy of Magistrates, will be declared the winner." The aged magistrate closed the book on the table in front of him and sat down.

Priest Sherwyn spoke again. "The governor of each district sponsors someone from that land as a representative if he feels they have enough to offer the kingdom. At this current Shoginoc, four districts have presented themselves for judging."

Sherwyn motioned to the groups in the center of the hall, and gave the district representatives a moment to bow to the crowd.

"This is how we will proceed. Each district will make a presentation. At the conclusion of the last presentation, the Hierarchy of Magistrates will meet and select the victor," Sherwyn said. "Lots were drawn, and the district of Lewyol was selected to go first, followed by Donigi, Grenoa, and then Erd. Governor Elric, the floor is yours."

For the next several minutes, Governor Elric presented a large chest full of exquisite ceramic items that were handcrafted in his home district. Each item was worth a small fortune, and the collection together was impressive indeed. At the end of the presentation, a large man in his mid-twenties was introduced as the suitor from the district of Lewyol. While somewhat handsome, he had large, bushy eyebrows that appeared to have merged in the middle of his forehead. The crowd's applause quickly faded, eager to see the next presentation.

Donigi's offering consisted of items from the sea: polished shells, pearls, and various other treasures that were available to the seacoast district. The suitor presented was another young man, appearing to be in his early twenties. While pleasant to look at, his smile displayed front teeth that looked to have cut down trees at some point in time. The crowd made a polite showing of approval, and it was obvious he was an improvement to the previous candidate.

What gave the district of Grenoa distinction was that the governor was also the suitor. The tall and lanky man had recently been appointed from his home district when the previous governor had died of old age. Because he was unmarried, he was given the chance to be the suitor in the Shoginoc. Grenoa was the district furthest southeast and was mainly desert. Nonetheless, the district put together a fine showing, with polished animal bones inlaid with precious stones being the main theme. The crowd reacted quite favorably.

"And finally, Governor Abrecan from the northern district of Erd," Priest Sherwyn intoned. "What do you bring to the Shoginoc?"

Abrecan stepped forward from his group, revealing a large chest behind him. He clapped his hands, and two of his entourage opened it. Inside were all manner of silver items, polished and gleaming. People in the hall shifted their positions and craned their necks to get a better look. After pausing a moment to allow the crowd to absorb the offering, Abrecan clapped his hands again. Members of his party came forward, revealing an additional chest full of silver treasures that were even more striking. A collective gasp escaped from the crowd. Traditionally, one chest was presented. An offering of two was unprecedented.

Taking advantage of the moment, Abrecan introduced the suitor from Erd. Daimh was dressed in a similar fashion as those around him, yet he stood out among his peers. His chiseled jaw and high cheekbones were among his many attractive features. His body rippled with muscles bulging under his tunic. Smiling, he displayed a set of brilliant white teeth and a pair of dimples, eliciting *ooh*s and *ah*s from the young women in the crowd.

Interrupting the crowd's reaction, Priest Sherwyn spoke up. "It is now time for the hierarchy to decide. Magistrate Seanan, if you would, please."

The eldest of the hierarchy stood and started walking to the far left of the hallway, followed by the other four members. Sherwyn said, "Magistrate Seanan, we start on the right."

Seanan stopped. After looking around in a confused manner, he headed to the other side of the hall.

King Kenrik leaned over to Princess Eliana and whispered, "Poor Magistrate Seanan. He's always had trouble with the difference between left and right."

The members of the hierarchy said nothing as they walked from group to group, carefully inspecting the offerings before finally leaving the hall to debate the matter.

"While the hierarchy decides," Sherwyn said, "please stay in your places."

The room began to buzz with conversation. King Kenrik leaned over again and said, "There shouldn't be much debate. I've never seen a treasure like Governor Abrecan has brought."

Eliana looked at the group from Erd and saw Daimh staring at her with a leering smile. This was not happening the way it did in the stories. He was handsome, no denying that, but there was something unpleasant about him. She whispered, "Father, the suitor from Erd disturbs me."

The king glanced at Daimh. "Oh? The crowd seems to favor him."

"Yes, but what about what *I* want?" Eliana asked almost urgently.

Using his most regal tone, the king replied, "This is your duty—your responsibility. This is what you were born for. You will be the queen." Softening his voice, he added, "It may not seem fair, but it is the way things have been done for generations. It took a little while for your mother and I to be comfortable around each other. It may take time, but you will adapt."

Her father's statement hit Eliana hard. Her mother and father didn't fall in love on sight? Why had her father waited until now to reveal this? Why didn't he tell her before what to expect?

"Father—"

Any further conversation was interrupted when the hierarchy returned to the hall. Magistrate Seanan walked over to Priest Sherwyn and handed him a folded note. The priest opened it, glared at the hierarchy for a moment, and then addressed the crowd. "The Hierarchy of Magistrates has decided."

CHAPTER 4

N one of the feasts Rinan had attended previously could compare to this. The banquet hall of the castle had tables laid end to end that ran the full length of the large room. All manner of meats, vegetables, and drink were available to the guests. Governors from all seven districts were in attendance, each with several others from their respective lands. Guardians lined the walls, dressed in a fashion suitable to the area they represented.

Wearing the gold and blue of a royal guardian, Rinan stood almost directly behind Eliana. From his vantage point, he could clearly see the company from Erd, who had been seated next to the royalty—the customary position for those selected at the Shoginoc.

To Eliana's left was Daimh, who seemed to be oblivious to anyone other than the princess. Rinan tried to relax but found his shoulders continually tensing up. Throughout the dinner, he had noticed Daimh ogling the princess. Rinan could tell Eliana was being polite and doing her best to keep a conversation going, but Daimh often lost track of the topic, and appeared to find any excuse to touch the princess.

"Your hair is magnificent." Daimh reached out and ran his fingers through Eliana's golden locks. She smiled, although Rinan thought he saw her flinch.

"Thank you. I can tell you got your dark hair from your father," she said. Rinan wondered if she was trying to direct Daimh's attention elsewhere.

"Oh, yes, I suppose," Daimh said. "Ah, my dear, allow me." He grabbed his napkin and leaned over, dabbing it against the corner of Eliana's mouth. It was another obvious attempt at physical contact, as there was simply nothing to wipe away.

The dinner continued for the next half an hour. After dessert had been

29

served and largely completed by the crowd, King Kenrik stood, quieting those in attendance.

"I thank you all for coming. Once again, I congratulate the district of Erd for being selected by the hierarchy." Raising his chalice, he said, "To peace in our kingdom!"

"To peace in our kingdom!" the crowd echoed.

⊰❉⊱

After the feast, Daimh insisted on escorting Eliana to her room. Since he refused to take no for an answer, Eliana acquiesced, even agreeing to take his arm. The princess insisted that Rinan accompany them, telling Daimh that she didn't go anywhere without her personal guardian. Looking Rinan over with distaste, Daimh reluctantly agreed.

Walking down the hallway toward her room, Daimh said, "When I become king, one of the first things I will do is commission new tapestries for the castle. Look how old some of these are. Dreadful."

"I'm rather fond of many of these," Eliana said. "They've been here as long as I can remember."

Daimh waved his hand dismissively. "Oh, we'll keep them somewhere. We just need new ones that are more exciting."

"Where would you propose we keep the old ones?" Eliana asked.

"I don't know. I've never really concerned myself with details. We'll have a servant take care of it." Stopping, Daimh motioned to one of the tapestries. "Look at this one. How boring." He sniffed loudly, then turned and continued down the hallway.

Rinan glanced at the tapestry Daimh found so unappealing. The title read "Rain and Sunshine."

"Here we are." Eliana let go of Daimh's arm and opened the door to her chambers. He started to follow her in.

She turned and placed a hand on the large man's chest to stop him. "Where are you going?"

He blinked stupidly. "What do you mean?"

"This is *my* room." Eliana frowned. "You will be sleeping downstairs."

"But we should get to know each other better," Daimh said. "After all, we will be married soon enough."

"Until we are married, you will sleep in your room, and I will sleep in mine," she said firmly.

The finality in her voice seemed to be lost on him.

"Surely you are joking." He pushed her hand away, taking another step into her room and causing her to back up.

Before Daimh could proceed further, Rinan grabbed his arm and stopped him. Daimh whipped his head around, and Rinan stared him in the eye.

"Let me show you to your room." Rinan's voice was hard as steel.

Daimh shook free of Rinan's grip. "How dare you touch me! Who do you think you are?"

"I am the personal guardian of Princess Eliana," Rinan said. "And she has made it clear that you are not welcome into her room."

"Rinan, you shouldn't handle Daimh that way," Eliana said. "After all, he's going to be king." She addressed both of them. "We are all tired. It's been a long day. I'll see you tomorrow."

She stepped into her room, closed the door, and locked it from the inside.

Daimh narrowed his eyes at Rinan. "We'll see how long you remain her personal guardian after I become king." He spun and stomped down the hallway.

Stunned, Rinan watched the future king walk away. The woman Rinan loved was going to marry a man who didn't deserve her, but when he had tried to defend her, she had rebuked him. Balling his hands into fists, Rinan thought about Priest Sherwyn's counsel. *Well, he wanted me to stay to see if my sense of duty would override my feelings,* Rinan thought. *I guess I have my answer.*

⇥✦⇤

Anemone, who had been waiting in the princess's room for the feast to end, came up behind the princess to help her with the buttons that ran down the back of her dress. Before the nursemaid could undo more than a couple of buttons, Eliana turned and collapsed into her arms. The embrace triggered the tears Eliana had been holding in. Anemone didn't say anything, but just held Eliana close as she sobbed, her body shaking as she cried.

After several moments, Eliana said in a quivering voice, "I can't do this. I know this is what I'm supposed to do, but I can't."

"I know it won't be easy, dear—" Anemone started, but Eliana cut her off.

"No. I can't. I just can't." She pushed herself away from her nursemaid.

"Eliana…"

Looking around the room, the princess said, "There has to be

31

something I can do." Her gaze settled back on Anemone, and her eyes got bigger. "Yes, that's it."

"What's it?" Anemone asked, clearly puzzled.

"You never had to marry. You gave your life to service and became a nursemaid. You had a choice."

"Eliana, there is a big difference between you and me," Anemone said.

"Just because I'm the princess doesn't mean I can't make choices in my life. I can't marry a man I don't love!"

Anemone put out her hand to touch Eliana's arm. "In time, you could learn to love Daimh."

Brushing away the nursemaid's hand, she said, "No. I could never love that man. He's arrogant and self-centered. He wants to replace all the tapestries. He thinks he can do whatever he wants. He's not..." she paused.

At this moment, she realized why over the last several months she had been dreading the Shoginoc. She had been taught her whole life that this was her duty and had even found the idea somewhat romantic, but something had changed recently, something significant and wonderful. Glancing over to the closed door and lowering her voice, Eliana said, "I'm in love with Rinan."

⇥✦⇤

Anemone spent several hours talking with the princess. Eliana came to the conclusion that rather than marry Daimh, she would renounce the crown and become a nursemaid, even though she was in love with Rinan. She saw that as her only option. She knew that being a royal guardian meant everything to Rinan. She couldn't imagine him renouncing his position for her, and if she couldn't marry for love, she would not marry anyone.

Nothing Anemone said could change the princess's mind, although the nursemaid did manage to convince her to sleep on it before she acted. Once Eliana appeared to be asleep, Anemone went straight to Priest Sherwyn for help. Fortunately, the priest was still awake when she knocked on his door. He ushered her in and offered her a chair.

Anemone pulled her hooded gray cloak tightly around her and said, "Princess Eliana is about to make a big mistake."

"How so?" Sherwyn asked.

"She's considering renouncing the crown. We must stop her."

"Oh dear." Sherwyn sat back in his chair and frowned. "This isn't good.

No, this isn't good at all." He paused. "As for stopping her, I'm not sure how we could do that. We can't force her. That much is clear in the Tome of Laws. Everyone gets to choose for himself—or herself. However, they must live with the consequences of their choices."

Anemone sighed. "She's such a stubborn girl. I don't know how to change her mind. She says she can't possibly love Daimh because she loves Rinan. But since she doesn't see marrying Rinan as an option, she wants to become a nursemaid."

The priest's eyebrows arched. "The princess claims to be in love with Royal Guardian Rinan?"

"So she says, but she's not expressed that to him."

"Interesting." Sherwyn rubbed his hand over his bald head. "Does Princess Eliana realize that if she renounces the crown, Daimh will still become king?"

"Yes, although I don't see that being much of an issue for Eliana," Anemone said, staring off at nothing in particular. "She has no interest in power or the status of being one of the royalty. When she was very young, she liked the idea of being queen. After growing up, however, she realized this made her different. She'd often complain that her responsibilities kept her from being herself. However, she's always kept up with her studies—the savants have seen to that." Anemone sighed. "I'm afraid that if we tell Eliana someone else will be the ruler, it won't convince her."

Sherwyn folded his hands on his lap. "Without Eliana on the throne, I fear there will be serious consequences for the kingdom."

"Oh?" Anemone said, her eyes wide.

"For several years, there have been disturbing reports from the district of Erd." Sherwyn leaned forward. "The people in Erd seem to fear Abrecan. I secretly sent in one of the clergy to investigate, and he was killed in what was described as an 'unfortunate accident.' Lady Calla has not been seen for several months—her disappearance occurred soon after a public disagreement with her husband."

Horrified, Anemone said, "I had no idea. Why hasn't the Hierarchy of Magistrates done something about this?"

Sherwyn sighed. "Abrecan is smart, and he covers things up too well. I have a suspicion that the magistrate of Erd has been doing Abrecan's bidding. Caldre could be convincing the hierarchy that everything is under control."

"I can't believe what I'm hearing." Anemone shook her head.

"I wish it wasn't true," Sherwyn said, clearly frustrated. "But now you know why it's important to place Eliana on the throne so King Kenrik can advise her. The true power of the crown belongs to the heir."

Anemone shrugged her shoulders. "I don't know what to do."

Sherwyn stood and went to his table. "I don't know either, but perhaps I can find a solution."

⚜

The first light of dawn entered Eliana's room. Despite promising Anemone to sleep before she acted, sleep had eluded her. Anemone had offered Eliana some plyese tea that had helped her sleep in the past, but the princess couldn't bring herself to drink it. She had too much on her mind and didn't want to sleep until she had thought it out. With each passing moment, it became clearer to her how she felt about Rinan and that she could not possibly marry Daimh. She knew speaking to her father about this was useless, since he was adamant that she must marry who was chosen.

The princess's room had three doors—one led to the hallway, one to the room where her personal guardian slept, and one to the room where her nursemaid lived. All the doors could be locked from inside her room to give her privacy, although she only kept the door to the hallway locked.

She looked over to the door that led to Anemone's room. The princess knew Anemone had left during the night. Apparently her efforts to feign sleep had fooled her nursemaid. Anemone had returned a few hours later, and that was the last Eliana had heard from her nursemaid all night. Here, in the early morning, Eliana could sense no movement from Anemone's room. She got up, put on her robe, and walked quietly over to the door that led to Rinan's room. She knocked once, and then again. When she didn't get a response, she cracked opened the door. Rinan wasn't there. His room appeared as if it had been vacant all night. Thinking back, Eliana realized she hadn't heard Rinan come back to his room.

A sudden thought occurred to her. Certainly Daimh wouldn't have done anything to him. She knew Rinan was dedicated to protect her—he showed that last night in preventing Daimh from entering her room. She had told Rinan to stop what he was doing because she didn't want him to get into trouble. She was grateful he had stepped in, but such actions could only lead to unfortunate consequences.

Her fear turned into panic. She crossed the room to Anemone's door and knocked. A moment later Anemone opened it, rubbing the sleep out of her eyes.

"Get dressed. I fear something dreadful may have happened to Rinan."

╾╬╾

"I never thought it would end like this," Rinan said. "But, as Priest Sherwyn likes to say, 'We must live with the consequences of our choices.'"

He didn't get a response, but he wasn't really expecting one. After all, he was alone in the stables, and the horse he was talking to seemed content just to listen.

Rinan finished placing the last of his rations in the saddlebags. He had roamed the castle all night, trying to decide what to do. The more he thought about it, the more he was convinced he couldn't stay. "I'll be right back." He patted the horse. "Captain Wayte should be up by now, and I can give him the news that I'm leaving."

Turning, Rinan discovered Eliana and Anemone at the entrance of the stable. The princess had her hands on her hips and was staring at him.

"Leaving to go where, Royal Guardian Rinan?" Elian asked sternly, her chin lifted.

"Princess, w—what are you doing here?" he stammered.

"We searched the castle for you all morning. Fortunately, we found someone who saw you heading to the stables." Eliana took several steps toward him. "But don't answer my question with a question. I asked you where you were going."

"I can't stay, Princess," Rinan said quietly. "I'm resigning and returning home."

"But why?" she asked, her voice losing the firmness it had before.

He wanted to tell her that he loved her, but he couldn't. It had been inappropriate to grab Daimh the night before, but sharing his feelings with her could only make the situation worse. Rinan hoped his answer didn't sound as weak to her as it did to him.

"You no longer have need of me. Your future husband will protect you. Word has it he is an expert swordsman. I fear that my desire to keep you safe will interfere with your marriage to Daimh. You made it clear last night that I was in the way. I think it would be best if I were not around."

"You're willing to resign as a guardian for me?" Eliana asked. The hardness in her eyes softened with the tears that started to form.

That was not the reaction Rinan expected. "Yes, Princess. I want you to be happy. My resignation is the only way I can bring that about."

Eliana reached out and took him by the hand. "That's not the only way, Rinan."

"I'm not sure I understand …"

Anemone, who had remained quiet to this point, chose this moment to speak. "Eliana, you should tell him."

Looking back at Eliana, Rinan asked, "Tell me what?"

Eliana took a deep breath. "After the Shoginoc and spending time with Daimh, I realized I can't marry a man like that. The last few months you and I have spent together have been the happiest I've ever known. What I'm trying to say, Rinan, is that I love you." She closed the gap between them and embraced him.

He tensed, unsure how to react. Had he heard right? The woman he loved had just told him she loved him too? Not only that, but she was embracing him. After feeling more miserable than he had in his entire life, this seemed too surreal to be true.

She rested her head on his chest. "Oh, Rinan. I'm sorry. I am so sorry."

Her tone of voice and her touch pushed Rinan passed his initial shock, and he returned her embrace. Then her last words sank in. "Sorry for what?" he asked softly.

Looking up into his eyes, she said, "I should have realized it sooner and told you."

It seemed as though she wanted to say something else. Although her mouth moved, no sound came out, but instead, tears started flowing from her blue eyes. Rinan put his hand behind her head and pulled her close, allowing her to cry.

After a moment, he said quietly, "You've been talking to Priest Sherwyn, haven't you?"

"Why?" Eliana asked between sobs.

He ran his fingers through her hair. "He's the only one I told that I was falling in love with you. I thought he wouldn't tell anyone."

Eliana pulled away so she could look at him. "Rinan, I haven't been talking to him."

"Then how did you... Oh."

The two of them stood there for a moment, not saying anything. Rinan wanted to say more but was unsure how to start.

Before either of them could break the silence, Anemone said, "I think we all need to see Priest Sherwyn."

⇥✠⇤

Rinan and Eliana followed Anemone in silence as the servants scurried around the castle in preparation for the day's activities. When they arrived at the priest's chambers, Anemone knocked on the door.

"Come in," said a tired voice.

The three entered the room to find Sherwyn hunched over his table. His bloodshot eyes revealed that he had not slept much during the night. Around him were various books and parchments, and the candle on the desk had burned down nearly its length.

"Priest Sherwyn," Anemone said, "you look as if you've not slept a wink."

Stifling a yawn, the priest stood and motioned for the three of them to sit down. "That's because I haven't. I was looking for a solution to a particularly complex problem."

"Ah, and have you had any success?" Anemone asked.

Smiling, he said, "I believe I have." He turned to Eliana. "I understand you are having doubts about marrying Daimh."

Glancing at Anemone, Eliana now understood where her nursemaid had gone the night before. "Yes. I can't marry that man."

"Eliana," Sherwyn continued, "forgive me for speaking so plainly, but Anemone has informed me that you are in love with Rinan."

"Yes, that is true."

Sherwyn shifted his attention to Rinan. "And Rinan, also forgive me if I am betraying any trust, but you confessed to me your feelings for Eliana. Do you still feel this way?"

"Actually, I just told her moments ago," Rinan replied, and Eliana could tell he was as confused as she was by the priest's questions.

Sherwyn motioned to the books and parchments around him. "I spent the night looking for a way to deal with a situation like yours. Under normal circumstances, the two of you could renounce your positions and marry."

Eliana felt Rinan tense up next to her. "But these are not normal circumstances, are they?" he asked.

"No, they are not," the priest answered.

"I'm not sure I understand," Eliana interjected. "And with respect, Priest Sherwyn, you don't need to tell me the consequences. I understand it means that I won't be queen. I've thought this through and have accepted it."

"Princess, I believe it is of the utmost importance that you become queen. I fear for the kingdom if you step down."

Eliana frowned. "I don't see how I could possibly have any effect on the kingdom."

"Princess, let me explain," For the next several moments, the priest told about Abrecan and the problems in the district of Erd. The more he spoke, the more alarmed Eliana became.

"I understand your concern. I'm not trying to avoid my responsibility to the kingdom." Her chest started to tighten. "At the same time, I simply can't marry Daimh. I love Rinan. I…I don't know what to do."

The priest smiled. "That is the exact 'complex problem' that I mentioned earlier. What if I told you I've found a way where you two can be married, and you can both still keep your titles?"

Eliana and Rinan looked at each other. Both had the same light of hope in their eyes. Turning back to the priest, she said, "I would say you have our attention."

⇥⧘⇤

Lit with dozens of candles, Eliana's room was quite bright, despite the late hour. Rinan and Eliana stood side by side, each dressed in simple white attire. They faced Sherwyn, who held an old tattered copy of the Tome of Laws. Anemone stood off to one side, holding a handkerchief to her face, wiping away tears.

"Please face each other," Sherwyn instructed. "Take each other by the right hand."

Eliana smiled as she turned to face her husband-to-be. Rinan's gray eyes sparkled, even in the candlelight. He didn't possess Daimh's striking appearance, but he was infinitely more attractive to her.

When she reached out and took his hand, she tried not to tremble but couldn't help herself. If Rinan noticed, he made no indication, perhaps because he seemed to be trembling as well.

Priest Sherwyn read from the tome. Although Eliana heard the words, she couldn't focus on their meaning. Instead, her thoughts kept drifting to how lucky she was to be marrying such a wonderful man. Any thoughts of the challenges they would face in keeping their marriage secret were drowned by the overwhelming joy she felt at the moment.

When asked if they would take each other in marriage, they each responded with a quiet, but sincere "I do."

At the conclusion of the ceremony, Sherwyn said, "You may now begin your life together with a kiss."

Eliana realized this was to be her first kiss. Throughout her life, she had envisioned what it would be like. Never had she pictured a moment like this, but as she leaned in to kiss Rinan and their lips met for the first time, she couldn't imagine anything more perfect.

CHAPTER 5

Priest Sherwyn was nervous. His plan to keep Eliana from resigning required a lot of care and planning, and, a bit to his dismay, a little luck. Fortunately, luck had been on his side thus far.

It had been two weeks since Rinan and Eliana's wedding. The future queen claimed she was not feeling well, which gave her and Rinan the excuse they needed to stay sequestered.

During that period of time, there had been a buzz of activity preparing for the royal wedding. The main hall had been set up for the ceremony, which would take place at sundown with an elaborate banquet to follow.

Occupying Sherwyn's thoughts at the moment was the ceremony itself. He had gone over it several times with Eliana. She was the key for this to work. If the wedding ceremony wasn't done exactly as outlined in the Tome of Laws, it wouldn't be binding. The trick was to perform the ceremony incorrectly without anyone noticing. What made this more difficult was that Magistrate Seanan would be the witness, insuring it *was* performed properly. However, Sherwyn's plan had succeeded thus far, and he hoped his luck would hold out a little bit longer.

❖

Eliana had butterflies the night she married Rinan. On the day of her wedding to Daimh, she had butterflies again—but this time for a different reason. She had practiced her part in the farce over and over, and hoped it would go as planned.

When the musicians started to play, she took her father by the arm and started walking down the aisle toward the dais. Her path was covered with rose petals that had been laid down by several daughters of noble families. The hall was lined with the most prominent families of the kingdom, all

39

smiling and watching as King Kenrik escorted the bride.

Priest Sherwyn stood at the end of the aisle, his golden robe a contrast to the dark crimson outfit Daimh wore. The handsome man appeared as if every servant in the castle had spent time grooming him. Governor Abrecan stood beside his son, a smile of self-importance on his face. Magistrate Seanan also stood on the dais, right next to Priest Sherwyn, his eyes darting back and forth between the approach of the king and princess and those who stood on the dais with him. Rinan was off to the side, standing against the wall. As she approached, Eliana noticed her husband's jaw was tightly clenched.

When they arrived at the dais, King Kenrik helped the princess step up, and then took his place behind her.

Using his loudest voice, Priest Sherwyn began the ceremony. This time, Eliana was able to listen to what the priest was saying. She reflected upon the words and how they related to her and Rinan. She could never honestly make such promises to Daimh.

Several times during the ceremony, Eliana sneezed. Word had spread throughout the castle that she had been ill, and it was hoped that the audience would believe the sneezes were a symptom of what had kept her out of the public eye recently. She could feel the butterflies in her stomach start to flutter even harder as the ceremony came to its conclusion.

"Please face each other," the priest instructed. "Take each other by the right hand."

Anticipating this part of the ceremony, Eliana reached out and took Daimh by the *left* hand before he could act. She spared a glance at Magistrate Seanan, who simply smiled at her. During the Shoginoc, her father had explained that the magistrate struggled with distinguishing between left and right. Aware of this as well, Sherwyn had incorporated it into the plan. It seemed to have worked, since Magistrate Seanan didn't correct her. Daimh gave no indication that he had noticed the switch either; Eliana hoped it was one of those details with which he couldn't be bothered. Governor Abrecan and King Kenrik were unable to see what Eliana had done from where they stood, and she hoped no one in the crowd was aware or close enough to notice.

Priest Sherwyn continued and asked Daimh if he accepted Eliana as his wife.

"I do," he said, but not before Abrecan gave him a sharp poke to prompt his response.

"And do you, Princess Eliana, accept Daimh as your husband?"

"I…" She sneezed loudly as she said "don't." She had practiced this many times during the last two weeks. She had perfected the sneeze to make it sound like she said "do," when in fact she was saying the opposite.

Priest Sherwyn jumped right in after the sneeze and finished reading from the Tome of Laws. Upon completion, he announced, "You may now begin your life together with a kiss."

Eliana looked up at Daimh, who licked his lips in anticipation. He leaned down toward her. Just as their lips were about to touch, she sneezed again.

⠤⠿⠤

"You look really beautiful," eight-year-old Alana said, looking at Queen Eliana with admiration.

"Why, thank you." Eliana smiled. She knelt down next to her young cousin. "Are those new earrings you're wearing?"

"Yes!" Alana beamed, proudly displaying the gold and sapphire jewelry. "The king himself gave them to me to wear today."

Reaching out and touching them lightly, Eliana said, "They are very nice. And I must say you did a marvelous job with the rose petals."

Alana blushed. "My father made me practice. He said how proud his big brother was going to be of me."

Eliana kissed Alana lightly on the forehead and then stood. "Well, you tell my uncle that he should be very proud of his little girl. Both my father and I were very pleased."

Alana nodded and then ran off to her father, who was talking with men from other noble families.

The banquet hall was still alive with activity, though the sun had set long ago. Unlike the ceremony, where only a select few were allowed to attend, the reception was open to anyone in Bariwon.

After the wedding was the coronation. It was a simple event, where the crown was transferred from King Kenrik to Queen Eliana. Before the coronation, Eliana had changed from her formal wedding gown into an elegant white dress. She knew she would be busy greeting the people of the kingdom, and the simpler dress would allow her to move among the crowd with greater ease.

King Daimh spent most of the reception with a drink in his hand, and at times, with a drink in *each* hand. As the night wore on, he became more intoxicated. Anemone was keeping a close eye on him, and when she sensed that he had drunk about as much as he could handle, she gave him a cup of her plyese tea, telling him, "This will help relax you for your important evening."

He gulped down the offering and shortly began exhibiting its effects. Anemone quickly summoned Queen Eliana, who saw Daimh's condition and took the next step in the plan.

"It's getting late," Queen Eliana said to King Daimh. "We should be headed to bed."

Through somewhat glazed eyes, Daimh muttered, "Uh-huh."

Anemone led the way to the door, with the queen and king close behind. Rinan brought up the rear, his hand resting on the hilt of his sword. Upon reaching the door, the newly crowned leaders of Bariwon turned to the crowd. As was tradition, they waved and said, "To peace in our kingdom!" Although when Daimh said it, it sounded more like "To peas in our kingpin!"

The crowd echoed the declaration, and then cheered as the young couple left the main hall.

※

King Daimh stumbled while entering the royal bedchamber. It was the largest bedroom in the castle, housing a huge bed with a mattress of down feathers, several wardrobes, a gilded mirror, and a round oak table surrounded by padded chairs. The room had several wrought-iron sconces that lit the room quite well, though it was dark outside. It had most recently been the bedroom of King Kenrik, but when his daughter was married and then was crowned queen, he became a councilor—just like his father, Philip, had done. Councilors had their own rooms in the castle, which, while large, didn't compare to the royal bedchamber.

Anemone helped steady Daimh and guided him to the bed. Eliana stood just inside the door, with Rinan outside, keeping watch. Daimh sat down on the edge of the bed, inhaled deeply, and promptly fell backward.

Anemone approached the bed, and after looking at Daimh for a moment, motioned to Eliana. The queen closed the door and walked over. "Is he asleep?"

"Oh, yes, and he will be for quite a while."

Anemone unfastened the clasp on her gray hooded cloak, removed it, and handed it to Eliana.

"Are you sure you'll be fine?" Eliana asked, donning the cloak.

Anemone smiled. "Yes, my dear. If I can handle a strong-willed young woman, a man like Daimh won't be much of a challenge."

Eliana gave her nursemaid a hug. "Thank you for everything." She placed the hood over her head, headed for the door, opened it, and stepped out into the hallway. Rinan was still there, watching.

"It's still clear, but it won't be for long. Let's get you out of here."

The new queen pulled the robe tightly around her and keeping her head down, Eliana started off to the room where she had grown up—the room she now shared with her true husband.

⊱⊰

Rain drops pelting the window were the first sounds King Daimh heard upon waking. He forced one eyelid open, even though doing so made the pounding in his head worse. Coming to his senses slowly, he realized where he was. He reached out his hand and felt for his new bride.

She wasn't there.

He rolled over and found that he was alone in the bed. Grunting, he forced his other eye open and looked around the room. Anemone was sitting in one of the padded chairs, her hands folded on her lap. She smiled at him.

"Where…?" Daimh mumbled.

"Oh, Eliana was up at first light, Your Majesty, as she is every morning. I'm sure she is still downstairs eating breakfast. She didn't want to wake you. You were sleeping very soundly."

Propping himself up on his elbows, Daimh tried to recall anything from the night before. He had a vague impression of coming into the room, but for the life of him couldn't remember anything after that. He looked down and found he was wearing a sleeping tunic. He didn't remember changing his clothes.

"Did she say anything before she left?"

Anemone responded, "Queen Eliana said last night couldn't have gone any better."

Daimh furrowed his brows. "Oh?"

"Oh, yes. She said you were something else."

"I'm sure I was, although I'm not sure I remember…" Daimh scratched his head.

"My king," Anemone exclaimed, "certainly you aren't saying you don't remember your own wedding night."

"Uh…"

"If I may be so bold as to offer advice, Your Majesty, I would strongly suggest that isn't something you should admit to anyone. You don't want your new bride to find out and to believe it wasn't a memorable evening."

"Well, I, uh…"

"And how would you feel if word spread through the kingdom that you were too drunk to remember what happened on one of the most important nights of your life?"

Daimh's eyes grew wide. "No, that can't happen!"

"Perhaps you'll remember more after you wake up. In the meantime, I would recommend that you keep this between us. I promise not to tell anyone, Your Majesty."

Daimh felt relieved. "Thank you."

"You are more than welcome. Anything I can do to help the kingdom."

⊰⧣⊱

"This is outrageous!"

Councilor Abrecan sat across from Councilors Kenrik and Philip. With fists clenched, the former governor of Erd pounded the table.

Raising an eyebrow, Councilor Kenrik said, "Abrecan, while this type of behavior may have been permitted in your district, it is not acceptable here in the castle."

Abrecan took a deep breath, held it for a moment, and then exhaled. "My apologies," he said through clenched teeth, "but the situation is still outrageous."

Councilor Kenrik clasped his hands on the table in front of him. "The queen says she is not feeling well. Out of concern for the king, she feels it best that she stay away from him."

"But it has been nearly two months! The couple is expected to produce an heir," Abrecan said, pointing a finger across the table. "Explain to me how that will be possible if Eliana refuses to be in the same room with Daimh."

Councilor Philip spoke up. "You must remember that the young couple hardly know each other. Eliana understands her duty. She will produce an heir. We must give her some time."

Abrecan folded his arms. "Fine. I'll talk to my son and settle him down. The Festival of Gratitude is only a few weeks away, and both the queen and king are expected to attend. Let's hope she is feeling better by then."

⊰⧣⊱

Since the time of the so-called wedding between Eliana and Daimh, Bariwon had experienced unseasonable storms. Days would pass without the sun shining directly on the land, and even when it did manage to break through the clouds, it was fleeting. On this morning, the sun was shining brightly for the first time in weeks. It was excuse enough for Eliana and Rinan to leave the castle and head to the nearby countryside for some fresh air.

They had taken a lunch with them to the tree where they had first picnicked back in the spring. Eliana believed it was the perfect time to share the wonderful news with Rinan.

"Rinan, I have something to tell you," Eliana began, fidgeting the way she did when she was excited about something.

"Oh? What's that?"

She smiled at her husband and took him by the hand. "Anemone believes we are going to have a baby."

At first, Rinan looked stunned. It was wonderful news, to be sure, but he didn't seem to be able to speak. He took Eliana in his arms and held her close. When they parted, both had tears of joy in their eyes.

"Do you know what this means?" Eliana asked.

"Yes! It means that you no longer have to make excuses to stay away from Daimh. As far as anyone knows, he fathered the child on your wedding night. This is wonderful!"

Sighing contently, Eliana said, "I know. I'm so happy."

"Although…"

"Yes?"

Rinan pursed his lips. "We haven't really talked about how we are going to raise this child. After all, he or she will believe Daimh is their father."

"Actually, I *have* thought of that," Eliana said. "I discussed it with Priest Sherwyn some time ago. He said he had considered that point before we were married, and has a solution. He insisted I not give it a second thought until I became pregnant. We'll talk to him soon."

A light rain started to fall. The young couple looked up to see a storm moving in quickly. The sun was still shining brightly for the moment, but the rain started falling with more enthusiasm.

"The sun's playing hide-and-seek," Eliana commented.

Rinan looked at his wife. "What's that?"

"The sun's playing hide-and-seek," she repeated. "It's a saying I made up as a child when the sun was out, but it was raining. You would think that the sun would be hidden by the rain."

"Or perhaps the sunshine is so beautiful, the rain wants to be part of it," Rinan suggested.

Raising her eyebrows, Eliana said, "The first time we came here, I accused you of not having an imagination because you couldn't see the objects the clouds were making. It seems I was mistaken. Rinan, I do believe you have an imagination after all."

CHAPTER 6

"I'll do it," King Daimh said.

Everyone in the main hall paused and looked at Queen Eliana. Her blue eyes narrowed at the king and then at his father, Councilor Abrecan. This wasn't the first time Daimh had volunteered to do something that would make him the center of attention.

After a moment, she said, "All right. Take the bowl to the king so he can pull the name."

Priest Sherwyn looked into the large crystal bowl that held seven folded pieces of paper. On each was written the name of a different district. Bowing to the queen, Sherwyn crossed the short distance between the two thrones and held out the bowl for King Daimh.

The king reached in and pulled out one of the papers. He unfolded it, and after silently reading what was written, he announced with a flourish to the court, "For this year's Festival of Gratitude, the royalty will be visiting the district of Lewyol."

The members of the court all applauded politely as Daimh put the paper back in the bowl and casually mixed up the contents.

"How fitting that Lewyol was selected," Sherwyn said. "After all, they did put on quite a showing at the Shoginoc. It will be nice to honor them at the festival."

Murmurs of agreement echoed in the hall.

"It's settled then," Eliana said. "As tradition states, we'll leave for Lewyol before dawn tomorrow. If I'm not mistaken, we should be able to arrive there before dark."

Priest Sherwyn nodded. "Yes, barring some unseen event, you should make it by nightfall."

"Excellent. That will give us a few days with the good people of Lewyol before the actual festival. I look forward to seeing their surprise when we arrive." Eliana stood and said to the court, "Thank you all. To those of you not coming with us to Lewyol, I wish everyone a safe and happy festival."

⇥✠⇤

A dozen horses rode in two columns down the wide road that led from the castle to the district of Lewyol. The company consisted of King Daimh, Queen Eliana, Councilors Philip, Kenrik, and Abrecan, and seven royal guardians. The king, queen, and councilors were dressed in the traditional colors of gold and blue, with heavy cloaks embroidered in highly detailed patterns. The royal guardians wore decorative chainmail armor with finely sewn tabards that prominently displayed the emblem of Bariwon. Even the horses were dressed up—the chain mail that hung just below their knees was all but covered in a thick cloth sewn in the kingdom's colors.

The trip started with Queen Eliana and King Daimh riding side by side just behind two of the guardians, with Rinan directly behind the queen. Aside from the weekly courts that were held, this trip was the first time Eliana had been in close proximity to Daimh since their wedding. She felt awkward with him, giving short answers and not trying at all to keep the conversation flowing. Daimh seemed oblivious to Eliana's cold shoulder and kept chatting away.

"You will, of course, be moving back into the royal chamber once our child is born," Daimh said out of the blue.

This caught Eliana somewhat off guard. "No, I won't," she said simply.

Daimh cocked his head to one side. "I don't understand."

Eliana took a deep breath. "Has no one explained this to you, Daimh?"

"Explained what?" He still sounded confused.

Eliana looked away and straight ahead at the road in front of her. "In the Tome of Laws, it states that either a husband or wife can claim the right of separation if they have cause. They would still be married, but would live in different houses, or in our case, different chambers of the castle."

He blinked stupidly. "And?"

She turned back to face him. "Daimh, I've claimed the right of separation. I can't believe no one has told you this."

"I still don't understand," he said. "I remember someone mentioning something about that, but I thought they had to be joking. Why would you want to be separated from me? What possible cause do you have?"

After taking another deep breath, Eliana said, "Daimh, I don't love you. In fact, I hardly know you. But it is my duty to the kingdom to marry whoever wins the Shoginoc and produce an heir. So, we are married, and I am carrying the heir to the kingdom. I have fulfilled my duty."

"But we are talking about *me*," Daimh said, his face starting to get red. "Any woman in the kingdom would be a fool not to want to be with me. And what are the people in Bariwon going to think about me when they find out?"

Eliana sighed. "Daimh, there is much more to being attractive than physical looks or how people perceive you. If you can't understand that, then you will never understand why I claimed the right of separation."

For the next few hours, neither Daimh nor Eliana said anything, though she glanced at him occasionally. He rode straight up in the saddle, staring ahead with a hard look in his eyes. She hated having to be so direct with him, but it seemed the only way to get through to him—a trait he must have gotten from his father.

After a quick break in the late afternoon, Councilor Abrecan requested that King Daimh ride with him for a while to discuss the festival. It wasn't unusual for Daimh to be coached by his father before public events. Eliana was relieved that Abrecan had given her a reason to change traveling companions. Councilor Philip seemed glad to take King Daimh's spot next to his granddaughter. They chatted off and on about the festival and other subjects as they rode. Although there were periods of silence between them, it was a comfortable silence, a refreshing change from when she rode with Daimh.

The entourage was still an hour or so away from the town of Lewyol, although they had passed by several villages along the way. The forest-lined road was fairly flat, with a few rolling hills breaking up the monotony. At times, the company was so quiet while they traveled that the only sound was the jingling of chain mail. The sun was just setting when a light snow started to fall, prompting Eliana to break the silence that had prevailed for the last several minutes.

"Oh, look!" She stretched out her hand and caught a few of the snowflakes as they floated down from the overcast sky. The white lasted a moment before it melted against the blue velvet of her glove. Within moments, the flakes became larger and more frequent.

"I suggest you pull up your hood." Councilor Philip nudged his horse closer to the queen. "We wouldn't want you getting a chill on the way to the festival."

"You are right—I should get more bundled up. It wouldn't be good for

49

the baby if I were to catch cold."

"On that subject, how are you feeling?" Philip asked.

Eliana donned her hood as she answered. "I'm doing well. Anemone tells me that in a couple of months I shouldn't be traveling. I was a little sick to my stomach in the mornings at first, but that stopped several weeks ago. My body is showing I'm with child, and my expanding middle can be uncomfortable at times, but aside from that, I'm fine."

Smiling at her, Philip said, "That's wonderf—" His words were cut off as he pitched forward in his saddle. His hands lost their grip, and he slid off his horse to the ground.

Time seemed to slow down. At first, Eliana didn't understand why her grandfather, who was an able horseman, would fall. But as she watched him slide to the ground, she saw an arrow sticking prominently out of his back.

"No!" she cried.

The sounds of more arrows slicing through the air were followed by shouts and screams of pain from the rest of the traveling party. Eliana felt strong hands grab her from behind and pull her to the ground between the two columns of horses. She panicked at first, but calmed a little when she realized it was Rinan who held her.

"Stay between the horses!" he ordered. "They've been trained not to panic when under attack."

Eliana nodded, then looked around. The rest of the entourage had dismounted and stood between the horses. Three more of her traveling companions were on the ground, each with arrows in them. Two were guardians—one was trying to pull an arrow out of his shoulder, while the other wasn't moving. In shock, she realized the other person who had been hit was her father. Abrecan and Daimh were by his side.

"Father!" she screamed and started to go to him.

Rinan grabbed her. "No! Stay here, it's not safe. Look after your grandfather." Crouching, Rinan worked his way back to Councilor Kenrik.

Kneeling next to her grandfather, Eliana took his head in her hands. His sightless eyes told her it was too late to help him.

Rinan returned to her side. "Your father is alive, but hurt badly. He stands a chance if we can get him into town soon. How is your grandfather?"

Blinking back tears, she looked up. "He's gone."

Captain Wayte's shouting interrupted Rinan's response. "Guardians, to arms! Here they come!"

The arrows had stopped. Peeking under the armor that covered the horses, Eliana could see men dressed in yellow and brown charging the road from the trees. Sounds from all around told her they were coming in from different directions. With all paths cut off, even if her group was to mount their horses and make a run for it, chances were they would be cut down before they got very far.

"Stay between the horses," Rinan said again as he removed his sword from its scabbard. "If I see an opening and tell you to make a run for it, get on your horse and ride to town as fast as you can. Stay low in the saddle and don't look back."

Rinan stepped out from the row of horses and took several strides toward the charging men. The other five remaining guardians did the same, each in a different direction.

Eliana found herself holding her breath as the distance between the attackers and defenders closed.

⊰⧺⊱

The charging man's face was covered in soot, his white teeth bared in a snarl as he raised his sword to attack. Holding his sword in a defensive position in front of him, Rinan assessed the situation. The man in front of him was followed by two more, several paces back. Their rivet-studded armor was made of leather, making it easier for them to move while giving up some protection. Rinan noted the vulnerable spots and steeled his resolve—he would not let any of these attackers get to Eliana. He simply would not.

When the lead attacker swung his sword at Rinan, instead of trying to stop the blade, Rinan deflected it off to the side, letting the man's momentum carry him forward and past him. Spinning, Rinan sliced the man across his hamstring, crippling him and sending him to the ground howling in pain. Rinan completed the spin and faced the two other men charging him.

One of the onrushing men stopped in his tracks, while the other kept the charge. The second man attacked. Feigning a parry, Rinan ducked below a wild swing, then brought up an armored hand and hit his opponent hard in the throat. The man dropped his sword and reached for his neck, trying to breathe through his crushed windpipe.

The remaining foe was more cautious than the others. Smiling wickedly, he approached slowly.

"Those two were fools," he growled. "I am not a fool. And you, guardian, are dead." The attacker reached behind him and pulled out a dagger, the sharp edge gleaming even in the dim light of the overcast sky. With a sword in one hand and the dagger in the other, he moved in.

Avoiding jabs and thrusts, Rinan tried to get in a clean cut at his opponent. This man was more skilled than the others, and each blow Rinan made was stopped, deflected, or avoided.

The two danced in combat for several moments, neither gaining the advantage over the other. Rinan could hear the clashing of metal on metal around him, but didn't dare take his eyes off his opponent to see how his fellow guardians were faring. He knew the longer this fight took, the more Eliana was at risk. He had to try to put an end to it quickly.

An idea struck him as he fought off the latest onslaught. He faked a thrust to the left, opening his right side to his attacker's dagger. The move worked as the man in yellow and brown attempted to stab Rinan's side. Anticipating the move, Rinan grabbed the wrist that held the dagger and twisted, causing the smaller blade to fall to the ground. His attacker yelped in pain and took a step back, wringing his hand free from Rinan's grip. Pressing the attack, Rinan drove the man back further.

After regaining his bearings, the man stopped Rinan's approach and began to counterattack. Rinan allowed a particularly strong blow to knock him off his feet. In his roll away from the man, Rinan grabbed the fallen dagger but kept it behind him as he stood. He slumped, feigning an injury. The attacker, seeming to smell an impending victory, gloated from several steps away. "Time to die," he said.

Glaring into the man's eyes, Rinan grimaced, and then threw his sword straight up in the air. His opponent looked puzzled as he watched the weapon fly upward. Rinan used the distraction to throw the dagger with his other arm. It flew true to its mark, catching the man in the neck. Rinan caught his sword by the hilt on its way back down.

The man reached to pull the blade out, but the damage was done. Watching him fall to the ground, Rinan said, "I guess you can be fooled after all."

-}‡{-

Eliana sat on the ground and held her grandfather. The numbness she felt had less to do with the cold and more with what she had just witnessed. Daimh and Abrecan were hunched over her father and the other guardians who had fallen.

Part of her realized she was no longer hearing the sounds of battle. After carefully laying her grandfather down, she stood and peeked around the horse.

Captain Wayte was motioning for two of the guardians to search the nearby trees. Another of the guardians was checking the fallen attackers. Rinan was by Wayte's side, sheathing his sword. Relief flowed over Eliana when she realized her true husband was safe.

Walking quickly back to the horses, Wayte headed to where Councilor Kenrik lay, while Rinan came over to Eliana. "Are you hurt?" they asked each other at the same time. Both shook their heads.

Eliana wanted desperately to hold Rinan, to tell him she loved him and that she was glad he was safe, but of course she couldn't do so in front of the others.

"Let's check on your father," he said.

Wayte was kneeling down by the former king. The guardian's face was as white as the snow that continued to fall around them. He looked up at the approaching queen and shook his head.

Taking a few steps forward, Rinan then said, "What happened? I saw his wound. It was serious, but we should have had time."

Abrecan stood up and looked Rinan in the eye. "Apparently the wound was more serious than you thought. There was nothing more that could've been done."

Something in Abrecan's tone seemed off to Eliana, but she couldn't place it. She still had not fully come to the realization that she had just lost both her grandfather and her father.

Rinan turned to her. "Let's get you to your horse. The others will take care of your family."

❦

"There appear to be no others in the trees or surrounding areas," reported Guardian Dougal, who was roughly the same size as Wayte but had darker skin. "The attackers are dead, except the one Rinan crippled."

King Daimh, Councilor Abrecan, and Guardians Wayte and Rinan stood next to the covered bodies of the fallen. In addition to Councilors Kenrik and Philip, one of the guardians was also killed in the initial attack.

"How many attackers were there?" Abrecan asked.

"Eleven in total," Wayte answered. "This does not make any sense. No one knew we were coming this way. And if they did find out, why send so few? Those that attacked us were quite skilled, but they were no match for royal guardians."

Wayte turned to Rinan and Dougal. "Bring the one Rinan injured. Let us get some answers."

Rinan nodded and he and Dougal returned a moment later with the prisoner. They put him on the ground in front of Wayte, but before Wayte could say anything, Abrecan stepped forward and thrust his sword into the prisoner's chest. The man looked at Abrecan with shocked eyes before he died.

Wayte grabbed Abrecan and shoved him against a horse. "What have you done?"

"I suggest you let me go, Captain Wayte," Abrecan said calmly, "unless you want to be tried for assaulting a councilor."

King Daimh moved in, grabbed Wayte by the neck, and started to pull him away. Instead of struggling against the taller man, Wayte relaxed and said, "Please release me, Your Majesty."

"Good decision, Captain," Daimh said. "You're in enough trouble as it is."

Rinan spoke up as the king let go of Wayte. "Councilor Abrecan, explain yourself."

Abrecan straightened his ruffled cloak. "I was making sure justice was served. The man was part of a band of attackers who killed members of the royalty. He deserved to die."

Wayte pointed a finger at Abrecan. "That was not your decision to make!"

Abrecan bowed his head slightly and turned to the king. "Your Majesty, was I mistaken on the correct action to take?"

"Of course not, Father. If you hadn't killed him, I would have."

"You see? The king agrees with my actions, and it is *his* decision to make," Abrecan said smugly. "It's unfortunate that I had to be the one to carry it out. If only Guardian Rinan wasn't so lacking in combat skills, I wouldn't have had to finish the man off."

"What?" Wayte exclaimed. "Not only did Guardian Rinan defeat three of the attackers, but he probably saved your life as well."

Abrecan smirked. "If you say so."

"I would have stopped them," Daimh said. "If Rinan could stop them, they would've been no match for me."

"I suggest we be on our way," Rinan interrupted, ignoring the slights against him.

"Well, it's obvious we are not safe here in Lewyol. We need to turn back," Abrecan said. "Until we know where this threat came from, we need the protection of the castle."

Still somewhat red in the face, Wayte seemed calm enough to see the logic in the suggestion. "Agreed. We need to go back to the castle. And you will have to answer for your actions here today, Councilor."

Abrecan headed toward his horse, but turned to stare at Wayte. "I'd be more worried about *your* actions if I were you. Perhaps on the way back, you can think of a good way to explain how the royal guardians allowed two councilors to be killed."

※

The ride back to the castle was quiet. The snow had stopped falling, and the moon shone down through parted clouds. The illumination reflecting off the newly fallen snow was enough for the party to see their way along the road.

Arriving back in the castle in the early morning hours, the party stabled their horses as Guardian Dougal was sent ahead to wake Priest Sherwyn and the Hierarchy of Magistrates.

Queen Eliana, eyes red and puffy from the tears she had shed for her father and grandfather, was escorted back to her room, where Anemone attended to her. Priest Sherwyn took care of the bodies of the fallen and prepared them for a funeral.

With the sun rising behind a gray sky of clouds, word of the terrible events spread around the castle and then quickly beyond. Messengers were sent to each of the districts, summoning the governors to the castle for not only the funerals, but also to discuss how to deal with what had transpired.

After the customary three-day mourning period, former kings Philip and Kenrik were laid to rest. The slain guardian was buried in a separate ceremony.

Underlying the grief was a tension that came from the attack itself. People from the kingdom were crying for justice, although it was unclear who was to be held accountable.

King Daimh, at Councilor Abrecan's prompting, announced that a court would be held as soon as possible to discuss what had happened and how to handle it.

※

"Things couldn't have gone better." Abrecan's face was illuminated by the flickering candle on his table. "Not only were Kenrik and Philip dispatched, but when all is said and done, I will look like the hero. Yes, things turned out quite nicely."

The raven-haired Caldre, newly made magistrate over the town that surrounded the castle, sat across from Abrecan, his sharp nose tilted upward in arrogance. "And your son was unaware that any of this was going to happen, correct?"

Waving a hand in dismissal, Abrecan said, "Oh, yes, yes. He can't be trusted with such intricate plans as these. My son understands that I'm looking after his best interests and that he needs to do what I tell him. He did, after all, follow the instructions to say that Lewyol was selected, regardless of the actual name on the paper."

"Very good. What would you like me to do next?" Caldre asked.

Abrecan leaned back in his chair and steepled his fingers. "Wait a few days, so as not to raise suspicion, and then retrieve the coin we paid the mercenaries. They didn't have it on them, so I'm betting it's hidden at the inn where they were staying before the attack. Talk to the innkeeper—make sure he knows what to say if anyone starts asking questions. In fact, I want you to stay in Lewyol to keep an eye on things, at least until my grandchild is born. We'll tell people you are looking into the attacks."

Caldre nodded. "Excellent plan. Is there anything else you want me to do before I leave?"

"Tonight, go to the local taverns and spread rumors that the attackers were acting under the order of the governor of Lewyol. Suggest that Governor Elric felt slighted by losing the Shoginoc and wanted revenge." Abrecan picked up the drink in front of him, and after taking a swig, pointed at Caldre. "Also say that you heard *I* had to kill the final attacker to protect the king and queen."

Caldre smiled in understanding. "Those rumors will be all over the area by tomorrow. It should make court very interesting."

Abrecan took another drink. "Yes, it will, won't it?"

CHAPTER 7

"**B**ut that is not what happened!" Captain Wayte shouted. The main hall was abuzz with whispers after the outburst. Councilor Abrecan had just recounted his tale of how the last remaining attacker had to be killed to protect the king and queen; that it was Captain Wayte's poor judgment that put them in danger.

It had taken two weeks to assemble all the governors for the court, including the newest governor from Erd, former guardian Eadward. With the Hierarchy of Magistrates and savants watching over the proceedings, Daimh sat upon his throne, with Councilor Abrecan next to him. Queen Eliana's throne was empty. Abrecan had suggested she be excused so she could continue to mourn her father and grandfather, and Eliana had readily agreed.

"Did you not bring the attacker within striking distance of King Daimh?" Abrecan asked Wayte.

"Yes, but—"

"Yes or no will do," Abrecan interrupted. Then he turned to the Hierarchy of Magistrates. "What is the acceptable punishment for someone who kills or attempts to kill a member of the royalty?"

Magistrate Seanan conferred with his fellow magistrates before he answered. Opening the book in front of him and turning the pages, he found the passage he wanted. He read, "*Anyone who kills or attempts to kill a member of the kingdom shall be punished, up to death, as decided by the king or queen.*"

"Then my actions were justified, since the king agreed he should have been put to death," Abrecan stated. "And I consider that matter to be closed."

Wayte began to protest again but was silenced by King Daimh. "That will be enough. My father said the matter was closed."

Looking at the others in attendance, Wayte searched for support.

57

However, everyone shied away from his gaze.

Councilor Abrecan continued, "In addition, Captain Wayte, it has been generations since there has been such a tragedy in our kingdom. The throne recognizes your excellent service record, so, instead of punishment, all we are asking is for your resignation." He glared at Wayte. "Unless, of course, you would like us to review your actions further."

Squaring his shoulders, Wayte stared hard into Abrecan's eyes. "I serve the kingdom of Bariwon. From what I can see here today, the spirit of the kingdom died with Councilor Philip and Councilor Kenrik. I hereby resign."

Wayte spun on his heel and walked from the hall. Abrecan scowled, then turned his attention to the rest of those in attendance.

"It's no wonder such a tragedy happened, with a man like Wayte in charge." Raising his voice to a more instructional tone, he said, "Now, let us discuss how we will respond to the attack. Governor Elric of Lewyol, step forward."

Savant Bertram paced back and forth, nervously chewing one of his fingernails. He was unsure why he had been summoned, and in light of recent events, his mind raced with possibilities. Only a few months ago, he was studying in his home district, blissfully unaware of what the future held for him. He never had ambitions of becoming a savant; he only wanted to learn as much about everything as he could. The history of Bariwon especially interested him. He had studied the Tome of Laws ever since he could read. In addition, he was fascinated by the circumstances behind its writing. His focused studies had given him vast knowledge that had earned him the right of his current position.

Former King Kenrik had brought him to the castle to replace a savant who had retired due to old age and a failing memory. Bertram hadn't had an easy time since he moved to the castle. It seemed the other savants didn't take him seriously at first due to his young age, and as they got to know him, they realized how intelligent and knowledgeable he was, and therefore they resented him. The guardians were closer to his age, but Bertram was all elbows and knees, and his skinny frame made him feel uncomfortable around the more physically mature young men.

When he was not teaching the younger nobles, he kept to himself and his books. He attended court as required, but he sat in the back and never uttered a word unless asked.

Keeping all this in mind, Bertram couldn't possibly imagine why Queen Eliana would summon him to her quarters. He knew the queen didn't share a room with the king, meaning she had chosen the right of separation after she had become pregnant. While this was allowed in the Tome of Laws, it had not been put into practice for several generations. He was pondering why the queen would choose this option instead of just resigning before she got married, when the door opened. The queen's personal guardian stood there, motioning for the savant to enter.

Taking a deep breath, Savant Bertram nodded and stepped into the queen's room.

⊱❋⊰

"And what do you make of all this?" Queen Eliana asked.

"Pardon me, Your Highness?" Bertram had just told the queen everything he had seen and heard in the recent court where Governor Elric had been arrested for plotting against the throne.

"What is your opinion of how King Daimh handled the situation?"

The savant fought the urge to chew on one of his fingernails. "I'm not sure I'm the one to be asking. There were more experienced savants and magistrates in attendance."

Folding her hands in her lap, the queen said, "Yes, that is true, but I'm asking *your* opinion." Then she smiled at Bertram. He knew the smile was probably to help him feel more comfortable, but in reality, it made him more nervous. Not only was she the queen, but she was also stunningly beautiful. Attractive women always made him uneasy.

He pondered the situation for a moment. Was she checking up on the king? It wasn't a big secret that the queen and king's marriage was strictly a formality. Arranged marriages were something Bertram had wondered about as he studied the history of the kingdom. Why had the authors decided to include this in the Tome of Laws? He had some ideas, but there seemed to be a piece of the puzzle missing. He had always been good with puzzles, but at the moment, he was struggling to figure out why the queen had brought him here. Unable to form a response based on what he thought the queen wanted to know, he decided to be as truthful and frank as possible. He brought his chin up, trying to gain strength from the posture.

"Actually, King Daimh had very little to do with any of the decisions that were made. He just sat there and smiled at the crowd, only speaking to back up something his father said. Councilor Abrecan did most of the talking."

Queen Eliana narrowed her eyes. "I see. Do you feel Councilor Abrecan made the correct decisions?"

Bertram took a moment before answering. "To be honest, I felt like he took some liberties. Nothing he did or said was strictly against any laws, but they could be interpreted different ways."

Queen Eliana and Guardian Rinan exchanged a meaningful glance after his response. Turning back to Bertram, Queen Eliana prompted him to continue.

"For example, Captain Wayte technically didn't break any laws. True, he was in charge during the attack, but nothing he did, from all the reports that were given, was illegal. It almost seemed as though Councilor Abrecan got him to resign out of frustration."

"And?" The queen motioned for the savant to keep going.

"Well, the situation with Governor Elric was a bit odd. Anyone suspected of a crime can be detained until it's sorted out. However, just because the attack happened in Lewyol and the attackers wore the district's colors doesn't mean Governor Elric had anything to do with it. But Councilor Abrecan was quite adamant that the governor was to blame. He is even sending Magistrate Caldre to Lewyol to investigate."

"And what was Councilor Abrecan's explanation of why he put Governor Eadward in charge of Lewyol, as well as Erd?" the queen asked.

Bertram frowned as he thought back. "He didn't really say—just that Governor Eadward would be watching over the district of Lewyol from now on."

The queen smiled warmly at him again. "You've been very helpful. I have just one more question for you. According to your studies of the Tome of Laws, if the king and queen disagree, which of them has the final say?"

Bertram brought his hand to his mouth and chewed on the nail of his pinky finger as he thought, this time unable to help himself. "It hasn't happened much, to my knowledge. But the Tome of Laws is pretty clear that the birth heir maintains the controlling vote. Since you are the daughter of the former king and queen, that means you would, Your Highness."

Queen Eliana stood. "That's what I thought. Thank you so much for coming, Savant Bertram. You've been most helpful."

⋆✦⋆

"I can't believe Governor Elric had anything to do with this," Eliana said after Bertram had left the room.

"Why do you think that?" Rinan asked, taking the seat just vacated by the savant. He admired how well his wife was handling the situation, despite her recent loss. Eliana had agreed to let Daimh hold court because she hadn't expected anything more than formal reports to be issued, and the pain was still too fresh to hear a retelling of how her father and grandfather had been murdered. She certainly hadn't expected any action to be taken. Had she known, she would have attended herself, despite whatever pain it would have caused.

Eliana shook her head. "I've known Governor Elric since I was a young child. He's like an uncle to me. He and my father were very close friends. I don't believe he would be capable of such actions. Abrecan, however..." Her voice trailed off and she shook her head.

"Are you suggesting that Abrecan plotted to kill your father?" Rinan asked, an edge in his voice.

"Don't tell me you haven't thought the same thing," Eliana said.

Rinan balled up his fists. "I've thought over a lot of possibilities. And yes, I have considered Abrecan's role in all this. It just makes me so angry. I don't know how you can be calm when I feel like I want to jump out of my skin."

Eliana leaned over, then opened Rinan's fists and held his hands. "I know. You're a man of action. You've demonstrated that before. However, we must be careful. Abrecan is working within the law, and any action we take could end up doing more harm than good. We need to handle this with words, not swords. Growing up in the castle, I've learned that words can be as powerful as any sword."

Rinan exhaled deeply. "Fine. I will try to be calm. What do you plan on doing next?"

Eliana grimaced. "I'm going to show Abrecan just how sharp words can be."

⇥✦⇤

The following morning, the residents of the castle awoke to a blizzard. The howling winds created moans and unearthly sounds throughout the castle. Snow drifts several feet high were found in the courtyard, inspiring everyone to stay indoors as much as possible. Inside the main hall, a cold draft of air could be felt, despite the roaring fires in the room's several hearths.

"Thank you all for coming, although it seems the weather gives you few options for travel today," Eliana began.

The setup was the same as for the previous day's court, with the exception of Eliana's attendance. She sat up straight in her throne, dressed in a warm but regal gown.

"Thank you for allowing me an extra day of mourning," she said graciously. "Court will now continue."

Abrecan coughed into his hand. "Pardon me, Your Highness, but until we conclude the investigation, there is no more to discuss. You need not worry about the unpleasant details—the men are taking care of it."

Eliana's response matched the chill in the air. "Councilor Abrecan, it was *my* father and grandfather who were killed in the attack. I have a vested interest in the subject at hand. In addition, I am the queen, and it is my responsibility to preside over court when it is held."

"Be that as it may," Abrecan said, "there isn't anything to discuss. We've taken care of everything that can be done to this point."

"Including throwing Governor Elric in the dungeon?"

"The attacks happened in Lewyol. Elric is responsible for that district, and he is being held, yes."

Addressing the rest of the members in the hall, Eliana said, "And the king and queen are responsible for what happens in Bariwon. Since the attacks happened in Bariwon, does that mean we should be thrown into the dungeon as well?"

"Don't be absurd," Abrecan scoffed.

"Then why is Governor Elric in the dungeon?"

Speaking in a voice one would use while talking to a small child, Abrecan said, "Your Highness, evidence points to the governor's involvement. I believe it is best to keep him detained until we can prove he is guilty. The king agrees with me, so the matter is settled."

For a moment, Eliana didn't respond. She looked around the hall, judging the reaction of those in attendance. Several in the audience avoided her gaze, while others looked at her with anticipation.

Eliana motioned toward the Hierarchy of Magistrates. In a firm, unwavering voice, she said, "Magistrate Seanan, please see that Governor Elric is removed from the dungeon. Take him to a room in the castle and keep him guarded, but make sure he is fed and kept warm. In addition, please find Captain Wayte and beg him to return. Offer our apologies. We'll need his help to find out who was behind the attacks."

"What?" Abrecan bellowed. "There is no need! I'm already sending Magistrate Caldre to look into the matter. Wayte has resigned! You can't do that!"

Giving him a hard stare, Eliana said, "I believe I just did, *Councilor* Abrecan."

"Your Highness, you are obviously still not thinking straight. It is understandable, due to recent events. But the decisions have already been made with the king's approval," Abrecan countered.

Eliana refused to back down. "According to the Tome of Laws, the heir to the throne has the final say when there are disagreements. I have taken your opinion under advisement, and I disagree with it. Now that we've established that point, I do not expect to have to remind you in the future. Is that clear?"

"But—"

"Councilor Abrecan, is that clear?" Eliana asked, her voice as loud and strong as it had been all day.

Abrecan's response was to fold his arms, scowl, and give an almost imperceptible nod.

❖

Caldre tightened the knot on his ponytail, pulling his raven black hair tight against his head. There wasn't anything wrong with the ponytail before, but Caldre found himself fiddling with it when he was anxious.

He had worked for Abrecan for many years, and during that time, he had seen the former governor get angry, but today was different. Today Abrecan was humiliated, not only by a woman, but in front of a large crowd of important people. In the past, Abrecan had shouted and acted out physically. The quiet and cold manner Caldre saw now was something new, and he wasn't sure how to react to it.

They had been sitting in silence for the past several minutes. Caldre had come to the councilor's room as he did every night, to discuss the day's events and to plan for the future. Tonight when Caldre was ushered in, Abrecan hadn't said anything. He merely sat at the room's only table, folded his arms, and stared off into nothingness.

Caldre began several times to speak, but the words caught in his throat. He didn't want to further anger the man sitting across from him, so he sat and waited.

"It's unfortunate, really," Abrecan said, finally breaking the silence.

Caldre jumped a bit when the councilor spoke, and hoped he hadn't noticed. "What's unfortunate?"

Abrecan turned his head and looked Caldre in the eyes, though the faraway look remained. "She's really quite lovely. It will be a shame to have her killed after she gives birth to my grandchild." Abrecan sighed in what seemed to be frustration. "However, we need to proceed carefully. The queen will be very careful after the attacks on her family. She doesn't go anywhere without her personal guardian." Abrecan stared off into space again. "You should have seen Guardian Rinan during the attack. He's quite formidable. While he's around, it will be hard to get to the queen."

"So we need to remove Rinan from the picture," Caldre said.

"And there is more." Abrecan's voice was still distant. "My son was an embarrassment today. He just sat there during court, not saying anything. It made him look weak. When he looks weak, *I* look weak. We need to show the people he is someone to be feared."

Caldre thought for a moment. Various plots popped into his mind only to be dismissed after a flaw was discovered. He needed to get rid of Rinan while at the same time making the king look strong—and he had to do it without the action being traced back to Abrecan. But how?

A moment of inspiration struck and Caldre's eyes lit up. "I have an idea."

CHAPTER 8

Vashti knelt on the floor, hemming a new gown for Eliana, who did her best to hold still. The silver needle slid unexpectedly through the fabric, pricking Vashti's finger. "Ouch!" the seamstress exclaimed.

Looking back over her shoulder, Eliana asked, "Are you all right, Vashti?"

The elderly lady wrapped her finger in some spare fabric that was close by. "Oh, yes, yes. No need to worry about old Vashti, Your Highness. It seems my age is starting to catch up to me. It's been a long while since I've pricked myself. I'll be fine. Let's finish up here."

"If you're sure…"

"Yes, yes. I'm fine. Let's change the subject. Have you heard from Captain Wayte yet?" Vashti asked, returning to the hem.

Eliana looked out the window. A recent blizzard had stopped and moved on, and in its place the sun shone down on the white-covered kingdom. "Not yet. As you know, it took us a while to find him once he left. He's been in Lewyol for nearly two months. I was happy he agreed to come back. I believe he returned primarily to conduct the investigation. If anyone can find out who killed my family, it will be him."

Vashti clucked in agreement. "Yes, yes, he's a good man. Have you and your husband come up with names for the child yet?"

Before she caught herself, Eliana almost said that Rinan wasn't sure about a name. Even after all these months, she struggled when people referred to Daimh as her husband. "To be honest, I've not seen much of the king, or his father, for that matter, for a couple of months, although I have heard they are planning to attend the upcoming sparring contest."

"Yes, yes, they will be there. Of that I'm sure."

"Oh, and how do you know?"

Vashti laughed lightly. "I promised to keep it a secret, Your Highness. The king has a surprise for you."

"Hmm. I'm not sure I'm in the mood for surprises." Eliana smoothed out her dress in front of her. "I'm a bit nervous about having a sparring contest after the tragedy, but word has it that several guardians have requested that we start them back up. I understand the people's need for distraction and desire to return to familiar events, but I'd feel better if Captain Wayte was back with his findings first."

"Oh, I think you'll see it is the right choice. But remember, I promised to keep it a secret." Vashti stood up. Turning the queen around, she admired her work. "Yes, yes. That's better. It looks like I need to get to work on making some more dresses for you. The baby is getting so big now. Where has the time gone? It's almost hard to believe in a month we'll have a new prince or princess."

⋆⋕⋆

The hall was filled to bursting for the sparring contest. It was customary for a member of the royalty to select the contestants. Usually, the victor from the previous week was chosen to battle against a new contender. At times, the victor was on assignment, so the king or queen would decide who would get the honor of competing. Queen Eliana had made the opening remarks to the crowd and was about to announce the contestants when the king interrupted her.

In a loud, powerful voice, Daimh addressed the crowd. "This is the first sparring contest held since the tragedy that fell upon Bariwon. To show you all that the kingdom is in good hands, I am going to participate. It will be an honor for you to witness such an event."

Before Eliana could respond, the crowd roared enthusiastically. Normally, only royal guardians sparred in the contest, although there had been the rare occasion when a visitor, like a governor or one of the guardians assigned to the various districts, participated.

King Daimh smiled. "I take it you all approve." Another cheer came in response.

Taking off his fur-lined cape, Daimh revealed that he had dressed for the occasion. Although his clothing was similar in style to what guardians wore on days of the sparring contest, it had been trimmed with silver and crimson embroidery down the sleeves. Eliana noticed the trim was Vashti's work. It was obvious Daimh had been planning on competing for a while—long enough to commission the work from the seamstress.

After walking to the center of the combat area, the king stopped, turned to the crowd, and said, "In addition, I am going to allow you to choose my opponent. Suggestions?"

The crowd erupted, with people shouting names to the king. After cupping a hand to one ear dramatically, Daimh said, "Ah, I hear Royal Guardian Rinan's name quite a bit. Then Rinan it shall be."

The room had been abuzz with excitement before, but this statement added fuel to an already blazing fire. Rinan had never been defeated in these weekly contests—and he had been a favorite of the crowd.

Eliana wanted to protest but knew if she did, it would hurt all that she had done in the last few days to raise the spirits of her people. Instead, she turned to Rinan, who was already preparing himself. She noticed his gray eyes were filled with determination. Before he could head down the stairs of the dais, Eliana grabbed his arm.

She whispered, "Rinan, be careful. I'm not sure what they're up to, but it can't be good."

Not taking his eyes off Daimh, Rinan replied in a low voice that only she could hear. "Don't worry. I won't hurt him…well, maybe a little."

❖❖❖

Rinan was in trouble, and he knew it.

There was a saying in Lebu about situations where any option led to an undesired result: "Sometimes when climbing a tall tree to escape a bear, you can find yourself stuck with no way down."

When he first heard his name selected to compete against the king, he felt a swell of energy. He wanted very much to knock the smugness off Daimh's face. But in grabbing the wooden broadsword that was used in sparring, he remembered the lesson Eliana had taught him the night he confronted Daimh. Although he wanted very much to take out his frustrations on the king, he knew he had to be careful. Abrecan had obviously planned this out, although Rinan wasn't sure to what end.

His mind raced as he took his place on the floor. If he won, how would Abrecan twist it to his advantage? Perhaps the councilor could say that Rinan wasn't respectful or had hurt the king enough that he should be removed as a guardian. But if he lost, Abrecan might claim Rinan was too weak and shouldn't be protecting the queen. Unsure which way to proceed, Rinan figured he'd best turn his full attention to the tall man standing in front of him, who at the moment seemed very bear-like.

"Begin!" Eliana commanded.

Daimh raised his sword and took three purposeful steps forward, swinging at Rinan. In defense, Rinan parried the cut, but the sheer force of the blow nearly knocked him off his feet. Instead, he took a step back, giving up ground to keep his balance.

The king kept advancing, with Rinan doing his best to fend off the blows. For the first few moments, he was completely on the defensive. He knew Daimh was strong and had studied swordplay for much of his life.

After a few more blows, Rinan realized that the king wasn't treating the situation as only a sparring contest. Daimh kept taking swipes at Rinan's head and midsection rather than attempting to take advantage when he was off balance. One exchange of blows brought the two combatants close together. In a low voice, Rinan said, "Your Majesty, the object is to knock your opponent off his feet."

With a feral grin, Daimh said, "If you're unconscious, you'll be off your feet." He shoved Rinan hard in the chest.

The shove pushed Rinan several feet away. The king angled his sword low and moved forward while starting an upward swing. Rinan's memory sparked from when Eadward had used a similar tactic. He maneuvered his sword to parry the blow so both swords were above their heads. The parry worked, and Rinan found himself in the position he wanted. Pivoting his hips, he brought up a leg and kicked Daimh as hard as he could in the stomach.

The effect was not what Rinan had hoped or expected. The sensation was much like kicking a stone wall. Stunned by the result, his attention lapsed long enough for Daimh to twist his wrists and wrench the sword out of Rinan's grasp.

The large wooden sword clattered to the ground by Daimh's feet. Kicking the sword across the floor out of Rinan's reach, Daimh shouted, "Yield now!"

Rinan took a few steps back. "No, I don't think I will."

Turning to the crowd, Daimh shouted, "This is the man who is supposed to protect your queen! He lacks the judgment to know when he is beaten. Do you feel she is safe while in his care?"

While the king's attention was diverted, Rinan ran to the closest wall. The crowd parted, allowing him in. He jumped up and removed one of the banners that lined the hall. Next, he unlatched the cloth that displayed the standard of Bariwon and handed it to a spectator, then walked back to the combat area carrying an eight-foot staff of solid wood.

Daimh turned to face Rinan. "What do you think you are doing?"

Rinan held the staff in front of him. "I'm finishing this contest."

Grabbing the hilt of his sword with both hands, Daimh laughed and started toward Rinan. Instead of trying to stop the blows the king offered, Rinan batted them away. Using the longer reach of the staff, he counterattacked by smacking Daimh across the shins and back.

Daimh's attacks became more furious, making them easier for Rinan to counter—and offering more openings to exploit. After a particularly wild swing, Rinan cracked Daimh across the hands, causing him to drop his sword. Using the end of the staff, Rinan pushed the sword out of Daimh's reach.

Watching Daimh nurse his hands, Rinan asked, "Do you yield?"

The king responded with a growl, then charged Rinan. The guardian side-stepped and ducked under the lunge, tripping Daimh with the staff as he passed. The king's balance was compromised and he sprawled forward. Rinan stood and spun, and swinging the staff as hard as he could, spanked the king across his backside. The blow was enough to cause Daimh to fall flat on his face.

He moved to stand up when Eliana declared, "Enough! The contest is complete!"

Daimh turned and glared at her, then pointed to Rinan and roared, "He cheated!"

"Royal Guardian Rinan came up with another way to win the fight, one which didn't violate the rules, which is why he is the perfect man to be my personal guardian," Eliana said not only to Daimh, but to the rest of the crowd as well.

Councilor Abrecan moved down to where his son stood. Gesturing to Rinan, he said, "You've made a mockery out of this contest." Then Abrecan took his son by the arm and stormed out of the hall.

◈

Rinan rotated his arm, trying to ease some of the pain in his shoulder.

"Are you sure you will be all right?" Eliana asked.

He nodded. "Yes, I'll be fine. One thing about Daimh—he's very strong."

"Let's get you back to our room and have Anemone take a look at it anyway, just to be safe."

Rinan agreed, and the young couple headed for the staircase that led to the third floor. Upon reaching it, they both noticed Abrecan standing at the top, with his arms folded and a scowl on his face.

Ascending the stairs, Eliana asked, "Is something the matter, Councilor?"

Abrecan pointed at Rinan. "I want him removed from the castle."

"Oh?" Eliana said, her voice strong. "And why is that?"

"The king's reputation was quite damaged by today's events," Abrecan said, staring hard at Eliana. "The king is very sensitive about how he is perceived by the people. Removing Rinan will go a long way in repairing Daimh's image."

"And on what grounds would you have my personal guardian removed?" Eliana continued to climb with Rinan behind her.

"On what grounds?" Abrecan threw his arms up in disgust. "How can you even ask that? After what he did today to the king, I should have him thrown in the dungeon. I'll settle for just having him resign."

Reaching the top of the stairs, Eliana said firmly, "Councilor Abrecan, Rinan did nothing against the rules. I confirmed this with the Hierarchy of Magistrates after the contest. No one forced Daimh to compete—he said it was his idea. I'm sorry your son was embarrassed, but that isn't grounds to have a guardian removed."

"Then what do you suggest we do to restore the king's reputation?"

A smile played across Eliana's face. "Well, for starters, I wouldn't let Daimh compete against Rinan again."

❖

"The Rabid Dog," read the large sign over the door. To emphasize the point, the sign also depicted a dog's face with a foaming mouth. "Lovely," Captain Wayte muttered.

He dusted off his shoulders where the lightly falling snow had gathered before he entered the inn. It wasn't the largest he'd visited during his investigation over the last few months, but the common room was bigger than most, with staircases on either side that led to second-story rooms.

An unkempt innkeeper stood at the bar, using a soiled rag to wipe down a spot-stained mug. Wayte wondered if the man wasn't actually making the mug dirtier. Flashing a grin of rotted teeth, the man asked, "Gitcha drink, Captain?"

"I am fine, but thank you for offering. I would, however, like to ask you a few questions." Wayte walked to the bar and took a seat.

The innkeeper grunted. "Yeah, fine. Whatcha need?"

Glancing around, Wayte noticed the room was fairly empty. A hunchbacked barmaid was sweeping the wooden floor, and in the corner sat a man in a grungy cloak with his head resting on a table, snoring softly. "Do you remember if a fairly large group of men stayed here a few months ago?" Wayte asked.

The innkeeper put down the mug he had been drying and grabbed another. "Kinda hard to miss 'em. A dozen or so men, very rowdy, demandin', and poor tippers."

Wayte nodded. "And do you recall why they were staying at the inn?"

"Didn't say." The innkeeper paused to blow his nose with the soiled rag, and then continued wiping the mug. "Jist come in one day, gave us a buncha trouble, and then left in the middle 'o the night. Weird thing is, they's ain't never come back, even though their stuffs was still here."

"Ah, do you mind if I were to look at what was left behind?" Wayte asked.

"Bah! Don'tcha understand plain speakin'? I says their stuffs *was* here. When they's didn't come back, I sold their stuffs. They'd never did pay for the rooms, so I don't feels bad sellin'. It was mainly junk, nothin' special."

Wayte drummed his fingers on the bar. "Hmm. Was there anything out of the ordinary about the men?"

"Well, they's was boastin' about 'ow Govern'r Elric wuz gonna make 'em rich, but I never did hear whys. Oh! And they's asked if they's could clean the fireplace. I told 'em I wouldn't pay 'em to do it, but they's did it anyways."

Captain Wayte stood. "Thank you again for your time. You have been most helpful. If you remember anything else, please let one of the local guardians know, and they will get word to me."

As Captain Wayte left the room, he heard the innkeeper mumble, "Another poor tipper."

Magistrate Caldre opened the door behind the bar, walked over, and dropped a sack of coins on the counter in front of the innkeeper.

"You did excellently," Caldre said. "Remember, if anyone else comes back to ask about the men, tell them the same story."

"Not hard to remember. Was all true, 'cept the parts 'bout Govern'r Elric. I thinks they's says it was Govern'r Abrecan."

Caldre shook his head. "No, you must be mistaken. I suggest you remember it as Governor Elric, like I told you. Is that clear?"

The innkeeper simply nodded, then lifted the rag and blew his nose again.

—※—

"It was just as you suspected," said Royal Guardian Dougal, taking off the grungy cloak he had been wearing. "Caldre was there and bribing the innkeeper, who overheard the men saying Governor Abrecan was going to make them rich."

Balling his fist and pounding it against the wall, Wayte said, "I knew it. That is the proof we need."

Dougal looked out the window of the inn where Wayte was staying. "I would have been back sooner, but I didn't want to risk suspicion."

Wayte patted him on the shoulder. "No, you did fine. Did anyone follow you here?"

"Not a chance. I worked my way through three inns before I came here. At the last one, I snuck through a back door. If I was being followed, they should believe I am still among the crowd in that common room."

"Very good. We will let Caldre believe he has fooled us. That way, he will not harm the innkeeper—we need him alive to testify." Wayte motioned to his riding outfit that was laid out on the bed. "Get dressed in my clothes and make it fairly obvious that you are headed back to the castle. If you keep your face hidden and wear my gloves to hide your darker skin, they should believe you are me. When you get back to the castle, find Rinan and tell him what we discovered. Do not tell anyone else—I am not sure who else we can trust."

"And what are you going to do?" Dougal asked, sitting down and taking off his boots.

Wayte blew out a deep breath. "I am going to make sure Caldre leaves. Once he does, I am going to visit the innkeeper again, but this time, with an invitation to the castle he cannot refuse."

CHAPTER 9

Eliana woke to a distant tapping. Opening her eyes, she looked around the room, noting it was still dark outside. Next to her, Rinan stirred but then rolled over, swinging one arm over her. She sighed in frustration. Eight months into her pregnancy, she had trouble enough getting comfortable, and it seemed even the smallest of noises kept her from sleeping. She tried taking several deep breaths to relax, but then heard the tapping again.

"Hmm...what?" Rinan mumbled.

"You heard it too?"

He sat up in bed and reached over to the side, where his sword was propped against the wall. "Yes, but I'm not sure what it was," he said groggily. "I'll check it out."

Eliana held on to his arm. "Wait a moment. Let's see if we hear it again."

The young couple remained still and listened quietly. For several moments, they strained to hear more tapping, but all was quiet—they could only hear each other breathing.

The silence stretched out until Eliana said, "Perhaps you should go take a look."

"Sure, I'll be right..."

A firm knock on the door caused them both to jump. After Eliana realized the knock had come from the door to Anemone's room, she exhaled the breath she had been involuntarily holding.

Rinan picked up his sword and walked over to the door. Unlatching the lock, he opened the door a crack. "Yes, Anemone?"

"Are you two going to sleep all day? I thought you'd be up by now," the nursemaid said.

"What do you mean? It's still dark outside." Rinan opened the door farther, and Anemone walked into the room and over to the window.

She opened the curtains and revealed a sky of heavily swollen clouds that almost completely hid the light of the sun. "Believe it or not, it *is* morning. It appears a storm blew in last night and seems to be content with hanging over the castle."

Rinan followed Anemone to the window and looked out. "I don't think I've ever seen a storm like this. The clouds are so dark and thick—they almost appear hostile."

"Well, storm or not, the queen needs to have her breakfast." Anemone walked over to Eliana's wardrobe and opened the doors. "It's my understanding that the king and his father are already at the table, awaiting you."

Eliana swung her legs over the edge of the bed and sat up. "Now that is odd. I don't recall Daimh or Abrecan ever joining us for breakfast before."

Assembling the queen's outfit, the nursemaid said, "That's because they haven't."

Rinan frowned. "I don't like it when they surprise us. It usually means they're up to something."

The tapping sounded again as Eliana stood. "Anemone, do you know what's making that noise?"

"Yes, they are hanging the new tapestries."

Rinan and Eliana looked questioningly at Anemone. "What new tapestries?" they asked at the same time.

⋅⟩╬⟨⋅

Councilor Abrecan sat majestically on a horse, his chin tilted up and shoulders squared. One hand had a tight grip on the reins while the other held a sword covered in blood.

"Unbelievable," Rinan muttered, standing in front of the newly hung tapestry that depicted the scene. "Isn't this where 'Rain and Sunshine' used to be?"

"Yes," Eliana said, her voice somewhat distant. "It was here."

Bending down, Rinan read the plaque under the silver-and-crimson trimmed tapestry. "It reads, 'Councilor Abrecan saves the life of King Daimh.'" Rinan straightened and looked up and down the hallway. "Funny, I don't see a tapestry of what actually happened."

Two servants farther down the hall were hanging another tapestry. The one they had removed had been dumped unceremoniously on the floor. The taller and thicker of the servants stood on a stool with a hammer in his hand, pounding on a large iron spike sticking out of the wall.

Eliana crossed the distance purposefully, with Rinan right behind her. The second servant, a balding, stout little man, saw them approaching and tugged on the pant leg of his partner.

The servant with the hammer stepped off the stool and bowed. "Good morning, Your Highness."

Even though she was upset, Eliana managed a warm smile. "Good morning, Gilroy and Blaine. May I ask who instructed you to hang these new tapestries?"

The two servants glanced nervously at each other. "We got our orders from Councilor Abrecan, Your Highness," Gilroy said, fidgeting with the hammer. "He wanted new spikes put in for them."

Eliana moved in front of the tapestry, with Rinan following to stand a little behind her. The scene depicted Daimh standing in a battlefield, surrounded by bodies. The king held a large, ornate sword with a gem-inlaid hilt. The title read, "King Daimh, Master Swordsman."

"I see," the queen said. "And did Councilor Abrecan specify which tapestries to remove?"

"Yes, he was quite clear as to which ones to take down," Blaine answered.

Motioning to the ground, Eliana said, "This tapestry depicts the authors of the Tome of Laws. They are more important to Bariwon than any one particular king or queen. It was placed here at the top of the stairs to be a prominent reminder of what these wise men did for all of us. I want you to put it back."

Bowing again, both servants responded with "Yes, Your Highness."

Eliana exhaled deeply and turned to head down the stairs.

"Rinan!" someone shouted from down the hallway.

Both Rinan and Eliana stopped and saw Royal Guardian Dougal jogging toward them, gesturing for Rinan to wait. Rinan walked back to meet up with his fellow guardian, leaving Eliana to wait for him at the top of the stairs. At the same time, the servants had grabbed the tapestry that depicted King Daimh and were pulling on it to take it down. They were stopped when one of the hanging loops got stuck on a spike.

"Dougal, why are you wearing Captain Wayte's uniform?" Rinan asked, eyeing his fellow guardian from head to toe.

"It's a long story," Dougal said, somewhat out of breath. "I just got back. I have important news for you from the captain."

Gilroy stood on the stool to free the tapestry. Blaine yanked hard just as it was freed from the spike, causing Gilroy to topple backward off the stool. The sound caught Rinan's attention, and he turned just as Gilroy crashed into Eliana, making her lose her balance. She reached out to grab the banister, but missed and tumbled down the stairs. Her head and back repeatedly hit hard against the stone before she came to a rest at the bottom of the stairs, her body contorted awkwardly.

Rinan all but flew down the stairs after her, Dougal close behind. Kneeling beside his fallen wife, Rinan lifted her head gently. She was breathing, but unconscious.

"Get Anemone—and hurry!" he told Dougal.

⋆⁂⋆

"Pick her up carefully and get her to a bedroom," Anemone instructed, her heart racing. Gilroy and Blaine went to lift the queen, but Rinan stopped them. "No, we'll take her," he said, motioning to Dougal to help him.

Anemone addressed the crestfallen servants. "Go get Priest Sherwyn. Tell him to come here quickly."

The two guardians lifted Eliana gently and carried her broken form to a bedroom just down the hall from the end of the stairs. She was still unconscious, and her breathing was becoming shallow. Anemone instructed them to place her on the bed.

"Dougal, stand outside and don't let anyone in except Sherwyn," the nursemaid said firmly. "I don't need to be distracted by any of the nobles."

Rinan stood next to the bed, holding his wife's hand, and looking toward Anemone for guidance. For the next few moments, she examined Eliana. She felt the queen's head and grimaced at what she discovered. "I won't lie to you, Rinan," Anemone said. "She is hurt very badly. I'm not sure there is anything that can be done."

"There must be something…" Rinan said, his eyes pleading.

The door opened and Priest Sherwyn stepped in, closing the door behind him. "Oh, dear," he said as he saw Eliana on the bed.

⋆⁂⋆

Dougal stood outside the door, stoically looking over the crowd that had gathered in the hallway.

"I'm sorry, but Nursemaid Anemone made it clear that no one else was to enter," he said to Councilor Abrecan, who had arrived right after Priest Sherwyn. Abrecan was flanked by King Daimh and Magistrate Caldre, the latter looking rather tired and disheveled.

"Ridiculous. We need to know what's happening. Is my grandchild all right?" Abrecan blustered.

Dougal matched Abrecan's stare. "Your concern for the *queen* is touching, Councilor. I'm sure Anemone will give us information when she can. Right now, she doesn't need any distractions."

Caldre stepped forward. Tilting his head to one side, he looked Dougal over. "Royal Guardian Dougal, why are you wearing Captain Wayte's uniform?"

The guardian felt the blood drain from his face. When he regained his composure, he said, "Now is not the time, Magistrate."

"You realize there is a law against impersonating a higher-ranking guardian, correct?" Caldre folded his arms and sneered.

Standing up straighter, Dougal said, "I am not at liberty to discuss this subject at the moment. When Captain Wayte returns, he will explain."

Caldre's eyes lit up with understanding. He nodded and motioned for Abrecan to follow him away from the crowd. Dougal saw Caldre talking to the councilor and motioning adamantly with his hands. Abrecan turned to look at Dougal and glared.

Abrecan and Caldre walked down the hall and out of sight. In the meantime, the group of nobles and servants that had gathered was consoling the king. He, in return, was assuring them that even if something happened to the queen, the kingdom was in good hands. To Dougal, it seemed the king was feasting on the attention.

Dougal thought he heard crying from behind the thick oak door he guarded, but the sound of the people surrounding him was loud enough that he couldn't be sure. After several moments, everyone's attention turned to see Councilor Abrecan walking back to the area with Caldre and a couple of guardians in tow.

The crowd parted to allow them in. Abrecan pointed to Dougal and said, "Guardians, take him to the dungeon for impersonating Captain Wayte. Make sure he speaks to no one." Dougal noted that the two guardians with Abrecan were both from Erd. He started to say something, but Abrecan interrupted him. "Not a word!"

The guardians took Dougal by the arms and forced him away from the door.

"Now, let's see what is going on," Abrecan said, reaching for the door.

Before he touched the handle, the door swung open and Priest Sherwyn came out. His eyes were red and puffy and his shoulders slumped. "I'm sorry to announce that Queen Eliana and her unborn child are dead."

❧❦❧

"Remember me?" Captain Wayte asked.

The innkeeper looked up from the tip jar and eyed him. "Ya, wuz only yesterday. Kinda hard to forgit when the capt'n o' the guardians comes a visitin'."

"I guess that is true," Wayte said. "And speaking of the truth, I would like to ask you if you remember anything differently from when we last spoke."

Wayte sat down at the bar. In the morning hours, there were several patrons sitting at the tables to eat breakfasts the hunchbacked barmaid was serving. No one else was sitting at the bar, but at that time of the day, the captain mused that most of the regulars were still sleeping off the effects of the night before.

The innkeeper paused for a moment, then picked up the tip jar and put it in front of Wayte. "Maybes I remember somethin', and maybes not."

Looking down at the ceramic jar that held a dozen or so coins, Wayte nodded. Then, in a quick motion, he stood and grabbed the back of the innkeeper's head and slammed it against the bar, causing the tip jar to fall to the floor. It shattered and spilled its contents, much to the joy of the people in the common room, who moved to snatch the coins.

Wayte leaned over the bar. Grabbing the innkeeper's arm and twisting it behind his back, Wayte said in a menacing voice, "Here is your tip— unless you want to spend the rest of your life playing bartender to rats in the castle dungeon, you will tell me who was actually behind the attacks on the royal family."

❧❦❧

Something was wrong. Wayte could not quite put his finger on it, but something was definitely not right. Riding down the street to the castle gates, leading the bound and gagged innkeeper on a horse behind him, Wayte puzzled on why he felt uneasy. Even though the streets were generally quiet during the evening hours, it was quieter than normal. The only sound was the snow crunching under the hoofs of the horses. Come to think of it, Wayte didn't recall seeing anyone since he had entered the town that surrounded the castle.

As he approached the castle gates, Wayte was stopped by several guardians. They were dressed in armor trimmed in crimson and silver, with the symbol of Erd on their breastplates. Wayte recognized the man standing in front as Sullivan, a guardian Wayte himself had defeated in the Mortentaun years ago, earning Wayte the right to be a royal guardian and sending Sullivan back to Erd as a guardian for that district.

"Hail," Wayte said. "Where are the guardians I assigned to watch the gate?"

Sullivan spoke up, his dark eyes glaring. "They've been called to other duties. Councilor Abrecan told me and my men to watch the gates tonight." The guard's gravelly voice matched the scars and pockmarks on his face.

Wayte frowned. "What other duties were they called to do?"

"Can't say. However, we've been told to bring you to Councilor Abrecan when you arrived."

The other three guardians lowered their hands to their weapons.

Looking down at them from his mount, Wayte said, "Yes. I am sure Abrecan is anxious to see me. However, he will have to wait until I have spoken to the queen."

"That's not gonna happen," Sullivan said. "I guess you've not heard that the queen died this morning."

A shiver ran up Wayte's spine. Had he heard correctly? "What? No… How?"

Stepping forward, Sullivan ignored Wayte's question. "So as I said, you are to come with us, Captain. We'll take care of your prisoner."

Wayte pushed back the grief he was feeling for Eliana. He had more immediate issues at the moment. He sat up straight in the saddle and addressed the men in front of him. "You are guardians of Bariwon, but you are not royal guardians. You hold no authority here. I decline your invitation to meet with Abrecan. However, you can inform him that I will be addressing him soon enough."

The four men backed away slowly. Sullivan said, "I was told you would probably say something like that. Have it your way." With that, he lifted one hand and motioned.

Archers who had positioned themselves above the gate on the castle walls let their arrows fly. Neither Wayte nor the innkeeper had time to react before they were peppered with arrows.

�⋅✦⋅

"Nadia, you never cease to amaze me." Kelvin rubbed the stubble on his chin. "Just when I thought you could not cook a more perfect supper, you find a way."

Removing the empty plate from in front of her husband, Nadia looked at him with smiling gray eyes. "And you, my love, only compliment me when you want something."

Kelvin feigned a hurt look. "Are you suggesting I can't give my wife an honest compliment without expecting something in return?"

"I'm not suggesting it, I'm telling you straight out." Nadia turned her back to him as she finished taking the dishes to the sink.

He stood, walked up behind his wife, and wrapped his arms around her waist. Then he kissed her neck and said in a quiet voice, "You know, since you are already up and in the kitchen, I told the boys at the tavern I'd bring some of your famous tarts to the card game tomorrow."

"I knew it!" She elbowed Kelvin in the ribs, then turned around and mussed his jet-black hair. "Well, I suggest *you* get cooking. All the ingredients you need for the tarts are in the cupboard."

A firm knock on the front door of the log house caught the couple's attention. "Now, who would be visiting us at this hour?" Nadia asked as Kelvin went to the door.

He lifted the latch and opened the door to the last face he had expected to see.

"Rinan!" Nadia ran to the door and ushered him in. He was dressed warmly, with a large backpack hanging from one shoulder and a bundle in his arms.

"Hello, Mother and Father."

"What are you doing home, Son?" Kelvin took the backpack from Rinan after he closed the door.

"It's a long story," Rinan said, his voice echoing the fatigue on his face. Unwrapping the layers of the bundle, he said, "I'd like to introduce you to my son."

"Your son?" Kelvin exclaimed. "How is that possible, Rinan?"

Nadia elbowed past her husband and put her arms out. Rinan let his mother take the child. "Let's not worry about that now," she said. "Let's get you warm and fed."

Rinan sat down heavily on a chair by the table. His father sat next to him, putting a hand on his shoulder. "Rinan, are you all right, Son? You look terrible."

"Father, I…" Rinan started, but he couldn't continue. Instead, he buried his head in his arms on the table and began to cry.

CHAPTER 10

Alana didn't want to be inside. It was finally getting warm again, and she would much rather be outside, but she was stuck sitting in the classroom with her least favorite savant, studying her least favorite subject.

There *were* some subjects Alana liked. She enjoyed learning about flowers and trees. She also liked to learn about the weather. Those were things she could see and feel. Not like this class. Not like studying the Tome of Laws.

Every noble child was instructed to read and study the Tome of Laws from a very early age. In fact, it was the first book Alana had read all the way through—not by choice, of course.

By age nine, she had read it several times, but now they were studying it more in detail. Savant Bertram was nice enough, but he was very quiet and always seemed to be chewing on one of his fingernails.

That day they had been studying about the Shoginoc. Her teacher said it was important because of what had happened recently to Queen Eliana. Alana was sad that her cousin had died last month—she had liked her.

Addressing the class, Bertram said, "Since no heir was born from Queen Eliana and King Daimh's union, can anyone tell me who will be the next to take over the throne, and when?"

There was no reply.

"No one knows?" the savant asked.

Again, there was no reply from the class of young nobles.

"The answer is that twenty-one years from now, there will be another Shoginoc. Until that time, King Daimh will rule Bariwon. Students, you should know that. It's written in the books before you."

Those students who weren't looking elsewhere in the room gave Bertram blank stares.

"Alana, will you please read from chapter eleven, paragraph nineteen?" Bertram asked, sounding mildly frustrated.

Taking her eyes from the golden sunlight shining through the window, Alana looked down at her copy of the Tome of Laws and turned to the correct chapter. Finding the requested paragraph, she started to read: *"When the firstborn child of the king and queen reaches the age of twenty-one, he or she shall become the new king or queen. The former king and queen will become councilors to the newly crowned leader of Bariwon. An arranged marriage will selected by a Shoginoc. In the spirit..."*

Bertram interrupted her. "Wait a moment, Alana. You missed a word when you turned the page. Please try again starting with 'An arranged marriage.'"

Sitting up straighter, Alana started reading again. *"An arranged marriage will selected by a Shoginoc. In the spirit..."*

Bertram stood and walked over to Alana, who stopped reading. "You did it again. Let me show you where you are making the mistake."

The savant looked at her book and flipped the page over and back a few times. "Oh, wait. That's odd." He furrowed his brow and walked over to his desk. He scanned through his book. Alana could hear him say, "That's strange. I've read this passage over and over, and I've never noticed that."

Bertram stood there for a moment and puzzled over his book. He started chewing on a fingernail.

That's really disgusting, Alana thought, and looked back out the window.

⟨⟩

Rinan sized up what was before him, his practiced eye looking for weaknesses. He formulated a plan, tightened his grip, and brought the ax over his head and then quickly down, chopping his target neatly in two.

"Nicely done," Kelvin said. "The log never stood a chance."

Turning his head to look at his father, Rinan asked, "Are you making fun of me, Father?"

Kelvin grinned. "Yes, a little. Ever since you were young, you could never do simple chores around the farm without turning them into some sort of battle or quest. I knew from an early age that you were bound to be a guardian."

Rinan placed another log on the chopping block. "Yeah, and we all know how that turned out."

"Actually, we really don't. Your mother and I have respected your wish to tell us what happened when you were ready, but Son, it's been over a month."

"Well, I'm still not sure I'm ready to talk about it," Rinan said, chopping another log in two. "I've had a month to think about what happened, and I've come to realize I made some pretty big mistakes."

A light drizzle started to fall, the drops gathering on the leaves of the tall trees that stood above the farm.

"People, as a race, seem to be good at making mistakes." Kelvin started to gather up the firewood scattered around the area. "The key is to learn from the mistakes and not repeat them. I've made some pretty big ones in my life, as well."

"Nothing compared to mine, Father." Rinan shook his head.

"Try me."

Rinan placed the head of the ax on the ground and leaned on it for support. "Did you marry someone in private without the consent of her family, father her child, and then fail to protect her when she needed you the most?"

At first Kelvin didn't say anything; he just looked at his son as the rain started to fall harder around them. "No, Son, I can't say that I did."

Rinan set up another log for chopping. "I think it is safe to say those are mistakes I will not repeat."

❖❖❖

Thunder shook the windows of the castle's main hall, and rain pounded heavily against the roof, but the members of the court scarcely noticed.

Priest Sherwyn was in attendance, along with the Hierarchy of Magistrates, the savants, and the heads of the noble families. Even though courts were generally held once a week, this was the first since the queen's death the previous month.

Sherwyn had dreaded this day. He believed he had done all he could to prevent Abrecan from taking power, but he had failed.

Councilor Abrecan sat on the queen's throne, with Daimh next to him on the throne belonging to the king. "It has been a trying several weeks for all of us," Abrecan said once everyone was in place. "My son is stricken with grief, and so I will conduct this court."

It seemed to Priest Sherwyn that Daimh appeared more bored than grieving. "The investigations into the recent tragedies that have plagued my kingdom are complete," Abrecan continued. "Magistrate Caldre, to whom I've assigned these investigations, will report the findings."

The sharp-nosed magistrate stood. He paused a moment, and Sherwyn knew Caldre was making sure all eyes were on him before he started.

"The attacks on the royalty which ended in the deaths of Councilors Kenrik and Philip were indeed ordered by Governor Elric. He was upset over losing the Shoginoc and ordered the attacks as revenge. Elric has been put into the dungeon until we can plan his execution. Governor Eadward of Erd has been given charge to watch over the district of Lewyol."

The reaction in the hall varied from person to person, but Sherwyn thought the underlying reaction was shock. If Caldre noticed, he made no indication and continued with the report.

"The death of Queen Eliana has been ruled an accident, even though there are still some suspicions that one or both of the servants involved may have been working for Elric. To ensure that no more accidents take place in the presence of these servants, they have been banished from the castle."

People in the hall started to move in their seats and glance at each other, as if they wanted to see if they were the only ones who couldn't believe what they were hearing. Sherwyn's eyes met Seanan's, but the elderly magistrate merely gave him a helpless look, then turned away.

Caldre sniffed loudly before he continued. "Captain Wayte was killed in self-defense. Guardian Sullivan had been instructed to escort Wayte to Councilor Abrecan upon his arrival. However, Wayte refused, and when Sullivan insisted, Wayte became hostile. Sullivan had no choice but to defend himself. Guardian Sullivan was not only justified, but because of his brave actions, he is being promoted to captain of the guardians."

Some people were now shaking their heads in disbelief. Caldre took notice and stopped talking.

Councilor Abrecan spoke up. "Is there something any of you want to say?" The tone in his voice was clear that comments were not really what he sought. The room quieted again. "Magistrate, continue."

"Royal Guardian Dougal was found impersonating the captain of the guardians. While this offense is not punishable by death, he will be spending the rest of his life isolated in the dungeon. In addition, Royal Guardian Rinan has abandoned the castle. He seems to have disappeared soon after the queen's death. He is officially being removed as a guardian for his failure to protect the queen. He, too, has been banished from the castle."

Sherwyn noticed Abrecan sit up straighter when Caldre began the next part of the report.

"Finally, no heir was produced from the marriage of King Daimh and Queen Eliana, so another Shoginoc will take place this summer. A new queen will be selected so that an heir can be born."

A quiet voice came from the back row where the savants sat. "Excuse me, but that isn't correct."

Everyone turned to look at Bertram. Sherwyn saw the young savant's shoulders shrink when he noticed all the attention he got.

"What did you say?" Abrecan asked. Even Daimh was paying attention now.

Bertram stood up and said, "You are mistaken. The next Shoginoc will be held in twenty-one years."

Abrecan's face started to turn red. "Who are *you* to tell us that we are mistaken?"

Bertram missed the point of the councilor's question and responded, "I am Bertram, a savant here in the castle. The Tome of Laws clearly states that if no heir is born of the queen and king, a new Shoginoc will take place twenty-one years after the queen or king was crowned."

"But the queen died before the heir could be born!" Abrecan blustered. "And my son has every right to marry again. Therefore, their offspring will be the heir."

Bertram nodded and then said, "Yes, King Daimh is allowed to remarry, but his wife will not be queen, and their firstborn child will not be the heir."

Abrecan gripped the arms of his throne, his crimson face looking like an overripe tomato. "What are you talking about?"

Priest Sherwyn was amazed at Bertram's calm reaction to Abrecan's obvious contempt. The savant was either very brave or just oblivious to the councilor's tone and body language. Knowing what he did of Bertram, Sherwyn assumed it was the latter.

"Two hundred and eighty-four years ago, a similar situation happened, except it was the king who died," Bertram explained. "The queen remarried, but her husband was never called the king. They had five children, but the oldest was not considered heir to the throne. Twenty-one years later, a Shoginoc was held, and the man and his wife who were chosen became the new queen and king."

Magistrate Seanan stood up, looking even frailer than he had at the last court. Sherwyn knew Seanan had been very fond of Eliana and her family, and the aging leader of the magistrates had taken their deaths especially hard.

"Bertram is correct," Seanan said. "I remember the story. One of the authors of the Tome of Laws was still alive at the time, if I recall correctly. They wanted to have another Shoginoc after the king died, but the author said that is not what the law would allow."

Abrecan's glare shifted from Bertram to Seanan. "Why not?"

Magistrate Seanan nodded his head toward Bertram. "The savant can explain it better than I."

"Well?" Abrecan asked.

Bertram looked around the hall, his expression blank. At first Sherwyn wasn't sure if the young savant was going to say anything, but then Bertram spoke up with a confidence in his voice that took Sherwyn somewhat by surprise.

"Over three hundred years ago, a terrible disease called the nislles swept over the land, killing many, including all of the royalty. Since there was no clear heir, there were battles over the throne. Many more lives were lost. When King Roderick eventually came to power, he wanted to make sure nothing like this would happen again. That is why he commissioned five wise elders to write the Tome of Laws."

"I wasn't looking for a history lesson, Savant," Abrecan interrupted. "Tell me why a Shoginoc is against the law."

Bertram seemed undaunted. "I was getting to that, Councilor. One of the main reasons for the Tome of Laws is to look after the good of the common person in the land. The laws were designed to prevent corruption among the rulers. One way to do that was to regularly select a new leader. The people of Bariwon were in favor of the idea, but wanted to keep a king or queen in place—something with which they were familiar."

"Your point?" Abrecan was visibly becoming more frustrated.

Bertram cocked his head to one side. "Don't you see? If there was another Shoginoc because the new queen or king died before they could produce an heir, a corrupt person, perhaps someone who lost in the Shoginoc, would just keep killing off the royalty until he got what he wanted. Making the Shoginoc happen twenty-one years later would prevent that."

Abrecan narrowed his eyes, then sat back in his chair and folded his arms. For several moments he didn't say anything. He looked at Magistrate Seanan and then at Savant Bertram. The red in his face slowly faded, and he nodded his head. "I was unaware of that view on the law. Thank you for your opinion on the matter. So it appears we wait twenty-one years to see who the next king will be."

Sherwyn was surprised by Abrecan's reaction. *What was he up to now?*

"We can't call this child 'baby' forever." Nadia slowly rocked the infant in her arms. "Can you imagine how his friends would tease him?"

Rinan stared into the fireplace, watching the dancing flames. "We hadn't decided on a name. We had several ideas, but we hadn't picked one. We thought we had more time to decide."

Nadia didn't press her son for details; she was relieved he was beginning to talk about it at all. Over the last few days, she had gathered that his wife had been in an accident that caused her to go into early labor and that she had died during childbirth. Rinan still blamed himself for not protecting her, although Nadia pointed out that accidents happen, and sometimes there was nothing that could be done.

The crackling fire and the rain falling on the roof were the only sounds that filled the room for the next several moments. Then Kelvin asked calmly, "How did your wife's family react to the accident?"

Rinan didn't say anything at first—he just kept staring into the fire. Finally, he said, "I'm sure you knew that her mother, father, and grandfather had both died previously. Eliana had aunts and uncles, but they—"

"Wait a moment," Kelvin interrupted. "Your wife's name was Eliana? As in *Queen* Eliana?"

Rinan looked from the fire to his parents. "I told you I was in charge of protecting her, so I thought you knew that when I spoke of my wife, I was referring to Eliana. We married in private, and the marriage between her and King Daimh was a sham."

"We heard that the child had died. Who else knows that the child actually survived?" Kelvin asked, his voice taking on a more urgent tone.

"Just me, Priest Sherwyn, and Eliana's nursemaid, Anemone. They were the only two in the castle who knew Eliana and I were married. They won't tell anyone."

The baby in Nadia's arms started to stir. She began rocking him again, but then said, "Rinan, you should hold him." She held out the bundled child to her son.

Looking somewhat uncomfortable, Rinan did his best to rock the baby as his mother had.

"Does anyone else know you came here?" Kelvin asked.

"No... I don't think so. Why?"

Kelvin blew out a long breath. "Son, you're not safe here."

Rinan looked up from the baby in his arms. "What?"

"I know you have a lot on your mind, but consider this—if the king finds out this child survived, he's going to think you kidnapped *his* child. If he finds out the truth, that you are the father, well, how do you think he will react?"

Rinan's face went pale. "I didn't think—"

"Did you bring anything with you from the castle?" Kelvin interrupted.

He paused for a moment as if in thought. "Aside from my clothes and my son, I only took my sword and my wife's copy of the Tome of Laws. I thought it was important that our child learn to read, and it was the one book I could take quickly when I left."

"May I see it?" Kelvin asked.

Rinan nodded, then got up and retrieved the book.

His father took it from him and opened the cover. "See, the opening page has the symbol of royalty on it. There are some words here—can you read these?" He pointed to the text and the symbol of royalty drawn next to it.

Rinan leaned over and read, *"This copy of the Tome of Laws belongs to Eliana, daughter of King Kenrik and Queen Lareyna."*

"It would be best if this page wasn't left in," Kelvin said. "With the page gone, the ownership wouldn't be in question, and it's one less thing that can be used against you."

Kelvin ripped the page out, and Rinan looked as if part of his soul was being torn away. "I never meant for any of this to happen," he said dejectedly. "I can't let my mistakes hurt anyone else. But I don't know what to do."

"Tevoil," Nadia said abruptly, snapping her fingers.

Kelvin nodded. "Yes, that would work."

Rinan looked puzzled. "Tevoil?"

"I had a cousin, George was his name, who used to live in the district of Tevoil," his father said. "He passed away recently, and because he had no family of his own, we were given ownership of his farm. We were going to give it to you when you retired. It's far back in the forest. You and your son could make a life for yourselves there. No one will think to look for you in Tevoil, and we certainly won't tell anyone."

Rinan looked down at his son. The baby had his mother's blonde hair and blue eyes. "But I don't know anything about raising a child. I don't know if I can do this."

"You'll manage. He's a good baby," Nadia said. "Have you noticed how he likes to hear the rain? The other day, the sun was shining brightly. He was being fussy, but out of nowhere came a light rain, even though the sun was still shining. It was amazing—he calmed right down."

Rinan felt a warm sensation wash over him when he considered what his mother had said. "That's it." He smiled down at his son.

"What's it?" Nadia asked.

"You've helped me realize what I should name him," Rinan said. "My son's name is Rayne."

CHAPTER 11

Three Years Later

"What is it supposed to be?" Governor Eadward asked, clearly confused.

Garth stood proudly next to his latest tree sculpture. "What do *you* think it is?"

Eadward furrowed his brow. The tree had been meticulously trimmed, the two main branches intertwining in a complex pattern. "I honestly have no idea."

Garth looked at Eadward, at the tree, and then back at Eadward. "It's 'joy!'"

Eadward crossed his arms and frowned. "You can't sculpt joy."

"But—" Garth motioned to the large tree next to him "—I did."

Blinking in disbelief at the gardener, Eadward said, "I've been the governor of Lewyol for over two years now, and I still do not understand you people."

"You don't like it?"

The portly governor waved a hand to dismiss the notion. "No, no. It's fine." Indicating the area around him, he said, "Everything in my garden is fine. I just don't understand why anyone would put so much effort into, well, a tree."

"Do you feel my efforts were wasted?" Garth asked.

"Not wasted," Eadward replied, "just misdirected. You can't sell the tree, and you aren't making any money from showing off the tree, so why spend all that time on something that won't bring you any gain?"

Garth wiped the dirt off his hands, "Ah, you do not see the tree after all."

"D–don't see?" Eadward stammered. "It's right here in front... bah! Never mind." With that, Governor Eadward turned and walked out of the garden, shaking his head.

Iolanthe loved her husband, Garth, but even she had to admit he was a little off. It was as if he looked at life with eyes that saw things differently than everyone else. He was smart enough to have been a savant and strong and quick enough to have been a guardian, but instead, he chose the life of a gardener.

He was quite good at it—he really was. Garth's work had been noticed several years ago by Governor Elric and had made such an impression that he was asked to design and care for a garden at the governor's house.

Recently a noble visited the garden and was very impressed. Word spread quickly among the more affluent people in the kingdom, and the garden had become one of the distinguishing attractions in all of the district of Lewyol. Anyone who traveled through the area made it a point to stop by and see it. Ironically, Governor Eadward once discouraged the effort put into the garden, but since it had become popular, he now took credit for it.

The garden reflected Garth's quirky personality. The curving paths that ran through the garden often led to isolated spots where a person could sit and think—at least, that was her husband's intention. Even though the garden wasn't terribly large, it was big enough that you could get lost if you were not paying attention to where you were going.

On one occasion, some visiting nobles had lost their daughter for a time in the garden. They called upon Garth to help find their young child. To hear him tell of the incident, he took a moment to walk the main path that led to each end, turned around, walked roughly a third of the way back in, took several side paths, and found her sitting under a large, sculpted tree, humming lightly to herself and looking at the greenery around her. The nobles were relieved, and when they asked how Garth knew where to find her, he said, "Because if I was a little girl her age, this is where I would go."

He always said things like that. That was part of his charm, but it confused people who didn't know him.

When they had their first child, there had been quite the discussion on what to name the baby. Iolanthe had a few ideas, but Garth didn't seem interested in any of them. They still hadn't decided when their baby boy arrived. Holding the newborn in her arms, Iolanthe said to her husband, "If you don't decide on a name, I'm going to pick one."

"No need," he had said. "It's obvious what he should be named."

"Oh? And what is that?" she had asked.

"Oakleaf."

So, they had a two-and-a-half-year-old running around named Oakleaf. The name actually fit somehow, although Iolanthe couldn't explain why.

And now, as she was about to give birth to their second child, she wondered what they would name the baby. She had brought it up once before, and Garth's response was, "Yes, I'm curious to know what the baby's name will be as well."

Another intense cramp, followed by a desire to push, let Iolanthe know she wouldn't have to wait much longer to find out.

⁂

Bertram flexed his fingers, trying to ease the stiffness in his hand. He glanced at the candle on his desk and noted it had melted quite a bit since he checked it last, but this was nothing new. He often lost track of time when he was writing. Each savant was required to spend time every day copying books to be used by future generations. He was currently working on chapter eleven of the Tome of Laws, and, as instructed, was being very careful to make sure he was copying the text word for word. When he reached paragraph nineteen, he again noticed what seemed to be a missing word. He read the words again carefully to make sure.

It said, *An arranged marriage will* (turning the page) *selected by a Shoginoc.*

When he had discovered this anomaly a couple of years ago, he had checked several books, and they were all the same. It was possible that a savant from years ago had made a mistake and then it was diligently copied for years. Because the missing word was between pages, Bertram could see how the omission had been made. Or perhaps that is just the way it was written, but somehow he didn't think that was it. Everything else in the book was written very properly, so it was hard to believe the authors would miss this.

The oldest copy in the library was ninety years old. He had checked that one, and it matched the other books. Perhaps there was an older copy of the Tome of Laws stored somewhere in the castle that he could check. But where would he start to look? Looking down at his fingernails, he tried to find one that hadn't been chewed on recently as he puzzled over the issue.

⁂

The room was huge. It was so large, in fact, that it made Bertram feel rather small in comparison. The walls were lined with shelves that ran to the ceiling, two stories high. Rolled-up tapestries were scattered around the floor. Many were in front of the shelves, sometimes stacked two or three high.

"If what you seek exists," Magistrate Seanan said, motioning to the room, "it would be in here."

Bertram whistled. "What *is* this room?"

"It's where things go that are deemed too valuable to destroy, but too old to be of any real use," Seanan said. "Funny thing is that no one comes here except to put things in. Well, no one in my memory until you."

The young savant looked around, wondering if it was worth the effort to sort through the contents just to satisfy his curiosity. "Any idea where I should start looking?" he asked the elder magistrate.

"Well, there seem to be more books on the right side." Seanan pointed to the left half of the room. "But I'm not aware of any rhyme or reason to how things were placed in here."

Bertram took a few steps into the room. Near the ceiling were windows that let in bright beams of sunshine, dust visibly swirling in a mist. Turning in a circle, he tried to decide where to begin. Nothing grabbed his attention, so he decided to start at the top shelves and work his way down.

He grabbed a ladder. "Thank you again for your help, Seanan. This may take a while."

The elderly savant chuckled. "Oh, yes, I'm sure of it. It would take years to go through everything in this room."

⋯⁂⋯

Anemone touched the guardian's hand, and even though she did so gently, the young man flinched in pain.

"Just relax," she said, taking his hand again. "It appears your index finger is broken. Let me guess—it was from today's sparring contest."

The guardian bit his lower lip and nodded.

Anemone sighed as she retrieved a length of cloth from one of the dresser drawers and proceeded to wrap the guardian's first two fingers together. "It may never be the same," she said while tying off the cloth, "but at least this will help it heal somewhat straight."

Leading him to the door, the nursemaid said, "No more contests for you for several weeks."

As she let the guardian out of the room, Anemone was surprised to see Priest Sherwyn waiting for her. "Sherwyn, what brings you here? Are you in need of care?"

The bald man smiled sheepishly before he stood up and came to the door. "I'm afraid that I am."

"Come in, come in."

Sherwyn thanked her upon entering the room.

"So, what can I do for you?" Anemone asked, looking at the priest from head to toe.

He held out his hand. "I was walking down the stairs and slipped. When I grabbed the railing, I was able to catch myself, but not before getting this sliver under my fingernail."

"Well, at least it isn't an injury from one of the weekly contests." Anemone frowned. "I swear that ever since Captain Sullivan took over, the contests have become more violent. Poor Royal Guardian Benjamin even lost a finger off his right hand last week."

Sherwyn grimaced. "I heard about that. Have you also noticed a change in how the guardians are acting?"

Anemone inspected the priest's fingernail. "Yes, I have. It's as if they are no longer focused on helping others, but are more interested in flaunting their supposed power."

"I'd say that is an astute assessment," Sherwyn said. "And since Councilor Abrecan has nearly doubled the number of guardians in the last few years, it seems you can't go anywhere without being harassed by one of them."

The nursemaid went to the hearth and removed a pot of warm water. "When I went into town the other day to get more blankets and bandages, I saw a guardian backhand one of the local merchants. From what I could tell, the merchant was complaining about his taxes being nearly doubled, and when he grumbled about it, the guardian hit him. Of course, when the issue was brought up in court, Abrecan supported the guardian's actions."

Sherwyn hung his head. "I've heard similar stories."

She poured the warm water into a bowl, then moved the priest's hand into it to soak. "The tricky thing about slivers is that once they get imbedded, they can be hard to get out. If left unattended, they can cause a sickness that spreads throughout the body."

"I tried everything I could to get it out, but nothing I did seem to make a difference," he said.

Anemone smiled. "Sometimes it takes something you wouldn't expect to solve the problem. We'll soak your hand in warm water until it becomes wrinkled, and then soak it in cold water. You'll find the sliver will eventually be expelled by your body."

Seven remarkably beautiful young women stood in a line, each smiling her prettiest smile. They wore long dresses of a similar cut, each a different color to reflect the girl's home district.

"Welcome, everyone!" Abrecan said to the crowd assembled in the large field usually used for the yearly guardian competitions. His greeting was answered with cheers, though not at all exuberant.

"Today we will find out who will have the honor of marrying your own King Daimh."

Another half-hearted cheer seemed to be largely ignored by Abrecan.

"Congratulations again," he said, turning to the women in front of him. "You were selected as the most beautiful women in your districts. It is a great honor for you to meet the king and have a chance to become his wife."

The women tittered nervously.

"I know you are all anxious to meet King Daimh. Remember, he will be selecting a bride based on the impression you make on him. Good luck to all of you."

Abrecan stepped back and motioned with his hand. A couple of guardians opened the flaps of a large crimson tent. Wearing his crown of gold with sapphires and holding an ornate ruby-studded silver scepter, King Daimh strutted onto the field. A group of minstrels broke into song as the king walked.

To OUR great King Daimh, we sing!
Of HIM, we spend time boas-ting!
His deeds are renown,
He honors the crown.
He IS quite sublime—our king!

The seven young women all stood a bit taller, several arching their backs slightly as the king approached. Daimh flashed a grin, his deep dimples showing prominently.

"Hello, ladies," he said. "I have two simple questions for each of you. First, what is your name? And second, why do you think I should choose you?"

The king started with the woman on the far right, whose bright orange dress indicated she was from Grenoa.

"My name is Azalea, Your Majesty." The red-haired beauty curtseyed slightly. "You should choose me because with your help, I will make Bariwon a better place to live for everyone."

Daimh moved down the line, the candidates' answers varying from wanting to help rule the kingdom to being a devoted wife, and one even commented that she had always wanted to live in the castle.

Reaching the end of the line, Daimh sized up the woman before him. Her long, flowing dark hair cascaded over her vibrant green dress. She was physically more mature than the rest of the ladies, with full lips and curves in all the right places. She just looked at Daimh with her dark eyes and smiled, revealing dimples that rivaled the king's.

After they looked at each other for a moment, Daimh said, "And you? What are your answers?"

"Oh! My name is Nicole." She paused, then smiled even brighter than before. "And I want to marry the most powerful, respected man in all of Bariwon."

⊰⊹⊱

"Have you noticed that Nicole looks quite a bit like your son?" Caldre motioned to the newly married couple, who stood in the hall surrounded by younger nobles.

Councilor Abrecan nodded. "Yes, I've heard that from a few different people."

Several nobles were speculating that the beauty from the district of Regne was chosen because Daimh was so infatuated with his own looks that he chose a female version of himself. However, Caldre thought better of mentioning it and held his tongue.

After looking around the hall, which was decorated even more elaborately than the last wedding reception, Caldre said, "It seems there are not as many people here as when Eliana and Daimh were married."

"Meaning?" Abrecan voice took on a harder edge.

"Nothing, nothing," Caldre said quickly. "Just merely an observation. Perhaps they are all busy with the harvest."

Abrecan's jaw tightened noticeably. "Yes, yes, that's the reason. Just as well. Less people we have to feed."

"At least this is almost over. Planning and executing the contest to find a bride for your son took quite a bit of our time and attention."

"It will be worth it," Abrecan said. "After he failed in the contest with Rinan, Daimh lost a lot of confidence. For some odd reason, he turned to the minstrels and became interested in the songs they sang and the plays they put on. But he was still under foot too much. With his little bride to keep him busy, I can stop babysitting him." Abrecan turned to Caldre and poked the magistrate in the chest. "Make sure Nicole understands that her job is to keep my son happy—and out of my hair."

⋆⋆⋆⋆⋆

Three Years Later

Oakleaf sat on a large wooden chair, his elbows resting on his knees and his chin cupped in his hands. The five-year-old's spiky blond hair was even more messy than normal, an indication of the late hour.

His younger sister slept soundly in a chair next to him. She had wanted to stay up as well, but her two-and-a-half-year-old body had different ideas.

"Daddy, when is the baby in Mommy's tummy going to come out?" Oakleaf asked, watching his father pace back and forth in front of the door to his parents' bedroom.

Garth stopped and looked at his son. He blinked once, then again. "When do *you* think the baby will get here, Son?"

Oakleaf started swinging his legs that were not quite long enough to reach the floor. "I don't know, but this is taking forever."

Garth snapped his fingers in agreement and started pacing again.

Trying to pass the time, Oakleaf started to count how many times his daddy walked back and forth. When he reached forty eleven, he heard a baby crying in the other room. His daddy stopped and looked expectantly at the door. After several moments, the nursemaid opened it and said, "You can come in."

Oakleaf jumped out of his chair and ran to the door. He followed his daddy inside to see his mommy lying in her bed, holding a little baby with a full head of dark hair.

"And what is the name of this son, my love?" Iolanthe asked, looking at Garth with weary eyes.

"A son." Garth smiled. Bending down, he looked carefully at the latest addition to his family. Then he straightened. "Snapdragon."

Looking down at the small person in her arms, Iolanthe said, "Yes, of course. My little Snapdragon."

Oakleaf walked up to the bed, rested his head on his mother's arm, and looked at the baby.

"Say hello to your brother, Oakleaf," Iolanthe said.

Oakleaf reached out tentatively and touched the baby's small head.

"Hello, Snapdragon."

Garth held up a hand. "Don't go anywhere—I want to get your daughter."

Iolanthe gave him a look that said, "Where am I going to go?"

Garth left the room and returned with the dark-haired little girl in his arms.

"Look, sweetheart," Garth said to the three-year-old, who was rubbing sleep out of her dark eyes. "It's your new brother, Snapdragon."

Bringing her closer the baby, Garth said, "And Snapdragon, I want you to meet your sister. Her name is Sunshine."

⊰∦⊱

It took all the strength of Rayne's six-year-old arms to block the sword coming at him. But at least he had blocked it. That was something.

"Good," Rinan said. "You watched my eyes and saw where I was going to attack. Just like I've been trying to teach you."

"It hurt my hands, Father," Rayne said. He was used to hard work. But doing the chores around the farm didn't hurt as much as when his father sparred with him.

"It hurt your hands because you tried to stop my attack completely instead of deflecting it. You tried to absorb all the force of my blow, and that's why your hands hurt. This time, try to knock my sword to the side." Rinan set his feet and prepared to attack again.

Rayne didn't focus on his father's practice wooden sword, but instead tried to watch his father's overall movements: where his feet were placed, how his shoulders were set, and most of all, his eyes. The eyes gave away everything, or so his father told him.

Instead of the attack coming in waist-high, Rinan's sword arced low. Rayne anticipated and brought his own wooden sword down to block. This time, when the swords connected, Rayne twisted his wrists a little, causing his father's sword to be redirected enough that it wouldn't harm him. His father was right; his hands didn't sting as much this time.

"Very good," Rinan said. "That's enough for now. I'm sure you're hungry."

Rayne was. They had been up at first light, like every morning. They had been working on fortifying the roof to their home—the only home Rayne had known. As his father explained it, the home had been left abandoned by a relative and given to them. Even after living there for six years, it seemed there was always something to be fixed or improved. Maybe some of the items had to wait for Rayne to get older, and that's why they'd been working so hard lately.

They were sparring in an alcove a short walk from their home. It was one of Rayne's favorite places to go. There was a canopy of leaves which kept out the harsh summer sun. A stream of cool, clear water ran nearby. In a word, it was peaceful.

Between two roots of a large oak tree, Rinan sat and beckoned his son to sit by him. Their lunch consisted of bread they had baked last week, green apples from trees they tended, and jerked beef that his father had gotten from Rayne's grandparents during their last visit.

"When are we going to see grandfather and grandmother again?" Rayne asked when he sat.

Rinan's brow creased. "Not for another while."

"Why? I miss them." Aside from his father, Rayne's grandparents were the only people he had ever met.

"We just need to be...careful is all."

"But why?"

"There's a lot of bad out in the world. Not everyone is as nice as your grandfather and grandmother. Careful and prepared people survive."

It wasn't the first time Rayne had heard his father talk about being careful. Whether it be sparring or working on the farm, his father would always warn him to be careful. "I always try to be careful, father. Really, I do."

Rinan's frown was replaced with a forced grin. "I know you do. Enough of that for now. Finish your lunch. We can spar some more before we need to get back to the roof. You're getting better each time you pick up your sword."

⋇

Governor Eadward rested his hand on his plump belly while he waited to be summoned to see Abrecan. As a guardian, Eadward was always active—especially while serving as Princess Eliana's personal guardian. She was an energetic young woman, and he found that after following her around all day to keep her safe, he was exhausted. It got to the point where he simply couldn't keep up with her, and if he couldn't do that, he couldn't protect her. But since he'd retired and become a governor, he spent most of his time sitting, and in turn, his body had gotten fat.

In the end, Eliana had died at too young of an age. It was too bad. He had been grooming her to be the perfect match for Daimh. With what Abrecan had planned, they would need the queen's support, even if she didn't fully understand the larger scheme. Her death had delayed the plans, but now it seemed Abrecan was ready to start again.

The room that had been given him to stay in the castle was decorated lavishly, more so than when had served as a royal guardian. Then again, much had changed in the years since Eliana's death. At this very moment, workers were replacing the conical roofs on the towers. Instead of blue, red slate was being used. Eadward guessed most people wouldn't understand the significance, but he did.

A knock at the door startled Eadward from his musings, and he cursed himself for being surprised by something he should have been expecting. "Come!" he called out.

Instead of a servant, Abrecan entered the room. This was something Eadward had not expected. Standing clumsily, he said, "Councilor Abrecan, forgive me. I was expected to be summoned to your chambers."

Abrecan closed the door. "Sit down before you fall down."

"Yes, of course…" Eadward said, feeling warmth come to his cheeks. No one but Abrecan spoke to him with such disrespect.

The de facto leader of Bariwon sat in a chair padded with red velvet across from Eadward. "What have you learned?" Abrecan asked.

"As you know, the northern mountains are enormous. Every expedition we've sent to find a way to scale them has failed, sometimes resulting in death."

Abrecan let out a huff. "Then they aren't trying hard enough."

"I wish that was the case," Eadward said carefully. "But a young man I trust—Crescens is his name—is very trustworthy. My family has known his for generations. He went with the last group. Before even seeing the tops of the mountains, it became more difficult to breathe. It became so bad that they had to stop and come back down."

"That makes no sense," Abrecan said. "It isn't as if they were going underwater. How can there be no air at the top of the mountains?"

Eadward didn't know. The best he could do was guess. "Well, water comes from clouds and there are almost always clouds covering the tops of the mountains. Maybe there is too much water in the clouds and it prevents them from breathing?"

For a moment, Abrecan said nothing. He simply stared at Eadward like that was the most idiotic thing someone had ever said.

"Or not…" Eadward said.

"Well, keep sending men until you do find something," Abrecan said. "Our ancestors once found a way to the other side. I want to know what's there."

CHAPTER 12

Fourteen Years Later

"The sun's playing hide-and-seek," Rinan said, squinting through the raindrops at the beams of light that had broken through the clouds.

Rayne set down his crate of vegetables in the horse-drawn cart. "What's that, Father?"

"Just a phrase your mother would use when it was raining but the sun was out." Rinan patted his twenty-year-old son on the back.

Rayne looked up at the sky. "I don't get it."

"It means...well, I guess it would be hard to explain. It's just one of those things she would say."

Picking up another crate off the ground and lifting it onto the cart, Rayne repeated, "'The sun's playing hide-and-seek.' I'll have to remember that."

Rinan walked to the house to bring over the last of the crates. He glanced back at his son, who was a good twenty paces away, and got an idea. He reached into a crate and selected a fist-sized onion.

"Hey, Rayne!" he shouted as he threw it at his son.

Turning, Rayne saw the round object coming rapidly toward his head. He reached out and caught it before it could hit him.

"Another test?" the young man asked, throwing the onion back to his father.

Rinan caught the onion at chest height and smiled. "Always. You can never let your guard down. Life-changing events can happen when you least expect it."

Rayne walked toward his father to help with the last of the crates. "I doubt much will happen on our trip to town."

Rinan wagged a finger at his son. "You never know. I haven't spent your whole life teaching you how to fight and keep your reflexes sharp just for the Mortentaun. These skills may come in handy when you least expect it."

"Well," Rayne said, lifting up a crate and walking back to the wagon, "we are the only people here on the farm, and aside from the rare trips to Grandma and Grandpa's house or into town to sell our crops, we don't see anyone else. So unless something happens on the visits, I don't see why you are always pushing me to be on my toes."

"Sometimes you just need to trust that your father is looking out for you. Understand?" Rinan put the last of the wares into the cart. "Now, untie the horse while I finish tying up the canvas cover."

Rayne walked around the cart and undid the leather straps that kept their horse in place. A flash of lightning, followed by booming thunder, startled the horse, causing him and the cart to lurch backward. Rinan cried out when the wagon backed up over his lower leg. He fell to the ground and watched as Rayne looked back at him. Moving quickly, Rayne urged the horse forward, pulling the cart off his father. He tied the horse back up, then rushed to his father's side.

Rinan grimaced in pain. "See? What did I tell you? I let my attention slip for a moment, and now I've got a broken ankle."

"You didn't have to break a part of your body to prove your point, Father," Rayne said, helping him back to the house.

"Perhaps not, but I doubt this is a lesson you or I will soon forget."

⋗⧻⧻⋖

"Have you seen your brothers?" Iolanthe asked.

Not looking up from her book, Sunshine responded, "Of course. Every day."

Iolanthe rolled her eyes. "I mean, do you know where your brothers are?"

"Let me guess," Sunshine replied. "You need help with something and they aren't around."

"Yes, I noticed we are almost out of candles. We need to get some more, but I have to start working on dinner so it will be ready when your father gets home."

Nodding her head toward the window, Sunshine said, "It seems to me that Oakleaf and Snapdragon have the ability to sense when something needs to be done, and find a way to occupy themselves with other activities."

Iolanthe looked out the window to the field in front of the house, where she could see her sons sparring again with large wooden swords. She worried when her twenty-year-old son sparred with his brother, who was five years younger. Oakleaf was always careful, but accidents could and did happen.

Opening the front door to the wood-framed house, Iolanthe yelled out, "Boys! I need you to go into town and buy some candles."

Oakleaf lowered his sword. "But Mom, the Mortentaun is just a few months away. I really need to practice. Send Shiny. I'll bet she's not doing anything but reading."

Snapdragon took that moment to swipe at his big brother's legs, but Oakleaf blocked his blow.

Iolanthe looked back inside at her daughter. "Sunshine..."

She slapped her book closed. "I'll spare us the argument of why this isn't fair and just go."

⟡⟡⟡

"Ah, Sunshine! Welcome, welcome," Chandler said cheerfully when the seventeen-year-old beauty entered his candle shop.

"Well met, Chandler." She lowered the hood of her cloak.

Peering through the misty window, the candle maker asked, "So, is it still raining outside?"

Sunshine shrugged. "Hard for me to say, since I'm inside now."

"Yes, well, uh, go ahead and select what you would like. I was going to close up soon, but take your time."

Sunshine went to the back of the store and picked out the candles her mother wanted. She was placing them in her wicker basket when the door opened. Three guardians, tunics and leggings wrinkled and spotted, barged into the shop, laughing loudly. Two of the guardians were obviously twins. They were nearly copies of each other, aside from a scar that ran down the cheek of one of them. The third guardian was a bit taller and more muscular, with an overbite protruding from what could be called a sad attempt at a mustache.

"Hello, guardians." Chandler's voice was less cheerful now.

"Take what you want," the bucktoothed man told his fellow guardians.

Chandler cleared his throat. "Guardian Zubin, I don't believe I've met the other men with you."

Zubin started picking up various candles and then tossing them back after examining them, breaking some in the process. "Yeah, they're new. Just came down from Erd. This here's Thomas, and that there's Thomas."

103

Sunshine came around a shelf with her full basket to face the guardians. "Did you say you were both named Thomas?"

The Thomas without the scar looked at Sunshine from head to toe and smiled. "My mum and dad had only picked out one name, so when my brother here came along after me, instead of trying to think of a new one, they just named us the same."

"I see." Sunshine pursed her lips. "I can imagine it would make it easier to call you both to dinner." She headed to the counter where Chandler was waiting.

"Whoa," said the Thomas with the scar as Sunshine walked by them. He grabbed her arm.

Turning to face him, she said, "I'm not a horse." She shrugged away from his grip and then turned her back on him.

Scarred Thomas said to Zubin, "Did she just insult me?"

Before he could answer, Sunshine turned around and said in an overly sweet voice, "Oh, no, my big tough guardian. I didn't insult you. If I were to insult you, I would say something along the lines of, 'You may find saying "whoa" will work better on a horse than on a human, you muscle brain.' But I wouldn't insult a so-called protector of the people." She smiled brightly at the three men, curtsied, and then continued walking to the counter.

The guardians stood there looking at each other while Sunshine paid Chandler for the candles and left the shop.

Zubin followed after her. "I think she did insult you that time, Thomas. Let's go."

⋆⫘⋆

The horse clip-clopped on the curving road that led to the town of Lewyol in the district of the same name. Although Rayne and his father lived in the district of Tevoil, Lewyol was actually the closest town to their farm. Rayne sat up straight on the bench of the cart, his eyes searching the trees around him. He had promised his father he would stay alert and was trying his best.

This was the first time Rayne had taken the trip alone. He knew the way quite well, and his father insisted that he go before any of the food could spoil. The break in his father's ankle was pretty bad—bad enough that he didn't think he could handle the trip into town, but not so bad that he couldn't be left alone for the couple of days Rayne would be gone.

The rain had turned to a light drizzle for most of the day-long trip, though the sky had remained overcast. Apparently, it hadn't rained as hard this close to town, as the dirt road was damp, but not muddy.

Rayne had stopped only twice during the trip. Once was to drop off a crate to Dulcie, an elderly lady that lived on the Tevoil-Lewyol border. Whenever he and his father went into town, they always stopped and gave her some of their harvest. When Rayne was old enough, he had asked his father why they did this when they could sell the crops for money. His father simply said that some things were worth more than money.

The second time he stopped, Rayne moved several large branches that had fallen in the road. He noticed that one of the branches was fairly straight and solid. Using his small belt knife, he was able to strip off an eight-foot-long staff he would give to his father to help him walk around while his ankle healed.

After several more hours of traveling, Rayne came around a large bend and could see the town ahead of him. A certain sense of excitement kicked in. He wasn't really nervous about being without his father—instead, he felt a sort of freedom.

He guided his horse-drawn cart down the wide street, looking carefully at the shops and inns that lined the road. The merchant who bought their crops was more toward the center of town, fairly close to the governor's house.

Approaching his destination, Rayne's attention was drawn to a tall, dark-haired, young woman about his own age who had exited one of the shops. Their eyes met for a moment before she started walking purposefully down the side of the road, carrying a large basket in one hand. Right behind her, three guardians came out of the shop and began to follow her. The tallest of the three said something Rayne couldn't make out. The attractive brunette stopped, turned to face them, and said something in return. The guardians caught up to her, and the lead one reached out and grabbed the basket. They struggled for a moment before the basket dropped to the ground, spilling its contents.

Rayne brought the horse to a stop as the young woman placed her hands on her hips in defiance. The guardians closed in on her.

⋆✦⋆

Sunshine was still fuming when she left the shop. It was frustrating enough that she had to do her brothers' work, and she was definitely not in the mood to deal with the guardians' behavior.

Her mother had told her that the guardians hadn't always been the bullies they were now, and at one time were treated with respect. It was only when King Daimh had taken over that things had changed.

Sunshine realized at a young age that she was what others would consider to be pretty, much like her mother. But in addition, she had gotten her intellect from her father. Spats with her mother often ended with Iolanthe rolling her eyes and saying, "Sunshine, you are definitely your daddy's daughter."

Because of her looks, she often got attention she didn't want. Over the last couple of years, as she changed into a woman, she found men looking at her strangely and making what she considered rude comments. It seemed that the guardians were the worst of the lot.

Upon leaving the store, she noticed a horse-drawn cart coming down the road, driven by a young man dressed in simple clothes, with bright blond hair protruding from under a straw hat. Their eyes met for a moment, and she thought she saw him smile slightly. It wasn't the type of smile she was used to seeing from men—it actually seemed sincere. But chances were, he was just like the rest of them, and all she wanted now was to get home and back to her book. She tightened her grip on the basket and started to head for home when she heard the guardians come out of the shop behind her. She had planned on just ignoring them until she heard Zubin say, "Hey, you may be pretty, but you have a mouth on you."

Spinning around, Sunshine said, "Yes, I do. It's good for eating, breathing, and saying things like 'goodbye now, I'm going home.'"

Zubin closed the distance between the two of them and grabbed her basket. She tried to pull it away from him, but instead she managed to drop it, causing the candles to spill out on the ground.

She placed her hands on her hips and glared at the men in front of her.

"You won't leave until I tell you," Zubin said, a leer playing across his face. "And maybe not even then."

Sunshine held out her hands in front of her, indicating for them to stop, and said loudly, "Keep away from me!"

"Or what?" Zubin asked, taking a step closer.

She'd had run-ins with Zubin before, but he had never been this forceful. Perhaps he was trying to show off for the new guardians. She wondered if any of the shop owners would come to her aid if she yelled for help, though she hadn't seen anyone really stand up to the guardians except for her father. She thought about making a run for it, but doubted she would make it very far. Still trying to figure out what to do, she saw Zubin's head snap forward.

What had just happened? She noticed a large onion lying on the ground not far from Zubin's feet. Looking beyond, she noticed the young man she had seen earlier. He was standing up in the cart, holding another onion in his hand.

"What the…?" Zubin said, rubbing the back of his head. He turned around and looked at the culprit. The brothers Thomas were already moving toward the cart, drawing their swords.

⭙

Now, that may not have been the smartest thing I could have done, Rayne thought, watching the guardians approach him with swords drawn. Why had he done that? He hadn't really thought about it, he realized. He had simply reacted when he sensed the young woman was in trouble. He doubted throwing more onions would be enough to stop the three advancing men.

He glanced around for something he could use to defend himself. His belt knife would do little good against three men with swords. But the knife *did* remind him of the wooden staff he had made earlier. He grabbed it and jumped down from the cart, then took several steps toward the guardians.

"You are in a lot of trouble, farmer," growled the buck-toothed man.

One of the other guardians said, "You tell him, Zubin!"

Holding out the staff in front of him, Rayne said, "Look here, guardians. Just let the young lady over there go on her way, I'll go on mine, and we'll put this behind us. There is no reason for this to result in violence."

"Bah! It was *you* who hit me in the head, so I'd say the violence has already begun," Zubin said. "Thomas, bring him here."

The two men on either side of the taller guardian advanced on Rayne. Spinning the staff in front of him, Rayne moved to his right, closer to the guardian who sported a long scar down one cheek.

The scarred man rushed in, swinging his sword high. The skills Rayne's father had taught him kicked in as he parried the blow high with one end of the staff, and then quickly brought the other end around low, sweeping his opponent off his feet. The guardian hit his head hard on the ground and lay still. Sensing the other man coming in from behind, Rayne thrust the staff backwards, catching the man hard in the chest and knocking the wind out of him. He went to the ground, clutching his chest and trying to breathe.

"Arrrggghh!" Zubin yelled, charging.

Rayne brought the staff up just in time to block the sword that was aimed for his head. He brought the staff around, but Zubin jumped back out of the way. Zubin regained his balance and lunged in, his sword aimed at Rayne's heart. Sidestepping, Rayne instinctively swung the staff at Zubin's head, connecting solidly with a satisfying crack. The bucktoothed guardian's knees buckled and he dropped to the ground.

Rayne spun around to the other two, but they were holding up their hands defensively. They stood up, sheathed their swords, picked Zubin up, and dragged him out of the street. Heart pounding, Rayne watched them go before looking over to where the young lady stood with her arms folded, wearing an expression he couldn't read.

Walking over to her, Rayne asked, "Are you all right?"

She nodded her head and continued to look at him strangely.

Not sure what to do next, Rayne knelt down and started to gather up the candles that had spilt out of the basket.

"More heroics?" she asked.

Rayne stopped and looked up at her. "I'm sorry, what?"

"It's not enough that you saved me, but now you're saving the candles from getting dirty?" She knelt to help him.

Rayne looked into her deep brown eyes, and for a moment, couldn't think of anything to say. When he realized he was just staring at her, he lowered his eyes back to the ground. "I'm just trying to help."

She considered him for a moment. "I believe you."

He put the last of the candles in the basket. "Um, well, there you go. Will you be all right getting home?"

She stood. "I don't see where the guardians have gone. Although I don't live far from here, it would probably be best if I had company."

"Well, I need to sell my crops first." Rayne rubbed his hand along his jaw as he thought. "It shouldn't take very long. The merchant is just down the street from here. I'll be happy to escort you home once I'm done."

"I'll wait with you." She smiled. "Thank you."

"And by the way, my name is Rayne." He extended a hand.

Taking his hand in a firm shake, she said, "Well met, Rayne. My name is Sunshine."

"Sunshine? Are you making fun of my name?"

"No. Are you making fun of mine?" She looked at him innocently and batted her eyelashes.

Rayne raised his hands in protest. "No, not at all. I've just never heard of a name like Sunshine before."

"Ah. If you find my name odd, wait until you meet my brothers."

CHAPTER 13

The sun was just starting to set when Rayne and Sunshine pulled up to her family's house. He took notice of the bushes and trees around the house that had been trimmed into odd shapes and patterns.

They hadn't seen the troublesome guardians while selling Rayne's wares, or on the trip to the house. The conversation while traveling was, at times, confusing to Rayne. Sunshine was very pleasant and easy to talk to, but every once in a while she would say something that left him speechless.

She invited him into her house and found the rest of her family sitting around a large wooden table. By the looks of things, dinner was just beginning. Sunshine introduced Rayne as someone who helped bring the candles safely home. Her mother immediately invited him to stay for dinner.

Having limited experience with social customs, Rayne found himself uncomfortable at first with the people he had just met. Sunshine's mother and two brothers seemed nice enough, but her father was a little odd—he would say things that reminded Rayne of Sunshine's confusing statements, only Garth said them more frequently.

After the food had been served, Sunshine started recounting the tale of what had happened in town, when her father stopped her to clarify a point.

"An onion, you say?" He raised his eyebrows at Rayne.

Sunshine said, "Oh, yes. Right to the back of Zubin's head. It was quite the amazing throw."

"How far away was he?" Snapdragon asked with a mouth full of food.

Before Rayne could answer, Garth said, "That hardly matters. I do wonder, though…"

Sure he was going to be asked why he threw the onion, Rayne tried to

109

come up with an answer. The fact was, he didn't quite know. His father had always taught him to be aware of danger and to act on instinct, so perhaps that was what had happened. Ready to explain that to Garth, Rayne was surprised once again by the question he was asked.

"Why not a turnip? Or perhaps a potato?" Garth asked.

Everyone at the table stopped eating and looked at Rayne expectantly.

Blinking back at them, Rayne thought for a moment before he responded. "Well, I guess an onion seemed appropriate at the time."

Garth nodded his head in acceptance and returned his attention to the food in front of him.

Iolanthe asked, "What happened after you hit Guardian Zubin with the onion?"

Rayne tried to downplay the fight. "Well, they took exception to my actions and wanted to discuss it further. After a brief exchange, they decided to leave."

"That doesn't sound like Zubin," Oakleaf said. "The man is a bully. He wouldn't have left you alone, unless..." Oakleaf looked at Rayne carefully. "What did you do?"

"Well, I, you see, I—"

"He beat them up," Sunshine said.

Garth and Iolanthe nearly choked on their food.

"You beat up three guardians?" Iolanthe asked.

Feeling uncomfortable with all the attention, Rayne said, "Well, I scared them away more than beat them up. They weren't hurt too badly, I think."

Iolanthe turned to her husband. "Governor Eadward isn't going to like this. You need to talk to him about what happened."

Garth snapped his fingers in agreement.

"You know the governor?" Rayne asked.

Sunshine's father shrugged. "He sometimes stays at the house where my garden is."

Confused, Rayne looked at Iolanthe for clarification.

"My husband is the gardener for the governor's estate," she explained. "The garden is well liked and appreciated around Bariwon. Over time, the governor realized this made him look good, and so he treats my husband well. He allows us to borrow books from his library for Sunshine to read, and he tends to keep the guardians away from us."

"Yeah, but Shiny seems to have a knack for upsetting them," Snapdragon said. He stuck his tongue out at his sister.

Iolanthe gave the youngest child a sharp look. "That's enough, Snapdragon."

"How could you have beat up three guardians?" Oakleaf asked incredulously. "These men are trained how to fight."

After taking a drink of water, Rayne said, "My father has been teaching me how to fight since I was little. I guess all his teaching worked. He wants me to become a guardian, although I'm not sure that's what I want."

"Why not?" Oakleaf asked. "I've been preparing hard for the Mortentaun next spring. I think it would be a great adventure to become a guardian."

"Next spring, eh? That's when I would be participating," Rayne said.

"I don't think you'd fit in, Rayne," Sunshine said. "All the guardians I've met are selfish pigs."

Oakleaf whipped his head around to look at his sister. "What does that say about me?"

Sunshine didn't missed a beat. "Oh, you'd fit in very well."

Rayne became more comfortable as the evening passed. At first, he wasn't sure what to think about how Sunshine and her brothers interacted. Over time, it became clear that the siblings were often joking with each other and were not seriously antagonistic. It had always been just him and his father on the farm, and during dinner Rayne wondered what it would have been like to have brothers and sisters around while he was growing up.

With dinner finishing, he said, "I want to thank you all for dinner. I should get to the inn."

"Nonsense," Garth said.

"Excuse me?"

Iolanthe reached across the table and patted Rayne's hand. "He means that after defending our daughter, the least we can do is put you up for the night. There's space in the boys' room. We wouldn't think of making you go to an inn."

"Well, if it wouldn't be too much trouble." Rayne glanced at Sunshine.

The brown-eyed beauty gave him a smile while her mother said, "No trouble at all."

⇥✣⇤

The last thing Zubin remembered was the farmer jumping out of the way of his attack. After that, he could only recall waking up in his room with the brothers Thomas looking over him. Although his head was hurting, nothing seemed to be broken. He was a bit dizzy when he stood, but he wouldn't allow that to keep him from finding this farmer and making him pay.

He was used to people cowering before him, and when they didn't, it made him angry. Plus, assaulting a guardian was against the law, and Zubin couldn't wait to arrest him. Guessing their attacker was in town to sell his crops, Zubin figured that checking with the merchants in town would be a good place to start.

The three guardians went from shop to shop, looking for information. Soon after the sun had set, they came to one of the last shops in town, The Pantry. The door was locked, with dim lights visible through the closed window shutters. Zubin pounded heavily on the door. After a brief pause, he pounded again. Soon after, it opened a little.

"What's all the ruckus about?" asked an elderly woman's voice through the crack.

Zubin pushed the door open and barged into the shop, nearly knocking over the gray-hair woman. "You took your sweet time answering, Theresa."

She stepped back. "I—I'm sorry, guardians. I didn't know it was you."

"I'll let it pass this time." Zubin looked around the shop carefully. "Did you buy some food today from a young, blond-haired farmer?"

Theresa's eyes opened wide. "You mean Rayne?"

Scarred Thomas scoffed, "What kind of name is that?"

Zubin smacked him on the chest. "Never mind that. Theresa, do you know where this Rayne is now?"

"Is he in some kind of trouble?" asked the store owner, looking worried.

Scarless Thomas pointed a finger at her. "Yes, and you will be too, if you don't tell us where he is."

"I...I don't know, honestly." She backed up even more. "But he must be at one of the inns. He's from Tevoil, and that's too far away to make it home by dark."

Zubin took a step closer. "Where in Tevoil?"

Theresa backed up to the wall. "I'm not sure. It can't be too far into that district, or they wouldn't come here to sell."

"Fine, we'll check the inns. If you see Rayne again, tell him the guardians are looking for him."

⇾✦⇽

Zubin walked out of The Rabid Dog Inn and blew out a long breath. This was the last of the town's inns they had visited, and there had been no sign of Rayne.

"Are you sure we checked every inn?" asked Scarred Thomas.

"Yeah," Zubin said, frustrated. "No one has seen him—even the hunchbacked innkeeper in there says she hasn't seen him. He probably knew we were going to come after him and risked the journey home at night."

"So what do we do now?"

Zubin set his jaw and thought a moment. "First thing in the morning, we are going to Tevoil. We'll find him."

Scarless Thomas spoke up. "What about Sunshine? Are we going to let her get away with treating us like she did?"

Zubin got an unpleasant look on his face. "Well, Governor Eadward has told me to stay clear of her family, but she likes to come into town alone sometimes. Next time she does, we'll be waiting. She can't tell the governor if she can't speak."

⟶❉⟵

Dulcie tottered over to the window when she heard the hoof beats. She thought it must be Rayne returning from Lewyol. He was such a nice young lad. He and his father had dropped off food ever since her husband passed away those many years ago. She had baked a nice pie last night and hoped to give it to Rayne to take home to share with his father. It wasn't much, but it was the least she could do for them.

Looking out, she was surprised to see it wasn't Rayne after all, but three men wearing guardian uniforms. Going to the door and opening it, she waved and said, "Well, hello! Welcome, welcome! It's been a while since I've had a visit from the guardians."

In her old age, her eyesight was starting to fail her, but she could still see well enough to function. She did wonder, however, if her sight was getting worse, because two of the young men appeared to look almost exactly alike each other. But it was the third man who spoke up as he dismounted from his horse.

"Hail, Grandma," he said. "Do you know this area very well?"

Dulcie chuckled. "I'm pretty sure you're confused. I'm not your grandmother—I never had any children. But to answer your question, I've lived here all my life, yes."

"Do you know a farmer named Rayne?" asked the guardian in front of her. "He's from this area."

Smiling, Dulcie said, "Oh, yes! Sweet, sweet Rayne. He lives with his father on a farm around here."

He turned to his companions, and she thought she saw him grin. "How

113

do we get there?" he asked her.

Dulcie thought it over a moment. "You know, in all the years I've known those two, they've never said. I'm guessing it is fairly close." Her eyes lit up. "It's possible they moved to George's old farm. It would make sense. I started getting visits from them not long after George died."

"Tell us how to get there," he ordered.

"Just follow the main road that leads to Tevoil," she said. "You will see a lake along the way. Take the small road that branches off from the main road after you pass the lake. It's not much farther from there. If that's not the right place, then I don't know where they live."

The man got back on his horse. "Excellent. We'll be on our way then."

Dulcie waved again. "Say hello to them for me."

The three men rode off without responding.

Going back into her house, she thought, *I'll need to make more pies if I keep getting all these visitors.*

⊹✣⊱

Rinan pulled out a blank parchment and thought about what he should write. With his ankle broken as it was, he was unable to do much more than hop around the house on one foot. While that was enough to do the basic activities of the day, it was also very tiring.

By the late afternoon, he didn't have the energy to do more than read a book, or write in his journal. It was his father's idea that he should write down his thoughts regularly—he said it would help him figure out things in his life better, and it had. He was careful what he wrote; he didn't want Rayne to accidentally find out things about his past that might bring him harm.

Rinan didn't cringe as much anymore when he thought about the past. He realized he had been very young and caught up in a situation that was bigger than he could understand at the time. He had loved Eliana very much, but over time he realized that marrying her privately was the wrong decision, even if it was for the supposed greater good. Living a lie had been a constant strain on both of them. The saddest part was that the lie was designed to prevent Abrecan from taking power, and in the end, he had done just that. Rinan had chosen a path, and it led to a place he hadn't expected. At least Priest Sherwyn was right about that.

Rinan had always tried to be honest with his son, up to the point of revealing who his mother really was. He simply told Rayne he met his mother while he was a guardian and that she died in childbirth. Rinan still worried that Abrecan or Daimh would find out he was the father of

Eliana's child, and that the baby had survived. On the rare occasion when someone came to the farm, Rinan always reached for the sword he kept hanging on the back of the door, thinking that maybe the guardians had finally caught up with him. Some twenty years had passed, and no guardians had ever come to take his son away. However, both Anemone and Sherwyn knew the secret, and so, assuming they were still at the castle, there was always the possibility that the truth could come out.

With Rayne in town alone for the first time, Rinan couldn't help but be nervous. He had taught his son well, and knew he could handle himself, but Rinan would feel a lot better once Rayne returned.

Rinan lifted his quill, dipped it in the ink bottle next to the parchment, and started writing down his feelings. Sounds from outside the house caught his attention. Hearing the sound of hoofs on the road made him believe at first that Rayne had returned, but the sounds were not quite right. They were too fast for a horse pulling a cart, and then Rinan realized he was hearing more than one horse.

His pulse quickened as he stood up from the table and hopped over to the window. What he saw made a shiver run down his spine—three guardians were dismounting from their horses. Taking a few more hops over to the front door, Rinan grabbed his sword and removed it from its scabbard.

Opening the door, Rinan faced the three younger men, each with swords drawn. He thought he saw surprise on their faces when they saw that he was armed. The surprise didn't last long before the guardian in the middle motioned to the other two and ordered, "Get him!"

❈

Rayne awoke to see Snapdragon standing over him, eyeing him intently. This was disconcerting, since it took Rayne a moment to remember where he was and why there was a young man in his room.

"Ah, you are awake." Snapdragon smiled. "Mom said breakfast was about ready and wanted you to have some before you left."

Propping himself up on his elbows, Rayne said, "That's very kind of her."

He noticed shafts of light shining through the window across the room, and realized that for the first time in recent memory, the sun had risen before he had. He sat up from the pallet they had made for him and reached for his boots. "I slept longer than I intended."

"Maybe if you hadn't been up so late with Shiny, you wouldn't have been so tired," Snapdragon said, a smirk playing across his face.

Rayne laced up his boots. "It wasn't that late, was it? I mean, we were just talking."

"Uh-huh, sure," said the younger boy. He wrapped his arms around himself and made kissing noises.

Rayne stood up to take a playful swipe at Snapdragon, but the boy dodged out of the way and ran from the room. "We did nothing of the sort!" Rayne called out, following him. "Your sister and I were only…"

Stopping in his tracks, Rayne saw that the rest of the family was around the table, looking at him.

Iolanthe stood and put her hands on her hips. "You and my daughter were only doing *what?*"

Rayne's eyes opened wider, and he could feel his face start to turn red. He looked at Sunshine, who had a mischievous grin on her face. "We were only talking," he said somewhat timidly.

"You should have at least tried to get a kiss out of her," her father said. "She could use a good kissing."

Oakleaf and Snapdragon broke out in laughter. Iolanthe picked up a muffin and threw it at her husband, while Sunshine looked embarrassed for the first time since Rayne had met her.

"What?" Garth said. "Her best friends are books. It's nice to see her spend some time with something other than words on paper."

After a wonderful breakfast with Sunshine's family, Rayne thanked them again for all they had done. He followed Garth out to the back of the house, where his horse had been tied up for the night.

"My sons took care of your horse and cart this morning," Garth said. "You should be set for the trip home."

Rayne checked the horse's harness and was satisfied that the cart had been securely attached. "It was wonderful to meet you and your family," he said as he guided his horse around the house.

"It was, wasn't it?" Garth smiled.

When they arrived at the front of the house, Rayne saw Sunshine at the door, holding a wicker basket in her hands. Garth took Rayne by the arm and said, "Watch out for the guardians on the way home. They can be dangerous." He patted Rayne on the back, and then went inside the house.

Sunshine walked up, holding her basket out in front of her. "We've packed you a lunch for your trip."

Taking it, Rayne said, "Thank you very much."

They stood there awkwardly for a moment before he said, "If I decide to go to the Mortentaun, maybe I'll see you. I guess you'll watch your brother compete."

Sunshine looked thoughtful for a moment. "Well, I wasn't looking forward to it, but I am now." She took a quick step forward and kissed Rayne on the cheek. He took a step back and noticed her smile. Over her shoulder, he saw her mother and two brothers standing just inside the house, each with his jaw dropped. Her father, however, was smiling as broadly as Sunshine.

⊱❖⊰

Driving home, Rayne couldn't stop thinking about Sunshine. Her smile and dark brown eyes were simply intoxicating. Maybe he would consider going to the Mortentaun if for no other reason than to see her again. Even better, perhaps they could squeeze out a few more crops to sell before the winter so he could go back and see her sooner than next spring.

He was still musing over excuses to go back to town when he arrived at Dulcie's house. Even though he had left late from town and was anxious to get home to check on his father, he decided to stop by and say hello.

"Rayne! It *is* you!" Dulcie greeted him warmly. "How was your trip into town?"

After getting down from the cart, Rayne walked over and gave the elderly lady a big hug. "It was…eventful."

"Oh? How so?"

Rayne thought for a moment about how much he should tell her. Maybe it would be best if she didn't know that he'd had a run-in with the guardians, so he answered cryptically, "I met some interesting people."

"Hold that thought a moment," Dulcie said. "I have something for you." She went back inside her house and returned holding a pie. "I baked this for you and your father. There's probably enough for your visitors."

A shiver went down Rayne's spine. "What visitors, Dulcie?"

"Oh, three guardians came by here a couple of hours ago, asking about you," the elderly lady said. "I thought you may have already been by, so I told them how to get to your farm. That is, of course, if you live at the farm George used to own before he died."

Rayne felt a sense of dread wash over him. On one of his visits to see his grandmother and grandfather, they had mentioned something about a cousin George and how he had owned the farm before his father took it over. "I must be off, Dulcie. Thanks again for the pie. Be well." With that, he urged on his horse to hurry home.

Pushing the horse to go as fast as he dared, Rayne wondered what action he would take after he arrived at the farm. What would the guardians do once they found he wasn't there? Would they be waiting for him? What would they do to his father?

He knew his father could take care of himself, but a broken ankle would make things difficult. He tried not to panic. He needed to stay focused and keep paying attention to where he was going. The guardians could be waiting for him at any point along the road.

Rayne picked up the trail left by the guardians' horses once he left the main road that was just beyond the lake. He slowed as he came closer to his home. When the log cabin finally came into view, Rayne noticed three horses roaming free and eating the grass around the farm. There was no other sign of the guardians.

Rayne brought the horse to a stop, then reached back into the cart and grabbed the wooden staff he had used the day before. Then he stepped down from the cart and took some tentative steps toward the house.

The front door was wide open. Gripping the staff tighter, Rayne sneaked forward, his heart pounding heavily and his eyes scanning the area. He stopped when he saw a body lying on the floor in a pool of blood just inside the house.

CHAPTER 14

At first, Rayne couldn't make out whose body was lying on the floor inside the house. As he crept closer, his eyes started to adjust to the light, and he noticed the body was wearing a uniform.

He stepped up on the porch and cautiously looked inside. The scene before him made his blood turn ice cold. Aside from the body he had already noticed, there were two more guardians sprawled on the floor, each lifeless. At the table in the center of the room sat his father, hunched over with his back to the door.

Rayne rushed to his father's side, stepping over the bodies of the fallen guardians in the process. He reached out tentatively, but stopped short when he realized his father wasn't breathing. Feeling the strength leave his legs, Rayne grabbed a chair and sat down.

From his current angle, he could verify that these were the same guardians he had encountered in Lewyol. Each sported many wounds, several of which were definitely fatal. Looking back and forth between the twins, Rayne grimaced when he realized their wounds made it impossible to tell which of them had a scar before the battle.

Satisfied that none of the guardians posed a threat, Rayne turned his attention to his father. Rinan's head lay on the table, one arm wrapped around his middle, the other hand still holding a quill and resting on a parchment.

Rayne slid the parchment from under his father's hand and read what he had written. The top part of the page was in his father's practiced handwriting.

My son has been gone from me today. I didn't realize how much I would miss him when he left, but it is something I need to learn to accept. I have done my best to teach him to be a good person. I want nothing more than for him to become the guardian I could not be—to serve the people and make Bariwon a better place. It is my hope that he never backs down from what is right, even when that is the hard decision to make. Perhaps one day, I'll be able to tell him more of my past. I wish I hadn't ...

The entry ended there. Further down on the page were more words, except there were splotches of blood next to the letters.

They found me. I don't know how. Rayne, if you read this, burn the farm. Go to my parents. Become a guardian. Don't tell anyone who your father was. I love you, my son.

The words on the page became blurry as Rayne blinked away the tears in his eyes.

⇥❈⇤

The first thing Rayne did was to bury his father in an alcove of trees where they would go to spar, have picnics, or just to talk. It was one of Rayne's favorite places, and it was far enough from the farm that he thought his father's grave would go undisturbed.

After that, Rayne went back to the farm and packed up the few possessions he thought his father would want him to keep. There was his father's copy of the Tome of Laws—it was the only book they owned, and his father had used it to teach him to read. There was also Rayne's few belongings, like clothes and a bow and quiver with several arrows he and his father had made. Lastly, Rayne wondered what to do about his father's sword. It had always been hung on the back of the front door, and aside from the Tome of Laws, it was the only item his father had kept from his days as a guardian.

Rayne had found the sword propped up against the table by his deceased father. After cleaning off the blood, Rayne returned the sword to its sheath, and in the process, noticed an engraved crest on the blade just above the hilt. He had seen this symbol before in Lewyol, and if he recalled correctly, it was the crest of the royalty. In addition, there were two engraved swords crossed just below the crest, with the letters "PGPE" followed by a date.

Rayne didn't know the meaning of the symbol or of the letters, but he did understand that the sword meant a great deal to his father. He imagined his father would want him to keep it.

He visited his father's grave one last time. Standing over the gravesite, Rayne couldn't help but wonder why his father didn't want anyone to know who he was. He loved his father very much, and although they didn't always see eye to eye, Rayne respected him. He couldn't possibly imagine what his father had done to cause himself such shame.

Perhaps his grandparents knew. Maybe they could explain why his father thought the guardians were after him. He knew his father had been a guardian many years ago, but his father didn't speak much about it, aside from a few occasions while he was training Rayne to fight.

Rayne scattered dry hay all over the inside of the house, making sure he covered the bodies of the dead guardians. Using flint and steel, he lit the home on fire. He watched long enough to make sure the whole house would be consumed, then climbed aboard the cart and turned the horse toward his grandparents' home.

⋖⊰╫⊱⋗

Alana didn't really care if she got lost—part of her was actually hoping she would. Wandering through the governor's garden in Lewyol was one of her favorite activities. She took every opportunity to leave the castle and come here, so when her husband said he needed to visit Governor Eadward, Alana jumped at the chance to go with him. For her, spending time in the garden was much more than a physical experience—it was an emotional one. It allowed her to think and reflect without the constant distractions at the castle.

The leaves on the trees showed signs of autumn. Some trees seemed to be fighting the changing of the season by remaining green, while others appeared to have embraced it by turning various shades of orange and red.

Strolling around the corner of a hedge, Alana came upon an older man on his hands and knees. "Garth, what are you doing down there, old friend?"

The gray-haired gardener finished removing some weeds that were growing in a flower bed of yellow roses before he looked up. "Ah, Lady Alana. Looking to get lost again?"

She smiled. "Something like that. It gives me an excuse to stay here longer."

Garth stood and wiped the dirt from his hands on his apron. "You've been getting lost here for years. Considering how many times you've visited, that is quite the achievement."

Alana bent down to smell the roses. "Yes. I remember the first time I came here many years ago. I started wandering and found a beautiful spot where I sat and admired the garden. It was only after you brought my parents that I heard someone use the word 'lost.' I thought that was funny, because I didn't feel lost. So, if coming here to relax and enjoy this wonderful garden means to get lost, then yes, that is my intention."

"Who got lost?" asked a voice behind Alana.

She turned to see Garth's daughter, Sunshine, standing in the path behind her, holding several books in her arms.

"No one yet, but Lady Alana hopes to soon," Garth said.

Sunshine nodded her head. "A noble goal."

"It's good to see you again, Sunshine," Alana said. "I see that at least someone is making good use of the governor's library."

Glancing down at the books, Sunshine said, "Yes, we tend to keep each other company."

"With all the reading you do, you probably know more than most of the new savants we have at the castle," Alana said. "If you ever need more books to read, let me know and I'm sure I could get you some from the castle library."

Sunshine's eyes lit up. "You could?"

"Oh, yes. I'm sure the books from the castle would enjoy the company too."

"That's very kind of you, Lady Alana," Garth said.

Alana shrugged off the compliment. "Think nothing of it. As a noble, I have the right to take any book I want, and many of them are just collecting dust. I would love to see them be put to good use."

"Alana! Alana!" shouted someone from the other end of the garden.

"It's my husband," Alana said, her shoulders slumping a little.

Garth started walking toward the sound. "Don't worry. I'll help your husband look for you. However, it may take us a while, since you are lost in the garden. The last place I'd think to look is the southwest corner."

Alana reached out and squeezed Garth's arm. "Thank you," she said before she headed southwest.

⇥✢⇤

In the storage room, Bertram sat on top of a rolled-up tapestry, holding a glass object in his hand and peering at it curiously.

"What did you call it again?" Priest Sherwyn asked.

"A prism," the savant answered.

Sherwyn rubbed his hand over his bald head. "A prison? What could you keep locked in something so tiny?"

The savant chuckled. "No, not 'prison.' It's a 'prism,' with an 'm' at the end. But you are right in one regard—it does keep something inside it."

"Oh?"

Bertram stood and walked over to a narrow beam of light shining down through a lattice that covered one of the upper windows. Extending a hand, he held the prism out so the light hit one side of the pyramid-shaped glass. The result made Sherwyn gasp.

On the opposite wall shone a light pattern of various hues. "A rainbow!" Sherwyn said, astonished. "This prism holds a rainbow? How is that possible?"

"I'm not sure. When I found it, there was a note that simply said, 'Hold this prism up to a beam of light to display the rainbow.' I'm guessing that is why they put the lattice on that window above, to produce the right light. It's one of many mysteries I've run across here in this room."

Sherwyn walked over to the light pattern and examined it closer. "If I recall, Magistrate Seanan told me you started coming here many years ago looking for something dealing with the Tome of Laws."

"Yes. I never found an answer to that puzzle, but with all the things here to explore and with all my many duties, there are still a number of areas I've not searched."

Sherwyn turned back to the savant. "Speaking of your duties, they will be changing soon."

"What do you mean?"

"Magistrate Seanan is very sick. Anemone doesn't know how much longer he'll be with us. It's time for him to step down from the Hierarchy of Magistrates. He wants *you* to take his place. He asked me to tell you."

Bertram nearly dropped the glass pyramid. "Me? But I'm not a magistrate—I'm a savant."

"Savants have become magistrates in the past. It isn't unheard of," Sherwyn said. "And I daresay you know the law better than anyone. Over the years, your insight on the Tome of Laws has been of great value. You've helped clear up issues that have become, well, muddy at times."

Bertram returned the prism to the shelf and shook his head. "I don't think Councilor Abrecan will approve of this. I've heard that he wants Magistrate Caldre on the hierarchy."

Sherwyn smiled. "Councilor Abrecan doesn't have to approve. The magistrates are independent from the royalty—you know that. In fact, Abrecan is the reason you were chosen."

"I'm not sure what you mean." Bertram sat down again on the tapestry.

Sherwyn sat next to him. "You recall that twenty years ago, Abrecan tried to hold a Shoginoc to find a wife for Daimh. You stopped that. The next Shoginoc is less than a year from now. Seanan and I have been talking about it for some time. We both want you there to make sure that Abrecan doesn't interfere. He needs to be removed from power."

"I'm not sure what I can do," Bertram said, starting to chew on a fingernail.

Sherwyn patted Bertram. "Just make sure the Tome of Laws is followed. It's kept the peace for centuries when we've done as it says."

"Someone will need to replace me," Bertram pointed out. "And I've not been impressed with the recent savants who have been selected."

Sherwyn chuckled. "I've thought of that too. I was asking around recently if anyone had a suggestion for a new savant, and I got quite an interesting response from one of the nobles."

⟨⟫⟩

Kelvin bit into the tart and was rewarded for his efforts. The tangy berries complimented the light, sugary glaze perfectly. "Delicious. Absolutely delicious," he said, taking another bite.

Nadia looked up from her sewing. "Don't pat yourself on the back too hard, or you may knock the tart out of your hand."

Kelvin took another tart off the table and playfully ran it back and forth under Nadia's nose. "It's your fault I can make these at all. Had you not forced me to make these years ago, you'd still be the master of tarts. Don't be jealous that I can make them better than you."

"You certainly *cannot* make them better than me!" Nadia said in mock anger.

"Oh? Is that so? Prove me wrong then." Kelvin took the tart away and held it protectively.

Nadia wagged a finger at her husband. "Oh, no, no. I'm not falling for that trick again. You play on my pride, and to show you I'm better, I make up a whole new batch of tarts. You then sample the whole lot for 'judging reasons.'"

"Then you acknowledge that you can do no better, and I remain the champion!" Kelvin raised both hands above his head in triumph.

Grabbing a rolled-up pair of newly darned socks, Nadia said, "I'll show you who is champion!" She went to throw the socks, but Kelvin ducked and made a beeline for the door as fast as his old legs would take him. He opened it and ran outside, hearing Nadia in pursuit. He had taken half a dozen steps when he spotted a horse and cart coming down the road to their farm. Squinting, he tried to make out who it was.

He came to a stop just as he felt the socks hit him in the back of the head. Nadia came up beside him and said, "It looks like Rayne."

Kelvin blinked in confusion. "No, it doesn't. There isn't a cloud in the sky."

"No, I mean it looks like our grandson, Rayne." She pointed to their visitor.

"Oh, yes, I see him now. But where's Rinan?"

The older couple waited patiently. When their grandson got within shouting distance, Nadia called, "Hello, Rayne! This is a surprise. Where is your father?"

Rayne didn't respond right away, but when he climbed off the cart, he spoke. "Grandmother, Grandfather, something terrible has happened."

They led him into the house, and after the three of them sat at the table, he told them what had transpired. After the initial shock wore off, Nadia broke into tears, while Kelvin became stiff and stoic.

"Why were the guardians after him?" Rayne asked.

Nadia and Kelvin exchanged a glance before either one of them spoke. "We don't know," Kelvin said. "Your father said he made some mistakes while he was a guardian. Perhaps…"

"Well, do you at least know why he didn't want anyone to know he was my father?" Rayne asked.

Nadia wiped tears away with a handkerchief. "On his visits, it became clear that he wanted you to become the guardian he failed to be. Perhaps he didn't want anyone to judge you or your abilities based on your parentage."

"But if I enter the Mortentaun, they'll ask where I'm from. What do I say?"

"You tell them the truth," Kelvin said. "You are from Lebu. You may have grown up in Tevoil, but you live here now, with us."

Rayne leaned forward and put his head in his hands. "This all seems like a nightmare. I can't believe he is gone."

Nadia stood up and embraced her grandson from behind. "We helped your father when he needed us, and we'll help you. Don't worry, Rayne—we're here for you."

It was agreed upon that he would be given Rinan's old room. The rest of the day was spent cleaning out the various items that had been put in the bedroom over time and moving Rayne's things from the cart to the house. After Rayne had gone to bed for the night, Nadia said to her husband in a quiet voice, "I'm not sure I feel good about lying to Rayne. Maybe we should tell him about what Rinan did and about his real mother." Kelvin shook his head. "We promised Rinan that we wouldn't reveal that to Rayne. It's for his protection. You know how badly Rinan wanted Rayne to become a guardian. Let's honor our son's last wish and do whatever we can to help. Knowing the truth at this point in time will only complicate things. Perhaps later, when the time is right, we'll tell him."

CHAPTER 15

Three Months Later

Savant Bertram tried to distract himself by doing some transcribing, but his thoughts kept drifting back to what was going to happen later at court. Despite his misgivings, he had resigned himself to the fact that he would not be a savant much longer. He had read what the duties of a magistrate were, so he was familiar with what his daily tasks would be.

What he wasn't sure about was how many of his responsibilities would require him to deal directly with Councilor Abrecan. Over the years, Bertram had felt that Abrecan didn't particularly like him. He mentioned this to Sherwyn once or twice, and the priest had told him not to worry—Abrecan treated most people that way. When Bertram had been asked to clarify some minor disagreements about the law, he had done so quickly and logically. Still, it seemed that more often than not, Bertram's input seemed to upset the councilor.

There had been no full-blown confrontations between him and Abrecan, aside from the discussion many years ago to determine when the next Shoginoc would be held, and even then, it wasn't a heated argument. Not long after the death of Queen Eliana, there had been a few out-and-out arguments between Councilor Abrecan and various people in the castle. Bertram didn't believe it to be a coincidence that the people who argued with Abrecan often ended up missing or convicted of crimes that were serious enough to have them executed or thrown in the dungeon for life.

At the same time, Bertram always felt the duty to stand up for what was right—he just did so in a more tactful and less confrontational way. He avoided the councilor as much as possible, but he knew that would be more difficult from now on, and that is what made him the most nervous.

Once he became one of the Hierarchy of Magistrates, he would be even more visible in Abrecan's eyes. He just hoped this new visibility didn't cause *him* to disappear.

-»✠«-

"Have you been inside the castle before?" Alana asked Sunshine as they approached the gates.

Sunshine nodded. "Yes, many years ago."

Alana snapped her fingers. "Oh, that's right. Your father was given an award here for his work on the governor's garden in Lewyol. I remember that. That *was* a number of years ago—you must have been small at the time."

"I was. However, I do remember it quite clearly."

Alana chuckled. "Chances are, things have changed quite a bit, but I'll let you discover that for yourself."

Sunshine followed Alana over the lowered drawbridge that crossed a wide moat. They walked under the raised portcullis and into a large chamber.

The first thing that struck Sunshine was how ornately everything was decorated. The walls were lined with tapestries that all looked fairly new. Most of them contained images of men Sunshine figured to be Councilor Abrecan and King Daimh, from the clothes they wore and the crowns on their heads. At the end of the entrance chamber stood two large wooden doors, closed, with guardians on either side. An older, bald man wearing the robes of a priest stood at the doors and smiled as they approached.

"Sunshine," Alana said, "this is Sherwyn, the castle priest."

Sunshine curtseyed. "It's a pleasure to meet you, Priest Sherwyn."

"And I, you." Sherwyn nodded.

"Now, Sunshine," Alana said, "as we discussed, this will be a very important day. The court will be starting soon. The introductions of the new savants will happen toward the end, so we'll sit patiently until it's our turn."

"Understood," Sunshine responded.

"This should be quite interesting." Sherwyn straightened the mantle draped around his neck. "Since you will be the first female savant the kingdom has ever had, I suspect this will cause quite a stir."

Sunshine felt very tiny when she walked into the hall. The roof must have been five stories high, with arched, stained-glass windows running its length. Banners displaying the colors and crests of the different districts lined the walls. A wide, red carpet ran from the doors to a raised platform at the other end. The platform, which was bigger than Sunshine remembered—couldn't really be called a dais as much as a stage. In the very center, two large and elaborately crafted thrones sat on a raised section of the stage. On either side were two smaller thrones, lower than the others and back a pace or so. Even lower than that sat a large table off to the left, positioned at an angle so it faced both the thrones and the rest of the hall. Hanging thirty feet down from the ceiling behind the stage were two huge tapestries. The one on the left depicted a man who Sunshine guessed was Abrecan, from the graying hair, while the one on the right had to be the king. Both were posed proudly and held weapons in their hands.

Alana and Sherwyn walked down the red carpet, with Sunshine a step behind. On either side of the carpet were rows of chairs and benches that looked like they could be moved to face either the stage or center of the hall.

Despite the amount of people the room could hold, only the first several rows were occupied today. Sunshine deduced from their clothing that most were nobles. One section was full of people she guessed to be savants. Several of them were just a few years older than she, and one man actually looked younger.

An older, sharp-nosed man with dark hair pulled back into a ponytail caught her eye next. He was staring at her with an all-too-familiar look. She wasn't sure who he was, but there was something aside from the expression on his face that bothered her.

Alana stopped at one of the benches near the front and motioned Sunshine to go in first and have a seat. Priest Sherwyn walked up to the stage, and after climbing some stairs off to the side, took a seat at the large table.

After a few moments, Sunshine turned to Alana, who had sat down next to her, and whispered, "It really works."

"What really works?"

Sunshine motioned to the hall and the large tapestries. "The setting. The ridiculously large tapestries, the gaudy, oversized thrones, all of it—it's designed to intimidate."

Alana looked around and was quiet for a moment. "I'd never really thought of that, but it does make sense. The fact you figured that out just goes to show me I made the right choice in sponsoring you as a savant."

The door behind them opened again, and four men dressed in long black robes with padded shoulders walked toward the stage. They sat down at the table, leaving the chair closest to the thrones vacant.

"The royalty is next," Alana whispered, "although we may have to wait a little while. Abrecan likes to make a dramatic entrance."

Sunshine waited patiently with her hands folded in her lap. She reflected on how she was feeling at the moment. She wasn't nervous, but she was definitely anxious about what was going on around her.

When Alana had asked Sunshine if she would be interested in becoming a savant, only her father didn't think the request was a joke. There had never been a female savant, but as they discussed it, her father pointed out that there had to be a first time for everything.

Sunshine knew she would miss her family, but the opportunity to come to the castle and have access to its vast library was too appealing. She knew she would be expected to teach and perform other duties, but she would also have time to read.

One thing she knew was that her time in the castle would definitely be more interesting than life in Lewyol.

⊰⧣⊱

Councilor Abrecan reached up to make sure his crown was straight. Satisfied, he was about to motion for the guardians to open the doors and let him into the main hall when he heard someone approaching from behind.

"Greetings, Father," King Daimh said. "Now that I'm here, we can enter."

Turning to face his son, Abrecan narrowed his eyes. "What are you doing here, Daimh?"

"What do you mean? Is court not being held today?"

"Yes, but you *never* attend court," Abrecan said.

The king smiled. "Ah, but today is different. Word has it the new tapestries have been completed, as well as my new throne. Also, I heard that something important is going to happen. I want to be here so people can see me in my new throne in front of my new tapestry when the important news is given. I've invited the minstrels to attend so they can write a song about it."

Abrecan frowned. "Where did you hear such a rumor?"

Waving a hand dismissively, Daimh said, "Oh, I don't remember —a guardian or servant, probably."

"But didn't you and Nicole have plans today to view the latest play the minstrels are performing?" Abrecan moved between Daimh and the doors that led to the main hall.

Daimh sighed. "Oh, yes, and I'm sure it will be magnificent! It's about how I saved your life when Councilor Kenrik was killed. But once I heard that something important was going to happen today, I told the minstrels to put off the performance until tomorrow."

"I'm sure court will bore you, Son. I'm sure Nicole can find something for you two to do."

Daimh rolled his eyes. "Doubtful. And after all these years of failing to bear me any children, I don't think she's capable of doing so. I've grown fond of her, and I can't imagine being with anyone else, even if she is overly sensitive about what people think of her. She actually fainted this morning when she found a gray hair. She'd be with me now if the nursemaids were not attending her."

Folding his arms, Abrecan said, "Daimh, there is no need for you to come to court. I can take care of any issues that arise."

"Oh, yes, I'll let you deal with any of the unpleasant details." Daimh admired his reflection in the polished armor of one of the guardians. "I'm not here for that. I'm here so my subjects can see their king. It will be a special honor for them. Now let's go in. I'm tired of waiting."

⇥✦⇤

The blaring of trumpets sounded from behind and to the right of the stage. Sunshine watched as two large doors were opened and in strutted two men, both wearing crowns and carrying scepters. The older of the two went first and took a seat in the left-most throne, which Sunshine guessed should be for the queen. The younger and taller man followed after, and stood looking carefully at the throne on the right for a moment before he sat down with a large grin on his face.

"I proclaim this court to start!" King Daimh announced, flashing his dimples.

Everyone sat quietly for a moment, seemingly unsure how to react to the king's statement.

"As you can see," Abrecan said, "the king has decided to treat you all by attending court today. Priest Sherwyn, if you would." And with that, Abrecan motioned to the table on the left.

Priest Sherwyn stood and said in a loud, clear voice, "Court will now begin. We recognize that Magistrate Seanan is absent due to illness. We will first hear reports from the various districts and from the captain of the guardians. After that, any new castle savants will be presented, followed by a special announcement from the magistrates."

Sunshine listened as the representatives from the different districts gave brief reports. When the representative from Lewyol stood, Sunshine found herself curious as to what would be said about her home district.

"There are no major concerns to present to the court," the representative said. "However, to follow up from a previous report, Guardians Zubin, Thomas, and Thomas are still missing. Their replacements have arrived and have assumed their duties."

Sunshine felt a chill run down her back. She hadn't been into town since her run-in with the guardians. Her father thought it best she not go for a while. She'd heard that the guardians who harassed her were replaced, but she didn't know why. She couldn't help but think it had something to do with Rayne. She had not seen or heard from him, and she wondered how he was doing.

Her thoughts were still focused on what could have happened when the captain of the guardians stood to speak. "To address the issue in Lewyol, I recently received word from some of my men that the missing guardians had an altercation with a farmer from Tevoil. They searched the area of Tevoil and were directed to a farm further into the district. They discovered it had been burned to the ground. There were human remains among the ashes, although they were unable to determine how many bodies. It is assumed that the guardians found the farmer in question, killed him and his family, and then burned the farm down. Although we do not know all the details, I'm sure they were justified in their actions. When they return to duty, I recommend that they are honored."

Sunshine was stunned. She hadn't known Rayne for long, but had liked him very much. She couldn't believe that killing him and his father could be justified. She sat, unaware that the captain had finished and that Sherwyn had stood to introduce the next part of the agenda. She snapped out of her reverie when Alana elbowed her in the side and then stood up.

Following the noble, Sunshine walked to the end of the red carpet in front of the stage. Alana stood tall, elevated her chin slightly, and said in a regal voice, "King Daimh, Councilor Abrecan, I am proud to sponsor Savant Sunshine, from the district of Lewyol."

Abrecan's jaw dropped. Daimh sat up straight and moved to the edge of his throne. Pointing to Sunshine, the king said, "That's a woman!"

Whether in shock from hearing about Rayne or something else, Sunshine didn't think before she responded, "Very good, Your Majesty. You got it right on the first guess."

Abrecan's jaw dropped even more, and he looked like he was about to say something, but he was interrupted when his son exclaimed, "Yes, I did, didn't I? Good of you to notice. I must say, you are much prettier than the rest of the savants we have here. We welcome you to the castle."

Abrecan turned his head sharply and stared at his son. He didn't say anything, but then turned his attention to the magistrates. "There must be some mistake! A woman can't be a savant. Am I correct?"

The hierarchy glanced at each other blankly for a moment before they looked out to the crowd. "Savant Bertram?" one of them asked.

A tall, thin man stood. "Although it has not happened before, there is nothing in the Tome of Laws that prevents it."

"Then it is settled," King Daimh said. "This is a very important day in the history of Bariwon! We've witnessed the very first woman to become a savant. What a wonderful song this will make!"

He eyed the minstrels, who all nodded emphatically. Returning his attention to the young woman before him, the king said, "Welcome to the castle, Savant...er, what was your name again?"

Alana spoke up before Sunshine could say anything. "Sunshine, Your Majesty. Her name is Sunshine. And thank you very much." Alana curtsied, with Sunshine following her lead, and then walked back to their bench and sat down.

⊰╪⊱

Priest Sherwyn did his best to hide the smile on his face. When Alana had first told him about Sunshine and how she would make an excellent savant, he couldn't help but think how this would unsettle Abrecan. The councilor seemed to have very little regard for anyone of the female gender; in fact, he had proven many times over the years that he thought women were inferior to men. To have the king trump his father by accepting Sunshine so readily was priceless—and just what Sherwyn was hoping for when he hinted to the king's guardians that the king should be at the next court. However, the joy Sherwyn got from watching Abrecan squirm was fleeting. The next part of the court could prove to be dangerous, and it was Sherwyn's responsibility to set the wheels in motion.

"Next on the agenda is an announcement from the Hierarchy of Magistrates." He stood and unrolled a piece of parchment. "Since Magistrate Seanan is unable to attend, he asked me to read the following statement: *'I, Magistrate Seanan, am very ill and do not have any illusions that I will be on the face of the land much longer. To this end, I have chosen to step down as a member of the Hierarchy of Magistrates. After much consideration, I have chosen a new member of the hierarchy.'*

Sherwyn paused and spared a glance around him. Councilor Abrecan was looking at him expectantly, King Daimh was staring off into space and looking bored, Magistrate Caldre was tightening the knot on his ponytail, and Savant Bertram looked like he was going to be sick.

After clearing his throat, Sherwyn read, *"'I am pleased to announce that the newest member of the Hierarchy of Magistrates is Savant Bertram.'"*

For a moment, it was very quiet in the main hall as the announcement sunk in. The silence was short-lived as the hall exploded in objections and cheers.

"Quiet!" Abrecan thundered, standing up.

The court quickly followed the councilor's command.

"Let me see that," Abrecan ordered.

Sherwyn walked over and handed the parchment to the councilor. Abrecan read over the letter several times before he said anything.

He turned to the rest of the hierarchy. "I see that you all signed the document as witnesses. Are you sure that Seanan said Bertram?"

The other members of the hierarchy nodded in confirmation. Abrecan handed the parchment back to Sherwyn, but not before he had squeezed it tightly in his hands, crumpling the edges.

"Welcome then, *Magistrate* Bertram," said Abrecan in a cold voice. "And on that note, I call this court to an end."

⤙⧧⧉⤚

Sunshine followed Alana through the castle, up several flights of stairs, and then down a long corridor to the room she was told would be her new home.

Alana opened the door. "That went better than I expected. It was a good thing the king was there and so willing to accept you. The fact that you are so beautiful didn't hurt things, either."

Alana walked into the room. "The castle will provide everything you need, but the items you brought with you have been moved here. I hope you'll find it satisfactory."

Looking around the room, Sunshine saw that it was perfect. There was a fireplace big enough to keep the room warm and to provide light to read by. The wardrobe was opposite a bed that looked quite comfortable. Next to the wardrobe sat a small table with a couple of thick books on top. Although it was everything Sunshine could have hoped for, she didn't feel the joy she had anticipated.

Alana must have noticed something was wrong. "Is there a problem with the room? I hoped you'd be pleased."

Sunshine shook her head. "Please don't misunderstand. I *am* grateful. It's better than I could have imagined."

"Then what is the matter?" the noble asked. "You look as if you just received bad news."

Sunshine walked to the table and picked up one of the books. "Do you remember during court today the report about the missing guardians from Lewyol?"

Alana walked over to Sunshine, put her arm around her, and said, "Yes, I remember. Did you know them?"

"I did, yes, but that isn't the reason I'm...well, I'm not sure how to describe how I feel." Sunshine carefully opened the pages of the book. "The guardians were bullies. They were threatening me one day, and the farmer from Tevoil defended me. I took him home to my family and he had dinner with us. He was very kind and wonderful—he was unlike anyone else I had met. And now because of me, he's..."

She couldn't say any more. Alana pulled Sunshine close and embraced her, letting the young woman cry.

CHAPTER 16
Two Months Later

The arrow flew straight and true, and despite a strong wind, hit its mark dead center.

"Very impressive," Kelvin said. "Even your father would have had difficulty with that shot."

Rayne reached into his quiver and pulled out another arrow. The winter sun reflected off a layer of new-fallen snow, causing both Rayne and his grandfather to squint at the target—a painted bull's eye on the side of a large oak tree forty paces off. "Thanks, Grandfather. He always said I had uncanny aim with a bow and arrow."

Cupping a hand over his eyes, Kelvin turned to look at his grandson. "You've been practicing every day since you got here. Last summer when you and your father came to visit, you told me you weren't too sure that you wanted to become a guardian. It appears you've changed your mind. Is this all because of your father's note?"

Rayne fit the arrow into the bow. "His wish for me to become a guardian does play a part, but it's more than that."

"In what way?"

The young man raised the bow and eyed the target. "I've had a lot of time to think. If it meant that much to my father, there must have been something to it. He always said the guardians were here to serve the people, but from what I saw in Lewyol and what I've heard from you, there are some who have lost sight of that. Father spent his whole life teaching me not only to fight, but to be a good person. Over time, I've come to realize that becoming a guardian is something I want to do after all."

Kelvin smiled. "I'm glad to hear that. You can't live your life based on other people's expectations."

"And"—Rayne pulled back the string—"there's someone from Lewyol I want to see at the Mortentaun this spring."

Changing his focus to the target, Kelvin said, "Well, it sounds like there are several reasons why you are training so hard. You'll need to practice sparring, and I'm way too old for that. But I know someone who can help you."

Rayne let go of the bowstring, and the arrow raced toward the tree. It struck the target right next to the previous arrow. "I'd be very interested in meeting this person. Thank you, Grandfather."

→❈←

Explain why *this* plan failed," Abrecan said, sitting at the table in his room, holding a drink.

Caldre wasn't sure which was more frustrating—the fact that Abrecan didn't seem disturbed by this latest failure, or that his plan to frame Magistrate Bertram had failed again.

Throwing his hands up in the air, Caldre said, "I don't know why it failed. It should have worked. What man wouldn't take payment for such a seemingly innocent favor?"

"And then you would have caught him in the bribe and had him removed, correct?" Abrecan looked smug.

Caldre nodded. "Of course. *I* should be on the hierarchy, not him. I'm sure if we can get Bertram removed, I could pressure the other four old fools to select me to take his place. Are you sure I can't just have him killed?"

"It's not that simple." Abrecan frowned. "Bertram doesn't leave the castle, ever. We've tried to lure him out so he could meet an unfortunate end, but he won't go. We don't have any power to make him leave, either. If he were to be murdered in the castle, it would reflect very badly on us. There was quite a backlash when Queen Eliana died here—I don't need to remind you of all the headaches that caused, and that actually *was* an accident."

Caldre reached back and tightened the knot on his ponytail. "Yes, I remember how people didn't feel safe in the castle and it took a long time to calm their fears."

"Why not get rid of one of the other hierarchy members?" Abrecan asked.

"Because it was Bertram that got my spot, and so *he* must go. In addition, over the last few months, the new head of the hierarchy,

Magistrate Aldous, has become very impressed with Bertram. If another spot were to open up, I think Bertram could persuade Aldous to exclude me. After my several attempts, I suspect Bertram knows I'm out to get him."

A solid knock on the door made Abrecan stand and say, "You will drop any more plans to get rid of Bertram, at least for now. You will instead help me with another important matter."

Caldre realized now why Abrecan wasn't getting upset—it didn't really matter if Caldre was on the hierarchy or not. Unless Abrecan felt like he personally benefited from something, he showed little interest in it. It was obvious now that Abrecan already had something else in the works.

As he walked to the door, Abrecan said, "This should be the man that holds the key to my future." He opened it and said, "Ah, Governor Eadward. Welcome! How was your trip?"

⇥✣⇤

"And this is the room I told you about," Bertram said, trying to keep his voice from cracking. Sunshine gasped softly when she entered the large room. It was nearly as long as the main hall, though the ceiling was not nearly as high. Bookshelves lined the walls and ran down the center. The shelves contained not only books, but various objects of different sizes and materials. Rolled-up tapestries were scattered around the floor, leaving just enough space to walk around.

"I thought you were embellishing, but obviously you were not."

Bertram took a few tentative steps into the room and pointed to the top of a bookcase by the door. "That's where I started looking, oh, I'm guessing before you were born. Over the years, I worked my way around the room and I've discovered many interesting things, but never the answer to my original question."

"Did other savants help you look?" Sunshine asked, following Bertram into the room.

He shook his head. "No, none of them did. In fact, you are the first savant to ask me about the seemingly missing word in the Tome of Laws."

Sunshine frowned. "I find it hard to believe that none of the other savants discovered the error when transcribing."

"To be fair, I didn't notice it either, at first," Bertram said. "It was only when I was teaching the young nobles one day that I discovered it. I have learned over time that most people's minds fill in the missing word automatically when reading the passage."

After taking a few steps further into the room, Sunshine turned around in a slow circle, looking both high and low at her surroundings. "When was the last time you were here, Magistrate?"

"Ah," he said, avoiding her gaze. "It must have been weeks ago. Between overseeing the training of the new savants and learning my duties as a magistrate, I've been quite busy. I'm glad you came to me with your question about the omitted word. It reminded me of this place. I miss coming here."

"And you wouldn't mind if I spent time looking around?" Sunshine asked, taking a pyramid-shaped glass object from one of the shelves and peering into it.

Bertram paused before he answered. He had always enjoyed this room because it was away from everyone else. Only the late Magistrate Seanan and Priest Sherwyn knew he spent time here. But when Sunshine came to him, on a suggestion from Priest Sherwyn, he realized that he was being selfish and should share this room with someone else. Soon after Sunshine was titled a savant, it became apparent she was very bright and curious, reminding him of himself when he was younger. She also wasn't interested in the power or fame that many in the castle sought, so Bertram felt that if he would share the knowledge of this room with anyone, it would be her. If only he could relax in her presence. After all these years, beautiful women still made him nervous.

"Oh, no. Not at all," he said finally, probably sounding less convincing than he intended. "I'm glad someone else has taken an interest in this room. There are many things to be learned here. Take, for example, the prism in your hand. The overcast sky won't allow you to use it today, but on the next sunny day, follow the instructions next to where you found it. You'll be in for a pleasant surprise."

Sunshine smiled at Bertram. "Thank you."

"Thank me for what?" he asked, shying away from her.

She returned the prism to the shelf. "Thank you for showing me this place. Not only that, but thank you for making me feel welcome to the castle and for taking me seriously."

Bertram blushed at the compliment. "You are more than welcome. When I came here, I felt the same way you do now, but for other reasons. Please let me know if you have questions about anything you find in here, or if you find the answer to the question that brought me here in the first place. I fear my duties will keep me from spending any time here for a while."

Sunshine smiled and nodded. "I promise."

※

Governor Nash of Lebu laughed heartily. He slapped his knee while tears ran down both cheeks into his snowy-white beard. Then, the thickly built man clapped his hands together and quoted, "'Because the sun only comes out during the day!' Yes, very funny. I hadn't heard that one. Very funny indeed!"

Kelvin bowed slightly. "I see you haven't lost your sense of humor since you became governor."

"Ah, just the opposite." Nash motioned for Kelvin to take a seat next to his desk. "I've found I need my sense of humor now more than ever. But I'm sure you didn't come just to tell me a joke, old friend. What brings you here?"

Kelvin crossed the room and sat in the padded chair. "When my son Rinan wanted to become a guardian, you taught him what he needed to know from your days as a guardian. Thanks to your help, he did quite well in the Mortentaun."

"Ah, yes, Rinan." Nash sat down, leaned back, and placed both hands behind his head. "He was a natural, that one—quick as lightning and surprisingly strong for someone of his build. I heard a rumor that he left the castle not long after Queen Eliana's death, rest her soul."

Kelvin nodded. "That's correct. Rinan moved to a different district and had a son."

Nash's eyes lit up. "Why, that makes you a grandfather, you old dog! How is Rinan doing?"

"Rinan's dead. He passed away a few months back."

The governor got up from behind his desk and sat down in a chair next to Kelvin, then put his muscular arm around him. "I'm so sorry to hear that. Having buried two children myself, I know the pain you feel. What of your grandson and Rinan's wife?"

Kelvin thought a moment before he spoke again. "Rinan's wife died during childbirth. My grandson, Rayne, is the reason I came to see you."

Looking intently at Kelvin, Nash said, "Why's that?"

"Rayne desperately wants to become a guardian like his father. I've seen him training, and I believe he has as much talent, if not more, than Rinan. He would make an excellent representative for our district in the Mortentaun, but he could use your help."

Nash smacked Kelvin hard on the back, nearly knocking him out of the chair. "Absolutely! We have a few young men here in town who have been getting together to train. I've been overseeing their work, and we'd love to have Rayne join us."

"Thank you, Nash," Kelvin said. "One last favor, if I may?"

"Anything."

Kelvin looked straight into the governor's eyes, making him see how serious he was. "Rinan didn't exactly leave the castle under the best of circumstances. That's why I've not mentioned this before. I'd rather not go into details, but I fear there may be those at the Mortentaun who will judge less than favorably if they knew that Rayne was Rinan's son. Could we simply tell people that Rayne's father has passed on and he is now in my care?"

Nash looked searchingly at Kelvin for a moment before he responded. "You are one of the most honorable people I've ever met. I trust you on this and will respect your wishes—on one condition."

"What would that be?"

A big grin split Nash's face. "If I recall, your wife made the best tarts I've ever had. Next time you come, you must bring some."

⇥✦⇤

Two Months Later

Priest Sherwyn took in a deep breath, held it for a moment, and then exhaled slowly. In the sixty-five years he'd been alive, he'd discovered that this was one of his favorite times of the year. He often took walks to stretch his legs, and on his way out of the castle today, he had bumped into Anemone and invited her to come along.

They walked to a slightly sloping hill that was a fair distance from the castle. The hill had one large tree standing majestically at the summit. Sherwyn looked closely at the tips of the tree when they arrived. Buds were definitely starting to form.

"Do you see them? The buds on the trees?" he asked Anemone.

The nursemaid used her cane for support as she leaned forward and squinted. "Yes, I believe I do."

He took another deep breath. "You can even smell a difference in the air. It gives me hope."

"Hope? Hope for what?"

Sherwyn smiled. "Every year, the snow comes and makes the world a cold and inhospitable place. But no matter how hard it snows or how cold it gets in any given winter, new life always comes again in the spring. There is always hope, no matter how bad things get."

"And you hope this year will make things better, correct?" Anemone asked, tightening her gray, hooded cloak around her.

"This year holds definite promise," Sherwyn said. "Twenty-one years have finally passed, and a new king and queen will be chosen in the summer. Daimh's reign as king, or probably more accurately, Abrecan's reign, has been difficult."

Anemone nodded in agreement. "Do you ever wonder if we did the right thing with Rinan and Eliana?"

"I wonder that all the time," Sherwyn said. "And I've come to the conclusion that we made a mistake. Doing something wrong, even for a perceived greater good, can only lead to bigger problems. I can't say for sure, but had Eliana stepped down as queen, she'd probably still be alive. I've not heard from Rinan since he left. I can only hope he has lived a happy life."

Anemone looked at Sherwyn with tears forming in her eyes. "Yes, I've come to the same conclusion. Is there anything we can do to atone for our actions?"

The priest reached out and gently touched one of the branches. "You never know what opportunities will be presented. In the meantime, we should just try to do what is right, and for the right reasons."

⋆⋇⋆

Lady Linden came up to her husband, who was standing with his arms folded, surveying the scene in front of him. She had been attracted to Nash when they first met, not long after he retired from being a guardian. He was a jolly man who always seemed to find the brighter side of things. She rarely saw him as serious as he was at the moment, and that was enough to bring her concern.

"What is it, Nash?" she asked, rubbing his back.

The large man looked at her and gave her a familiar smile. "Just lost in thought, my dear. Nothing's wrong—just the opposite." He nodded his head toward the open field, where four young men were sparring with large, wooden broadswords. A thin, blond-haired man was in the center, with the other three surrounding him. He was moving quickly, effectively fending off each attack from the other three.

"Is that Rayne?" she asked, peering closely.

Nash chuckled. "Aye, it is. He's something special. I have no doubt he has the skill to become a guardian. But it's more than just his skills with a blade."

Resting her head on her husband's shoulder, Linden said, "Yes. He's a sharp boy. Very polite, and he has a good head on his shoulders. He'd make a nice change of pace from the guardians we've been getting recently. This will reflect well on the district, and you."

"You know I've never worried about trying to impress the castle—at least, not since Daimh became king." Nash stroked his beard. "But I do hope Rayne will have a positive impact on his fellow guardians."

"Aren't we getting ahead of ourselves?" Linden asked. "After all, he needs to do well at the Mortentaun to become a guardian."

"Bah!" Nash said. "Unless someone sabotages the Mortentaun, Rayne is a shoo-in."

CHAPTER 17

A light spring breeze washed over Rayne. He closed his eyes, drew in a deep breath, and then exhaled slowly. Tilting his head up and then opening his eyes, he saw high, white fluffy clouds floating in a clear blue sky. The sight was calming, while the noise around him had the opposite effect. Standing in a line surrounded by thousands of people was something Rayne had not experienced before, and it was unsettling. Even when he had gone into town with his father, there weren't crowds like there were today, the first day of the Mortentaun.

His grandfather stood beside him as they waited to register. The training over the last few months with Governor Nash had gone well, with the former guardian picking up where his father had left off. Rayne felt as physically ready as he could be, but his emotions were running a bit stronger than he would like.

"Next!" called a button-nosed man sitting behind a table with a quill in one hand.

Rayne and Kelvin stepped forward to the edge of the table. Not looking up from the parchment in front of him, the man asked, "Name?"

"Rayne, spelled R-A-Y-N-E."

The man looked as though he was stifling a chuckle. "If you say so. What district?"

Rayne looked at his grandfather, and Kelvin nodded.

"Lebu," Rayne said.

After writing down the information, Button Nose asked, "Father's name?"

Kelvin spoke up before Rayne could say anything. "His father is no longer with us. Rayne is my responsibility now. You can put down Kelvin as his sponsor."

"Fine, fine." The man noted it on the parchment. "Go to the staging area marked for your district and wait for your name to be called."

"Thank you very much," Rayne said. "By the way, can you tell us where the contestants from Lewyol are gathering?"

Bringing his head up for the first time, the man looked at Rayne and Kelvin and said, "Not my job." Then he looked past them and shouted, "Next!"

⋯⁂⋯

"You could use a good kissing." Sunshine smiled roguishly.

Bertram blinked a few times and nearly choked on his words. "Wh—what did you say?"

"It's something my dad said to me once when I got too involved in my books," she explained, still smiling. "It was his way of saying, 'Don't forget there are other things in life aside from reading.' I've never seen you leave the castle, and you hardly leave your chambers. It's the first day of the Mortentaun, for heaven's sake! Come with me and Alana. My family will be here, and I'd love to introduce you."

Sunshine's warm smile almost melted Bertram's defenses. Over the last few months, he and Sunshine had developed a mentor-student relationship. He had no illusions about anything romantic, but they definitely had a close friendship. Under Priest Sherwyn's advisement, Bertram kept a low profile and stayed away from others as much as possible. But with Sunshine, he found a kindred soul—someone else who thirsted after knowledge.

He had no desire or reason to leave the castle; he felt safer inside its walls. He had never explained this to Sunshine because he didn't want her to develop the same fears.

Bertram slowly shook his head. "I've far too much work to do. But please, go, have a good time. Perhaps you can invite your family to the castle. I'd be interested in meeting your father—he seems to be quite an interesting person, from what you've told me."

"Bertram, please?"

He gulped. "Perhaps another day. I have much yet to finish."

"All right then," Sunshine said in an overdramatic tone. She turned to leave, but then stopped. "Oh, by the way, I was sitting on one of the rolled-up tapestries last night reading an interesting book about the weather patterns in Bariwon. It was late and I was getting tired. I accidentally dropped the book when I started to doze off. When I went to pick it up, I happened to glance at the bottom shelf behind the tapestry.

There were several books down there, and it appeared that one may be an older version of the Tome of Laws, but with the dim lighting, I couldn't tell for sure. I tried to get it out, but was unable to because the tapestry was blocking the way, and it was too heavy for me to move by myself. Perhaps if you gave me a hand later, we could move it together."

Bertram's eyebrows shot up. "Could you tell how old the books were?"

Sunshine shrugged. "Not for sure, but they did look older than most of the books I've come across."

"Yes, by all means, come see me when you return," Bertram said, excited about the idea. "It may be just like the other copies we've come across, but you never know."

⊰⧉⊱

Bouncing up and down on the balls of his feet, Rayne anxiously awaited the officiator's command. Glancing to his left and his right, he sized up his competition. The group included everyone from his district, as well as those from the district of Donigi. In all, about forty young men stood on a line, awaiting the word to start the race.

The sprint was the first event of the day—a quick run of about two hundred paces. Rayne noted that there were several young men who looked built for speed, while some of the others would definitely do better in the events designed around strength.

Flexing his fingers in an effort to relax, Rayne tuned out everything around him, aside from the officiator and the goal line.

"Go!"

Pushing off with his right foot, Rayne started to run toward the goal. Within the first fifty paces, the runners started to separate. By the halfway mark, Rayne found there were more people behind him than in front. A thin, wiry man who wore a purple armband with the number 6 written on the side had started to leave the pack behind. Knowing he couldn't catch the faster man, Rayne focused instead on running as fast as he could.

Crossing the finish line, he ran on a bit further, and then turned back to see that the majority of the group was behind him. Taking in deep gulps of air and walking around, he worked his way back to the staging area for his district. His grandfather was waiting for him with a big smile on his face.

"Well done, Rayne!" Kelvin patted his grandson on the back. "We'll await the official announcement, but from what I saw, you were near the front."

Rayne noted the officiators conferring at the judging table. While he waited, he stood on his tiptoes and tried to look over the crowd. He had spotted the large, yellow banner of Lewyol indicating where their participants were gathered, but they were on the far side of the field. He'd not been able to go over and see if he could find Sunshine yet, but as he understood it, there would be a chance during the middle of the day, when participants could leave to get something to eat.

"Attention, please! Attention!" shouted an officiator who had stepped onto a small platform. The crowd quieted, and he continued. "In the first running of the sprint, number 6 from Donigi is awarded five points for winning the race. The following are awarded three points each for finishing in the first five."

Rayne knew he had done well and hoped he was one of the first five. He was a fairly fast runner, and he needed these points to help him advance to the next day's events. When the officiator called out number 17 from Lebu, he double-checked to be sure that was his number and breathed out a sigh of relief.

"Atta boy, Rayne!" Kelvin said, embracing him. "Three points. Great start to the Mortentaun!"

⤜✠⤛

Sunshine saw the yellow banner of Lewyol blowing in the breeze. "This way, Alana," she said, heading toward the spot where her family was to meet her.

"I'm sure you're looking forward to seeing your family, but try not to run over anyone on the way." Alana lifted the hem of her skirt and walked quickly to keep up with the young savant.

Slowing down, Sunshine said, "Sorry. I didn't think I would miss them as much as I have."

"It's quite all right." Alana smiled. "They aren't going anywhere. We'll find them."

Winding through the crowd, Sunshine searched for her family, and her heart leaped when she spotted her mother and younger brother sitting in the wooden stands. Within moments, they saw her too and made room for her and Alana to join them.

"Mom, Snapdragon!" Sunshine's voice quivered as she gave them each a quick hug. "It's so good to see you. Did I miss anything?"

Iolanthe shook her head. "Not really. There have been a few races already, but Oakleaf's group is still to come."

Sunshine looked down at the field and craned her neck, trying to spot her brother in the sea of young men. "I don't see him."

"Try looking with your eyes open, Shiny." Snapdragon pointed. "He's there, by Dad. He's been assigned the number 12."

Iolanthe pinched Snapdragon's arm. "You haven't seen your sister in months, and already you start with the teasing? Be nice!"

Looking rebuked, Snapdragon said, "Sorry, Shiny. I'll be nice. I missed you."

She smiled lopsidedly. "Well then, maybe you should improve your aim."

⁘

Rayne pointed to the young man with spiky blond hair near the front of the race. "See, Grandfather! I'm pretty sure that's Oakleaf. He's the brother of Sunshine, the girl from Lewyol I told you about."

"Ah. And if Oakleaf is here, Sunshine should be here as well."

Rayne responded with a quick nod of his head.

"Well, just don't let the thought of that young woman distract you," Kelvin said. "There's a lot of the Mortentaun yet to go, and you need to stay focused."

The race ended, and soon the officiator declared the results. "Five points to number 21 from Grenoa, the winner of the race. Three points each to the following: 5 from Grenoa, 3 from Grenoa, 19 from Grenoa, 12 from Lewyol, and 2 from Lewyol, for finishing in the first five. One point goes to everyone else, except for the last five men to finish the race, who get no points."

Cheers and groans from the crowd followed the announcement.

The officiator held up both hands, then said, "We will now prepare for the second event. This is a longer distance race, starting here, going around the castle, and ending up back here. We will stagger the starting times. Will the participants from Lebu and Donigi please come to the line?"

"Pace yourself, Rayne," his grandfather said. "Don't try to keep up with the fastest runner at the beginning—let him tire himself out."

⁘

When the participants from Tevoil were called for the long distance race, Sunshine was suddenly flooded with emotions. Rayne was from Tevoil, and if he was still alive, surely he'd be one of the men walking to the starting line. The thought of his death also reminded her that Zubin and the Thomas twins were still out there somewhere. A chill ran down her back at the realization that they may have been found and could possibly be here at the Mortentaun.

"What's wrong, dear?" her mother asked.

Sunshine realized her shoulders were slumped and she was staring at the ground. She sat up straighter and put on a smile. "Nothing. I was just reminded of something unpleasant."

"Anything you want to talk about?"

"No, not now. Perhaps later—let's watch the race." Sunshine turned her attention back to the field.

"All right. Let's think of happier things," Iolanthe said. "Do you see Rayne down there among the participants from Tevoil? I looked during their first race and didn't see him."

"Rayne? Who is that?" Alana asked.

Before Sunshine could say anything, Snapdragon blurted, "Oh, he's just a farmer Shiny's in love with, that's all."

Alana's eyes grew wider. "You mean, *that* farmer from Tevoil?"

Sunshine didn't say anything; she just gave Alana a hard stare, shook her head, and then motioned subtly toward her mother.

Iolanthe smiled. "Oh, yes. I'm sure Sunshine has told you about him, Alana. He is a really nice boy."

Alana paused and then said cautiously, "Yes, we've talked about him. I just didn't recall hearing his name before."

"We'll talk about that another time," Sunshine said, trying to change the subject. "I think Oakleaf's group is about to be called."

⊰⊱

Grandfather was right, thought Rayne as he spotted the finish line in the distance. *Pacing myself was the best way to approach this.*

Not long after the race started, the man who won the sprint took off at full speed. By halfway around the castle, he had slowed considerably, as did all the others who had tried to keep up with the early leader. After clearing the castle and heading back to the finish line, Rayne, who had been keeping a steady pace, was near the front of the pack. He was side by side with two other men as they approached the end of the race. Rayne felt he had a burst of speed left in him, but didn't want to use it too early.

The crowd started cheering as the three of them raced closer to the finish line. When they were all roughly one hundred paces away, Rayne decided it was now or never, and made his move.

Right away, the man on his left matched his pace, while the man on the other side started to lag behind. What started with forty men was now a two-person race. Rayne knew he was already ensured three more points regardless of who won, but he also knew that some of the next events that required brute strength would be a struggle for him, so it was important that he get as many points as he could in the events he was better at. He was neck and neck with the other young man as they approached the finish line. The cheering of the crowd was nearly deafening. Giving everything he had, Rayne all but dove over the finish line, and then collapsed. He looked on the ground next to him and saw that the man he had raced against had done the same. "Who won?" Rayne asked, trying to catch his breath.

Panting heavily, his opponent responded, "I have no idea."

⊰❋⊱

"Bah. Could you see what happened?" Snapdragon asked Sunshine.

She stood on her tiptoes, but still couldn't see over the people in front of her. "I didn't see. It sounds like it was a close finish, though."

The people in the stands slowly started to sit down when the officiator took his place on the platform. Holding up both hands, he waited for the crowd to quiet down. "After conferring with the judges, we have agreed that the finish from the first group was too close to determine who won. Therefore, both 15 of Donigi and 17 of Lebu are being awarded five points."

"Wish I could have seen that," Snapdragon said, pouting and sitting down on the bench with his arms folded.

Iolanthe sat down next to her son. "After lunch, we'll see if we can't get a closer spot."

"You may want to stand up now, Snap," Sunshine told him. "It looks like the next group is headed to the finish line."

⊰❋⊱

The officiator stood in front of a large wooden board that listed the top point holders after two events. He announced that number 13 from Erd was in first place with ten points, having won both events in his group. Rayne's eight points tied him for second place with number 24 from Regne.

"I'm proud of you, Rayne." Nadia gave her grandson a big hug. "You're doing very well."

Rayne blushed. "Thank you, Grandmother, but the two events after the lunch break are not really my forte."

"Maybe not," Kelvin said, "but you've definitely earned the right to compete in tomorrow's events—and you will do well in those."

"Your grandfather's right," Nadia said. "Just do your best. I've prepared some lunch at our camping site. Let's rest up and get you something to eat."

Rayne stepped back away from his grandparents. "I'll be right there. I would like to see if I can find someone first."

⇥✠⇤

"You're all invited to join us in the castle for lunch," Alana said to Sunshine and her family. "I'm sure you're interested in seeing where Sunshine lives."

Iolanthe responded quickly. "That would be wonderful! Are you sure it won't be too much trouble?"

Alana waved a hand dismissively. "No trouble at all. I made arrangements with the castle servants yesterday to set up a table for me and some guests in the eastern courtyard. It's nothing compared to the governor's garden in Lewyol, but it's quite nice this time of year, with the budding of the trees and flowers."

"Then we accept," Iolanthe said. "Don't we, dear?" she asked Garth.

"Apparently so," he replied.

"And congratulations to you, Oakleaf," Alana addressed the tall young man standing next to Garth. "Six points after two events is very impressive."

"Thank you," Oakleaf said, nodding.

Alana turned toward the castle. "Let's be off then!"

⇥✠⇤

Rayne wove his way through the crowd, trying to keep Lewyol's yellow banner in his sights. People had come down from the stands to visit with the participants, so it was slow going.

When he arrived at the Lewyol staging area, he looked around but didn't see Oakleaf or any members of his family. Rayne stopped a participant with a yellow armband. "Excuse me. I'm looking for Oakleaf. I believe he's competing from your district."

"Yeah, Oakleaf," the young man responded, looking around. "He's here, but I don't see him anywhere right now."

"Would you do me a favor when you see him?"

"Sure."

Still looking around and hoping to spot Sunshine, Rayne said, "Could you tell him that Rayne was looking for him?"

"Rayne? Is that your name?"

Used to hearing this question, he simply nodded in confirmation.

"Yeah, I guess I can do that."

Rayne clapped his fellow participant on the shoulder. "Thank you. And good luck in the Mortentaun."

⇢✦⇠

"What do you think you are doing?" Iolanthe exclaimed.

"I'm thinking about exactly what I'm doing." Garth continued to snap off small twigs from a tree in the courtyard. "Would you rather I not think about my actions?"

Iolanthe sighed. "I mean, this isn't your garden. Come sit down and eat with us. Let the castle gardeners take care of that."

Garth placed the twigs he had broken off into a neat little pile at the base of the tree before walking to the table and sitting down with his family and Alana.

"Where is your husband, Alana?" Iolanthe asked, but not before she gave her husband a jab in his ribs with her elbow.

Alana didn't look up from her plate where she was cutting her meat into bite-sized portions. "He's involved in judging the Mortentaun. He'll be quite busy the next couple of days, yet another reason I'm happy to have you all here as my guests."

"Ah, Sunshine! There you are!" Bertram said, entering the courtyard.

Sunshine stood. "Magistrate, hello. This is a surprise. Come, meet my family." She made the introductions, and then asked Bertram, "I take it you were looking for me?"

Bertram positively beamed. "Yes, I was. I couldn't wait for you to return. I had a servant help me move the tapestry, and I found the book you told me about. It was indeed a copy of the Tome of Laws. From the cover, lettering, and binding style, it definitely looks to be older than any of the other copies we've come across."

"Did you open it yet?" Sunshine asked.

Bertram shook his head. "Not yet. Since you were the one who found it, I wanted you to be there."

"Mom, Dad, I know I've not seen you in a while, but would it be all right if I joined you later?" She stepped away from the table. "I promise you a full tour another time."

Iolanthe looked disappointed for a moment, but quickly put on a smile. "Absolutely. We understand you have duties here."

⇥✦⇤

Kelvin and Nadia sat across from Governor Nash and Lady Linden on small blankets surrounding a larger one where all manner of food had been laid out. They were listening intently to Nash recount a story of when he had been a guardian.

"Captain Reynold had gotten after me once again for sleeping in late," Nash continued. "So, he made it very clear that if I was not up when the first light of dawn shone through my window, I'd be docked a week's pay."

Linden interrupted. "Ah, I should try that. You still stay up way too late. So much so, I can't get you up in the mornings."

The group laughed, but Nash ignored the comment and continued the story. "We had a card game planned for that night and I knew I'd be up late, so the thought of getting up early the following morning was, well, unappealing. So, I had a stroke of genius and had some of the castle servants brick up the window."

"You did not!" Nadia said, laughing.

Nash sat up a bit straighter. "I most certainly did! And the next morning when Reynold came to check on me, I was fast asleep in the dark room. To my surprise, he didn't really get mad. He said I had followed the letter of the law, albeit not the spirit of it. He told me that since I was so interested in sleeping during the day, he'd give me a new assignment—guardian in charge of the night watch. And so that is why I have a hard time getting up early, even to this day."

"Excellent story, Nash." Kelvin reached for a loaf of bread. Included on the blanket were several neatly stacked tarts. Nash reached for one, but Linden slapped away her husband's hand. "Not until we've eaten the rest of the meal!"

Feigning a hurt look, Nash said, "If I wanted to be treated rudely, I would've accepted the king's invitation to eat in the castle."

"Won't the king be upset if one of the governors doesn't join him?" Nadia asked. "Don't get me wrong, I'm glad you're here."

"I'm glad I'm here too." Nash glanced toward the castle. "I don't particularly care what the king thinks. He and his father have caused me nothing but headaches. I'm glad the Shoginoc is this year. We need a new king."

After swallowing a chunk of bread, Kelvin asked, "Are you going to sponsor anyone from Lebu in the Shoginoc?"

Nash shook his head slowly, causing his long, white beard to swish back and forth. "I wish I had someone to sponsor. Lebu is mainly a farming district without any real valuable resources, aside from the strong wood we provide to the other districts. Anything we find that would be considered a treasure is taken from us in taxes. We just don't have the means to put together a good showing at the Shoginoc."

"Speaking of a good showing, here comes Rayne," Linden said.

He walked over to them and sat down next to his grandmother. "This is an honor, Governor Nash and Lady Linden. If I knew you were going to join us, I would have been here sooner."

"Bah!" Nash said. "Don't worry about that. We're proud of how well you're doing so far."

"Thank you," Rayne said to both the governor and his grandmother, who was handing him some food from the blanket.

"Did you find who you were looking for, Rayne?" Kelvin asked.

"Not yet, but hopefully after today's events, I'll run into her."

CHAPTER 18

"Where is Governor Nash?" Abrecan asked Caldre, scanning the length of the table one more time.

Caldre looked around the main hall before answering. "He was invited—all the governors were. There are empty chairs down at the end, so it seems he didn't come."

"Make sure you find him and that he understands where he needs to be for the next banquet," Abrecan said firmly.

"Absolutely."

The guests were just finishing their first course and were waiting for the main entrée to be served. The rest of the governors were in attendance with their spouses. King Daimh sat at the head of the table by his wife Nicole, with Councilor Abrecan and Magistrate Caldre sitting to their right.

"I think the Mortentaun is going very well, Your Majesty," said the governor of Regne to King Daimh. "It is a credit to you and your father."

Daimh grinned. "Yes, the Mortentaun has been enjoyable so far, although, I think tomorrow's events will be more to my liking."

"Then you will be in for a treat, Your Majesty," Governor Eadward said. "My nephew, Ivor, is in first place after this morning's events. He's quite good at hand-to-hand combat, so the sparring contests tomorrow should be rather entertaining."

❖

Rayne eyed the large rock in front of him. It was somewhat round in shape, and any rough edges had been worn away with time and use. He bent his knees, then placed both hands under the rock and lifted, focusing on using his legs and not his back. Getting the rock to his waist took a great deal of effort, but he knew he was already in better shape than some of the others. His group had drawn numbers for the first event of the afternoon. Rayne had pulled a number in the middle, and so he had the chance to watch the others' attempts. While some of the larger men had no trouble with the rock, a couple of the participants of slighter build were unable to lift it at all.

After putting one leg behind the other for balance, Rayne lifted the rock up to his shoulders. The strain on his muscles made him want to drop the rock there and then, but he forced himself to remain steady. He leaned on his back leg slightly and then shifted his weight forward, using all his energy to throw the rock out onto the field. It didn't travel far, but it traveled far enough. He could see it had landed beyond several of the colored metal spikes the officiators were using to mark the throws of the various participants. The crowd cheered as Rayne walked off the field and back to where his grandfather was waiting for him.

"You knew that was going to be the hardest event for you, and you did just fine." Kelvin shook Rayne's hand. "I dare say you are guaranteed at least one point."

Rayne looked back to the field in time to watch a rather large man pick up the rock as if it weighed no more than a pumpkin and then hurl it over all the other markers. "I'm glad that's over. It required very little strategy—it was more a matter of brute strength."

⤖✦⤙

"Are you sure, Snapdragon?" Iolanthe asked.

The sixteen-year-old nodded furiously. "Yes, I'm sure that was Rayne who just competed."

"But it doesn't make sense. Lebu and Donigi are competing now. Rayne is from Tevoil."

Folding his hands across his chest and glaring at his mother, Snapdragon said, "I know that. But it really looked a lot like Rayne."

"It may have looked like him, Snapdragon, but it couldn't have been," Alana said softly.

Snapdragon didn't use the same defiant tone he had with his mother, but he was still quite adamant when he said, "Maybe he moved to Lebu. It would explain why we've not seen him with the group from Tevoil."

Alana sighed quietly and paused. "Sunshine will be upset by what I'm about to tell you, but you should probably know. That can't be Rayne, because he and his family were killed by some guardians last fall. I'm sorry to be the one to tell you. He obviously made a strong impression on your family."

Iolanthe's face turned ashen. "Oh, no. He was such a wonderful young man. Poor Sunshine must have been crushed. Rayne was the first boy in whom she had ever taken an interest."

"Sunshine was quite upset when they announced in court what had happened to Rayne, yes," Alana said. "But over the last few months, she's been very diligent in her work at the castle. I've wondered if she didn't dedicate herself to her work to help distract her from thoughts of Rayne. The mention of him earlier today must have brought back all sorts of sad feelings. I'm not surprised that she jumped at the chance to help Bertram instead of coming back here."

⋙⋘

The large book had been bound in a deep brown leather cover with the faded gold-inlayed words "Tome of Laws" written upon it. The page edges were rough and yellow, and they looked almost brittle in places.

"Are you ready?" Sunshine asked.

Bertram nodded. "Yes. Let's see when this copy was written."

He carefully opened the front cover. On the front page below the title was the date when the book had been transcribed. It was earlier than any of the other copies they had found, but it was the note below the date that caught Bertram's attention.

It read, *Let it be known this is a copy from the original Tome of Laws.*

"Oh my," Sunshine said.

Bertram thought for a moment. The original Tome of Laws had simply fallen apart over time. When it was first written, only one copy was made. Any other copies were forbidden for fear of mistakes and errors that came from transcribing. But over time, copies had to be made because there was no way to preserve the book from the effects of age. That is how savants had first come about—they were brought to the castle to make copies of the Tome, and they had done so meticulously as to avoid errors. Savants took on other responsibilities over the years, but this was still their primary duty.

"Bertram?" Sunshine pulled lightly on his sleeve.

"Hmm, what?"

She smiled. "Are you just going to stare at the book, or are you going to check for the missing word?"

"Of course. Sorry. I was just lost in thought."

"It's all right. This is been a long time coming for you. I can understand if you want to take a moment."

Bertram shook his head. "No, we've waited long enough. But we must be careful. The pages are going to be fragile, even though it seems that at least some of the pages are made from thicker parchment than what we use now."

He reached down and gently turned the pages. "Let's see now. Chapter eleven, paragraph nineteen. Ah, here it is. *The former king and queen will become councilors to the newly crowned leader of Bariwon. An arranged marriage will...*" Bertram paused and then said to Sunshine, "What happens if we turn the page and we find the same error as the rest of the books? It will be quite disappointing."

"If that's the way it is, that's the way it is, but we aren't going to know until you actually turn the page."

"True..." Bertram closed his eyes and turned the page. He slowly opened his eyes, then looked at the top of the page and read, *"selected by a Shoginoc."*

Unable to hide his disappointment, Bertram felt his shoulders slump and the strength leave his legs. "Oh, well. I guess that's that."

"May I?" Sunshine said.

Bertram took a step back, found a tapestry to sit on, and watched as Sunshine slowly turned the pages back and forth. He had really hoped this would solve the problem of the seemingly missing word, but just like every other attempt, it hadn't.

"Uh, Bertram?"

"Yes?" He was unable to hide the disappointment in his voice.

Sunshine motioned him to come back to the table. "There's a reason some of these pages seem thicker than the others, see? There are two pages stuck together."

Bertram stood and went over to the book. Squinting, he noticed that the edges of the page were uneven in places, and it did appear that two pages were stuck together. "Yes, that's right. Some of the earlier ink they used would become sticky over time if it wasn't used sparingly."

"These are quite stuck together," she said. "I'm not sure how we can get them apart without ripping the paper."

Bertram rubbed his hands together. "It's possible. I've done it before, but it will take some time. Run off to a seamstress and get us a needle."

Rayne squared up his body, trying to get the staff he was holding behind his head to rest evenly on his shoulders. From each end of the staff hung baskets filled with rocks. The officiators explained that each basket was made to be the same weight by using a large balancing scale.

The last event of the day required the participants to race the same two hundred paces as they had in the first event, but this time carrying the heavy baskets.

Waiting for the officiator to make sure everyone was ready, Rayne again sized up his competition. The man who had won the rock-throwing contest looked comfortable, while the man who had won the first sprint looked like his knees were about to buckle.

"Go!"

Keeping his back straight once again and letting his legs do the work, Rayne found himself starting to fall behind the pack. A quarter of the way in, he took a quick glance to either side. Many of the men were treating the event as a sprint, hunching over and running as fast as they could. The sprinter had already fallen over and was out of the race.

By the halfway mark, Rayne started to catch up to the crowd. Some of the men who had done well in the rock-throwing contest were starting to cramp up and were slowing down.

Rayne felt his legs aching from the strain, but he still felt strong enough to push on. As he closed in on the finish line, several men collapsed from exhaustion or slowed down so much they were moving at a snail's pace. The man who had won the rock-throwing contest had already finished, well ahead of the rest of the group.

Rayne crossed the finish line, made sure he was clear of any other of the participants, and then lowered the baskets to the ground. Looking around quickly, he noted that he had finished in the top five and therefore earned three more points. All that was left was to walk off the cramps forming in his legs and then wait until everyone else had competed.

-»¥¦«-

Standing in the middle of the field with all the participants, Rayne waited anxiously for the officiators to finish posting the final results from the first day's events. He had no doubt that he had done well enough to qualify for tomorrow, but he wondered where he would place in the overall standings. The last race had been run with another strong showing from number 13 of Erd. One of the officiators climbed a ladder next to the wooden score board. Rayne's guess was correct as number 13 from

Erd was the first to be posted with a total of twenty points. Number 24 from Regne was listed next with fourteen points, followed by Rayne with his twelve points.

The board held enough space for the top sixteen participants. Each of these men would qualify for the next day's events. After watching the officiator place number 12 from Lewyol in the sixteenth position on the board, the crowd cheered and the participants started to move off the field back to their districts. Approaching the Lebu waiting area, Rayne felt a hard slap on his back.

"Rayne, my boy, well done! Well done indeed!" Governor Nash said. "I don't believe anyone from Lebu has placed that high in the first day's events since, well, I guess since your father."

"Thank you, Governor," Rayne said. "I couldn't have done it without your help."

"Bah! Now you're just being modest. You understand what doing so well means, right?"

Furrowing his brow, Rayne thought a moment. "Well, aside from qualifying for tomorrow's events, I'm not sure."

Nash laughed. "Ah. I don't know if I should be happy or sad for you when I tell you the news then."

"Oh?"

"The highest-scoring participants are invited to have dinner with the king in the castle," Nash said. "Of course, 'invited' may be misleading. It's more like 'required.'"

Rayne looked over to where the participants from Lewyol were gathered. "Do I have time to go find someone first? I was hoping to meet up with her after today's events."

"Afraid not." Nash shook his head. "After I skipped lunch with the king today, he sent a couple of his guardians to remind me to be there tonight as soon as possible after today's events. You'll have to catch up with her later. I've already told your grandparents so they won't be worried."

⊰╪⊱

"Have we met before?" Caldre asked Rayne as they were introduced.

"I don't believe so, Magistrate," Rayne said politely.

Caldre narrowed his eyes and looked at the young man carefully. "You seem very familiar to me—are you sure you've not visited the castle before?"

"I'm sure, Magistrate."

"Very well then. Go ahead and have a seat. The king and his father will be out shortly."

Rayne thanked Caldre and then found his seat at the table next to Governor Nash and Lady Linden. Leaning over, Nash asked in a whisper, "What was that all about?"

Rayne glanced over to where Caldre was being introduced to one of the participants from Erd, a thickly built man with dark hair and a fairly large, bulbous nose.

"I'm not sure, exactly," Rayne said. "He thought that we may have met before, but I'm sure we haven't. Perhaps I remind him of someone."

"Perhaps," Nash said, exchanging a meaningful look with his wife. "But not to worry. Let's enjoy the meal. Just remember to stand when the king arrives and be seated when instructed. The king's father will probably have some words for me because I missed lunch today, but I can handle it. It would be best if you kept quiet and didn't speak unless you are addressed."

"Understood."

❖

Bertram wiped his brow once again, trying to make sure no drops of sweat fell onto the paper before him. Although the spring evening was cool, he was sweating profusely as he slowly worked the needle back and forth in an effort to separate the pages that were stuck together.

He and Sunshine had taken turns throughout the afternoon with the painstakingly slow process, but they had made steady progress and were nearly finished. The pages had indeed been stuck together due to the excess of ink. They had agreed not to read what they had uncovered until the pages were completely separated. It was tempting, and Bertram found himself catching snippets of words and phrases here and there, but he tried not to concentrate on them. What he had seen were mainly names and dates, which led him to wonder what it was about these people that made them important enough to be included in the Tome of Laws.

"Almost done, Bertram. Nice and easy," Sunshine said, sounding as tired as Bertram felt.

And just like that, the needle slid past the last stuck part and allowed them to open up the pages.

"All right, here we go," Bertram said nervously. He turned to the page before and read: *When the firstborn child of the king and queen reaches the age of twenty-one, he or she shall become the new king or queen. The former king and queen will become councilors to the newly crowned leader of Bariwon. An arranged marriage*

161

will…" He turned the page and read, *"not be allowed for the heir to the throne. History has shown us that such arranged marriages have caused conflicts between noble and powerful families in the kingdom. We include several examples of problems that come from these types of arranged marriages."*

The majority of the hidden two pages listed names, dates, and situations where arranged marriages caused issues or conflicts. Nearing the end of the last missing page, Bertram read, *"Each person of the kingdom will be allowed to marry whomever they desire, regardless of rank, wealth, or ties to noble families. This includes the king and queen. If the king or queen does not marry, or if he or she does marry and is unable to produce an heir, a new king or queen will be chosen twenty-one years after the crowning of the king or queen. This new leader will be …"* He turned the page and read the next paragraph. *"selected by a Shoginoc. In the spirit of competition that is part of the history of the kingdom, each district will have the chance to participate. Whoever brings to the kingdom the most worth, as decided by the Hierarchy of Magistrates, will be declared the winner. Twenty-one years is to be the standard period of time that any leader will be on the throne, and therefore, the Shoginoc will be used to select a new leader for the kingdom if an heir is not produced in a timely manner."*

Bertram stopped and looked at Sunshine, his face pale. "Do you understand what this means?"

Her eyes wide, Sunshine responded, "Yes, it means the Shoginoc has been performed incorrectly for generations."

⊰╪⊱

"Nash, why don't you just ask someone?" Linden asked, walking next to Rayne and following her husband down a passage in the castle.

He didn't stop or look back. "Because I'm not lost. I'm just exploring a little."

Linden looked at Rayne and rolled her eyes. He tried to suppress a smile but wasn't very successful. Taking two quick steps forward, Linden grabbed her husband by the arm. "Nash, it's been many years since you've been this far into the castle. I think we're going in circles. It wouldn't hurt to ask someone where your old quarters are. I'm as interested as you to see if the window is still bricked up, but we've been roaming for a while now."

Nash threw his hands up in disgust. "It's just that they've changed or moved all the tapestries, so I don't have any markers to remind me which way to go. Or the markers I do recall are not where they were before."

"Well, it doesn't look like many people come down here very often,"

Linden said. "Perhaps we should turn back."

"I have a better idea," Nash said. "Rayne will stay here. We'll go on a bit further. If we don't find it in the next few minutes, I'll shout and Rayne will help us get back."

Before his wife could object, Nash strode off down the hallway.

Rayne looked around and noticed several tapestries hanging from the walls. One off to his left, next to a door, depicted a large tree on a sloping hill with the castle in the background. It looked like it had been hung hastily, and there wasn't a plaque indicating what it was about. He found the scene peaceful, but somewhat haunting.

His reflections were interrupted when the door next to the tapestry suddenly opened.

❖

"We have to take this information to the leaders," Sunshine said. "Wouldn't you agree?"

Bertram chewed on a fingernail before he responded. "Yes, they need to be told, but we need to figure out the right time to tell them. Perhaps it would be best if we waited until after the Mortentaun is over."

"Actually, since all the governors are here, this would be the perfect time," Sunshine exclaimed. "This is so exciting! We're experiencing history."

"I suppose we are," Bertram said hesitantly, "but I think we should tell the hierarchy before we tell the rest of the court."

"All right, you stay here and I'll go get them," she said, heading to the door.

"You want to go *now?*" Bertram asked.

"Why wait?"

Before responding, Bertram glanced down and then back at Sunshine. "Very well, but please be careful and don't tell anyone else until we get the hierarchy here to discuss this. Understand?"

Sunshine gave Bertram her best smile. "Why are you so worried? This is wonderful. I'll be fine."

She finished walking across the room and opened the door quickly. As she stepped out into the hallway, any thoughts of the Tome of Laws or the hierarchy vanished.

CHAPTER 19

Rayne and Sunshine stood there a moment, neither one speaking. "Sunshine!" Rayne said once he got over his initial shock. "What a surprise!"

He noticed her eyes grow wider and saw her take a step back. Putting up his hands, he said, "I'm sorry, I didn't mean to startle you."

Sunshine, who Rayne suspected was never at a loss for words, didn't respond. Instead, she started to tear up. She blinked and looked at him again as if with new eyes.

"What's the matter?" Rayne asked.

She shook her head, then swiftly came to him and embraced him tightly, resting her head on his chest. "Nothing is the matter. Just the opposite," she said, her voice shaking.

Rayne had thought so much about her over the past few months. He couldn't believe he'd not only found her, but that they were in each other's arms. "I tried to find your family at the Mortentaun today," he said, "but I kept missing you. Did you get the message I left for your brother?"

Sunshine took a step back, then reached down and clasped Rayne's hands in her own. "No, I haven't seen my brother. But Rayne, you must understand—I thought you were dead. I was told the guardians found your farm and that you and your father had been killed."

Rayne gasped. "Who told you that?"

Sunshine looked up and down the hallway. "Not here. Come with me," she said, then led him back into the room.

Sunshine brought Rayne inside and closed the door. She introduced him to a tall, thin man.

"Tell us what happened," Sunshine said.

Rayne eyed the magistrate warily.

"You can trust me, Rayne," Bertram said.

Sunshine nodded emphatically. "Magistrate Bertram is a good person, Rayne. I trust him. Please tell us what happened."

Rayne sat down on a rolled-up tapestry next to Sunshine, across from where Bertram sat. "Fine, but first, I have to know. What are you doing here in the castle, Sunshine?"

"You don't know?" She sounded surprised. "Rayne, I'm a savant. I thought you knew, else why would you be in the castle?"

Bertram interrupted. "Obviously you two have some catching up to do. Rayne, why don't you go first?"

Rayne nodded. He told them what had happened to his father at the farm and how he had moved to Lebu to live with his grandparents. He downplayed how well he had done in the Mortentaun, but Sunshine wouldn't let that slide, complimenting him on scoring high enough to be invited to the castle.

After Rayne explained how he had ended up in the hallway moments ago, Bertram clasped his hands together. "Rayne, I must ask. Why were the guardians after you and your father?"

Sunshine spoke up and gave the magistrate a quick accounting of what happened in town the day she met Rayne. She finished by saying, "Bertram, these were bad men. They were threatening me. I still shudder when I think about what they would have done to me had Rayne not stopped them. I can't deny I'm relieved they are not still out roaming the kingdom. What Rayne did was a selfless act."

"I understand why you are asking, Magistrate," Rayne said, stiffening. He turned to Sunshine. "Bertram is a magistrate, Sunshine. He's committed to uphold what is found in the Tome of Laws. It's against the law to strike a guardian, isn't it, Magistrate?"

"Yes, it is."

"But Bertram!" interjected Sunshine. "Can't you see that—"

She stopped when the magistrate held up a hand. "You need not worry. The law states that guardians are not above the law. If two or more people are willing to testify that any action against a guardian was in self-defense, or defense of the helpless, that overrides the law against striking a guardian."

Bertram looked squarely at Rayne. "In fact, that may be one of the more noble acts I've heard of in quite some time."

Rayne shied away from the compliment. "Thank you, Magistrate. I'm sure many others would have done the same, had they been there."

"Perhaps at one time they would have…" Bertram said softly, casting a glance at the Tome of Laws lying on the table next to him.

"Rayne!" came a muffled shout from behind the door.

He stood quickly. "Governor Nash! Please excuse me a moment." He dashed to the door, jumping over the various objects and tapestries strewn about. He opened the door to see Nash and Linden in the middle of the hallway. They both turned at the sound.

"Rayne, my boy!" Nash said, somewhat out of breath. "What are you doing in there?"

Rayne bowed. "My deepest apologies, Governor. I hadn't intended to leave the hallway."

Linden stepped forward. "Are you all right? You look different somehow."

Rayne felt a presence behind him. "It's my fault," Sunshine said as she moved next to him. "I dragged Rayne into the room. I'm sorry if that caused any problems."

Nash peered back and forth between Sunshine and Rayne. "Rayne, is this the person you have been looking for all day?"

He nodded, his cheeks turning red. Sunshine smiled and took Rayne by the hand.

"Ah," said Nash and Linden at the same time.

After everyone was introduced, including Magistrate Bertram, who had joined them, Rayne and Sunshine were given a few moments alone before going their separate ways for the evening. Bertram remained in the hallway with the governor and his wife, while Sunshine and Rayne returned to the room.

"It's funny how life is, isn't it?" Sunshine asked.

Rayne smiled. "Yes. I didn't think I'd run into you here, but I'm glad I did."

She took him by the hand again. "I'm glad you did too. After I thought you were dead, my life changed. All I focused on was my work here. And now…"

"Yes, I know. There are a lot of things to talk about," Rayne said. "But the governor made it clear we needed to leave soon. Will you be able to attend the Mortentaun tomorrow?"

Sunshine nodded and gave Rayne a smile he felt all the way down to his toes.

⊰⊱

"You appear to be quite taken with him," Bertram said after Rayne left.

"I am," Sunshine said. "When I heard he was dead, I tried to forget all about him, but seeing him today brought all those feelings back."

Bertram gave her a fatherly smile. "And he seems quite taken with you, too. However…"

Sunshine raised her eyebrows. "However what?"

"You do understand that he is here competing to become a guardian, correct? While savants and guardians assigned to districts are allowed to marry at any time, royal guardians are forbidden to marry during their term of service. If Rayne does well enough in the Mortentaun, wouldn't that pose a problem?"

Sunshine didn't say anything for a moment. Bertram could see her thinking, and her features revealed that she wasn't happy with the conclusions she was drawing.

"Yet," Bertram said, trying to make his voice cheerful, "royal guardians only have to serve a minimum of two years before they can resign. Granted, many serve much longer than that."

Sunshine straightened up and looked at her mentor. "When I met Rayne, something between us just clicked. It's hard for me to describe exactly what I mean by that. At the time, he wasn't sure he wanted to be a guardian, but he is here and doing well, so I can't help but think that something may have changed. If he wants to be a guardian, I'll support him." She sighed. "You must understand that when I thought he was dead, part of me felt dead as well. To see him alive—well, it has awakened something inside me. If he does become a royal guardian, I'd be willing to wait for him, as long as it takes."

Bertram looked at her searchingly. "I imagine you would."

"However, I haven't forgotten my duty here. I'll go fetch the rest of the hierarchy."

Bertram shook his head. "No, no. It's getting too late for that now. Go ahead and retire for the evening. I want to look over the Tome some more. I'll gather the hierarchy tomorrow."

Sunshine cocked her head to one side. "Are you sure this news can wait?"

"This information has been lost for many years," Bertram said, placing a hand on the Tome. "It can wait one more day."

⇥‡⇤

The morning sun shone brightly, matching Sunshine's mood. She had slept better than in recent memory and got up at the first light of dawn. She took some extra effort getting ready for the day's activities, making sure her dress and hair were just so.

When she met up with Alana for breakfast in the courtyard, she caught herself humming a little tune her father used to hum when he was in a particularly good humor. During breakfast, Sunshine told Alana she had run into Rayne the previous evening, and then she explained everything that had happened, including the embrace she and Rayne had shared. The two young women giggled together in excitement.

After a satisfying meal, they made their way out of the castle, through the town, and to the field where the Mortentaun was being held. The area was already abuzz with activity. A couple of bards were spinning tales to the crowds that gathered around. Merchants had set up tents and were peddling their wares, with one inventive merchant hauling fruit in a large basket strapped to his back. Alana found this man especially intriguing and stopped him.

"Ah, my lady," the man said, glancing at the ring of nobility Alana wore. "How may I help you?"

Alana reached for her coin purse. "Instead of people coming to you for business, you go to the people, I see. Very ingenious."

He nodded at the compliment. "May I get you something? I have fresh strawberries and also apples from last season."

"I'd love a few strawberries. May I get you something, Sunshine?" Alana asked.

She peered into the basket. "An apple would be lovely, thank you."

Alana paid the man for the items and he went on his way.

"Thank you for the apple," Sunshine said, holding it closely.

"You're welcome."

They worked their way through the crowd toward the banner of Lewyol. The participants were still gathering, so when Alana and Sunshine found her family, Oakleaf and her father were still among them.

"Ah, Shiny! How nice of you to come cheer me on," Oakleaf said somewhat sarcastically. "But of course, I know the real reason. You found out Rayne is here and doing well."

"What?" Iolanthe gasped. "I thought—"

"It appears we were given faulty information," Alana interrupted. She pointed to the scoreboard. "Rayne is, in fact, number 17 from Lebu."

"I knew I spotted him!" Snapdragon said excitedly. "See, I told you."

Iolanthe smiled. "Very well, Snap. You were right. I'm sorry for doubting you."

Sunshine went to her older brother and gave him a hug he was clearly not expecting. "Leafy, I'll be cheering for you too, you wooden head. It's good to see you."

⊰⊱

"It's fairly straight forward," Kelvin told Rayne as they walked toward the field. "The morning event will test your ability with a bow and arrow, while the afternoon event is designed around hand-to-hand combat."

Rayne craned his neck to one side and then to the other, trying to work out the kink he had awakened with this morning. He had slept well, even though falling asleep was a bit trying. He kept thinking of Sunshine, but would then chide himself for not staying focused on the Mortentaun. Sleep eventually did overtake him, and he had slept so soundly that when his grandmother woke him, he found he had slept with his neck in an awkward position.

"Now, about the first event," Kelvin continued. "You are shooting at a target that has three circles. The outer circle is blue, the middle is red, and the bull's eye is yellow. Each of the sixteen participants will shoot in the opposite order of their points. This means you will go third to last—a good place to be."

Rayne nodded. "Got it."

They arrived at the field and could see the officiators setting up the target. Kelvin pointed to it. "After everyone shoots, the two that are the furthest from the bull's eye will be eliminated. The target will then be moved back ten paces and the remaining participants will shoot again. Any questions?"

"Just one." Rayne straightened his tunic. "How do I look?"

⊰⊱

Oakleaf was the first to go, since he placed sixteenth overall the day before. Sunshine stood by her family and cheered as her brother went to the line and took aim. The crowd quieted in anticipation of the shot. Oakleaf let the arrow fly, and from Sunshine's position, it appeared to hit in the inner yellow circle, just off center. Oakleaf raised his arms enthusiastically while the crowd applauded his excellent shot.

Each participant took turns making the same shot, all of them hitting the target, most of them at least hitting inside the red circle. None had done better than Oakleaf when Rayne stepped to the line.

When Rayne was introduced, Sunshine cheered just as hard as she had for her brother. She thought she saw him spare a glance in her direction before he took aim. The crowd quieted and Rayne took his shot. It hit the very center of the bull's eye, inspiring the crowd to congratulate his good shot with extra applause. The second-to-last participant's shot hit within the red circle, bringing the large man from Erd to take his turn.

"He won every event in his division yesterday," Snapdragon told his sister. "I hear that had never been done before. I can't wait to see how he does here."

Sunshine sized up the man. Although he didn't seem as tall as his fellow participants, he was definitely more muscular. The man didn't seem as comfortable with the bow as the rest, and Sunshine's observation was validated when his shot went wide, not even hitting the target.

⇥╬⇤

"Well, that was a disappointment." Councilor Abrecan frowned. "You said your nephew was better than that, Eadward."

Eadward's red face betrayed the calm response he tried to give. "Ivor is strong and quick, and very good in combat, but he doesn't see well at long distances. Don't worry, Councilor, he will demonstrate his abilities later this afternoon."

Abrecan made a rude noise. "I would hope so. How many are left from Erd?"

Caldre rose from his seat next to the councilor and took a closer look down at the field. "It appears eight of the remaining fourteen are from Erd. There is still a good chance that most of them will become royal guardians."

"Fine. Captain Sullivan tells me he'd prefer that his guardians come from Erd," Abrecan said. "They seem to understand better how things are run. Caldre, perhaps you could find a way to make sure more men from Erd do well."

Caldre thought for a moment. "It's probably too late for me to do anything for the morning competition, but I think I can come up with something for the afternoon event. If I may have your leave?"

"Of course," Abrecan said, waving away the magistrate.

⇥╬⇤

Rayne squinted at the target that had been moved eighty paces away from the shooting line. Fortunately, there wasn't a morning breeze to speak of, which meant Rayne didn't have to compensate for wind.

He had hit the center, or very near the center, in every shot he had taken so far. Now that there were only four participants left, Rayne found himself focusing more on the task at hand, and less on his surroundings. It wasn't easy because one of the four remaining participants was Oakleaf, and that was a constant reminder that Sunshine was looking on intently. The other two men were from Erd, both large and not particularly friendly.

Oakleaf went first again. As the crowd silenced around him, he took aim. Just when he was about to release the bowstring, one of the men from Erd coughed loudly. It was enough to have an effect on Oakleaf's shot, and for the first time during the competition, he missed the yellow bull's eye and hit the red.

Visibly upset, Oakleaf turned to face his opponent and was about to say something when Rayne stepped in. "That was a good shot, Oakleaf. You nearly hit the bull's eye from this distance. Any of us would be hard-pressed to do that well."

Oakleaf sent Rayne a questioning look, but Rayne glanced quickly at the other two men and hoped Oakleaf understood. One of the men appeared a bit nervous now, licking his lips and fidgeting with his bow. The other man, the one who had coughed, still waited confidently.

The nervous participant took his place, took in a deep breath, and tried to steady his quivering hands. His shot went wide, hitting the outer blue ring.

When the next man from Erd stepped up, the officiator at the line said to Oakleaf and Rayne, "I don't want to hear any noise out of you two."

The man from Erd looked at Rayne and Oakleaf and gave them a smirk. He turned back to the target and took his aim. Just before he was about to let go, a burst of wind came whipping across the field—enough to cause the man's shot to go even wider than that of his fellow participant from Erd.

"No fair! The wind blew that off course!" the contestant shouted, waving his arms in disgust. "I demand another shot!"

The officiator looked nervously at the grandstand where King Daimh and Councilor Abrecan were sitting. "I'm sorry, but interference from the elements does not constitute reason for a second shot."

With the wind still blowing fairly hard, the man threw his bow to the ground and said, "Fine! No one will be able to get off a good shot in this wind."

Rayne took to the line and aimed carefully. He felt the wind on his face, adjusted slightly, and let his arrow fly. The crowd erupted when it hit the bull's eye dead center.

"Good luck, Oakleaf," Rayne said, slapping the young man from Lewyol on the back.

Oakleaf fitted the arrow in his bow. "Thanks. You too, Rayne."

The target had been moved back another ten paces, and fortunately the wind had died down to a light breeze. The crowd was on its feet now as the last two men prepared for their final shots. Oakleaf set himself, took his time to aim, and then fired. It was by far his best shot of the day, hitting what appeared to be the center of the bull's eye.

Rayne was the first to shake Oakleaf's hand in congratulations. The crowd was still cheering when Rayne set up for his turn. After selecting an arrow from the quiver provided, Rayne took a deep breath and brought up his bow. His mind went back to a practice with his father when he had been faced with a similar shot. His father had gone before him and made a nearly impossible shot to beat. At the time, Rayne had said, "There isn't even a point for me to take the shot. There is no way I can beat you, Father." Rinan had said something Rayne had never forgotten. "There will be times when it appears you cannot win, but those are the most important times to try your best. Never give up, even in the face of a seemingly impossible situation. It is often the effort that makes all the difference."

Rayne smiled at the memory and released the bowstring. His arrow flew true, but hit just to the right of Oakleaf's shot, giving Sunshine's brother the victory.

The crowd exploded in reaction to such a fine display of marksmanship and cheered heartily as Oakleaf and Rayne walked off the field together, waving to the crowd.

CHAPTER 20

Magistrate Aldous arched an eyebrow at Bertram. "I don't think it would be possible to gather the rest of the hierarchy today. Most of them are still at the Mortentaun."

Bertram sighed. "Yes, of course. I can see that it would be difficult. But what I've discovered—"

"Is something we'll all be interested in, I'm sure Bertram," Aldous said, giving the younger man a warm smile. "But you need to learn that there is more to life than books and studying. Come, join us. You may find that you will actually enjoy the experience."

Bertram shook his head, more dramatically than he intended. "I don't think so. I have duties here."

Aldous stood. "Nonsense. I'm the head of the Hierarchy of Magistrates, and I'm relieving you of any duties you feel obligated to do for the rest of the day."

The sound of cheers caused both men to look out the window of Bertram's room.

"You see?" Aldous said. "That is the sound of happy people."

Bertram folded his arms. "It's not that I think I wouldn't enjoy it. It's just that I'd rather not be around certain individuals."

"Like who?"

Bertram absently started chewing on one of his fingernails. "I feel uncomfortable around the royalty. And then there is Magistrate Caldre…"

Aldous sighed. "Caldre is just overly ambitious. Don't worry about him. As for the royalty, they hold no power over us, nor we over them. We are both bound to follow the Tome of Laws."

"When I say something in court that Councilor Abrecan doesn't like, he looks as if he wants to do me physical harm."

"Nonsense," Aldous replied. "You're letting your imagination run away with you. You've never backed down from stating what you thought was right—that's one reason you were chosen to be on the hierarchy."

Bertram bowed his head. "Yes, that's true. I don't know what comes over me sometimes."

"Well, don't give it another thought. We'll convene the hierarchy first thing tomorrow. In the meantime, it sounds like the morning event is coming to a close, and I don't want to miss any more of the Mortentaun. Will you join me?"

Bertram took an involuntary step back. "Perhaps, when I'm done here."

"All right, but don't take too long. There are wondrous things to see and do there."

With that, Aldous left the room, but left the door open.

When Bertram felt Aldous was far enough away, he closed the door, selected a book from his collection, and sat down on his bed with his back toward the window.

⊰✦⊱

Rayne sat next to Sunshine in the courtyard, holding her hand under the table. During the mid-day break between events, Alana had once again invited Sunshine's family to join her at the castle for lunch. Sunshine asked if she could invite Rayne and his grandparents, and Alana easily agreed.

Rayne was amazed how well his grandparents got along with Sunshine's parents. It was as if they were old friends meeting up after years apart. Across from Rayne sat Oakleaf, sporting on his tunic the marksmanship pin he had won that morning. During the last event, Rayne and Oakleaf seemed to have developed a bond of friendship, almost an "us against all of them" approach to the rest of the participants.

"It was quite the exciting event this morning," Alana said to Rayne and Oakleaf. "Both of you should be quite proud."

"Thank you, my lady," they said in unison.

"Yeah, I thought for sure Rayne was going to win," Snapdragon said. "Who'd have thought Leafy would save his best shot for last?"

"Now, Snap, you're going to make Rayne feel bad." Iolanthe scooped an extra helping of spinach onto his plate.

Rayne wiped his mouth with a napkin before he spoke. "Actually, I'm not upset. It was a really good event, and Oakleaf won fair and square. Since I didn't win, I'm glad Oakleaf was the victor."

"But what happens if you two get paired against each other in the hand-to-hand combat event this afternoon?" Snapdragon asked. "Are you going to take it easy on him, Oakleaf?"

Garth reached over to Snapdragon's plate, picked up a large forkful of spinach, and shoved it in his youngest son's mouth. "Obviously, Snap needs something to fill the void he calls a mouth."

Snapdragon's expression was priceless and inspired laughter from the table.

"It's interesting you should bring that up, Snapdragon," Rayne said. "Before we left for lunch, Oakleaf and I got to see the bracket set up for the event this afternoon. We're in different divisions, so the only chance we'd have to fight against each other is if we are the final two."

"Well," Kelvin said, "I have seen Rayne in training, and I have no doubt he'll do quite well this afternoon. If Oakleaf can fight as well as he can shoot, we very well may see these two battle it out for the title."

-⋗‡⋖-

"And the weapons in this barrel are to be used for the non-Erd participants if you see me stand and motion to you with my handkerchief," Caldre instructed. "Is that clear?"

The officiator charged with setting out the weapons for the event peered into the barrel. "What's different about these?"

Caldre's cold stare made it clear that such questions were not to be asked.

"All right, all right," the officiator said, raising his hands defensively. "I'll do as you command."

"Just remember to look up into the grandstands before each contest." Caldre pointed to where King Daimh and Councilor Abrecan were already seated. "It would be unfortunate if you neglected to do so."

-⋗‡⋖-

"Alana, how does this event work?" Sunshine asked.

Her friend pointed down to the field to where a large circle, twenty paces wide, had been drawn on the field using crushed chalk. "It's rather simple, really. Each participant will start in the middle of the circle. Various types of weapons are placed on the outer edges. When the officiator gives the word, the men run to the outer edge in opposite directions, choose their weapon, and then rush to face each other. Sometimes the officiators will add or take away different weapons between events to see how well the men can adapt. As long as the item is

175

in the circle when the match starts, it's fair game. The object is to knock the other person off his feet, force him out of the circle, or get him to yield."

Sunshine frowned. "It seems a bit barbaric, doesn't it?"

"Yeah, it does. Isn't that great?" Snapdragon said.

Sunshine suddenly felt a bit queasy. Even though she had heard the weapons were made of wood, there was a good chance people could get hurt. She searched for Rayne in the crowd of participants and spotted him next to her older brother. They seemed to be talking and pointing to the circle, probably discussing strategy.

"Sunshine? Are you well?" asked her mother, putting her arm around her. "You look pale."

Sunshine took her eyes off the field. "Yes, I'm fine. Let's just hope the same can be said about Rayne and Oakleaf after this event."

⇥‡⇤

Rayne watched intently as Oakleaf and his opponent walked to the center of the circle. He noticed the officiators placing various weapons on the edge of the combat area. The crowd had been allowed to come close to the circle, standing only a few steps outside of it. One section had been set aside for the participants, where Rayne stood now.

Oakleaf's opponent was a wiry man from Regne with jet black hair. The two moved to the middle of the circle, and the officiator gave them their final instructions, whereupon both participants nodded in understanding. After taking a few steps back, the officiator raised one hand in the air, then paused a moment for dramatic effect and dropped his hand swiftly.

The participants raced quickly to opposite edges of the circle. Each man grabbed a sword and a shield and then turned to face the other. Moving carefully toward the center, Oakleaf initiated the attack. His blows came quickly and solidly. The other man did his best to fight him off, but he was put on the defensive so early that he had backed out of the battle area before he realized it.

Upon his return, Rayne congratulated Oakleaf, and together they watched the next several matches, awaiting Rayne's turn. The match before Rayne's caused quite the reaction from the crowd. It involved the man who had scored the most points in yesterday's competition. Rayne heard others refer to him as Ivor, designated as number 13 from Erd.

As soon as Ivor's match started, he did something very odd. Instead of racing to his edge of the circle, Ivor quietly followed his opponent to the edge and then shoved him out of bounds before he knew what had happened. The people from Erd cheered while just about everyone else booed his actions. The officiators gathered together, discussed the situation, and then quieted the crowd.

"The participant from Erd did nothing against the rules, and therefore is the victor," the officiator said. He waited for the boos and the scattered cheers to settle down before he continued. "As long as the participants use only what is found in the circle when the match starts, they can use anything at their disposal to achieve one of the goals."

Ivor strutted off the field as Rayne and his opponent approached the center of the circle. Rayne recognized his opponent as the man who had won the two strength competitions the day before. He stood a head taller than Rayne, and his arms appeared to be as thick as Rayne's legs. Rayne looked up at the man as the officiator gave the instructions. He had been taught several different methods of combating a stronger or taller opponent, but he wondered which to use against someone taller *and* stronger.

The other unknown was which weapons he'd be given—he wouldn't know what was available until he got to the edge of the circle. He offered his opponent a smile, but didn't get one in return.

The officiator lowered his hand, and Rayne raced to the edge. He was hoping to find a staff, but was only given a two-handed broadsword as an option. He picked it up and turned to face his opponent.

From watching the rock-throwing and rock-basket events, Rayne knew the man was strong and had good endurance. Rayne didn't remember him doing well in the bow-and-arrow event, so chances were his dexterity wasn't that good, and perhaps that was something Rayne could exploit.

When they arrived at the center of the circle, Rayne waited for the man to initiate the first attack. He didn't have to wait long as his opponent swung his sword hard, but not very quickly, and Rayne was able to parry it easily. The man offered several more blows, each coming in at predictable angles and easily deflected. Rayne then decided to go on the offensive. After another strong but slow blow, Rayne riposted, quickly slashing at the man's legs and smacked him hard against the shins.

Looking more upset than injured, the man lunged forward, swinging harder than ever. Rayne again riposted, this time hitting his opponent hard on the arm with the flat part of the blade.

The pattern of wild swings, followed by Rayne's quick responses, continued for several more moments. Rayne kept backing up slowly, keeping an eye on the chalk edge in his peripheral view. When he was as close to the edge as he dared go, he waited for the next blow. Instead of trying to block the swing, Rayne ducked low and to his left, allowing the cut to swish harmlessly over his head, but causing his opponent to overextend himself and lose his balance. The taller man lurched forward and stepped over the line.

The officiator immediately told the men to halt and declared Rayne the winner.

❄

The second round started with Oakleaf quickly defeating his opponent. This time they were not given any weapons, and Oakleaf was able to wrestle the man to the ground.

When Ivor walked onto the field, the crowd again reacted strongly, some cheering and some booing. He and his opponent were each given a morning star—a weapon that was basically a ball attached by a chain to a handle. A real morning star would have sharp spikes on the ball, but this wooden version did not.

Ivor's opponent attacked first, bending low and swinging for the big man's legs. The chain wrapped around one of his ankles, but before his opponent could yank on it, Ivor jumped backwards, pulling the man forward and off his feet. Before the officiator could stop the match, Ivor strode forward and kicked the fallen man hard in the ribs.

Rayne passed Ivor on his way to the center of the circle, noticing the smug look on his face. Trying not to think about what he would do if he faced Ivor, Rayne sized up his current opponent. The man wore a red armband, indicating he was from Erd. He was roughly the same size and build as Rayne, with intense, dark brown eyes and a neatly trimmed goatee. Once again, Rayne's warm smile was answered with a chilly glare.

Upon the officiator's command, they ran to get their weapons. Rayne couldn't help but grin when he noticed he was given the option of a sword or a staff. Having experienced firsthand how effective a staff could be, he chose it. Rayne was also betting that his opponent would select a sword. He picked up the staff and spun around to see that his opponent had indeed selected a sword and was racing toward him. Rayne took several steps forward, then set himself and allowed the other man to come to him.

The participant from Erd barked out a laugh when he saw the staff in Rayne's hands. This obviously boosted his confidence, and he charged hard. Using the full length of the staff, Rayne easily fended off the attack.

The two men exchanged blows, but Rayne was able to keep the other man at bay while letting him do all the work. After several minutes, Rayne sensed his opponent was tiring and took advantage. Following an almost desperate advance, Rayne parried the swing and quickly brought the other end of the staff around, smacking the man hard on the forearm, causing him to drop his sword. The man looked shocked and was clearly in pain.

Rayne knew his opponent couldn't pick up the fallen sword without becoming vulnerable. He took some slow steps away from Rayne, raising his hands defensively. Instead of pressing the attack, Rayne lowered the staff and asked, "Do you yield?"

Looking behind him to see how far away his other weapon was, the man must have realized there was no way to reach it without opening his flank to Rayne. Lowering his head in defeat, he spoke loudly enough for the officiator to hear. "I yield."

⋆⧓⋆

"Something about that seemed familiar," Caldre said to Abrecan.

Abrecan nodded curtly as he stared hard onto the field. "How many from Erd are left?"

Caldre stood to get a better look at the scoreboard. "At the start of the third round, there are four men left. Two are from Erd, one is from Lewyol, and one from Lebu."

"I see," Abrecan said. "I was hoping for a better showing. I thought you were going to arrange that, Magistrate."

Still standing, Caldre pulled out his handkerchief and waved it several times until he was sure the officiator had seen the signal. Caldre turned back to the councilor and the king. "I have. You'll see." He sat back down and put his handkerchief away. "I'm still trying to recall why that last match was familiar. Something about a man with a sword fighting against a man with a staff…"

"Just drop it, Magistrate," King Daimh said harshly, gripping the armrests of his chair so tightly his fingers turned white.

⋆⧓⋆

Sunshine's anxiety spiked significantly as she watched Oakleaf and Ivor walk toward the middle of the field. She only knew Ivor's name because Snapdragon had worked his way down into the crowd to get a closer look and heard people cheering for him. Unable to get close enough to see the

179

matches, her younger brother had returned to the stands with his family.

Oakleaf had done well so far, but it seemed that Ivor was a formidable fighter, and she didn't want to see her brother get hurt.

"I'm not sure I can watch," Sunshine said.

Iolanthe put her arm around her daughter. "You don't have to if you don't want to."

"What?" Snapdragon exclaimed. "How can you *not* watch?"

"Snap…" his mother said reproachfully.

The crowd erupted in cheers as the contestants raced to the edges of the circle to retrieve their weapons. Both selected two-handed broad swords. They worked their way back toward the center, swords at the ready. Ivor swung first. Oakleaf brought his sword up to block, and as the two wooden blades connected, Oakleaf's sword shattered.

Obviously stunned, he was distracted just long enough for Ivor to let go of the sword with one hand and punch him, knocking him to the ground. Oakleaf brought his hands to his face and pulled them away slick with blood flowing from his broken nose. Ivor stood above him, sword raised. Even though Oakleaf had been knocked off his feet and the match was over, Ivor was going to keep attacking. Before Ivor could inflict more injury, the officiator stepped in and placed a hand on his chest to stop him. Ivor stared threateningly at the officiator a moment but then backed away, swinging the sword victoriously over his head.

⊰⬥⊱

Rayne didn't get a chance to check on Oakleaf because he was due up next. He walked onto the field, carefully looking around. A man standing up in the king's box caught his attention. It was the sharp-nosed man he had met at the castle the day before who thought Rayne looked familiar. What was his name again? Colder? Callous? Something like that. Whatever his name was, Rayne remembered he was a magistrate. He was waving a white handkerchief. Usually that meant someone was surrendering, but why would he be doing it?

Glancing around, Rayne saw one of the officiators looking at the magistrate as well, and nodding. While this seemed odd, it wasn't as strange as what had happened to Oakleaf's sword in the last match. It didn't seem possible that even Ivor could swing hard enough to destroy the wooden blade. But what Rayne needed now was to focus on the matter at hand—and that was the man in front of him. Unlike the other participants Rayne had faced, his opponent wasn't all that muscular.

Rather, he was lean and spry. Rayne had watched him closely during the event and sensed they had similar strengths and weaknesses.

Once again, the officiator instructed the combatants and signaled them to start. Rayne rushed back to his edge of the circle and saw his options: a shield and a short sword. Picking up the sword, he noticed it felt too light in his hand, and a quick inspection of the blade revealed where it had been hollowed out. The shield also seemed flimsy, with the nails that held the leather strap to the wood nearly pulled out. Perhaps this was one of the tests, but he didn't think so. He doubted his opponent from Erd was given the same poor quality of weapons. He turned and faced the center of the circle and saw his opponent was already on his way.

Instead of rushing out to meet him, Rayne stood at the edge, shield up and sword at the ready. His opponent didn't seem fazed by Rayne's actions and continued running toward him. When he got within a few steps, Rayne dropped the shield and sword on the ground, crouched down, lowered his shoulder, and let the other man's shock and momentum work to his advantage. The man was completely surprised by the move. Rayne was able to duck under his opponent's shield and sword and plant his shoulder in the man's stomach. He pushed up with his legs and flipped the man over him and into the crowd. Several rows of people were knocked down in the process, and Rayne was already helping them up when the officiator came over and somewhat hesitantly declared him the winner.

⇥⧲⇤

"Did you see that?" Snapdragon cheered. "That was brilliant! Rayne totally caught him off guard."

Sunshine wrung her hands nervously. She wanted Rayne to do well, but not *too* well. If he did well enough, he would become a royal guardian, and he wouldn't be allowed to marry. She knew it was selfish of her, and of course, she would wait for him to retire if he became a royal guardian. Right now, however, she just didn't want him to get hurt.

"Why didn't he use his weapons?" she asked.

Alana chimed in, "I am wondering that too. It was very odd."

Iolanthe had left the stands to check on Oakleaf. She hadn't returned yet, so Sunshine was still anxious to know her brother's condition.

Alana shielded her eyes from the sun and squinted at the scoreboard. "I can't see from here, Snapdragon. How many more rounds are there?"

Snapdragon didn't even look at the scoreboard. "This is the last match. It's Ivor against Rayne."

-»╬«-

Standing next to his grandfather, Rayne waited for the officiator to call him onto the field.

"Grandfather," he said just loudly enough for Kelvin to hear, but no one else, "I think someone tampered with Oakleaf's weapon and also mine from the last round."

Kelvin nodded. "I was thinking the same thing, but I'm not sure there is anything we can do about it. After all, the officiators work for the king."

"I saw the magistrate sitting up by the king wave his handkerchief to an officiator before my match," Rayne said. "Do you think it was some sort of signal?"

Kelvin rubbed his chin for a moment. "Perhaps the king wants the participants from Erd to do well, so much so that he is willing to give you and Oakleaf inferior weapons. You could say the magistrate is waving the white flag because he is surrendering to the fact that his men can't win in a fair fight."

-»╬«-

The officiator stood in the center of the circle and raised both hands, quieting the crowd. "It all comes down to this. The winner of this match will automatically become a royal guardian. After this event, the officiators will tabulate the scores, then announce the rest of those who have earned the rank of royal guardian from this year's Mortentaun."

He motioned for Rayne and Ivor to come forward. At that same moment, a man carrying a basket full of apples and strawberries on his back accidentally stepped in front of Ivor, who reacted by shoving the man out of the way. The merchant fell over and spilled his wares all over the ground. Rayne felt the urge to assist him, but Kelvin was already there, helping the man out of the circle. Rayne glanced up at the grandstand and again noticed the magistrate waving the white handkerchief.

The officiator said, "You both know the rules, so no point going over them again. May the best man win."

"Oh, I will," Ivor said, giving Rayne a shove in the chest. Rayne didn't react, but instead set himself for the officiator's signal.

The officiator raised a hand above his head, waited a moment, and lowered his hand.

Ivor spun and raced back to his weapons. Instead of heading to where his weapons were, Rayne ran toward the edge where he and Ivor had entered.

Rayne reached where the merchant had fallen. He caught his grandfather's questioning look before he bent down and picked up a large, solid apple that had spilt out into the circle. He spun toward Ivor who had selected a wicked looking two-handed mace, set himself, and threw the apple as hard as he could. The timing was perfect—the apple hit Ivor in the face just as he was turning toward Rayne. The apple exploded in a shower of pulp and peel. Ivor's head snapped backward sharply, and he stumbled back a few steps, but didn't fall down. Instead, he wiped the apple residue off his face, gripped the hilt of his mace tightly, and started moving toward an unarmed Rayne.

⇥⧉⇤

"Where is he going?" Snapdragon screamed when Rayne didn't move toward his weapons.

Sunshine didn't answer. She only hoped Rayne knew what he was doing. When she saw him hit Ivor in the head with an apple, her eyes went wide, but then she noticed the giant man's reaction and smiled. But he didn't go down, so she grabbed onto Snapdragon's arm, squeezing him hard. She buried her face into his shoulder, and for the first time this afternoon she could not force herself to watch.

⇥⧉⇤

Rayne looked to where his weapons lay a dozen paces away. They were more than likely useless, but he would have felt a bit better with something in his hands. He was considering his options when the officiator raced in and stood before Ivor, stopping him. It took Rayne a moment to realize that the crowd standing by Ivor's weapons was making extra noise and pointing to the ground. The officiator motioned Rayne to approach, which he did.

Again, the officiator raised his hands to get the crowd to quiet down. Rayne expected the officiator to declare Ivor the winner because Rayne had used the apple. He was ready to argue that the apple was a fair item because it was in the circle before the match started. The rules clearly stated that anything could be used that was found in the circle as long as it wasn't added after the match had begun.

To his surprise, the officiator said, "Number 13 from Erd stepped out of the circle after being hit with the apple, which makes number 17 from Lebu the winner!"

CHAPTER 21

"And these will be your quarters," Captain Sullivan said brusquely to Rayne and Oakleaf. "Someone bricked up the window years ago. You'll just have to live with it."

The room's furnishings consisted of two beds, both worn and lumpy. At the foot of each bed were large trunks, the only real storage the room offered. Against one wall there was a small table with a large bowl that held some water. A mirror hung above the table, lit by candles in sconces.

"Go ahead and put your belongings in the trunks," Sullivan said. "You'll be fitted for guardian uniforms tomorrow. Until then, wear your nicest clothes. Dinner with the royalty will be in about an hour, so make sure you are ready when summoned."

With that, Captain Sullivan walked away, leaving Rayne and Oakleaf alone in the room. The two new guardians stood there a moment, looking around.

"Which side do you want?" Rayne asked.

Oakleaf, his nose still swollen, nodded to the left. "I'll take this one, though neither look like much of a choice."

Rayne set down his packs and opened the trunk. He first put in his father's sword and then his copy of the Tome of Laws. Covering both with a dark brown canvas blanket, he made it look as though the canvas was the bottom of the trunk, effectively hiding his father's possessions. Next, he unpacked his clothes. "Well, at least we will get to be together. I'd hate to be forced to live with Ivor, or any of the other new guardians."

Oakleaf, starting to unpack as well, agreed. "Do you find it odd that we are the only new royal guardians who aren't from Erd?"

Rayne shrugged. "Not really. When the officiators posted that the two of us and four participants from Erd won, I wasn't too shocked. In fact, I heard someone say that had we not won today's events, all of the new royal guardians would have been from Erd."

"That doesn't seem fair." Oakleaf frowned. "So far, I've not been impressed with how things have been run. Perhaps my expectations were too high. I have been working toward this for the last few years, and now that I'm here, I guess I'm disappointed that my reality and my dreams aren't quite matching up."

Rayne reached over and slapped Oakleaf on the shoulder. "Give it a chance. We're just getting started. After all, how many people get the opportunity to have dinner with the royalty?"

They finished unpacking and were talking about the day's events when their door burst open, causing both of them to jump. In the doorway stood a thickly built man with narrow eyes and a very pronounced crooked nose. He wore the uniform of a guardian, trimmed in crimson and silver.

"Git up," he said. "Time fer dinner."

Rayne stood up and extended a hand. "Hello. My name is Rayne, and that's Oakleaf."

The guardian didn't take Rayne's hand. Instead, he gave a hard stare that switched between Rayne and Oakleaf. "Wut kinda names are those?" the guardian scoffed.

"Furst a woman savant named Sunshine and now yous two. Wut ever happened to proper names like Cameron?"

Oakleaf stood up. "I take it that's your name."

Royal Guardian Cameron nodded sharply. "Yeah. By the way, wut happened to yours nose? Ah, wait—yous the one that Ivor beat up. Ha ha! Chances are yous be lookin' like me from here on out," he said, pointing to his own nose.

Rayne noticed Oakleaf wasn't amused, and he decided to jump in before Oakleaf said anything to get himself in trouble. "You said it was time for dinner, right? We should be going then."

"Aye," Cameron said. He turned and walked down the hallway, with Rayne and Oakleaf following.

After walking down a series of hallways, they arrived in a large chamber and stopped in front of two huge wooden doors. The other men chosen as royal guardians were standing at the door already, their escorts beside them. Rayne spotted Ivor right away and couldn't help but smile when he noticed Ivor was sporting quite the black eye.

Ivor shouldered his way past the others to stand in front of Rayne. The large, bulbous-nosed man looked down at Rayne's tunic and grimaced. "I see you're wearing the pin you were awarded for the combat event," he said, poking Rayne in the chest just above the pin, a miniature replica of two crossed swords. Ivor turned his head to include the rest of the new guardians and said loudly, "Although it would be more appropriate if it showed an apple instead of swords."

Ivor laughed heartily, and the other guardians soon joined in. Rayne looked down at the pin, smiled, and then looked back up at Ivor. "Perhaps it should. But at least I'm able to hit a target at a distance."

The guardians laughed again, but stopped quickly when Ivor spun and glared at them.

When Captain Sullivan entered the chamber, his dark eyes narrowed. "What's so funny?" he demanded.

The guardians all became silent and Cameron stepped forward. "Nuthin,' Cap't. Just a bit 'o fun 'fore dinner."

"I see," Sullivan said, then turned his attention to the rest of the guardians. "Let me make one thing clear to you new royal guardians. You've earned the right to be worshiped by the commoners. However, when around me or the royalty, you will be quiet and speak only when spoken to. That clear?"

"Yes, sir," they said in unison.

Sullivan nodded. "Very good then. Let's go in and have dinner. And remember, anyone who causes problems for me will live to regret it."

⭒⧓⭒

"My compliments on a wonderful dinner," Governor Eadward said, taking a seat. After dinner, Governor Eadward, Magistrate Caldre, and Councilor Abrecan had retired to Abrecan's room.

Caldre sat down next to Eadward. "Yes, the Councilor made some excellent choices for dinner tonight."

"Yes, yes, enough with the pleasantries." Abrecan looked uncomfortable with the positive comments. "Let's discuss how things are progressing for the Shoginoc."

Eadward sat up straighter. "I've been able to procure several valuable items from both Erd and Lewyol, but most of the silver from Erd has been mined out and sent to the castle, and Lewyol hasn't had much to offer."

"It needs to be a formidable showing," Abrecan said. "There has to be no doubt that it is the biggest offering. You should have been able to do that by combining the resources of two districts. Did I make a mistake by appointing you governor of both Erd and Lewyol?"

Some of the color drained from Eadward's face. "You didn't make a mistake. We've tried very hard, but the commoners don't seem particularly interested in supplying us with what we need. How do you suggest I inspire them?"

"It's not my responsibility to inspire your commoners," Abrecan said bluntly.

Caldre cleared his throat. "If I may make a suggestion?"

"What is it, Caldre?" Abrecan seemed annoyed at the interruption.

"There are a number of valuables in the castle that are gathering dust and won't be missed if they are removed," Caldre said. "The items could be polished and added to Eadward's offering."

Abrecan leaned back in his chair and steepled his fingers as he thought. "That's not a bad idea. I'm surprised *I* didn't think of it."

"Shall we proceed then?" Caldre asked.

"Yes, yes. Make sure it's enough to make a difference." Abrecan focused his attention on Eadward again. "And remember our agreement, Eadward. In return for giving you the throne, you will do what I say and not make any decisions unless they are cleared through me first."

Eadward nodded. "Understood."

"Excellent," Caldre said. "Since that is settled, may we discuss something else, Councilor?"

Abrecan stifled a yawn. "What is it now, Caldre?"

Absently pulling on his ponytail, Caldre said, "I have a plan to unseat Bertram."

"Not another plan." Abrecan sighed dramatically. "Tell me what you have in mind. I'm curious to see how this one fails."

Caldre tried to ignore the lack of support, but he couldn't hide the frustration in his voice. "I've not been able to remove the magistrate because he stays fairly isolated. However, I've noticed that someone has gotten close to him."

"Who?"

"The new savant, Sunshine," Caldre said. "Bertram has taken her under his wing."

Abrecan's attention perked up a bit. "Are they involved romantically?"

Caldre snorted. "Oh, no. Not in the least. He's more like her mentor."

"Ah. That would make more sense—he's rather ugly. Sunshine, however…even I have noticed her. She's quite stunning."

"Yes, she is," Caldre said. "As you know, I've never married. I think it may be time. Sunshine would make a wonderful prize with which to be seen, and I could use her to get to Bertram."

Abrecan raised his eyebrows a bit. "And how do you plan on wooing her?"

"Everyone has a price," Caldre said. "She obviously loves knowledge, so I'll offer her fewer duties so she can study more. I'll start by asking her to be my personal assistant."

Abrecan looked doubtful. "And if that doesn't work?"

"Then I'll see that she gets more duties so she has less time to read," Caldre said. "And if that fails, I'll threaten to take away something she cares for more than books."

⇥✦⇤

Rayne and Oakleaf were awakened when Cameron barged into the room, looking none too happy.

"Git up," he commanded. "It's bad enough I gots stuck training yous two, but even worser that I gots to git up early too. Meets me at the front gates as soon as yous can."

The two new guardians got ready and rushed to the front gates, asking servants along the way the quickest route there. They arrived at the front gates in plenty of time, but Cameron still harassed them about being slow.

"Where are yours uniforms?" Cameron asked, folding his arms in front of him and looking at Rayne and Oakleaf with distain.

"Captain Sullivan said we would be fitted for uniforms today." Rayne stood as straight as he could.

Cameron looked doubtful. "Oh, he dids, dids he? You better nots be lying to me."

Oakleaf, not standing nearly as straight as Rayne, responded, "Why would we lie to you?"

"Because yous may want me to git in troubles with the Cap't." Cameron pointed a finger at them.

Rayne and Oakleaf exchanged a quick questioning look, but neither said anything.

"Never minds abouts the uniforms for now. Yous will start learnin' to read laters today."

"I already know how to read," Oakleaf bragged.

"As do I," Rayne said, trying to sound less boastful than his companion.

Cameron's expression soured even more. "Oh, so now yous thinkin' yous better than me 'cos yous knows how to read already?"

"Uh, no," Rayne said carefully.

"Whatevers." Cameron shook his head. "This mornin' yous will be inspectin' anyone enterin' or leavin' the castle. Makes sure no ones brings nothin' dangerous inside and no one leaves with stuff that don't belong to thems."

"Understood," Rayne said, and Oakleaf nodded.

"And don't tries nothin'. I'll be checkin' in on yous from up theres." Cameron pointed up to the archer's tower by the front gate. "Any questions?"

"Yes, sir, I have one," Rayne said. "Where do the guardians in the castle live once they get married?"

Cameron gave Rayne a blank stare. "Wut?"

Rayne tried again. "In Lewyol, guardians who got married were given a house by the governor. I was wondering what arrangements are made for royal guardians."

Again, Cameron didn't say anything for a moment. Then he broke out in laughter. "Wut's yous talkin' about? Royal guardians can't git married, least not untils they retire. Now quit wastin' my time and git to work." He walked away, still laughing.

"What's wrong, Rayne?" Oakleaf asked. "You look pale."

Rayne didn't respond—he was still in shock. Why hadn't he known before? Perhaps he just assumed they could marry because guardians throughout the land were allowed to. Plus, it wasn't mentioned in the Tome of Laws.

This knowledge impacted Rayne in more than one way. The most obvious was that he wouldn't be able to court Sunshine. Did she know about this? Is that why she wanted to talk to him? How could he work here in the castle, with her so close, and not be able to be with her?

But even as disheartening as that was, it was the next thing he realized that was the most disturbing. His father had been a royal guardian, and he had gotten married. Perhaps *that* was the mistake his father had referred to—getting married when it wasn't allowed. What would cause him to do that? His father was one of the most honorable and truthful people he had known. If that was the mistake his father regretted so much, Rayne himself was a result of this mistake. He wasn't sure how he felt about that, but it did give him reason to pause.

"Rayne?" Oakleaf poked him in the shoulder. "Hey, are you there?"

Rayne glanced at Oakleaf without turning his head. "Did you know royal guardians couldn't get married?"

"Well, yeah. You mean you didn't? I thought you were just messing with Cameron."

"No," Rayne said quietly. "I didn't know."

-»‡‹-

A week passed, and Cameron had kept Rayne and Oakleaf very busy. It was called their "training" period, but it seemed like they were given all the duties and tasks of the older guardians. This meant long days of almost nonstop activity, followed by short nights on lumpy beds.

The swelling in Oakleaf's nose had gone down, and it did indeed look like it would be crooked from that time forward. As time passed, the young man from Lewyol was becoming more disenchanted with being a guardian. It was fairly obvious that the new guardians from Erd were not given as much work as Rayne and Oakleaf.

At one point, Oakleaf even said that had Rayne not been there, he would have probably resigned. Rayne, on the other hand, was no stranger to hard work from his life on the farm. While the days were long and the work hard, Rayne accepted it and actually enjoyed it.

He had started developing a good rapport with many of the servants, as well as several of the nobles and savants in the castle. In addition, the hard work sometimes helped him keep his mind off the rule that he was forbidden to marry. However, no matter how hard he tried, there were any number of things that would remind him and cause him to become troubled again. Despite being exhausted after working all day, sleep seemed to elude him, and he often woke in the middle of the night thinking about Sunshine. He desperately wanted to talk to her. He had seen her in passing and could tell she wanted to talk, but they couldn't find a time to get together. At night he would think about what he'd say to her, but nothing sounded quite right.

After the first full week, Captain Sullivan finally gave Rayne and Oakleaf the night off after dinner. Oakleaf chose to spend his time trying to catch up on some sleep, while Rayne was able to get a servant to find Sunshine and ask her to meet him in the eastern courtyard.

When Sunshine entered the courtyard, Rayne stood by a large sculpture of King Daimh, looking at it distastefully. "That's the same reaction I had when I first saw it," she said.

Rayne turned and smiled when he saw her. "It seems a bit, well, much, doesn't it?" He nodded his head slightly toward the statue.

"No more than just about everything else in the castle. You can't go anywhere without seeing some tribute to either the king or his father."

"Yeah, I've noticed," Rayne said. "But enough about them. How are you doing, Sunshine?"

She smiled again, and Rayne felt a warm tingle throughout his body.

"I'm the one who should be asking you," she said. "It seems Cameron has been running you and Oakleaf ragged."

"He has." Rayne motioned for Sunshine to follow him to a stone bench. After sitting down, he said, "But it's been worth it, now that you're here."

"Thank you," she said. "I've been hoping to talk to you for some time."

"I know. I've wanted to talk to you too."

Sunshine's countenance changed. Her normal cheerful expression was replaced with something that could only be described as seriousness. "Rayne, at one time you said you weren't sure you wanted to be a guardian, but—"

"But here I am."

Sunshine nodded. "Yes, here you are. When we first met, I felt something for you I hadn't really felt before. I found myself thinking about you often after you left. Even when the chance came along to become a savant, I still only considered it to be a temporary situation, depending on how well you did in the Mortentaun."

She reached out and took Rayne by the hand. "When I thought you'd been killed, I felt as though part of me died as well. I threw myself into my duties here. When we met in the castle, I felt all sorts of different emotions. I was so happy to see that you were alive! I think you were happy to see me as well."

Rayne's heart ached when he thought of what she must have been feeling when she thought he was dead. He squeezed her hand. "I was *very* happy to see you."

"That brings us to now." Sunshine took a deep breath. "To put it simply—where do we go from here?"

He paused a moment before responding. "Well… I'm not sure. When my father died, he left me a note asking me to become the guardian he hadn't been. I loved my father very much and I wanted to make him proud. But as I trained, I started to understand why he was asking what he did. He wanted to serve people and make Bariwon a better for everyone. Something happened to him—I'm not sure what—and he felt like not only did he *not* make it a better place, but he had made things worse."

"I can only imagine how hard his death was on you," Sunshine said, caressing his hand.

"It was hard. After he died, I had a lot of time to think. A big part of me has a yearning to do something important. It's hard to describe. I'm sure it was something my father felt as well—a desire to make a difference."

"And by becoming a guardian, you hope to be able to make a difference," Sunshine said.

"That's it exactly."

Sunshine swallowed hard. "How long do you plan on serving?"

"I hadn't really thought about it in those terms. I guess as long as it takes for me to make a difference."

Sunshine slowly removed her hand from Rayne's. "I see."

"What's the matter?" he asked, noting that Sunshine looked disappointed.

"You know that royal guardians aren't allowed to, well..."

"Yes, I know that we're not allowed to marry. Actually, I just found out a few days ago. Had I known, I—"

Rayne sat up straight, turned, and faced Sunshine, who appeared as if she was about to cry. "Sunshine, I couldn't stop thinking about you after we met. Even during training, I was looking forward to seeing you again at the Mortentaun. Meeting you in the castle was one of the happiest moments in my life."

He reached out and took her hand again. She seemed hesitant to give it, but acquiesced. "I want very much to court you, but if I'm not allowed to marry, I don't see how it would be possible."

"Well, we're not allowed to court officially, but there isn't a law preventing us from being friends. I would be willing to wait for you to retire," she said, and to Rayne, it sounded like she was trying to be brave. "You would be worth the wait."

Rayne had felt a weight pressing down on him, and suddenly it lifted a little. She was willing to wait for him! Was he being selfish? Was it fair for him to ask her to do that? "Are you sure that—"

"I'm sure," Sunshine said, sounding completely confident in her response.

Rayne slid over next to her and slipped his arm around her. She put her head on his shoulder, and they sat there for a while in silence.

⟐

Bertram wasn't sure what type of response he'd get when he announced what he and Sunshine had discovered. He thought the reaction would likely be a strong one, with different people shouting all at once. Instead, it was almost eerily quiet in the main hall after he spoke.

Looking at faces in the crowd, which included the governors of the districts as well as the usual court members, Bertram thought he understood why. Many of those in attendance were offspring of arranged marriages, and several were in arranged marriages themselves. Apparently the realization that they should have been able to choose for themselves came as a shock.

Abrecan finally broke the silence. "And you are sure about this?"

Bertram nodded, looking down and not meeting the councilor's stare. "Yes, I had the other members of the hierarchy verify the validity of the book, and they've all signed a proclamation to that fact."

"I see," Abrecan said. "This is quite an interesting find. But I don't see how it will affect the upcoming Shoginoc. So far, all the people who have declared the intent to participate are already married, so it is a moot point."

Priest Sherwyn stood up from the table where he sat by the members of the hierarchy. "I believe that if someone else declares an intent to participate in the Shoginoc who isn't married, this would apply to them."

Abrecan scoffed. "I find that to be highly unlikely. The Shoginoc is in a couple of months. Anyone who was seriously considering participating would have declared by now."

Bertram interjected, "Actually, anyone can declare his intent up until the Shoginoc ceremony begins."

Right away, Bertram realized he had made a mistake. Abrecan's expression made it plain that he was not happy with Bertram's clarification, especially in front of all of the governors. Once again, he felt the all-too-familiar urge to rush back to his room and close the door behind him.

⊰⫛⊱

"Thank you, Guardian," Anemone said. "It's a refreshing change to have someone actually help me carry the supplies to my room."

Rayne shrugged. "It's my pleasure. Are you telling me that the other guardians don't help you?"

Anemone chuckled. "More like *won't*. That wasn't always the case. Before Abrecan took over, guardians used to be nice."

"Abrecan took over? Don't you mean King Daimh?"

She chuckled again. "Oh, yes, Daimh is the king," she said sarcastically. "Sometimes it's hard to tell."

Rayne stopped and looked at the elderly nursemaid questioningly. "Forgive an old woman, Guardian," she said. "You are new here, and I shouldn't bog you down with such unpleasantness."

Anemone squinted, took a step closer to Rayne, and stared at him. The invasion of his personal space made him feel uncomfortable, but instead of stepping back, he simply asked, "Is something the matter?"

"It's just that for a moment there, you seemed quite familiar to me," she said. "Have we met before?"

Rayne considered telling her that his father was a guardian years ago. While he never thought there was a strong resemblance between him and his father, anyone who knew his father well could perhaps perceive the relationship. But Rayne remembered his father had warned him not to tell anyone who he was. The nursemaid was one of the nicest people Rayne had met thus far, and he felt like he could trust her, but he kept his father's wish.

"I don't believe we've met, no," he said.

Anemone leaned in even closer. "Are you sure? There's something very familiar about your eyes."

Now that *was* odd. Of all of his features, his eyes were the least like his father's. If his blue eyes didn't come from his father, perhaps they resembled his mother's. Although his father talked about his mother's personality and how much he loved her, he never really talked about where she came from or who her parents were. It wasn't that Rayne hadn't asked—he had. But his father had always skirted the issue. Rayne realized that since his father had married while he was a royal guardian, perhaps his mother had been a servant here in the castle. If that was the case, it was possible the nursemaid had known her.

Rayne's curiosity about his mother fought against his plan to keep his family history a secret. "Perhaps—" he began to say.

"Yes?"

Rayne decided against saying anything after all. "Perhaps you saw me at the Mortentaun or when I was at the castle dinners."

Anemone looked at him doubtfully. "Perhaps, Guardian."

"Rayne," he said. "Please call me Rayne."

CHAPTER 22

"You requested my presence?" Sunshine asked after she had been ushered into Magistrate Caldre's room.

The sharp-nosed man stood and gave her a smile she found disturbing. "Yes, my dear. Please, please, have a seat."

He motioned to a padded bench next to a large window that overlooked the town below.

Sunshine hesitated a moment before she walked over and chose the far edge of the bench. She sat up straight with her hands folded on her lap.

Caldre sauntered over and sat next to her. He rested one arm on the windowsill and again gave her a smile that made her want to shiver in disgust.

"So, what can I do for you, Magistrate?" Sunshine asked, using a serious tone.

"Relax, relax. I know you must be nervous being around such an important person, but there is no reason to be so tense."

He put his hand on her shoulder. She fought off the urge to bat it away—instead, she tried to ignore it was there. He massaged her shoulder gently. "See how tight your muscles are? Perhaps you would like a drink to help you relax."

"I'm not thirsty."

Caldre continued to massage her shoulder. "As you wish. Let me know if you change your mind. I do have some of the finest drinks from around the kingdom."

"I'm quite fine, Magistrate," Sunshine replied.

"Caldre. Please call me Caldre."

Sunshine nodded. "As you wish, Magistrate Caldre. Once again, what may I do for you?"

"You are direct." He moved his hand from her shoulder toward her

195

neck. "I admire that. It is a good trait. It means you are confident, and confidence is very attractive. Not that *you* need confidence to be attractive, of course."

Sunshine didn't flinch. "Thank you, Magistrate. Now, I don't mean to sound rude, but I have duties awaiting me. So, if you wouldn't mind telling me why you asked me here…"

"Actually, your duties are the reason I wanted to talk to you," he said. "I understand you love to read, and I imagine all your responsibilities as a savant give you precious little free time. I would like to present to you an opportunity that will lessen your duties so that you will have more time to spend as you wish."

The hair on the back of Sunshine's neck stood on end, and not only because Caldre's hand was nearly touching her there. "What offer?"

"I am in need of a personal assistant." He leaned in closer. "Someone who will help me with, well, whatever my needs are."

His hand was now on the back of her neck, and Sunshine felt him pulling her to him. "I'll have that drink now," she said suddenly.

Caldre appeared somewhat startled and let her go. He nodded with a leer on his face, then walked over to a cabinet full of bottles of different shapes and colors.

"What can I get for you, my dear?" he asked, reaching for a couple of silver goblets studded with what looked to be rubies.

Sunshine stood and moved to the middle of the room. "Water."

Caldre froze in place. Still facing the cabinet, he said, "Water? Are you sure? I have much more exotic things."

"I'm sure you do, but I prefer something a little less pretentious."

Caldre filled one of the goblets from a water pitcher on the table next to the cabinet, then filled the other goblet with a red liquid. He turned around and handed Sunshine her drink.

She took the goblet, gulped down the water, and handed the empty goblet to the magistrate. "Thank you. I will consider your offer."

After curtseying slightly, she departed, leaving Caldre standing in the middle of the room holding both goblets.

-)∦(-

Bertram looked at Sunshine and sighed in dismay. Glancing down, he noticed that his fingernails had all been chewed down to almost nothing over the last few days. He knew it was a nervous habit, but it offered him some small comfort in a time of great anxiety.

So far nothing had happened to him as a result of his comment at the most recent court, but Bertram remembered all too well how Abrecan responded when someone disagreed with him—especially in public.

After all, Abrecan's wife, Lady Calla, had never been heard of again since being sent to their summer home. Bertram felt Abrecan's anger would certainly come forward again under the right circumstances, and often the person to carry out the unpleasant mandates was Magistrate Caldre. To that end, Caldre had been rewarded handsomely. Not only had he been made magistrate over the town of Bariwon that surrounded the castle, but he had also been given a luxurious suite. Abrecan seemed to support Caldre in whatever he wanted, so upsetting Caldre was akin to upsetting Abrecan.

As worried as Bertram had been before, he was even more worried now—and not for his own well-being. "To be honest, Sunshine, I'm not sure what Magistrate Caldre would do if you refused his offer," he said glumly.

Sunshine stood at the window of Bertram's room, the afternoon light shining behind her. "What could he do?" she asked almost defiantly. "I've done nothing wrong."

"Sadly, I've discovered that to Caldre and Abrecan, it isn't a matter of what is right and what is wrong. It's more a matter of what's better for them. If you make things hard on them, they make things worse for you."

"Would they banish me from the castle?" Sunshine asked, the resolution in her voice lessening.

Bertram folded his arms. "Possibly. Or they could find something you care for and take it away from you."

Her eyes widened. "They wouldn't hurt my family or—" she looked as though she caught herself before saying a name "—anyone else. Would they?"

"I wouldn't put it beyond them," Bertram said.

Sunshine started pacing back and forth in front of the window. "This is so unfair! I don't know what to do." She stopped. "Wait. I know something I can't do. I can't accept his offer."

"I don't blame you," Bertram said.

"I'm sure this will make him angry. What then?"

Bertram opened his arms wide and motioned to the room around him. "I think you are beginning to understand why I don't leave my quarters unless absolutely necessary."

⊹

Alana walked with Sunshine down the long hallway after they finished their evening meal with the royalty, savants, and several members of the Hierarchy of Magistrates.

"You seem rather distracted tonight," Alana said. "Something wrong?"

Sunshine gave Alana a forced smile. "I have a lot on my mind, and I would like to talk about it, if you have some time later."

"Of course, dear. You know you can talk to me about anything." Lowering her voice a bit, Alana asked, "Does it have something to do with Magistrate Caldre? I noticed him staring at you in an odd manner during most of the meal."

Sunshine looked around and noticed that two of the magistrates were several paces behind her, while a few of the other savants were in front. "I'd rather wait to talk about—"

She was interrupted when a couple of guardians rounded the corner, running at full speed, and plowed into her and Alana, knocking them both to the ground. Sunshine looked up to see what had happened, and noticed Guardians Ivor and Cameron standing over them, looking perturbed.

"Yous needs to watch where yous goin'," Cameron said to the two ladies.

Alana tried to get back on her feet, but struggled to do so because her legs were tangled in her long, flowing dress. "Watch where *we* are going?"

"That's right," Cameron said, either ignoring or missing the inflection in Alana's voice.

Sunshine saw a hand extend to her and turned to see Rayne.

"Please forgive my fellow guardians," he said. "They seem to have left their manners back in their rooms."

With Rayne's help, Sunshine and Alana got back on their feet. Sunshine smoothed out her savant's robes, while Alana inspected her own clothing.

"Thank you," Alana said. "It's nice to see that at least one of the royal guardians remembered to bring their manners with him." Reaching up to her ears, she exclaimed, "Oh! My earrings! They must have fallen off when we were knocked down."

The other savants and the magistrates joined them in searching the floor for the missing earrings.

"They're gold with sapphire inlaid in the middle. I'd hate to lose them. They were a gift from King Kenrik," Alana explained.

"Here's one," Rayne announced, holding it up to Alana. Sunshine thought she saw Cameron pick something up off the floor and put it under his tunic as they continued to look, but wasn't sure enough to accuse him.

After several more moments, Alana said, "Oh, dear. Those were my favorite pair. I can't imagine where it might have gone. If any of you find it, please let me know."

"We'll continue to look," Rayne said.

Alana glanced around one more time. "All right, thank you." She smiled at Rayne before turning to Cameron and Ivor. "Next time, Guardians, I will discuss this with Captain Sullivan."

"No needs to git hims involved." Cameron looked nervous. "I was trainings Ivor here, and yous got in my way. Next times, yous just be more careful."

Alana rolled her eyes. "Sunshine, let's go."

Sunshine squeezed Rayne's arm. "Thank you, Guardian Rayne, for your help." She gave him a wink and walked off with Alana.

⇥※⇤

Caldre examined the envelope in his hand. "The seal has been broken."

"That so?" Guardian Cameron said indifferently. "Wuz probably that servant that gaves it to me to give to yous."

Opening the envelope and removing the card from inside, Caldre read the simple message that was written in flowing script:

Magistrate Caldre,

Thank you for your offer, but I must decline. I feel there are much more qualified people who would serve you better as an assistant. I will continue to work and study so that one day I will be worthy of such an honor.

Sincerely,
Savant Sunshine

Caldre crumpled up the note and threw it into the fireplace, where it caught fire from the embers.

"I'm guessin' that wuz bad news," Cameron said.

Caldre almost lashed out at Cameron, but held back. Who was Sunshine to refuse him? Her refusal only made Caldre want her more. He *would* have her. And once he had Sunshine, he would use her against Bertram. But how to get to her?

"Cameron, what do you know of Savant Sunshine's friends here in the castle?" Caldre asked.

Cameron scratched his head for a moment. "Wells, her brother is a guardian here. Alsos, I thinks there is somethin' betweens her and Guardian Rayne. And she spends lots o' time with Magistrate Bertram. I tries to gets her attention once, but she gaves me no never mind."

Caldre nodded. "That will be all."

Cameron turned to leave the room, but stopped when Caldre said, "Oh, and one more thing, Guardian. Next time you deliver a personal note to me with the seal broken, I'll see to it that a part of *you* gets broken."

⇥❖⇤

"Guardian Rayne! Excellent. I'm glad it's you," Anemone said, waving as he approached her.

There were several assignments that Rayne enjoyed, and helping Anemone or the other nursemaids was one of them. Smiling, he said, "It's good to see you again, Nursemaid. How are you today?"

"Call me Anemone, please. You've known me long enough." She took Rayne by the arm. "And I'm feeling as well as a woman of my age can feel, I suppose."

"I'm happy to hear that," Rayne responded. "Where are we off to today?"

Anemone pointed a spotted, crooked finger toward the main road that led to the heart of the marketplace in town. It was just after mid-day, and while it had been sunny all morning, afternoon clouds had started to roll in. "I'm in need of more bandages. Those darn guardians keep getting cuts from all their fooling around with swords."

"I'd be happy to get them for you," Rayne said. "There's no need for you to make the trip."

Anemone patted Rayne's arm as they walked. "Ah, in that you are wrong. If I don't keep moving, these bones of mine will stop working altogether. And I'm not quite ready for that just yet."

"Understood." Rayne flashed another grin.

"There you go again," Anemone said. "Every time you take me somewhere, I can't shake the feeling that I've met you before. You seem so familiar to me—especially your smile."

Rayne tensed up a bit, but tried to force himself to relax. In the weeks he'd been in the castle, several people, mostly the older residents, had remarked how he looked familiar to them. Up to this point, he had been able to dodge any probing questions on why that may be.

"Well, I have helped you many times, and we've taken several trips into town together," he said slowly, "so it's no wonder I seem familiar to you."

Anemone scoffed. "It's more than that."

They continued walking down the street, chatting idly about how spring was transitioning into summer with its longer days and warmer temperatures. As they approached their destination, a light rain started falling.

Looking up, Rayne noted that the sun was still shining even though the rain clouds had arrived. "The sun is playing hide-and-seek."

Anemone stopped abruptly. "What did you say?"

Rayne nodded toward the sky. "The sun is playing hide-and-seek. It's raining even though the sun is still shining."

"Where did you hear that?" Anemone asked, eyeing Rayne carefully.

Rayne shrugged. "It's something people say."

Anemone shook her head slightly. "No, they don't. I've not heard that saying for many years. Tell me, Rayne, where did you hear it?"

"My father said it once on our farm in Tevoil. He said it was something my mother would—" Rayne stopped talking. He had been very careful up until now not to mention his father and mother to anyone, but here he was, telling Anemone. He felt like he could trust her, but still felt he had said too much.

"Your mother would say?" she prompted.

Rayne tried to urge her to start walking again, but Anemone wouldn't move. "Also, you said you grew up in Tevoil, but you represented Lebu in the Mortentaun, didn't you?"

"I did." Rayne wondered how to explain it. A lesson his father had taught him over and over again was, "Always tell the truth, Son. It's much easier than remembering what you lied about." He hadn't lied—he had just avoided answering the questions. He decided to be honest with Anemone, at least until he could find a way to change the subject.

"My father died last year," Rayne said after a pause. "We lived in Tevoil at the time. After he died, I moved to live with my grandparents in Lebu.

Technically, they were my sponsors for the Mortentaun, so I represented Lebu."

"And did your mother move with you as well?" Anemone asked almost anxiously.

Rayne shook his head. "No, my mother died long before that. If it's all right with you, I'd rather not talk about this."

"I'm sorry for asking such personal questions. But if you will indulge me, I have just one more."

Rayne considered the old woman before him. In the time he had known her, he had seen her treat the servants and commoners with respect, and she would always go out of her way to help someone. Rayne felt she was a good person, and he couldn't imagine her intentionally hurting anyone.

"All right, one more question," he agreed.

"How did your mother die?" Anemone asked.

Rayne looked away from the nursemaid and up at the clouds that continued to move over the town. "I didn't even know her. My father told me she died giving birth to me."

Anemone nodded. "Thank you, Rayne. Now let's get inside before we get too wet."

❧❦❧

Councilor Abrecan grinned like a cat that had a mouse cornered. Governor Dylan of Donigi noticed and didn't care for the expression

"So, Governor Dylan," Abrecan began, "I understand your district has decided to sponsor someone for the Shoginoc. Don't you think it's a bit late for that? After all, the Shoginoc is only a week away."

Looking around the room, the governor noted many expensive items. The tapestries on the wall had to be recent commissions, since the depictions of the councilor included the gray hair that now dominated his head.

Dylan considered his response carefully. "Yes, Councilor, I know it seems very last minute. But understand this—I have been training a young man to replace me as governor. He's shown quite the aptitude for leadership. I think he would make an excellent king, but we didn't think we would be able to gather enough items to compete at the Shoginoc. However, fortune struck, and we recently came across an oyster bed that had been overlooked for years. It was discovered quite by accident. What we found was an amazing cache of pearls—some so large as to take your breath away."

Councilor Abrecan narrowed his eyes. "And you think you have enough of these pearls to make a credible showing at the Shoginoc?"

Dylan nodded emphatically. "Oh, yes. Pearls are one of the rarest items in Bariwon—each is very valuable. The collection we have is quite impressive indeed."

Abrecan picked up a pear from the table in front of him and started slicing it into sections with a sharp knife. "And is your sponsor married, Governor Dylan?"

Dylan eyed the knife in Abrecan's hand. "No, he isn't. But as I understand it, that no longer makes a difference—he would be able to marry anyone he wanted."

Placing the pear slices on a plate, Abrecan said, "Yes, that's true, thanks to Magistrate Bertram's discovery." He held up the knife and used it to motion toward Dylan. "There isn't anything I could say that would persuade you to change your mind about participating, is there, Governor?"

"Why would you want to change my mind?" Dylan asked, looking at the knife and not at the councilor.

Abrecan chortled. "It's no secret that you've been critical about me and my son, although you've not been man enough to do it to my face."

"Councilor, I—"

"I have left you alone in your district," Abrecan interrupted, "because you have always paid your taxes on time, although I wonder why we haven't received part of these pearls in taxes. In addition, the reports of your insolent attitude have always bothered me. Your insistence in participating in the Shoginoc has taken things too far."

Governor Dylan slid his chair back from the table and stood. "Are you threatening me, Councilor?"

Abrecan gave Dylan another cold grin. "No, Governor, it is you that are a threat to me."

In one swift motion, Abrecan took the knife and stabbed himself in the back of his other hand. He let out a howl of pain, which caused the guardians to rush into the room.

"Arrest him!" Abrecan shouted, holding his bleeding hand prominently. "He just attacked me!"

CHAPTER 23

"**D**id you see this tree when it was in full bloom this spring?" Sherwyn asked.

Anemone squinted up at the large tree, noting that the blossoms were all gone and the summer leaves had grown in. "I didn't. Unlike you, Sherwyn, I don't make it out to this hill very often."

"Well, I'm glad you decided to join me today," he said. "What inspired you?"

Anemone removed a wool blanket from the bag she had slung over one shoulder. She laid it on the ground and sat down, motioning Sherwyn to join her. "I needed to talk to you, and it had to be someplace where we couldn't be overheard."

Sherwyn frowned as he sat down beside her. "You don't think it's safe to talk in my room, or yours?"

The nursemaid shook her head. "I couldn't take the risk. After the shocking news of Governor Dylan's attack on Councilor Abrecan, I'm leery about many things in the castle."

"Understandable," the priest said. "Although, I'm not entirely sure I believe Dylan did it."

Anemone considered Sherwyn carefully. "You aren't?"

"I heard Dylan was going to enter his district in the Shoginoc. It seems more likely to me that the councilor did something drastic to prevent another entry."

Anemone sighed. "And the Hierarchy of Magistrates won't do anything about it?"

"What can they do?" Sherwyn shrugged. "It's Abrecan's word against Dylan's. And Abrecan was stabbed—that can't be disputed."

"It's possible that Abrecan stabbed himself. I wouldn't put it past him."

"Be that as it may, it seems that after Governor Dylan was arrested, his sponsor had a closed-door discussion with Abrecan, and soon after, it was announced that Donigi withdrew. That means that only Erd, Regne, and Lewyol will be competing. That doesn't bode well for Bariwon."

Anemone cocked her head, her flowing gray hair cascading off to one side. "How so?"

Priest Sherwyn took a deep breath. "Think about it. Erd and Lewyol are both governed by the same man—Governor Eadward, who is the candidate for both districts."

"But what of Regne?" Anemone said.

"Lady Nicole is from Regne. Not long after she was chosen to become Daimh's wife, her father was made magistrate over Regne. He's the candidate the governor of Regne has selected. It appears that Abrecan has thought of everything."

Anemone shook her head. "No, not everything."

Sherwyn eyed her carefully. "What do you mean?"

"I think I've discovered something wonderful. Have you met Guardian Rayne?"

Rubbing his hand over his bald head, Sherwyn thought for a moment. "I believe so. He's new, right? Bright yellow hair? He seems very nice."

Anemone nodded emphatically. "That's him. Does he remind you of anyone?"

"Hmm. I've not really been around him much, but if I recall, he did seem familiar to me."

Anemone sat up straight. "Let me give you some clues. In addition to his blond hair, he has bright blue eyes. He was born twenty-one years ago. His father's parents live in Lebu. His mother died during childbirth."

"Are you suggesting he's Eliana's son? It might be nothing more than a coincidence. If I recall, Rinan was from Lebu, but we don't know where he went after he left."

"Rayne said he grew up in Tevoil, but after his father died, he moved to Lebu." She waved her hands in front of her. "But more importantly, when Rayne escorted me to town yesterday, he used a phrase Eliana made up when she was younger for when the sun was out, but it was raining. I've not heard anyone else say that but Eliana. He must have heard it from Rinan, who heard it from Eliana."

"I don't know, Anemone. It seems a bit of a stretch. How could you prove this? You said Rinan passed away."

"We need to send someone to Lebu to see if they can find out," Anemone said. "I asked around this morning, and it was Governor Nash who personally trained Rayne. He would know who Rayne's grandparents are. I'm sure they know the truth."

Sherwyn rubbed his hand over his head again. "Why not ask Rayne directly?"

"I almost did," Anemone said. "But as soon as he mentioned his father and mother, he became very quiet. It was obvious this was not something he would talk about easily. Plus, we'll need someone else's word on it."

"Someone else's word about what?"

Anemone smiled excitedly. "That Rayne is actually the heir to the throne."

⊰❋⊱

Alana waited patiently to be escorted to see the governor. When Priest Sherwyn and Nursemaid Anemone first came to ask her for a favor, she was understandably curious. Alana had known them a long time and knew they had been loyal to her uncle, King Kenrik. Over the years, she would often go to Sherwyn for advice on how best to deal with one political issue or another, and he always gave her good counsel. Sherwyn and Anemone clearly felt they could trust Alana as well, because they invited her to take a walk with them outside after dinner and told her what they suspected about Rayne. Both the priest and the nursemaid were getting on in age, and neither was up to the task of traveling to Lebu and back before the Shoginoc. Sworn to secrecy, Alana had arranged for a guardian to accompany her to see Governor Nash. After arriving in Lebu, they went directly to the governor's house. The wait to see the governor was a short one, and soon Alana was ushered in, with the guardian waiting outside.

"Ho ho!" Governor Nash chuckled when Alana came in. "Well, isn't this a surprise. It's not often I get visited by a member of the nobility."

Alana gave Governor Nash a polite hug and a quick kiss on either cheek. "It's good to see you again, Governor. I always enjoy your visits to the castle—your sense of humor is such a refreshing change from what I have to deal with day to day."

Offering her a seat, Nash sat down next to her on a large, comfortable couch. "That's kind of you to say," he said. "Did your husband come as well?"

Alana's mood changed at the mention of her husband. "No, he's still back in the castle," she said a bit stiffly.

"Is something the matter with him?"

"No, he's fine. He has claimed the right of separation," Alana said.

"When it was revealed that arranged marriages were not condoned by the Tome of Laws, many of the people who were forced into arranged marriages made the same claim."

Nash patted her on the knee. "Oh, my dear. I'm so sorry."

"Don't be," Alana said. "Ours was a loveless marriage. We never had any children, and we spent most of our time apart, so things haven't changed much." She squared her shoulders. "But that's not what brings me here today. I need to ask you something, to be kept just between you and me."

"Of course," Nash said.

"I understand you helped train Guardian Rayne."

Nash nodded. "Oh, yes. He is one of the most talented fellows I have ever trained. I dare say he's even more talented than his father."

Alana sat up straighter. "You knew his father as well?"

"Of course! I helped train him too—right after I retired from being a guardian myself," Nash said, pounding on his chest for emphasis.

"And who was Rayne's father?" Alana asked, trying to sound casual.

Nash frowned. "Has Rayne done something wrong?"

"No, actually, just the opposite. He has been an exemplary guardian. He's impressed many people."

"Then why ask about his father?"

Alana leaned in a bit closer to Nash and said conspiringly, "That's why I was sent here. It's important."

Nash leaned back and rubbed his long, white beard before he answered. "I promised Rayne's grandparents I wouldn't reveal Rayne's parentage before the Mortentaun. They felt it may cause him to be treated unfairly. Even though it's after the Mortentaun, I'd rather not betray that trust until I've spoken with them."

"I understand and respect that," Alana said. "Would you be kind enough to summon them? And the sooner, the better. Time is of the essence."

⊰╪⊱

Cameron dangled the golden earring in front of the young lady. She stood, mesmerized, and eyed it carefully.

"I takes it yous like?" Cameron said.

Arlie nodded her head. "It is very nice, yes."

"That's there a real sapphire," the crooked-nosed guardian said, pointing to the large blue gem inlaid in the gold. "Maybe I gives yous this if yous gives me somthin' in return."

The fawn-eyed young woman furrowed her brow as she looked between the beautiful piece of jewelry and the leering guardian.

"What do you want now, Guardian Cameron?" asked a large man brusquely as he entered the store from the back room.

Cameron quickly put the earring under his tunic. "I don't thinks I likes how yous talkin' to me, Barclay."

Spreading his arms open to the room around him, Barclay said, "Unless you're here to buy some furniture, I'm going to ask you to leave."

"I'm heres to collects yous taxes," Cameron declared.

Barclay walked over to his daughter and put his arm around her shoulder. "My left foot, you are. I already paid my taxes this month."

"Then I tells yous I'm heres to collects again," Cameron said. "But I can be nice and forgits about that if yous lets me spend time with yous daughter."

Barclay gave Cameron a hard stare. "Over my dead body."

Cameron sized up the large, barrel-chested woodworker in front of him. "Rayne!" he shouted. "Gits in heres!"

Rayne ran into the store and looked between Guardian Cameron, the shop owner, and his daughter. "What's the matter?"

Cameron pointed to Barclay. "He's refusin' to pays his taxes."

"I don't understand, Cameron," Rayne said. "We were here earlier this month."

Cameron drew his sword. "He's goin' to pays his taxes because I says so." He brought his sword up and pointed it at Barclay. The shop owner, to his credit, didn't react.

Drawing his sword as well, Rayne walked up to the counter. Instead of pointing it at Barclay, he put the tip under Cameron's chin. "Guardian Cameron, I tell you he has already paid this month. You are out of order. Lower your sword."

Cameron looked at Rayne in obvious shock. "What's do yous thinks yous are doin'?"

Rayne brought his weapon a little closer, causing Cameron's head to tilt up slightly. "I'm doing what's right."

Barclay and his daughter stared wide-eyed at the two guardians. Cameron glared at Rayne for a moment and then lowered his sword. "Yous will regrets this Rayne," he said threateningly before he turned on his heel and stormed out of the building.

⊷⊱✦⊰⊶

"Rinan," Kelvin said, "was Rayne's father."

Alana nodded. "Thank you. That's what we thought."

Kelvin pulled his wife closer to him on the couch in Nash's office. Nadia was crying softly, her head buried in her husband's shoulder. "This has been very hard on us over the years," Kelvin said in explanation.

"Aye, 'tis not easy living with a secret for that long." Nash addressed them from behind his desk. "But I'm not sure why that information would bring you all the way out here, Lady Alana."

"It will become clear momentarily," she said. "Kelvin, Nadia, did Rinan tell you who Rayne's mother was? Before you answer, let me assure you that this information will not be used against Rayne in any way. The people who sent me already know and have told me."

Nadia looked up at Alana and asked, "And who sent you, exactly?"

"Priest Sherwyn and a nursemaid named Anemone," Alana said without pausing. "They were present when Rinan was married."

Looking at her husband, Nadia nodded. Kelvin cleared his throat and said, "Rinan told us he had married Queen Eliana in private before she married King Daimh, and the marriage between the queen and king was a sham."

"What!" Nash stood up. "Why in the world would the castle priest allow such a thing?"

"It was actually the priest's idea," Alana said, "but it's complicated. It's sufficient to say that Sherwyn did it in an attempt to keep Abrecan from coming to power. Here is the important part. It appears that Councilor Abrecan has arranged it so someone loyal to him will become the new king of Bariwon."

Nash's face became as white as his beard. "Oh, dear, are you sure? I heard Governor Dylan was going to sponsor someone. I know Dylan, and like me, he has no love for Abrecan."

"Governor Dylan has been arrested for stabbing Councilor Abrecan," Alana said miserably. "Abrecan wanted to have him executed right away, but there is a law that states that no executions can take place against anyone who had been sponsored or is being sponsored in the Shoginoc."

Nash shook his head in disgust. "Dylan would never have attacked Abrecan. It's not in his character. But if someone loyal to Abrecan takes the throne, the new king can have Dylan executed."

Alana's eyes grew large as she realized the truth of Nash's words.

"Can Governor Dylan's sponsor still be part of the Shoginoc?" Kelvin asked. "After all, the sponsor did nothing wrong."

"He can be," Alana answered, "but it appears that Abrecan coerced the sponsor from Donigi into withdrawing from the Shoginoc. I'm not sure why he would agree to that. Fortunately, Dylan is still protected under the law until the Shoginoc is over."

"I don't see how any of this has to do with our grandson," Nadia said.

Alana smiled. "If Rayne is the son of Rinan and Queen Eliana, Sherwyn and Anemone believe he is the true heir to the throne."

Nash slapped his hand down on the table. "If that's so, that means Abrecan can be removed from power once and for all!"

Kelvin looked doubtful. "Do you honestly think they are going to accept that Rayne is the son of Queen Eliana?"

"With you two testifying, and Sherwyn and Anemone coming forth with what they know, there should be enough believable witnesses for the Hierarchy of Magistrates to act in removing Daimh from the throne. And with him gone, Abrecan will have no more power."

CHAPTER 24

Sheathing his sword, Rayne nodded to the woodworker and his daughter. "Please accept my apologies for Guardian Cameron's behavior. I will be sure to report his actions."

Barclay looked at Rayne searchingly. "This is the first time I've seen a guardian confront another guardian. I'll have to admit I'm surprised."

His dark-eyed daughter nodded her head in agreement while looking at Rayne with wonder. This wasn't lost on Barclay, and a large grin spread across his face.

"I'm very protective of my only daughter, Guardian Rayne." Barclay squeezed his daughter's shoulder for emphasis. "She has had many men try to court her, but until now, I've not found one I've been impressed with."

Rayne felt his cheeks grow warm. "That's very kind of you to say." Addressing Arlie, he said, "You are lovely. But alas, royal guardians are not allowed to court."

The disappointment on Arlie's face was unmistakable, but she managed to say, "Other ones have been asking me."

"Yes, and not all of them are as honorable as you, Guardian. Some feel the rules don't apply to them," Barclay said. "If I may make a suggestion, be careful in dealing with Guardian Cameron. He's a slippery one."

Rayne bowed slightly at the waist. "Thank you for the advice. But he has to learn that guardians need to follow the laws, just like everyone else."

Cameron was nowhere to be found when Rayne left the shop. He checked several of the nearby stores and inns, and none of the merchants had seen him. With the sun working its way down the sky, Rayne decided to head back to the castle and report to his captain.

Walking down the wide road that led to the castle, Rayne took a moment to consider the large structure before him. The three-storied building was surrounded by a high stone wall with only the one large gate. A tall tower rose from each corner, topped with a conical roof of red tile. Rayne had heard that the roof had once been a dark blue, but it was changed along with many other things in the castle since Daimh had become king.

Rayne approached the front gate and waved in greeting to the guardians who were on duty. Instead of waving back, they both moved toward him, hands on the hilts of their swords. Slowing down, Rayne asked, "Is something the matter?"

"I'm sorry, Rayne," said one of the guardians. "We've been instructed to place you under arrest upon your return."

Rayne raised his hands slowly. "I'm sure this is just a misunderstanding, but of course I'll cooperate."

⋆⫶⋆

Captain Sullivan stared hard at the two guardians before him. Cameron was smirking and standing casually, while Rayne was at attention, keeping his expression serious.

"I don't like this," Sullivan said. "No, I don't like this one bit." He clasped his hands behind his back and paced back and forth. "The people of Bariwon need to see the guardians as a strong force in the land. They need to know that the guardians are not to be questioned. What happened between the two of you today could seriously damage that." He stopped pacing and faced them again. "An example needs to be made here to show the people this type of behavior is unacceptable."

Pointing a finger at Rayne, Sullivan said, "As far as I'm concerned, you physically threatened a fellow guardian, and had Cameron not thought quickly, I have no doubt you would have spilt his blood."

Stunned, Rayne said, "But, Captain—"

"No!" Sullivan shouted, stomping a foot on the floor. "No! You will not say another word. You will be held in the dungeon until I decide what to do with you."

Rayne obeyed his leader's demand for silence and simply nodded.

"Guardians! Come in here!"

The door to Sullivan's room opened and two guardians came in, one of them Oakleaf. "Take Rayne to a cell somewhere very deep in the dungeon," Sullivan commanded.

⋆⫶⋆

Sitting in the dark on a damp, hard floor, Rayne smacked his fist against the wooden door of his dungeon cell in frustration as he thought about his options. Over the past few months, he had seen guardians do many things he considered inappropriate, but it seemed Captain Sullivan didn't care as long as the taxes kept coming in and King Daimh and Councilor Abrecan were happy.

It wasn't until Cameron pulled his sword on the merchant that something inside Rayne snapped. Some things are just wrong, Rayne knew, and he couldn't stand by and do nothing about it. Just as it had when he attacked the guardians in Lewyol, his sense of justice had overtaken his sense of self-preservation.

He realized that had he not acted in Lewyol, his father would probably still be alive. But what would have happened to Sunshine? He had done the right thing in defending her, and he had done the right thing in forcing Cameron to back off. Yet if these actions were right, why were there such negative consequences? To be fair, not all the consequences were negative. Even though Rayne's father had died, Sunshine was safe. Thinking about what the future held for him, Rayne hit the wooden door again, if for no other reason than to do something more than sit there.

"Hello? Hello? Someone there?" said a faint voice.

Rayne responded, "Yes? Hello?"

"There *is* someone here," the voice said. "It's been a long time since anyone has been put into the cell next to me. You must have done something very wrong to be this far back in the dungeon."

Rayne lowered his head to the bottom of the door. It had a small access panel that could only be opened from the outside. He had been given a meal and had been asked for his chamber pot a few hours earlier, and the exchange was made through this panel. The wood was thinner here, though even if anyone could break through the wood, the opening was too small to fit through.

"Who are you?" Rayne asked. "Have you been down here long?"

There was a pause, and for a moment Rayne wasn't sure if the other man had heard him. "I've lost track, but it seems I've been down here a long time—almost as long as I can remember. But I have to know—is Daimh still king?"

"Yes," Rayne said, "although the Shoginoc takes place in a couple of days."

"Thank you for the information," the voice said. "The servants who feed me won't talk to me. I'm sure they're following orders."

Rayne could hear the sense of dismay in the other man's tone.

213

"Why? What did you do?"

"Does it really matter?" The voice sounded bitter now. "I just did what I thought was right, and I ended up here."

The statement shook Rayne to his very core. He remembered something he was taught in his youth. "My father once told me to always do what was right, even if it wasn't the easy thing to do. He told me we may never see the results of our good deeds, but just because we don't see them, doesn't mean they are not there."

There was another long pause before the voice answered. "Your father was a very wise man. But tell me, what would he say about your current situation?"

"Well," Rayne said, "let's just say that I'm here because I was acting in a way I thought a guardian should act, and it seems that the captain is more concerned with appearances than what is right."

"You are a guardian?" The voice was a bit stronger now.

"Yes."

"It seems we have more in common than either of us had realized," the voice said. "I, too, was a guardian before I was put in here."

Rayne shifted his body so he could put an ear closer to the panel. "My name is Rayne. You never did tell me yours."

"It seems my name means little down here, but I see no harm in telling you," the voice said with a hint of sadness. "My name is Dougal."

⇥‡⇤

"And what can I do for you, Magistrate Bertram?" Captain Sullivan asked disdainfully.

The thin magistrate cleared his throat. "I understand we need to convene a hearing with the hierarchy, but as of yet, we have not received your request. With the Shoginoc approaching rapidly, time is short."

The pock-marked captain eyed Bertram for a moment before responding. "I'm not sure what you are talking about. Don't you have better things to do than to come to my quarters and ask me such things?"

Bertram glanced around the room. The well-crafted furniture was a stark contrast to his humble possessions. It seemed that Sullivan had been rewarded for keeping Abrecan happy.

"I understand you placed a guardian under arrest and then put him in the dungeon," Bertram said. "He has a right to be heard in front of the hierarchy within a day of the arrest."

Sullivan folded his arms and scowled. "Oh, yeah? Says who?"

"The Tome of Laws," Bertram said confidently. "Would you like me to read you the passage?"

"No," Sullivan said darkly. "No need. But tell me, how did you even know about this?"

Sunshine had come to Bertram in tears—Oakleaf had told her what happened to Rayne. Instead of saying something that would get either of them in trouble, Bertram responded cryptically, "Do you honestly think I wouldn't know about such things?"

Captain Sullivan considered Bertram a moment. "Fine, whatever. When do you want to have this hearing?"

"Right after the mid-day meal today," Bertram said. "I expect you and all the people involved to be there."

❖

Sunshine sat next to her fellow savants on a bench in the main hall, waiting anxiously for everyone else to arrive. During the afternoon meal, word had gotten out that there was going to be a hearing concerning Guardian Rayne. It seemed he was well liked by almost everyone in the castle aside from his fellow guardians, so this generated quite a buzz. The hall was as full as Sunshine had ever seen it for such a hearing. Most involved minor squabbles between the guardians and members of the kingdom. To her recollection, in every case, the guardians had won.

Sunshine reached down and squeezed the edge of her seat when Rayne was ushered into the hall. His hair was a mess, and his normally clean-shaven face had at least a day's worth of stubble. He no longer wore a guardian uniform, but was dressed in a simple cloth jerkin. Hoping he would turn around and look at the crowd, Sunshine offered her best smile in a show of support, but Rayne sat down on the front row and stared straight ahead.

The Hierarchy of Magistrates and Priest Sherwyn entered the hall, followed shortly by King Daimh and Councilor Abrecan. The minstrels who constantly attended the king followed directly behind the royalty. The proceedings were opened by Aldous, the oldest-ranking member of the hierarchy.

"We are here today to review the charges against Guardian Rayne," Aldous said, leaning heavily on the table in front of him and sounding slightly out of breath. "I've asked Magistrate Bertram to conduct this hearing."

Sunshine noticed Councilor Abrecan's expression sour as Bertram stood and thanked Aldous.

"Captain Sullivan," Bertram said, "what are the charges against Guardian Rayne?"

Sullivan stood. "Rayne is charged with attempted murder."

The collective gasp from the hall caused Councilor Abrecan to speak up. "You will all remain quiet, or I will have you removed."

Looking a bit pale, Bertram tried to regain his composure. "Who are the witnesses to this crime?"

Sullivan nodded to two guardians seated next to him, and they stood. "Guardian Cameron and Guardian Ivor will testify that Rayne drew his sword on Guardian Cameron and brought the blade to his throat. A wound to the neck is almost always fatal, so his intention could only have been murder."

Rayne raised his hand to get Bertram's attention.

"One moment, Guardian Rayne," the magistrate said. "You will get your chance to speak shortly."

Looking at Guardian Cameron, Bertram asked, "And why did Guardian Rayne draw his sword on you?"

The crooked-nosed man smirked. "I was collectin' taxes, jist likes I supposed to be doin'. The daughter o' the merchant wuz flirtin' with me, and I guess Rayne gots jealous. I hears rumors she and Rayne has somethin' goin' on."

Sunshine shook her head in disbelief. That couldn't be the case—Rayne wouldn't be involved with another woman, would he? *Of course not,* she chided herself. *This is just an attempt to make him look bad.*

"Anyways," Cameron continued, "he puts his sword up to my throat and says to me he's goin' to kill me if I don't back off. I backs off and wuz ables to escape 'fore he could hurts me."

Bertram stared at Cameron, then turned his head and asked Ivor, "And you saw all of this?"

The tall guardian from Erd simply nodded in agreement.

"And where are the merchant and his daughter, Captain Sullivan?" Bertram asked, glancing around the hall.

Captain Sullivan shrugged. "When we went to their store, it was deserted, and their neighbors said they must have left in the middle of the night because no one saw them leave."

"I see..." Bertram said thoughtfully. "Do you have anything to add?"

"What else needs to be said?" Sullivan asked harshly. "I consider this action to be attempted murder. Had Guardian Cameron not been so skilled in his escape, I'm sure Rayne would have killed him."

Bertram frowned. "That will be all, Captain. Guardian Rayne, please stand."

Rayne stood, and instead of slumping over and looking defeated, he stood tall, with his shoulders squared.

"Guardian Rayne, did you draw your sword and place it against the throat of Guardian Cameron?" Bertram asked.

In a clear, strong voice, Rayne stated, "Yes, I did."

The crowd reacted with gasps and several people saying, "Oh, no." Abrecan sat up straighter and glared at the people in the hall.

"And why did you do this?" Bertram asked.

"Guardian Cameron was attempting to collect taxes from the merchant, but we were there earlier in the month and had collected already." Rayne pointed at Cameron. "I was standing outside, per Cameron's order, and only entered the store when he called me in. He told me the merchant refused to pay his taxes. When I reminded Cameron that they had already paid for the month, he said he wanted them to pay again, and he drew his sword."

Cameron stood up and yelled, "That's not the ways it happened!"

Bertram didn't shy away from the outburst. "Guardian Cameron, you had your chance to speak. You will not speak again unless asked a question."

"But—" Cameron began, but he was silenced when Sullivan yanked him back to the bench.

"Continue please, Guardian Rayne," Bertram instructed.

Rayne nodded. "It's my opinion that Cameron was breaking the law and threatening the innocent merchant and his daughter."

Bertram's eyebrows furrowed. "But Guardian Ivor testified that he saw the whole thing and agrees with Guardian Cameron."

"Guardian Ivor wasn't there," Rayne said matter-of-factly. "I don't know where he was, but he was not in the building when this happened."

Ivor started to stand up, but Sullivan grabbed hold of his tunic and shook his head.

"What else would you add, Guardian Rayne?" Bertram asked.

Rayne turned and looked at Captain Sullivan and the two guardians. He then shifted his attention to Councilor Abrecan and didn't say anything for a moment. Sunshine couldn't see Rayne's expression, but whatever it was, the councilor appeared not to care for it.

"I became a guardian with an honest desire to help the people of Bariwon. However, it has become obvious that honesty is in short supply here. Consider the following points. If I truly threatened Cameron's life, do you think he would still be alive? And if he escaped my threat, do you think I would walk casually back to the castle and allow myself to be arrested? And what of the merchant? Isn't it convenient that the only two people who can verify my story have disappeared? And last, does anyone here who knows both Cameron and myself actually believe his story over mine?"

"No!" shouted a voice from the crowd. "I do not believe Cameron's lies!"

The voice came from an elderly lady who stood and pointed a finger accusingly at the crooked-nosed guardian. Sunshine knew her as Anemone, a nursemaid who had spent many years in the castle.

"Shut up!" Councilor Abrecan shouted. "You've been warned not to speak out. Guardians, get her out of here."

The guardians who stood against the walls moved toward the nursemaid. The crowd watched in stunned disbelief.

"Don't let them do this!" Anemone cried out, backing away from the advancing guardians. "Abrecan has caused nothing but problems all these years! Do not let him and his henchmen do this to an innocent man!"

Abrecan stood up and shouted even louder, "Shut up! Shut up! *Shut up!*" He motioned furiously at the guardians to grab her.

Priest Sherwyn came down the stairs and rushed toward Anemone. The nursemaid looked terrified as guardians came at her from different directions. When Sherwyn reached her, she clutched his arm for support.

"There's no need to be physical here, Guardians." Sherwyn held up his hands in a gesture of peace. "She will go with you quietly, won't you, Anemone?"

The nursemaid gave Sherwyn a questioning look but then nodded her head. Then a gruff-looking guardian grabbed Anemone's arm roughly and pulled hard, nearly knocking her off her feet.

"That's quite enough!" Sherwyn put a hand on the guardian's chest.

The guardian responded by slapping the priest's hand away and shoving him to the floor.

"No one else will interfere!" Abrecan screamed almost hysterically. "Guardians, arrest the priest as well!"

The remaining people in the hall sat very still while watching the guardians remove Anemone and Sherwyn.

"As for you, Rayne," Abrecan said, still seething, "the choice is clear what needs to be done." He addressed Bertram and the rest of the Hierarchy of Magistrates. "Read what the Tome of Laws says about someone who attempts to take the life of another."

"But, Councilor—" Bertram began.

Abrecan slammed his fist down on the armrest. "Read it!"

Bertram paused a moment, looking at Rayne briefly before he opened his copy of the Tome of Laws, and turned to the correct page. In a quiet voice, he read, *"Anyone who kills or attempts to kill a member of the kingdom shall be punished, up to death."*

"Louder!" Abrecan bellowed.

Bertram spoke up. *"Anyone who kills or attempts to kill a member of the kingdom shall be punished, up to death."*

Abrecan glared at Rayne while he asked Bertram, "And how many witnesses does it take to prove guilt?"

"Two."

Pointing to Guardians Cameron and Ivor, Abrecan said, "There are your witnesses. They are guardians, so their motives cannot be questioned. Now tell me, who makes the final choice of punishment once the person is found guilty?"

Bertram sat down, defeated. "The king or queen."

Abrecan stood and said to the crowd, "Such actions by a guardian are unacceptable, especially against another guardian. The people need to see that they are not allowed to threaten us. The punishment needs to be severe! Rayne must be put to death!"

The councilor turned to his son, who had the same blank look on his face as he did when court began. "Wouldn't you agree, Your Majesty?"

"Of course, of course," King Daimh said. "Are we done yet?"

CHAPTER 25

Sunshine sat alone in the main hall for a while after Rayne had been escorted back to the dungeon. One of her fellow savants asked if she was all right, but Sunshine didn't respond. She didn't react when she heard someone enter the hall and walk toward her. It wasn't until Magistrate Caldre sat down next to her that Sunshine finally acknowledged his presence.

"Oh, my poor dear," he said in his customarily nasal tone. "You look quite distraught."

Sunshine gave him a blank stare.

"It was dreadful what happened here today." With a sweep of his arm, Caldre motioned to the empty hall. "Guardian Rayne showed himself to be quite the able fighter. It's too bad he never learned how to adapt to his surroundings. He was always trying to be noble and such, and he ended up irritating his superiors. And of course, he should have learned never to get involved with a woman while being a guardian in the castle—very dangerous indeed."

This last statement helped Sunshine find her voice. "He was not involved with the merchant's daughter," she said coolly.

Caldre arched an eyebrow. "Who said anything about the merchant's daughter? Oh, no, my dear, you misunderstand." He poked her with a finger. "I'm referring to you."

"Me? What are you—"

"Tsk, tsk." Caldre wagged his finger in front of her face. "There's no use denying it. After you turned down the offer to become my personal assistant, I put you under observation. My sources tell me that you and Rayne spent a lot of time together."

Sunshine's pulse quickened. "So what? We've done nothing against the rules."

"No?" Caldre asked. "There are rules about courting."

"We are friends, Magistrate," Sunshine said defiantly.

The sharp-nosed magistrate nodded, then said in a patronizing tone, "Yes, of course. But that hardly matters now, does it? He is, after all, going to be put to death."

Sunshine gave Caldre a hard stare. "Is there a point to this conversation, Magistrate?"

"Direct as always. Very good. Very good indeed. I do have the ear of the king, and I may be able to persuade him to change his mind."

Trying not to show the spark of hope she felt, Sunshine asked, "You could arrange to set Rayne free?"

"Free? Oh, dear, no. Not free." Caldre shook his head. "Rayne has been found guilty. I can't change that, but I believe I could get the king to change the sentence to life in the dungeon. Of course, I would expect something in return for this favor..." He put his hand on Sunshine's knee and squeezed it suggestively.

She didn't remove it, but rather acted as if it wasn't there. "What specifically do you want in return?"

"Why, for you to be my bride, of course," Caldre said with a smile that repulsed her. "I would have settled for an assistant, but since you chose to play hard to get, I decided to increase my demands."

At this, Sunshine batted his hand away. "What makes you think I would agree to such a thing?"

Caldre's smile turned into a threatening snarl. "Before you decide, I suggest you realize that you are the only one who can prevent Rayne from being put to death."

He stood and loomed over her. "If he dies, it will be your fault. And that is something you will have to live with for the rest of your life. You have until tomorrow before the execution to give me your answer."

With that, he spun and marched out of the hall, leaving Sunshine alone once again.

After summoning the strength to make it to her room, Sunshine collapsed on her bed and began to cry softly. She wasn't sure how much time had passed when she heard a knock on her door.

Sure it was Magistrate Caldre, Sunshine got up, straightened her dress the best she could, and reached for the knob with the intention of letting him know exactly what he could do with his proposition.

Instead, she found her brother Oakleaf at the door. He appeared as crestfallen and miserable as she was. "Shiny, I just got in from making my rounds in town, and I heard what happened to Rayne."

She fell into his arms. "It's so unfair, Leafy. I don't believe for a moment that Rayne is guilty."

"I don't believe it either," he said, "but we don't have time to discuss this now. There are people we need to see."

Sunshine stepped back and wiped the tears from her eyes. "What people?

⊰╪⊱

The entourage of Lady Alana, Kelvin, Nadia, Governor Nash, and his wife Linden arrived at the castle the day before the Shoginoc. They arrived at the castle in the early evening with the sun just starting to set, casting long shadows in front of them as they approached the main gates. After being admitted by the guardians, Alana led them directly to find Priest Sherwyn. He was not in his room, and none of the servants had seen him recently. Fear gripped her heart as she wondered what could have happened to him. She and the others sought out Anemone, but were unable to find her, either.

Unsure what to do next, Alana took the group back to her room. She asked a servant to have meals sent up while they conferred.

After about an hour, a light knocking sounded on Alana's door. Thinking it was the servant with their meal, she opened the door to find Oakleaf with his sister Sunshine, both wearing serious expressions. Alana ushered them in quickly and closed the door behind them.

"What's the matter?" she asked.

Oakleaf nudged his sister. "You tell them."

Sunshine looked up with bloodshot, puffy eyes. "We have bad news. Rayne, Priest Sherwyn, and Nursemaid Anemone have all been arrested."

"Arrested?" Alana exclaimed. "Come in and explain what's going on."

Sunshine and Oakleaf walked into the crowded room and closed the door behind them. Sunshine recognized Governor Nash and his wife sitting at the table in Alana's room, and was surprised to see Rayne's grandparents next to them.

"Kelvin, Nadia," Sunshine greeted them. "I didn't expect to see you. What brings you here?"

Alana motioned for Sunshine and Oakleaf to have a seat on her bed. "We'll explain that later. Please, tell us what happened to Rayne, Sherwyn, and Anemone."

Nodding, Sunshine took a deep breath and then recounted what had happened. Her story was interrupted several times with Nash's outbursts and continued when Linden had settled her husband down.

When Sunshine finished, everyone sat in stunned silence for a moment until Nadia asked somberly, "When are they going to execute my grandson?"

Nash slapped his hand on the table. "They are *not* going to execute him. I won't allow it."

"And just what are you going to do?" Linden asked skeptically.

Nash blustered for a moment, and then said, "I don't know, but I must do something!"

Alana shook her head. "I'm not sure anything can be done. Once Abrecan makes up his mind about something, it is pretty much a foregone conclusion."

"There *is* something that can be done to spare Rayne's life," Sunshine said quietly.

Everyone looked at her expectantly.

"Magistrate Caldre said he could talk the king into changing the sentence to life in the dungeon if I were to agree to marry Caldre."

Nash threw his hands up in disgust. "Absolutely not! This is just like those weasels. What we need to do is find the merchant and his daughter to testify that Cameron was lying and Rayne was telling the truth."

Kelvin spoke for the first time. "He's right. Knowing Rayne, he would rather die than have you marry someone to save him."

"Sullivan reported that the merchant and his daughter disappeared in the middle of the night," Sunshine said. "It's doubtful we can find them before tomorrow."

Oakleaf jumped to his feet. "Maybe we *can* find them. I have an idea where to look."

⋖⧨⋗

Ivor counted out loud. "Forty-seven...forty-eight...forty-nine... fifty."

"Fifty what?" Oakleaf asked, coming down the rock steps into the dungeon.

Ivor stood up quickly, sword drawn, and then relaxed when he saw it was Oakleaf.

"Bah, it's just you," said the tall guardian from Erd. "I was just counting the drips of water I heard. Not much else to do. It must be really raining hard outside for water to be seeping in down here."

Oakleaf walked to the wall and placed his hand on it to feel the moisture. "Yeah, it's really pouring out there."

Ivor sat back down. "What are you doing here? I was told I had the night shift."

Thinking quickly, Oakleaf said, "The captain said he wanted extra protection for the dungeon. He didn't want anyone bothering the new prisoners."

Ivor scratched his head and looked suspiciously at Oakleaf. "You sure the captain said that?"

Oakleaf nodded toward the stairs. "Want to go ask him?"

"Nah, you know the captain doesn't like to have people question his orders." Ivor leaned his chair back against the wall. "It figures he would give the bad assignments to the new guardians. You might as well take a seat. It's going to be a long night."

Oakleaf sat down in the other chair in the antechamber outside the dungeon. For the next several hours, the two guardians sat mainly in uncomfortable silence. As the night dragged on, Oakleaf noticed Ivor starting to doze off. Although his head would bob up and down as he fought off sleep, Ivor eventually succumbed.

Oakleaf waited a good half hour to make sure Ivor was sound asleep, then removed the keys from the peg on the wall, trying cautiously not to wake his fellow guardian. After opening the door that led to the dungeon, Oakleaf grabbed a torch and headed in. He walked through the maze of passageways that made up the dungeon, looking carefully at the ground by each cell door. It wasn't until he had gone quite deep into the dungeon that he found what he was looking for. At the base of one of the doors, the moss and dirt had been pushed away as the door was opened. As a general rule, the doors were only ever opened to put someone in or to remove the dead prisoner.

Oakleaf opened the small door where the meals were delivered. "Hello! Hello in there!"

There was a moment before he got a response. "Yes, hello?" came a tired male voice.

"Who is this?" Oakleaf asked.

"What does it matter?" asked the voice. "Are you here to torture or taunt me?"

"Neither," Oakleaf said gently. "I know you were put in here recently. Please, tell me who you are."

There wasn't a response.

"Please sir, this is important," Oakleaf said. "I give you my word as a royal guardian. I mean you no harm."

"A fat lot of good a royal guardian's word is," said the man.

Frustrated, Oakleaf asked, "Is there anything I can say that will convince you to trust me?"

Again, no response.

"Fine, I'll see if your daughter is willing to help me."

"Wait!" the prisoner said. "Leave Arlie alone!"

Smiling, Oakleaf said, "So, you have a daughter then."

"You tricked me," the man growled. "Fine. My name is Barclay."

"Barclay, you know me. My name is Oakleaf. You know I'm not like the other royal guardians."

"Yes," Barclay said. "I thought you sounded familiar."

Oakleaf tried not to get too excited. He needed to stay focused on the task at hand. "Do you know why you were put in the dungeon?"

"No, not for sure," Barclay said bitterly. "They came in the middle of the night and brought us here. They wouldn't answer me when I asked, but I suspect it had to do with Guardian Cameron."

"You suspect right," Oakleaf said. "Can you tell me what you saw the day before you were brought here?"

"Why are you asking me all this?"

Placing a hand on the door as if to try to comfort Barclay, Oakleaf said, "Because I can help you, but first I need to know what you saw."

There was no sound from the cell for several heartbeats.

"Fine." Barclay went on to tell how Cameron had tried to force him to pay his taxes when he had already paid, and how Rayne had stepped in to prevent it.

"Were there any other guardians in the shop with you aside from Cameron and Rayne?"

"No."

"Would you be willing to testify about what you saw?" Oakleaf asked.

Barclay let out a harsh laugh. "Of course, if I ever got the chance. But I doubt I will."

Oakleaf stood, undid the lock, and opened the door. Barclay shielded his eyes from the light of the torch, then struggled to his feet with Oakleaf's help.

"Let's find your daughter," Oakleaf said.

They exited the cell, and Oakleaf again studied the floor for indications of recently opened doors. It didn't take them long to find the door and verify that Barclay's daughter Arlie was inside.

With the woodworker and his daughter in tow, Oakleaf made his way back toward the exit. He warned them to keep quiet so as not to wake Ivor.

Oakleaf noticed that the exit door was nearly closed all the way—shut tighter than he had remembered. Creeping to the door, Oakleaf pushed on it lightly and was startled when it flew open. Ivor stood before him, sword drawn.

"Captain Sullivan was right. He said to keep an eye out for you. You and Rayne were obviously friends, and he thought you'd try something stupid. It's probably why he wouldn't let us just kill Barclay and Arlie, to draw you out." The muscle-bound guardian pointed his sword at Oakleaf. "However, he also said if you actually tried something like this, I should kill both you and them."

⇥‡⇤

The sun fought its way up the sky, trying to peer through the swollen storm clouds without success. Despite the heavy rains from the night before and a light drizzle that still lingered, a large crowd started to gather outside the castle gates.

Excitement for the Shoginoc ran high, but when word spread that an execution would take place before the ceremony, it was as if fuel had been added to an already blazing fire.

Sunshine stood in the crowd, wearing a hooded cloak in an attempt to stay dry. Rayne's grandparents were with her, Nadia clutching Kelvin's arm for support.

Oakleaf never returned after he left the night before, so it seemed any hope of saving Rayne was lost. Sunshine wondered if it was too late to change her mind and agree to marry Caldre, but Nadia and Kelvin were both adamant that was not an option.

"There yous are. Magistrate Caldre has been lookin' fur yous," said a voice behind Sunshine. She turned to see Cameron staring at her, raindrops dripping from his crooked nose. She fought the instinct to slap him.

She stepped closer to Kelvin and leaned against him. "I'm sure he is," she said angrily. "You can pass on this message to him: Rain will fall from the sun before I would agree to his conditions."

Cocking his head to one side, Cameron looked like a confused, mangy mutt. "Wut?"

"That means no, you wooden head," said Kelvin, who had also turned to face the guardian. "Now get out of our sight."

Cameron's eyes flashed in anger, but after sizing up Kelvin and glancing around at the packed crowd, he slunk away.

Kelvin put an arm around Sunshine. "That was the right thing to do. I'm sure this is hard, but we can't give into such manipulation."

"Why does doing the right thing have to be so hard sometimes?"

Sunshine asked gloomily.

Nadia reached out and touched Sunshine on the arm. "It only seems hard in the moment. Time will tell that it was actually easier than living with making the wrong choice."

The crowd started to murmur with excitement as people walked onto the large platform that had been set up for the execution. Sunshine recognized Governor Nash and his wife among the governors of the other districts.

"I just wish we knew what happened to Oakleaf," Nadia lamented. "He was our only hope to save Rayne."

Sunshine felt a twinge of guilt when she realized she was so wrapped up in feelings for Rayne that she hadn't been as concerned that something may have happened to her brother. She wasn't sure what she would do if she lost both Rayne and Oakleaf. Could she live with the guilt of knowing she could have done something?

Her mind raced. Was there nothing that could be done? She had gone to Bertram the night before and he said his hands were tied—two witnesses testified what had happened. According to the Tome of Laws, that satisfied the requirements. There was no one else to testify for Rayne—only the missing merchant or his daughter could help.

Sunshine didn't want to believe Oakleaf had failed. Even though she often teased her brother, he was not one to give up once his mind was set on something. Unfortunately, they were running out of time. Perhaps if she couldn't stop Rayne's execution, she could delay it. But how? Her eyes searched the platform for inspiration. Once again she noticed Governor Nash, looking rather upset, sitting among his fellow governors. As she looked at each of them in turn, inspiration hit.

"I've thought of something," she said to Kelvin and Nadia. "Stay here. I'll be right back."

⇥✦⇤

"She says somethin' 'bout water becomin' sunlight," Cameron said.

Caldre sniffed haughtily. "What are you talking about?"

Wiping the rain out of his eyes, Cameron said, "I thinks she means 'no' by that."

Caldre balled his fists. "Fine! She will regret that until the day she dies." He pushed his way through the guardians who surrounded Rayne. They were just inside the castle gates, awaiting the signal to proceed to the platform. Making sure Rayne was still in chains, Caldre walked up to the prisoner and said, "You should know that I gave Savant Sunshine a way to save your life, but she refused. It seems she will never forgive you for betraying her trust with the merchant's daughter. In fact, I've heard she is actually looking forward to watching you die."

Rayne lifted his hands, causing the chains to rattle.

Caldre jumped back in fear, and several of the guardians surrounding Rayne grabbed hold of him.

"Settle down," Rayne said. "I wasn't threatening you, Magistrate, although it does show me how brave you truly are to be scared of a man in chains, surrounded by men with swords."

The calm, steady tone of Rayne's voice unsettled Caldre. "I was just...startled, is all."

"Yes, I'm sure," Rayne said. "But know this—Sunshine and I share something you will never understand. I don't believe your lies. You've lived so long telling them, I'm not sure you could speak the truth if you wanted."

Caldre felt the eyes of the surrounding guardians on him. Did he see doubt in some of their expressions? No matter. Rayne would soon be dead, and the guardians would be shown what happens to those who don't do as they are told.

Lifting his chin and looking down his nose, Caldre said, "It seems Sunshine and I have something in common. We'll both enjoy watching you die."

Not letting Rayne respond or waiting for the signal to proceed to the platform, Caldre walked briskly out of the castle. He was still fuming when he reached the platform stairs. How dare Rayne insult him!

When Caldre reached the top, he noticed everyone was seated where he or she should be, with the exception of Governor Nash. He was on the far edge of the platform, a good thirty paces away, kneeling down at the edge and talking to someone in a hooded robe. From his vantage point, Caldre couldn't tell who it was.

"Governor Nash!" he said firmly. "Return to your seat!"

Nash ignored Caldre at first, so he took a few steps toward the governor, the fury inside him building. Before Caldre could say anything else, Nash stood up and walked back to his seat. Quickly looking at the person in the hooded robe, Caldre caught only an indistinguishable glance before the figure melted back into the crowd.

Caldre took his seat, aware that he sat alone among the chairs set up for the royalty and the Hierarchy of Magistrates. The crowd looked at him expectantly, probably wondering why he was up there alone.

His embarrassment was short lived as trumpets sounded, announcing the arrival of everyone else. The hierarchy came first, dressed in their black robes and looking somber. Councilor Abrecan was next, smartly dressed in crimson with silver trim. Finally King Daimh arrived, smiling and waving to the crowd, who gave a polite cheer in return. His minstrels sang loudly as he entered.

King Daimh—master of the sword!
Of this we sing in accord!
Looks great on the throne,
Best king that we've known!
Forever he will be adored!

"Welcome, welcome," Daimh said loudly. "I've asked my father to oversee these proceedings."

He motioned to Abrecan, who stood and bowed to his son. Daimh was still in the process of being seated when Abrecan addressed the crowd.

"While it is unfortunate that we must put someone to death today, this shows that justice will be served. The person being executed today was once a royal guardian."

A collective gasp came from the crowd. Word had spread about an execution, but the details were always held until the day when it would take place.

"Yes, yes, I know," Abrecan said. "It's a tragedy that someone of such an honorable position would attempt to kill a fellow guardian. But we are here to show you that no one is above the law."

Waving a hand toward the stairs of the platform, Abrecan proclaimed, "Bring the prisoner forward!"

Several guardians came up the stairs, followed by Rayne, still in chains. Then came several more guardians, one of them carrying a large axe. He walked over to a large wooden block with a wicker basket off to the side. Rayne was brought to the block and forced down on his knees.

"Stop!" shouted Governor Nash, jumping to his feet.

Everyone in the crowd and on the platform froze for a moment before Abrecan broke the silence.

"What is it, Governor Nash?" Abrecan asked, clearly annoyed.

Nash walked to the center of the platform, then turned to face the crowd. "This execution will not continue."

Before he could say anything else, Caldre interrupted, "Governor, you are out of line! This man has been tried and found guilty. You cannot stop it!"

"But I can, and I am," Nash said forcefully. "You cannot execute Rayne because I am sponsoring him as the representative from Lebu in the Shoginoc."

CHAPTER 26

"Ivor, you don't want to do this," Oakleaf said, handing the torch to Barclay and then slowly raising his hands.

Ivor grabbed the hilt of his sword with both hands. "Oh, really? And who are you to tell me what I want?"

Oakleaf stepped back carefully, causing Barclay and Arlie to step back as well. "These people can prove that Rayne is innocent. If you stop us, he will die for a crime he didn't commit."

Ivor lowered his sword a little, looked thoughtful for a moment, and then said, "So, if I stop you, the man who humiliated me in the Mortentaun, in front of all of the important people in Bariwon, will die?" He raised his sword up into an attack position and smiled malevolently. "You don't make a very good argument."

Oakleaf stepped back and drew his sword just in time to block Ivor's attack.

"Go back the way we came! Look for an open cell door!" Oakleaf told Barclay, batting away another blow. The merchant and his daughter started down the hallway, with Oakleaf following them the best he could while fending off Ivor.

The narrow hallway made swordplay difficult at best. The swings had to be short and compact. Ivor even had to stoop in places where the ceiling dipped low. The group worked its way back through the passages, taking corners now and again. Oakleaf continued to fight defensively, giving up several chances he had to press the attack.

Ivor seemed to grow more frustrated. He was able to move Oakleaf back down the passageways, but wasn't able to do any real damage to his person.

"Quit running away and fight like a man!" Ivor shouted after yet another one of his attacks was deflected.

"What's the matter, Ivor? Upset that the sword I'm using hasn't been hollowed out this time and you are forced to fight fairly?"

The insult angered Ivor further, causing his blows to become more erratic. Several times, Ivor's wild swings would glance off the stone walls, causing sparks.

"Here!" Barclay said finally. "This door is open!"

Oakleaf allowed Ivor to push him back even a bit further down the hallway, driving them past the open doorway. Deciding it was time to go on the offensive, Oakleaf set his back foot and started to counterattack.

With both guardians unwilling to give up ground, the blows came fast and hard. Oakleaf noticed it seemed to be getting darker in the hallway. The torch Barclay held was the only source of light, which made the swordfight even more challenging.

"The torch is going out!" Barclay yelled.

"Light another one—quickly!"

"Where?" asked the woodworker.

"There should be one hanging on the wall nearby," Oakleaf said, ducking beneath another powerful swing.

"I'm not finding one!"

"Against the wall," Oakleaf turned his head quickly to see if he could spot another torch.

Taking advantage of Oakleaf's split attention, Ivor feigned high, but then quickly stabbed, impaling Oakleaf in his thigh just below the hip.

Oakleaf looked down at the sword and then up at Ivor's triumphant grin. He heard Arlie gasp. In the flicker of the dying torch, Oakleaf saw the open prison door behind the still-grinning face of Ivor.

Oakleaf dropped his sword. "Nice move."

Ivor put more force behind the sword, driving it deeper into Oakleaf's thigh. "You put up a good fight, but not good enough. Once I finish you and then kill the old man, I think I'll have some fun with the girl there."

"Over my dead body," Barclay said.

Ivor shook his head. "Nah, I'll take her a good distance away from your dead body first."

"I don't think so." Oakleaf's voice was raspy and labored.

With both hands on the hilt of his sword, Ivor leaned in closer, raised an eyebrow and said, "Oh yeah? And what are you going to do about it?"

Oakleaf summoned his strength and punched Ivor as hard as he could in the nose with his armored fist. Several of the metal links on his chain mail gloves split open with the impact. The taller guardian's head snapped backward, and when he looked again at Oakleaf with wide eyes, his once-bulbous nose was now at a funny angle. Oakleaf lowered a shoulder, spun slightly, and wrenched the sword from Ivor's grip. He lunged forward and caught Ivor in the chest with his shoulder, causing him to stumble into the open prison. Oakleaf grabbed the door and began to shut it as fast as he could. The door was almost closed when it stopped abruptly. Ivor had stuck his foot in between the door and the frame. Feeling the strength drain from him, Oakleaf doubled his effort, but he couldn't get the door to budge.

After handing the dying torch to Arlie, Barclay rushed in and kicked Ivor's foot, causing it to retreat and allowing the door to close tightly. Oakleaf fastened the lock just as the door shuddered from what could only be Ivor slamming against it from the other side.

With Ivor contained, Oakleaf's strength left him completely, and he sagged to his knees.

"Take it out," said the young guardian. Barclay grabbed the sword, and putting a foot against Oakleaf's chest, quickly yanked the sword free.

"We need to get you out of here," Barclay said.

Oakleaf nodded. "Light a new torch first. Hurry."

Both of the men looked toward the young woman, who was staring at them and holding the all-but-burned-out torch. Rushing to her side, Barclay took it from her and started searching for another torch to light.

"There!" Arlie said, pointing several paces down the hallway. Barclay ran toward the new torch and reached it just as it went out, leaving them in the dark.

"Oh, no," the merchant said. "I guess we'll have to find our way back in the dark. Do you think you can, Oakleaf?" Only silence answered him.

Feeling his way, Barclay stumbled over Oakleaf's leg. Kneeling down, he reached out and felt his leg, now wet and sticky. He noted that Oakleaf was still breathing, but he must have fainted from loss of blood.

Barclay removed his shirt and began ripping it into strips. "Father? What are you doing?" Arlie asked, moving toward the sound.

"I'm trying to stop the bleeding," he said, putting a folded part of his shirt against Oakleaf's thigh.

"What are we going to do now?" she asked. "How are we going to find our way out?"

"I honestly have no idea," Barclay said grimly, "but chances are, even if we find a way out of here, it will be too late to save Oakleaf or Rayne."

⇥✦⇤

"Is this everyone?" Abrecan asked, looking over the assembly in the main hall from his viewpoint atop the stage. After Governor Nash's declaration that he would sponsor Rayne in the Shoginoc, Abrecan demanded that royalty, savants, governors, and magistrates reassemble in the main hall to discuss the situation away from the open public.

Standing to the right of Abrecan, Magistrate Caldre squinted before replying, "It appears so."

"Fine," Abrecan said. "Now that we are away from the crowd, we shall look into the validity of Governor Nash's claim." The councilor turned to the five men dressed in long black robes. "Can Governor Nash prevent the execution of Rayne by sponsoring him? We know from the earlier situation with Governor Dylan that people can't be executed if they are involved in the Shoginoc. But the difference here is that Rayne's crime was committed *before* he was sponsored."

Magistrate Aldous stood slowly and said, "We will need a moment to discuss this." He sat down again and opened his copy of the Tome of Laws, as did the rest of the hierarchy.

Magistrate Bertram quickly flipped through his pages, got the other magistrates' attention, and pointed to a passage. All the magistrates read the passage and then spoke quietly among themselves for a moment before Aldous stood once again.

"The Tome of Laws says, and I quote, *'A day before the first Shoginoc, Governor Tristan was executed for murdering Lady Persephone. It was discovered later that Governor Raleigh was actually responsible for the death of Lady Persephone, and put the blame on Tristan in an attempt to prevent Governor Tristan from participating in the Shoginoc, therefore giving Raleigh a better chance for his district to be selected. To avoid this type of treachery, anyone participating in the Shoginoc may not be executed and will be allowed to participate. If the accused is proven irrefutably guilty after the Shoginoc, he or she will be stripped of all titles and subjected to the consequences of his or her actions.'*

Tapping his foot impatiently, Abrecan said, "And?"

Aldous blinked at the councilor for a moment. "That's all it says on the subject."

"Meaning?"

With his finger on the page before him, Aldous read again, *"Anyone participating in the Shoginoc may not be executed and will be allowed to participate."* Looking back up, he said, "It says nothing about when the crime was committed, but Rayne is participating in the Shoginoc, so it seems clear to us he cannot be executed."

"But he was already found guilty! Even if he were to win the Shoginoc, he would be stripped of his title and executed!" Pointing to Governor Nash, Abrecan demanded, "You will explain yourself."

Nash stood up, stroked his white beard thoughtfully, and then said, "I know Guardian Rayne. I spent many hours training him for the Mortentaun. It's simply not in his character to commit the crime of which he has been accused."

Caldre stamped his foot, then stepped in front of Abrecan and all but shouted, "But he himself admits to putting his sword to another guardian's neck!"

Nash pointed a thick finger at the magistrate. "That would not be a crime if Rayne was protecting the innocent. This, I know, *is* in Rayne's character."

Caldre threw his hands up in the air. "It doesn't matter! He's been convicted! Nothing can change that now."

"Not true," the governor said. "If the merchant and his daughter are found and they testify otherwise, Rayne must be set free."

This caused a bit of a stir among the crowd, but Caldre stopped it short by saying, "That won't happen."

"How are you so sure?" Nash took a step forward. "I understand that the merchant and his daughter simply disappeared one night. No one seems to know where they went. Well, that's not true. We actually have someone who believes they know where to find them and is retrieving them right now."

Caldre folded his arms. "That—that can't be true. No one saw them leave."

"Are you so sure, Magistrate?" Nash's voice grew more confident. "Isn't it possible someone knows where they are?"

Abrecan grabbed Caldre's arm and jerked him back a step. "So, Governor," Abrecan said smoothly, "your reason to sponsor Rayne was simply to delay his execution, correct? It's good of you be so concerned about someone from your district."

Nash gave a small chuckle before he responded. "Ah, no. That isn't the only reason, Councilor. I honestly believe that Rayne would make an excellent king. He's been taught correctly, and he strives to do what is right—and not just what suits him personally."

Abrecan didn't respond at first; he just stared down at Nash for a moment. "It doesn't really matter. Fine, he can participate in the Shoginoc. If you were actually able to make a good showing, you would have already sponsored someone else. There isn't a chance he will be selected. All you've done here is waste our time. The Shoginoc takes place in one hour from now. I think it is best that we keep Rayne under guard to prevent an attempt at escape. You are all dismissed!"

❧⚜❧

Barclay carefully moved Oakleaf away from the door that continued to shudder with what could only be Ivor trying to break it down from the other side. The imprisoned guardian was shouting for help and yelling obscenities, causing a stir among the other prisoners in the area.

"Father, can he break down that door?" Arlie asked. "He is rather big and strong."

"I'm not going to give him a chance," Barclay said.

He felt his way back to the door in the pitch black of the dungeon. He found it, then searched for the small opening at the bottom where food was given to the prisoners. Sitting down with his legs against the door, Barclay lifted the panel. This got Ivor's attention. Barclay felt the guardian's arm reach through in an attempt to grab him. But Barclay had anticipated this action and grabbed Ivor by the wrist with both hands. Making sure he had a firm grip, he pushed away from the door quickly with his legs, causing Ivor to lurch forward and smack his head hard against the other side of the door. Barclay felt Ivor's arm break in the process, and Ivor stopped moving.

Barclay let go of Ivor's arm, then stood and backed away until he bumped against a door directly across the hall. He slid down and sat, leaning against it.

A light but steady knocking on the access panel of the door he was leaning against caused Barclay to flinch. He started to scoot away but stopped when he heard a voice.

"What did he say?" Arlie asked from the darkness.

"I'm not sure," Barclay said, edging closer to the door. Finding the access panel, he put his ear against it and listened.

"I can help you," said the voice.

Turning to Arlie, Barclay said, "He says he can help us, but I'm not sure we can trust anyone down here."

"But *we* were put down here, Father. And we are trustworthy. Maybe they were also put down here when they shouldn't have been," she pointed out. "And we do need help."

"That we do," Barclay admitted. He carefully opened the access panel and asked, "Who are you, and how can you help us?"

"My name is Sherwyn. I am the castle priest."

Barclay harrumphed. "Excuse me if I don't quite believe you. Why would the castle priest be in the dungeon?"

"Councilor Abrecan was upset with me for standing up to him in a court where an innocent guardian was convicted of attempted murder," Sherwyn said.

"Which guardian?" Barclay said.

"Rayne."

Barclay felt his daughter reach out and touch his arm. "I believe him, Father. Who else down here would know about Rayne?"

"How could you help us?" Barclay asked, still cautious.

"I heard everything that happened out there. I can help in a couple of ways," Sherwyn said. "First, in the cell next to me on your right is Nursemaid Anemone. She will be able to attend to the guardian's wounds."

"And second?" Barclay asked.

"When I was brought down here, I memorized which passages they took. I can escort you out of the dungeon."

⁂

Despite the rain pounding relentlessly against the roof and windows of the main hall, the mood was anything but gloomy. In fact, it almost crackled with electricity while people waited anxiously for the Shoginoc to begin.

Sunshine sat among her fellow savants, wearing a simple white dress cinched about her waist with a blue and gold belt. As many people as could fit lined both sides of the hall, all facing the stage. Sunshine noted that many people were dressed in the traditional gold and blue, while there were pockets of others who wore crimson and silver.

The Hierarchy of Magistrates stood on the stage, waiting for the royalty to arrive. The Shoginoc participants stood in the center of the hall. Governor Eadward was surrounded by large men dressed in guardian uniforms. Three tables held their offering for the Shoginoc, draped with ornately sewn covers.

A smaller group from Regne was next. Their candidate was an older gentleman. What hair remained was still dark, and even from her current position Sunshine noticed his warm eyes. He bore a striking resemblance to Lady Nicole, which was only logical since he was her father. Only one covered table was by the group from Regne.

The last group consisted only of Rayne and Governor Nash. Despite protests from Nash, Rayne was constantly under guard and was not allowed to change from the clothes he had worn for the execution. He looked ragged and tired at first glance, but there was something about the way he stood and moved that displayed calm confidence.

Trumpets blared at the front of the hall, and the large oak doors slowly opened. The royalty entered and pompously moved to their positions on the stage. King Daimh sat proudly with his wife Nicole next to him, who was all smiles and waves. Councilor Abrecan appeared as arrogant as ever, looking down his nose at the people in the crowd. Captain Sullivan stood on one side of the thrones, with Guardian Cameron standing on the other side.

But it was Magistrate Caldre who caught Sunshine's attention. He wasn't a member of the royalty, so she wondered why he had followed the others. His eyes darted back and forth, nervously scanning the crowd as he walked to the front of the stage.

Caldre reached the edge and said loudly, "Welcome to a most special event in the kingdom—the Shoginoc!" The audience exploded in applause. Once the noise died down, Caldre continued to peruse the crowd as if he was looking for something in particular.

When it had quieted enough for him to speak again, Caldre announced, "Normally, the castle priest would be the master of ceremonies for the Shoginoc, but due to recent events, Sherwyn has been removed, and we are still awaiting word from the church on his replacement."

The members of the church who sat across the hall from Sunshine all appeared to be surprised at this announcement and even began to whisper among themselves.

"It has been just over twenty-one years since King Daimh was selected to marry Queen Eliana. Sadly, Queen Eliana died in a tragic accident before she could give birth to the heir of the throne," Caldre said. "Recent discoveries have shown us that arranged marriages are not what the authors of the Tome of Laws had intended, but that doesn't impact this Shoginoc.

"Magistrate Aldous has asked Magistrate Bertram to read from the correct version of the Tome of Laws which will explain how we will proceed."

Bertram looked over the large crowd, gulped, and then looked down quickly to the book in front of him. In a somewhat shaky but loud voice, he read, *"If the king or queen does not marry, or if he or she does marry and is unable to produce an heir, a new king or queen will be chosen twenty-one years after the crowning of the king or queen."*

Bertram sat back down quickly, rubbing his brow with the back of his hand.

Caldre stepped back up to the edge of the stage. "Three people have been sponsored for the Shoginoc from their respective districts." He motioned to the candidates in the hall before him. "They are Governor Eadward from both Erd and Lewyol, Magistrate Nicolas from Regne, and Rayne from Lebu." Again, the crowd applauded enthusiastically, and each of the candidates bowed in response.

"However, I should make it known that Rayne has been convicted of a crime and was only sponsored by Governor Nash so he could cheat death."

"Caldre!" Governor Nash barked. "You are out of line!"

The crowd's reaction was mixed. Some people were shouting at Governor Nash to quiet down, while others were shouting at Caldre. There was quite the din in the large hall.

⋆⋆⋆

"The castle is so empty and quiet," Arlie said, following the group down a long hallway. Sherwyn was leading the way, with Anemone and Arlie's father right behind him, while Arlie took up the rear.

Her father was carrying Oakleaf in his arms—no easy task, seeing how tall the guardian was. Fortunately, all the years of working with wood had made her father a very strong man.

"We are taking the back hallways," Sherwyn said, moving as quickly as he could for someone of his age. "We're lucky to have gotten to this point unnoticed—although that probably means everyone is at the Shoginoc."

A heavy silence fell over the group. If the Shoginoc had started, that meant Rayne's execution had already taken place. They turned a corner and went up a flight of stairs, and then stopped in front of an unremarkable door. "Wait here," Anemone said as she moved to the front, opened the door, and looked inside. She had a brief conversation with whoever was in the room, then opened the door the rest of the way. Stepping in, she motioned for them to follow her.

The room contained several beds, and the walls were lined with cabinets of all different sizes and shapes. In the room stood a woman Arlie guessed was in her mid-forties. She was working quickly on setting up one of the beds.

"This is Nursemaid Ophelia," Anemone said. "She'll help us."

Ophelia gave them a quick smile, and then said to Barclay, "Bring him here. Let's take a look."

Barclay brought the young guardian over to the bed and laid him down gently. The cloth Barclay had used as a bandage was nearly soaked through with blood.

Anemone and Ophelia examined Oakleaf. Arlie heard them mutter phrases like, "It seems to have missed any vital parts," "He's lost a lot of blood," and "Let's get his wound cleaned up."

The two nursemaids continued to work on Oakleaf for the next several minutes. He stirred once when they poured a clear liquid on the wound that looked like water but smelled like something you would find at a pub.

After putting clean bandages on him, Anemone turned to the rest of them. "Thank goodness Ophelia was on duty. She can be trusted and will look after Oakleaf. We believe he will be fine."

Arlie felt a sense of relief at the news. She had met Oakleaf a couple of times in town, and unlike her feelings toward most guardians, she was impressed with him. In addition, he had just saved her life, so she was truly happy he was going to be all right.

"We must hurry," Anemone said. "We need to get to the Shoginoc."

Sherwyn ran his hand over his bald head as he thought. "I don't see why. In fact, we should get as far away from here as possible."

"I didn't tell you!" Anemone said in realization. "I was too concerned about helping Oakleaf. Ophelia tells me that Rayne wasn't executed after all."

"What? Really?" Arlie said.

Anemone nodded. "Yes, Governor Nash was able to spare him by entering him in the Shoginoc."

"That was very clever of him." Sherwyn smiled. "And you are right— we need to get to the Shoginoc as soon as possible."

Barclay looked doubtful. "Won't we be stopped before we can get in?"

"I think I have a way," Anemone said. She walked over to an armoire, removed four hooded gray cloaks, and then gave one each to Sherwyn, Barclay, and Arlie. Donning one herself, Anemone said, "Just keep your hoods up and your heads down, and people should believe we are all nursemaids."

⊰╫⊱

Sunshine stood and looked over the scene, wondering if it would turn into something ugly. From the corner of her eye, she saw one of the side doors to the hall open. Several figures dressed in hooded cloaks entered and began to make their way through the crowd.

Others began to notice them as they moved to the center of the hall where the candidates stood. It appeared to Sunshine that Caldre hadn't noticed the newcomers yet, as he was engaged in a heated conversation with Magistrate Aldous.

Caldre turned his back on the hierarchy and moved to the front of the stage. He had begun to motion everyone to quiet down when he looked at the four hooded figures that had now reached the center of the hall. "Guardians!" He pointed. "Stop them!"

"Not until we are heard!" shouted one of the hooded figures, whose voice was familiar to Sunshine. Throwing back his hood, Priest Sherwyn revealed himself. Nursemaid Anemone showed her face next, while the other two remained concealed.

Glancing back at Caldre for his reaction, Sunshine noticed Councilor Abrecan jump to his feet. "What are you doing here, Sherwyn?" Abrecan demanded. "You were put under arrest!"

The crowd quieted and seemed to hold its collective breath for the priest's response.

Standing tall with his chin up and shoulders squared, Sherwyn declared, "We are here to make sure that the true heir is put on the throne."

CHAPTER 27

King Daimh watched with disdain. He had wanted his last day as king to be memorable, a day that the kingdom would look back on for years to come. People would say, "I was there the day our own King Daimh generously stepped down and became a councilor." He had told the minstrels this was to be his crowning achievement—the day he graciously pledged to help the new king in any way he could. He expected them not only to write a song about it, but instructed them to create a play based on today's events as well.

Instead, the ceremony had been abruptly halted when Magistrate Caldre insulted one of the participants. It was bad form, and Daimh told himself he must talk with Caldre about disrupting his final day as king.

But even worse was when one of the governors responded in kind. What was his name? Mash? The king never really bothered to learn their names. All that mattered was that *they* knew *him*. To disturb things even further, a priest dared to show up and cause problems. Hadn't this priest been taken away for some reason? And what did he mean by "the true heir to the throne"?

"You will not be allowed to speak here! Guardians, remove them at once!" Daimh heard his father command. Several guardians Daimh knew to be from Erd, and therefore loyal to his father, started to move toward the cloaked figures in the middle of the room. Daimh noted with some surprise that many of the older guardians remained where they were.

"This information is too important for the future of Bariwon," Sherwyn declared. "I must be allowed to speak!"

The governor who had taken a stand against Caldre was the first person to reach Priest Sherwyn and his group. He nodded at them, and then turned to face the stage and the guardians who continued to move in.

"I say let him speak!" shouted the white-bearded man. Turning to face the crowd, he raised his arms and repeated, "Let him speak! Let him speak!"

A vast majority of the crowd started to chant along with the governor. In addition, many from the crowd stepped into the middle of the hall between the advancing guardians and the priest.

"Move out of the way! Cut down any that try to stop you!" Abrecan shouted. Caldre was by his side and also threatening the crowd to move or die.

Daimh had seen enough. He stood and walked up behind his father and Caldre. Grabbing them both by the shoulders, he startled them into silence. This got the crowd's attention, and the guardians stopped. Everyone quieted down enough for Daimh to speak.

"I am still the king of Bariwon," Daimh said, his voice firm. "I will not have songs sung about how I allowed blood to be spilled at the Shoginoc. I will not be considered a fool for generations. If the priest does in fact have news of a proper heir, I, for one, want to hear it."

Abrecan looked as if he was going to explode with rage. "Daimh " he began to say.

"No, Father," Daimh said. "Not this time. Sit down, and we will listen to what he has to say."

Abrecan didn't move at first. He looked at his son for a moment, then out at the crowd. Not saying anything, he simply sat down on his chair, with Caldre following suit.

"Explain what you mean by 'the true heir to the throne,'" Daimh ordered the priest.

The people who had moved into the center of the hall backed off, allowing the elderly man to speak.

"Thank you, Your Majesty," Sherwyn said. "What I am about to confess will cost me my position with the church, and I'm most certain it will be cause for severe punishment."

The once-boisterous crowd had quieted so that only the rain falling on the roof could be heard in addition to Sherwyn's voice. "I am afraid, Your Majesty, that you are the victim of a terrible deception." The priest turned in a slow circle and said to the crowd, "As are all of you."

Daimh definitely did not like the idea of being deceived. What was the priest talking about? He folded his arms and furrowed his brow. "What deception?"

Sherwyn took a deep breath. Anemone patted him on the back in comfort. "You never married Queen Eliana," he said.

The crowd burst into gasps and a buzzing of conversations.

This didn't make any sense to Daimh. Surely the old man was losing his mind.

"You are wrong," Daimh said. "I was there, and it did indeed happen. You should know that—you were the one who performed the ceremony..."

"I performed the ceremony so it wouldn't be binding," Sherwyn said. "Eliana made sure you took her by the left hand, instead of the right, and she did not say, 'I do.' The two of you never kissed. She sneezed just beforehand."

Daimh tried to think back to the ceremony, but he couldn't recall many of the details. He was sure he had kissed her—or was he confusing that with his wedding to Nicole?

His father jumped out of his chair and shouted, "Sherwyn, why would you do such a thing?"

Daimh took hold of his father's arm and had him sit back down, which seemed to embarrass his father. Daimh was in charge here now, and he didn't need his father making things worse.

"I pretended to perform the ceremony, but did it incorrectly, because Queen Eliana was already married at the time," Sherwyn said.

Daimh continued to stare intently at Sherwyn while the crowd again reacted to the priest's latest statement. "What are you talking about?" Daimh asked evenly, still trying to puzzle it out.

Remaining straight and tall, Sherwyn said, "Queen Eliana was going to renounce her title rather than marry you. You see, she was actually in love with someone else." The priest took another deep breath before he continued. "I was fearful of having you and Councilor Abrecan take control of the kingdom. Everything I had heard about the conditions in Erd made me fear for the overall well-being of Bariwon. Looking at what has happened to the castle and the kingdom over the last twenty-one years, those fears of mine were justified."

A burst of anger cut through Daimh's confusion. Did he hear correctly? Did Sherwyn actually criticize how he had ruled Bariwon? How could he, after all the good Daimh had done? The songs written in Daimh's honor were proof that he was the best king Bariwon had ever had. At that moment, Daimh wanted to order the guardians to remove Sherwyn, but there were still too many questions unanswered. However, the priest must be made to know that he was only allowed to speak because of Daimh's good graces.

"You are on dangerous ground, Sherwyn," Daimh growled. "You will only be allowed to speak until I stop you. I suggest you continue recounting *your* mistakes for all to hear."

Sherwyn flinched, but then continued, "Very well, Your Majesty. I convinced Queen Eliana to stay so she and her father would remain in power. In return, she could marry the man she truly loved, and I would falsify the marriage between the two of you."

Now he knew the priest had lost his mind. Daimh had fathered a child with Eliana, even though he been unable to with Nicole. "But she was carrying my child when she died!" declared Daimh. "She wouldn't have been—"

It didn't happen very often to Daimh, and when it did happen, it was a shock. Based on what he was told here today, he actually was able to put the pieces together and come to a conclusion.

He turned his attention to Anemone. "The child wasn't mine, was it? You must have given me something on my wedding night so I wouldn't remember."

"That's right, Your Majesty." Anemone looked at the floor after she responded.

Daimh felt anger start to rise inside him as he saw his legacy slipping away. "You both have made me into a fool after all. Before you are taken away, answer me this. You said you were here to reveal the true heir. I don't see how that is possible, since Eliana died before she could give birth."

Anemone looked up. "After Queen Eliana's fall, she was very near death. I was able to remove the baby boy before she died and give him to the baby's father, who took him away from the castle."

"And who was his father?" Daimh demanded.

"Her personal guardian," Sherwyn said. "Rinan."

⊰⧉⊱

Until this point, Rayne had stood by, silently observing as the events unfolded around him. When Sherwyn announced there was an heir to the throne, he was understandably curious to find out who it was. Perhaps this heir would decide that Rayne didn't need to be put to death.

With Sherwyn's last statement, however, all other thoughts fled Rayne's mind. *His* father was married to the queen? That meant *he* was...

Wide-eyed, he looked at Sherwyn and Anemone, who nodded at him in response. His grandparents emerged from the crowd and walked toward him, smiling and nodding as well.

It was Governor Nash who spoke first after Sherwyn's announcement.

"Why, that would make Rayne the heir to the throne!" he exclaimed, slapping him hard on the back.

Stunned, Rayne simply stood there as the hall once again exploded in cheers and protests. Magistrate Caldre and Councilor Abrecan were back on their feet, shouting and pointing.

"Quiet!" King Daimh yelled. "Quiet! You will all be quiet!"

Turning to face the king, Rayne waited for the ruler of Bariwon to speak. But it was Abrecan who spoke next. Although doing so appeared to cause him pain, he asked his son, "If I may, Your Majesty?"

Daimh nodded curtly in response.

"This is all too convenient, Sherwyn," the councilor said. "There is no proof, aside from your word. And by your own voice, you've admitted to lying in the past to further what you consider to be best for the kingdom. It's obvious that nothing has changed."

Kelvin and Nadia had taken positions next to Rayne and Nash by this time. Kelvin said, "I will testify that what Sherwyn says is true, as will my wife."

"These are Rayne's grandparents," Nash explained.

Abrecan threw his hands up. "Not good enough. Even if these people are who they say they are, I won't accept that as sufficient proof."

"My father's sword and his copy of the Tome of Laws," Rayne said suddenly. "I have them both here. The sword has the symbol of royalty on it. I never understood why until now."

"Where are these items?" Nash asked.

"They're in a trunk, at the foot of my bed," Rayne said. "I hid them under a canvas blanket at the bottom when I came here."

Nash headed to the exit. "I'll go get them. But I'll need some help to find the room."

Alana came forward from her place among the nobles. "I'll go with you. I know where the guardian's rooms are. We'll find Rayne's."

"It's the room with the window bricked up," Rayne offered in way of help.

Nash smiled. "That's my old room! If Alana can get me to the general area, I'll know which one it is."

"I can do that." Alana exchanged a smile with Rayne, and then led Nash from the hall.

Caldre leaned forward in his chair. "If I may, Your Majesty, there is something important that makes all this a moot point."

"Yes?" Daimh asked.

Pointing a crooked finger at Rayne, the magistrate said to the crowd,

"Rayne was convicted of a crime, and even if he becomes the king, by law he will be stripped of his title."

His head still swimming from the revelation about his parents, Rayne was rudely brought back to reality with Caldre's statement.

"About that," Sherwyn said. "I suggest you hear what these people have to say."

The two figures next to Sherwyn and Anemone slowly removed their hoods.

"This is Barclay and his daughter Arlie," Sherwyn explained to everyone. "They are the people Rayne was protecting from Guardian Cameron. They will testify that Rayne drew his sword only to protect them."

"Impossible!" Caldre blustered, getting to his feet. "Are these people who they say they are, Cameron?"

Caldre turned to ask the guardian, but only found an empty space where Cameron should be standing. "Where did he—" Caldre started to ask.

"That's Barclay!" shouted a voice from the crowd.

"Aye, that's him!" another voice called.

Magistrate Aldous stood. "Is this true? Did Rayne lift his sword only in defense of the innocent?"

"Yes, sir," Barclay said. "Guardian Cameron was trying to collect taxes from us after he had done so only a short while before. He demanded payment and drew his sword when we refused. Rayne got him to back off."

"And what of Guardian Ivor?" Aldous asked. "He supports Cameron's story."

Barclay blinked and then looked at his daughter. "There was no other guardian there, Magistrate."

Bertram tugged on Aldous's sleeve and said something to him that the crowd couldn't hear. Aldous nodded, and then turned his attention back to Barclay.

"Tell us, Barclay, why didn't you come forth earlier?" asked the aged magistrate.

Barclay took a step forward and looked directly at Magistrate Caldre. "My daughter and I were taken in the middle of the night from our home and put in the dungeon. Large sacks had been put over our heads so we couldn't see who had taken us, but the voice of one of the men was definitely that of Guardian Cameron. He has a very particular way of speaking."

"That he does," Aldous agreed. "Magistrate Caldre, Captain Sullivan, what do you know of this?"

Caldre gave Sullivan a warning stare. "Nothing," the captain of the guard said. "It appears that Cameron was working outside our authority."

"You say you were taken, but here you are," Caldre stated. "No one escapes from the dungeon. How is that possible?"

Barclay shared a meaningful look with Sherwyn. "We were set free by Guardian Oakleaf."

"Impossible!" Caldre said. "I personally requested that Guardian Ivor watch over the dungeon. Oakleaf couldn't have gotten by Ivor."

"But he did," Sherwyn said. "However, not until he was nearly killed. We were able to get him to help, and he is being treated. It's our hope that he will live."

The knot in Rayne's stomach tightened. Oakleaf had done this for him! Rayne would never ask anyone to make such a sacrifice.

"And what of Guardian Ivor?" Caldre asked.

Barclay chuckled. "Let's just say he's resting uncomfortably in one of the cells he was guarding."

Before Caldre or Sullivan could protest, Magistrate Aldous interceded. "I've heard enough. Until a proper court can be held to clear Rayne officially, we will suspend the charges against him."

Rayne felt as though a dark, gloomy sky had suddenly been replaced by bright beams of sunlight. With Barclay and Arlie here to testify on his behalf, and with Cameron's disappearance, Rayne felt confident he would be cleared of the charges against him. He heard the crowd cheering, and for the first time he noticed Sunshine in the crowd. She was giving him a smile that almost made him melt. Barclay and Sherwyn shook Rayne's hand, while Anemone and Arlie each gave him a quick embrace.

At that moment, Nash and Alana returned. Nash held Rinan's sheathed sword in his hand, and Alana carried the Tome of Laws. They walked directly to the stage and handed the items to the Hierarchy of Magistrates.

Bertram carefully removed the sword from its scabbard and placed it on the table before them. Each of the magistrates investigated the sword closely. They spoke quietly to each other, a couple of them flipping through their copies of the Tome of Laws and pointing to certain passages. They then opened Rayne's copy of the Tome and turned over the first few pages. Bertram frowned.

Everyone in the hall, including those on the stage, waited expectantly for the hierarchy to say something. Magistrate Aldous stood once again. He pointed to the sword. "We have determined that this is indeed the sword that would have been given to Eliana's personal guardian. While the Tome of Laws is bound in a fashion reserved for the royalty, it is missing the page that names the original owner. It appears to have been torn out. Since copies of the Tome of Laws are only given to savants, royalty, magistrates and governors, it is curious as to how Rayne would have obtained it, especially if it is indeed a copy only given to a member of the royalty."

Alana spoke up. "I verify that the Tome of Laws before you is indeed one given to royalty. Queen Eliana was my cousin, and I recall seeing a book just like that in her room on many occasions."

"Be that as it may," Aldous said, "there isn't any proof that it was Eliana's."

Anemone stepped forward. "I know how you can verify it was Eliana's. I was her nursemaid, after all. When she was young, her father and I found that she had drawn in her Tome of Laws because she felt it needed pictures. If the copy you have before you has passages circled with hearts and flowers drawn around them, it would have to be her copy. I believe it was in the chapter that discusses her becoming queen. If it is her copy, Rinan could have taken it with him when he left the castle."

Bertram turned the pages until he reached chapter eleven. His frown was replaced by a large smile. "Yes, it is just as you say."

The Hierarchy of Magistrates then consulted again in quiet voices before Aldous stated, "Based on the evidence, it is the opinion of the hierarchy that Rayne is indeed the son of Eliana and Rinan."

King Daimh sat down heavily on his throne, his wife Nicole looking at him with obvious concern. Abrecan sat down and grabbed the armrests of his chair, while Caldre looked stunned.

"However," Aldous continued, "that does not make him the heir to the throne."

Governor Nash's voice boomed over the noise of the crowd. "What are you talking about?" he asked. "Rayne should be king! He is the only one here who carries the true blood of kings!"

Aldous shook his head slowly. "I'm sorry, Governor, but the Tome of Laws is quite clear on this point. The heir is the offspring of the queen *and* king. While Rayne's mother was the queen, his father was not. Daimh was officially crowned as king. Only a child of Eliana and Daimh would be the heir."

"Then this changes nothing!" Abrecan exclaimed. "The Shoginoc must go on, correct?"

The head of the Hierarchy of Magistrates merely nodded in agreement and sat back down. Caldre took that as a cue and jumped to the front of the stage. "Then let us continue. Everyone not involved with the Shoginoc needs to leave the center part of the hall."

Nadia gave her grandson one last quick hug, while Kelvin squeezed Rayne's arm in support. Sherwyn, Anemone, Barclay, and Arlie moved to the side closest to Sunshine and the rest of the savants.

"Lots were drawn earlier, and we'll first see the presentation from Regne, followed by Lebu, and then conclude with the joint districts of Erd and Lewyol," Caldre instructed. "Governor Uaithne, the floor is yours."

The representative of Regne came forward, swishing his verdant cape behind him. His beard was trimmed in a fashion that outlined his strong jawline. As was tradition, members of his entourage opened a large brass chest, which contained various items made from a combination of wood and metal. Each item appeared to be meticulously handcrafted.

"I am sponsoring Magistrate Nicolas, father of Lady Nicole, to be the next ruler of Bariwon," Uaithne said. "He will make a most excellent king."

The crowd clapped politely at the presentation.

"And now, Governor Nash," Caldre sneered, "you may go."

Unabashed, the large ruler of Lebu stepped forward. "I have no box full of pretty rocks to show off," he said loudly, "but what I *do* have to offer is what I consider to be quite the treasure. Rayne is one of the finest men I've ever known. He comes from a good family. He always thinks about others before himself. *This* is the kind of person we need on the throne. To that end, I wish for you all to hear from him." With a wink at Rayne, Nash stepped back and allowed Rayne to speak.

Standing unflinching for a moment, Rayne gathered his thoughts while everyone looked on expectantly. So much had happened so quickly, and his mind was racing. Not only did it look promising that the charges against him were going to be dropped, he had also learned the identity of his mother. And now, here he was in the Shoginoc, being asked to give a speech. He knew he had no chance to win—Governor Nash had nothing to present except him. Perhaps, however, he could use this forum to address the problems he had discovered during his time as a royal guardian.

"I have no desire for power or wealth," Rayne said quietly and somewhat cautiously. "I grew up on a farm with my father, and we learned to live off what the land provided. We were blessed not only to have enough for our needs, but we were able to share with others."

Rayne gestured to the other participants. "These men have more experience in games of power. I, on the other hand, only have the knowledge I have been taught. My father always taught me to do what is right, no matter who's watching, or if you don't always see the end results of your actions.

"Very recently I was facing execution, and even though I was sad that my life would soon end, I had the knowledge that I had done the right thing, and for the right reason."

Rayne motioned to the Hierarchy of Magistrates and continued, his voice becoming stronger and more confident. "My father had me study the Tome of Laws growing up. It was the one book we owned. We would read and discuss it often. The Tome of Laws shows a pattern of declaring a law, followed by the reasoning behind the law. It isn't the words of the law that make it important, but the spirit of it.

"Laws of good intention are really of no use unless there are good people to enforce them," Rayne said. "In my time as a guardian, I have seen people twist and turn the laws to the point where they have lost their spirit."

Opening his arms wide, Rayne said firmly, "I implore whoever is chosen today to keep in mind the spirit of the law as they rule over our once-great kingdom of Bariwon. Help return it to the way it should be—a kingdom of peace."

As he stepped back, Rayne was surprised to hear thunderous applause and cheers from the people in attendance. Even the Hierarchy of Magistrates was standing and clapping vigorously.

"Enough, enough," Caldre said, trying to regain control over the crowd. "We have one more participant. Governor Eadward, the floor is yours."

⇥✦⇤

Sunshine's knees felt weak after Rayne's speech, but she fought the urge to sit down. Everyone in the crowd was on their feet, and if she wanted to continue to observe the proceedings, she needed to remain standing. The last several moments had been a rush of emotion for the young savant. Rayne was no longer in danger of being executed, and would probably be freed. Of course, she was shocked to learn that Rayne was the son of Queen Eliana. With all of that and the moving speech he had just made, Sunshine was emotionally overwhelmed.

The total lack of material offering from Governor Nash gave Rayne no chance to be selected, but she believed he knew that and instead used the opportunity to encourage change for the better. She wondered how all this new information would affect their future. Would Rayne stay on as a guardian? There was really no way of telling until the official court was held to clear him of the charges.

Rayne turned and gave Sunshine a smile just as Governor Eadward stepped up to address the crowd.

"Before I present the wondrous treasure I have to offer today," Eadward said pompously, "let me respond to Rayne's comments." The governor pointed a finger at Rayne. "I knew Rayne's father. In fact, his father took over for me as Eliana's personal guardian. Instead of doing what was right, his father selfishly used his influence to seduce Eliana and convinced her to break the very laws he had sworn to uphold. Rayne speaks pretty words, but he is the result of that forbidden and unlawful union and cannot be trusted."

Eadward turned away from Rayne and strutted forward. "I, however, faithfully served as a royal guardian for many years before I became the Governor of Erd and then Lewyol. Here is what I offer!"

Members of Eadward's group opened three large, silver chests and displayed quite a number of silver and crystal items. Sunshine squinted a little to make sure she was seeing things correctly. On top of one of the piles were two silver goblets studded with rubies. Their design was fairly unique and looked familiar to Sunshine. It was with a feeling of outrage that Sunshine recognized these goblets as those she had seen in Caldre's room.

Several in the crowd showed signs of approval at the riches offered. Using that as momentum, Eadward continued, "I am sponsoring myself in this Shoginoc. I will make the people of Bariwon do as they are told. There will be peace, by force if necessary. I can think of no one else who deserves to be king more than I."

He stepped back with a flourish and waited for the crowd to respond. His face turned an unpleasant shade of crimson when he received only scattered applause.

Caldre stood. "The magistrates will now decide."

The hierarchy left the stage, with Bertram helping the elderly Aldous down the stairs. They started on the right side, where Governor Uaithne stood proudly next to his offering.

After briefly looking over the items, they moved onto Governor Nash and Rayne. Bertram offered Rayne his hand and said something only the two of them could hear. The hierarchy chatted with Nash for a moment before moving on.

Stopping at Eadward's group, Sunshine noted that several of the hierarchy stood with their arms folded and were frowning slightly. After spending the least amount of time with Eadward, the five magistrates walked out of the hall to debate the matter.

Sunshine found herself tightly gripping her robe, and then tried to force herself to relax. The crowd was shifting and fidgeting, anxiously awaiting the return of the hierarchy. They didn't have to wait long before the men returned, climbed back upon the stage, and handed a note to Caldre.

Caldre opened the note and read it, his face void of any expression. He looked up and said, "The next king of Bariwon will be Eadward."

CHAPTER 28

Alana stood silently among the crowd after Caldre announced that Eadward had been selected as king. Immediately after Caldre spoke, Eadward raised both hands above his head and let out a loud cheer, though he was in the minority.

"No."

Eadward stopped and turned toward the sound of the voice.

Alana turned to face the stage as well and saw Magistrate Bertram standing, his hands placed firmly on the table before him. In the years she had lived in the castle, she hadn't gotten to know Bertram very well. He tended to keep to himself, although she had noticed that he did have a close relationship with Sunshine. Bertram was often nervous and shied away from people when they spoke to him, but Alana knew that when the magistrate felt particularly strong about something, he could be persistent.

"Ignore the magistrate." Caldre waved his hand in Bertram's direction. "It's obvious that Eadward offered the most riches and is therefore the winner."

"No," Bertram said more forcefully. "I will not allow this to happen."

"What?" Governor Nash shouted. "Let what happen?"

Alana noticed that unlike Bertram, Nash always spoke his mind.

"Eadward was not selected by the hierarchy," Bertram said.

Caldre held the paper up. "This? You mean this? I knew you were joking when I read it. Eadward is clearly the winner. Any fool can see that."

"Whose name is on the paper?" Nash demanded.

Alana felt the crowd swell up around her. She began to fear that things might become violent.

"Rayne was chosen to be the new king," Bertram stated.

The crowd's cheers overrode the protests from Abrecan, Eadward, and their supporters.

"Let me explain!" Bertram tried to shout, but his voice was lost in the sea of sounds.

"Quiet!" Daimh boomed, causing the crowd to settle down. "I don't understand. Governor Eadward is offering more than Rayne."

Bertram spoke firmly and clearly. "The Tome of Laws says, quote: 'Whoever brings to the kingdom the most worth, as decided by the Hierarchy of Magistrates, will be declared the winner.'"

Pointing to Eadward's offering, Bertram smiled. "It doesn't define the word 'worth' in a material sense. Over the years, that is what it has become. But Rayne reminded us of the spirit of the law. To that end, we see in Rayne someone who brings to the kingdom the most worth— someone who is willing to lay down his life for what is right, without any thought of gain for himself. *This* is the kind of person we need to rule Bariwon!"

✦⧣✦

Three Weeks Later

"Do you think enough time has passed?" Caldre asked, obviously worried.

Abrecan continued to stare at the fire that blazed in his modest room's hearth. "It doesn't matter," he said in a quiet but hard voice. "I won't allow this to continue any longer."

"But I don't think—" Caldre started to say.

"That's right," Abrecan cut him off sharply. "Don't think! You just do as I say. Had you done your job correctly, Eadward would be king, and I wouldn't have had to move out of my room to this oversized wardrobe."

Caldre didn't say anything after the rebuke. He just sat up straight in his chair and waited for Abrecan to continue.

"It's bad enough they took down all the tapestries of me," Abrecan growled, "but to lower the taxes and ask us to do some of the chores the servants would do is ridiculous. Plus, we haven't had a decent feast since Rayne became king."

He blew out a sigh of frustration. "And even more terrible is the king's new bride. It sure didn't take him long to marry her. She's even worse than he is—always being overly nice to the servants and guardians. Rayne and Sunshine don't have the slightest idea how to rule, and they won't listen to my advice."

Abrecan stood from his chair, walked over to his bed, and reached under it to remove an ornate sword. "I'm tired of the games and being subtle. I am going to take back this castle. Tomorrow after the king's first court, I want you to free Ivor from the dungeon, then the two of you will go to Erd and gather as many men as you can and bring them back here."

"I'm not sure—" Caldre started to say.

Abrecan shut him up with a sharp look.

"Are you sure you don't want me to leave earlier?" Caldre asked after a long moment.

Abrecan shook his head. "No. Word has it something eventful is going to take place at court tomorrow. It could raise suspicions if you were absent." Swishing the sword back and forth in the air, Abrecan said, "For too long, Bariwon has been ruled by words from a book. No, it ends here. I will take back this kingdom by any means necessary."

⊰⊹⊱

Rayne squeezed Sunshine's hand as they stood in front of the newly hung tapestry. "I think it was a wonderful idea to put it here in the hallway by our room," he said. "I've liked this from the first moment I saw it."

She reached out to lightly touch the fabric. "It was hung outside the storage room for the longest time, but people here in the castle tell me it was one of your mother's favorites. I thought you'd enjoy having it closer to our room."

"I wish I knew what it was titled," Rayne said. "Perhaps something about the large tree on that hill. Or maybe it's something about spring or summer. I don't know."

Sunshine moved her hand to the clouds depicted on the horizon. "I wonder if the storm is arriving or leaving."

"I would hope leaving," he said. "Although I enjoy the rain, I've become rather fond of sunshine."

His wife looked at him with a smirk on her face. "That has got to be one of the sappiest and most wonderful things you've said to me. How you managed to pull that off with one sentence is amazing."

"Your Majesty," Governor Nash said, bowing. "Pardon the interruption, but we've done as you have asked. Court is ready, and I must tell you, Councilor Abrecan is none too pleased."

Rayne turned to the governor. "I'm sure he isn't. Thank you, Nash. You've been a big help with this inquiry. And were you able to secure Daimh, Sullivan, and Caldre as well?"

Nash nodded his head. "Yes, Your Majesty. They are waiting in the main hall with Abrecan."

"Thank you again," the king said. "We'll be right there." He kissed his wife on the cheek. "Today we take a big step in setting things right."

⌁✦⌁

King Rayne sat next to Queen Sunshine on the modest dais in the main hall. Servants and crafters had worked almost nonstop since the coronation to change the main hall back to how it had been before Daimh became king.

Beside the thrones sat the Hierarchy of Magistrates, minus Aldous, who had passed away a few days following the Shoginoc. The castle priest's seat was also vacant. In front of the king and queen sat Councilor Abrecan, Councilor Daimh, Magistrate Caldre, and Captain Sullivan. The four men were surrounded by guardians dressed neatly in blue and gold.

"We have much to do in this, our first court," Rayne said. "We will be selecting a new member of the Hierarchy of Magistrates, as well as announcing who the church has selected as the castle priest, but first, we need to take care of some unpleasant business."

"This is an outrage!" Abrecan said. "You have no right to treat us this way."

Rayne leaned forward in his chair and stared at Abrecan. "You will remain quiet, Abrecan, unless you are asked to speak."

Addressing the rest of the people in the hall, Rayne said, "While I was in the dungeon, I had the opportunity to get to know one of my fellow dungeon mates. He told me the very interesting story of why he was imprisoned. I have had him released, cleaned up, and asked him to attend this court." With that, one of the side doors opened and a bone-thin man was escorted in by two guardians.

"This" —Rayne motioned for the man to come to the dais— "is Dougal. He was a guardian years ago. He helped former Captain Wayte, rest his soul, investigate the deaths of Councilors Kenrik and Philip."

Rayne watched Abrecan and Caldre carefully as he made this announcement. He noticed their eyes open wide in surprise.

"Dougal, will you please tell us what you and Captain Wayte found in your investigation?" Rayne asked once the former guardian reached the dais.

Pointing a gnarled finger at Abrecan and Caldre, the nearly toothless man said, "They were behind the deaths of Kenrik and Philip."

"You have no proof!" Abrecan shouted, trying to stand up, but one of the guardians put a hand on his shoulder to prevent him.

"We had two witnesses ready to testify," Dougal said, "but you killed one of them when Captain Wayte returned, didn't you, Sullivan?"

Sullivan leaned away from Caldre and responded, "I was, just... well, I was just following orders."

"And I was thrown in the dungeon before I could say anything," Dougal said.

Abrecan threw his arms up. "But it doesn't matter! You have no proof aside from Dougal's word. You need at least two witnesses."

Rayne nodded his head in agreement. "Yes, that's true." He motioned toward the door and again it opened. This time a very old hunchbacked woman was led in by Governor Nash.

Caldre turned white as a cloud. "No!" he said under his breath.

"And who is this?" Abrecan demanded.

"This," Rayne said, coming off his throne and helping the woman to a chair near the dais, "is the barmaid of the inn where Kenrik and Philip's killers stayed the night before the attack. Dougal dressed in rags and pretended to be asleep when Caldre showed up at the inn. This barmaid was there too, cleaning the inn. Caldre paid off the innkeeper to say that it was Governor Elric, not Abrecan, who was behind the plan."

Caldre shook his head. "No, she would be dead by now."

"But I ain't be dead, eh?" she said, her cloudy blue eyes glaring at Caldre. "I may be old, but I still remember that day. Hard to forget when the killings of kings was talked about."

"But why didn't you come forth before?" Bertram asked.

She shook her head. "I was afraid. The owner never came back. I took over the Rabid Dog Inn and hoped every day they wouldn't come for me."

The fear on Caldre's face was unmistakable. "I was only doing as I was told. Abrecan was behind all of this."

In response, Abrecan reached out and grabbed for Caldre but was stopped by the guardians.

"Magistrates?" Rayne said when Abrecan was under control. "What say you?"

The hierarchy spoke quickly among themselves, and then Bertram stood. "We find Abrecan, Caldre, and Sullivan guilty of murder. Following someone's orders is not reason enough to commit such a heinous crime."

"No!" Abrecan shouted. "I ruled this kingdom. You would have all been lost without me! Do you think my idiot of a son could have ruled Bariwon? You cannot do this to me!"

Rayne nodded to one of the guardians, who put a gag over Abrecan's mouth and held him down in his chair.

"Your Majesty," Bertram said, "it is up to you to decide their fate."

Rayne sat back in his chair. Sunshine reached over and took his hand in hers.

"Killing them will do nothing to bring back the dead," Rayne said finally. "Instead, I sentence Abrecan, Caldre, and Sullivan to spend the rest of their lives in the dungeon."

Abrecan struggled even harder, while Caldre and Sullivan slumped in their seats.

"As for you, Councilor Daimh," Rayne said, "I honestly believe it when I hear from others that you didn't know what was going on."

Daimh shook his head. "I didn't."

"To that end, I give you the chance to retire to your home district with your wife, never to return to the castle. Do you accept?"

Cocking his head slightly to one side, Daimh paused a moment, then asked, "Where would I live?"

"From what I understand, your mother is still alive and well, and is living in a nice house by a lake in Erd," Rayne said.

"But I was told she was sick and I couldn't see her," Daimh said.

Looking at Abrecan, Rayne said, "You were misinformed."

⟶✦⟵

Nursemaid Ophelia's heart leaped when she heard Oakleaf say, "I'm thirsty."

Smiling, she rushed to the bed where the young guardian lay. "Of that I'm sure. You've been asleep a long time."

Oakleaf had lost a great deal of weight and looked gaunt. This was the first time he had spoken since he had been injured. "How long? Did Barclay and Arlie—"

"Shhh. There is much to tell. Be assured that everything is fine, though. Everyone is safe and well."

Oakleaf let out a contented sigh. "That's good," he said, his voice cracking.

"You've had a lot of people checking on you," Ophelia said. "One particular young lady has been here every day for hours on end reading to you and talking to you."

His eyes lit up. "Arlie?"

The nursemaid nodded. "She should be here soon, if she follows her pattern. I'll let her fill you in on what you've missed."

❖❖❖

Sherwyn closed the door to his room in the castle for the last time. He was carrying a small satchel filled with the last of his meager possessions.

"You weren't going to leave without saying goodbye, were you, old friend?" asked a familiar voice from down the hallway.

The priest looked up and smiled as Anemone approached. "Of course not. I was actually on my way to see you."

"So, what did the church decide?" she asked.

He shrugged. "They were too merciful, in my eyes. They asked me to step down as the castle priest, but have offered me a chance to live out my days at the head monastery. It could have been much worse."

"Yes, it could have," Anemone said.

"And what of you?" Sherwyn asked.

The nursemaid smiled. "I, too, have been treated mercifully. They asked me to step down, and Ophelia has been promoted to head nursemaid. I'm allowed to stay in the castle as a nursemaid."

"I'm going to miss our talks," Sherwyn said. "You've been a good friend."

Anemone reached down and squeezed his hand. "And I always will be."

❖❖❖

Dougal looked at himself in the mirror and couldn't help but smile. King Rayne had asked him to be captain of the guardians not long after Captain Sullivan had been put into the dungeon. As the king had explained, Bariwon needed someone who remembered what it truly meant to be a guardian. Dougal had initially declined, concerned that all those years in the dungeon had made him physically weak, and he wasn't sure he would be able to fulfill the duties of a captain. But King Rayne had insisted, and Dougal had finally agreed.

He had just put on his captain's uniform. Although the man in the mirror looked old and weak, he smiled. The irony of the moment wasn't lost on Dougal. He had been thrown in the dungeon for wearing the captain's uniform, and here he was many years later wearing one again. Except this time, *he* was the one putting people in the dungeon.

❖❖❖

"Wut's wrong wit yous?" the crooked-nosed man asked Kelvin. "Can'tcha sees I'm still thinkin' here?"

Rayne's grandfather nodded. "By all means, I'm not trying to rush you. I was just reminding you it was your turn."

His opponent peered down at his cards, then reached down to grab one of the tarts from the table. Kelvin responded by pulling the tray out of reach. The man looked up, made an ugly face at Kelvin, and then looked down at his cards.

"I tell yous wut," he said. "If I wins this hand, I not only gets the coins on the table, but also the rest o' them tarts."

Kelvin folded his arms and looked skeptical. "Oh? And what do *I* get if I win?"

"I let yous walk out o' here unbroken," the man said threateningly.

Not intimidated, Kelvin unfolded his arms. "It's still your turn."

The man seemed to think for a moment. "Fine. I'm sure I got yous beat." He laid his cards down on the table.

Kelvin revealed his cards.

"Hah!" the man said, reaching out to gather up the coins, but paused when Kelvin pulled the tarts even further out of reach.

"That was a nice hand, Cameron," he said.

Cameron's eyes widened. He jumped to his feet, causing his chair to fly out from behind him and crash to the floor. "How do yous know my name?" he demanded, pulling out a knife he had hidden under his tunic.

Still seated, Kelvin said, "I've known for the last few days. I recognized you from when I was at the castle."

Pointing the knife at the older man, Cameron said, "Eh? If yous known who I wuz, why waits until now to say so?"

"I was waiting for them to arrive," Kelvin said, motioning toward the door of the tavern, where four royal guardians dressed in gold and blue walked in with their swords drawn.

CHAPTER 29

Nine Months Later

"The sun is playing hide-and-seek," Rayne mused.

Sunshine arched an eyebrow at her husband. "What's that?"

He pointed to the castle. From their viewpoint on the hill, the overcast sky had parted slightly, and clear light shone down on the blue-tiled, conical roofs of the towers.

"The sun is out, even though it's still raining," he said. "I'm told my mother made up that saying when she was younger."

Sunshine sighed a little and leaned back against the tree where they sat. "I would have liked to have met your mother. And I'm sure that our child would have liked to have met her as well." Sunshine patted the large curve of her stomach.

"You know—" Rayne placed a hand on his wife's belly "—we still haven't decided on a name."

"A name. Yes, I'm sure our child would like one of those."

Rayne kissed Sunshine on the cheek. "Every time I bring up the subject, you avoid it."

"Well ..." she said, "with me and my siblings, my father waited until after we were born to name us. He said he couldn't possibly know our name until he met us."

"Um," Rayne said carefully, "you realize that doesn't make a lot of sense, right?"

"Why not?" Sunshine asked. "After all—"

She stopped and scrunched her face.

"What is it, my dear?"

"I think it's best if we get back to the castle." She tried to stand up. "It appears we won't have to wait much longer to find out our child's name."

※

Rayne waited outside the door, pacing. Garth and Iolanthe sat holding hands on a bench and watched him walk back and forth.

"How long did you say this takes?" Rayne asked his parents-in-law.

"It will be over when the baby comes out," Garth said.

Iolanthe rolled her eyes. "You're not helping."

"But neither am I wrong," Garth pointed out.

"Perhaps you should go back and tend to the gardens, husband. After you turned down becoming a councilor, it was very nice of Rayne and Sunshine to ask you to become the castle gardener."

Garth nodded and went to stand up, but Iolanthe sighed and pulled him back down. "I was kidding, you wooden head. You wouldn't want to miss the birth of your first grandchild, would you?"

The door opened and Nursemaid Ophelia announced, "You may come in."

After taking a deep breath, Rayne walked in, followed closely by Garth and Iolanthe.

Sunshine lay propped up on a bed, looking worn out, with her dark hair sticking to her head. She was holding a child completely void of hair, but with dark eyes peering up at them.

"Well, hello, little one." Rayne approached carefully. When he reached the bed, he kissed Sunshine on her forehead and said, "She's beautiful. Or do I mean, he's handsome?"

"She's a she."

"Wonderful." Rayne gently took hold of one of the baby's tiny hands. "So, now that we've met, what's her name?"

Sunshine looked down at her baby and tilted her head to one side. "I... I'm not sure." She turned to her parents. "What should we name her, Dad?"

"It's obvious." Garth looked stunned that they even had to ask.

"Oh?" Rayne said. "Then would you be inclined as to tell us?"

Iolanthe quickly clasped her hand over her husband's mouth. He didn't push it away—he just moved his eyes to stare at his wife.

"Are you sure you want him to tell you?" Iolanthe asked.

Sunshine nodded. "I'm sure, Mom. So, Dad, what's your granddaughter's name?"

Iolanthe removed her hand, and Garth nodded out the window before answering.

"Rainbow," he said. "Her name is Rainbow."

Part 2

THE WAXING MOON

CHAPTER 30
Four Years Later

"The moon's going to be full soon," Creighton said, his voice echoing off the tunnel's walls. "Time's running out."

Kerr eyed his big brother. "Don't you worry. I'll get around to asking her."

"You better hurry," Creighton said. "She told me she was thinking about going to the Mortentaun with Keefe."

"That's not what I heard." Kerr laughed and then swung his pick into the rock wall in front of him.

Creighton leaned on his shovel. "Maybe she just didn't want to hurt your feelings, little brother."

"Now I know you aren't telling the truth." Kerr lifted his pick for another swing. "Since when hasn't she spoken her mind?"

Creighton smiled sheepishly. "Ah, you got me there. All right, so she said you're a looker. Aside from Keefe, you don't have much competition in this town."

"And I'll have even less if we can find a vein of silver." Kerr swung his pick again, driving it into the reddish rocks and bringing another shower of fragments.

The older of the two men wiped his brow. "Good thing King Rayne will let us keep what we find, at least a good portion. I still get burned up about what happened when father found that vein years ago. Abrecan took every last bit of it."

"Yeah, I'm not sad to see Abrecan gone. It's been what, four years now? I just wish we'd find something, anything, we can sell soon."

Creighton moved closer. He shoveled up loose rocks and dumped them into the wheelbarrow several paces behind them. "I know we've been at this for months, but we'll find something. I'm also thinking we'll have to put up another buttress soon."

Kerr nodded. "Aye, though this tunnel has held up well thus far. You know, I had a feeling when I woke up, like something was going to happen today."

"Was it a good feeling at least?" Creighton asked, putting another shovel full of rocks into the wheelbarrow.

"Yeah, it was a good feeling."

Kerr hefted the pick again. This time when the pick hit, it pierced the rock in front of him and stuck. He tried to pull it out, but it wouldn't budge.

"What's this then?" Creighton asked as he walked to stand next to his brother.

Kerr put a foot against the rock, spit into both palms, and grabbed hold of the pick again. "It's stuck, but not like I've seen before."

Creighton took hold of the pick as well, and they both pulled. At first nothing happened. Then suddenly the pick came free, but not until a section of rock came with it. The action caused several of the weaker stones above it to collapse, sending up a wash of dust that momentarily blinded the brothers.

"Are you hurt?" Creighton asked, coughing through the dust.

Kerr waved a hand in front of him. "Nah, just landed on my backside. You think we ought to clear out?"

"Not yet," Creighton said, moving forward. "It was just a small collapse."

Kerr came up next to him. The dust had cleared enough that the brothers could see. "Look there, that rock I pulled out—it's almost perfectly square."

Creighton wasn't looking at the rock, but at the area the collapse had cleared.

"That's because it's a brick, not a rock."

Kerr made a grunting sound. "A brick? What makes you think…" He looked up. Before them was a section of wall made up of similarly sized bricks, each one roughly the size of a large dog.

"What's a wall doing this far into the mountain?" Kerr asked.

Creighton took several steps back, grabbed a torch, and lit it from one of the lamps they used to illuminate the tunnel. "Let's take a look." He moved back to the wall and put the torch through the hole created by the brick they had removed.

"You think it's safe? What if it collapses on you?" Kerr asked as he grabbed his big brother's arm.

Creighton shook his arm free. "I have to see what's beyond this."

The hole was just large enough that Creighton could poke his head and shoulders through. Kerr waited anxiously, examining the rocks above to see if he could spot any cracks forming. The moments stretched on, and finally he tugged on his brother's shirt. Creighton pulled back from the hole and whistled as if in awe.

"What?"

"Beyond this wall is a large tunnel, four or five spans across," Creighton explained. "It goes on as far as I could see."

Kerr's eyes flicked back and forth between his brother and the hole. "Did you see any silver?"

"Nah, but that isn't what has me wondering."

"Wondering what?"

Creighton didn't respond at first. He focused on the opening, holding the torch between himself and their discovery, almost as if he was using the torch to defend himself.

"The cave in there is manmade. The floor, walls, and roof are all flat. They used thick stone columns as buttresses. Someone spent a lot of time and effort building it to last."

Kerr took a step back. "Where could it go? Nothing is beyond the northern mountains. They're impassable."

"Maybe that's why they built the tunnel—to find a way to get through the mountains, to find new lands."

Kerr rubbed his chin in thought before he spoke again. "If that's the case, then why brick it up? And how did it get this far into the mountain?"

"Well," Creighton said, looking up, "I'm betting we've been digging through a part of the mountain that was created by a landslide years ago. That's why we've made such quick progress. As for why they bricked it up…"

"Yes?" Kerr prompted.

"One would only brick up something like this for two reasons." Creighton grimaced. "To keep people from going in…or to keep something from coming out."

CHAPTER 31

It was something that had never been done before, and dwelling on such thoughts could keep it from happening this year. At least that's what Oakleaf kept trying to tell Snapdragon.

The two of them stood on the edge of a large circle, surrounded by thousands of people cheering Snapdragon's name. It all came down to this, the last event of the Mortentaun. Snapdragon had won every event up to this point, and he was only one win away from achieving what many thought was impossible: a perfect score.

However, Snapdragon didn't think it was impossible. That would mean accepting weakness and failure as an option—something he refused to do. He hadn't trained every possible moment with the finest guardians in Bariwon so that he could fail. He'd had more than his fair share of criticism from people saying he was bound to do well because as royalty he had an unfair advantage. Granted, he had trained with people who knew how to win, but in running the racing events, or throwing the heavy rock, or even shooting with the bow and arrow, he was out there by himself.

Alone.

Even now, as he prepared himself to compete against his final opponent, he saw some jeering faces among the cheering crowd. Well, he would show them.

He walked into the center of the circle, side by side with his opponent. Snapdragon looked up at the stands. His mother and father, also King Rayne, Queen Sunshine, and Princess Rainbow were all on their feet cheering. Snapdragon didn't believe for a moment that his four-year-old niece Rainbow understood what was happening, or how significant this situation was, but it was nice to see her enthusiasm.

After arriving in the center of the circle, the officiator who had been waiting for the contestants smiled and said, "Congratulations, you two, on making it to the finals. You both know the rules, so no point going over them again."

Snapdragon chanted the mantra in his head that he had used thus far—*Knock down, knock out, or knock around.* It helped him block out the crowd and stay focused on the task. He would win if he could knock his opponent off his feet, knock him out of the circle, or knock him around enough that his opponent yielded.

"Are you ready?" the officiator asked.

Snapdragon sized up his opponent one last time. He stood just a bit shorter than Snapdragon and was much thinner, and he had a goofy grin than never seemed to leave his face. Where Snapdragon had won his events by out-muscling his competition, the other man had won with speed and tactics. Snapdragon turned to the officiator and nodded.

After getting a nod from the other man, the officiator raised one hand in the air, paused for a moment, and then brought it down swiftly.

Snapdragon spun and ran to where his weapons were laid out. He had only a moment to choose one. The randomly selected weapons included a long staff, a two-handed wooden sword, and a large wooden mace. He grabbed the mace. Its leather-bound handle was attached to a larger block of wood, giving the weapon a good bit of weight.

He turned to see that his opponent had selected a staff. This didn't surprise Snapdragon, especially since King Rayne had successfully used a staff when he competed in the Mortentaun a few years ago. That event had become legendary and had made the staff a more fashionable weapon for guardians recently. Snapdragon figured the other man would select the staff, which was the reason he countered with the mace. He walked slowly but steadily back toward the center of the circle.

When they were within striking distance, the other man grabbed the staff at one end with both hands and swung it toward Snapdragon. Snapdragon jumped back out of the way, demonstrating remarkable agility for someone of his muscular build.

His opponent swung again, causing Snapdragon to jump back again. It was a good tactic—trying to get him to jump back out of the circle, and one that Snapdragon had expected.

Seeming to gain confidence, the other man grinned even wider and swung a third time, but this time Snapdragon reacted differently. He stepped forward and took the staff hard in his right side, just below his armpit. Though the blow was strong, the staff didn't pack much of a punch and Snapdragon was able to pin the staff between his body and right arm. He grabbed the staff with his right hand and then, hefting the club with his left, he swung down hard and broke the staff in two.

Snapdragon's opponent stepped back and stared at the broken staff.

Pointing his weapon at the man in front of him, Snapdragon said, "I suggest you yield."

⊰⊹⊱

The main hall was decorated elegantly in soft gold and blue tones for the meal that followed the completion of the Mortentaun. Governors from each district were in attendance, as were all the members of the royalty, most of the royal guardians, and the newly selected regional guardians.

King Rayne stood up from his place at the head of the main table, and the crowd fell silent. "What a wonderful Mortentaun this has been," he said. "Let me state once again how proud I am of my wife's brother Snapdragon. I have seen him work very hard and had no doubt he would do well this year, but to be the first person to post a perfect score has made this Mortentaun something special."

The crowd cheered and Snapdragon stood and took a bow, inspiring even more cheers.

Rayne waited patiently for the crowd to quiet before he spoke again. "I would also like to thank the servants for the wonderful feast they prepared to celebrate the closing of the Mortentaun."

Again, more applause from the crowd as the servants who lined the wall bowed appreciatively.

"Though announcements are usually done in court, I would like to take this moment to make one," the king said. "The last few years have been the most prosperous Bariwon has seen in many generations. Trade is flowing between districts, theft is down significantly, and there is a general sense of cooperation among the people of the land. All this is due in no small part to the work of one man—Captain Dougal."

The captain of the guardians tipped his head in acknowledgement.

Rayne motioned to the elderly man. "Captain Dougal has done a remarkable job teaching and inspiring both the regional and royal guardians to fill their positions with the best intentions. Gone are the guardians that would use their positions for personal gain. And Dougal has done this all despite being wrongfully imprisoned for over twenty years. He has reestablished what it means to be a true guardian."

The crowd then cheered for Dougal, though the attention seemed to embarrass him.

"Therefore," the king continued, "it is my sad duty to announce that Dougal is leaving our service. His time in the dungeon has taken its toll, and it is our wish that he spend the rest of his life in comfort. And so, it is my pleasure to announce that Fallon has been selected to be the next captain of the guardians."

Fallon, a solidly built man with a broad chest and a thick, bushy mustache, stood at the king's prompting. His steely blue eyes scanned the crowd, seemingly taking in every detail.

"But enough with the business of the kingdom for now." Rayne smiled. "Let us enjoy the rest of the evening."

In the corner of the main hall, musicians started playing a happy melody as the crowd resumed eating and talking.

"I can't tell you how proud I am of you, Son," Iolanthe said to Snapdragon, who was seated across from her. "Isn't that right, dear?" she asked, elbowing Garth in the ribs.

Garth turned his head from watching the musicians. "Yes, your mother is very proud."

"And?" Iolanthe elbowed her husband again.

Garth looked searchingly at his son. "Snap, you've worked hard for many years to get to this point. Now that you're done, are you happy?"

Snapdragon furrowed his brow and paused before responding. "I don't think that I *am* done, Dad. I think this is just another marker along the way."

The elderly gardener nodded. "Then I'm proud of you as well."

"Hey, I'm proud too!" Rainbow said, her four-year-old voice a little louder than her parents might have preferred. "And look what I can do!"

She closed her eyes and with her left hand reached up and touched her nose with her index finger. "Tada!"

The people around her laughed and clapped appreciatively at the trick, to which Rainbow responded by saying, "Thank you, thank you," and then took a little bow.

"You taught her that trick, didn't you?" Queen Sunshine asked her other brother.

Oakleaf nodded. "Aye. She's a sharp one."

"Thank you for the compliment," King Rayne said. "She's almost a bit too smart for her own good. You've been a big help raising her, Leafy, and I'm sure you'll do a fine job with your own son."

Arlie, holding her and Oakleaf's newborn son, said, "He's already been a great father to our little Rowan."

"Speaking of family," Iolanthe said, "it's a shame your grandparents aren't here, Rayne."

His cheery expression clouded a bit. "I hear my grandfather hasn't fully recovered from the illness he caught this past winter. I wish they would have agreed to move to the castle once I became king, but they said they were happy with their home and friends back in Lebu." Rayne shook his head, then turned back to Snapdragon. "So, Snap, are you ready for your training as a royal guardian?"

"I am," he said confidently.

Sunshine appeared a bit surprised. "Oh? Aren't we a bit cocky, eh, little brother?"

"Not cocky," he responded, sounding defensive. "I'm just confident I can handle whatever Captain Fallon throws my way."

⊰≹⊱

Melanie walked carefully down the dungeon stairs. The stone steps could be slippery if they were wet, which happened when the rain was heavy enough that it seeped inside. Thankfully, today was not one of those days. Still, it was difficult work, especially when carrying a tray full of food for the prisoners. Upon reaching the dungeon entrance, she was stopped by a couple of guardians.

"Hello there, Melanie," one of them said. He was a happy fellow by the name of Asher. He had always treated her nicely, despite the fact that most servants were ignored while under Abrecan's reign. That had changed when Rayne became king—he had made sure everyone was treated with respect. While most of the people in the castle embraced this, there were those who struggled with it, like Asher's companion for the day. Stuart was a grizzled old veteran who had been a royal guardian for more than eighteen years. He seemed to have a permanent scowl on his face, and the servants joked that the reason he served as a royal guardian for so long was because no woman in her right mind would want to marry him.

"Royal Guardian Asher, Royal Guardian Stuart," Melanie said in greeting.

274

Asher stepped forward. "All right then, let's see what's on the menu today."

Melanie went to lift the lid covering the tray when Stuart spoke up. "Can'tcha just let one of these servants through without harassing them?"

"You know the instructions from the king. Everything that comes in and out of the dungeon needs to be inspected," Asher responded.

"It's all right, Royal Guardian Stuart, he's just doing his job," Melanie said and then lifted the lid.

Stuart grumbled something under his breath while Asher looked through the meals.

"Everything looks to be in order," Asher said. He moved to unlock the main dungeon door. "Remember, no talking to the prisoners. Also, report anything they say to you."

"Saints!" Stuart said, then sat down on his chair with a huff. "You don't have to tell them every time they bring stuff here."

With a patient smile, Asher said, "Yes, I do. You know that."

"I don't mind," Melanie said, setting the lid back on the large tray. "We all have our duties to uphold."

Asher opened the door and motioned for Melanie to go in. "Well said."

Melanie nodded to the guardian as she passed him and entered the dungeon. The way was lit by evenly spaced sconces, but even if it hadn't been, she knew her way quite well. She heard the door close and lock behind her. There were moans and shouts from prisoners when they heard her go by. She had learned to ignore them over the years. She was there to feed certain prisoners, men in the far end of the dungeon.

Upon reaching her destination, she set the tray down by the small access panel at the bottom of the door. She knocked on the door twice, waited a beat, and then knocked three more times before opening the panel.

"Ah, Melanie," a voice said from inside the cell. "It's been a while since you have fed me."

Melanie absently pushed a lock of her black hair behind her ear. "It couldn't be helped. They randomly assign us our chores for the day."

"I don't blame *you,*" the voice responded smoothly. "I truly appreciate what you do for me."

Melanie felt her cheeks grow warm. "I do what I can."

"So tell me, were you able to receive a message from our mutual friends?" the voice asked.

She lifted the lid of the tray, then picked up one of the meals and handed it through the access panel. "I did hear back from them, yes."

"And what did they say, my dear?"

Melanie smiled. "The exact message was, 'Our forces are gathered and are ready. What are your orders, Abrecan?'"

⭑⚽⭑

The scream made both Snapdragon and Blythe turn their heads.

"This way," Snapdragon said. He started to head down one of the paths between the rows of tall shrubbery.

Blythe grabbed his friend's arm. "Don't think so. Think that came more from the left." His normally cheery face was lined with concern.

"Trust me," Snapdragon responded. "My father made this maze and I've spent a lot of time here. The left path looks to be the fastest way there, but it isn't. We go right."

Blythe shook his head. "Not so sure."

"Fine. You go left and I'll go right," Snapdragon said, feeling frustrated.

"Nah. Not supposed to split up."

Snapdragon drew his sword. "I'm not waiting." He started running down the path to the right.

Leaves from the thick bushes brushed against Snapdragon's wide shoulders as he ran. He took corners sharply until he was nearly where he thought the scream originated. Ahead was a little clearing in the maze where a tall tree grew in the center. The clearing had no other exits. He came to a stop just before the last corner. He took a deep breath and peeked around the edge of the shrubbery into the clearing.

Captain Fallon stood with his back to the tree. He had one arm around the waist of a young woman while holding a knife to her neck with his other arm. She had fiery red hair and a splash of freckles across her nose. Her clear green eyes held a look of defiance, despite the fact that she was being held at knifepoint. Snapdragon had seen the redhead around the castle wearing the gray cloaks worn by nursemaids.

Snapdragon wasn't sure if Fallon had seen him or not, but either way, he decided a bold approach was best. He stepped out from around the corner and pointed his sword directly at the captain of the guard, who was still a dozen paces away. "There's no place for you to run. Let the girl go."

"I think you've misjudged the situation," Fallon said, a false smile playing under his thick mustache.

Snapdragon took a few steps forward. "I don't think so. If you hurt the girl, you will suffer a very slow and painful death. Let her go right now, and I'll make sure you aren't hurt on the way to the dungeon."

Fallon's smile grew larger. "Nice try."

"I'll show you a—"

Snapdragon's response was cut short when he felt a hard blow to the back of his head. He felt his knees start to buckle and fought to stay conscious, but lost that battle and fell face first on the ground before him.

⊰╫⊱

Opening his eyes took as much effort as Snapdragon could summon. Four blurry objects hovered over him in front of a deep blue background. The objects slowly came into focus to create the faces of Fallon, Blythe, the redheaded young woman, and another new guardian Snapdragon had met but couldn't remember his name.

"Help him up," Fallon instructed.

The other two guardians grabbed Snapdragon by the arms and brought him over to the large tree in the center of the clearing. As he sat up against it, Snapdragon started to speak, but was interrupted by Fallon.

"Let's see, what did we learn today?" Fallon asked. He held up a hand and pointed to his index finger. "Well, first off, you showed up without your companion. I've told you to stick together no matter what. The two of you together are much stronger than the two of you apart."

He pointed to his next finger. "Second, you didn't make sure the rest of the area was clear before you came in. Your attacker was right up against the wall as you strode in."

"Third, did you consider that my orders were to kill the woman, regardless of whether or not I lived? People will die for what they believe in." Fallon pointed to a third finger.

Snapdragon shook his head. "It wasn't fair. You tricked me. Things were not as they appeared."

"Oh?" Fallon knuckled his mustache. "How so?"

Snapdragon tried to sit up straighter. "You told me the trial would involve you and a hostage. There was no talk of you having help. Also, you picked an especially beautiful girl to hold hostage. You wanted me to be distracted by her."

Fallon laughed. "Yes, she is quite pretty. I've found Seraphina to be very useful in tests like these. New guardians tend to do stupid things around pretty ladies."

Seraphina smirked and curtsied.

"As for things not being as they appear, that's often the case," Fallon said, this time without any humor. "That is what I want you to learn. But just as that can be an obstacle to you, you can also use it to your advantage.

I want you to think about that." Fallon's smile returned. "Granted, with the blow you took to the head, thinking may be a bit of a strain for you. Go back to the castle." With that, Fallon turned and headed out of the clearing.

Seraphina stood over Snapdragon, considering him for a moment. "By the way, I'm not a girl. I'm a woman. I'd remember that if I were you."

⇥✠⇤

"Yeah, that's quite the nice goose egg you have there, Brother," Oakleaf said while inspecting the back of Snapdragon's head. "Let me go get you something for it."

Oakleaf reached for his crutch and started to hobble toward the door. Snapdragon had grown used to seeing his older brother with the crutch over the years, but it was still a sad reminder that his brother would never walk without it.

"No, it's fine," Snapdragon said. "I want to feel the pain and let it remind me of how I failed."

Oakleaf looked back over his shoulder. "Failed? You?"

"Now don't make it worse by teasing me," Snapdragon said more tersely than he intended. "It's bad enough that I messed up my first training exercise. I don't need you rubbing it in."

Oakleaf turned around and hobbled back to the bed where his brother rested. He sat down on the edge and punched Snapdragon in the shoulder. "There was a time when all you did was tease me. That's what brothers do. But ever since I was injured, you've been overly nice to me. Snap, I'm still your brother. That hasn't changed."

"Sure it has," Snapdragon turned his head so he was looking at the wall. "You're a hero. Everyone knows you for what you did. If it wasn't for you, Rayne would have never become king. Innocent people would have died, and the kingdom would be under the rule of one of Abrecan's minions. You aren't my brother. You're a legend."

"A legend?" Oakleaf scoffed. "Does a legend need a stick of wood to be able to get around? Does a legend have to retire from being a guardian because he can no longer support himself with his own two legs? Snap, I'm still me. I'm still your brother. Sure, things have turned out differently than I thought they would be, but I'm happy. I have a beautiful wife and a wonderful baby boy."

Snapdragon didn't try to hide the bitterness in his voice. "Yes, everyone admires you and adores you for what you've done and sacrificed. Some of us have to work for our successes."

"Ah." Oakleaf rolled his eyes. "That's what this is about. Snap, you don't have anything to prove to anyone."

"Easy for you to say. Keep in mind I have a sister who is queen and a brother who is a legend."

Oakleaf sighed. "Again with the 'legend' talk. Listen, you didn't fail today. You learned. If you got nothing else from what I taught you while you were preparing for the Mortentaun, I hoped you'd at least understand that we learn more from our mistakes than from our successes. Don't be afraid to fail—but learn when you do."

"Just leave me alone," Snapdragon said. He rolled onto his side with his back to his brother.

"Fine, if that's what you wish," Oakleaf responded. "Just remember that tomorrow, court is being held and you are expected to attend. Pull yourself together by then."

⊰⊱

The field to the southwest of Erd Proper was often used for training young men intent on participating in the Mortentaun. Combat skills were honed, battle tactics drilled over and over, and older, retired guardians worked with the younger men on all the other aspects of being a guardian. It was the perfect place for Eadward to gather his forces—no one would question what all the armed men were doing.

After it was discovered that many of the items he had offered in the Shoginoc were from the castle, he claimed ignorance and resigned in shame as governor. Eadward then slinked back to Erd, accepting the fact that his attempt at glory had failed. He had been sitting in a dark corner of a pub, drinking away his sorrows, when a man dressed in a hooded cloak had sat down next to him.

The man offered Eadward a chance at redemption, something the former governor didn't think was possible. He was understandably doubtful of the offer until the man removed his hood to reveal that he was Crescens, the assistant magistrate of Erd.

That meeting had happened three years ago. It had taken that long to find men he could trust, and to recruit even more. But he finally felt he had the numbers he needed to take back the castle for Abrecan.

Eadward walked back and forth in front of the men on the field, who stood at attention as he spoke. "Many of you served with me in the castle when I was a royal guardian. Others of you served under me while I was governor of both Erd and Lewyol. The rest of you know me by my well-earned reputation. The time is soon at hand. I am a man of my word— and I *will* see that Abrecan is freed."

The men cheered as one.

CHAPTER 32

C rescens licked his fingertips and then used them to slick down his dark hair. He inspected his outfit, making sure the silver-embroidered, deep red tunic and matching leggings were clean and wrinkle free. He put on his best smile and entered the magistrate's room.

Selene didn't look up from her desk upon his arrival, which gave Crescens a moment to admire her. She had a properly sharp nose and high cheekbones. Her full lips rarely smiled, but when they did, the action caused his pulse to race—not that he would let it show, of course. As assistant magistrate of Erd, it was his responsibility to carry out the magistrate's orders, not to fawn over her like a puppy dog.

He closed the door behind him and took three purposeful steps toward her desk—just far enough to be respectful, yet close enough that he could address her properly.

Selene spent several more seconds reading the document in front of her before she looked up. "Report."

"Yes, Magistrate." Crescens bowed. "The message was sent to Abrecan through our trusted channels. We aren't certain how long it will take to get a response. They continue to randomly rotate the servant's duties in the castle. But between Melanie and Ciar, he should get it soon and then we'll get his confirmation."

Selene stood and walked to the window. She looked down on the town of Erd, which surrounded the governor's palace. Placing her hands behind her back, she asked, "And Governor Wardell is none the wiser?"

"No." Crescens shook his head for emphasis. "The king's puppet is unaware of the forces we're gathering."

The magistrate looked up from the town toward the northern mountains. "It's almost time," she said softly.

-⇥✦⇤-

Snapdragon stood side by side with the other new royal guardians, and tried not to stare in Seraphina's direction. The stunning redhead sat with the other nursemaids, smiling and looking up at King Rayne as he welcomed everyone to court.

Snapdragon tried to listen to his words, but he couldn't keep his eyes off Seraphina. This was something Oakleaf had warned him about. Royal guardians were not allowed to marry while in service, though the regional ones were. When Snapdragon asked why some guardians could and others couldn't, Oakleaf shrugged and said that was the way it was—and that royal guardians needed to be careful about falling in love.

King Rayne's father, Rinan, was a tragic example of two people falling in love—in their case a royal guardian and the princess—and what happened when they tried to keep it secret.

Despite the history and the warnings from others, Snapdragon was enthralled with the young nursemaid. He had asked around and found out she was a couple of years his elder and had been a nursemaid for the last several years. Granted, she was still in training, but she was considered a nursemaid nonetheless.

"The first item on the agenda for today," King Rayne stated, "is a surprise from our royal crafter, Grant."

A rather large man with massive arms stood and bowed to the king. "Thank you, Your Majesty," the royal crafter said in a rich, full voice. "As you know, by order of the king, the main hall was renovated over the past few years. Gone are the large, intimidating features that Abrecan had put into place."

Snapdragon looked around the spacious hall and noticed that the changes made it feel welcoming and even cozy.

"My apprentice, Bearach, has a knack for mechanics," said Grant, motioning to a similarly built younger man sitting next to him. "While we rebuilt the front doors to the hall, the floor was also being replaced. Bearach came up with an idea and we built it."

King Rayne smiled. "Oh, yes? And what did you do, Bearach?"

The crafter's apprentice stood. "With your permission, Your Majesty, may we open the front doors to the main hall?"

"But of course," the king said, appearing more curious by the moment.

Bearach motioned to the guardians standing by the doors. The doors opened smoothly and silently at first, but it seemed the guardians had to push with a bit more effort to open the doors wider. When the doors reached the walls that ran along both sides of the entranceway, there was an audible *clank*. The guardians looked at each other in surprise when the doors remained solidly in place.

"Thank you," Bearach called to the guardians and then turned back to the king. "Now, if you would, Your Majesty, please have a seat on your throne."

Rayne nodded and then smiled at Queen Sunshine, who was already seated in her throne next to the king's.

Once Rayne sat down, Bearach said, "If you will please reach under the right armrest, you will feel a handle of sorts. It has been bound with leather. Hold it and pull it down toward the floor, if you would."

The king nodded and reached under the armrest. He appeared to find the handle easily enough, and with a little effort he was able to pull the handle down. The recently opened doors to the main hall closed by themselves, and many observers gasped.

"Magic!" someone shouted. Others echoed the statement.

Bearach held his hands up as if to calm the crowd. "It's not magic! We know there is no such thing. Mechanics—I used mechanics!"

King Rayne stood. "Please, everyone, please."

The crowd quieted almost immediately.

"Bearach, that was quite amazing," Rayne said. "Would you please tell us how you did that?"

Bearach beamed. "Well, without going into too much detail, each door is attached to a curved metal bar that is somewhat flexible. If you look at the top of the doors, you can see them."

Rayne squinted at the doors and nodded.

"Imagine the metal is like a bow string," Bearach said. "When the doors are opened, it's like pulling back on the string. Once the doors reach the wall, there are hooks that latch into metal hoops at the top of the door. The hooks are on a hinge which lifts up and goes into the hoops when the doors are opened all the way."

Pointing to the handle on the throne, Bearach said, "The handle is attached to a thin but durable chain that runs under the stone floor and up the walls. It gets a bit tricky here to explain, but it's enough to say that moving the handle lowers the hoops, releasing the hooks and thus allowing the doors to close."

Queen Sunshine spoke up. "Bearach, that is brilliant! Where did you get such an idea?"

The crafter's apprentice bowed before he responded. "I took elements from different things I've seen and… well, I put them together."

"You are to be commended, Bearach," Rayne said. "The ability to look at different objects and find a new, creative use is something I would encourage more people to do—with one thing in mind."

Grant stepped next to Bearach and asked, "What would that be, Your Majesty?"

"Let me answer that by asking Bearach a question," Rayne responded. "Tell me, why did you make it so I could close the doors from my throne?"

The young crafter glanced at Grant before he said anything. Grant nodded in encouragement.

"Um, well, I thought you would like to be able to do that." Bearach seemed to have lost his confidence. "You could use it to impress visitors."

Rayne rubbed his chin while listening. "Yes, I could do that. Do you think it may also inspire fear in them, as it did to several folks here?"

"Perhaps," Bearach said, appearing even more uncomfortable, "if that was your intention."

Rayne smiled. "Please do not feel that I am discounting your work. It is amazing. But tell me, why were we making the changes to the hall in the first place?"

Bearach's eyes grew wide and he didn't answer.

"Rayne, just tell him your point," Sunshine said in a playfully chastising tone.

The king nodded. "Abrecan made great efforts to inspire fear in those around him. Fear as a leadership tool can be effective, at least in the short term. I've been taught and have seen firsthand that people are led better by inspiration, rather than intimidation."

The king motioned to the hall around him. "I wanted this hall to be a place where people felt at ease. I wanted them to be able to talk and learn without being distracted by the flaunting of power that Abrecan brought to this castle."

"Your invention is brilliant, as we've stated," Sunshine interjected. "And perhaps next time you'll spend less time deciding if it *could* be built and more time deciding if it *should* be built."

Looking crestfallen, Bearach bowed again. "Of course. I will heed these words of wisdom."

Snapdragon carefully considered his sister and her husband after Bearach had sat down and they had moved onto the next matter on the court's agenda. Snapdragon wasn't sure he fully agreed with their opinions. Why not do something if it could make life easier? He pondered this thought throughout the rest of the afternoon.

⇥✦⇤

Ciar frowned at Melanie. "Are you sure?" he whispered.

His fellow servant nodded and then took him by the arm and led him to one of the guest rooms in the castle.

"Safer to talk here," she said quietly. "We've come too far to fail now. We need to be more discreet."

He glared down at her. "But are you sure that's what Abrecan said? We can't risk it. The timing has to be perfect."

Melanie matched his glare. "I know. You don't have to keep reminding me. Abrecan said for us to wait just a little bit longer. I don't know why. I thought he would be anxious to get out of the dungeon."

Ciar blew out a long breath and started to pace. "For over four years we've had to keep up this charade. Abrecan would go insane if we told him of all the changes Rayne has made. The sooner Abrecan is freed and the castle is back in his hands, the better."

"I've had more of a reason to miss him than you have," Melanie said bitterly. "No one understands him like I do. He has told me that himself. Not his estranged wife, not his idiot of a son, not even that failure, Caldre."

"Has he told of his plans for Caldre once they're freed?" Ciar asked. "He wouldn't tell me."

Melanie shook her head. "He's not told me, but I'll bet that's something Abrecan has spent much of his time planning—how to respond to Caldre's mistakes. Let's make sure we are successful in our portion of this plan. Whatever Abrecan is planning for Caldre, I'm sure it will be painful."

⇥✦⇤

"All right then," Captain Fallon said. He stood in front of the new royal guardians. "Today is going to be a different type of training. You've all shown me you are able to handle yourselves physically, but let's see if there is anything rattling around in those heads of yours."

Snapdragon groaned inwardly. He was a royal guardian, not some savant! He had trained in all manners of combat. Why must the captain insist on these mind games?

Fallon started to pace back and forth in front of the new guardians. "I'm guessing some of you may feel this to be a waste of time. You're men of action, right?"

A chill ran down Snapdragon's back. It was as if the captain was reading his mind.

"Well, even the strongest foe can be defeated by good tactics and smart thinking. Remember that."

He stopped to face them and smoothed his mustache. "You are all to return to your quarters. You'll each find a set of clothing provided for you. You are to change into this clothing with special attention to make sure people won't see you as guardians. I want you to do whatever you can to behave the way you are dressed. Act the part. Return here within the hour."

This is getting better and better, Snapdragon thought sarcastically as he headed back to his room. Blythe walked alongside him, his usual lopsided grin on his face.

"Wonder why he's having us change out of our uniforms," Blythe mused. "Gotta be something undercover. Should be fun!"

Snapdragon harrumphed. "Why test us in the Mortentaun on our physical prowess if we are expected to think like savants?"

"Don't know about that," Blythe said. "The combat events used lots of strategy. Supposed to use our heads, right?"

Snapdragon harrumphed again.

Upon reaching their room, Blythe was delighted to find a merchant's outfit laid out for him, complete with a highly embroidered coat.

The farmer's clothes set out for Snapdragon looked like they had been dragged through the mud. The breeches and tunic were threadbare, and the straw hat appeared to have housed birds at one point.

Blythe laughed when Snapdragon finished putting on the farmer's clothes. "Looks like you got into a wrestling match with a pig and lost. Well, almost. Ah! Here we go."

Previously unnoticed on the side of Snapdragon's bed was a small bucket that appeared to be full of mud. Blythe lifted the bucket and handed it to his roommate.

"You've got to be kidding," Snapdragon said.

Blythe's smile grew even bigger. "Heard the captain, didn't you?"

⊰✛⊱

Snapdragon tried to avoid people's stares as he walked from his room back to where Captain Fallon was waiting by the castle's front gates. Servants, nursemaids, savants and even a member of the Hierarchy of Magistrates gaped when he walked by, but he tried to pay them no mind. The outfit was bad enough, but the dried mud on his hands and face made Snapdragon even more embarrassed.

In contrast, Blythe was strutting like a peacock, smiling and waving at everyone he saw. By the time they finally reached the front gates, Snapdragon was in a foul mood.

"Very good," Fallon said upon seeing them. "Guardian Blythe, you look very much the merchant—all puffed up and full of himself. And you, Guardian Snapdragon, it appears you've just walked off the farm after a long morning's work."

Fallon reached into a satchel hung over one shoulder, pulled out a bag of coins, and handed them to Blythe. Then he addressed both Blythe and Snapdragon. "Though the competition is over, the Mortentaun festival is still in full swing and will be for another week. You'll find all sorts of activities going on, some of which are against the law. Your task is to find anyone that is trying to take advantage of the people, or perhaps you will catch a cutpurse or two. Remember to act like you are dressed. The sharper criminals will spot you as a guardian if you carry yourself like one."

Blythe and Snapdragon nodded.

"Guardian Blythe, go ahead. Return at nightfall and report." Blythe saluted sharply and headed toward the castle gate.

"As for you, Guardian Snapdragon," Fallon said, a hint of a smile playing across his lips. "You'll have a bit of a different approach. After all, a farmer would most likely attend the festival for one of two reasons. First, to look for a wife, or second, because his wife nagged him into taking her. In your case, it'll be the second of the two."

"Sir?"

Fallon looked beyond Snapdragon. "Ah, here she comes now."

Snapdragon looked over his shoulder. His jaw dropped when he saw Seraphina walking toward them, dressed in farmer's attire.

When she reached Snapdragon, she took him by the arm and asked, "Are you ready to go, sweetie?"

⊰✛⊱

"You need to relax," Seraphina said. "After all, you're supposed to be a farmer taking his beautiful bride to the festival."

Quite aware of her arm hooked around his as they approached the festival, Snapdragon said, "Well, Captain Fallon said as a farmer I would only be taking my wife to the festival because she nagged me to go."

Seraphina laughed. "Fallon said that, did he? That old stick-in-the-mud. Are you saying that a farmer might not actually enjoy spending time with his wife?"

"I... well, er, I—" Snapdragon stammered.

"Let's pretend instead that we are madly in love and that you want to impress your wife by showing her a good time at the festival." Seraphina patted Snapdragon on the arm. "Please try to relax."

Snapdragon took a deep breath, held it for a moment, and then exhaled. "All right, I'm relaxed."

"Ha! You are not," Seraphina chided. "What's making you so tense? I watched you in the Mortentaun. You looked more relaxed then, even when you were about to face someone in combat."

"Yeah, but those were all men I was facing," Snapdragon said, not really meaning to vocalize it.

Seraphina stopped and faced him. He felt his knees weaken as he looked into her big green eyes. "Now you listen to me, Snapdragon," she said. "You can't go all goofy every time you are around a woman. I'm betting Fallon knows this, and *that* is why he picked me to go with you. Aside from trying to help you, sending me with you sounds like his sense of humor." She turned back to the road leading to the festival and they continued walking.

"You've known Fallon for a while then, eh?" Snapdragon asked, trying to change the subject. "Are you and he...?"

Seraphina laughed again. It was one of the most beautiful sounds Snapdragon had ever heard. "There you go being goofy again. Fallon is like, well, I would say like an uncle to me. Let me explain. My mother died when I was very young. My father died when I was ten."

"I'm so very sorry," Snapdragon said softly. "I didn't know."

"It was a long time ago, but thank you for your concern," Seraphina responded. "Anyway, after my father died, I was taken in by one of the local nursemaids here in town. When I was sixteen, she arranged it so I could study in the castle with other nursemaids. Now normally you need to be eighteen, but she said I was ready and Abrecan was more than willing to have me in the castle."

Snapdragon felt her shudder when she said the former councilor's name.

"So, I've been in the castle as a nursemaid for the last six years," she said. "Let me tell you, there's been such a difference since your sister's husband took over. He's a very good king. And your sister is simply wonderful."

Snapdragon sighed. "Yes, they are well loved and respected by everyone."

Seraphina looked at Snapdragon inquisitively, but then appeared to decide it was best not to ask. Instead she continued, "I met Fallon when I first came to the castle. He's an honorable man and very dedicated to being a guardian. I wasn't surprised at all when he was made captain. He looked out for me while Abrecan was still in power. He's that way. He looks out for everyone."

"At times I feel like he's singling me out," Snapdragon said. "It's as if he doesn't like me. Case in point, Blythe gets to dress up in nice clothes and strut around the festival, while here I'm caked in mud and looking a step up from a beggar."

"Oh? And you consider having to accompany me a punishment, do you?" Seraphina asked playfully.

Snapdragon shook his head in protest. "No, I didn't mean that. I just mean…"

Stopping again, Seraphina blinked at him and tilted her head to one side. "Then you like to be with me. Is that it?"

He felt even weaker in the knees than before. "No fair. You're doing it again."

She tilted her head to the other side and cooed, "Doing what, Snapdragon?"

"Bah!" he said, throwing his arms up in the air.

She giggled. "Fine, fine. I'll stop. But you really need to learn how to control yourself when a woman is toying with you."

Snapdragon reluctantly let her take his arm again. "I wonder if it's too late to become a priest," he mumbled.

❖

The crowd buzzed around the large field, moving from event to event. Merchants and peddlers offered "the finest wares Bariwon has to offer." There were games of skill, strength, and chance, many of which were patterned after the events of the Mortentaun.

But it was the minstrels that drew the largest crowds. Snapdragon and Seraphina stood among many others listening to a tall, lean man with a long, graying beard. He was dressed in brightly colored clothing, some colors that had no place being part of the same outfit. A large hat, upended on the ground in front of him, held several coins from appreciative spectators from previous performances.

He held a lute in his hands almost lovingly as he peered out into the crowd. "Welcome one and all! It is my pleasure to present to you a tale of romance, danger, and heroics! It is called 'The Ballad of Oakleaf the Bold.'"

Snapdragon bowed his head and shook it. He turned to walk away, but Seraphina stopped him. "I want to hear this," she whispered.

"But—" he started to say, but was interrupted by the first chord from the lute.

Please lend me an ear one and all,
A wondrous tale for young and old,
'Twill make you laugh and make you bawl,
The Ballad of Oakleaf the Bold!

The minstrel sang of how Oakleaf was nearly killed while heroically saving Arlie and her father, and in doing so, freeing Rayne from the false charges against him and allowing him to become king. Snapdragon felt like he would be sick as the song progressed. He wanted desperately to walk away, but Seraphina had a firm grip on his arm and had her feet solidly planted. Even though she probably weighed half of what Snapdragon did, for some reason he doubted she would be easy to move.

At last the ballad ended with people cheering and throwing more coins into the minstrel's hat. As the crowd dispersed, Seraphina said, "Oh, that was simply wonderful, wasn't it?"

"Sure, it was splendid," Snapdragon responded flatly. "But it isn't what we are here for."

Seraphina pulled him a bit closer, and with her eyes shifting back and forth, whispered, "Are you sure? Perhaps his song enchanted people to throw money into his hat. Maybe you should arrest him."

"Can't you be serious for a moment?"

Snapdragon led her away from the minstrel. They walked for a bit before finding themselves in a nearly deserted path on the edge of the festival.

"Step right up! Step right up!" shouted a plump little man standing on a large wooden box. He was wearing a long, earth-toned cloak that was wrapped around him so tightly that he appeared to be a tiny hill with a head stuck on top of it. "Come be impressed at the amazing mind powers of Gordon the Great! Let me bewilder you with my powers of perception!"

Snapdragon guided Seraphina over to him. "Let's see what this is all about."

"Ah, wonderful. Wonderful!" Gordon said when they arrived. "You've come to be amazed and confused by Gordon the Great."

"Yes," said Seraphina, sounding somewhat unconvinced. "Amaze and confuse us."

He wagged a finger in front of their faces. "Aha! Skills like mine are not for everyone. Let me ask you, can either of you read?"

"Yes, I can," Snapdragon stated matter-of-factly.

Seraphina elbowed Snapdragon in the ribs and Gordon's eye-brows shot up in surprise.

"Oh, and how did a farmer like yourself learn to read, my good man?" Gordon asked suspiciously.

Without missing a beat, Snapdragon said, "Surely you've heard that Queen Sunshine has established reading schools in every town in the kingdom. Anyone is allowed to attend and learn. The missus here said she wouldn't marry a man that couldn't read, so there you have it."

"Ah, a demanding one there, your wife," Gordon said. "And she is pleasing to the eye, even covered in all that dirt and grime."

"And this spoken from a man who looks like he's buried under a mound of dirt," Seraphina said dryly.

Gordon chuckled. "Ah, she's a fiery one as well. But enough! There is the matter of the game. Here's how it works. You pay me two silver coins. After that, I'll write your exact age on this paper before me. If I do so correctly, I keep the silver coins. If I fail, I'll give you back the two coins and give you two more in addition."

"But how can you be sure I'll tell you if you are correct?" Snapdragon asked.

Gordon spread his hands in front of him. "Why, I'll have to trust your honor, my good sir. Do we have a deal?"

Snapdragon and Seraphina exchanged looks. She shrugged.

"All right then, we have a deal," Snapdragon said.

Gordon smiled and rubbed his hands together. "Excellent. The two silver coins, please."

Snapdragon reached into the bag of coins Fallon had given him. He retrieved the money and noticed that Gordon was eyeing the rest of the purse's contents.

Upon receiving the coins, Gordon said, "All right, my good man, please stand over there so I can take a good look at you."

Snapdragon moved to the area where Gordon had indicated. The little man looked him up and down. While he did so, a couple of men moved behind them to watch what was happening.

Glancing over at Seraphina, Snapdragon noticed her hiding a smile behind her hand.

Gordon took out a scrap of parchment. Dipping a quill into a bottle of ink set up on a tall table next to him, he wrote something down on the parchment and folded it in half.

"Are you ready to be amazed and confused?" Gordon asked theatrically.

Snapdragon nodded.

Gordon handed him the parchment. "Take a look and you'll see I was as good as my word. I have written down your exact age."

After unfolding the parchment, Snapdragon cringed as he read the words "*Your exact age.*" He glared at the little man, "You cheated."

"What did it say?" Seraphina asked.

He held the parchment up for her to see.

Gordon stood up as tall as his frame would allow. "My good sir! You have no right to say such things. You must admit you are amazed."

"But I'm not confused," Snapdragon growled.

Gordon's countenance darkened. "Ah, no. That's the next part."

With that, he motioned to one of the men standing behind them. The larger man grabbed Seraphina, clasping a hand over her mouth. Before Snapdragon could respond, the other man reached down and yanked on the end of a rope that had been hidden in the dirt. The rope had been tied in a noose of sorts that circled Snapdragon's legs. The noose tightened, tying his legs together. He tried to move, but lost his balance and fell to the ground. He lifted himself up with his arms just in time to see Seraphina being dragged off into the woods by the two men, with Gordon following behind as fast as his little legs would carry him.

CHAPTER 33

Snapdragon looked around for help, but there was none to be found. Gordon had picked a good place for the kidnapping. Snapdragon sat up and reached down to untie the noose. The knot was fairly complex and would take him some time to undo—moments he probably didn't have. Once in the woods, the men could disappear quickly.

He worked as fast as he could and finally got free from the rope, then ran in the direction the men had taken Seraphina. Fortunately, it had rained the previous evening, and the tracks were easy to spot at first.

Three sets of tracks were distinguishable, with long furrows here and there where Seraphina must have been dragging her feet. The path they took was fairly straight, which led Snapdragon to believe that they were headed for a specific location and not trying to lose anyone that would follow them. But why?

The forest was dense enough that he couldn't see too far ahead, but not so thick that he was slowed down by fighting through branches. After several minutes of chasing after them, Snapdragon heard a scream that was quickly muffled. He knew he wasn't far behind them.

Suddenly, Snapdragon remembered he wasn't armed. What would he do once he caught up to them? He slowed down a bit and scanned the area. He spotted a section of a tree branch on the ground and picked it up. Part of the wood had rotted out and the branch didn't have much weight to it, but it was better than nothing.

He continued on, but more cautiously, trying not to make noise as he closed in. He heard the men but couldn't see them, and was unable to make out what they were saying. He moved closer until he was able to observe them. They had stopped in a clearing and stood looking in Snapdragon's direction.

He got a good look at the other two men for the first time. Both were large, but neither seemed particularly muscular. One of them held Seraphina around the waist with a knife at her throat. In her mouth, they had stuffed what looked to be a large handkerchief.

The other man was holding a long sword that appeared as if it had seen better days. Snapdragon could see that it was rusted in places. As for Gordon, he stood behind both of the men and was peering around them in the direction they had come.

So they were waiting for Snapdragon. Why weren't they running away? Was this another one of Fallon's tests? It seemed too similar to the captain's recent test in the bush maze. But if Fallon wanted to see if Snapdragon could learn from his mistakes, so be it.

Instead of charging in headfirst, Snapdragon paused a moment and formulated a plan.

⊰☖⊱

Snapdragon stepped out into the clearing, arms wide and hands empty. The man holding Seraphina grabbed her a bit tighter, while the other man moved into a fighting stance.

"Stop," Gordon spoke up. "Wait a moment. He isn't a threat."

Snapdragon took a step closer. "I'm here to make a deal. Let my wife go and I'll give you all the coins I have with me." He reached down and undid the pouch tied to his belt.

Gordon narrowed his eyes and appeared to size up Snapdragon. "What makes you think it's the money I'm after? Perhaps I want the girl instead."

"I saw you eyeing my coin pouch," Snapdragon said, hefting it in one hand. "By the looks of you and your men, you need money more than you need the company of a woman. And, I must tell you, she's quite a handful."

Snapdragon looked at Seraphina, hoping she would reveal something to help him pass Fallon's latest test. Her eyes held the same defiant look as the last time she was held prisoner, but there was something else as well— something he couldn't quite place.

"Well, I think you aren't seeing things clearly," Gordon said. "What if I want both your money *and* your wife?"

Snapdragon reached behind him and pulled out the makeshift weapon—the tree branch—he had tucked in his belt. "To get both, you'll have to pry the pouch from my cold, dead hand. And I promise you I won't go down without at least one of you going down with me."

"Just give him the bloomin' girl for the money," growled the man holding Seraphina. "You ain't payin' me enough to risk gettin' killed."

After a dramatic sigh, Gordon said, "Fine, fine. Throw me the pouch and I'll release her."

"No," Snapdragon said firmly. "Release her, and when she is halfway to me, I'll throw it to you."

Not waiting for Gordon to haggle any further, the man holding Seraphina released her and shoved her toward Snapdragon. When she was halfway to him, Snapdragon threw the money pouch in a high arc toward the men. It landed with a solid *thunk* on the ground in front of them just before Seraphina reached Snapdragon and pulled the gag from her mouth.

The two men with Gordon exchanged excited glances as he picked up and opened the pouch. He poured the contents into one hand. Instead of coins, there were only small rocks.

"Where's the money you promised me?" Gordon demanded.

"I promised you all the coin I had on me. I buried the coins in the forest behind me and filled the pouch with rocks." Snapdragon smirked. "Who is amazed and confused now?"

Gordon looked at Snapdragon with pure hatred.

"All right," Snapdragon said. "Did I pass Fallon's test this time?"

"This isn't a test," Seraphina said breathlessly.

Gordon frowned. "Fallon? As in Captain Fallon? What's going on here?"

Snapdragon looked from Seraphina to Gordon and then back again. She shook her head.

Standing up straight and holding the makeshift weapon in front of him, Snapdragon said, "I am Royal Guardian Snapdragon, and you are all under arrest for kidnapping."

"Get him!" Gordon screamed.

The two henchmen tensed up for a moment, looked at each other, and then ran off into the forest in opposite directions, leaving Gordon standing alone with a handful of rocks and an empty pouch.

Snapdragon didn't attempt to pursue either of the other men, but rather looked right at Gordon. "All right, use your powers of perception to figure out how this is going to end."

❖

"And then Gordon told you where you could find the other two men?" asked Blythe, his smile even wider than normal.

Snapdragon nodded. "Yeah. It didn't take much persuasion."

"Heard you went with Seraphina," Blythe said with a hint of jealousy. "Bet that was fun."

"She's a very fascinating person—although she was rather shaken up after the whole affair with Gordon. She was uncharacteristically quiet on the way back. Once we got to the castle, she didn't say anything before she made a beeline toward her room. I was hoping she'd at least thank me for saving her."

"Weren't you scared when you realized it wasn't a test?" Blythe asked. He seemed reluctant to swap his merchant's coat for his uniform, but they had to change for dinner.

Snapdragon put on his guardian tunic. "Not really scared. More like resolved. These men were honestly trying to do harm. I sincerely think they intended to take both the money and Seraphina. That's why they didn't try to take it from me at first. They wanted to draw us away from the crowds. Even with all King Rayne has done, there are still folks like that out there."

"It's the reason we are here, friend."

"So, what about you? Anything interesting happen?" Snapdragon asked.

Blythe pulled his boots on. "Nothing as exciting as you. Had a boy try to steal my coins from off my belt, and there was a man who tried to sell me 'genuine pearls' from Donigi, which were no more than smooth, round rocks painted white, but that was about all."

"Well, I'm glad you weren't in mortal danger," Snapdragon said, putting on the last part of his uniform. "We'd better hurry if we're going to get anything good for dinner. It'll be nice to spend the evening with the other guardians after such an eventful day."

Blythe stood and opened the door to their quarters. He stepped into the hallway. "Don't you remember? Meeting with Savant Waylon tonight after dinner to study geography."

Snapdragon groaned. "Oh, yeah, that's right. So much for a night of relaxation."

⤛✦⤜

Savant Waylon looked at the roomful of guardians with disdain. "Anyone?" he said.

"What was the question again?" a guardian behind Snapdragon asked.

Waylon sighed dramatically, his chubby face drooping in obvious disappointment. "I asked what you thought would be the most important thing we needed in Bariwon."

"More desserts after dinner!" one guardian chimed in.

"How about letting royal guardians marry?" another added.

"Nah, how about two extra hours of sleep a night!" added yet another.

Waylon slapped his hand on the table in front of him to quiet the laughter.

"Roads!" he said. "We need more and better roads!"

Folding his arms, Snapdragon echoed skeptically, "Roads."

Waylon's eyes lit up. "Yes, roads! Roads will allow easier travel through the kingdom. Smoother, faster travel will allow farmers, merchants, and traders to sell their wares to a larger area, allowing for more profits and greater distribution of goods!"

"I don't understand," Blythe said.

Waylon rolled his eyes. "Every year we get reports of food spoiling because farmers were unable to sell all of it. At the same time, there are districts like Grenoa that often suffer from hunger because they are unable to grow enough food."

Snapdragon raised his hand. "This is all interesting, but why tell us? Why not tell the king? Aren't we here for a geography lesson?"

Waylon appeared to consider the questions, then said carefully, "Well, there are those in this room who might have a better chance of convincing the king."

Snapdragon sighed. "Listen"—he turned to address the rest of the room as well—"please do not treat me any differently than any other guardian. Any of you. Yes, my sister is the queen and her husband is the king. But I'm tired of people trying to use that to their advantage or use it against me."

The room was quiet for a moment before Waylon said, "Yes, of course. My apologies. Let us get on with the lesson."

Moving to the wall behind him, the portly savant pulled down a cloth, revealing a map of Bariwon. "This, my good men, is a copy of the most accurate map of Bariwon," Waylon said proudly. He looked disappointed at the lack of interest shown by the guardians.

With a long stick, he pointed to the middle of the map. "This is where the castle is located. It was purposely built in the center of the kingdom." Waylon turned back to the guardians. "We know there are other kingdoms in the world, yet we don't have any fear of invasion. Can anyone tell me why?"

No one responded.

"Here," Waylon said, pointing to the western coast, "is the western sea. High cliffs run the length of the coast, with the exception of Aecon Bay.

The outer part of the bay has sharp rocks that tear up the bottom of any ship that enters. Closer to shore, the bay is very shallow and wide, so no large ships can enter or leave. There are no known ways to sail a ship into Bariwon. While this acts as protection for us, it also prevents us from building and sailing ships that can travel any measurable distance."

Pointing at the bottom of the map, Waylon said, "These are the southern wastelands. The deserts there are too dry and hot to support life. No one that has set out on an expedition into the wastelands has ever returned."

"To the far east are the vast marshes." The savant moved his pointer. "They are as much of a natural barrier as the southern wastes. There are very few settlements close to the marshes. It is a mystery as to why, but most people become very ill when they spend any amount of time close to these wetlands. There are stories of an occasional person from other lands crossing the marshes, but they are near death from the travel and speak differently than we do, so we have been unable to learn anything from them. I suppose it is fear more than anything else that keeps people from traveling through the marshes.

"And lastly are the northern mountains," said Waylon. "Anyone from Erd can tell you how majestic they are. They are so high that people who have tried to climb them report they have had a hard time breathing before they get near the top. When the tops of the mountains are visible through the clouds—which is rare—they are covered in snow, even during the warmest time of the summer. What lies beyond them is a total mystery."

Waylon set down the pointer and addressed the guardians in a serious tone. "For better or worse, we are isolated from the rest of mankind. Therefore, it is important that we have peace in our land. Our ancestors knew this, and that is why we say, 'To peace in our kingdom,' at the end of every event."

He put both hands on the table and leaned forward. "That is why there are guardians. You are to ensure the peace in our land. Recently, there were those who forgot that and used their positions of power to better suit their own wants."

Up to this point, Snapdragon hadn't understood why the new guardians were made to attend these types of classes.

He was now beginning to understand.

⚜

Eadward's face turned red like it always did when he was upset. He had tried his hand at cards while he was a royal guardian, but he almost always lost. And most of the time it was to one of his fellow guardians, Nash. One day, after losing especially badly, Eadward confronted the plump guardian and accused him of cheating. Nash just laughed in his jolly way and said, "Your face is an open book. Everyone knows when you have a good hand or when you are bluffing. It's not my fault you can't keep your emotions under control. It would do you good to learn."

Right now was one of those times when Eadward wished he could hide his emotions. "Did Abrecan tell you why he wanted us to wait?" he asked through gritted teeth.

Selene responded coolly, "No, though I have a good guess why."

Eadward stomped around her office, trying to calm down. "And what's your guess?"

The magistrate of Erd sat at her desk, put her hands on her lap, and said, "He is waiting for the right time. It makes sense. I would guess the Festival of Gratitude would be such a time. The king and queen and many of the royal guardians will be away from the castle, which will make it easier for our men to take over."

Eadward frowned as he considered the idea. "I'll admit that makes sense. But still, our forces are ready now. I know we could take the castle."

"It isn't enough to take it—we must keep it as well," Selene pointed out. "That will be easier with more men, men that we could lose in a bloody battle to capture the castle."

Eadward balled his fists. "But the Festival of Gratitude is months away."

"Perhaps another opportunity will present itself earlier," Selene said. "Keep your men ready. They may need to move at a moment's notice."

⇥✦⇤

The gentle breeze had a bit of a chilling effect on the top of the guardian tower, even though it was nearly summertime. Snapdragon leaned against the waist-high stone wall and gazed down. The town surrounding the castle was active—people walking down the streets that led to the main gates, with other roads running perpendicular to the main ones. He couldn't help but think of Savant Waylon and his excitement for roads. The savant had made a good point, and despite himself, Snapdragon did mention it to his sister.

Beyond the town were the farmlands. For some reason, the checkerboard patterns created by the farmers' fields had always fascinated Snapdragon. Here among nature in all its wonder, the patterns looked very unnatural. Snapdragon idly wondered when a bird flew over the farms if it noted that something was odd. Then again, would a bird even bother with such things?

"Thinking again, eh?" Blythe asked. He clapped Snapdragon on the shoulder.

"Aye, I was wondering what a bird might think when it flew over the farmlands."

"Believe you've been up here in the tower too long today if you're pondering such questions." Blythe laughed.

Snapdragon shrugged. "Perhaps. That does sound like something my dad would consider. Let's do something else to pass the time. You're always good with a story—tell me one."

"Story, eh? All right, let me think a moment." Blythe rested his arms on the wall and looked out over the land. After a moment, he pointed. "See that inn down there? The one with the red slate roof?"

"Aye."

"Father owned an inn like that in the town of Donigi, where I'm from. Across the road from our inn was another inn. They were the two biggest inns in all the town. As competitors, they were always trying to entice people to stay in their rooms.

"One trick they used was to bring in merchants and performers to set up displays or do performances in their common areas. Oh my, some of the things Father would bring in." Blythe shook his head and grinned.

Snapdragon couldn't help but grin as well. "Like what?"

"Well, there was one time when my father brought in a merchant who sold exotic animals. They were mostly just lizards and such from the southern wastes, though he did have a few turtles. Keep in mind that turtles are considered lucky in Donigi, so they sold quickly."

Blythe flicked a few pebbles off the tower wall into the moat below, then continued. "What was strange is that the innkeeper from across the street actually came into my father's inn and bought one of these turtles. It was the only time I recall him ever entering our inn.

"Father considered it a win of sorts that he got the other man to buy from his inn. These two had been fiercely competitive in everything since they were younger. Tell you this so you understand the significance of what transpired a couple of weeks later."

Snapdragon's eyes widened. "Oh, and what was that?"

"One morning, Father and Mother were setting up for breakfast when Mother screamed. She woke the whole inn. Placed on the bar was a rather ornate box. Mother was white as sand. Father didn't turn white after he opened the box. Instead, he turned red—bright red. Only turned red when he was very angry."

"So, what was in the box?" Snapdragon prompted.

Blythe's grin dissolved. "A dead turtle."

"A dead turtle?"

Blythe nodded. "Aye, a dead turtle. Understand that as lucky as a turtle is, a dead turtle is considered a bad omen. Naturally, Father was upset. Spent the next several days planning and plotting to get revenge on the other innkeeper. Never seen Father like that."

"That's terrible!" Snapdragon said. "What did he do?"

"One day another merchant came to town promising to sell exotic animals, but instead of coming to our inn, he went to the other inn. The other innkeeper gloated when word got out. Father stood outside his inn and just watched with his arms folded.

"A short while later the merchant returned with a dozen cows," Blythe said, grinning again. "The merchant took them into the inn, despite the innkeeper's attempts to stop him. Eventually the cows were removed, but not until they had left, let us say, a rather unpleasant mess behind them."

Snapdragon slapped the wall and laughed. "So it was your father that arranged the cow merchant, right?"

Blythe nodded again. "That's right. Heard it took quite a while for the smell in the common room to go away. But that isn't the end of the story."

"No?"

"There was a woman in town who was rather old and not thinking right. Everyone in town kept an eye on her, to keep her out of harm's way if nothing else. Often this woman would shop at Father's inn. Coming in a few days after the cow incident, she asked my father if he got the broken turtle she brought back."

Snapdragon clapped a hand over his mouth. "Oh, no."

"Aye, she had bought a turtle and just kept it in the box, never feeding it or taking care of it. When the turtle died and started to smell and change color, she brought it back because she thought it was broken."

"So your father had gotten all upset and planned his revenge for no good reason at all?"

Blythe flicked another rock off the wall. "Aye. From that point on, my father tried to do the right thing and not jump to conclusions. It was then that he started the talk of me becoming a guardian. Think maybe he wanted me to be a better person than he saw himself. And so here I am."

"Well, I for one am glad you are here," Snapdragon said. "You are the only one who has never really treated me differently because of my family."

Blythe flashed him another goofy grin. "Well, after you beat me in the Mortentaun by breaking my weapon with your mace, thought it better to be on your good side. In fact— Wait, what's that?"

Snapdragon looked where Blythe was pointing. A man with a long, flowing red cape flapping behind him was racing his horse toward the castle, nearly running over people along the way.

"Think we should sound the alarm?" Blythe asked.

Reaching for the mallet propped against the tower bell, Snapdragon said, "Anyone going that fast through town toward the castle must have a good reason—or perhaps an evil one."

Snapdragon raced down the tower stairs after ringing the bell. He knew that the guardians at the front gate would have no idea why the alarm had been sounded. He tried to yell down to them, but the distance was too great. Blythe agreed to stay up top while Snapdragon ran to tell them about the man on the horse.

Sprinting through the halls toward the front gate, Snapdragon nearly ran over a few servants. When he arrived at the front gates, he spotted the man at the far end of the main road. "There!" he shouted and pointed.

The other two royal guardians spun around and drew their swords. Snapdragon knew the archers would be ready on the towers.

To Snapdragon's surprise, the man pulled the horse up before he reached the guardians. His face dripped with sweat, and his horse had worked up a lather.

"Move out of the way!" the man said in an Erd accent. "I must see the king!"

None of the royal guardians budged, but Snapdragon asked, "What's so important, then?"

The man on the horse gave them a horrified look. "The people in the town of Procep. They're all gone!"

CHAPTER 34

King Rayne briskly entered the main hall. Instead of taking a seat on his throne, he went directly to the man in the red cape and shook his hand. "I hear you have something to tell me. Please have a seat."

On other occasions, Snapdragon had noticed that many of the older people in attendance frowned when the king sat on the edge of the dais where the throne was placed. They had grown up in an era when the leaders of Bariwon followed a certain protocol. King Rayne's personal approach seemed to be more effective, but many still struggled with it—including, it appeared, the man in the red cape. At first he continued to stand at attention, but Rayne motioned for him to sit down. After a long pause, he did so.

"Now tell me…" Rayne said, prompting the man for his name.

"Rudyard, Your Majesty."

Rayne nodded. "Rudyard, please tell me what is happening."

Rudyard glanced around the room as if he was uncomfortable with the number of people present. Snapdragon had escorted the man, after making sure any weapons he had were removed, to the main hall while one of the guardians at the front gate had gone to get the king. Those in the hall included Captain Fallon, several savants, and a few of the Hierarchy of Magistrates.

"You can speak in front of these people," the king said. "They can all be trusted."

"As you say, Your Majesty," Rudyard bowed his head slightly. "I am an aide for Governor Wardell of Erd. Returning from the Mortentaun, we encountered one of the guardians assigned to Erd. He and his horse had been traveling without rest for two days and were near complete exhaustion. He reported that he had been to Procep as part of a routine visit and found something very strange."

303

Narrowing his eyes, Rayne asked, "What did he mean by strange?"

"The people were no longer there."

"I don't understand. Where would they go? Perhaps they came to the Mortentaun."

Rudyard shook his head. "Not likely, Your Majesty. Although only fifty or so people live in the village, it's right against the northern mountains and fairly isolated. They don't have enough horses to carry all of them to the Mortentaun, and it's too far to walk. Plus, there are other factors."

The king rubbed his chin. "What factors?"

"The guardian told of doors wide open, half-eaten meals left on tables, clothing still hanging on drying lines, and such," Rudyard said.

"Has the nislles returned?" a savant asked, worry lining his face.

Snapdragon had heard about the nislles when he was young—it was something adults used to scare children into being good. 'Better eat all your vegetables or you may get the nislles!' was something his mother had told him on more than one occasion. But like most such stories, the heart of it came from something that actually happened. Snapdragon had learned that centuries ago, a sickness that came to be known as the nislles killed a vast number of people in the land. It left the kingdom without a leader or anyone who had a rightful claim to the throne, which in turn led to a bloody struggle for power. The result was the system they had now. The Tome of Laws was written by the survivors to ensure there would never be a void of power again. But Snapdragon believed every adult in the kingdom secretly feared that the nislles might return one day to kill their loved ones.

Rayne said confidently, "It couldn't have been the nislles."

"How can we be sure?" the savant asked.

"Queen Sunshine is an avid reader and quite the scholar in her own right. Remember that she was the first female to become a savant. She has told me stories of the nislles, based on her readings.

"If it was the nislles, there would be dead bodies remaining. It took several days for someone to die, and only after intense suffering. These people would know if they were going to die and would have at least sent someone to get help. They wouldn't have left meals uneaten and clothes out in the weather."

The savant nodded, keeping his eyes low. "Yes, of course."

Rayne turned to Rudyard. "So, if not the nislles, then what?"

"I honestly do not know, Your Majesty," he said. "But these people left very abruptly for some reason—either by their own free will, or by force."

Rayne frowned. "If what you've told me is true, it doesn't sound as if they left of their own accord."

"Yes, Your Majesty," Rudyard said.

Stroking his chin, Rayne remained quiet for several moments. The crowd remained quiet as well. Finally, the king stood, and Rudyard quickly stood beside him. "I say we prepare for the worst of all scenarios," Rayne said. "If these people were indeed taken, it was by a powerful force. However, I'm not willing to sacrifice one or two guardians to investigate this further."

"But Your Majesty," Rudyard exclaimed. "Certainly we must do something!"

Rayne gave the man from Erd a tight smile before speaking again. "You didn't let me finish. I'm not willing to send one or two guardians to investigate. Instead, we will send a formidable force of our own."

⊰❈⊱

Ciar tried to act like he normally would when delivering food to the dungeons, but his heart was racing and he could feel beads of sweat forming on his brow. He had to remain calm—he couldn't let the guardians in the dungeon suspect anything was out of the ordinary.

He stood quietly while they inspected the food and instructed him not to talk to the prisoners. He had made this trip many times over the last few years, but it was nothing like today. Today he had historic news.

Making his way back to Abrecan's cell, Ciar thought how best to tell his leader. It should be done respectfully—something worthy of the words he was about to utter. Only a few in the kingdom were privileged enough to understand the importance of the message, and Ciar was honored to be one of them. Not even Melanie had been told.

After opening the small access panel at the bottom of Abrecan's door, Ciar blurted, "The people of Procep have disappeared!"

He cringed at how he had presented such momentous news, but alas, it was too late.

"Are you sure?" Abrecan responded, hope seeming to ooze into his voice.

"Yes!" Ciar all but shouted. Lowering his voice so as not to be overheard by others, he said, "The report just came in. They said the people of Procep were all missing."

There was a drawn-out pause.

"And what was Rayne's response to such a report?" Abrecan asked carefully.

Ciar smiled. "He is sending a large force from the castle northward to investigate."

"How large a force?"

Ciar scratched the back of his head. "I wasn't present at the meeting. But I overheard a couple of the savants talking afterward. They said it was going to be a 'formidable force.'"

Another pause. When Abrecan responded this time, it was with an authoritative tone that Ciar hadn't heard from him since he had been placed in the dungeon. "It seems the legends may prove to be true after all. It is a sign—a sign that I am destined to rule. Tell them the wait is over. We act now."

⤞⫟⤝

"Uncle Snap!" Rainbow shouted. She ran across the room with her arms spread.

Snapdragon went down on one knee and scooped up his niece, giving her a kiss on the cheek when she wrapped her arms around his throat. He pretended to choke a bit as she squeezed him tightly. She relaxed a little but didn't let go. Snapdragon stood, lifting the girl.

"How come you don't play with me anymore?" Rainbow asked, sticking out her lower lip.

Queen Sunshine looked up from the chair where she had been reading. "Now, now, sweetheart," she said, "your uncle is an important man. I'm sure he'd love to play with you, but he's busy with royal guardian duties."

Rainbow furrowed her brow. "Who makes you do all that stuff?"

"Captain Fallon is the one who tells me what to do," Snapdragon said as he bounced Rainbow lightly in his arms.

"And who makes Captain Fallon do stuff?"

Snapdragon laughed. "Well, I guess that would be your daddy."

Looking at her mother, Rainbow said in a serious tone, "Mommy, we gotta have a talk with Daddy about this."

"All right, we'll talk to Daddy," Sunshine said, smiling. "In the meantime, why don't you go play with your dolls so your uncle and I can chat for a moment?"

Rainbow pouted again. "You always have grownups that want to talk to you, Mommy."

"I promise when I'm done, we'll play dolls, all right?"

"All right, Mommy," Rainbow said, then released Snapdragon enough that he could let her down.

Indicating an open chair next to her, Sunshine said, "So, Snap, this is a surprise. What brings you here?"

He looked around the royal bedchamber as he sat down. The decor was elegant without being pretentious. But that described his sister. It seemed she had taken on the mantle of being queen almost effortlessly. His sister's dark hair matched his, though Snapdragon's shortly cut hair had some natural waves to it. The main difference between them, aside from their gender, was that Snapdragon's eyes were blue compared to her darker, brown eyes.

"Well, Shiny, I guess you've heard about what happened in Procep."

Glancing down at Rainbow, Sunshine said, "Yes, I've heard."

"Then you've also heard what your husband has in mind?" Snapdragon asked, taking the hint and keeping his voice light in front of his niece.

Sunshine sat up straighter. "In part, yes. I understand that there will be a number of people going for a little trip."

"I'll be going with them," Snapdragon said.

"Can I come too?" Rainbow asked, still playing with her dolls and not looking up.

Sunshine gave Snapdragon a knowing stare and nodded toward her daughter. "Ah, not this time, sweetheart. But we're planning on taking you with us this year to the Festival of Gratitude."

"All right, Mommy."

"I just wanted to thank Rayne for allowing me to go," Snapdragon said. "I was afraid I'd be left out because I'm your brother."

"Snap, Rayne had nothing to do with that. Captain Fallon selected you to go. And I know my husband well enough to say that he wouldn't interfere in such a manner. You are your own man. I'm sure you were selected because Fallon wanted you along."

Snapdragon turned and looked out the window. "I'm not so sure. Maybe he was afraid that if he excluded me, you and Rayne would be upset."

Sunshine laughed lightly. "You wooden head! You get chosen to go, so you think the king made it happen. If you hadn't been chosen, you would think it was because Fallon didn't want to make the king upset. Is it possible you were chosen regardless of who you are related to?"

He looked back at Sunshine with one eye closed. "It's possible."

"Then go do what you need to do."

Snapdragon and Sunshine stood and embraced. "All right, thank you, Shiny," he said. He reached down and tousled Rainbow's hair. "See you later, you."

Rainbow jumped up and gave Snapdragon's leg a hug. "Bye-bye, Uncle Snap. I hope you find where those people went."

Sunshine and Snapdragon exchanged startled looks.

"Well, Rainbow," Sunshine said, "it looks like your daddy and I need to be more careful what we discuss around you."

❈

Snapdragon had just finished closing up his last saddlebag when he felt a hand on his shoulder. He turned around and was somewhat startled to see Captain Fallon. The captain had never greeted him so informally.

"It looks like you're all ready to go," Fallon said, looking over Snapdragon's horse.

Snapdragon nodded. "Yes, sir, I am."

"Excellent. As you have noticed, this little expedition of ours has turned into quite the procession."

Snapdragon looked at the group of people actively preparing for the trip. Captain Fallon had selected a dozen royal guardians. Someone had brought up that the men would need to be fed, so several servants dressed in simple leather armor were mounted with pack horses in tow. And of course, if there were people who needed to be attended to, nursemaids were required. Snapdragon smiled a bit to himself as he noticed that Seraphina was one of those selected for the trip. "What if the houses needed to be fixed or armaments made?" someone had asked. So the royal crafter Grant and his assistant Bearach were loading up a cart with all manner of tools and raw materials. Strangest of all was Savant Waylon, who sat awkwardly on a horse with his nose in a book. Why he was going along, Snapdragon had no idea. Lastly was Rudyard, still wearing his red cape proudly as if to say, "Yes, I hold an important position in Erd."

"I didn't expect to have so many…different…types of people along for the trip, Captain," Snapdragon said carefully.

Fallon's steely blue eyes scanned the group quickly. "To be honest, neither did I. We don't know what we'll be facing up there. Was it a herd of wild animals? A band of ruffians? Even worse, something we haven't considered? Having all these people on the journey concerns me, but there are things that are out of my hands. And that is why you are here."

"Sir?"

Fallon gave him what Snapdragon guessed was his best attempt at a fatherly smile. "I am bringing you and Blythe along primarily to protect the non-guardians in this group. If things turn ugly, you and Blythe are charged to get these people to safety and protect them with your lives. Let me and the other guardians take care of the rest. Do you understand your orders?"

Snapdragon felt his chest start to roil with anger, but he tried to look calm. "Yes, sir. Blythe and I are to play babysitters."

Fallon grimaced. "Well, I wouldn't put it that way, and neither should you. This is an important responsibility. Granted, it may not be as glorious as you perceive it, but it's the one you've been charged with. I expect you to do this without complaint. Am I clear?"

"Clear as light through water, sir."

Queen Sunshine stood by her husband in their chamber. Through the window, they could see Fallon and his group preparing to leave for Procep.

"Who in the group knows of your plan, aside from Fallon?" she asked softly.

Still looking out the window, Rayne said, "Grant, the crafter."

"Is there no one else you can trust?"

"There are plenty of people I trust. It isn't about trust. It's about being cautious."

She put an arm around his waist. "When do you leave?"

Rayne pulled her close to him. "Oakleaf has already started to gather the rest of the guardians that are going. We should be ready by tomorrow night. Your brother wishes he could go with us, but his leg..."

Sunshine nodded. "He just doesn't want anything bad to happen to you. Neither do I. Are you sure that *you* have to go? Won't people notice you are missing? After all, we're not sure how long you will be gone."

"I'm sure there will be questions eventually, but that is where you need to dazzle them with your beauty and wit," the king said, trying to sound playful.

Sunshine's only response was to squeeze him tighter.

Fallon's group left the castle after the morning meal. The procession drew curious looks from the villagers who lived in the area around the castle. The king had told Snapdragon it was just a matter of time before word spread of what had happened in Procep. Having the villagers watch Fallon lead an expedition party north would hopefully give the townspeople peace of mind that something was being done.

Snapdragon and Blythe were near the back of the group, followed only by two older royal guardians charged with making sure no one sneaked up on them.

The first day the group was relatively quiet, and Snapdragon assumed everyone was anxious about what they would face when they arrived in Procep. He caught Seraphina turning around a few times to look at him. When their eyes met he would offer his warmest smile, but she would quickly turn away.

They hadn't spoken since the festival. Snapdragon inquired casually about her, but he mostly heard she had been uncharacteristically quiet since the event. He wanted to make sure she was all right, and he hoped she didn't somehow blame him for her being taken at the Mortentaun festival.

At the end of the first day, Fallon and the group were to spend the night at an inn in the town of Lewyol. Although Lewyol was not in a direct line to Procep from the castle, it was the largest town within a day's journey. Fallon had wanted to stay at an inn the first night because he knew there would be nights when they would have to camp in the wild. Staying at the inn also meant fewer provisions had to be taken along, so they needed a smaller number of pack horses, which tended to slow travel.

Having grown up in Lewyol, Snapdragon knew several people in the town and was greeted warmly. Once they had stabled their horses, the travelers settled into the common room, where servers were rushing around preparing meals.

People tended to group together based on their responsibilities, much to Snapdragon's disappointment. He had hoped to sit at a table with Seraphina, but before he could make his way to her, Rudyard clasped him by the arm and said, "Please join me."

Blythe followed along as Snapdragon sat down at a table.

"So tell me, guardians," Rudyard said in his thick Erd accent. "What think you of our situation?"

Blythe eyed the food being served. "Think it's going to be interesting what we will find. Bet it was a group of bandits who took them. Hoping for a ransom, perhaps."

Rudyard growled. "You think Erd is nothing but a bunch of evil people running around looking to cause harm, do you?"

"No," Blythe said. "Isn't what I said at all. Although—"

"Although you've all thought that, haven't you?" Rudyard said harshly. "Let me tell you that the people of Erd were none too happy under Abrecan's rule and were even less happy once his son became king. But blaming all of Erd for the acts of a few men is unfair."

"Although," Blythe continued calmly as if the red-caped man had not spoken, "it's apparent that's the way you must feel. Think you're putting your own thoughts on others."

Rudyard stood quickly. "Oh, so now it's *my* fault that the people disappeared?"

"Enough!" Snapdragon stood and put his hand on the hilt of his sword. "That's not what he said! You are out of line!"

Rudyard considered Snapdragon briefly before he slammed his hand down on the table and started to laugh. "It appears Fallon was right about you."

"What do you mean by that?" Snapdragon asked tightly.

"Relax, relax." Rudyard chuckled. "Captain Fallon just wanted to see how you'd react if I were to play an angry, bitter man from Erd. He said you'd react the way you did, though I bet him you would have taken it a step further and had me on the floor with your sword at my throat. It appears I have misjudged you."

Rudyard reached into the money purse tied to his belt and removed a silver coin. "Hey, Fallon!" he called to the captain, who was sitting two tables over. "You win!"

He flipped the coin end over end and Fallon snatched it out of the air. The captain nodded his head at Snapdragon.

"Another test then?" Snapdragon asked across the room, realizing everyone was watching.

Fallon stroked his mustache and responded loudly enough for Snapdragon to hear, "We're all being tested every day. Most of us just don't realize it."

⊰⊱

Selene walked so smoothly she almost glided. She kept her chin up and her shoulders squared, even under the most trying of circumstances. This was one of many things Crescens adored about her. So when she sat down hard on her chair and hunched over at the messenger's news, Crescens found it unsettling.

"You may leave us," Selene instructed the messenger. "Speak of this to no one else."

The man nodded and made a quick exit from the room.

"Magistrate, are you all right?" Crescens asked, after closing the door.

Selene stared down at her shaking hands and didn't respond. Crescens had never seen her like this—and it scared him. He waited for several uncomfortable moments before he asked, "Would you like me to fetch a nursemaid?"

Shaking her head briskly, the magistrate whispered, "No."

What had affected her so? All the messenger had said was that Procep, a small village up against the northern mountains, had been deserted for no apparent reason. In response, the king had sent an entourage north to investigate. The message also said that Abrecan wanted to move now on the castle. This was something they had been preparing and planning for, so Crescens thought Selene would be elated. But here she was, acting as if the moon had just fallen from the sky.

"Shall I fetch Eadward to tell him the good news?" Crescens asked.

This statement must have snapped Selene out of her stupor, for she looked up at him with eyes blazing. "Good news?"

"About Abrecan wanting us to move now."

Selene seemed to regain some of her composure before responding, "Yes, yes. Go find Eadward and bring him here. Mention nothing of Procep, however."

Confused but knowing better than to question her orders, Crescens simply bowed.

⊷⊰❈⊱⊶

Hail the size of peas fell early in the morning as the group awoke and ate breakfast. After finishing his meal, Savant Waylon stood by the window and frowned, causing his droopy jowls to sag even further. Curious, Snapdragon stood beside the man and looked out the window. White dots bounced up and down on the ground, and then finally settled, covering the area in an almost snow-like veneer.

"It's a bad omen." Waylon made an odd gesture with his hands.

"The hail?"

Waylon repeated the gesture. "There are those who believe that hail is actually little bits of the moon breaking off and pelting the land. These are the same people that believe the moon is an indication of what to expect."

"How so?"

Waylon made a fist and held it up in front of the guardian. Snapdragon looked at the savant inquisitively, wondering what he had said to cause the older man to react that way.

"This represents the full moon," Waylon said. "It is a sign of power and strength. People born under a full moon are considered to be favored."

He cupped his hand into a *C* shape. "This represents the waning moon. It is a sign of weakness and failing."

"And this," he said, closing his fingers into his palm, but leaving his thumb curved and extended, "represents the waxing moon. It is a sign of change and growth."

Snapdragon frowned. "And what is the sign of the new moon?"

Waylon made an open circle with his hand. "This," he said with a shudder. "It is considered to be bad luck. People born under a new moon are thought to be cursed, or at the very least disfavored."

"And the gesture you made?"

Waylon looked a bit sheepish. "A silly superstition, I'm sure." He made is right hand into a fist. With his left hand, he made the symbol of the new moon by moving his fingers and thumb in a circular shape. He then hit his left hand with his right so that both his hands were now fists. "I would surmise it means getting rid of the bad luck with good."

Snapdragon made the gesture, but used his dominant left hand as the fist to crush his circled right hand.

Waylon gasped. "No! Never do that with your left hand. Those that believe these superstitions also think left-handed people are cursed."

"Oh, really?" Snapdragon arched his eyebrows. "And what people are these?"

Waylon glanced over at the rest of the travelers, who were finishing up their morning meals. "It's primarily people who live up north, in Erd."

Snapdragon looked outside again. "So having pieces of the moon fall off means it is falling apart—losing strength."

Waylon nodded.

"No wonder you'd say hail is a bad omen."

CHAPTER 35

The hail had stopped, though the sky remained canopied in gray. The company was on the move again, heading almost directly north from Lewyol. The goal was to reach the outskirts of the district of Erd within a couple of days, which meant they would have to camp on the side of the road for at least one night.

After a quiet morning of travel, the group stopped in a village for the midday meal. They didn't stable the horses or unpack, but stopped only long enough to buy food to take with them.

The village consisted of several farms plus a main road with shops lining the sides. A modest inn was the village's focal point, though it was too small to hold everyone in the company.

"We will be leaving before the sun reaches its peak," Fallon said when the company came to a stop. "Please make your purchases quickly."

Snapdragon squinted up at the sky. Though the clouds hid the sun, he couldn't imagine they had but a few moments to shop. He looked around and spotted a small shop with a boar on the sign above it. After dismounting and tying his horse to a tree, he said to Blythe, "I'm in the mood for pork. Want to join me?"

"Nah. Think I'll find me some bread and maybe some pastries."

"All right, I'll meet you back here soon."

Snapdragon made sure he had his coin purse, then headed to the shop. Despite the village not being very large, the residents took good care of their buildings. The paint was fresh and the road was clear of any deep ruts or holes.

"It's a good start," a voice said behind him.

He turned his head and saw Savant Waylon walking behind him, appearing to admire the road.

"How's that?" Snapdragon asked out of courtesy.

Waylon waved his pudgy arm in front of him in a sweeping motion. "These villagers understand how to take care of a road. People in the area know this and prefer to take this route when traveling from Erd to Lewyol. It brings business to these shops."

"Again with you and roads," Snapdragon said lightly.

Waylon looked defensive. "This is proof I'm right!"

"I didn't say you were wrong."

They arrived at the shop and entered. There was a salty smell in the air mixed with the aroma of roasting pork. Snapdragon felt his mouth starting to water, and by the looks of it, Waylon was reacting the same way.

A woman in her middle years was standing behind a counter, wrapping up a food order for another guardian who had arrived first. The guardian paid her, and then nodded to Snapdragon and Waylon on his way out.

"Hello then, what will it be?" the lady asked in a slight Erd accent.

Waylon walked up to the counter and practically drooled over the different options in front of him. Snapdragon looked on, amused, when the door to the shop opened again. In came the three nursemaids, all laughing until they spotted Snapdragon.

Ophelia was the oldest. Snapdragon knew her as the nursemaid who had treated his brother, Oakleaf, when he'd been injured while rescuing Arlie and her father. Next was Anissa, whose hair was just starting to turn grey. Snapdragon knew little of her except that she was one of Seraphina's teachers. And then there was Seraphina, who looked away from Snapdragon as soon as their eyes met. She said something to the other two nursemaids, then hastily left the shop.

"Just get me the same thing you are getting," Snapdragon instructed Waylon, handing the savant his coin purse. He smiled at the other nursemaids and then hurried out the door.

He spotted Seraphina just down the street with her back to him. "Seraphina!" he called.

She glanced back at him but kept walking away. He jogged and held the hilt of his sword so it wouldn't sway too much. "Seraphina," he said softly when he caught up to her. "Please, wait."

Whether it was his tone or the "please" that got her to stop, Snapdragon wasn't sure. She faced him and said, "Yes, Guardian, what can I do for you?"

"I don't understand," Snapdragon said. "Did I do or say something to upset you?"

She folded her arms, and her green eyes flashed with anger. "How can you ask that?"

315

"By opening my mouth and letting my tongue flap, I suppose," Snapdragon replied, realizing he sounded vaguely like his father for a moment.

Seraphina's expression relaxed slightly. "I'm not a helpless old maid," she said finally.

He blinked a few times and then looked at her from head to toe. "Far from it."

"I'm not talking about physically." She folded her arms in front of her. "I mean I can take care of myself. I don't always need someone to come to my rescue."

"Listen, Seraphina, I'm sorry. I didn't mean to let them take you back at the festival, it's just—"

"That's what I'm talking about!" she said, her nostrils flaring. "*You* didn't let them take me. *I* let them take me. If you hadn't come, I would have found a way to get free. But no! After people in the castle heard about what had happened, they kept asking me, 'What was it like to be rescued by Snapdragon?' or, 'Wasn't it lucky that Snapdragon was there to save you?' I'm tired of people thinking I always need to be rescued."

With that, she spun around and walked back toward the horses. Snapdragon stood and watched her go, aware that someone was coming up behind him.

"What's that all about?" Waylon asked in a muffled voice.

Snapdragon turned slowly and noticed the stout savant had a mouth full of food and his arms were full of wrapped packages.

"It's nothing," Snapdragon said. "Just women being women, you know?"

Waylon shrugged. "Here's your lunch." He handed Snapdragon several packages.

"All this?" Snapdragon asked, juggling the items.

"Well, you said you wanted the same thing I was getting."

⋑⧣⧫

"Here, this will work," Fallon pointed to a large open field.

With the northern mountains on the horizon, the large, grassy field surrounded by tall pine trees was a breathtaking sight—and a welcome one to the weary travelers. Captain Fallon had driven them hard through the afternoon and early evening. Snapdragon had wondered how soon they would stop, noting that the summer sky was starting to darken.

The servants went to work quickly to create a large pit in a central area where a fire would be built. Tents were pitched with the openings facing the fire, while the nursemaids started preparing the evening meal.

In a shorter time than Snapdragon thought possible, a roaring fire was cooking dinner for the company. Snapdragon sat on one of the wooden logs the guardians had dragged over for seating, pulled out his sword, and started sharpening it.

Through a gap in the tents, he saw Bearach pushing an ankle-high branch into the ground. The crafter's apprentice then got up, walked twenty or so paces, and put another branch into the ground. After that, Bearach walked another twenty paces around the outside of the camp and put in another branch.

Snapdragon got up and walked over to where Bearach was placing yet another branch. "Hey there, what are you doing?"

Bearach looked up and wiped his hands on his trousers. "Trying something."

Snapdragon looked back in the direction Bearach had come and saw that these ankle-high branches had been placed nearly all the way around the camp. For the first time, Snapdragon noticed that each branch was forked, creating a Y shape.

"Trying what?" Snapdragon asked.

Bearach walked a few more paces beyond Snapdragon and placed the last branch into the ground. "Give me a hand and you'll see."

"All right then."

The crafter removed a pack from his back and pulled out a loop of thin rope. "This is very tightly wound and strong," he said. "It's not cheap to get, but it's well worth it."

He unwound the rope a bit, then handed the main loop to Snapdragon. "Hold this for a moment, please."

Taking the free end, Bearach knelt down and tied it to a forked branch in the ground. He motioned for Snapdragon to give him more rope as he walked to the next branch, where he looped the rope around the top of the branch and then moved on to the next one. As soon as the rope ran out, he pulled out another length, tied it to the loose end, and then moved to the next branch. Four lengths of rope later, the camp was surrounded by this ankle-high rope, pulled fairly tight. Bearach stood back and nodded satisfactorily.

"Yes, that will definitely keep beavers and raccoons out of the camp," Snapdragon said carefully,

Bearach harrumphed. "We aren't done."

"No? Are we going to build a fence to keep out dogs and wild pigs, too?" Snapdragon chided.

Bearach rolled his eyes then reached into his bag and pulled out a tightly wrapped leather bundle. He unwrapped it to reveal several round metal objects with hoops attached to them. The crafter picked one up and shook it.

"A bell," Snapdragon said. "And of fine workmanship, I must say."

Bearach actually smiled a bit. "Thank you. I've been working on these for a while." He knelt down again and fit the loop of the bell over one side of the fork in the branch. Walking to the next branch, he put another bell on it.

"Pull on the rope there," he directed Snapdragon, pointing to the middle of the two branches.

When Snapdragon did so, the branches moved enough for the bells to jingle.

"A warning system, then?"

A grin split the crafter's face. "Exactly. I wasn't sure how big the camp would be, so I have enough ropes and bells for an area twice this size. If someone or something tries to enter the camp at night, they will trip on the rope and alert the guardians on watch."

"It's a very good idea," Snapdragon said. "However, I see just one flaw."

Bearach's grin faded. "What would that be?"

"If someone gets up in the middle of the night to, well, answer the call of nature in the woods, the whole camp will know, won't they?"

⊰❈⊱

That night, clouds blotted out the light from the waning moon and the stars. King Rayne was waiting while Oakleaf finished preparing his horse. The stables were all but deserted, with just the two of them and one more person Rayne trusted.

"I double checked. Abrecan is still in his cell, as are Ivor, Cameron, Sullivan, and Caldre," said the other man hiding in the shadows. "We've been randomly rotating the servants who feed them, plus we check to make sure nothing is smuggled in, so I doubt Abrecan is even aware of what's happening."

Rayne nodded while he put on his riding gloves and checked again that he had his bow and sword handy. "That's good. Make sure you keep a close eye on them while we're gone."

"Why not just kill them to be sure?" Oakleaf asked, sounding like he was half joking, half serious.

The man from the shadows gasped. Rayne reached down and smacked his wife's brother on the shoulder. "You aren't helping by saying things like that."

"Maybe not, but it would be one less thing we needed to worry about," Oakleaf retorted.

"Do you remember the last thing Abrecan said when he was put into the dungeon?" Rayne asked.

The man from the shadows answered, "He said that he would have his revenge. That people would come for him, and he would rule Bariwon again."

"Exactly," Rayne said. "There is no question in my mind that there are people still loyal to him. How many royal guardians retired soon after Abrecan was imprisoned? Quite a few, right? Did some stay behind, hoping to see him freed? You'll have to admit it's quite possible. While he's alive, we stand the chance of his supporters slipping up and revealing themselves. It wouldn't be easy to free Abrecan from the castle. There really isn't any hope of him escaping, not with all the precautions we are taking. Killing him outright would make him a martyr in his followers' eyes, and who knows what they would do then. No, it's best to keep him alive while we seek out those who would try to free him."

"Do you still think the disappearance of Procep's residents may be a ruse to leave the castle undefended?" Oakleaf asked.

"I think that is one of many possibilities," Rayne said. "But Rudyard was assigned by Governor Wardell, a man I trust. Sadly, I think there *is* something dangerous going on in Erd, and I intend to find out what it is."

Oakleaf nodded. "Well, the castle is defended as well as it can be. I did as you asked and got many of the retired guardians to agree to come and stay here. The rest of the royal guardians, as well as those from surrounding areas, will be meeting you by daybreak—out of sight of any that would suspect what we are doing. The extra supplies you asked for are already there."

"Well, that's good. We've made quite the showing with Fallon and his entourage so people know we're responding. They just don't know how big of a force we're responding with," Rayne said.

"Do you have any other orders before you leave, Your Majesty?" the voice asked from the shadows.

"Keep a close eye on my wife and daughter—keep them safe," he said. "And thank you again for all your good advice, Bertram."

319

‑⊰❋⊱‑

King Rayne traveled due north from the castle. He was dressed in a simple, brown hooded cloak and leather armor. At first glance, he would appear to be one of the travelers that frequented the town around the castle, and that was the way Rayne wanted it. Oakleaf had begged him to travel with a guardian, but Rayne knew that would bring unwanted attention. After all, he had been a royal guardian himself before he was king, so he was far from defenseless.

Fallon had been ordered to find out what happened in Procep, and to do it in a way that would be visible to the people of the land. Having nursemaids, servants, and crafters go with the group would most certainly increase that visibility.

Rayne had also instructed them to spend at least one night in Lewyol. Abrecan had assigned Eadward to be the governor over both Erd and Lewyol, so Rayne thought that there might still be those loyal to Abrecan residing there. Having a show of force in the district might convince those still loyal to Eadward and Abrecan to think twice.

Former governor Eadward still lived in Erd as far as Rayne knew, though he had resigned when it was discovered that many of the items he had offered in the last Shoginoc were actually from the castle, and not new offerings from the districts he represented. Eadward claimed his men gave him the items and that he had no reason to doubt they were from his districts. There was no proof Eadward had known about the deception, so he was allowed to go free, but who knew what the man had been up to since he resigned, and there were no reports of him from the magistrate of Erd.

Ahead of Rayne was a grove of trees, the place where the guardians were gathering. Dawn was just starting to break, allowing him to see shapes move among the clump of large pines. *I made it just in time*, Rayne thought.

The plan was to camp there during the day, gather the rest of the men, and move out in force after dark.

‑⊰❋⊱‑

Fallon's group awoke just before dawn and ate their morning meal before they packed up. Snapdragon had taken his turn as guard over the camp. He was allowed to get some sleep before and after his shift, but breaking up a night's sleep like that always made him weary the next day.

In addition, he wasn't afforded the luxury of sparring or running while on the trip. While preparing for the Mortentaun, he had spent hours each day working on honing his combat skills or developing his muscles. All those recent hours on a horse's back were starting to take their toll.

"We should be there before the sun sets if we push hard," Snapdragon heard Rudyard report to Captain Fallon when the group was ready to leave.

The group moved forward just as the first light of dawn appeared. As the sun rose in the east, dark clouds appeared from the northwest. Since the travelers were heading toward the northern mountains, they could very well move directly into the storm's path.

Uneasiness lingered among the group as they knew they would reach their destination by day's end, and that they might have to face whomever or whatever had taken the people of Procep.

By midday, the mountains loomed closer, with the dark storm clouds advancing. The group ate the midday meal on the move, breaking only long enough to feed the horses.

Chatter among the group was minimal, mainly due to the guardians paying sharp attention to their surroundings and asking others to talk softly. The land was covered in premature twilight by late afternoon. Though the threat of rain was in the air, the storm held off.

"There it is," Rudyard said. He pointed off to the left from their present course as the group neared the foot of the mountains.

The village of Procep sat unceremoniously up against the mountains. There were small, thatched-roof houses set about in a pattern akin to a small child leaving his wooden blocks scattered on the floor. There didn't appear to be a main road that ran through the village, just a path of sorts that led into the heart of the houses. Snapdragon glanced at Waylon, who was looking down at the ground, muttering something and shaking his head in apparent disgust.

There was no movement in the village ahead of them, nor were there any lights shining in windows. Clothes hung from ropes strung between trees or houses, as had been reported.

Captain Fallon slowed the group down and said something to the two royal guardians that rode up front, sending them off at a gallop in opposite directions around the small village.

Motioning, Fallon sent two more guardians into the center of the village. These two moved in more carefully, swords drawn. Four more guardians fanned out from the group, scanning the area with longbows in hand and arrows fitted in the drawstrings.

The guardians behind Snapdragon were faced away from the village, bows drawn and watching the area from which they had just come.

Clenching his horse's reins tightly, Snapdragon wanted to do more than keep an eye on the rest of the group, making sure they didn't do anything foolish. He wanted very much to be doing something more active, like going into Procep, and was frustrated that he had to sit back and watch.

The two guardians that had gone into the village went from house to house, never getting off their horses. After an extensive search, they returned and reported something to Fallon that Snapdragon couldn't hear.

The other two guardians that had encircled the village returned shortly, but again Snapdragon couldn't hear their report.

Curious, Snapdragon leaned forward a bit in his saddle, hoping to pick up a few words here or there, but without much luck. Still straining to hear, he felt the wind start to pick up. It was soft at first, but then started to grow in intensity.

"There!" someone shouted.

The four front guardians with bows all swung toward the west, and one of the guardians let an arrow fly toward something that was most definitely moving.

"Hold!" Fallon commanded as the arrow successfully pinned a roughly knitted dress to a tree.

"It's just the wind," Fallon called. "Do not fire!"

The clothes that only a moment before had been hanging motionless were now dancing in the wind, making the village almost appear to come alive before their eyes.

Fallon turned and faced the rest of the group. "The village is indeed deserted. It is as Rudyard has told us."

Rudyard raised an eyebrow at the captain as if to say there should not have been any doubt.

"There is no obvious threat here, although there do appear to be several caves nearby in the mountains," Fallon said. He looked up at the sky before continuing. "It is getting too dark to investigate further tonight. I know this may seem odd to some of you, but we'll be staying in the village tonight. Please respect the villagers' possessions. I'm still hopeful that we will find these people and bring them back here. We'll be posting double the usual number of guards tonight."

As the group fell into formation, Snapdragon said to Bearach, "So, do you have enough rope and bells to surround the village?"

Three hundred or so men stood before King Rayne, looking at him expectantly. They had come ready to do battle, which was exactly what he wanted. He had given them their separate orders, which they all agreed to without question, though at least half of the men appeared surprised by what the king had assigned them to do. The sun had just set, and they were ready to move.

"You have all been handpicked for this mission." Rayne sat on his horse while addressing his men. "While life in Bariwon seems to be as good as it ever has been, I fear there are those who would act on their own selfish desires to the detriment of our kingdom."

He paused a moment to be certain all the men were focused on him. Then, in a loud, strong voice, the king stated, "We cannot let that happen. We *will not* let it happen! To peace in our kingdom!"

"To peace in our kingdom!" the men echoed in reply.

⇥✦⇤

Snapdragon studied the man in front of him, or to be more precise, he studied what the man held in his hand.

"Going to wait all night, or are you going to pick?" Blythe said.

"Fine." Snapdragon reached out and plucked a twig from the man's hand.

Blythe slapped Snapdragon playfully on the back. "About time you picked us a good watch."

"Bah!" said the other guardian, who was holding the short straw. "Fine, you two get first watch. We'll relieve you in the middle of the night."

The group had made it into the village and settled into several houses before the rain finally came. Though the houses in Procep were simple, they were made solidly enough to keep out the elements.

Snapdragon donned a thick leather cloak to keep the rain from soaking him to the bone, then stepped out into the rainy night. The water was coming down in sheets, and there was a growing stream running through the center of the village.

Blythe followed closely behind in his own leather cloak. "Don't like it here." He shivered. "Think something bad happened."

Snapdragon headed to the edge of the village, intent on walking the perimeter. "There was no blood, no sign of a struggle, not even tracks we could find. I think that is more unsettling than anything else."

"On that we agree." Blythe cupped a hand over his eyes and looked toward the towering mountains. "Not even enough light here to see the mountains—just a big, dark, black void. Like there's something there, just beyond our ability to see it."

The two young guardians walked around the village for the rest of their shift, not seeing or hearing anything out of the ordinary. When they were finally relieved, they headed back to the house to which they were assigned. After warming themselves in front of the fire, they quickly fell asleep.

⊰⊹⊱

Traveling at night was slow going. One of the men with Rayne was a guardian named Aaron. His assignment for the last couple of years was to travel through the district of Erd and then report back every few months. No one in the group knew this region like Aaron did.

Rayne had elected to take back trails, away from populated areas. Unlike Fallon's group, Rayne's contained only guardians—there were no nursemaids, servants, or the like. Traveling only at night and through wilder areas was a safe way to keep from being discovered. By Aaron's best guess, they would arrive in Procep a day after Fallon's group.

⊰⊹⊱

The smell of bacon cooking was the first thing Snapdragon noticed when he woke. He felt more rested than he had in a couple of days, though his legs and backside were still a bit sore from riding so long.

Prying one eye open, Snapdragon saw Blythe still fast asleep on a bed on the other side of the modest house. Even sleeping, he had a silly grin on his face.

Snapdragon sat up slowly, stretched, and looked for his boots. Blythe awoke at the sound of Snapdragon moving around and then rolled over on his stomach, muttering something about still being tired.

The door burst open at that moment, causing both Snapdragon and Blythe to leap to their feet, each holding a sword they had kept by their beds.

Waylon stood at the door, his pudgy face turning white at the sight of two royal guardians pointing swords at him.

"I didn't mean to startle you," the savant said. "I thought you were already up."

Snapdragon lowered his sword. "Perhaps it would be best if you knocked next time."

"Agreed," Blythe said.

324

"You've not heard then, I take it?" Waylon asked excitedly.

Snapdragon and Blythe shook their heads.

"I went for a walk this morning." Waylon held his hands up defensively. "I know, I know, Captain Fallon already told me how foolish it was. But I couldn't miss the chance of seeing these ore mines up close. I didn't think I would be allowed later."

There was a drawn out pause before Snapdragon said, "And?"

"Oh! Sorry, forgot you don't know," Waylon said. "One of the caves leads to something most extraordinary—a tunnel that leads deep into the mountain."

CHAPTER 36

Oakleaf looked down on the town that surrounded the castle. Word had spread quickly about what had happened in Procep, and the people had become especially restless when Fallon's group left the castle.

There had been more activity than normal in the town, with people bustling back and forth. Far more people were visiting the inns and markets by the castle entrance than normal. At the gate to the castle, its only entrance, four guards stood just outside the raised portcullis. At least eight archers were in the towers above. While these tasks were usually rotated, that wouldn't be the case for the next several days. Only men Oakleaf trusted were allowed to watch over the castle entrance.

Oakleaf felt Rayne was playing a dangerous game, while at the same time, he saw the wisdom in it. If Abrecan's supporters tried to use this time to free their leader, they would be in for an unpleasant surprise.

⇥✛⇤

"Be very careful here." Grant pointed up. "It wouldn't take much to knock down these support beams and bring the whole cave down on us."

Captain Fallon nodded as he inspected the wooden beams. "You're the crafter. You know more about these things than I do. Is it safe to bring our horses through here?"

"Why would you want to do that?" Grant asked with a frown.

"Follow me." Fallon went to the end of the cave, where the remnants of a large brick wall remained. Holding his torch in front of him as he walked, he stepped past the brick wall and into a larger, man-made tunnel.

Grant, Snapdragon, Bearach, and Blythe followed carefully behind him.

"Take a look here." Fallon crouched down so the torch was right above the cobblestone floor.

"Ah," Bearach said right away.

Snapdragon puzzled over what he saw, or rather, what he wasn't seeing.

"I don't understand." Grant scratched his head.

Fallon looked back at them with a grimace. "Perhaps your apprentice can explain."

The large crafter turned his head and raised an eyebrow at his young assistant. "Well?"

Bearach pointed. "Who knows how long this tunnel has remained deserted. According to Savant Waylon, there is no mention of such a tunnel in any book he has read. We have to assume it has been many, many years. Look at the ground—what do you see?"

"See cobblestones is all." Blythe leaned down for a closer look.

"Exactly," Bearach said, nodding.

Grant grunted. "I still don't get it."

"Wait!" Snapdragon interjected. "If this tunnel hasn't been used for a very long time, why are the cobblestones so clean?"

Bearach snapped his fingers, then pointed at Snapdragon. "You got it. Something, or a great many somethings, have been through here recently. The reason we don't see tracks in the dust or dirt is because someone wiped them clean."

Fallon stood. "I believe the people from Procep came through here. There are stables in the village, but no horses. I have to believe they took their horses along with them."

"But where did they go?" Blythe squinted into the darkness.

Fallon folded his arms. "That's what I intend to find out."

⇥✦⇤

Fallon's group lined up in a single file before the cave entrance. Everyone walked beside his or her horse, or in Grant and Bearach's case, beside their wagon. The tunnel beyond the mine was much wider and higher, though it would be slow going because of the darkness.

As usual, Snapdragon and Blythe were near the rear of the procession, watching over the non-guardians. Grant and Bearach were near the front.

Bearach had fastened two large wooden beams to the back of his cart, pointed straight up. To the top of these beams the young crafter had wrapped oil-soaked cloth which, when lit, would make two very large torches.

"Here we are in the back again," Snapdragon muttered, watching the first few guardians enter the cave.

"Least we got to be in the tunnel with Grant and Bearach," Blythe pointed out.

"Aside from being in charge of protecting the crafters, I'll bet Fallon did that just to make sure we felt included."

"Worked." Blythe grinned. "Definitely felt included."

The group slowly and carefully went one by one through the mine and into the tunnel. By the time Snapdragon and Blythe entered, the large torches on the crafter's wagon had already been lit.

The tunnel went straight into the mountain as far as Snapdragon could see. It widened enough that Fallon could position bow-wielding guardians on either side of the wagon, and the tunnel was tall enough that they could once again travel on horseback. Blythe and Snapdragon were given the order to ride on either side of the nursemaids, servants, and Savant Waylon. Traveling was a bit easier now, but Fallon took his time, stopping often to check the tall stone buttresses or to study the floor.

The clip-clop of the horses' hooves echoed in the tunnel when the group was on the move. Without a sky above them to help gauge the time, Snapdragon wasn't sure how long they had traveled before they stopped for the midday meal.

Soon, the group was on the move again. Not long after, they came to a bend in the tunnel. From what Snapdragon could tell, they had been heading almost due north, but now the tunnel turned almost directly west. In addition, there was a noticeable breeze blowing toward them, causing the torches to flutter.

Captain Fallon stopped the group and said something loud enough for the group to hear, though it was a bit tough to make out due to the echo off the tunnel's flat surfaces. "Stay here," he instructed. "Five of us will check ahead."

The captain went ahead with four guardians, two carrying torches. Snapdragon watched as the scouting party continued on and then seemed to slowly rise from the ground. Others must have noticed this, as several people around him started whispering and shifting around nervously.

Bearach said loudly, "It's just the tunnel angling up. It may be taking them to the surface."

The group calmed down a bit, and indeed the scouting party did continue to move upwards until they were no longer in view.

After several moments of waiting, Bearach got down from his cart and walked over to one of the stone buttresses. He was studying it intently when Waylon joined him.

Snapdragon eased his horse forward. "And here," he heard Bearach say when he was close enough. "See how they interlocked the stones? If I'm not mistaken, that's the same method used in the castle walls."

Waylon leaned in closer. "Hmm. I'm not so sure."

"I've studied architecture some, and this is an old and unique design," Bearach said.

"Meaning what?" Snapdragon asked.

Bearach and Waylon shared a glance before Bearach stepped toward Snapdragon and said, "Meaning that it is more than likely that whoever built the castle also built this tunnel."

"But why wouldn't we have heard about this tunnel before?" Snapdragon questioned.

Waylon shrugged. "A lot of records and history were lost when the nislles came. We are still putting bits and pieces together of what came before."

Snapdragon frowned. "I would think that there would be at least some mention of this tunnel. After all, this must have taken a long time to build, and there had to have been a reason for it."

The crafter looked at the wall, using his finger to trace the distinctive interlocking stones. "I have an idea why we've not heard of it."

"And what would that be?" asked Waylon warily.

"Someone decided it should be kept hidden."

Snapdragon heard Fallon and the other guardians returning before he saw them.

When Fallon got close to the group, he said loudly, "The exit to the tunnel is not far from here. It leads to a mountainous area with narrow canyons that run off in different directions. There's no indication which way the people went, but there is an area not too far beyond the exit where we can set up camp."

In short order the group was once again on the move. The tunnel did indeed slope up gently, and before long there was light in addition to that of the torches. Snapdragon heard a collective sigh of relief from the group when they first spotted the exit and the dark reddish sky beyond. The sun was just setting when Snapdragon emerged from the tunnel.

The captain's description was accurate, but it didn't convey the majesty of the landscape. The mountains were very rocky, with scraggly shrubs growing here and there. It seemed as if everything, including the path on

329

which they came out, was made of a deep red stone. There were several small canyons, each not much wider than ten paces, that led in different directions—none of them appearing to be especially hospitable.

One of the nursemaids turned to look back at the tunnel and Snapdragon saw her face pale. Craning his neck, he, too, looked back at the entrance.

A large, curving archway stood out very prominently against the mountain face. Along the curve of the archway were letters formed in an odd manner that read:

Nie SyLL eSSe

In addition, white stones had been placed into the dark red earth at the mouth of the tunnel in the shape of an open circle.

Captain Fallon didn't stop but continued to lead the group into a canyon to the north of the tunnel entrance. After several sharp turns, the path opened up into a clearing. Several more small canyons branched out from the clearing in different directions, as if the clearing was the hub of a wheel.

The group efficiently set up camp once Fallon instructed them to do so. After helping set up the tents, Snapdragon again aided Bearach in setting up his rope and bell warning system.

"Captain Fallon wants the camp kept in tight, so we won't need as much rope tonight," Bearach said.

He and Snapdragon went about putting the Y-shaped sticks into the ground. Then Bearach walked over to the canyon they had come from and removed another bag from his pack. He untied the opening, reached in, and pulled out a handful of small white rocks. He leaned down and placed the rocks in the shape of an arrow pointing back the way they came. The white rocks were a stark contrast against the deep red earth.

"With the mountains so high, it's going to be hard to see where the sun is most of the time," Bearach explained. "I would imagine it could be very easy to get lost in these canyons. It wouldn't hurt to leave some markers behind."

⇢⧚⇠

Crescens entered the palace's main hall. It was vacant aside from Selene, who stood by the far window. She appeared to be staring at the northern mountains. She hadn't heard him approaching, which was fine by him. It gave him more time to look upon her without her noticing.

He heard her saying something quietly, something with a chant-like quality, perhaps a mantra. Then she made an odd gesture with her hands, hitting them together as if she was clapping, though no sound was produced.

When he got a few steps closer, she finally heard him and slowly turned around.

"Magistrate," he said in greeting.

Arching one eyebrow, Selene said, "Yes, Crescens? Do you have something to report?"

He bowed. "Yes, Magistrate. Eadward and his men are on their way to the castle. They are traveling in small groups, dressed like common folk. Word has it that many are headed to Bariwon with the news from Procep spreading. They are looking for protection."

Selene smiled briefly. "And is there any more news from Procep?"

"None that I've heard," Crescens said. She had acted so differently since she had heard about Procep. He had been patient, letting her tell him when she was ready, but this was so unlike her. It had him concerned. "Is there anything I should be listening for in particular?"

She considered him carefully as if she was debating what to tell him. He wanted her to tell him everything and had tried hard to earn her trust, yet he knew there were secrets she kept to herself.

"No," she said finally. "Just report anything you hear, word for word. Leave nothing out."

⇥✦⇤

Snapdragon tried in vain to get comfortable. Blythe had pulled a straw that gave them the middle-of-the-night guard watch, meaning Snapdragon would try to force himself to fall asleep as soon as possible. But attempting to do so only made it harder to sleep, which led to frustration and even less chance of dozing off.

He and Blythe elected to sleep out under the stars, as did a few other guardians. They hadn't pitched all the tents in an attempt to keep the camp size smaller. Savant Waylon was about to enter his tent he was sharing with the crafters when Snapdragon saw him look up at the sky and then make the moon gesture with his hands.

Snapdragon noted it was going to be a new moon tonight, something Waylon had said was unlucky or a bad omen. Snapdragon didn't believe in such things, but seeing another person so distressed by it couldn't help but make him uneasy.

It was a clear night, with dazzling stars filling up the sky. The stars didn't offer much light, but it was enough that Snapdragon could make out the shapes of tents and the other guardians sleeping on the ground.

Yawning deeply, Snapdragon again shut his eyes and tried to relax. His father told him the trick to falling asleep was to let your mind wander— thinking too hard about one subject often led to fitful sleep and unpleasant dreams.

Snapdragon took several deep breaths and imagined he was relaxing on a sloping, grassy hill on a warm spring day without any cares in the world. This picture was constantly interrupted by thoughts of the people of Procep, his anger at being treated like a lesser guardian in Fallon's eyes, and even by images of Seraphina's smile.

Time passed, though Snapdragon wasn't sure how long. He thought he heard the jingling of bells, but the sound stopped as quickly as it had started. For a moment he considered opening his eyes to investigate, but it was probably nothing. There were other guardians on watch who would sound the alarm if there was anything to worry about. Perhaps the ringing was his imagination, or perhaps he was dreaming.

Snapdragon sensed movement, and it took him a moment to figure out if he was still dreaming before he decided to do something. Rolling onto one side, he pried his eyes open to see Blythe staring at him, his usual goofy grin on his face. But there was something not right with his eyes— they lacked their usual spark.

Feeling something move by his feet, Snapdragon laid on his back and propped himself up with his elbows.

A dark mass against the field of stars loomed over him. Reacting on instinct, Snapdragon kicked up and out with his legs, causing an audible "oof" from whatever it was and sent it sprawling backwards.

Snapdragon grabbed the sword he had kept beside him and jumped to his feet. He blinked several times, trying to adjust his eyes to the darkness. The mass he had kicked was actually a man with some sort of item in his hand.

"Blythe!" Snapdragon shouted. "Get up! To arms!"

A shriek echoed off the mountain walls, followed shortly by more shouts, some in a language Snapdragon didn't recognize. The man before Snapdragon advanced on him, but even in the dark, Snapdragon was able to fend off the attack and shoved the man away.

"Blythe, get up!" Snapdragon shouted again, kicking his friend.

The kick caused Blythe to roll over on his back and stare straight up into the sky. Snapdragon's vision had adjusted enough to let him see that the young guardian's throat had been cut from ear to ear—a permanent smile mocking the one Blythe usually wore.

With Snapdragon distracted, his attacker plowed into him, knocking him off his feet. His sword spun out of his hand from the impact, and Snapdragon found himself on his back with the man pinning his arms and shoulders to the ground.

The silhouette of the man's blade appeared above his head and moved quickly toward Snapdragon. Pushing hard against the ground with his legs, Snapdragon flipped the attacker over his head.

Snapdragon got back to his feet and swiftly retrieved his sword. He didn't hesitate and impaled the attacker as he tried to get back to his feet, fatally wounding him.

With the immediate threat before him gone, Snapdragon looked around the camp. He spotted Captain Fallon on the other side of the camp, fighting off several men. Snapdragon headed toward him to help, but Fallon noticed him and shouted, "No! Protect the others! Do your duty!"

Pausing for the briefest of moments, Snapdragon fought the urge to run to the aid of his captain anyway. He doubted Fallon would survive against so many men.

Snapdragon spun and headed toward the nursemaids' tent. All around him, guardians were now engaged in battle, and none appeared to have seen the two men nearly at the nursemaids' tent door.

Leaping over the bodies of fallen enemies and comrades, Snapdragon sprinted toward the tent but knew he wouldn't arrive in time. The nursemaids screamed when the men threw open the tent door. One of the men entered, and abruptly one of the screams came to a stop.

In desperation, Snapdragon threw his sword at the man still outside the tent. It caught him in the lower back and knocked him to the ground. The man in the tent came back out when he heard his companion go down. By then, Snapdragon had arrived and tackled the other man. Kneeling over him, Snapdragon pounded him with his fists several times in the head until the man stopped moving.

He turned to face the other attacker and realized the man was dead. The sword had pierced him in the spine, probably killing him instantly. Grabbing the hilt of his sword and pulling it free, Snapdragon looked at the nursemaids. Anissa was on the ground with her throat slit, while Seraphina and Ophelia clung to each other.

More guttural shouts came from the far side of the clearing, and Snapdragon could make out dozens upon dozens of dark shapes descending upon the camp.

"We can't stay here," he said. "Follow me!"

The nursemaids got to their feet. Close to the nursemaids' tent was the crafters' and Waylon's tent. Grant was outside, holding a heavy hammer in his hands. Bearach was stuffing things in his backpack, while Waylon stood by him, hugging himself tightly.

"Get them out of here!" Grant commanded. "I'll hold them off until you can get away."

Snapdragon again fought the urge to argue. "Let's go!" he said to the nursemaids, Bearach, and Waylon. "Bearach, you go first. I'm right behind you."

"Go where?"

Snapdragon pointed ahead with his sword. "Down one of these canyons. We need to find a place to hide."

⇥⧧⇤

Grant watched Snapdragon hesitate only a moment before following his orders. After making sure that the guardian had gotten the survivors to go with him, Grant waded into battle.

Swinging his weighted hammer, he crushed the ribs of an attacker who had started to follow Snapdragon. While Grant was not quick, he was very large and strong.

He saw Captain Fallon and a few of the other guardians making a stand by the mouth of one of the canyons. They were woefully outnumbered. At that point, Grant realized the wisdom of Rayne's idea of sending a larger force.

Fallon and his men were holding off the enemy for now, but were losing ground. Grant worked his way along the edge of the camp, trying to get behind the attackers to help his comrades.

He was attacked twice and was able to fight them off, but not before he suffered several wounds, including a deep gash in his left thigh.

Suddenly he found himself where he wanted to be. The strange men were still rushing in from a side canyon, but Grant was behind and to the side of them. He was about to let out a lusty battle cry to help Fallon when he saw the captain fall. He was too late. Grant stepped back and heard a crunching sound. Looking down, he saw he had stepped on the arrow Bearach had made of white rocks.

Another guardian fell, then another, and Grant realized it would be fruitless to try to help them now. Convincing himself he was not a coward, but rather that he was doing the best thing to help, Grant turned and ran for the tunnel, going as fast as his injured left leg would take him.

⋗⧣⧣⧤

Bearach was running in the opposite direction of the attacking horde. The nursemaids and Waylon did their best to keep up, with Snapdragon right behind, constantly looking over his shoulder.

One of the attackers had broken away from the camp and was giving chase. Snapdragon knew they wouldn't be able to outrun him, so he prepared to stop to take the man on. When the man got within ten or so paces, Snapdragon stopped and spun around. He felt something brush by his ear and then heard a *thunk* behind him. Focusing solely on the approaching man, Snapdragon set himself with his sword held high over his left shoulder, the point angling down slightly.

He was able to size up his attacker for the first time. He had a shaved head with a long, pointed beard. He was bare-chested and wore some type of breeches made from hairless animal skin. The strange man was brandishing a large club.

Timing his swing, Snapdragon crouched and sliced deeply into the man's stomach before he could bring his club down. Satisfied he no longer posed a threat, Snapdragon went back to his companions to find them hunched over Ophelia.

Seraphina was in tears, and understandably so, as Snapdragon noted a long knife embedded in the back of the older nursemaid's neck. Ophelia wasn't moving or breathing.

"There's nothing we can do for her," Snapdragon said tightly. "We must keep moving."

Seraphina stared at him with her deep green eyes, then nodded and got up to follow Bearach once again. The crafter continued to head toward the nearest canyon, with Snapdragon doing his best to run along in the dark while frequently looking back over his shoulder to see if they were being followed.

They entered the mouth of the canyon and hugged the left wall as it curved slightly to the west. Soon, Snapdragon could no longer see the camp behind them, which gave him a bit of comfort because it meant his group couldn't be seen, either.

Waylon slowed down, puffing dramatically.

"Bearach!" Snapdragon called, just loud enough for the lead man to pause and look back. The savant was holding an arm around his ample middle and trying to stay on his feet.

"I... am... sorry," Waylon said breathlessly. "Too... much... time... reading."

"I know you're tired, but we must keep moving."

Waylon bent over, facing the ground. "I... need... a... moment."

Grabbing him by the arm, Snapdragon said firmly, "We must keep moving."

Bearach came over and took the savant's other arm. "Aye, we aren't safe here."

They helped the man put one foot in front of the other. He was too big for Snapdragon to carry, but at least they were moving again, even if it was at a walking pace.

Soon, they heard the sound of flowing water. The canyon opened up to a small river that ran north to south, while the canyon continued due west. At the sight of the river, Waylon dropped to his knees and buried his head in the cool water. He was joined by the others, who knelt down to take a drink. After doing so himself, Snapdragon rolled over onto his back, taking in deep breaths.

"This can't be happening," Seraphina said quietly. "This must be a bad dream."

Snapdragon saw the redhead pinch her arm, as if trying to wake herself from a nightmare. Growing up, he'd had vivid dreams—dreams that felt real, even after he had awakened. This *had* to be one of those dreams. The guardian closed his eyes and pinched himself, hoping to awaken from the awful events that had just taken place. After pinching himself, he sat up quickly, taking in a deep breath. He first looked up into the night sky, seeing the same stars he had fallen asleep under in the camp. But then he heard the sound of the river. Turning his head, he saw that his companions were still at the river's edge. This wasn't a dream.

"Do we keep on the path?" Bearach asked.

Snapdragon shrugged. "We have no idea where it leads. These rock faces are too steep to climb. But we can't stay here. In the morning, they will have no problem following our tracks."

"Then what do we do?" Seraphina glanced back the way they had come. "Do we cover our tracks somehow?"

Snapdragon looked around and thought for a moment. Even in the dim light of the stars, he could see a rock jutting above the river several dozen paces away. It appeared to be a man–and-a-half's height off the ground.

If they walked in the river, it would effectively hide their tracks, though a smart tracker would realize that and follow them down the river. They needed a way to throw off the attackers.

Snapdragon glanced at his companions. Waylon seemed beyond exhaustion. Seraphina was staring at him intently, while Bearach was adjusting the strap on his pack.

"Bearach, do you still have the bag of white rocks with you?" Snapdragon asked.

Bearach nodded.

"All right, I have an idea."

Snapdragon had them each take one step beyond the river and onto the canyon floor to the west. From there, he had Bearach make a circle, several hand spans wide, with the white rocks. After that was completed, he had them all leap backwards into the shallow river. Waylon struggled with this part a little, but was assisted by Bearach and Snapdragon.

The group then headed down the river to the rock overhang. Snapdragon boosted up Bearach first, and then easily lifted Seraphina to where Bearach could lift her the rest of the way. Waylon was a bit more of a challenge, though between Snapdragon lifting and Bearach pulling, they were able to get the savant on top of the overhang. Snapdragon jumped high enough to grab Bearach's outreached hand and then pulled himself up the rest of the way.

The overhang was several paces wide with the edges curving up, creating a bowl-like structure. Waylon lay on his back, still panting. Seraphina sat next to him, hugging her knees. Bearach and Snapdragon lay on their bellies, peering over the rock edge to the way they had come.

"Who are these people?" Seraphina asked. "Why would they want to kill us?"

"Perhaps they see us as invaders," Snapdragon said, scanning the darkness.

"But we didn't do anything to threaten them—we were just sleeping," Seraphina said angrily.

Waylon sat up a bit. "Being on their lands may have been enough provocation."

"Perhaps," Bearach said. "But that's all beside the point. What do we do now?"

Snapdragon faced his companions. "We wait here until the party that will track us arrives."

"Why? Didn't you tell us we had to keep moving?" Waylon asked.

"The best thing to do right now is stay hidden," Snapdragon said. "We have no idea where we are. These canyons are like a maze. The path back to the tunnel is blocked by our enemies. There may be another way back, but we can't look for it while we are exhausted and people are tracking us."

"So, are you saying they won't find us here?" Seraphina asked skeptically.

"If I'm right, they will stop looking for us once they get to the river," Snapdragon said. "Until then, we need to rest and be as quiet as possible."

⤙‡⤚

The wound in Grant's thigh was worse than he had thought. He had been able to limp his way to the tunnel entrance, but noticed he was bleeding pretty badly, leaving a trail of blood. He was fairly certain none of the attackers had seen him, but when the sun came up, they would be sure to notice his bloody tracks.

He sat down and bound his thigh the best he could, grimacing at how deep and wide the cut was. He tried to stand up, but found he could no longer put any weight on his leg.

"Sheep dip," he cursed, falling to his knees.

He looked back over his shoulder, back to where he could still hear the screams of battle. He tried to stand again but with the same result. Resigned to the fact that he couldn't walk, and knowing he couldn't hop back to Bariwon, Grant did the only thing he could do. He started to crawl.

⤙‡⤚

Snapdragon saw the first tracker right after dawn. The sky was just starting to brighten, though the sun wouldn't shine down on them until midday, due to the high mountain walls around them. The man was similar to those Snapdragon had seen the night before. His head was shaved and he had a long, pointed beard with a streak of green running down its length.

He was bare-chested and wore dark brown breeches with what looked like leather boots. When he reached the river's edge, he looked up and down the river, and then stepped forward, heading west. Behind him were two more men, both bald with beards, but these two held weapons, and each had a red stripe in his beard.

Snapdragon peeked over the edge of the overhang. The first man crossed the river and was about to step on the shore when he stopped suddenly. He smashed his hands together in a gesture similar to the one Waylon made to ward off bad luck. The two men with weapons rushed up to the shore, but they also stopped and made the same gesture. Exchanging glances, the three men spun around and splashed loudly across the river and then sprinted back the way they had come.

Snapdragon lowered himself from the edge and said to his companions, "They're gone—and I don't think they'll be tracking us any longer."

CHAPTER 37

"Why would they stop following us?" Seraphina asked. "What did you see?"

Snapdragon lowered himself from the ledge. "Waylon, back at the inn when you taught me about the moon symbols, you said it was people from up north who believed such things, correct?"

Waylon nodded, causing his second chin to bounce.

"And on the way here, Bearach mentioned the tunnel had been built in a similar manner to the castle, correct?"

Waylon nodded again.

"So, you think the people that attacked us are related somehow to the people in Erd?" Seraphina asked incredulously. "I heard them shouting last night, and I couldn't understand them."

"Language is a living thing," Waylon said suddenly.

All three of the savant's companions looked at him questioningly.

"Language changes over time," he said, taking on the tone he used when teaching classes back at the castle. "Certain words are added or taken away or even have their meanings changed as time passes. If a language is written down, it tends to change more slowly. If these people are indeed relatives of the people of Erd, it's possible that their language has changed enough that we can't understand it."

Waylon's eyes lit up as he appeared to realize something. "Remember what it said over the tunnel when we came out? 'Nie syll esse.' That could very easily mean 'None shall pass.' In fact, now that I think about it, many of the older writings we find are very loose in their spelling. And who knows how their dialect could have changed over time."

"So what if they are related to the people in Erd?" Bearach asked. "Why do you think they won't be following us anymore?"

Snapdragon answered, "Remember at the tunnel entrance—remember the white circle? Everything around us is deep red. The white symbolizes something important to them. I took a chance that they still held the old traditions Waylon told me about."

The savant nodded. "I understand now. You suspected that these people might be superstitious enough to be scared off by the symbol of the new moon, based on what I told you."

"Exactly, and it seemed that was the case," Snapdragon said. "They saw the symbol Bearach had made with the white rocks and that our tracks stopped there, and it really spooked them. They made hand gestures similar to what you showed me, Waylon."

The savant's expression changed into one that Snapdragon couldn't quite read. "Oh, dear," he said. "We may be victims of bad timing. Last night was a new moon. If they do, in fact, hold onto the old superstitions, having strangers appear on their land last night, especially if they saw us coming from a forbidden tunnel, would be considered a very bad omen indeed."

"How can you all be so heartless?" Seraphina asked. "People died back there—people that were my friends!"

No one spoke for several uncomfortable minutes. Snapdragon had lost a dear friend in Blythe. Maybe it was the sense of survival that took over. Maybe he just didn't want to think about it. Thinking about it made him angry and made him want to fight. Part of him wanted to rush back to the campsite and kill as many of the attackers as he could. But he knew that would only get him killed, and without him, Seraphina, Bearach, and Waylon wouldn't stand a chance.

"I'm sorry, Seraphina," Bearach said softly. "You're right. We've not been respectful of the fallen. We've all lost people we were close to. Grant was like a father to me. I don't think I've realized he's…"

Bearach turned away from them, but not before Snapdragon noticed tears in the young crafter's eyes.

"I agree. We need to mourn those who have fallen," Snapdragon said quietly. "But unless we are careful, we'll be joining them. I'm sorry if I seem 'heartless,' as you said, but understand it is my duty to protect you, and I intend to get us home."

"And how do you plan on doing that?" Waylon asked. "As you've stated, the only way we know back to the tunnel is blocked by those men that attacked us last night."

Snapdragon lifted himself back up to the top of the ledge and peered over the side. "Then I'll have to find a different way."

He lowered himself from the rock overhang into the river. The water actually felt refreshing against his boots, cooling his feet as he walked up the river. He slowed as he approached the intersection where the trackers had been a few hours previous. He wanted to make sure they didn't come back with larger numbers before he set off to see if he could find another way back.

He had three options. He could continue up the river, follow the path back to where his group had been attacked, or follow the path where Bearach had placed the white stone circle. Going down the river was not an option, since just beyond the overhang the river dove under a steep rock face.

Upriver seemed to be the opposite direction of the tunnel home, while the path with the white stone circle Bearach had made appeared to run parallel to the face of the mountain that contained the tunnel. Perhaps following the path would give them a chance to double back later.

Snapdragon's instincts told him the last thing he should do was follow the path back to the camp. But at the same time, he knew that he could get back to the tunnel if the way was clear. Pulling out his sword, he turned toward the campsite.

The canyon headed in an easterly direction, with occasional twists and turns. Snapdragon was careful to ease around the corners to make sure he saw anything before it saw him.

At last he turned a corner and saw their campsite from the night before. The area was bustling with activity. Men, all bare-chested with shaven heads, had taken down the tents and replaced them with a different type of shelter. A few dozen of these triangle-shaped shelters were set out in no particular pattern. They consisted of what appeared to be animal hides sewn together and stretched across a square frame. These frames were then leaned against a singular post sticking out of the ground and tied off at the top, probably to keep them from blowing away.

The focus of the activity was on the other side of the camp, far enough away that Snapdragon couldn't see what was going on. One thing was sure, however—this way home was still blocked.

Moving as quietly as he could, Snapdragon worked his way back to the river and continued on the path beyond Bearach's white stone circle. This part of the narrow canyon had many twists, and with the high mountain walls, Snapdragon couldn't use the sun to keep track of the direction he was headed. Eventually the canyon opened into a clearing. It looked deserted, so Snapdragon took a chance and entered it. He was able to see the sun and reorient his sense of direction.

The valley only had two exits. One was the direction from which he came; the second was a slightly wider canyon to the northwest. It wasn't very long, and Snapdragon thought he could make out open plains beyond. Knowing he shouldn't get too far away from his companions, and realizing he might wander for days without ever finding another path back, he headed back down the winding canyon and then down the river to the overhang. By then it must have been mid-afternoon—a point reinforced by his stomach growling.

Once he arrived at the overhang, Snapdragon called out just loudly enough for his companions to hear.

Bearach peeked over the edge. "Did you find a way back?"

Snapdragon shook his head. "I'm afraid not. But we can't stay here forever, and there is a clear path for us to follow. I suggest we be on our way."

"All right then," Bearach said, then disappeared back over the edge.

The next thing Snapdragon saw was Waylon's feet dangling over the rock. The savant slowly inched his way forward until he sat on the edge of the overhang. He looked down at Snapdragon. "Now what?"

"Turn around and let Bearach lower you down," Snapdragon instructed. "I'll help lower you the rest of the way."

After several awkward moments, Waylon was on the ground. Seraphina was next, and Snapdragon was very careful where to hold her as he helped her down. His hand slipped once and he accidentally grabbed her backside, but he moved his hand as quickly as he could. She smirked at him when he set her on the ground.

Bearach swung over the edge and, refusing Snapdragon's help, dropped the rest of the way, creating a splash when he hit the river.

"We're going to keep along the path we took last night," Snapdragon said. "It was clear of people. We'll need to find a place to build a fire tonight, and we will need to eat something soon if we hope to find a way back."

Bearach pulled his pack off his shoulder. "I can help with that. I grabbed several things from my tent last night before we left." He rummaged around in the pack and pulled out a cloth wrapped in twine. He untied it to reveal several strips of dried meat. Snapdragon could see Waylon's mouthwatering at the sight.

"How much of this do you have?" Snapdragon asked.

Bearach searched through his pack again. "I have four more of these. They each have ten strips."

"All right, one strip each for now," Snapdragon said. "We need to make them last."

Seraphina pulled the hood of her cloak over her head. "Can we get moving, please? These shadows and the cold water on my feet are chilling me to the bone."

"Of course." Snapdragon took a big bite of dried meat.

"Same order as last night?" Bearach asked with a mouth full of food.

Snapdragon nodded, and they set off with the crafter first in line, then Seraphina, then Waylon and Snapdragon.

When they arrived at the intersection, Bearach motioned to the white rock circle and asked, "Should I pick these up? Maybe we'll need them again sometime."

"Not a bad idea," Snapdragon said, "but be quick about it. I don't feel safe here."

Snapdragon saw Bearach freeze in place and realized he was looking back the way they had come. Spinning with his sword in hand, Snapdragon saw several of the bald men standing on the other side of the river. Before he could react, he felt something hit him hard in the head. It dazed him enough that he fell to his knees. Trying to blink away the stars before his eyes, Snapdragon looked back at the men to see one of them let loose another rock from a sling. *He must be a very good aim* was the last thing Snapdragon thought before he fell.

⇥✦⇤

"Weren't you just here?" Guardian Stuart asked, eyeing Ciar carefully.

Ciar nodded. "Aye, that I was. Crazy schedule Oakleaf has us on. I never know what I'm going to be doing next."

Stuart's companion at the dungeon entrance was leaning back on his chair and looking bored. Ciar didn't recognize the older guardian, but there had been fewer guardians in the castle since Fallon and his men had left, so it was possible this was one of the guardians who seldom had dungeon duty.

"You know the rules," Stuart said. He lifted the lid off the food tray briefly and peered inside. "In you go."

Ciar didn't say anything as Guardian Stuart let him into the dungeon and then closed the door behind him. Ciar had been lucky so far—had Guardian Asher been there, he most certainly would have been suspicious of Ciar having been down here so recently. The servant with whom Ciar traded assignments had been glad to switch and promised not to tell. No one liked to feed the prisoners. No one except Ciar and Melanie.

After finding Abrecan's cell, Ciar opened the small access panel.

"Abrecan," he said. "It's me, Ciar."

"Ciar, tell me what is going on." The commanding and forceful tone of the former councilor's voice startled Ciar.

"The castle is poorly defended without Fallon and his men. The cripple Oakleaf is in charge. There is a surge of people coming to Bariwon Proper upon hearing the news of Procep, which is perfect because it will allow Eadward and his men to prepare without drawing attention to themselves."

"Excellent. And what news is there from Procep?" Ciar could hear the smile in Abrecan's voice.

"None so far. But you do believe it has to do with the legend, correct?" Ciar asked.

"Why wouldn't it? The timing can't be a coincidence. My freedom will coincide with the freedom of our long-lost brothers north of the mountains. It is fate."

-⟫✦⟪-

A terrible pain in the side of his head was the first thing Snapdragon felt when he awoke. He scrunched his forehead, trying to ease the pain, and felt dried blood crack when he did. The next thing he realized was that he was sitting up, leaning against a post of some kind, with his hands tied behind his back.

Prying open his eyes, Snapdragon looked around. Bearach and Waylon were tied up in a similar fashion, with the crafter to Snapdragon's right and the savant to his left. Both had gags in their mouths and were looking at Snapdragon with fear in their eyes.

The three of them had been placed at the edge of the camp, backs to the canyon where they had been captured. Scanning the area, Snapdragon saw no sign of Seraphina, but what he did see made his blood run cold.

At the far end of the camp, near the canyon that led to the tunnel, lay the bodies of his group—or at least what was left of them. They had been put on display, and from what Snapdragon could see, unspeakable things had been done to them.

The camp seemed nearly deserted. There were only a few of the bald men roaming around, busy taking down the shelters. Several horses were saddled in a nearby pen. Snapdragon knew if he could get free and get to the horses, he could make a run for it. But why would they leave the horses here if most of the men had left? It didn't make any sense. He also noticed that his sword and Bearach's pack were at the edge of the makeshift stable.

One of the bald men with a red stripe in his beard said something unintelligible when he noticed Snapdragon had woken up.

A slightly larger and heavier-set man appeared to answer him.

Snapdragon strained to understand and thought he actually recognized part of what they were saying. The smaller of the two men pulled out a short, curved knife and approached. He was flanked by two more men, each with a red stripe in his beard.

Snapdragon strained against the ropes tying his hands together, but couldn't break the knots. He bent his knees, bringing his feet closer to him. The man with the knife stayed out of range of the guardian's legs and instead circled around behind him.

One of the other men went to Waylon, while the other stood next to Bearach. The bearded men all pulled curved knives from their belts and placed the tips below the left eyes of both of his companions.

The man behind Snapdragon said something that sounded like a warning, using some words that sounded like "friends" and "suffer".

The guardian felt the ropes on his hands being cut. When they were free, Snapdragon brought his arms forward carefully and stretched them to ease the ache.

The other two men made dramatic gestures with their knives, indicating that if Snapdragon acted in a hostile manner, Bearach and Waylon would be seriously injured or killed.

Feeling a hand grab his shoulder and then lift, Snapdragon realized they wanted him to stand up. He stood slowly, so as not to give the impression he was about to do anything aggressive.

He was then shoved in the back, toward an open space. The area had a large circle drawn in the dirt and had been cleared of any shrubs or bigger rocks. Dark patches of ground were scattered around the center of the circle, and as Snapdragon was moved even closer, he realized the patches were areas where large amounts of blood had been spilt.

The man behind Snapdragon kicked him in the back of the legs, sending the guardian to his knees. Another bald man, this one with a blue stripe in his beard and his nose pierced with some sort of dark stone, strode forward and started chanting in low, guttural tones.

Snapdragon's mind raced. How could he escape? His companions were still being held at knifepoint, and anything he did could have disastrous consequences for them. He still saw no sign of Seraphina. The man with the blue-striped beard flicked a few droplets of water on Snapdragon's face, chanting something indecipherable. He then nodded to the man behind Snapdragon.

The guardian was pushed to the ground and kicked hard in the ribs until he rolled over. Once on his back, Snapdragon felt thick ropes looped around his wrists and then pulled tight. Then, ropes were tied to his ankles in a similar fashion. Next, two of the bearded men brought four horses out of the stable and toward the circle.

They took the ends of the ropes and tied each one to a different horse. With a sickening realization, Snapdragon understood what they had done to Fallon and the rest of his traveling companions.

Blue Beard walked back into the circle and flicked more droplets on Snapdragon, chanting even louder. Snapdragon took in a deep breath, looked up at the midmorning sky, and realized he was about to die. He felt a sense of sadness wash over him. It wasn't that he felt remorse for anything he had done, but more of what he wasn't going to be able to do. He wanted to be a father someday. He loved being around his niece Rainbow and his nephew Rowan. He wanted to fall in love, to get married, and share his life with someone. He also felt a powerful desire to make a difference in the world, and he didn't believe he had yet accomplished all that he could.

The chanting from Blue Beard kept speeding up, and Snapdragon perceived a pattern in what he was hearing. It wouldn't be much longer.

Suddenly, the chant stopped. Snapdragon tensed up, expecting to feel the horses start to move in different directions.

For a moment, nothing happened. Then a cry of hysteria echoed off the canyon walls.

Snapdragon craned his neck to look up at Blue Beard. He was screaming and staring at where Waylon and Bearach were tied up. Tilting his head up so his chin touched his chest, Snapdragon saw what had scared Blue Beard.

Walking toward the campsite, arms spread wide open, was Seraphina. Her riding dress was gone and she was only wearing her white shift. Her bright red hair cascaded over her shoulders and her face and hands were ghostly white—whiter than they should have been.

Glancing around, Snapdragon saw that all of the men were gaping at Seraphina as she approached, some of them visibly quaking. One of them made the moon gesture with his hands.

The men who were standing over Waylon and Bearach backed away from Seraphina as she approached. Not letting the opportunity pass,

Snapdragon worked his wrists back and forth to loosen the ropes that bound him.

He had freed one hand and had the other one almost free when Seraphina reached the edge of the camp. She tilted her head back, opened her mouth, and let out a dreadful scream. At the same moment she flung her arms forward. White powder flew from her hands, swirling in the air around her.

The bearded men turned and ran in the opposite direction. The horses started to stir as well, and Snapdragon was able to get his other hand free just before the horse it was attached to bolted.

Reaching down, Snapdragon quickly removed the ropes from his ankles, keeping a close eye on the skittish horses to which he was stilled tied. Once free, he jumped up and turned to where the bearded men had run. They were all still running away, nervously glancing over their shoulders.

Snapdragon sprinted to the makeshift stable and grabbed his sword. Satisfied that the bearded men were still fleeing, the guardian went to Bearach and Waylon and cut the ropes that bound them.

Seraphina had stopped screaming and ran toward Snapdragon. When she reached him, she hugged him tightly, and then stepped back. Tears started streaming from her eyes, staining the white powder she had used to cover her face.

Next, she hugged Bearach and Waylon, the savant awkwardly returning her embrace when it was his turn.

"What in the world—" Bearach started to ask.

Shaking her head, Seraphina said, "No time. We need to leave. Now!"

Snapdragon looked around for his options. Only three of the horses remained—the others had scattered when the men had.

"Quickly, mount up!" Snapdragon commanded. "Waylon, you get on that one. Bearach, take that one. Seraphina and I will take the black one."

Bearach ran over and grabbed his pack, then helped Waylon get onto the tall horse.

Snapdragon grabbed his sword, climbed on the horse, and offered his hand to Seraphina. She looked like a sad jester with her tearstained cheeks and white-powdered face and hands. She climbed up, sat behind Snapdragon, and put her arms around his waist.

"Bearach, take the rear. Waylon, follow right behind me," Snapdragon said. "We are going to make a run for the tunnel home. Let's just hope we can get through."

He faced his horse toward the canyon entrance, which still bore the white stone arrow, and kicked his horse into a run. He felt Seraphina squeeze him tighter when the horse began to gallop.

Hope of getting home started to build as the canyon entrance drew closer, but the feeling disappeared when a large man on a horse emerged from the canyon. He had broad shoulders and, like the rest of his companions, was bald. But his beard was even longer than the other men's, with a blue stripe, a green stripe, *and* a red stripe. In addition, his ears had been pierced with some sort of gleaming black rock that ran from his lobes through the tops of his ears, giving him a demonic appearance.

Behind him were ten or so men on horseback, with several dozen armed men on foot.

Snapdragon pulled back on the reins, stopping his horse abruptly.

The broad-shouldered man grinned unpleasantly. He said something to his men that sounded like a chastisement. Snapdragon understood the words "not an ancient" and "only a woman." Whatever trick Seraphina had used to spook away the men obviously didn't fool this man. He pulled out a long, jagged sword and urged his horse toward Snapdragon and his companions.

CHAPTER 38

The leader didn't charge toward Snapdragon's group, but instead inched his horse forward. His intense gaze never left Snapdragon, and the young guardian thought the look on the other man's face was similar to that of a cat when it knew it had a mouse trapped.

"Go!" Snapdragon shouted to Bearach. "Back the way we came!"

The crafter turned his horse around. Waylon managed to follow, and both took off at a gallop back toward the canyon that led to the river.

Snapdragon spun his horse around and started after his companions. He glanced over his shoulder and saw the bald-headed men in pursuit, the one with three stripes in his beard leading the way.

Snapdragon guided his horse to where one of the shelters was being taken down. He reached down and grabbed one of the sides that had been untied from its post.

"What are you doing?" Seraphina hissed.

He lifted the square of tightly pulled animal skins so he had a good grip on it. "Trying to slow them down."

Fighting against the wind, Snapdragon angled the square so that the edge was facing the direction they were heading and the large, flat surface was parallel to the ground. He looked back over his shoulder and saw the leader gaining on them, only a few horse lengths behind, with his sword held high over his head and a grin on his face.

"Hang on!" Snapdragon told Seraphina, then threw the square at the leader.

The man was close enough that he didn't have time to react. The square edge hit him in the chin, knocking him off his horse. The other bald men reined in their horses to help their fallen leader.

Snapdragon looked ahead to see Bearach enter the canyon with Waylon right behind him.

"That was amazing!" Seraphina said. "You hit him right in the chin!"

"I was aiming for his horse."

They entered the canyon and Snapdragon had to slow his horse down a bit to navigate the twisting path that led to the river. Once they arrived, Bearach and Waylon were on the other side of the river, moving slowly and looking back toward them.

"Now where?" Bearach called.

Snapdragon pointed to the canyon on the other side of the river. "Through there! There is an opening not far beyond. When we get there, let me take the lead."

Bearach nodded and kicked his horse in the ribs.

Upon crossing over the river, Snapdragon noticed that the white rocks Bearach had laid in a circle were gone. He would ask Seraphina about it later.

The canyon soon opened to the valley Snapdragon had visited earlier. When he passed Waylon and Bearach, he gestured toward a wider canyon to the northwest and urged his horse toward it.

As they approached the wider canyon, Snapdragon could see the open plains beyond. A large river ran roughly east to west not too far beyond the mouth of the canyon. Deer and elk roamed in the open, grassy plain, many drinking from the river.

Where there was drinkable water and wildlife, perhaps there was a town or village where Snapdragon and his friends could take refuge. He had read about people that roamed from place to place, taking what they needed along the way. They had been quite common during the period after the nislles. The bald-headed men reminded him of these roamers, so perhaps any people they found would be enemies to their pursuers. It was the best Snapdragon could hope for at the moment.

Entering the wide canyon, he glanced back to see Waylon behind him, with Bearach not far behind. In addition, Snapdragon saw the bald-headed men just entering the valley, with the broad-shouldered man again leading the way.

Snapdragon focused again on the plain ahead of him. He angled his horse toward the eastern side, scanning the area for any signs of civilization. His heart sank when all he saw was open range.

"What is that?" Seraphina all but shouted in his ear.

He looked back and saw her pointing at something in the distance to the west of them.

It looked like a hill on the horizon, but what was odd was that it seemed almost triangular in shape. In addition, there was nothing near it—no mountains, buildings, or other structures.

"I don't know what it is." Snapdragon turned his horse toward it. "But we're going to find out."

The guardian pushed his horse as hard as he could, glancing back now and again to make sure Bearach and Waylon were keeping up. The crafter seemed fine, but the plump savant had a look of pure horror on his face as he hung on for dear life.

The triangular hill came closer into view as the horses galloped on. It sat on the opposite side of the river, and there appeared to be a low bridge of sorts that would allow them to cross over the swiftly moving current.

Upon closer inspection, Snapdragon saw that the hill wasn't a hill at all, but rather a structure built of large gray stones stacked on top of each other. He had no idea why it had been built here in the middle of a plain, or how the large stones got there. But one thing he saw gave him a glimmer of hope. At the base of the pyramid was an archway. It looked to be about five paces wide, and it was tall enough for a horse to enter.

Glancing back again, Snapdragon felt his heart race even faster as he saw the bald men gaining ground. He looked back and forth between the pyramid and the oncoming enemies and estimated he and his companions would arrive just ahead of the men chasing them.

He counted ten men pursuing them, aside from the broad-shouldered leader. Snapdragon had trained in combat much of his life, including how to deal with multiple attackers. He could successfully fend off two or three men at a time, but there was no way he could take on eleven.

But he wouldn't have to if he could make it to the archway first. The fairly narrow opening would bottleneck the attackers and allow him to take them on in smaller numbers. The odds that he would be able to kill them all were still slim, but if he was going to die, at least he'd destroy as many of them as he could before he fell.

The bridge was in full view now. Like the pyramid, it was made of gray stone, with one major exception. Near the top curve where it ramped up, Snapdragon saw that white stones had been inlaid in the gray ones in a curving pattern. When his horse's hooves struck the rock and they started climbing the bridge, he noticed the curving white stone pattern continued up over the zenith of the bridge. It wasn't until Snapdragon was on top of the bridge's highest point that he noticed the white stones were inlaid in the shape of an open circle.

He turned his attention to the pyramid before him. It stood at least as tall as the highest towers in the castle. This close he could see smaller openings further up the pyramid, leading to flat outcroppings. There was no sign of recent activity in the area, and grassy weeds grew near the opening.

Snapdragon stopped his horse and motioned for Bearach and Waylon to go through the archway. The two men slowed their horses and entered the pyramid. Soon, they were enveloped by the darkness of the structure's interior.

Snapdragon jumped off his horse, leaving Seraphina still mounted. He quickly led the horse into the opening, unable to see where the other two men had gone. He spun and readied his sword to face the oncoming pursuers.

To his surprise, the bald men had stopped on the other side of the bridge. Aside from the broad-shouldered leader, they were nervously shifting around, some of them making the moon gesture with their hands.

The leader stared at Snapdragon loathingly. He shouted something the guardian couldn't make out and then spat on the ground before him. Giving Snapdragon one last glare, he turned his horse and started leading his men away from the pyramid.

⇥⧫⇤

Eadward kept his head down as he followed two of his men to The Bull's Horns Inn. It was a three-story building with a huge hearth in the common room. While all of the inns in the town surrounding the castle had become more docile since Rayne had become king, The Bull's Horns still held an air of the good times—the times when Abrecan had run the kingdom and the people of Bariwon knew their place.

Eadward had picked two especially large former guardians to accompany him. Both were formidable and, he had to admit, rather ugly. They would draw attention away from him. He was too well known, and being spotted could ruin everything.

During the daylight hours, his men had waited in nearby inns. They had made good time in the darkness of last night's new moon and had staggered their arrivals enough as to not cause suspicion.

One of the men talked to the innkeeper about a room, while Eadward and the other man waded into the crowd. Even at midday, the common room was packed. It seemed many had come to the area after the news spread about Procep.

People spoke in subdued tones about what could have caused it. The most popular theory was that the nislles had returned, and that it once again threatened to wipe out the population of Bariwon. Eadward smiled when he heard such rumors. Something most definitely was returning to change Bariwon forever, but it wasn't the nislles.

The innkeeper and the guardian seemed to have come to an agreement on a room. Motioning with his head, Eadward's man indicated for them to follow.

Avoiding eye contact with any of the inn's patrons, Eadward followed the large man up a set of solidly built stairs to a second-story room that contained three beds.

Eadward walked to the window and stared out at the castle that loomed not far from where they were. "Perfect," he said.

⊷⊰⊱⊶

Darkness. It was a darkness so thick it seemed to press down on Snapdragon, adding weight to his weary legs, which were threatening to give out from underneath him once he entered the pyramid.

"What happened?" Seraphina's voice came from somewhere ahead of him.

He looked back over his shoulder to the plain beyond the pyramid and saw the bald men continuing to ride away.

"They left," Snapdragon said with relief.

Bearach's voice pierced the darkness. "They left? Why?"

"Because of the bridge," Waylon answered. "Didn't you see the open white circle when we rode over it?"

"No, I didn't." Bearach sounded defensive.

Snapdragon's eyes had begun adjusting to the lack of light, and he could make out the shapes of his companions. They were standing beside their horses, facing him, though he couldn't see much beyond them.

"This place must be sacred to them," Snapdragon said. "Why else would they not want to cross over the bridge?"

Waylon's reply was just above a whisper. "Perhaps it wasn't because it is sacred. Perhaps it was fear that held them back. These are superstitious people."

"This place looks deserted," Seraphina said. "What could they be afraid of?"

Snapdragon saw Waylon shift uncomfortably, and he could now make out the chubby man's features. "Superstitions are often based on something—a real thing—to be afraid of."

"Just because the pyramid looks deserted, doesn't mean it is," Bearach pointed out.

Snapdragon squeezed the hilt of his sword, which was still in his hand. "Bearach is right. Perhaps it's best that we leave the pyramid until I can scout it out some."

Waylon looked back over his shoulder and shuddered. "I think that's a good idea."

⇥✦⇤

The sun was making its way toward the mountain ranges to the far west of the plains. Bearach had taken care of the horses, moving them out of the pyramid to a grassy area by the river. Wild game grazed nearby, seemingly oblivious to Snapdragon and his companions. For the first time since the attack, they were able to let down their guard a little.

Waylon sat cross-legged at the base of the pyramid, appearing to try to memorize every detail. Snapdragon warned the savant not to let curiosity get the best of him and to stay out of the pyramid until it could be investigated.

Seraphina was sorting through the saddlebags, taking inventory of their supplies. She still wore only her white shift, though she had washed the white powder from her face and hands. Despite his earlier warnings to Waylon, Snapdragon let curiosity get the better of him, and he approached the young nursemaid.

"Find anything useful?" he asked, looking over what Seraphina had placed on the ground.

She motioned to the items. "There are a few blankets, some dried food, flint and steel, and several bladders we can fill in the river."

"Have you found anything to wear?" he asked.

Seraphina looked up at Snapdragon, smirking. "I should probably put something on, shouldn't I?"

"Only if you want me to be able to concentrate on getting us back home," Snapdragon said teasingly.

For the first time since he had met her, Snapdragon thought he actually saw her blush. "There are tunics and breeches in here, though they are all made for a guardian. I'll find a way to make them work."

"Speaking of clothes, why are you only wearing your shift? And what happened back in the camp?" Snapdragon asked more bluntly than he intended.

Bearach looked up from tending the horses, and even Waylon took his eyes off the pyramid for a moment.

Seraphina didn't answer at first. Instead she reached into a saddlebag and pulled out a light brown tunic. She slid it over her head and harrumphed when she saw that it fell below her knees. Next, she took a short length of rope and tied it around her waist, effectively making a dress out of the oversized shirt.

"Once you were knocked down, Snapdragon, they also knocked out Bearach and Waylon," she said.

Snapdragon noticed Waylon rubbing the back of his head at the comment.

Looking down, Seraphina said, "I didn't know what to do. I ran—I ran down the canyon, but soon one of them followed me. Unlike the others, who had red or green stripes in their beards, he had a blue stripe. He caught up with me and grabbed the back of my cloak. I lifted my arms in the air and let the cloak slide off of me, but my riding dress came off as well, leaving me in my shift."

She brought a hand to her long red hair. "He first looked at my hair and said something that sounded like a curse. He then noticed my white shift and took off running back the way he had come, screaming hysterically. Unfortunately, he was still holding my cloak and dress when he ran away."

She hugged herself around her middle. "I didn't know what to do. We had run far enough down the canyon that I couldn't see what had happened to the rest of you. It took me a little while, but I gathered enough courage to come back to where you had fallen. When I finally got there, you were all gone, and the only thing that remained was the circle of white rocks."

"I'm still unclear why—" Snapdragon started to say.

"Let me explain," she interrupted. "I got to thinking that something about my appearance really scared the man with the blue beard. Maybe they don't have women with red hair here. We know that the color white holds some sort of meaning for them. Whatever it was, I thought perhaps it was something I could exploit."

She reached down and picked up a fist-sized stone. "I gathered the white rocks from the circle and, using a larger rock, pounded them into a white powder. They have rocks like that where I grew up, and I remember watching my father crush them down to powder. What he used them for,

I'm not sure, but that's beside the point." She took the stone in her hand and rubbed it against her other hand for emphasis.

"After I crushed them all, I used water from the river to moisten my face and hands and applied the powder. I teased out my hair the best I could. My reflection in the water told me I looked different enough that it might startle them sufficiently to allow you to escape."

"But the scream… and the flinging of the white powder?"

"It was a bit over the top, I know, but I wanted to get their attention. Apparently it worked."

Snapdragon reached out and gently touched her arm. "That was very brave. You saved our lives."

"Consider us even," Seraphina said, then turned back to sorting the items in the saddlebags.

⋆⊰❈⊱⋆

Snapdragon peered up from the base of the pyramid. He held his sword in his left hand and a makeshift torch in his right. He could almost feel Bearach, Seraphina, and Waylon's eyes on him as he stepped into the archway.

Of all their options, they all agreed the pyramid would be the safest place to stay. It was cold comfort, considering they knew nothing about the structure. Seraphina had actually given Snapdragon a quick hug before he headed in to investigate.

Standing just inside the archway to let his eyes adjust, he moved the torch back and forth slowly a few times. The archway led to a fairly spacious open chamber, with the ceiling angling up to roughly twice the height of a normal-sized man. A steep set of stairs led up from the far side of the chamber, roughly twenty paces away. It appeared to be the only exit from the chamber, aside from the archway that led outside.

Snapdragon walked to one of the side walls and saw drawings carved into the stone, with characters below that looked like a form of writing. Snapdragon narrowed his eyes a bit at the drawings. At first glance it seemed that they told a story. While that did pique his curiosity, his goal was to determine if the area was safe, and ancient pictures and words didn't pose much of a threat.

Taking a quick but deliberate walk around the chamber, Snapdragon verified that the pictures and words surrounded the room and that the only discernible way further into the pyramid was the steep stone stairs.

Putting the torch before him, Snapdragon carefully ascended the stairway. After about twenty steps, the stairway ended at a small hallway that ran perpendicular to the stairs. Looking right, then left, Snapdragon decided to go left. The hallway didn't go far before he came to another set of stairs going up, these doubling back the way he had come.

He looked up the stairs but couldn't see the end of the stairway. Again, he slowly started to walk up the old stone steps. On the seventh step up, the stone gave way beneath his foot, and the edge where his heel rested tilted down quickly. He heard a solid thump behind him but didn't turn around to see what had made the sound, because the rest of the steps started tilting down as well. The angle of the stairs was steep and Snapdragon started slipping backwards. Instinctively, he placed his hands against the stone walls on either side, but slowing his slide proved to be tricky, considering that he was still holding his sword and torch. He then jammed his feet into the corners where the ramp and walls met, bringing him to an abrupt halt.

Feeling his heart pounding in his chest, Snapdragon looked back over his shoulder down the stairway. He saw what had made the noise behind him when the stairs had tilted. Opposite to the end of the stairs, long, sharp spikes now protruded from the wall. Whatever triggered the steps to tilt must have also pushed the spikes into place. Had he not stopped himself from sliding down, he most certainly would have been impaled.

Upon further inspection, Snapdragon found that the spikes extended the width of the hallway, so even if he were to slowly work his way back down, he wouldn't be able to go back the way he had come.

That left exactly one way for him to go. He estimated the distance between the two walls and had an idea. He placed one foot flat against the wall and inched it up until he felt he could put his weight into it. Then he leaned his torso toward his sword hand, opposite of where he had moved his foot. Taking a deep breath, he pushed off with his foot, putting his back up against the wall. He flung his other foot forward so it was planted next to the other one. It wasn't pretty, but with his legs and back holding him in place, he was able to free his hands.

First, he sheathed his sword, emptying his left hand. Next he considered the torch. Scaling his way up the passageway would be next to impossible while holding the torch. He considered holding it in his teeth, but the torch wasn't very long and that would bring the flames dangerously close to his head.

Looking again up the passageway, he realized he had gone far enough that he could see where the ramp that used to be stairs ended. He didn't see any other option, so he threw the torch. It flew end over end and landed on the level area above the ramp, bouncing around a bit before finally coming to a stop right at the edge. Had he missed his target and the torch gone down the ramp, he wasn't sure he would have been able to grab it as it went by.

He took one foot off the wall and bent it under him against the wall behind him. From there, he was able to shift his weight to where he could place a hand on either wall. Moving his feet back down to the corners between the walls and ramp, Snapdragon started to climb up the ramp.

The progress was slow, and he tried to take his mind off his straining muscles by focusing on the torch. Inch by inch, he worked his way up, trying to note any other traps along the way.

He started to think of what he would do once he reached the top. What other surprises awaited him? But then he chided himself. While he should be wary of what lay ahead, if he lost focus and slipped, none of that would matter.

The torch loomed closer, giving him hope he would make it to the top soon. He watched the dancing flames and used it as his inspiration to keep going, despite the fact that his arms and legs were starting to quiver from effort.

He nearly lost his grip when the torch rose from the ground and appeared to float in midair for a moment. Gathering his wits, Snapdragon looked *beyond* the torch and caught a glimpse of a figure holding it before the person quickly moved away, leaving Snapdragon in the dark.

CHAPTER 39

With a renewed sense of determination, Snapdragon forced his way up the ramp. It was his left hand that first caught the edge of the wall, indicating he had reached the top of the ramp. He got a firm grip on the edge and pulled himself up, then quickly drew his sword and assumed a fighting stance.

Quite aware that there could be more traps awaiting him, Snapdragon looked around and noticed a flickering light bouncing off a far wall. Reaching out with his right hand, he found the wall. He moved up close against it then went forward.

The light was all but gone now, yet Snapdragon was able to judge the distance, and he bounded toward it, taking large leaps to help reduce his chance of stepping on something he shouldn't. His last leap was a bit off and he crashed into the wall, but didn't lose his balance. Whoever or whatever had taken his torch had gone to his right, and he could see the light just fading from view. However, it was above his head, which probably meant one thing—another staircase.

Snapdragon had an idea and reached back to the wall opposite where the stairs ended. Running his hand along it, he didn't feel any holes or other openings that spikes could go through, so perhaps this staircase wasn't a trap. Not having much of a choice, he stepped up once, and then again, judging the distance between the stairs. He took a deep breath and started bounding up, taking several steps at a time.

He had nearly reached the top, by his best guess, and was proved right when his leap landed him a bit lower than he expected. He looked quickly left and then right, and didn't see any fading, flickering light from the torch, though he saw something better—dim sunlight.

He stopped and looked down both hallways. Following the pattern he had seen so far, the stairs he had just climbed led to a hallway that ran perpendicular to the stairs. On either end of the hall were staircases that led upwards. Creeping toward the light, Snapdragon stopped abruptly when he noticed that the wall opposite the end of the stairs leading to the light was filled with round holes from top to bottom.

Snapdragon backed up and went the other way. When he reached the other end of the hall, he indeed saw another stairway, this set without the holes on the accompanying end. Squinting up the stairs, he couldn't help but smile. More sunlight was visible, coming in from the right side.

With his sword in front of him, he climbed as quietly as he could. Reaching the seventh step, he purposefully stepped over it. When he neared the end of the stairs, he felt a cool breeze on his face. At the top, he peered around the edge toward the light.

There was a curved archway about ten paces away that led to an outside platform—one of the platforms near the top of the pyramid he had noticed earlier. Standing on the far side of the platform was a figure. After the utter darkness he had experienced in the tunnels, the bright sunshine made it hard to see clearly at first. But soon it became apparent that it was a man, slightly built and wearing roughly cut animal skins over his shoulders and as a sort of loincloth.

The man held the torch in one hand, but his other hand held onto something protruding from the wall at the top of the other staircase. The man was looking down the booby-trapped stairs, and he appeared to be anxious.

Snapdragon quietly took a few more steps, all the while keeping out of the man's view. He took another quick glance around the corner and didn't notice any obstacles between him and the other man. He rushed around the corner, sword at the ready, and yelled, "Hey!"

The figure turned his head. His dark brown eyes widened in fear. The man had unkempt, frizzy dark brown hair and a scraggly beard. He paused only a moment before heading down the stairs.

Snapdragon raced across the platform to the other staircase. To the left of the archway was a handle or lever of sorts, and Snapdragon realized this was what the other man gripped earlier.

Acting on a hunch, Snapdragon grabbed the stone handle and again yelled, "Hey!"

The frizzy-haired man looked over his shoulder and back up the stairs, then stopped abruptly when he saw Snapdragon's grip on the stone handle. Turning slowly around with his hands up in the air—one holding the torch and the other empty—the man said something unintelligible, but the tone of his voice and his body language told Snapdragon that he was surrendering.

Again the man spoke softly, then slowly ascended the stairs. Snapdragon made his sword very visible to the man as he approached, while continuing to keep a firm grip on the lever.

"That's far enough," Snapdragon said firmly when the man was but a few steps away.

The man paused, tilted his head to one side, and said something that sounded like, "Yooo spak Rrrifnaherrd?"

"Rifnaherd? I don't know what that means," Snapdragon replied.

The man pointed to his mouth. "Rifna Erd. The language of the Rifna Erd."

Snapdragon motioned for the man to come the rest of the way up the stairs. He let go of the handle and backed off when the man got close enough, but continued to keep him at sword point. The man kept a respectful distance, still holding the burning torch as he joined Snapdragon on the platform.

"Who are the Rifnaherd?" Snapdragon asked.

The man put his free hand to his forehead and pulled back his hair so it lay flat against his head. "The men who shave their heads. The men who were chasing you."

Snapdragon eyed the man warily. "How do you know they were chasing us?"

The man released his hair. He then opened his arms expansively and said, "I see a great many things from up here."

"If you see so much," Snapdragon said, "tell me, why didn't they follow us over the bridge?"

The man gave Snapdragon a look of absolute bewilderment. "What do you mean? Why would they cross it? They had no mylnohe with them."

Snapdragon noticed that getting a sense of the frizzy-haired man's speech was becoming easier, and obviously the other man understood Snapdragon well enough. Still, Snapdragon didn't understand the full meaning of everything. He shook his head and said, "This isn't getting us anywhere. Why did you take my torch, and what does that lever do?"

Again the man looked perplexed. "You have not been sanctified. You should not be here. As for the lever, pull it down to see for yourself."

"I have a better idea," Snapdragon said, stepping away from the lever. "I want you to do it."

The man shrugged, then walked over to the lever and pulled it down.

Snapdragon heard the same *thunk* he had when he was on the tilting steps, and peering down the stairway, he noticed these steps were now angled as well. Obviously, it hadn't been something Snapdragon had triggered. "You caused the other staircase to do this, didn't you?" he said to the man. "That could have killed me! Why did you do that?"

"You have not been sanctified," the man said in a tone one would use when trying to explain something to a small child or an idiot.

Snapdragon thought for several moments, then said, "My name is Snapdragon. What may I call you?"

The man bowed at the waist. "I am called Sverre."

"Sverre," Snapdragon said, though saying the man's name was like speaking with a mouthful of food. "We meant no disrespect by crossing the bridge and entering this pyramid."

"Temple," Sverre corrected. "This is the Temple of the New Moon."

"Temple," Snapdragon said reverently. "My apologies. We were simply trying to escape from the Rifnaherd."

Sverre nodded. "Yes, the Rifna Erd are unclean."

"We will happily leave if you can show us a safe place to hide from them," Snapdragon said.

This time, Sverre shook his head. "There is no safe place to hide from the Rifna Erd. They kill or enslave any who are not like them."

"But you are not Rifnaherd," Snapdragon pointed out. "They have neither killed nor enslaved you."

Sverre spread his arms. "I am not hidden."

Snapdragon sighed. "But you are safe here."

Sverre pulled the lever back up, causing the stairs to go back into place and creating the *thunk* that Snapdragon imagined to be the spikes going back into the wall.

"I am sanctified," Sverre said.

"We can't stay here, and if we leave, the Rifnaherd will find us. What do you suggest we do?"

"You must become sanctified."

⇥✠⇤

Grant stopped to rest. It had been slow going through the tunnel, especially in the dark. He hadn't traveled far, but at least he was out of sight of the tunnel entrance. His hands and knees were torn up quite badly from having to crawl, but he had to return to Bariwon. He was one of the few that King Rayne had confided in, and he needed to tell what he had seen. Grant doubted anyone had survived the attack by the strange bald men. He choked back his grief for the fallen—especially Bearach. The young crafter had become like a son to him.

Strange noises from behind made Grant tense up. He listened carefully but couldn't make out exactly what was causing the sound. It almost sounded like someone taking a chisel to stone, but that didn't make any sense. The entrance to the tunnel was wide open—they wouldn't need to clear a path.

Then he heard voices. Many voices.

Grimacing, Grant returned to his hands and knees and continued to crawl toward his homeland.

⇥❖⇤

Sverre led Snapdragon back down through the temple, and Snapdragon noted that the man took the paths where the traps didn't exist—at least the ones of which he was aware. Sverre had given the torch back to Snapdragon and led as if he instinctively knew the way. Snapdragon had no doubt that the man could find his way around without a torch.

Upon exiting the temple, Snapdragon found his companions waiting anxiously.

"We heard you shout," Seraphina said. "And then we saw you up there on the pyramid. We thought you were shouting at us, but then realized you weren't when he joined you." She nodded at Sverre, obviously unsure what to think about the man.

"Sverre here is a resident of this place," Snapdragon said.

"It is as he says," Sverre stated.

Waylon, Bearach and Seraphina all appeared startled when Sverre spoke.

"And obviously he understands our language," Snapdragon pointed out.

Sverre shook his head. "No, not your language. The language of the Rifna Erd. You are not Rifna Erd, so it is not your language."

Snapdragon thought he saw something in Waylon's eyes—recognition? Yet he wasn't sure and Waylon didn't say anything.

Anticipating his companions' questions, Snapdragon said, "There are things to explain, yes. But right now, we need to do something if we are to be allowed to stay here in the Temple of the New Moon to hide."

"Temple of the New Moon, you say?" Waylon asked, glancing up at the large structure before him.

"Yes," Sverre said. "Only the sanctified can reside in the temple."

Waylon nodded solemnly. "And how exactly does one become sanctified?"

"You must immerse yourself in the water," Sverre said, pointing to the river that ran beside the temple. "And be observed by one who is sanctified."

"That's it?" Seraphina asked, already moving toward the river.

Sverre held his hand up. "Wait. You must immerse yourself without the restrictions of this world."

Seraphina placed her hands on her hips. "Meaning?"

"I do not know how to be clearer," Sverre said, clearly perplexed. "You still have the restrictions of this world."

Sverre grabbed a hold of the animal skins that covered his shoulders.

Snapdragon's eyebrows shot up. "You mean without clothing? Naked?"

"Yes, as you entered the world, so shall you re-enter the world," Sverre said.

All four men turned and looked at Seraphina. Her response was to roll her eyes. "Fine," she said, starting to undo the rope that held her oversized shirt in place. "But not until you all turn around."

Sverre shook his head. "I must observe or you will not be allowed to enter."

"How convenient," Seraphina mumbled before waving at Snapdragon, Waylon, and Bearach to turn around.

The three of them did as requested, and as Snapdragon did so, he couldn't help but notice the big grin on Sverre's face.

⊰❖⊱

Fortunately it was during the warmest part of the day when all four of them finished Sverre's process of sanctification. Whether it was just the cool water washing away the dirt and grime he had gathered over time, or something else, Snapdragon felt very refreshed and rejuvenated after his turn in the river.

Snapdragon kept a close eye on Sverre. The man had, after all, tried to kill him, so who knew what else he was capable of.

"You are now able to enter into the temple," Sverre said, then turned and walked back toward the archway.

"Wait!" Waylon said, who was still drying off from his turn in the river. "I have so many questions. Who built this temple? What are you doing here?"

Stopping and holding up a hand for silence, Sverre said, "Your thirst for knowledge will be quenched. Follow me and you shall have all you can drink."

Sverre strode into the temple, heedless of the darkness inside. Snapdragon stayed right behind him, holding a new torch Bearach had fashioned while the rest of them had taken their turns to be sanctified. Seraphina, Bearach, and Waylon followed closely behind.

Once he reached the middle of the chamber, Sverre turned and faced them. Spreading his arms wide, he said, "Here is the knowledge you thirst."

Dumbfounded, Waylon said, "I don't understand. I don't see anything."

Sverre's response was to walk back toward the archway that led outside. He stood just to the left of it and put his palm against one of the square bricks. He leaned in and pushed against the rock, creating a clicking sound followed by the sounds of rock scraping against rock.

Soon the chamber started to become lighter, then lighter still until clear blue shafts of light shone through openings in the chamber's vaulted ceiling.

"Incredible," Bearach breathed, walking over to the stone Sverre had pushed. He studied it a moment. "It must be counter-balanced somehow, but to do so with only rocks that would open the other outlets... I can't even imagine the precision it would take to make that happen."

Bearach looked back into the chamber. "Plus the effects of time. It's a wonder these work at all. Aha!" He hurried to a corner that was darker than the rest, then stopped and looked back up and around. "There should be light here as well, based on the pattern of the rest of the chamber."

Sverre nodded. "You are wise. That corner has been dark for generations, no doubt due to the will of the one who surveys all."

"It did have light at one time?" Seraphina asked.

"So it is said. But that is not where to begin to quench your thirst." Sverre walked to another wall and pointed. "Here."

The four companions followed Sverre and looked to where he pointed. Snapdragon recognized the stone-carved pictures he had seen before, but still couldn't read the writing.

"What does it say?" Waylon said.

Sverre blinked a few times. "What people speak Rifna Erd, but not the true language?"

Snapdragon tightened his grip on his sword while the frizzy-haired man considered them a moment. Sverre *was* unpredictable, and Snapdragon wasn't sure if not speaking this "true" language was as serious an infraction as not being sanctified.

After a tense moment, Sverre turned back to the wall and said, "If you do not know the true language, then I will tell you the story of the Rifna Erd and the Tular Tevoil."

⟡

One of King Rayne's dear friends was Governor Nash of Lebu. Nash, a former royal guardian, had once been in charge of the castle's night watch. Nash had told Rayne how all those years of being awake at night had made him grow accustomed to sleeping during the day, which Rayne was trying to do now. It felt so unnatural to rest while the sun was up. He would have to ask Nash about that when he saw him again.

However, during times like these, Rayne knew he should get rest when he could. By Guardian Aaron's best guess, if they left at dusk, they would arrive in Procep by morning. And once they arrived, they would return to a somewhat normal sleeping schedule. At least, that was Rayne's hope. It would wholly depend on what they found in Procep. Rayne tensed as he thought again about what they might find, but then chided himself. Worrying would not help him sleep—and sleep was what he needed.

CHAPTER 40

Sverre pointed to the first scene that had been chiseled into the stone wall: a castle. Snapdragon felt the hair on the back of his neck rise when he realized it was the castle in Bariwon.

"Before the time as we now mark it, a great ruler lived in a temple built by the design of the Tular Tevoil," Sverre explained.

Snapdragon noticed that his companions also recognized the castle, and he saw Bearach mouth the word "Tevoil." Was it a coincidence that the Tular Tevoil shared a name with one of the districts of Bariwon? Sverre either didn't notice their reaction or didn't care and continued on, going from scene to scene around the chamber.

"Tular Tevoil and Rifna Erd worked together to build the mighty temple. Tular Tevoil the mind, Rifna Erd the arm. Once it was completed, they built a tunnel, known as the Pendeltune, between lands, only to discover that the new lands were already possessed. The people of the new lands were simple and true and came to admire and welcome them."

Pointing to a picture of a large, bald man sitting on a horse, surrounded by more bald men with weapons, Sverre said almost sadly, "Rifna Erd came to rule over the true people and forced them and the Tular Tevoil to build this mighty temple where we stand today. Many lives were lost during this dark time."

Sverre smiled as he pointed to the next picture and said proudly, "But the Tular Tevoil and the true people of the land joined forces and, knowing the fears of the Rifna Erd, caused the temple to be a terrifying place full of secret traps and dark places. But most of all, they renamed the temple after the new moon, the thing the Rifna Erd feared most."

The next picture showed the temple, but on one side was a large open circle that seemed to be made out of fire. "It is said that Rifna Erd was so shaken by the betrayal that he left the temple and roamed the land, killing any that would not follow him," Sverre went on. "For many a season, Rifna Erd stayed away from the temple."

"I'm sorry to interrupt," Seraphina said, "but was Rifnaherd a man or a group of people?"

Sverre looked at the nursemaid. "Yes."

Snapdragon took this vague answer to mean that Rifnaherd was a man, and that the people who followed him were called by his name.

"Wait a moment," Bearach said. "Is it Rifnaherd or Rifna Erd?"

Sverre gave the crafter a puzzled look. "I do not understand."

"Rifnaherd or Rifna… Erd?" The pause between words was clear.

"Ah," Sverre said. "It is Rifna… Erd, as I have said all along."

Snapdragon looked at his companions. Bearach and Seraphina seemed surprised by the connection, but Waylon did not. Perhaps the savant had learned about the Rifna Erd in his studies.

Pointing to the next picture, Sverre continued, "Tular Tevoil and the true people became one, intent to return through the Pendeltune to live among the people of the first temple. But after traveling to the Pendeltune, they found a message written into the stone that said 'Nie syll esse,' which meant that something bad—something very bad—had happened in the land of the first temple. After much debate, it was decided that they would travel through the Pendeltune anyway, but they found it had been sealed up."

"If they did not return to the land of the first temple, as you call it, where did they go?" Snapdragon asked.

Sverre moved to the next panel, near the corner. "With Rifna Erd roaming the land, there was no safe place for the Tular Tevoil to go, except perhaps to the rumored Itamunno Kael. It was a story passed down from generation to generation of the true people, and unknown to the Rifna Erd."

Then the frizzy-haired man declared, "And that is all you are to know."

"What?" Waylon said. "But there's more to the story—more engravings on the wall."

"The story ends here, by the will of the one who surveys all." Sverre motioned to the top of the chamber where no light showed through, unlike the rest of the room.

"But we can look at the engravings using a torch." Waylon sounded bewildered.

Standing in front of the next picture, Sverre folded his arms and said, "No, you cannot."

"Let me understand," Bearach said. "If light were shining here, you would proceed?"

"But light does not shine here," Sverre said matter-of-factly.

Bearach walked around the chamber, looking up at the openings where light was shining through. He came back to the dark corner, pointed up, and asked, "Sverre, may I please try something here?"

The frizzy-haired man stood motionless for a moment. Then, without saying a word, he stepped out of the way.

"Snapdragon, do you think you could support me on your shoulders?" Bearach said.

The guardian sized up the crafter. Though he was a good head shorter than Snapdragon, he was bulky in a muscular way, and probably weighed almost as much as Snapdragon. Before responding, Snapdragon glanced at Seraphina, who was looking at both of them skeptically.

"Absolutely," Snapdragon said, hoping he sounded more confident than he felt.

He got down on one knee and used the wall as a support, then let Bearach climb up. With his feet planted solidly on Snapdragon's shoulders, and Snapdragon holding onto Bearach's ankles, the guardian slowly stood up.

"Throw me the torch," Bearach instructed Waylon.

The savant looked at the torch, then up at Bearach, and paused.

"I'll do it," Seraphina said. She took the torch from Waylon, then stepped back and gracefully tossed it up. It arced perfectly so Bearach was able to grab it without causing Snapdragon to lose his balance.

Bearach held the torch up to the top of the chamber. "Take two steps away from the wall and one step to your left," he directed.

Snapdragon did so carefully. For several drawn-out moments, nothing happened. He felt his legs start to quiver, and then he felt Bearach's weight shift.

There was a loud clicking noise, followed by the sound of rock scraping against rock. Soon the corner that had once been dark started to brighten. Bearach jumped off Snapdragon's shoulders and said, "That should do it."

Wanting to rub his aching shoulders, but not in front of Seraphina, Snapdragon watched as Bearach put away the long belt knife he wore.

"A section of rock had broken loose over time and was wedged in there, preventing it from opening," Bearach explained.

Sverre looked at the crafter strangely. "You have done the unthinkable."

Snapdragon wasn't sure if that was a good thing or not, so he took a step between them.

"For your deed, you will be told the rest of the story," Sverre said.

Snapdragon slapped Bearach on the shoulder in congratulations.

Sverre went to the next engraving. "The Tular Tevoil were able to decode the clues left behind by the ancient ones, and they found Itamunno Kael. With Rifna Erd still away, Tular Tevoil and the true ones—now all known as the Tular Tevoil—changed their language to what the true people spoke to confound the Rifna Erd. However, the language of the Rifna Erd is still taught for the time when we will return to the land of the first temple."

"That explains why we can't understand the writing below the engravings—it's written in their other language," Waylon whispered.

"The Tular Tevoil created two secret paths to Itamunno Kael, where they built their city, keeping watch over the Pendeltune, waiting for the day they could return."

"But I thought you said there was no safe place to hide from the Rifna Erd," Snapdragon said. "But these Tular Tevoil you speak of are hidden."

Shaking his head, Sverre said, "No, not hidden. The Rifna Erd know where they are, just as they know where I am."

"But why do the Rifna Erd not kill the Tular Tevoil, or you?" Seraphina asked.

Sverre sighed. He explained as if he was talking to little children, "Knowing where a place is and knowing how to get there are two different things. As for me, only the mylnohe ever cross the symbol of the new moon, but even then, most fear to do so. None have come close to the Temple of the New Moon since I was selected."

They came to the last engraving—words inscribed with vertical lines to the right of the words.

"These are the names of those selected before me," Sverre said. Then, pointing to the word at the bottom of the list, he said proudly, "And this is my name."

Waylon reached out and touched the engraving. "These lines next to your name are newer than the rest. What do they represent?"

"How many new moons I have been here."

Waylon's eyes grew big, and he mumbled something under his breath that to Snapdragon's ears sounded like counting.

"You've been here for over two years," Waylon announced. "How much longer are you to be here?"

"I have completed nearly half my responsibility," Sverre said.

Waylon whistled in admiration.

"While I'm sure all of this is interesting to some of you," Seraphina said, "how exactly does this help us get home?"

"That depends," Sverre said. "Where is your home?"

Seraphina walked back to the first engraving and pointed to the castle. "We come from here—what you call the land of the first temple."

Sverre took several steps back and looked at each of them one at a time, a mixture of fear and excitement on his face.

"Are you saying the Pendeltune is open? That it is safe for the Tular Tevoil to return?"

"There is a tunnel that runs below the mountains that is open, yes," Snapdragon responded. "I assume it is this Pendeltune you speak of. But as for it being safe to return, the Rifna Erd are preventing us from going back—unless you know of a different way."

Sverre rubbed his hands together excitedly. "One of the two secret passages to Itamunno Kael opens in the canyons not far from the Pendeltune."

Bearach harrumphed. "But with the Rifna Erd out there by the tunnel entrance, is it safe for us to go to this passage—or the Pendeltune as you call it?"

"Most definitely not!" Sverre sounded shocked at the question.

Waylon, Seraphina, Bearach, and Snapdragon looked at Sverre expectantly for a moment, waiting for him to say more.

Finally Seraphina spoke up. "Well then?"

"There are *two* passages to Itamunno Kael." Sverre said impatiently.

Another long pause.

"And...?" Seraphina prompted.

"And?" Sverre repeated.

After letting out a long breath, Seraphina asked, "And where is the second passage?"

Sverre grinned. "Now that you have asked, I can show you."

Seraphina looked at Snapdragon and threw her hands up in the air. He gave her a knowing smile and shrugged his shoulders.

Sverre walked over to the foot of the stairway that led upwards. Snapdragon cringed, recalling how the last time he climbed stairs in the temple, he had nearly lost his life.

Pointing to Bearach, Sverre said, "Come over here."

The crafter furrowed his brow and slowly approached the spot where Sverre stood.

"Put a hand here and a foot there," Sverre instructed, pointing to two bricks that looked indistinguishable from the ones around them.

Walking to the other side of the entryway to the staircase, Sverre placed a hand on the rock wall in front of him and purposefully placed a foot in a certain spot.

"When I tell you to, push into the wall first. Then, when you hear the sound, press down with your foot."

Bearach nodded.

Snapdragon grabbed Seraphina's and Waylon's arms and pulled them back, away from the stairway.

"Now!" Sverre commanded.

Bearach pushed into the wall, as did Sverre. There was an audible *click*, and then Bearach and Sverre stepped down hard.

The floor before the stairway appeared to collapse down slowly. Inching forward, Snapdragon could see it hadn't collapsed, but rather formed a stairway, this one leading down.

"Amazing," Bearach said quietly.

"It takes two people to open the path on this end, and I cannot do it unless a sanctified person requests it," Sverre said. "And now, we shall go to Itamunno Kael."

⋅⊰✦⊱⋅

Walking through the streets surrounding the castle was becoming more difficult. Ciar doubted there were this many visitors in town during the Mortentaun. People cluttered the streets in search of food, entertainment, and even work. A common topic of conversation was the fear of the nislles returning, while other visitors spoke of legends of people from afar waiting for their chance to invade the kingdom. Ciar was one of the few who knew the truth.

The story had been passed down through his family, and it was only told to those old enough to understand the seriousness of keeping it secret. If Abrecan was correct about why the people of Procep had disappeared, Ciar wouldn't need to keep the secret to himself much longer.

After finally reaching his destination, The Bull's Horns Inn, Ciar elbowed his way into the common room. It was nearly time for the midday meal, so patrons of all types were crowded in, yelling for service.

This was one of the seedier inns in the town, which made it a perfect meeting place. The message Ciar had received stated that Eadward was staying here. Following the directions he had memorized—they were never written down—Ciar worked his way up the stairs and to the door of Eadward's room.

As he had been instructed, Ciar knocked twice, waited a beat, and then knocked three more times. The door creaked open a little, and a large man with rather unpleasant features looked down at the castle servant.

"Wutcha want?" the man asked.

Ciar responded by balling up his right fist. Then, after making an O shape with his left hand, he smashed his right hand into his left, causing the O to collapse.

The large man grunted and opened the door to let Ciar in.

Eadward was facing the window, hands clasped behind his back. It had been a few years since Ciar had seen his cousin, and he was amazed at how well Eadward looked.

"Ciar," Eadward said without turning to face him, "how long before you'll be ready?"

"I was about to ask you the same question."

The former governor turned and sized up Ciar. "You look tired. Is this too much for you to handle?"

Ciar tried not to scowl. His cousin had done him a favor by getting him employment as a servant in the castle those many years ago, and Eadward had never let him forget it. "Not all of us are destined for greatness," Eadward had once told Ciar condescendingly. "But do as you're told and one day even *you* may be worth something."

Well, Ciar thought, *that time is nearly at hand.*

Standing up straight and squaring his shoulders, Ciar responded, "I'm fine. I've been busy planning Abrecan's escape. I need only two more days—at the most—for everything to be in place."

Edward turned back to face the window. "That will do. The rest of my men will be in place by then."

⁓※⁓

Bearach and Snapdragon double-checked that all the provisions were secure on the horses, while Waylon and Seraphina spoke with Sverre at the entrance to the temple.

"Do you think he's telling us the truth?" Bearach asked just loud enough so Snapdragon could hear him.

Without looking over his shoulder, Snapdragon responded, "No. At least not as *we* see the truth. Remember that he tried to kill me for not being 'sanctified,' as he called it. In what other ways have we violated their customs? Where does that lower tunnel actually lead? Is it another trap?"

Bearach faced Snapdragon. "If you feel this way, why did you agree to go with him?"

"Do you see another option?" Snapdragon asked wearily. "Because I don't. At least he's letting us take our horses with us. We just need to be very careful. I want you to take up the rear. Keep a weapon handy. I'll stick next to Sverre, and we'll have Seraphina and Waylon stay in the middle."

Bearach grunted. "I really don't like this."

"Neither do I." Snapdragon clapped Bearach on the shoulder. "Neither do I."

⊰⧙⊱

Despite Sverre's insistence that there was no need for torches, Snapdragon wouldn't back down, so each of his party held one as they descended the steps. The passage was just wide enough for them to walk single file, and just high enough that the horses could walk without having to lower their heads.

After they all entered the tunnel, Sverre reached to his right and pushed against part of the wall. A loud noise behind him made Snapdragon want to spin around, but he fought the urge and instead drew his sword and pointed it at Sverre.

Bearach yelped in surprise and shouted, "The stairway just went back up!"

Looking quizzically at the point of Snapdragon's sword, Sverre said, "Of course. We do not leave the passages open."

"Now listen here, Sverre," Snapdragon said harshly, "you *will* tell me when you are about to do something. Understand? No more surprises."

Sverre blinked at Snapdragon. "Are you suggesting I leave the passageway open for any to enter Itamunno Kael?"

"No," Snapdragon responded, no longer trying to hide his frustration, "but remember that you tried to kill me not long ago, and I want to make sure that doesn't happen again."

Sverre looked at Snapdragon, then beyond him to the people and horses that followed. "If I wanted you all dead, it would already be so. Now, I am going to turn around and take a step with my right foot, then my left. Is this permissible to you?"

Snapdragon sighed. "Just tell me before you do anything more than leading us to our destination."

Without saying another word, Sverre turned and started walking down the passageway.

Several hours into their journey, Snapdragon felt a tap on his shoulder. Looking back, he saw Seraphina holding a dried meat stick in her hand, offering it to him.

"Thank you," he said, not wanting to take his eyes off her, but knowing he must keep a close watch on Sverre.

"You're welcome," Seraphina said softly before returning to her place in line.

Sverre walked on confidently, with the rest of them following closely behind. A few moments later, Sverre stopped.

"We are here," he announced.

Snapdragon reached out with his torch to look beyond Sverre, but saw nothing but more tunnel ahead of them.

"We are where?" Snapdragon asked.

"Here," Sverre said again.

Waving his torch around him, Snapdragon said, "This is Itamunno Kael?"

Sverre let out a laugh that to Snapdragon sounded a bit hysterical.

"You wanted me to tell you when I was about to do something," Sverre said. "Well, I'm about to."

He jumped into the air, stretching his body so it was parallel to the ground. His feet hit the wall solidly to Snapdragon's right, while his hands smacked hard against the wall to the left.

Just ahead and to the left, the wall sank into the ground, revealing a stairway. Fresh air rushed in, causing the torches to flicker. In addition, light coming from the stairway brightened up the tunnel.

"Sverre!" Snapdragon growled. "You were supposed to tell me what you were about to do *before* you did it."

The frizzy-haired man let go of the wall and swung his feet down beneath him. "No, you told me to tell you when I was about to do something. Now, let us go up to Itamunno Kael."

After climbing a long set of stairs, Sverre emerged into the sunlight, followed closely by Snapdragon, then the rest of the group with their horses in tow. Snapdragon gasped and heard Seraphina do the same.

"It's beautiful," she breathed.

Framed by giant, jagged mountains, a crystal-clear lake was surrounded by dwellings that appeared to be made out of white marble. Between many of the dwellings were rows of green vegetation, and in several places, Snapdragon saw pens of animals. But it was the image of the deep blue

376

sky, the clear lake, and the white, almost pristine, structures that took his breath away.

After taking several steps away from the group, Sverre turned and faced them. "It has been a long time since the Rifna Erd have gone to such lengths to find the way to our home," he said darkly. "You have all been trained well and have even broken your vows to let your hair grow and cross over the Symbol of the New Moon. This means to me that the Rifna Erd are planning something unlike we've seen before."

At that moment, several dozen men dressed in white robes and holding long spears emerged from nearby dwellings.

Before Snapdragon could protest, Sverre said, "It's my intention to find out from you just what they are planning."

CHAPTER 41

H is sword still drawn from following Sverre through the tunnel, Snapdragon made a quick evaluation of the men in front of him. Unlike Sverre's, these men's faces were all clean-shaven, and their hair was neatly trimmed. Despite the robes they wore, Snapdragon could tell the men were muscular, though they didn't appear comfortable holding spears. The horses Snapdragon and his companions brought along would be of no use—there was nowhere to go.

"Drop your weapons," Waylon urged his companions.

Bearach let out a sharp bark of a laugh. "I don't think so."

"I think we should," Seraphina whispered.

The crafter shook his head violently. "I've been chased, captured, nearly killed several times, and now trapped again. I'm not going down without a fight."

"Please," Waylon said.

Snapdragon had enough training to realize this was not a fight they could win. There was no place to go, and back down the tunnel was a dead end. Without saying a word, he threw his sword several paces in front of him and spread his arms wide to indicate he was not a threat.

"What are you doing?" Bearach hissed.

Looking over his shoulder, Snapdragon said quietly, "Living to fight another day."

Waylon came forward, arms spread wide as well, though the action caused a bit of a chuckle from Sverre.

Seraphina was next, mimicking Snapdragon and Waylon. Several of the robed men stared at Seraphina before refocusing their attention on the group as a whole.

After several tense moments, Bearach said, "Fine!" and threw his belt knife and pack on the ground before him.

"That was a wise decision," Sverre said. "I suggest you continue to be wise and tell us exactly what the Rifna Erd are planning when we put you to the question."

"But—" Seraphina started to say.

Holding up a hand, Sverre said, "Not now. I will not hear any more of your lies. You will be more willing to tell the truth when... properly encouraged."

From behind Sverre, walking along the water's edge, came three more men. Two of them were armed and dressed in a similar fashion to the spear-wielding men, though their robes seemed to have a slight purple tint. The man in the middle also wore a robe, though it shimmered in the sunlight, changing from white to a deeper purple. He wore a strange, flat, triangle-shaped hat that fit his head snugly.

The man in the strange hat was a good head shorter than his armed escorts, though the way he carried himself gave him an air of authority. He said something as he approached, of which Snapdragon recognized only the name "Sverre."

Sverre responded in a respectful but somewhat defensive tone.

When the man who appeared to be the leader arrived at Sverre's side, he scrutinized Snapdragon's group. After a moment, he said something again to Sverre.

The wild-haired man bowed his head slightly and responded in a quiet tone. This time Snapdragon understood the words "Rifna Erd."

"I am Merton," the man said. "I am the ruler of the Tular Tevoil."

Like Sverre, his accent was thick, but Snapdragon could understand him if he listened carefully.

"I am Snapdragon," the guardian said, "and these are—"

"Did I ask your name?" Merton interrupted.

Sverre's eyes grew wide, as did those of the spear-wielding men.

Instead of responding, Snapdragon simply gazed at the man as if to say, *Fine, I won't speak unless asked, but neither will I cower before you.*

"You will all be put to the question," Merton said, "but first your horses will be taken and put with our livestock. And then you must become sanctified before you are allowed to enter Itamunno Kael."

Seraphina groaned. "But we were already sanctified by Sverre before we were allowed to enter the Temple of the New Moon."

Merton looked at Sverre sharply, and the wild-haired man cringed.

"The process was not complete," Merton stated.

He motioned, and two of the original men in white robes with spears left the ranks and headed to a nearby dwelling. Two other men came forward and led the horses away.

"You will immerse yourself in the lake without the restrictions of this world, and when you arise, you will be dressed in new robes," Merton instructed.

Leaning over and sniffing Sverre, Merton said, "That includes you."

Seraphina threw her hands in the air and walked down to the lake. She undid the rope that held her oversized tunic in place.

By the time she reached the water's edge, the two men had returned and placed white robes on a rock near the lake. As Seraphina went to lift the tunic over her head, all the men quickly turned their backs to her, including Sverre.

"Don't I need to be observed by one who has been sanctified?" she asked angrily.

Without looking back at her, Merton said, "No. It is inappropriate for men to watch women be sanctified."

"Oh, really?" Seraphina said feistily. "Then why did Sverre tell me he had to watch and did so?"

Merton's shoulders tensed, while Sverre's slumped even more.

"That is something Sverre and I will discuss later," Merton said harshly.

⊰⊱

"Are you sure it was wise to humiliate Sverre like that?" Snapdragon asked Seraphina.

She smirked. "Served him right for all he's put us through."

The four companions from Bariwon sat around a stone table in a windowless room, all dressed in white robes. On the table before them was a modest meal of green beans and some kind of cooked meat. Glass goblets held what appeared to be water.

"Do you think it is safe to eat this?" Bearach asked.

Waylon looked up with a mouthful of food and said in a muffled voice, "I hope so."

"As both Sverre and Merton said, they are going to be 'putting us to the question' later. If they wanted us dead, they could have done that at any time before now," Snapdragon pointed out.

Bearach nodded and began eating.

"What do we tell them?" Seraphina asked.

"The truth," Waylon said quickly. "Tell them the truth. It may not be what they want to hear, and they will probably act as if they do not believe you, but whatever you do, tell them exactly what has happened to the best of your ability."

The rest of the group looked at the savant, and Snapdragon thought Bearach and Seraphina looked as stunned as he felt. Waylon was speaking to them as if he was back in the castle and instructing them—not like the scared scholar he'd been recently. Snapdragon paused for a moment at that thought. Why exactly had Waylon come along on the expedition? No one seemed to question it, but now Snapdragon was wondering if they should have.

"Waylon's right," Bearach said. "If we all tell the truth, our stories will match. And Grant used to say, 'Tell the truth always. It's much easier than trying to remember which story you made up before.'"

They finished the meal in short order, no one leaving anything to waste. It had been a while since they had eaten a substantial meal, and they took advantage of it.

The room had four beds lined up against the wall and a modest hearth in one corner. Even though it was one of the warmer times of year, it would get chilly at night this high in the mountains. A small fire provided just enough heat to make the room the perfect temperature.

Waylon yawned loudly and eyed one of the beds. "I think I'm going to lie down for a bit." He stood and moved to one of the beds.

Bearach yawned as well. "I think that's an excellent idea. Do you think we should leave a guard awake?

Snapdragon nodded his head toward the door. It was solid rock, just like the rest of the walls around them. It had been perfectly balanced to open on a central axis point, something Bearach marveled at once again, and it was clear it had been barred shut from the outside.

"I don't see leaving a guard awake doing us much good," Snapdragon replied. "We may as well get some rest while we can."

In response, Waylon started snoring loudly.

"Like any of us is going to get any rest having to listen to that all night," Seraphina muttered.

Snapdragon was too exhausted to sleep. It was an irony he had faced several times before, especially after a full day of combat training. His body ached in so many different places, and his mind raced as he thought over the events of the last few days. He could still picture Blythe in the moonlight, eyes that would never see anything again staring up, the ear-to-ear cut of his throat mimicking his constant smile. Of all the people who had died that night, Blythe was the one Snapdragon had been closest to. He could have imagined them being lifelong friends, even after they had retired and had families of their own.

He felt a stab of guilt. Why had he survived and not Blythe? He tried to push the thought out of his mind, but it kept returning.

Waylon had stopped snoring loudly, but Bearach made up the difference. In the rare silence between the two men snoring, Snapdragon thought he heard Seraphina sniffling. From the glowing embers of the fire, Snapdragon could make out the nursemaid's form. On the bed directly across from him, she lay on her side with her back toward him. He saw her body shudder and realized she was sobbing.

Snapdragon walked over to her bed, knelt down, and said, "Is there anything I can do?"

Seraphina's crying ceased, and for a long moment she didn't move or say anything. Feeling awkward, Snapdragon thought about what to say next, but he didn't want to make things worse. Just as he was about to go back to his own bed, she said softly, "It's all right to cry."

She rolled over and faced him. She reached out, took his hand in hers, and brought it to her face. He could feel the wetness of tears on her cheek, and something hard inside him seemed to melt. He rested his head on the edge of her bed and took a deep breath. She kissed his hand softly and then said gently, "It's all right."

Snapdragon exhaled raggedly, tears coming to his eyes. Part of him wanted to hold back, and it was as if Seraphina sensed that. She kissed his hand again. And with that, Snapdragon started to cry for the first time in his recent memory. It wasn't long before Seraphina joined him and he felt her reach an arm around him so he was nuzzling her neck. For a long moment they remained like that, Snapdragon kneeling on the floor next to Seraphina's bed, crying and mourning for those they had left behind. Eventually, he started to relax, and soon his sobs turned into regular, deep breaths.

⇥✦⇤

The sun's first rays were just coming over the horizon when King Rayne and his men spotted Procep. Guardian Aaron had been invaluable so far—not only had they reached Procep without being detected, but Aaron had also told Rayne about the history of places they had passed. Rayne had studied the basic history of Bariwon, but Aaron was full of stories from the locals. Many of these stories Aaron dismissed as tall tales, but Rayne had been told by his wife—who was quite the scholar in her own right—that legends and these "tall tales" were often based on something real.

The story behind Procep was a bit of a mystery. While a small village existed there now, people from the area claimed they were always digging up remnants of a larger town that would have covered an area ten times the size of Procep. Most of the savants in the castle dismissed these discoveries as the villagers trying to sell pieces of rubbish at high prices by inventing a story to go along with them.

The village itself was unremarkable; it looked like any number of villages that dotted the area. But something was wrong. Where was Fallon's group?

"Do you see any movement in the village?" Rayne asked Aaron.

The well-traveled guardian scratched at his thick beard. "No, and there isn't any smoke coming from the chimneys or anyplace else close. At this time of day, they would be up and making the morning meal."

"Is it possible we beat them here?" Rayne asked, frowning.

Aaron shook his head. "Not unless something delayed them along the way. But the path they took was well traveled, so I doubt it was because of the terrain."

"I don't like this. No, I don't like this one bit." Rayne looked at the men gathered behind him. All seemed tense, and many had their hands on their weapons.

"Send the scouts into the village. Have archers fan out to cover them," Rayne instructed Aaron. "Let's find out what happened here."

⋙✦⋘

The note Rayne held in his hand certainly looked like Fallon's handwriting. But more importantly, it used a key phrase at the end they had agreed upon to ensure that anything being communicated wasn't written under duress. It read:

Villagers not here when we arrived. No sign of them leaving. Tunnel discovered in one of the mineshafts. Going to explore. Will send back messengers in a few days. To peace in our kingdom!

Fallon

"And you found nothing else, aside from this note?" Rayne asked.

Guardian Aaron shook his head.

"Well then," Rayne said, "it appears we set up camp here and wait."

⇥✢⇤

Snapdragon awoke a while later, still kneeling by Seraphina's bed, his head resting against her neck. Without a window in the room, it was hard to tell what time it was, though he felt he had slept for several hours. He lifted his head, causing Seraphina to awaken. She raised herself up on one elbow, and they looked deeply into each other's eyes. There was an unspoken message there, one of mutual trust and understanding.

He felt his heart quicken and his cheeks turn red when he realized the position he was in. He was still a royal guardian and not allowed to court. But what if they didn't survive? Surely he would be forgiven for living for the moment.

At that instant, a loud noise by the door startled the others awake. Snapdragon sat up quickly, nearly dragging Seraphina out of bed because she still had her arm around his neck.

"What are you two...?" Bearach started, and then seemed to decide it was better to leave the question unasked.

Waylon, still rubbing sleep out of his eyes, said, "What's that? Did I miss something?"

The stone door spun open and Snapdragon could see daylight in the hallway outside. Two young women dressed in matching white robes carried in trays of food. They were flanked by a couple of spear-wielding men who were keeping a sharp eye on the prisoners.

The food was placed on the table, and the dishes from the night before were retrieved. Neither of the servers looked at the captives directly and seemed relieved when they left the room.

One of the men holding a spear said in the thickest accent they had heard yet, "You have but a short time before the questioning." Then he and the other man departed, and the door spun closed.

The prisoners quickly and quietly ate the morning meal. Bearach had looked back and forth between Snapdragon and Seraphina throughout most of the meal, acting like he wanted to say something, but he remained silent. As usual, Waylon was focused on the food before him.

Seraphina and Snapdragon exchanged meaningful glances time and again, but neither said anything.

Just as the captives finished eating, the door opened again. Merton stood in the hallway with his two protectors. Pointing to Seraphina, he said, "We will question the woman first."

Snapdragon stood up to protest, but the men on either side of Merton pointed their spears toward the guardian as if to indicate it was not open to debate.

Seraphina stood up, appearing completely composed. She walked around the table and faced Snapdragon. "I'll be all right," she said, reaching out to squeeze his hand. Then, with her head held high, she walked out the door.

Snapdragon wanted to rush after her, but he held back. As soon as she was clear of the door, it closed again, and the sound of it being barred shut sent a shudder through Snapdragon.

Waylon was the next to go, about two hours after Seraphina had been taken. Unfortunately, she wasn't returned to them, and Merton ignored Snapdragon's questions about where she was.

When Bearach and Snapdragon were alone, Bearach asked, "Just what happened last night with you and Seraphina?"

Snapdragon smiled. "What do *you* think happened?"

Bearach harrumphed. "It looked to me like you were trying to see if her bed was big enough for two."

"That wasn't it at all," Snapdragon said, feeling his face go red. "We were just, well, just…"

"Just what?" Bearach eyed Snapdragon carefully.

"Mourning together," Snapdragon said finally.

Bearach harrumphed again. "I see."

"We've been through a lot the last few days," Snapdragon said.

"That we have," Bearach replied in a softer tone.

They didn't speak much after that. When the door opened again, Bearach was selected to go. He gave a quick nod to Snapdragon and walked out the door with his fists clenched.

Alone in the room, Snapdragon paced the floor, wondering how his companions were doing. Waylon had insisted that as long as they all told the truth and their stories matched, they would be fine. So, Snapdragon repeatedly went over the recent events, making sure he had all the details.

When the door finally opened and Merton stood there motioning for him, Snapdragon felt a mixture of relief and fear.

"Before we take you to the questioner," Merton said, "I want to show you something."

Merton walked first, followed by one of the spearmen. Snapdragon went next, flanked by the other spearman.

The leader of the Tular Tevoil led them down a long passageway. Like everything else Snapdragon had seen thus far, the walls were made out of what seemed to be solid white bricks. They arrived at the foot of a staircase, and Merton paused only a moment before he ascended it.

The spiral staircase took them up what Snapdragon guessed were a couple of stories. He was proven right when they exited at the top of a tower, the tallest in the town that surrounded the lake.

"This is the legacy of the Tular Tevoil," Merton said, gesturing majestically with one hand. "We have had no murders in several generations. We live in peace and harmony. Each person shares with everyone else. There is no need for want. There are no poor. Everyone serves everyone."

Merton sighed deeply. "It should have been this way throughout all the land." This time he swept his hand to indicate the mountain range. "But the Rifna Erd made it impossible. Our deepest sorrow as a people is that we cannot leave this town. At our very core, we have the dream of returning to the land of the first temple."

He turned and faced Snapdragon. "You are not the first to try to trick us into thinking the way back was clear. Only two generations ago, the Rifna Erd sent up the sign of peace. We met with them at the Temple of the New Moon. They told us the way back to the land of the first temple was open. They offered us safe passage if we promised never to return and never to let anyone else come through the Pendeltune."

Snapdragon met the man's stare, not giving anything away. Merton was obviously very smart and wouldn't be telling Snapdragon this unless he had an ulterior motive.

Merton continued, "We pretended to debate the manner for quite some time, while we sent scouts of our own to the Pendeltune through the way not known to the Rifna Erd. The scouts discovered a large force of Rifna Erd there, prepared for battle. So you see, your plot to trick us is not an original one."

Unable to remain quiet any longer, Snapdragon said, "I don't know anything I can say that would convince you, aside from the truth."

Merton smiled thinly. "It isn't me you have to convince; it is the questioner."

With that, Merton spun and descended the stairs, the rest following in the same manner as before. At the bottom of the stairs, the leader of the Tular Tevoil took a different hallway. After about fifty paces, they came to another stairway heading down.

"The questioner is waiting for you." Merton pointed down the stairway.

Snapdragon said, "No matter what he says or does to me, I will only tell the truth."

Merton smiled again. "Of that I have no doubt."

Snapdragon went down the stairs and walked through the open door at the bottom. Sitting at a table on the far side of the room was a man with unremarkable features. The door was closed and barred behind Snapdragon, and for a moment he just stood there.

"You'll have to forgive my use of your crude language," the plain man said. "I may have to ask you the same question several times to make sure I understand what you are telling me."

Snapdragon nodded and then quickly looked around the room. There was a chair on the opposite side of the desk, and aside from a few sconces that kept the room lit, the room was as unremarkable as the man.

"Please have a seat so we can begin," the man said, indicating the chair in front of his desk.

Showing no emotion, Snapdragon walked over and sat down, keeping his shoulders squared.

On the desk in front of the questioner were several pieces of parchment—some blank, some written on in the odd characters Snapdragon had seen in the temple.

The questioner dipped a quill into a nearby bottle of ink and said, "Let us begin."

For the next hour, Snapdragon recounted what had happened over the last several days, starting with the discovery that a town near the tunnel had been deserted.

The questioner would stop him now and again, asking him to clarify points or repeat what he said. The plain man made no indication whether or not he believed Snapdragon; he simply took notes.

After Snapdragon had completed his account, the man set down his quill and looked up at the guardian. "That is the same story the others told me, with some slight variations due, no doubt, to their point of view of what they experienced."

"It's the truth," Snapdragon said.

"That is yet to be seen."

Reaching behind the desk, the questioner pressed on a brick. Just as in the Temple of the New Moon, this brick was apparently a pressure release of some sort, as the wall directly to Snapdragon's left slowly started to move down.

Standing up, Snapdragon saw a room beyond with a flat stone slab leaning against a wall, with restraints built in for hands and feet. Next to the slab was a table laden with all manner of wicked-looking tools. But what covered the slab itself and the floor around it made Snapdragon sick to his stomach.

It was blood, some of it still wet.

In addition, there were four large men holding spears, waiting for the wall to finish going down.

"Now we will discover the real truth," the questioner said. "I sincerely hope you do better than the ones before you."

"Meaning what, exactly?" Snapdragon said, spinning to face the questioner.

The man shrugged and looked at him blankly. "Meaning none of them survived the true questioning."

CHAPTER 42

"I feel as if you're not telling me everything," Crescens said.

The magistrate of Erd arched an eyebrow. "It's not like you to be so bold."

Feeling his face redden, Crescens tried to remain calm. He had told himself today was the day he would find out why Selene had been behaving so oddly lately. Knowing he had already crossed a line, he continued pressing her. "And it's not like you to be so... so... strange."

"Strange?" Her lips curled up a little.

Crescens could have kicked himself. "All right, perhaps that wasn't the best word to describe how you've been behaving. But you've been behaving differently ever since the news from Procep arrived."

Leaning back in her chair, Selene steepled her fingers while she appeared to consider his statement. After a long moment, she said, "You're right, I *have* been acting 'strange,' as you would say."

"With the utmost respect, Magistrate, I believe I've earned your trust and confidence," Crescens said. *And you've been haunting my dreams for years now,* he thought ruefully.

Selene motioned to a padded red velvet chair next to her desk. "Sit down, Crescens."

Her tone didn't give away whether she was upset with him or was about to confide in him. But he'd never been instructed to sit by her desk before.

"I suppose you have earned my trust." She sighed as he sat down. "And if I'm correct, you, as well as everyone else in Bariwon, will find out soon enough."

"Find out what, exactly?"

"Tell me," she started, "what do you know of the nislles?"

Crescens frowned. "Aside from the fact that it nearly killed everyone in Bariwon?"

"Aside from that, yes."

The assistant magistrate thought hard. This was his chance to get her to open up. But he honestly didn't know anything else about the nislles. Well, there was a story he had heard. It was his only hand, so he played it. "There was a rhyme we chanted as children. I didn't think much about it at the time, but now that you bring it up... let's see, how did it go?"

He pursed his lips and then started to recite:

From the north people taking
From the old man who whistles
From sleep none are waking
From the touch of the nislles.

He shrugged his shoulders. "I never understood what it meant. I thought it was just another children's rhyme."

"It's *not* just another rhyme," Selene said. "It's very significant."

"I don't understand."

She sat up on the edge of her chair and leaned forward with her hands clasped on the desk. "What I'm about to tell you, Crescens, you must never tell a living soul unless I give you permission. Do you swear to this?"

"I swear," he replied quicker than he should have. If he came across as too eager, she might reconsider telling him.

Selene took a deep breath. "Everyone in the kingdom is said to be a descendent of one of seven brothers, all sons of a man named Bariwon. These brothers' names are the district names as we know them today. Each brother was given dominion over part, or an aspect, of the kingdom. What they ruled over was distinguished by the title they were given. I only know two, those of the eldest brothers. One title was Rifna, and the other was Tular. Rifna is from the old tongue—it means something along the lines of 'below.' Now, that isn't to mean it was a lesser title; it was meant for one who ruled the ground and that below it. They were miners and stone crafters."

"And what did Tular mean?" Crescens asked.

She pointed to her head. "It meant 'extreme,' or 'on the far side.' There is even one interpretation meaning 'beyond.' It was an honorific title for one whose intellect was far superior to that of the others."

Crescens leaned in. "You said these were titles for the brothers. Which of the brothers were they?"

"Tular was the title for Tevoil. Rifna was the title for Erd," Selene stated.

390

This revelation set Crescens back. Erd, as in his homeland? Selene seemed to sense his confusion and continued.

"The descendants of Tevoil were known as the Tular Tevoil. The same was true for Erd's people—the Rifna Erd. They were the most powerful groups, or families, in the land. With the Tular Tevoil's intellect and the Rifna Erd's strength, they built the castle in Bariwon. They also built the palace here in Erd. Over time, the people became restless and wanted to expand, but there was nowhere to go. The natural boundaries of the land prevented it. That was, until the leader of the Tular Tevoil—a man who had a gap in his teeth and whistled when he spoke—came up with a plan to go beyond the northern mountains."

"Beyond?" Crescens said. "There is no way over or around the mountains."

Selene nodded. "True, so they decided to go under."

Crescens' eyes widened, but he didn't speak.

"With the hard work of the Rifna Erd, who were also known as the north people, and the Tular Tevoil's direction, a tunnel was built. 'The north people taking,' you see? Taking stones from the mountains. It seems hard to imagine a tunnel could be built, doesn't it?"

"That it does," Crescens said.

Selene's countenance darkened. "Soon after the tunnel was opened, a sickness began to spread across the land. How it started and how it came to be called the nislles, I don't know. But I do know that the Rifna Erd and the Tular Tevoil were blamed. Many people from these two groups fled through the tunnel to escape persecution, but some were left behind when the tunnel was bricked up and then closed off by a man-made landslide. From there, the story is well known. A bloody battle ensued because all of the ruling class was killed by the nislles. Roderick finally won and declared himself king. He commissioned The Tome of Laws, the book we still live by. To keep things somewhat familiar, each land area, what he called districts, was known by one of the brothers' names. However, he stripped away the titles, saying that all people were equal and should not be defined by their ancestors. However, those who were of pure Tular Tevoil blood or pure Rifna Erd blood kept that fact to themselves, still fearful of persecution. They would only pass on that knowledge of their bloodline to their most trusted children."

Something didn't make sense to Crescens. If what Selene was saying was true, how did she know?

She must have seen the puzzlement on his face. "You are wondering how I know all of this, right?"

"Aye," Crescens said carefully.

"My father, Abrecan's cousin, was a pure-blood Rifna Erd."

"So Abrecan knows this as well?" Crescens asked.

"Of course!" she stated as if it should have been obvious. "But he took it to mean he was special—that he was destined for greatness."

"But how do you know of the Tular Tevoil?"

"It's simple. My mother was a pure-blood from that line, though neither of my parents knew that about the other. They both confided in me and made me promise not to tell anyone, including the other parent. Each of the pure-blood families blames the other for their fall from grace."

Crescens leaned back in his chair. "This is almost too much to comprehend. But all of this doesn't explain why you have been acting differently."

"Doesn't it?" she asked, her eyebrows arching. "For generations people from both sides of my family have watched and waited—waited for the people north of the mountains to return. I never thought it would happen in my lifetime. When I realized what was happening, it came as quite a shock."

Crescens blinked at the magistrate a few times before responding. "But they haven't returned, or we would have known about it."

"You are missing the connection." She sounded almost disappointed in him.

"I'm sorry, Magistrate, I don't understand."

Pointing to the window that faced the northern mountains, Selene said, "While the tunnel was being built, a large town grew by the entrance. During the bloody war, it was all but destroyed. What remains there now is a small village—a village named Procep."

⸙

Seraphina was dead.

So were Bearach and Waylon.

Snapdragon had been charged with keeping them safe, and yet, despite all his training and best efforts, he had failed. Unlike his sister the queen or his brother the legend, Snapdragon wouldn't be the hero. Out of all those sent on the expedition, only he had survived, though he probably wouldn't survive for much longer.

The wall was still lowering, and it was only a matter of time before the four armed men would come for him. The questioner still sat in his chair, looking numbly at Snapdragon. Did this man have no soul? How could he be so passive about something like torture?

When the wall completely disappeared into the floor, the four men started moving toward Snapdragon, their spears pointed at him.

"Is there anything I can say that will change your mind?" Snapdragon asked the questioner.

"No."

Feeling a rush of adrenaline, Snapdragon said, "Then I guess it is time to *act*."

Before anyone else in the room could respond, he reached across the table and grabbed the questioner by the neck. The man was of a very slight build, so Snapdragon had no problem lifting him out of his seat and over the table. Positioning the questioner in front of him, Snapdragon kept one hand tightly clenched on the back of the man's neck, while he grabbed one of the man's arms with the other hand and pinned it up and behind him, almost to the point of breaking.

The four men with spears stopped abruptly. They looked at each other, and then one of them glanced back over his shoulder.

"Back off," Snapdragon commanded. "I'm not like the others. I've been trained for battle. If you try to take me, I promise you that this room will be covered in blood—and it won't be mine."

The questioner didn't say anything or even try to struggle. The spearmen again looked at each other, as if waiting for someone to decide what to do. Their indecision gave Snapdragon time to formulate the next part of his plan. Without much effort, he could easily break the questioner's neck and use his corpse as a shield against the men. The way they hesitated showed Snapdragon they were not used to real combat, and it was likely one of them would get brave enough to either thrust or throw his spear. If Snapdragon could get one of those weapons…

Then, from the corner of his eye, he saw a fluttering. He recalled one of the spearmen looking back over his shoulder. There was a white cloth hanging from the ceiling along one of the far walls of the torture room. Another fluttering, very slight—someone appeared to be back there.

Suddenly Snapdragon recalled the lesson Fallon had taught him at the inn on the way to the tunnel. What had he said again? "We are all being tested every day—most of us just don't realize it."

"Put down your spears and back off," Snapdragon ordered.

One of the men did so right away, while the other three still seemed unsure of what to do. The questioner remained placid in Snapdragon's grip.

"I said put them down!" Snapdragon shouted with such force that the rest of the men did so and backed off.

More fluttering from the white cloth. Good.

"Now," Snapdragon said calmly, "act like you are dogs."

The spearmen all looked at the guardian like he had gone mad, and for the first time, the questioner shifted. Snapdragon tightened his grip on the man's neck.

"I'm not going to ask you again," Snapdragon said.

The man that had dropped his spear first got down on all fours and started barking. The other three eventually did the same, though not with as much enthusiasm as the first man.

Even more fluttering, and Snapdragon thought he heard a whisper coming from behind the white cloth.

"All right," Snapdragon said, releasing the questioner, "that's enough. Come out from behind the curtain, Merton."

Slowly the white cloth was pushed to the side. Merton stood there next to another man that Snapdragon took a moment to realize was Sverre, clean-shaven with his hair cut.

Three of the four men stopped barking while the other one, the first one, seemed to be lost in the moment until one of his companions smacked him on the shoulder to stop.

"Sverre said you were different." Merton stepped forward. "He said you wouldn't be as intimidated as the others."

"I've told you the truth," Snapdragon said.

The questioner nodded his head, and Merton said, "You must understand that after waiting so long, and after the previous attempts of the Rifna Erd, we had to make sure. Fear tactics, like using animal blood on the table, often get people to change their story to the truth. How else would we keep the peace?"

"This was all a ruse then?" Snapdragon said, almost not wanting to hear the answer.

"Of course. Your companions are all safe, though each of them does believe that the rest of you were put to the question and didn't survive. The strong one—Bearach, I believe, is his name—actually broke the arm of one of the protectors before we were able to subdue him when he was told the news. He didn't change his story—none of them did. However, they all believe they will be tortured at some point. But not you. Would you really have killed these men if they had tried to take you?"

"It's good for them that we won't have to find out," Snapdragon said. "Unless, of course, you aren't telling me the truth now."

Merton said something to Sverre, who nodded and then went back to where they had been hidden. Snapdragon could see another room just beyond where the cloth had been hung.

"This is an exciting day for the Tular Tevoil," Merton said, rubbing his hands together. "A day long in coming."

Sverre came back into the room, escorting Seraphina. She saw Snapdragon, paused for a moment as if she didn't believe what she was seeing, then rushed across the room and embraced him. Snapdragon felt the tightness in his shoulders loosen when he knew for sure she was safe.

She looked up at him, tears of joy streaming down her face. Then, to Snapdragon's surprise, she stood on her tiptoes, leaned up, and kissed him on the cheek.

Merton interrupted, "Is this how she will greet the others as well?"

Both Snapdragon and Seraphina laughed at that, and she stepped away.

"Bring us to them and we'll find out," Snapdragon said, winking at Seraphina.

Merton told them to follow him.

Snapdragon was sure he'd find Waylon curled up and crying. Once again, the hefty savant surprised him by sitting almost serenely in the middle of the floor of what could only be described as a prison chamber, legs crossed and arms relaxed by his sides.

"Ah, there you are," he said in greeting.

Snapdragon noticed Merton frown at Waylon's behavior, as did Sverre and the protectors that accompanied them.

Seraphina was the next to enter the chamber, and without waiting for Waylon to stand, she leaned down and kissed the savant on the top of the head. "It's good to see you alive." She looked up and winked at Merton, inspiring another deep frown from the man.

"Remember, I said that if we told the truth all would be fine," Waylon said, struggling a bit to stand up.

Snapdragon offered his hand to help. Waylon took it, and upon reaching his feet he said to Merton, "You understand that we are telling you the truth, yes?"

Merton nodded, still frowning.

"Then let us get Bearach so we can discuss what needs to be done next," Snapdragon said.

"He will not be as easy to get to," Merton said matter-of-factly.

Seraphina took a step toward Merton and his men. "Why not?"

In the same even tone, Merton said, "He proved to be a bit more... what is the word in Rifna? Ah... troublesome than the rest of you."

"Bearach!" Snapdragon called, his voice echoing off the stone pit's walls. "Are you down there?"

There was no response.

"Bearach!" Seraphina shouted. "It's all right. We are all safe!"

Again, no response.

The pit was deep enough that the sun's light didn't pierce the darkness at the bottom. Snapdragon couldn't tell how deep it was or what lay at the bottom. Turning to Merton, he asked, "How did he get down there?"

Merton nodded to Sverre, who responded, "Bearach went mad when we revealed the torture chamber to him. He charged the protectors and hurt some of them badly before we could subdue him."

Snapdragon narrowed his eyes. "How exactly did you subdue him?"

Sverre pantomimed a blow to the head and then passing out. "Subdued."

"All right, then how did he get down there?" Snapdragon asked, pointing to the pit.

"The same way you will be going down to get him." Sverre motioned to one of the protectors. The man reached into a satchel and removed a length of rope attached to some sort of harness.

The harness was a bit snug around Snapdragon's muscular chest, but it appeared to be well constructed, and it was attached to a rope thick enough to support his weight.

Merton refused Snapdragon's request for a torch and said, "He will not be hard to find."

With the pit behind him, Snapdragon held onto the rope with both hands and let the protectors start to lower him down. He noticed Seraphina was trying to hide her concern, while Waylon looked completely relaxed.

Similar to the exterior of the other buildings and structures Snapdragon had seen in the town, the pit's stone walls were fairly smooth, which unfortunately also meant they tended to provide any traction. He tried to keep his feet on the wall as he was lowered, but they kept slipping, and he eventually gave up and allowed himself to hang with his feet dangling.

A strong stench came from the pit, increasing as Snapdragon descended. At last his feet touched something, and as he put more pressure on it, he felt it give way under his weight. It felt like he had stepped on someone, and for a moment he feared it was Bearach, but something was not right about the way it reacted to his weight. The stench was now overwhelming, and Snapdragon fought the urge to vomit.

His other foot landed more solidly, and he was able to gain his balance. Reaching down to feel what he had first stepped on, it took but a moment to realize it *was* a leg, but one that had been decomposing for some time.

He wiped his hands on his robe and looked around the pit, but still couldn't see anything in the darkness.

"Bearach," he called out, his voice echoing off the walls.

No response.

Snapdragon crouched and turned away from the rotting corpse. He reached out with his hands, searching for the crafter.

What he found next was something he first thought was a smooth rock, but with more probing realized it was a skull. He dropped it, trying to remain calm. After a few more harrowing moments, Snapdragon bumped up against a more solid object. With relief, he realized it was Bearach. He found the man breathing and was still wearing the harness in which he had been lowered. The rope attached to Bearach's harness had been cut and wouldn't reach to the top of the pit.

Snapdragon tried to revive his companion but was unable to do so. Feeling Bearach's head, he discovered his hair was slightly sticky in the back, but mostly clumped together with what Snapdragon guessed was dried blood. Apparently, the "subduing" of Bearach had been a bit more violent than Sverre and Merton had let on.

He removed the rope that was tied to his own harness and tied it to Bearach's. When he was satisfied it was secure, Snapdragon yanked on the rope twice and called up, "I found him! Pull him up!"

A moment later the rope became taut and Bearach began to be lifted out of the pit. Eventually Snapdragon could make out his friend's silhouette against the blue sky he could see above the pit.

Trying not to think of what else was down there with him, or why they were down there, Snapdragon kept his breathing steady. He could hear some conversations and more than once heard Seraphina's terse voice, though the distance and the echoing effect of the walls made it impossible for him to hear exactly what was being said.

Several maddening minutes later, Snapdragon saw the rope come over the edge. When it reached him, he quickly attached it to his harness and tugged on the rope twice. As he was pulled away from the rank bottom of the pit, he felt completely helpless. He could have easily been tricked and left down in the pit with Bearach. He chided himself for being manipulated.

At last, the edge of the pit came into reach. Not waiting for them to pull any more, Snapdragon grabbed the edge and deftly climbed out.

Bearach and Seraphina weren't there. Waylon remained next to Merton and Sverre and several of their protectors.

"Where are they?" Snapdragon demanded.

Waylon held up his hands. "Seraphina is attending to him. The blow to his head was worse than either of these men thought."

Undoing the harness, Snapdragon said, "I want to be taken to them."

"Of course," Merton said. "You will be taken to get cleaned up and fed before we start our discussion."

Snapdragon threw the harness to the ground. "And what discussion would that be?"

Merton and Sverre exchanged a meaningful look, and then the leader of the Tular Tevoil said, "The discussion of the exodus of my people to our rightful land."

Snapdragon and Waylon were taken back to the windowless room where they had spent the previous night. Though the door was closed behind them, it wasn't barred as far as Snapdragon could tell.

Bearach was lying on one of the beds, with Seraphina sitting next to him. On the floor was a ceramic washbowl, the water red from what Snapdragon assumed was Seraphina's cleansing of his wound.

"Will he be all right?" Snapdragon asked, going directly to Bearach's bed.

Waylon walked calmly to the other side of the room and sat down.

Not looking up from her patient, Seraphina said, "His skull wasn't cracked or broken, from what I could tell. As for whether or not he'll be all right, it may be some time before we know."

"He shouldn't have been so violent," Waylon said.

Seraphina spun around in her chair and snapped, "You are blaming *Bearach* for what happened to him? These... these people had me believing you all were dead and I was going to be next. I don't fault him for acting as he did."

"We were never in any danger as long as we told the truth," Waylon said in defense.

"How can you be—" Seraphina started to say, but she stopped abruptly when the wall opposite the stone door started to open.

Stepping between the opening wall and Seraphina, Snapdragon said, "What in the world?"

Wishing he had his sword with him, the guardian instead set his feet and prepared to spring at whatever came through what was apparently some sort of hidden passage.

When the wall had opened wide enough, a figure stepped through that shocked Snapdragon into momentary inaction. Dressed in a simple white robe like everyone else, a woman walked into the room. Her dark hair and deep brown eyes were a stark contrast to her fair white skin. She had high, firm cheekbones and full lips that were curved up slightly.

"Pardon the intrusion," she said, her voice light but firm. "I am Alethea, and I needed to speak to you before you were summoned by Merton."

Snapdragon looked behind her, but he couldn't see far into the passage. "Are you alone?" he asked.

"Are any of us ever truly alone?"

She kept her attention focused on him, and her even stare started to make him feel uncomfortable. She was strikingly beautiful, in a different way than Seraphina.

"Who are you that you have to sneak in here?" Snapdragon managed to say, and to his credit, he did so without his voice faltering.

Alethea took a step forward and smiled. "You need not fear me. I am here to help you."

He sensed Seraphina stand up and move next to him. "You'll forgive us if we don't believe you," she said.

Taking another step forward, Alethea ignored Seraphina and kept looking at Snapdragon. "Merton is not what he seems. Nothing here is as it seems."

"I guess that would include you then, eh?" Seraphina said, looping her arm around Snapdragon's.

"This is not the paradise Merton would have you believe it is," Alethea said, still looking directly into Snapdragon's eyes.

"I don't see this as a paradise," Snapdragon said. "There wouldn't be the threat of torture or bodies rotting at the bottom of pits in a paradise."

He felt Seraphina's gaze turn toward him, but he kept his eyes on Alethea.

The dark-haired beauty nodded and smiled again. "Very good. Thank the Zealous Star you see with opened eyes."

"But Seraphina is right," Snapdragon said, squeezing her arm. "Why should I trust you over anyone else here?"

Alethea turned her head a little and looked at Seraphina as if for the first time. She seemed to judge her quickly, and then she returned her attention to Snapdragon. "You shouldn't trust me. You don't know me. But there is something I can show you that will help you believe."

Snapdragon arched an eyebrow. "And what would that be?"

Alethea called back over her shoulder into the passage behind her. "Please come in now."

From the passage came a solidly built man with a strong jawline and a round nose. He was dressed in a well-worn tunic and breeches that looked out of place in their current surroundings.

"You need not worry, friend," the man said in a fairly thick Erd accent—but clearer than anyone else Snapdragon had met north of the mountains. "She's telling you the truth."

"Who...?"

The man stepped forward and extended a hand. "I should probably introduce myself. My name is Creighton. I come from the village of Procep."

CHAPTER 43

Snapdragon took Creighton's hand tentatively. The other man gave Snapdragon a hardy shake with a surprisingly strong grip.

"I'm Royal Guardian Snapdragon."

Creighton's eyebrows shot up. "Snapdragon? As in the Queen and Oakleaf's little brother?"

Snapdragon felt himself wince a little. "Aye, the very same."

The man from Erd looked at Snapdragon from head to toe. "Well, isn't that something? A royal guardian, eh? Guess we should be honored they would send you after us."

Creighton peered around the room. "Did they send just the four of you?"

"You don't know?" Seraphina asked suspiciously.

Glancing between her and Snapdragon, Creighton asked, "Know what, exactly?"

"First things first," Snapdragon said. "Let me introduce you to the rest."

Squeezing Seraphina's arm, which was still looped around his, Snapdragon said, "This is Seraphina. She is a nursemaid from the castle."

"I'm Savant Waylon," said the stout man, standing up. "And the man on the bed there is Bearach, a crafter."

Creighton's gaze remained on each of them as they were introduced, but lingered the longest on Bearach. "Ah, he's the one they put in the pit, eh?"

"Obviously you know something of us," Snapdragon said. "We need to talk."

"Yes, we do," Alethea put in, "but not here. It isn't safe for us here."

"We can't just leave," Seraphina blurted. "Bearach needs to rest, and Merton will expect to find us here."

Alethea looked at Snapdragon. "It isn't safe for Creighton and me here. You must come with us so we can talk. The door to this room isn't being guarded. If they come for you before you return, have the others tell them you went for a walk. We can release you at a safe place so it will seem you did."

"I'm going with you as well," Waylon said, stepping next to Snapdragon. Alethea ignored him.

"Snapdragon, I shouldn't leave Bearach," Seraphina said. "And I'm not sure I believe these people."

Creighton held up his hands, showing that they were empty. "You need not fear. I promise you we'll keep them safe. But he needs to know what I know."

"How would any of the people here know who my brother and sister are?" Snapdragon asked. "Plus, he talks like someone from Erd. I understand your concern, Seraphina, but I think I should go with them."

She let go of his arm. "Just be careful. I don't want to…" Her voice cracked and she shook her head, then turned and sat back down next to Bearach.

"I'll be back soon," Snapdragon promised her. Turning to face Alethea and Creighton, he said, "Let's go."

⇥✦⇤

The target set up on the far side of the castle's eastern courtyard had been peppered with arrows. Oakleaf watched as the archers practiced, giving advice when needed and congratulating those who had made difficult shots. He had kept them practicing during their downtime to keep them sharp. Rayne had left precious little behind in the castle for defense, so Oakleaf was determined to make sure his men were as ready as they could be.

"I heard you were a pretty good shot back in your day," one of the royal guardians said to Oakleaf. He was tall, with hair so blonde it was almost white. Barrfhionn was his name, though he claimed no one in the castle could pronounce it correctly. Most just called him "Barefin," which he said was close enough.

"Back in my day, Barrfhionn?" Oakleaf said, not attempting to hide the humor in his voice. "It was only a few years ago I was a royal guardian."

Motioning to the target, Barrfhionn said, "Ah, so do you still remember which way to hold a bow?"

Oakleaf's injury to his left hip had forced him to retire as a royal guardian, but he had kept up his skills with a bow and arrow. He practiced in private—his wife Arlie didn't want him thinking he was still a guardian, as she worried he might injure his hip even more severely, but he still enjoyed shooting. It took some adjustments to use a bow and arrow since he couldn't put much weight on his left leg, but he managed.

"Hmm. Let me see. I pull back on the stringy part, right?" Oakleaf asked, playing along with Barrfhionn.

The dozen or so men that watched laughed at the exchange.

Barrfhionn smiled and handed Oakleaf a bow and arrow. Holding them both in one hand because he was using his walking stick in his other, he hobbled to the mark where the archers stood.

He slowly set his feet, then let the walking stick drop to the ground. Its clattering on the cobblestones was the only sound now. All the men watching seemed to be holding their breath.

Oakleaf looked back at Barrfhionn. "Are you sure you want me to try this?"

"You don't have to," Barrfhionn said, looking ashamed that he had put his leader in such a position. "We all respect what you've done for the kingdom."

The men around him nodded in agreement.

Shrugging, Oakleaf said, "Well, it wouldn't hurt to try."

With that statement, the former royal guardian quickly brought up the bow, set the arrow, and fired in one seemingly smooth motion. The arrow flew true to its mark, dead center of the target.

The men stood in shock for a moment, then cheered loudly.

⇥⧱⇤

Alethea went first into the hidden passageway, followed by Snapdragon and then Creighton. Waylon brought up the rear. Once they were all out of the room, Alethea pushed on a well-marked stone, and the wall behind them closed. Snapdragon took one last look at Seraphina, whose back was to them.

"It's not far from here," Alethea said, leading on.

The tunnel wasn't completely dark, due to light coming from ahead and to the right. As they approached the illumination, Snapdragon saw that it led to a descending stairway. They walked on and the light increased. It was then Snapdragon realized it was sunlight, not firelight, which illuminated the area at the bottom of the stairs. He could also hear a number of voices ahead, some of which had the same Erd accent as Creighton.

Reaching the bottom of the stairs, Snapdragon was taken aback. They stood before a large cavern filled with at least two hundred people. At the far end was a huge gap that opened to the outside world. Dozens of dwellings, built mostly of rock and adobe, were laid out in the cave in an organized manner around a common area.

"What is this place?" Snapdragon asked.

"We call it Eddinh. Here we can live free from the rule of Merton and the rest of the Tular Tevoil," Alethea said, obviously proud of her home. "It is also a place safe from the Rifna Erd."

"Quite a sight, don't you think?" Creighton said.

Snapdragon nodded. "It's remarkable."

In addition to the dwellings in the large cave, Snapdragon noticed several holes in the walls, similar to the one from which they had just come. He assumed they led to other secret passages that went up to Itamunno Kael.

The people in the cave had noticed the small group and stood watching intently as they made their way toward the common area. Unlike the people in Itamunno Kael, these people smiled openly and seemed genuinely friendly.

It was fairly easy to figure out who was from Erd and who were native residents. The people dressed like Creighton were bunched together, though a few intermingled with the robe-wearing folks who Snapdragon assumed were from Eddinh.

Crossing the common area, Alethea led them into the largest structure in the village. Although it wasn't taller than any of the surrounding buildings, it was far wider. The front entrance had several stairs that led down to a wide-open main room.

In the center was a table shaped like a triangle. A man that resembled Creighton was seated at the table. Alethea motioned for Snapdragon to sit along one of the edges, where a bench ran the length. She sat on the other vacant bench while Creighton sat next to the man who looked like he could be his brother.

Snapdragon stepped over the bench and sat down, while Waylon had to sit down first and then swing his legs over.

"I have so many questions," Snapdragon said. "I'm not sure where to begin."

Alethea smiled. "It is understandable. Let me first introduce Kerr, Creighton's brother."

Kerr nodded.

"This is Snapdragon, a royal guardian sent to find us," Creighton said proudly.

Kerr looked stunned. "Are you Queen Sunshine's brother, by chance?" he asked in awe.

Glancing over at Alethea before he responded, Snapdragon said, "That I am."

If she was impressed by the statement, she didn't show it.

"And this is Waylon, savant of Bariwon," Snapdragon said, almost feeling bad that the man had basically been ignored up to this point.

Waylon said nothing—he just kept his face neutral and nodded.

"Now excuse me if I seem impatient, but I have to know what is going on," Snapdragon said. "Let's start with how you and your people got here, Creighton."

The man from Procep looked at Alethea, who said, "It is all right—you may proceed."

After clearing his throat, Creighton began, "My brother Kerr and I were digging in one of our local mines. Silver had been found around that area some time before, and we were hoping to find treasure. Well, I guess it could be said we found something much more interesting—a rock wall in the middle of the mountain."

Snapdragon folded his hands on the table in front of him and leaned forward.

"Well, we went back and told the people in Procep about it," Creighton continued, "and it was decided to clear away the wall to find out what was beyond it. Everyone pitched in and the wall was cleared away in no time. Kerr and I were then selected to see where it went."

Kerr interrupted. "We should have probably beckoned someone from the kingdom first, but it was so exciting and we didn't want to wait."

"So my brother and I packed our horses with supplies and went into the tunnel with torches," Creighton continued. "I'm guessing it is the same tunnel you came through."

Snapdragon nodded.

"So, anyway, when we got through to the other side, we were a bit spooked by the large white circle on the ground and the writing above the tunnel entrance, but we continued on. We hugged the mountains to the west but didn't see signs of anyone. After a few hours of traveling, it was starting to get dark, so we decided to make camp. But before we lit a fire, we found ourselves face to face with two strangers."

"Did they have shaved heads with beards?" Snapdragon asked quickly.

405

Creighton shook his head. "No, and from what I understand, thank goodness for that. These were Tular Tevoil scouts. Kerr and I had unknowingly passed by the hidden entrance that leads to Itamunno Kael. At first it was touch and go, especially when they realized we spoke the language of the Rifna Erd, or at least a form of it. But we convinced them of where we had come from, and thankfully they believed us."

Creighton took a deep breath. "They said it wasn't safe where we were camping, that the Rifna Erd were on the move and we needed to hide. And that's when fortune really smiled on us."

"How so?"

"These scouts were actually loyal to Eddinh, though they lived with the Tular Tevoil," Creighton answered. "Instead of taking us to Merton and his protectors, they brought us here to Eddinh."

"We have a secret way to the passage between the canyons and Itamunno Kael.," Alethea interjected. "Please continue."

"All right," Creighton said. "Kerr and I were taken to Alethea, where we told our story. After she discussed it with the other folks here, it was decided that we needed to bring our whole village here for our own safety. So we spent the night here, and the next day we hurried back to Procep and had people grab whatever they could at the moment and leave as fast as possible. I'm not sure exactly how they did it, but the scouts from Eddinh gave us some sort of device made from animal skins woven in with rough shrubs from the area. They told us to drag the device behind us to cover our tracks. They met us by the tunnel on this side and then brought us here."

"But why weren't you safe in Procep?" Snapdragon asked.

Creighton looked at Alethea, who responded, "Like he said, the Rifna Erd are on the move in the area. If they were to find Creighton and his village, the unspeakable would happen."

"But the Rifna Erd won't cross white circles," Snapdragon said. "I've seen that with my own eyes. It's taboo or something to them."

For the first time, Snapdragon thought he saw Creighton flinch. Apparently that was something the miner wasn't aware of.

"You are correct—most Rifna Erd will not. But the mylnohe, or the ones with the blue stripes, will cross the Symbol of the New Moon... if properly motivated," Alethea answered. "The current leader of the Rifna Erd is unlike what we've seen before. He doesn't seem to hold to the same traditions as his forefathers. The Rifna Erd have become much more unpredictable the last few years. We couldn't take the chance that Creighton's people would be taken by them."

"Don't take this the wrong way, for I'm glad you got them to a safe location, but what does it matter to you?" Snapdragon asked.

"Before I answer that, please tell us how you made it to Itamunno Kael."

Snapdragon considered his options. His gut told him that these people were telling the truth, though not as openly as they could be. But if he were in their place, he would be a bit guarded as well. Creighton was definitely genuine, so Snapdragon decided to heed Waylon's advice from before and tell the truth.

He told of the events that had brought him and his companions to this point. Several times, emotions ran high from the people in the room when they heard about what the Rifna Erd had done to the rest of the entourage, and again when Snapdragon told of the questioner and the threat of torture.

"Which leads to where you found us," Snapdragon concluded. "Although I find it a bit of a wild stretch to believe we just so happened to be placed in a room that has access to Eddinh."

"I was wondering if you were going to ask that," Alethea said, smiling a little. "Like the scouts that found Creighton, we have those who live among the Tular Tevoil who are loyal to us. We couldn't live down here without their support. One of the protectors assigned to you is one of ours. He made sure you were put in that room."

"All right, now that I've told you what you wanted to know, please explain why we and the villagers of Procep were brought here," Snapdragon said firmly.

"But of course," Alethea said. "For generations, the people of the Tular Tevoil lived in fear of the Rifna Erd finding them in Itamunno Kael. They dreamed of one day returning to the land of the first temple, or Bariwon, as you call it. But the way back was sealed with the warning of 'Nie syll esse' left for us. It was decided that we would only be able to go back if someone came through the Pendeltune first to let us know it was safe to return."

"But what does 'Nie syll esse' mean? We thought it might mean 'None shall pass,'" Snapdragon said.

"In a sense, that *is* what it means," Alethea said. "It was placed over doors or entrances of villages if there was a fatal sickness present."

"Of course!" Waylon said, entering the conversation for the first time. "Don't you see? I told you language changes over time, didn't I, Snapdragon? What is the name of the sickness that almost killed everyone in Bariwon?"

Snapdragon frowned a bit. "You are referring to the nislles?" Even as he said it, he made the connection.

"Exactly! 'Nislles' has to be a version of 'Nie syll esse,' shortened and changed over the years."

"So the reason the tunnel was blocked off was because of the nislles, then?" Snapdragon surmised out loud.

Waylon nodded. "It would appear so."

"Then what you are saying is that all of the land of the first temple is completely safe?" Alethea asked. "That it is safe for the people of Eddinh to go there?"

"If by safe you mean from the reason the tunnel was sealed, then yes," Snapdragon responded.

Creighton chimed in, "Thank goodness you figured that out. They kept asking me about that and we couldn't figure out what they meant."

"We need to get you back to your room soon," Alethea said. "You must not let Merton know it is safe to return."

"It's too late for that," Snapdragon lamented. "We told them everything we told you. And you still haven't explained why you live down here in secret from them."

"The Tular Tevoil were once as Merton probably explained them to be," Alethea said. "They were peaceful. Everyone shared with everyone. No one thought he was better than anyone else. A leader was selected only to help the people. But over time, it was found that this way of life only succeeded if the leader was benevolent. But the enticement of power is too much for some to withstand, so the leaders of the Tular Tevoil now live under the pretense of the old ways, though they rule by fear."

After motioning around her, Alethea went on, "Over the generations, the number of people living in Itamunno Kael was kept at an even level, meaning a child could be born only if someone in the Tular Tevoil died first. Parents were not allowed to have more than two children, unless the balance was off—then they were allowed to have more, though only through the permission of the leader. Any that opposed the leader were taken to the pit unless they renounced their opposition. Many chose to die in the pit instead."

"I take it that happens even to this day," Snapdragon said, trying not to shudder as he remembered his time in the pit.

Alethea nodded gravely. "Sadly, it does. This ancient cavern was forgotten over the generations, as it was built originally as a safe haven in case the Rifna Erd ever found how to get to Itamunno Kael. It was rediscovered only a generation ago, and kept a secret by those wanting to not live under the rule of the Tular Tevoil. Only the most trusted are brought here. We, too, have been looking forward to returning to the land of the first temple—to be free to live without fear of either the Tular Tevoil or the Rifna Erd."

"As you have stated," Snapdragon said, "time is short. Soon, Merton's men will come looking for us. What is it you want from me?"

"You cannot let Merton lead his people to the land of the first temple," Alethea said urgently. "Neither can you let the Rifna Erd find a way to get past the Symbol of the New Moon. Either way, you will bring destruction to your people—by the Rifna Erd through violence and terror, or by the Tular Tevoil through persuasion and uprising."

Snapdragon couldn't help but ask, "But what do we fear from the people of Eddinh?"

Alethea looked shocked at the question.

"Nothing," Alethea answered. "We want to live just as the people in Procep have described how they have lived."

"But again, I'm not sure how you expect me to keep both the Tular Tevoil and the Rifna Erd from going through the tunnel while allowing the people of Eddinh to do so safely," Snapdragon said.

"It will be a challenge, I know," Alethea said. "But until there is a solution, you must convince Merton not to leave."

Alethea and Creighton led Snapdragon and Waylon back to their room. Before opening the secret door, Alethea said, "If the others are already gone, we will take you a different way."

A rock was pushed, and the wall slid open to reveal Seraphina standing there with her hands on her hips and a scowl on her face.

"Did they come for us yet?" Snapdragon asked.

Seraphina shook her head. "Not yet. But I've been dying of worry since you left. I didn't think you'd be gone so long."

Entering the room, Snapdragon reached out for her, but she backed away. "I'm sorry. There was much to discuss."

"We must go," Alethea said. "We will be in contact soon."

She again gave all her attention to Snapdragon, causing Seraphina to bristle even more.

Waylon said nothing else but simply sat down on his bed. Alethea and Creighton left, closing the door behind them.

"Any change in Bearach?" Snapdragon asked, trying to break the uncomfortable silence that prevailed once the wall was sealed up.

Seraphina sat back down next to the crafter. "He opened his eyes and spoke for a moment. I told him everything was fine and advised him to rest. I'm surprised he didn't wake up when you returned." Then she all but demanded, "But what did they tell you?"

Snapdragon grabbed a chair and brought it next to Seraphina, then sat down and recounted what they had been told.

"So, basically, we are trapped again," Seraphina said when he finished. "We can't leave here for fear of the Rifna Erd, and we can't let the Tular Tevoil make it to Bariwon. Also, we are expected to believe these people from Eddinh."

Snapdragon sighed. "That about sums it up, yes."

"So what are we going to do?" the nursemaid asked.

Snapdragon thought for a moment before saying, "I honestly have no idea."

CHAPTER 44

"Well, I know what I'm going to do," Waylon said as he stood. "I'm going to find something to eat."

Snapdragon felt his stomach growl and realized he hadn't eaten since morning.

"I got the impression we would be fed when Merton summoned us again," Seraphina said.

"But who knows when that will be? And I'm hungry now," Waylon said as he walked to the stone door. He pressed against one edge, and the door opened smoothly on its center hinge, allowing him to pass.

Snapdragon didn't see any protectors right outside the door, but he doubted they would be far off. He wouldn't be surprised if Waylon returned shortly, empty-handed.

The savant closed the door behind him.

"He seems to be taking this whole situation better than I am," Seraphina remarked. "I'm not sure how he can be so calm during all this chaos."

Snapdragon nodded. "I agree. Since we arrived at Itamunno Kael, he's been acting, well, almost serene."

Bearach mumbled something unintelligible, shifting on his cot. The crafter then opened his eyes, and after a pause said, "Good to see you in one piece, Snapdragon."

Snapdragon clapped the crafter on the shoulder. "You too. How's the head?"

"Still part of my body," Bearach said, grimacing as he sat up a bit. "Though I doubt this ache will go away any time soon."

Seraphina put her hand on Bearach's chest and tried to stop him from rising. "You still need to rest."

The nursemaid's petite hand did little to stop the barrel-chested crafter from sitting up.

"I'm not going to be on my back when they come for us again," Bearach said determinedly. "I refuse to let them, or anyone, bully us around anymore."

"Bearach, there's been a new development," Snapdragon said.

"What happened now? And where's Waylon?"

Snapdragon explained what had transpired since Bearach had been "subdued," as Sverre called it. The crafter grunted again and again in response.

The door opened once more, and Snapdragon fully expected to see Waylon returning, but instead a tall, dark-haired protector entered and closed the door behind him. There was something familiar about this man, though Snapdragon couldn't say what. Perhaps he was one of the men who had led them here.

Seraphina stood. "Is Merton finally ready for us?" she asked, sounding annoyed.

"Not as of yet," the man said, his eyes darting around the room. "One of you has left. The fat one."

"His name is Waylon, and I'm pretty sure he wouldn't appreciate being called 'the fat one,'" Bearach growled.

The protector looked puzzled. "But doesn't that describe him?"

"Yes," Bearach conceded, "but that doesn't mean it's all right to refer to him that way."

"So, I should not describe someone or something the way it is?"

Seraphina shook her head. "That isn't what he is saying at all. It isn't polite to describe Waylon in such a way."

"Being fat is embarrassing where you come from? I don't understand. That is who he is."

Snapdragon stood up and took a step toward the protector. "I don't believe you came here to discuss what is proper to call someone. What does bring you here?"

The man looked at Snapdragon for a moment and then said, "Good. This is how we should talk. My name is Darius. Merton will be summoning you shortly, but I spoke with my cousin earlier and we both felt it was important that I introduce myself. It is a risk to do so, but what we are facing has no shortage of risk."

Snapdragon folded his arms. "Why is telling us who you are risky?"

"Surely Alethea told you about me," Darius said.

Is this another one of Merton's tricks? Snapdragon wondered. Alethea had said there were protectors who were helping the people of Eddinh, though she hadn't mentioned any of them by name—probably for their protection. Now that he looked Darius over more closely, he saw a definite resemblance to Alethea. The dark-haired woman had lived among the people of the Tular Tevoil at some point, so perhaps this was Merton's way of discovering if she had been in contact.

"And where would I have seen this Alethea?" Snapdragon asked carefully.

Darius paused. "She would have been with Creighton, a man from the town of Procep who is currently staying with the rest of his village in Eddinh."

A smile played across Snapdragon's lips. "You took a big chance there, Darius. But at the same time, you showed me you want my trust."

"I don't trust any of them," Bearach snapped. "Don't say any more."

"I understand your concern," Snapdragon said, turning to face his companion. "At the same time, I don't see us getting out of here without some help. We just met the people from Eddinh, but they are the only ones who haven't tried to kill us or threatened to torture us for information."

Snapdragon addressed Darius again. "I am grateful you took the risk to introduce yourself. What can you tell us of what will happen tonight with Merton?"

"The leader of the Tular Tevoil has demanded that a large feast be prepared."

"Told you so…" Seraphina mumbled.

"What was that?" Darius asked.

Grimacing at the nursemaid, Snapdragon said, "Never mind. Please, continue."

Darius nodded. "You will be presented among the most important people of the Tular Tevoil. There will be a discussion of how to best prepare for the mass exodus from Itamunno Kael to the land of the first temple."

"From what you know of Merton, what does he hope will happen upon the return of the Tular Tevoil?" Snapdragon asked.

"He expects to be welcomed with arms spread wide. He sees himself as the returning hero, awaited anxiously for generations," Darius said.

Bearach laughed out loud. "Well, he's in for quite the shock then, isn't he?"

"I do not think it would be wise to disappoint Merton. You of all people, crafter, know the results when he sees someone as a threat."

Bearach furrowed his brow and instinctively reached up to the back of his head. "I've been hit so much in the head recently—me and

Snapdragon both—it's a wonder we're still breathing. But, yeah, I get your point."

Darius stood up taller. "I came here to suggest that you do not contradict what Merton believes. He will not hesitate to use one of you against the others to get what he wants." His eyes fell directly on Seraphina after this last statement.

Snapdragon took a step closer to the nursemaid. "Your comments are well taken. Thank you."

"I must be off," Darius said. "There is much to attend to. I will be back after the dinner to discuss the next steps."

The protector of the Tular Tevoil then quickly exited, making sure the large stone door was firmly closed behind him.

"I don't like this at all," Bearach muttered. "There's too much to think about. Who do we trust? My head hurts enough without trying to figure all this out."

Snapdragon sat down next to Bearach's cot. "What does your gut tell you, Bearach?"

"To get as far away from here as possible."

"Mine's been saying that for a while as well. It just isn't that easy."

Seraphina said, "Well, my gut is telling me that we can't let the Tular Tevoil *or* the Rifna Erd invade Bariwon."

Snapdragon looked at her, impressed. "That's what I keep coming back to as well. Bariwon simply doesn't have enough guardians to fight off the large force that the Rifna Erd possess. And letting the Tular Tevoil back into Bariwon threatens the way of life for our people."

Bearach rubbed his forehead. "You aren't helping my headache."

⇥✦⇤

King Rayne had always thought of himself as a patient person. It seemed to be a good trait in a leader. The Tome of Laws taught that leaders often let their initial feelings dictate their course of action—more often than not, to less than desirable results. From what he had heard, Abrecan had been such a leader. Servants would say, "Watch out— Abrecan's in a foul mood! Better hide until he calms down!"

There were things that upset Rayne, but one of the many lessons his father had taught him was that feeling angry about something didn't justify a violent or angry response. In other words, if someone made him angry, it didn't give him the right to punch the person in the nose. And that is where being patient was valuable—it allowed him time to think before acting.

At this moment, however, Rayne found it very difficult to be patient. "Is there anything else our scouts have found?" he asked Guardian Aaron.

"No, Your Majesty. There is no indication of travel to or from the village, aside from what we have determined to be Fallon's group, and then the tracks that lead into the tunnel."

"So it seems that all of the people of Procep went into the tunnel," the king surmised. "But why would they do that?"

"I don't know," Aaron replied. "Let's hope that Captain Fallon and his men find out soon and send back a report."

-3‡&-

The sun was setting when Merton finally summoned Snapdragon, Bearach, and Seraphina. Waylon hadn't returned, which caused some concern, though the protectors insisted the savant was fine.

As they left the building where they had stayed, Snapdragon glanced up at the horizon. With the sun sinking just below the edge of the high mountaintops that surrounded Itamunno Kael, the sky was a deep violet. The lake mirrored the sky and shimmered with a distinct purple hue. In another time, under other circumstances, he would have stood and marveled at the view.

But, alas, the protectors didn't pause as they led the three companions to a large two-story building made from the same white stone as the rest of the structures in the town.

The high arch at the front of the building led into a spacious antechamber. Two giant stone doors on the far wall were opened to a large, spacious room that contained two long tables. Instead of individual chairs, benches ran along one side of each table. One table was slightly higher than the other and positioned so the people sitting at the higher table faced those at the lower table.

A wonderful aroma filled the room, and Snapdragon noticed the tables were laden with dishes of meat and some type of leafy green vegetable. He thought of how much Waylon would have enjoyed this meal, and wondered again where the savant was.

The higher table was filled end to end with various people, most of them older, with Merton sitting squarely in the middle. The lower table was empty aside from the three place settings Snapdragon assumed were for him, Seraphina, and Bearach.

"Sit down," Merton instructed, not rising from his seat.

Snapdragon remained near the door. "Where is Savant Waylon?"

Merton scowled. "He will join us shortly, though that is not the response I expected to our sharing our meal with you."

"Be careful," Seraphina whispered.

Smiling and spreading his arms wide, Snapdragon said, "My apologies. I am just concerned for my friend's well-being. We are most grateful for your hospitality."

Merton's features relaxed some and he motioned again for them to sit. The people sitting with him were dressed in the plain white robes that seemed common among the inhabitants of Itamunno Kael, but there was a definite shimmer to Merton's robe.

When the group from Bariwon had taken their seats, Merton said, "I do wish you spoke the true language instead of this crude form of speaking, but I cannot fault you for that. The true language is one of many things your people will learn from us upon our glorious return. We will eat before we discuss that subject further."

After he finished his brief speech, Merton ignored them and focused on his meal. Snapdragon did the same, fearing to talk during the meal in case that would break some sort of etiquette rule and set Merton off.

Snapdragon glanced at Bearach, who was being true to his word about remaining calm and quiet during the meal, regardless of what happened. It wasn't easy to get the large man to agree, but even he admitted he was worried about what they might do to Seraphina—or any of them, for that matter—to coerce the others into submission. Plus, as Snapdragon had pointed out, Bearach still needed to regain his strength to be ready for whatever happened.

When the meal was nearly over, Merton looked up and spoke. "Tomorrow we will start the preparations for our return to the land of the first temple. It will take us several days before we will be ready to leave. However, there are a few major points that we need to discuss."

"And these are?" Snapdragon asked politely as he could.

"First, I understand that you are related to the current ruler over the land of the first temple. Is this correct, Snapdragon?"

The guardian thought for a moment. He was sure he hadn't brought that up when he was being "interviewed" by the questioner. Perhaps one of his companions had. If so, there was no use denying it.

"It is as you say," Snapdragon responded.

"Excellent. Then you will arrange for an audience with him upon our return."

Snapdragon realized they might use him as a hostage if things didn't go the way they planned. "It will be done."

"Second, there is the matter of the Rifna Erd. Our scouts have seen them amassing in the area. Although one path from Itamunno Kael brings us to the canyons very close to the Pendeltune, we need to be certain we can pass unharmed."

Snapdragon fought the urge to frown. He wondered why they called the tunnel "the Pendeltune," but decided now was not the time to ask. "The Rifna Erd will be a challenge, yes."

"Since you have successfully escaped from the Rifna Erd, I place you in charge of keeping us safe during the exodus. You have tonight to formulate a plan, and you will present it to us tomorrow," Merton said, then looked expectantly at Snapdragon.

Snapdragon felt Bearach tense up next to him, but fortunately the man kept silent.

"I will have a plan for you in time," Snapdragon said confidently.

Merton actually smiled before continuing. "You have proven yourselves useful in various ways since your arrival. Despite the hostile nature displayed by two of you during the questioning, you have been redeemed in our eyes. Waylon has proven to be most trustworthy, and for that, you are in our good graces."

"If I may inquire now, where is Savant Waylon? We've not seen him in some time," Snapdragon said.

"He will be joining us shortly. He is finishing an assignment. We have two more things to discuss this evening." Merton turned his attention to Bearach. "Sverre tells me that you fixed the darkened corner in the Temple of the New Moon."

Bearach nodded.

"I have to admit, we have not kept up with the old traditions as we could have. The creators of this town were highly skilled in mechanics. Over time, items have broken down that we simply cannot fix. While it is not important for us to fix all of these before we leave, the entrance to the path that exits to the canyons by the Pendeltune must be repaired. As of now, it only opens wide enough for a single man to pass through. It needs to open wide enough for the carts and animals we are taking. Your task is to repair it before we leave. You have three days."

Snapdragon could tell the man next to him was on the verge of exploding. "He will be happy to help any way he can," Snapdragon said before Bearach could do anything foolish.

"For the last item of the night, we will now wait for Waylon to return."

At that point, several young men and women entered the hall and began to clear away the dishes. Other young people brought small helpings of a sweet berry dish. It was tangy, with just a hint of an herb Snapdragon didn't recognize.

Just as he was about done with the dessert, Waylon entered the room, flanked by two protectors.

"Waylon, excellent!" Merton stated. "Please join us."

Instead of sitting next to the people from Bariwon, Waylon took a seat on the far end of the higher table. Snapdragon could tell that Seraphina and Bearach were as surprised as he was.

"Waylon…?" Seraphina spoke up, leaving the rest of the question unasked.

The pudgy savant turned to Merton and asked, "If I may?"

Merton nodded.

"Friends, I cannot begin to tell you how wondrous all this is," Waylon began. "For generations we have kept the secret of the Rifna Erd and the Tular Tevoil, hoping one day for their return—never knowing they were waiting for *us.*"

"'We' who, Waylon?" Snapdragon asked.

"I am a direct descendant of Tular Tevoil," Waylon said proudly. "He had two sons—one he took with him, and one he left behind to watch over the first temple. When the nislles came and began to kill the population, the people blamed the Rifna Erd and the Tular Tevoil, even though they had nothing to do with it. It was simply a bad coincidence. But anyone related to either Tular Tevoil or Rifna Erd was hunted down and killed."

"It is a dark chapter in your people's history," Merton said with disgust.

Waylon nodded. "We went into hiding. Even when they built the wall to keep the Rifna Erd and the Tular Tevoil from returning, we kept silent. Over the years, all records of the tunnel and what happened were destroyed, and the subject was forbidden. A large landslide covered the wall to the tunnel and it was all but forgotten except by those of us that kept the faith."

Merton smiled at Waylon, as did the rest of the people at the higher table.

"But why didn't you tell us?" Snapdragon asked.

"I couldn't tell anyone until I spoke with Merton alone and knew he was going to accept me for my word," Waylon said. "I tried to see him at the questioning, but couldn't. It wasn't until this afternoon that I was able to get an audience, and even then it wasn't easy to convince him."

"I did not believe him at first, of course," said Merton. "Trust must be earned. I do not give it lightly."

Snapdragon grew more uneasy. "Waylon, what did you do to earn their trust?"

"You shall see soon enough." The savant smiled.

The protectors who had escorted Waylon opened a side door, and two more robed protectors entered, each holding a rope tied to the hands of a person following him.

At first the captives were hidden behind the protectors, but when they did come into view, Snapdragon's heart lurched.

It was Alethea and Creighton.

CHAPTER 45

Melanie smiled. "This will be perfect!"

"I'm not so sure," Ciar said, frowning.

It was late, and with his assignments completed for the day, he had come to Melanie's room. She had been anxious to talk to him.

"Well, I'm sure it will work." Melanie sounded defensive.

Ciar scratched his chin and looked down at the herbs on the table. She had gathered the stash over the last few days, stealing it in small doses from the Nursemaid's chambers. "What is it called?"

"Plyese. It's primarily used in teas—it has a calming effect. It can help you sleep."

"So, you expect the guardians on the night watch to sip this tea?" Ciar asked incredulously.

Rolling her eyes, Melanie said, "Of course not, you wooden head."

"Then what's it for?"

Melanie reached for the mortar and pestle next to the herbs. "Hand me a few of those herbs."

Ciar did so. Melanie took the plyese and put it in the mortar, which was basically a large bowl. She then used the pestle, a small, club-shaped tool, to grind the herbs into a fine powder. Ciar looked on skeptically. Then Melanie mixed the powder into a tankard she had set up. She lifted the tankard and handed it to Ciar.

"Take a whiff of this," she said.

Ciar sniffed the drink. "It's eggnog."

"Aye, and does it smell any different?"

Ciar sniffed again. "Not that I can tell. It just smells like... oh, what is it called? Ah—nutmeg."

"Now have a drink of it. Don't worry. It won't harm you."

Ciar took several gulps. "It tastes the same to me."

420

"Exactly! The nutmeg hides the smell and flavor of the plyese herb," Melanie said excitedly.

Ciar still didn't look convinced. He set the tankard back on the table. "So… your plan is to have the night watch drink the eggnog and get sleepy? I don't think that will work. They sleep during the day so that they can be alert at night."

Melanie sighed. "When made into a tea, plyese is used in small quantities. This is much more powerful."

"I'm still not buying it. The guardians are big men. I don't see how…"

Ciar didn't finish his sentence as his eyes rolled back in his head and he started to fall to the ground. Melanie was able to catch him and guide him to the floor so he didn't hurt himself.

Laughing, she whispered to an unconscious Ciar, "I told you it would be perfect."

⟶❄⟵

Snapdragon lay on his back in a well-furnished room. It wasn't the glistening stars beyond the glass window that held his attention, nor was it finding a way to prevent the Rifna Erd from interfering with the exodus of the Tular Tevoil. Rather, it was the expression on Alethea's face when she had realized that if Waylon hadn't betrayed her, Snapdragon would have.

"I'm glad you have already informed our host, Waylon," Snapdragon had said. "You saved me from having to do so."

At first, he had been unable to tell who was the most shocked—Alethea, Bearach, or Seraphina. Snapdragon had kept both his hands under the table while he spoke, and had given Bearach a firm grip on this arm and Seraphina a tight squeeze on her knee, hoping they would understand.

Merton had beamed to bursting when he saw the young woman's reaction to Snapdragon's words.

Snapdragon had struggled to contain the pure fire that roiled inside him. How could Waylon have done this, after Snapdragon had befriended the man and even saved his life? If anyone had the right to feel betrayed, Snapdragon did. But if he had learned nothing else from Fallon, rest his soul, it was to be patient and think a moment before he acted.

The hand had been played. Merton and Waylon held the highest cards—at least for the moment. That was not a battle that would be won there in the dinner hall. However, battles were often lost, and sacrifices made, for the larger good. Fallon had known that when he fought to the death, allowing Snapdragon to lead his group away.

"I'm glad you brought Creighton along as well," Snapdragon had continued. "He can tell you that he was basically taken hostage by the people living in Eddinh, and now that they have been liberated, they can go back to their rightful homes when the Tular Tevoil make their proud return."

Creighton's eyes had narrowed at Snapdragon's comment. Then, not looking at Alethea, he had bowed his head and didn't respond.

Snapdragon hadn't wanted to look at Alethea, but he couldn't help himself. It was the expression on her face at that moment that haunted him still.

Chiding himself for not focusing on a plan for the Rifna Erd, Snapdragon rolled onto his side, trying to become more comfortable.

After dinner, he and his companions had been given separate rooms in the main palace. Each was well furnished with a soft bed, a glass window, and a modest hearth.

Snapdragon's meager possessions had been left for him. His sword was propped against the wall next to the hearth. On an intricately carved table lay his armor and coin purse.

The Tular Tevoil didn't use coins or any other form of money. Everything was the property of the leaders, who gave to each person or family what they needed. The mere concept of money was as foreign to them as a pure communal economy was to Snapdragon.

His eyes rested on the coin purse. His father was not a rich man, at least not in the worldly sense of the meaning. Garth was extremely bright, and, as Snapdragon had grown to understand over time, also very wise. They didn't keep a lot of coins on hand, but there was something his father used to do with a coin. A trick. What was it?

Snapdragon's mind was starting to wander, which meant sleep was not far off. Perhaps a full, deep night's sleep would allow him to figure a way out of this predicament. Now, what was it with the coin his father used to do? To Snapdragon, it had seemed like magic at the time, though his dad had used it as a tool to explain that there was no such thing as magic, aside from what the good Lord above gave them, but that things may seem like magic when in fact they were simple misdirection.

Misdirection... misdirection...

The coin and misdirection...

⇥✦⇤

Grant had lost track of time. In the dark tunnel, he had no sense of day or night. Despite the injury to his leg and the exhaustion that all but begged him to lie down and rest, he kept crawling toward Bariwon.

The voices behind him had quieted, which led Grant to believe it was night. While part of his mind told him this would be a good time to sleep, a stronger part urged him forward. He had no doubt the strange men that had killed his companions would come through the tunnel; he just wasn't sure why they hadn't done so yet.

Regardless, once they started down the tunnel, they would catch up to Grant soon enough, unless he kept moving. Reaching deep inside himself for that extra effort, he kept crawling, praying he would get to the other side first.

⋙✦⋘

The sun had just risen above the mountaintops when Snapdragon sought an audience with Merton and his advisors. After waiting for a short period of time, Snapdragon was ushered into a spacious meeting room not unlike the white marble rooms he had been in before, though this one had various purple banners hanging from the ceiling.

Waylon was also there, dressed in the same fashion as Merton's advisors.

"Yes, Snapdragon," Merton said from behind his desk. "Have you a plan to deal with the Rifna Erd?"

Still standing, Snapdragon nodded, forcing himself to appear relaxed. When he had awoken this morning, it had come to him—a plan that just might work. "Yes, and it's important that I get started on it right away."

"If we agree to it, then you shall," Merton said flatly.

Snapdragon walked over to a small table and chair off to the side. "May I have a seat to give you a demonstration?"

Merton glanced at Waylon, who simply smiled.

"Proceed," Merton said.

Snapdragon sat at the table and rolled up the sleeves of his robe. He had not been allowed to change back into his armor while he was in town, as it would make him unclean in the eyes of the people. With the sleeves rolled up past his elbows, he removed a single coin from one of the robe's pockets.

"I know you don't use coins here in Tular Tevoil, but I want you all to take a close look at this one." He held it up for them to see, and one of the advisors, an elderly man nearly bent at the waist due to old age, came and took the coin and passed it around the room before returning it to Snapdragon.

"You all held the coin and felt its substance. It is real. Now, I'm going to make it disappear, but I can only do so if you all concentrate. If you don't, it won't work."

To Snapdragon's satisfaction, he had everyone's undivided attention, including Merton's.

Setting the coin on the table in front of him, Snapdragon picked it up with his left hand and then placed it in his right. Setting his left elbow on the table with his head leaning on his left hand for support, Snapdragon placed his right hand on his left forearm and started to rub it up and down, purposefully contorting his face to appear as if he were concentrating hard. After several rubs, the coin slipped out from under his right hand and clattered on the table.

Merton let out a snort of disgust, but before he could say anything, Snapdragon said, "One of you wasn't concentrating hard enough. I think it was you!"

He pointed at the elderly man who had passed the coin around. The man's eyes grew wide and he shook his head.

"All right, I'll try it again, but I need everyone to focus," Snapdragon said. Once again he picked up the coin with his left hand and then placed it in his right. Resuming the position he had used before, Snapdragon rubbed again, this time with more force.

Again, the coin slipped from under his right hand and landed on the table. "Waylon! It was you this time. You need to focus!" Snapdragon shouted. Every eye in the room turned to glare at the savant, including Merton's.

"Honestly, I was!" Waylon said, his cheeks turning red.

Snapdragon once again picked up the coin. "I almost had it that time. Please, everyone focus."

"Yes, focus, Waylon!" Merton snapped.

Snapdragon started to rub his right hand once more against his left forearm, this time going faster and faster until he quickly stopped and pulled his hand away, revealing that the coin was gone. He also held out his left hand and stood up to show that the coin was in neither hand, nor was it on his lap or up his sleeves.

He heard several people gasp, and each one looked bewildered. Before any of them could say anything, Snapdragon started shaking his arms wildly, then his hips. "I feel it moving inside me," he said dramatically. "It's looking for a way out!" He started shaking his legs. Grabbing hold of both sides of his head, Snapdragon then put out his left foot and shook it violently at them. "It's there! But it can't get out!" he said in a panicked voice.

Next his legs started shaking again, then his hips, and then his torso. "I think, maybe… maybe… ah… ah-choo!" He put both hands over his face and sneezed into them. He paused a moment, then slowly pulled his hands away to show them the coin sitting large as life in his right palm.

Everyone in the room stood, each staring at the coin in the guardian's hand.

"How…? Are you saying you are going to get my people out of here using magic?" Merton asked furiously.

Trying not to sound smug, Snapdragon said, "How would I do that? There is no such thing as magic. There are things that are real, and there are things that only appear to be."

Merton sat back down, and everyone else in the room followed him, aside from Snapdragon, who remained standing and looking down at them.

"Then how?" Merton asked, obviously expecting an answer without further delay.

"Misdirection," Snapdragon said. "The third time I picked up the coin with my left hand, I didn't place it in my right. I placed it in my ear. But you were all too busy to notice, because I had your attention focused where I wanted—not only on my right hand, but also on your own concentration. When you were all looking at my foot, I simply removed the coin from my ear and pretended to sneeze it out. But you all saw what I wanted you to see, allowing me to fool you."

Merton sat back and folded his arms. "Tell me how a simple trick like that will protect my people from the Rifna Erd."

"For me to do that," Snapdragon said, "I need you to tell me more about the time the Rifna Erd sent up the summoning signal at the Temple of the New Moon."

⇥❉⇤

Bearach lay on his belly, his face next to the stone wall. There was a lit lantern nearby and several small hand shovels that Snapdragon guessed had been used for gardening.

"Find anything yet?" Snapdragon asked when he got up next to the crafter.

Turning over and squinting up at him, the large man said, "Maybe…"

Snapdragon glanced around and saw several protectors watching over them. "Perhaps I should come down there and take a look."

Bearach grunted in approval and rolled back over.

Snapdragon lay down next to him and looked at what Bearach had been working on. The rock around the center hinge had been carefully dug away. Pointing to an area nowhere near the hinge, Bearach said loudly, "I believe it has something to do with the release mechanism. Let me show you."

He burrowed in deeper, and Snapdragon moved in right beside him.

"I found the problem back there at the hinge," Bearach whispered. "Simple problem to fix, but I got thinking, if I were to fix this right away, they might not have a reason to keep me around for long."

Snapdragon made sure he didn't look at the hinge. "How long would it take you to fix it?" he whispered.

"Not long at all," Bearach said.

"And how hard would it be to make it worse?" Snapdragon asked carefully.

Bearach smiled. "It would take me even less time."

"All right. Hold off for now, claiming you can fix it, but that it will require some time. I have another project, and I've convinced Merton that you are needed for it. But I can't go into what the plan is right now. We don't want to be overheard. Meet me at the tunnel entrance that goes to the Temple of the New Moon as soon as you can. Oh! And bring your backpack."

⊰⊹⊱

"You can fix the passage gateway?" Sverre asked Bearach when the crafter arrived at the tunnel entrance which led to the Temple of the New Moon.

Snapdragon eyed the muscular man, waiting for a response.

"Aye, it will take some time, but I can do it. I'll have it open in time for the exodus," Bearach said gruffly.

Snapdragon didn't blame Bearach for his foul mood toward Sverre. The man had tried to kill Snapdragon and then tricked them into coming to Itamunno Kael, where they were interrogated. At the same time, he needed Bearach's help with the situation they faced—and Bearach wouldn't do any good sitting at the bottom of the pit.

"Then we will be off," Sverre said, heading to the passageway.

"Where's Seraphina?" Snapdragon asked.

Sverre didn't look back but responded, "She will remain here to make sure that you both will be returning."

Bearach and Snapdragon exchanged a knowing look and then followed Sverre.

While traveling down the path, Snapdragon made note of the distance between the village and the entrance to the temple. They had made a fairly brisk walk of it, but it still took them several hours to reach the temple. If they were to ride on horseback, the time would be significantly shorter, though the tunnel was so low that a rider would have to crouch low over the horse's neck, provided he could get a horse to actually accept a rider in the confined space.

When they reached the end, Sverre opened the stairs that led up from the tunnel. Again, Snapdragon took special care to note how the release was done.

"Now that we are here, what did you need?" Sverre asked.

The main chamber of the temple was still well lit from the openings Sverre had activated when recounting the story of the Rifna Erd and the Tular Tevoil. Snapdragon walked over to one of the walls and scanned it for a certain drawing.

He pointed to it once he had found it. "Tell me about this."

The picture depicted the Temple of the New Moon with one side lit up with an open circle.

"Ah," said Sverre proudly. "That is a feature of the temple that was made to frighten away the Rifna Erd. It was built under their noses and was quite a sight, I am sure."

"So it's still here?" Snapdragon asked.

Sverre's eyebrows shot up. "It should be, but it has not been used since that one time. It is not likely to work."

Patting Bearach on the back, Snapdragon said, "Well, we'll see to that."

"It smells like some sort of ale," Snapdragon commented and then plugged his nose.

Bearach nodded. "If I'm right, it will catch on fire like ale as well. Just keep the torches back."

Sverre had led them up the stairs and into yet another secret passageway that had brought them to the room where they were now. There were torch holders on one side of the room, while on the other was a large, flat, circular stone, like a wheel lying on its side. It had two distinct removable sections—one on top and one off to the side. The one off to the side led into a trough of sorts that ran from the stone to the edge of the wall.

After removing the top of the stone, Bearach looked inside. A liquid seemed to bubble up from the ground deep below. Then it was drawn into a container and ran off to the left through a hole in the rock.

Bearach studied things for a moment and then grunted with satisfaction. He covered the top of the stone again and removed the section to the right. Little bits of the liquid seeped out time and again into the trough— until Bearach pushed down on a rock to the left. It appeared to have closed the opening that drew off the liquid, and the trough started filling up. When it was nearly half full, Bearach pulled up on the rock to the left and then covered the section to the right. Then the large man stepped back and said, "Hand me one of the torches."

Snapdragon asked, "Are you sure this is wise?"

Cracking a smile for the first time in Snapdragon's recent memory, Bearach said, "It's most definitely not wise, but that hasn't stopped me from trying things like this before."

Snapdragon handed him the torch and backed away, then watched as Bearach slowly lowered the torch to the trough. Just when Snapdragon thought nothing was going to happen, the fire leapt from the torch and then down the trough. It burned steadily, giving off some heat, but what was most remarkable was that it burned almost white.

"I've never seen anything like that," Bearach said, staring in amazement.

Snapdragon thought he heard Sverre curse some sort of oath in his native tongue.

"Any ideas how to get it to the outside?" Snapdragon asked.

Bearach seemed reluctant to take his eyes off the fire. "Of course. I believe we're near the top of the temple. At the end of the trough there's an outlet to the outside. It's blocked off, but I'll bet you it feeds the troughs outside. We should look outside to be certain, though."

Sverre led them to the outside ledge where he had first met Snapdragon. From there, Bearach climbed around the outside of the temple, inspecting the troughs. When he returned his face dripped with sweat.

"The troughs are mostly intact. It will take some time to repair them, but it's doable," he reported.

Sverre shook his head. "I do not understand. Why does it matter?"

"You'll see," Snapdragon said. "Now for the next question. Bearach, how hard would it be to make seven or eight holes in the rock here, roughly the size of a torch handle?"

Bearach knelt down and felt the rock. He removed a small pick from his bag and used it to chip away at the surface. "With a couple of strong men and some decent tools, it shouldn't take long."

"Explain to me why you would deface the temple so," Sverre all but demanded.

"You'll see," Snapdragon said once again, not trying to hide his smile. "But first we need to go back to the main chamber."

Once there, Snapdragon stood at the entrance of the temple and looked over the field beyond the bridge that spanned the river. It was wide open, and there was no place from which anyone could approach the temple without being spotted from some distance away. Though the sun had passed its apex, it was still high in the summer sky.

"All right, I've seen what I needed to and I'm ready to present my complete plan to Merton," Snapdragon announced. "Let's head back—there's much work to be done."

"I still do not understand!" Sverre said, clearly frustrated.

Starting back toward Itamunno Kael, Snapdragon's only response was, "You'll see."

⭑⭒⭑

Eadward eyed his cousin carefully. "And you're sure this will work?"

"Most definitely," Ciar said. "I know how powerful this herb is. It will work."

Ciar had remembered drinking the eggnog and then starting to disagree with Melanie, but then the next thing he recalled was waking up on the floor, sore from sleeping on the stone surface in an awkward position. If he'd had any doubts about using the plyese herb, they were gone now.

"And when can you put this plan into place?" Eadward asked.

Ciar spared a glance at the two large men Eadward kept as bodyguards in his room at The Bull's Horns. They both looked anxious to do something more than remain holed up at the inn.

"We just got our assignments for the next couple of days," Ciar replied. "I'll be serving dinner to the night watch tomorrow night. Melanie was able to switch her schedule so that she will feed the dungeon guardians the same night. She'll be able to free Abrecan and his men, and then, using less traveled hallways in the castle, we can get the prisoners to the entrance at dawn of the following day."

Eadward actually smiled. "Then that's when we will gather my men by the castle entrance. When they see Abrecan freed at the first light of dawn, it will give them the added courage they need to storm the castle. It's perfect."

"I'm glad you approve," Ciar said, happy to show his cousin he was more than just a castle servant.

Eadward's countenance darkened. "This is an event that will change the future of Bariwon forever. I'm putting a lot of trust in you. For once in your life, don't fail."

-)‡‡‡-

It was as if someone had kicked an ant's nest, Snapdragon mused as he walked among the people of the Tular Tevoil, who were hurrying back and forth in preparation for the exodus. He and Bearach were being led to Merton and didn't have time to stop and check on Seraphina.

They were brought to where Snapdragon had used the coin as an object lesson for his presentation of the plan. Bearach had offered to work on the passageway, but he was asked to remain.

"You have finished your plan then, yes?" Merton asked, sitting among the other rulers of the Tular Tevoil.

"Yes," Snapdragon answered. "And I'll need help from some of your people to make it happen, though they will still be able to join the exodus."

Sitting back and folding his arms, Merton said, "Proceed."

"Like I showed you with the coin, it'll be a simple misdirection," Snapdragon said. "We'll set the signals in front of the Temple of the New Moon for the Rifna Erd to gather. We need a chain of people within shouting distance of each other from here to there to announce when the first sign of the Rifna Erd arrives. We'll set up the signals one day before you are ready to leave."

"How does this protect us?" Merton sounded skeptical.

"The Rifna Erd don't know of the passage from here to the tunnel back to Bariwon. Based on what you told me, they will gather their people at the temple when summoned. They are, no doubt, aware that people have come through the tunnel and that we escaped them by hiding in the temple. They will expect that the meeting you have called will deal with just that topic."

Merton started to smile. "That will probably work. You are correct."

"In the meantime, you have scouts watching the tunnel entrance, right? Has there been any sign of the Rifna Erd by the tunnel?" asked Snapdragon.

"Not that we have heard, though we have not received any reports recently."

"And one last part," Snapdragon said, glancing at Sverre. "We can arrange to leave the Rifna Erd with a goodbye message they won't soon forget."

Sverre broke into a wicked grin and barked out a laugh. Merton asked him a question in their native tongue and Sverre responded in kind, causing all the Tular Tevoil in the room to smile and laugh malevolently.

"I believe that will work," Merton said, rubbing his hands together. "We will see that you get the men you need. And now for you, Bearach."

The crafter took a step forward, actually appearing nervous. Snapdragon wondered if they had gotten the passageway working and therefore no longer needed Bearach. Snapdragon was about to speak up and say he needed the man's help, but he didn't get a chance before Merton said, "We have another assignment for you, in addition to opening the passageway."

Looking relieved, Bearach said, "I have some work to do at the temple before the exodus, but of course, whatever you need."

Merton nodded. "Good. We need you to disable all the passageways from here to Eddinh. We have protectors standing guard over the people there, but we need them to help with the preparations to leave."

"I don't know where they all are," Bearach said.

"We have searched from inside the cavern and found them all, including the one that leads to the Pendeltune. We will show you."

Snapdragon took a step forward. "We'll need to bring the people from Procep up first. We don't want them trapped as well."

Shifting his gaze to Snapdragon, Merton said, "That will not be needed."

"I don't understand," Snapdragon replied.

"They have been corrupted by the people of Eddinh," Merton said flatly. "They are not permitted to return."

CHAPTER 46

"I'm done helping these Tular Tevoil!" Seraphina shouted. "Do you honestly believe they'll let us return with them? Do you honestly believe anything they say?"

Snapdragon took a step closer to the nursemaid, wanting to comfort her. She didn't back away, but neither did she come to him. "I believe it when they say they'll use you to get me and Bearach to do their bidding," he said quietly. "I also believe they'll take at least one of us back with them."

Seraphina nodded quickly. "It seems that being related to the king and queen gives you special privileges, even here."

Snapdragon often got angry at such comments, but he wasn't upset at Seraphina. He said her name softly.

Her face paled, and after a moment she said, "That wasn't fair of me. I'm sorry." Looking in his eyes, she seemed to silently beg for forgiveness.

"I understand you're frustrated," he said. "You have every right to be. However, I need your help."

"As you said when you came in to see me," Seraphina said, motioning to the guarded door to her room. "But you seem all too eager to help the Tular Tevoil with their plan to leave."

Snapdragon nodded. "I'm doing what has to be done."

He opened his arms and took a step forward to embrace her. She hesitated at first, but then acquiesced. With her head on his chest, Snapdragon whispered, "I'm sure we are being watched and listened to. I can't explain what I'm doing, but you've trusted me in the past with your life and I need you to do so again. If we get a chance, I'll tell you everything, but until then, please just do as I ask."

He let go of her and said loudly, "You'd be wise to help the Tular Tevoil as well. They'll play an important part in the future of Bariwon. These are good friends to have."

Seraphina's shoulders slumped. "Fine, tell me what I need to do."

⊰✦⊱

After leaving Seraphina's room, Snapdragon headed outside. Sverre fell into step beside him as soon as he left the building. The sun had just gone behind the mountains to the west, and even though night rapidly approached, the town was still full of activity.

"If this continues, we'll need an extra day before we'll be ready to leave," Snapdragon said.

Sverre frowned at him—something the strange Tular Tevoil man had been doing a lot. "I do not believe Merton will agree to wait one more day."

"Well, we wouldn't have to wait if I was getting the help I needed," Snapdragon spat back, not trying to hide his frustration. "And I've figured out why I was selected to be in charge of getting the Tular Tevoil back safely."

"And why is that?" Sverre asked, sounding wary.

Snapdragon spread his arms open wide. "Simple. No one else here thinks the way I do. You have all become soft. Sure, your leaders rule by fear, but aside from throwing people in a pit or threatening them with torture, you don't have any trained soldiers. Your protectors are nothing more than brutes with large weapons."

"You are presuming too much," Sverre said darkly.

Snapdragon barked out a laugh. "Am I? I think you've been trapped up here so long, fearing the Rifna Erd and waiting for someone to lead you back to your homeland, that you've given up hope of ever being able to liberate yourselves."

Sverre set his feet and folded his arms. "You have seen the Rifna Erd. They are too many and too powerful. If they were to ever find a way up here, they would kill us all. They are... what is it in your language? Barbarians."

"Exactly," Snapdragon said triumphantly. "And it takes a barbarian to think like a barbarian, right?"

Wide-eyed, Sverre shook his head, though the way his body tensed up confirmed Snapdragon's deduction.

"Although none of that really matters, aside from letting me do my job," the guardian went on. "You're assigned to watch over me, but you're also assigned to help me, correct?"

"Yes."

"Then get me the help I need so we can leave when Merton wants to."

Sverre sighed. "Tell me again what you need."

"I need a dozen men to act as a line of communication between here and the Temple of the New Moon. I need eight or nine women who can sew to work with Seraphina. I also need more men to assist Bearach on his fixes and changes to the Temple of the New Moon. And lastly, I need several corpses brought up from the pit."

"What? Did I understand you to say you need the bodies of the dead?"

Snapdragon looked at Sverre with steely eyes. "Do you want to distract the Rifna Erd or not? As you have said, these are barbarians, and we need to speak their language."

"I will not help you with the bodies of the dead. The other things, yes."

Snapdragon let out a long breath. "Fine. I will remove the bodies from the pit. Since you are so sick at the thought of it, perhaps you can get someone else to help me so you won't have to see them."

Sverre paused, appearing to be deep in thought, then said, "Could we use dead animals instead?"

"Do you want me to distract the Rifna Erd or not? They'll know the difference between human and animal remains."

"And there is no other way?"

Snapdragon folded his arms and frowned.

"Fine," Sverre finally said, "but only dead bodies from the pit."

⇒╫⇐

King Rayne sat on a wooden bench and stared at the mountains. He had sat there for hours, rubbing his chin while he thought. Growing up in Tevoil, he had been surrounded by trees. The tallest thing he had ever seen until now was the castle. He hadn't imagined anything as tall as these mountains. And he wasn't the only one. Several of his men mentioned having dreams of the mountains falling on them. Even now, during the early summer, the tops of the mountains were white with snow.

No wonder people considered these mountains impassable. Even if you could get near the top, the snow would be very deep. Still, what had inspired someone to dig under the mountain was beyond him. And why had he not heard of this tunnel before? It didn't make any sense. All he knew was that he had an overwhelming sense of foreboding when he looked north toward the mountains. He had felt that way since they had arrived.

The scouts still didn't have anything to report, and Aaron kept the men on high alert at the tunnel entrance. Still, Rayne was getting to the point where he needed to *do* something. Before he left the castle, Fallon had promised him that one way or another he'd send word—and that if he didn't, it meant it was too dangerous to do so. But if Fallon's group was in trouble, was waiting around making things worse?

Finally, Rayne came to a conclusion. *I'll give them one more day,* he thought. *And then we'll see for ourselves what is beyond these mountains.*

⇥⧉⇤

Bearach used a large hammer with a thick stone head and a sturdy wooden handle to hit the wedge.

"And this will hold, yes?" Sverre eyed the rock the crafter had just forced into the wall with the wedge.

"Aye, this will prevent the passageway from being opened on the other side—or from this side, for that matter," Bearach said, removing the wedge. "I've placed a smaller rock, using these tools, to disable the release mechanism. Unless someone knows exactly what I've done, they can't fix this."

Sverre pushed against the stone and grunted in satisfaction. "It is getting very late. How many more do you have to complete?"

Bearach gathered up his hammer, wedge, and sack of small rocks. "If your people found them all, there is just one more between here and Eddinh. And then there is the secret exit from Eddinh to the passage that leads from Itamunno Kael to the canyons by the tunnel, or Pendeltune, as you call it. That's how they found the people from Procep—it's a secret passage to your secret passage. In other words, there is a way from Eddinh that connects to the passage between the exit in the canyons by the Pendeltune and where the Tular Tevoil live. Got it?"

Sverre looked confused, but then his expression changed. "We should complete the exit to the outside passage next," he said, sounding like it was his decision. "We must show these people there is no hope of escape."

⇥⧉⇤

Protectors stood in a long line separating the people of Procep and Eddinh from Snapdragon, Bearach, and Sverre. Angry shouts assaulted Snapdragon, some in languages he couldn't understand.

"Traitors!" one voice rang out. "What part of your soul did you have to sell for your freedom?"

Snapdragon did his best to ignore the words, but deep down they bothered him. Unlike with Seraphina, he couldn't pull these people in close and whisper that everything would be all right—to relax and trust him. And the show they were putting on was having a profound impact on the protectors and Sverre. The dark mood in the cavern matched the increasing darkness outside.

Bearach made quick work of disabling the release for the passageway. Sverre insisted on trying to push it before they left and seemed satisfied it wasn't going to open.

The protectors slowly backed away from the crowd, their long, sharp spears pointed at the people of Eddinh and Procep. Sverre was the first one out of the passage and back to Itamunno Kael. Snapdragon and Bearach were next, followed by a line of protectors, the last few of them sprinting. Bearach quickly closed the door, placed a rock in the crack between the wall and the release mechanism, and started hammering a wedge into place when the door started opening again.

"Push up against it!" the crafter commanded. "Don't let them through!"

Snapdragon and several protectors ran to the door and strained to close it tightly so Bearach could secure the release lever. The shouts from the other side of the wall cut Snapdragon to the core, but he had to do this. The people of Eddinh and Procep had to be locked up.

One more heavy swing from Bearach locked the rock in place. He stood back, panting. "That was the last one. They can't come through now, and those stone doors are too heavy for men to break down."

⇥✦⇤

Selene's anticipation of Abrecan's release continued to grow. She had overcome her shock of learning about the people of Procep and the possibility of the people north of the mountains returning.

Knowing that King Rayne had sent people to investigate complicated things. What would they find? How would it impact her if the truth came out about her ancestors? It was at times like these she missed Abrecan. She needed his guidance—he would know what to do.

Reports from the castle had been as expected. The town around the castle, Bariwon Proper, was jammed with people, obviously looking for comfort from their king.

Oddly, King Rayne had sent his wife to address the people during court. It was said she was very charming and had a calming influence. But the king hadn't made an appearance. That was bad form—something Abrecan would never let happen. The people needed to see who was in charge.

Selene found herself pacing in her room. She had been so lost in thought that she had no idea how long she had been doing so. But it wouldn't be long now. In a few days, Abrecan would be on the throne and he would reward those that had stayed loyal.

❖❖❖

Snapdragon couldn't sleep. He had gotten up once to clear his mind, but he was under guard and wasn't allowed to leave his room. Sverre had promised him all the help he required for the following day's activities. As busy as today had been, the next would be even more so. Snapdragon knew he was playing a dangerous game. When training for the Mortentaun, he had learned that when in combat the actions you *didn't* take or the tactics you *didn't* perform were just as important as what you did. Sometimes, simply switching tactics could throw your opponent off guard and give you the victory. The trick was to know when to switch. Oakleaf called it being "momentarily misunderstood"—the moment when you had to make your move for it to have the greatest effect. But you had to set things up beforehand, and the effectiveness of the switch was only as good as the setup. And it was the setup on which Snapdragon was so desperately working.

So far things had gone remarkably well, despite how bad Snapdragon felt at seeming to betray the people of Eddinh and Procep. He had not considered that the people of Procep might not be allowed to leave, and he'd had to change his plan midstride. He thought he had found a way around it, but he wondered what other changes Merton would make in the bargain before the exodus.

Those troubling thoughts still remained when Snapdragon finally fell asleep.

Snapdragon was awakened hours later when the door to his room opened. Sverre stood there, the early morning sunshine silhouetting him.

"It is time to arise. I have assembled the people you have required."

Sitting up slowly and stretching animatedly, Snapdragon asked, "When do we begin?"

Sverre nodded his head to people out of Snapdragon's view. "Your morning meal is being brought in. We will give you a short time to eat and be ready. Do not delay."

⊰╬⊱

The dawn was crisp and bright. To Rayne, it felt like spring was giving him a goodbye present before it surrendered to summer. It wasn't cold, just cool enough that he needed to keep moving to stay warm.

Aaron had come to him at first light, as he did every morning. There was still nothing new to report. Rayne had heard a saying, "No good news isn't the same as bad news." But Rayne had waited long enough—it was time to *do* something.

"Send twenty scouts into the tunnel," the king said to Aaron. "Tell them I expect reports twice a day on their progress. Keep the rest of the men ready for battle."

To his credit, Aaron kept his opinions to himself, but his expression gave away that he had been anxiously awaiting this order.

"It will be done, Your Majesty."

⊰╬⊱

Ten of the strongest protectors stood at attention, each holding a stone hammer and metal spikes. Snapdragon did his best not to show that he recognized Darius, Alethea's cousin who had visited him earlier. Next to them were a dozen or so boys, probably in their thirteenth or fourteenth year, followed by seven older women.

"These are the men who will help Bearach at the temple," Sverre said, walking down the row. "The young ones will be the yellers between here and the Temple of the New Moon, while the revered ones will help with sewing."

Snapdragon nodded. "Very good. There's hope yet for us to leave on time."

Sverre shuffled his feet as if nervous.

"Where are Bearach and Seraphina?" Snapdragon scanned the area by the lake where they had gathered.

"They will be here shortly," Sverre said. "And for today, I will need to address my own affairs to prepare for the exodus. I am giving you a protector to... help you as needed."

438

Snapdragon knew the protector was nothing more than a reminder that he was being watched.

A very tall and muscular protector came up next to Sverre. "My name is Orrell."

"What's that you said?" Snapdragon asked, looking quizzically at the man.

"Orrell—that is my name. I will be watching over you."

Snapdragon looked at Sverre. "I don't understand a word he is saying."

"Why not?" Sverre asked. "You understand me."

Snapdragon did a quick shake of his head. "I can barely understand you. A good part of the time I'm guessing at what you are saying. There is something about his accent that I can't get around. Perhaps another protector from the ones you have chosen will speak better."

Sverre looked impatient. "What makes you think any of them will speak your crude language any better?"

"Well, it wouldn't hurt to try."

Not waiting for a response, Snapdragon went up to each man and asked him to repeat the phrase, "The quick brown fox jumps over the lazy dog."

Each time he frowned and shook his head until he came to Darius. Smiling, Snapdragon said, "Ah, this one I understand. What's your name?"

"Darius," the man said, scowling.

Snapdragon pointed. "At least he can be understood."

"Sverre, do not make me help this… outsider." Darius spat out the last word as if it was a piece of rotten fruit.

"You will do as you are told!" Sverre barked. "Orrell, you and Darius change places."

Snapdragon knew he had taken a risk in getting Darius to help him. The man had to think Snapdragon had betrayed his cousin, Alethea. Still, he needed someone who was not loyal to Merton and his kind, so it was a risk he had to take.

Facing the boys, Snapdragon said, "You'll need to spread out between here and the Temple of the New Moon in the passage below. Stand close enough to be within shouting distance. We need to know if there is any sign of the Rifna Erd while we're preparing."

A few of the boys didn't seem to quite grasp the concept until Darius explained it to them in their primary language.

Snapdragon then addressed the older women. "We need eight large white blankets or canvases made. Seraphina, who is an expert seamstress in her own right, will help you with what exactly needs to be done."

"I'm actually not a very good seamstress at all," a voice whispered behind Snapdragon.

He turned around and saw the nursemaid and the crafter standing there, flanked by two protectors.

"Just fake it," Snapdragon whispered through his teeth.

"Ah, here they are," he said loudly enough for all to hear. "Seraphina, Bearach—good. Seraphina, please take the women assigned to you and start working on the project we discussed last night."

Seraphina walked over to the women, followed closely by her assigned protector.

"And Bearach, these are the men who have been assigned to help you with the Temple of the New Moon," Snapdragon said.

The crafter harrumphed. "Well, we've got a full day of work ahead of us. Better get started."

Sverre stood with his hands on his hips, tapping his foot. "And what are you going to do?" he asked Snapdragon.

Snapdragon looked at Darius and said, "Are you as afraid of dead bodies as Sverre?"

⊰⊱

Snapdragon made sure the harness was snugly fastened and the rope securely attached. He reached for his torch. "Are you sure you're strong enough to lower me down?" he asked Darius.

"I am bigger than you, am I not?" the protector said. After glancing around, he added quietly, "That was smart of you, tricking Sverre to get me to help you."

As soon as they had been left alone, Snapdragon had quickly confessed to Darius that he was actually trying to help the people of Eddinh and Procep. It took some convincing, but he was certain Darius believed him and was willing to help. They both noticed Orrell watching them from afar, so Snapdragon had suggested they keep up the act that Darius was unhappy at being assigned as the guardian's protector.

"I'm just glad you are smart enough to have played it right," Snapdragon said almost in a whisper. "Had you been too anxious or willing to get me alone, I'm not sure Sverre would have allowed it."

"To be honest, the idea of getting dead bodies from the pit does not sound good to me. Is it really needed?"

"After I get them up here, I'll explain. I promised Sverre not to have the corpses taint this area, so I asked for blankets and ropes to tie up whatever parts I can find. I hope to be able to find several whole bodies.

I really don't want to have to piece them together from whatever I can find."

Darius looked at Snapdragon as if horrified.

"Trust me on this one, all right?" Snapdragon said, moving closer to the edge of the pit.

⇥✦⇤

Several hours later, thirteen bundles lay next to the pit, giving off a horrendous stench. Darius had done his job by bringing up each blanket Snapdragon had tied up and laying it on the pile.

Snapdragon was brought up at last, and he had just set down his torch and started wiping his hands on a clean blanket when he saw Sverre approaching.

"You need so many?" The man plugged his nose and kept a good distance from the bodies.

Snapdragon shrugged. "Some of the bodies were in pretty bad shape. I'll be lucky to have enough parts here to do what I need."

"And what is it you need to do?" Sverre asked, still shrinking away.

Walking to the pile and starting to undo one of the bundles, Snapdragon said, "Come here and let me show you."

"No!" Sverre practically shouted. "You must get these out of sight."

"Fine. Do you have a room where I can work then?"

Sverre paused and then spoke to Darius. The protector nodded in understanding.

It took several trips to an isolated building on the edge of town to relocate all the bundles. After carefully setting down the last one, Snapdragon motioned for Darius to close the door.

"Is this room safe?" Snapdragon asked Darius.

"Safe?"

"Safe from people watching us."

"Ah. Yes, obviously there are no windows, and there are no secret ways to listen in or to watch that I am aware of."

"Good!" Snapdragon rushed quickly to one of the bundles. Pointing to another bundle, the biggest one they had brought up, he said, "Quick! Undo the lashings on that one."

As fast as his fingers could fly, Snapdragon undid the knots he had recently tied, then opened the blanket. The corpse's eyes popped open and stared at him. He sighed in relief. "Alethea, you did great."

Darius's head whipped around to see his cousin sit up and push the blanket away.

"And what about me?" a muffled voice said, making Darius jump back from the bundle he had been untying.

Snapdragon nodded toward the form trying to fight its way out of the blanket. "Darius, will you please finish untying Creighton?"

CHAPTER 47

Grant thought he must be delirious. But then again, if he was, would he know it? Delirious or not, he was certain he heard sounds ahead of him in the tunnel, and he could make out pinpoints of light. Torches. They had to be torches. Had he gotten turned around? He stopped to listen, and what he heard sent fear through his heart. Unintelligible voices were coming from both behind him and in front of him.

The voices behind him were more distant, as they had been most of the time he had been crawling back to Bariwon. Grant guessed the bald men were being cautious and moving slowly, which worked to his advantage.

The pinpoints of light drew closer. He started to make out some of the words. These had to be Rayne's men.

"Over here," Grant tried to shout, but his voice cracked.

All the lights stopped moving at once. He had gotten their attention.

He called out again, this time more clearly. "Over here! It's me—Grant!"

A few of the lights moved closer, but most stayed back. Grant thought he heard strings being pulled back on several bows.

"How do we know it's you?" asked a deep voice.

Grant coughed and then, with all the energy he could muster, shouted, "To peace in our kingdom!"

❧❦❧

King Rayne felt numb. He had been standing a moment ago—he was sure of that—but now he found himself sitting on a chair next to a bed. Grant, whose wounds were being dressed, lay on the bed. He had just told Rayne about the attack.

"And you're sure that no one else survived?" Rayne asked quietly.

Grant shook his head. "I don't know how they could have. I saw Captain Fallon go down with several of his men. I was able to escape by good fortune, and if anyone else had escaped, I would've found them in the tunnel. I'm sorry, Your Majesty."

That meant Snapdragon was dead. How could the king tell his wife that her brother had been killed? Rayne wondered if he should have prevented Snapdragon from going. No, Snapdragon was a royal guardian, and it had been Fallon's choice to take him.

"And, Your Majesty," Grant continued, "I've no doubt these same attackers are coming through the tunnel as we speak. They were moving slowly, but they'll be here within a few hours."

"How many are there? Can the men I brought with me handle them?"

Grant grimaced as a dressing was tightened around his thigh. "I have no idea how many there were, or how many may be coming through the tunnel. I would prepare for the worst."

Rayne addressed the man who had just finished wrapping Grant's leg. "Go get me Guardian Aaron. On the way, alert all the men to gather at the tunnel entrance."

The man nodded and quickly left.

"Is there anything you can tell me about these attackers that will help us?" Rayne asked Grant.

"They didn't wear armor, at least none that I could see. They were very proficient with weapons, however. They conquered the camp by sheer numbers—they simply overwhelmed us. Aside from that, I'm not sure what else you want to know."

"I know you're a crafter and aren't trained in battle tactics, but is there anything else you can think of that will help us against these men?"

Grant paused as if in thought. Then his eyes lit up. "Actually, Your Majesty, I do have an idea."

⊷✦⊶

"Alethea?" Darius blinked at his cousin. "How...? What...?"

The protector shifted his attention to Snapdragon. "Was this part of the plan? There is no actual need for the dead bodies?"

Snapdragon shook his head. "We'll need to use them still, but the main reason for getting the bodies was a ruse to free Alethea and Creighton."

Still removing himself from the blanket in which he had been wrapped, Creighton asked, "How did you know we were in the pit? And why didn't they stop you from trying to free us?"

"They didn't tell me where you had been placed," Snapdragon said. "It was a guess, to be sure, and one I felt stronger about once I had gone to Eddinh and didn't spot you among the crowd. We didn't hear them because they were bound and gagged. I doubt very much that Sverre thought I would try to free you after I threw my lot in with Waylon after he betrayed us. But it was no coincidence that he had Orrell watching us, and Sverre himself checked on us once I came out of the pit. All he saw were dead bodies wrapped in blankets."

"I have to admit," Darius said, "once I heard about you betraying my cousin, I was sure you were going to betray me. I tried to make it to Eddinh, but by then all the passageways were being watched. You did not betray me, though. That is one reason why I did not come after you."

"As I briefly explained in the pit, before Creighton could choke me to death," Snapdragon said, "I had to pretend to follow Waylon or I would have probably been thrown in the pit as well."

"You were very convincing," Alethea said, her eyes narrowing. "I honestly believed you had lied to me. In fact, how do I know this is not part of another lie?"

Snapdragon saw the others tense up, awaiting his response.

"Think about it. What do I have to gain by freeing you? The people of Eddinh and Procep are locked up tight. I'm constantly being watched. It was a big risk to do what we did, and we still need to get you out of this room unnoticed. In addition, I can barely stand the smell in here as it is."

"How will you get us out of here if, as you say, you are constantly being watched? And where are we going to go from here?" Alethea asked.

Snapdragon smiled. "I am under observation. Darius is not. He will sneak you out of here tonight."

"Ah," Creighton said, "but you didn't answer her second question."

Snapdragon reached under his tunic and pulled out a pair of oddly shaped tongs. He handed them to Creighton, saying, "I need both of your help for a very important part of the plan."

⇥╪⇤

By the time Snapdragon left the room where the dead bodies were stored, it was mid-afternoon. Merton still planned to depart the next evening, which meant Snapdragon had a little over a day to finish his work.

Still escorted by Darius, he made his way to the passage that led to the Temple of the New Moon. A young man was standing at the entrance, looking proud in his white robe.

"I need to send a message to Bearach," Snapdragon said. "Are the other messengers in place?"

The young man nodded, though he seemed to struggle to understand. Darius must have noticed, for he asked the same question in their primary language.

This time the young man nodded more enthusiastically.

"Send this message, 'What is your progress, Bearach?'" Snapdragon ordered.

Facing down the passageway, the young man cupped his hands over his mouth and shouted the question. Snapdragon heard the question passed on by the next person in the human chain and thought he heard the third, though it was so faint he couldn't be sure.

"What do we do now?" Darius asked after they waited for a response from the passageway.

Snapdragon squinted up at the sun to gauge the time. "We still have much to do. We need to see how Seraphina and the rest of the seamstresses are progressing. Once they're done, we'll need to—."

"Holes done, ring done soon!" came a cry from the passageway.

Darius frowned at Snapdragon. "What does that mean?"

"It means he is ahead of schedule. Even so, it's going to be a long night." Turning back to face the messenger, Snapdragon said, "Now say, 'Set the signal!'"

The young man did so and the message was passed on.

"Signal? What signal?" Darius asked.

Snapdragon blew out a deep breath. "The signal to summon the Rifna Erd to the Temple of the New Moon."

⋅⊰╫⊱⋅

"You must put on your other clothes," Sverre said to Snapdragon. "The work you are doing is unclean, and you should not be wearing a robe."

Snapdragon looked down and saw that his once-white robe was covered in dirt from climbing in and out of the pit, as well as things that must have oozed from the body parts he had handled. "As you say. I will go back to my room straight away." He motioned to Darius.

Shaking his head, Sverre said, "No. I am done with my preparations. Darius is to return to his other duties—after he cleans up."

An anxious-looking Sverre had intercepted Snapdragon and Darius on their way to check on Seraphina and the other seamstresses.

Darius grunted. "Fine. I cannot stand to be around this outsider any longer." With that, he spun and strode off.

Sverre narrowed his eyes. "Where do we stand?"

"The modifications to the Temple of the New Moon are nearly completed. I've had Bearach set the signal to summon the Rifna Erd, so I expect we'll get a message in the next few hours that they are arriving, if what you told me is true about the last time this happened. The bodies are removed and are almost ready to be transported. I'll need a horse and a wagon."

Sverre crinkled his nose. "They will be provided."

"We need what the seamstresses have been working on, and I'll need sixteen spears like those the protectors use, and then I'll be ready to finish the work on the Temple of the New Moon."

Folding his arms and scowling, Sverre said, "I will not provide you with weapons."

Snapdragon sighed. "I do not need them as weapons—I need wooden staffs. They can be blunt on both ends."

After a pause, Sverre responded, "Those will be arranged."

"Good. Assemble what I need by the passageway that leads to the temple. We'll load the bodies last so you don't have to see or smell them."

"That would be wise."

Snapdragon glanced around the bustling town. "Now, where are Seraphina and the others working?"

⊰⧈⊱

Lying in a pile were seven canvases, each with one side bleached white and all roughly the size of a human man. The seamstresses, with Seraphina watching over them and giving orders, were working on the eighth and final one.

Seraphina looked up and smiled when she saw Snapdragon enter the room. He had changed into his armor and had cleaned himself up in the lake, so he looked almost presentable.

"They're just about completed." Seraphina motioned to the stack they had finished.

"These are what you require?" Sverre asked, lifting one of the canvases and examining it.

Snapdragon smiled, not taking his eyes off Seraphina. "Yes, they're lovely."

She blushed. "We'll be done with the last one soon, if you'd like to wait."

"There is no time," Sverre replied. "Finish your task and then tell the protectors outside the door to have these taken to the passageway where everything else is being gathered." He pointed to Seraphina. "You will then be taken to your room, where you will await the exodus. The rest of you will continue to help with the preparations."

"I could use Seraphina's help with the Temple of the New Moon," Snapdragon said.

Sverre smirked. "I am sure you could. But she will remain here for your return." There was no mistaking the underlying threat in his statement. Grabbing Snapdragon by the elbow, he said, "Now we will report to Merton. He is most interested in your progress."

Snapdragon took several deep breaths on the way to the building to which they had been summoned. There was a noticeable change to the town that surrounded the lake. People were packing up as if they never planned to return. While walking among the crowd, Snapdragon chanted the mantra in his head that he used during the Mortentaun. *Knock down, knock out, or knock around.* While he wasn't fighting today, the words reminded him there was always more than one way to win, and you often had to adapt and look for your opportunities as they came.

Upon entering the white-walled building, Snapdragon saw Merton sitting in his chair, hands gripping the armrests, which contradicted the calm look on his face. The rest of the elders sat along the wide table, with Waylon sitting on the far end, looking as pleased with himself as ever.

"Report," Merton commanded without any pleasantries.

"Everything is going according to plan," Snapdragon stated. "What we need for the temple is just about completed, and the messengers tell me that Bearach is almost done with his work as well."

"Meaning?" Merton said impatiently.

Not hesitating, Snapdragon answered confidently, "The signal should have been set to summon the Rifna Erd. If they follow the tradition from the last time a signal was set, they will gather to the Temple of the New Moon. This will distract them long enough that we will be able to make our escape down the passageway back to Bariwon."

"They will expect something to happen." Merton scowled. "Or they will perceive it as the trick it is."

Smiling, Snapdragon responded, "Oh, there will definitely be something happening at the temple to keep their attention."

"We have tested the doorway that Bearach was to fix, and it is still not working. I was clear that it must be ready."

"Bearach insists that the problem won't take long to fix, but I needed him for the other tasks first, or fixing the door would have been meaningless. When he completes his work at the temple, which will be tonight, he'll come here and complete the work on the door."

"We are still leaving tomorrow after the sun has set," Merton stated. "You must be ready then."

"We will be, but understand that we cannot leave unless the Rifna Erd come to the temple like you have told me they would."

Visibly relaxing, Merton said, "They will be there."

❖✣❖

"Rifna Erd approaching! Rifna Erd approaching!" shouted the messenger from the tunnel.

It was twilight, and Snapdragon had just finished loading the corpses onto the cart. Creighton and Alethea were still hiding in the room, looking rather ill from having been in close quarters with decomposing bodies. Snapdragon insisted Darius would bring them food and water and then set them free as soon as he could, so they needed to be patient a little while longer.

Snapdragon had wheeled the cart to the entrance of the tunnel when the message came. Sverre and several protectors—who stayed as far away from the dead bodies as they could—waited at the entrance. They all tensed up at the announcement of the approaching Rifna Erd, many of the protectors grabbing their weapons more tightly.

"We knew they were coming," Snapdragon said. "Or at least we hoped as much. This is a good sign."

The Tular Tevoil men didn't look convinced.

"Help me load the rest of the wagon. Then I need help lowering it down the stairs. Once at the bottom, I can hook it to the horse and take it from there."

Sverre nodded to the men around him, and each grabbed a canvas or a wooden staff and quickly placed it in the cart, giving a wide berth to the corpses.

Snapdragon took the reins of the horse, a chestnut mare, and, holding a torch in his other hand, started leading the horse down the stairs. A couple of the stronger protectors spun the wagon around and carefully backed it down the stairs.

When they had finally reached the bottom, Snapdragon had the men fasten the wagon to the horse and then allowed them to return to Itamunno Kael.

Snapdragon walked in front of the horse, leading her down the passage that ended at the Temple of the New Moon. Along the way, he passed the boys set as messengers. As their task was now completed, he sent them home.

It was probably approaching midnight when Snapdragon noticed a flickering light up ahead. Soon the shape of the stairs leading up to the Temple of the New Moon came into focus, and with it, the last messenger.

"Hello!" Snapdragon called out.

"Hello!" a voice responded.

Approaching the boy, who was clearly frightened, Snapdragon said, "Return home as fast as possible. Tell them I arrived safely."

The messenger nodded quickly and then ran down the tunnel.

"Is that Snapdragon I hear?" came a gruff voice from above the stairs.

Snapdragon led the horse up the stairs. "Bearach! Good to hear your voice again."

The crafter waited for Snapdragon to bring the horse and wagon up the stone steps and then gave him a firm handshake. He eyed the contents of the wagon and scrunched up his face.

"Did you get everything else we needed?" Bearach asked.

"I believe so. Did you get everything done here we discussed?"

Bearach broke into a big grin. "Oh, aye. And then some. Let me show you."

"Before that, what of these reports of the Rifna Erd?" Snapdragon asked, trying to peer out the opening of the temple.

Bearach walked to the entrance. "We noticed several scouting parties starting early this morning, but they kept their distance. It wasn't until we set the signals like we were told that we started to see a change."

After exiting the temple into the starlit night, Snapdragon took in a deep breath. Two large bonfires had been set ablaze in front of the temple, and twin plumes of dark smoke raced skyward. The bonfires were still burning, though Snapdragon imagined he would have to attend to them soon to keep them going. Looking beyond to the horizon across the river, he saw dozens of campfires burning. The distance was too far to make out any details, but that many campfires meant that a lot of Rifna Erd had come to the open plain, though they kept their distance.

"Could you tell how many there were before it got dark?" Snapdragon asked.

"I would guess a few hundred from what I saw, but it looks like more have come, based on the number of fires I can see now."

"And they've made no attempt to approach?"

"Not that I've seen, and we've been working near the top of the temple most of the day, so we've had a pretty good vantage point."

Snapdragon took another deep breath. "Well, let's get these supplies up top and you can show me what you've done."

⭰

With the help of the men who had been assigned to Bearach, the canvases, staffs, and bodies were quickly brought to the top of the temple.

"We made eight holes here," Bearach said. "Four on each side, about a hand span deep."

Snapdragon grabbed a staff and slid it into one of the holes, where it stayed with just enough give that it could be twisted. "Very good. Do you still have the lashings?"

Bearach pointed. "Aye, they're over there."

Snapdragon took another staff and placed it perpendicular to the staff he had put in the stone, roughly two-thirds of the way up. "The staffs need to be bound together like this," he instructed. "Then the canvases need to be attached so the white side is facing away from the river. The top of the canvas will be tied to the top of the staff here, with the sides fastened to the staff that is parallel to the ground."

The Tular Tevoil men looked confused until Bearach quickly put an example together for them to see.

"And what of the corpses?" he asked.

Snapdragon grimaced. "They get attached next."

⭰

Garth, Snapdragon's father, was a deep thinker and often pondered the mysteries of life while he went about the labors of the world. That was one reason he had chosen to become a gardener. It allowed him time by himself to work with his hands while his mind worked on any number of things.

Growing up, Snapdragon's father would often ask him to help with different tasks, and each time, Garth used it as a teaching opportunity. One of the more memorable times was when one of their horses had been about to give birth. Garth had felt it important that Snapdragon, Oakleaf, and Sunshine witness the event and help as they could.

Snapdragon, the youngest, tried to be brave and show his father he was not afraid. But as the "wonder of birth," as Garth called it, started, Snapdragon had to look away.

Later his father had sat down with him and said, "There are times in our life when we experience something which seems too much to handle. Part of our mind is screaming at us to run away, while another part stays calm, allowing us to shut out the screaming part. It takes time and practice to listen to the calm and ignore the screaming part of your mind, but if you develop this skill, you will succeed where others fail."

A few months later, one of their cows had a deep cut on her left hind leg. She was bleeding profusely, and Garth said if they didn't stop the bleeding, she would die. Snapdragon knew it was possible to sew up flesh, but couldn't imagine how they could do that with a cow. His father had him and his brother light several torches. He told Snapdragon the wound would close up if they could burn the two sides of the cut together. Since the cow would not like this, his father had told him that he, young as he was, would have to put the torch against the cow while Oakleaf, his mother, and his father tried to keep the cow from bolting. Snapdragon's mind had started to scream for him to run away, but he remembered his father's lesson and was able to fulfill his duty. The cow was saved.

Right now, part of Snapdragon's mind was screaming at him. Lashing parts of decomposing corpses to the canvas-backed rods was rather unpleasant, but he calmly went about it, while Bearach and the Tular Tevoil men watched on.

Working only by starlight and the faint light coming from the waxing moon, Snapdragon fashioned together eight mostly completed bodies. He didn't quite have enough parts, but he made do.

"Those will not last long in the sunlight or with the birds," one of the Tular Tevoil said, hiding his mouth and nose behind one hand.

"They won't have to—just until tomorrow night," Snapdragon answered. "Now, let's get down and make sure that these are positioned right."

Bearach came forward, smiling. "Ah, one thing first."

"Yes?" Snapdragon asked.

"I told you I had completed the ring for the burning oil, right?" Bearach said, beaming.

Snapdragon nodded. "Aye, though we can't afford to test it tonight. I need it to be a surprise."

"I figured as much," the crafter said. "I also added a couple more troughs, and from what I see here, it was a good thing I did."

"Oh?"

Bearach pointed to the edge of the platform on which they stood. "I extended the troughs along the edge on both sides of this platform where you've hung the bodies. When these are filled with oil and lit, the top of the temple will be quite illuminated, I would imagine."

Snapdragon looked at the recently built troughs. Smacking Bearach on the back, he said, "Is there anything you can't figure out?"

⊰✦⊱

As he stood at the base of the Temple of the New Moon, Snapdragon looked up at the eight silhouettes at the top of the temple. With the dark side of the canvases facing the river, Snapdragon was convinced that while the Rifna Erd would notice them, they wouldn't be able to see the bodies behind the canvases.

"They are hidden quite well," Bearach said. "I'm not sure exactly what you have planned, but I can't wait."

Snapdragon shook his head. "I'm sorry, but you won't be here to see it." Addressing the rest of the Tular Tevoil men that were there, Snapdragon said, "You must all return to Itamunno Kael to prepare for the exodus. I alone am to remain behind."

"What?" Bearach barked. "You—" he pointed to the dozens of campfires "—against all of them? Did you get hit in the head again?"

Snapdragon laughed. "Someone needs to be here for the meeting." He poked the crafter in the shoulder. "You need to finish the repairs on the escape route. Merton is quite worried that it won't be functioning when it's needed."

Bearach peered at Snapdragon. "Aye, it would be a problem if it were not to open when needed. I'll get to that and leave you here alone, against my better judgment. But tell me, just what are you planning on doing?"

Turning to face the gathering Rifna Erd, Snapdragon said, "I told Merton the Rifna Erd would be distracted, and believe me, they are about to be distracted in a way that will give them nightmares for generations to come."

CHAPTER 48

"There's one more project I need your help with before you go," Snapdragon told Bearach when they reentered the antechamber of the temple.

"Oh, and what would that be?"

"Remember how two people are required to open the stairway to Itamunno Kael from the temple? Can you fix it so only one person can do it?"

Bearach frowned and walked over to the release points. "There are actually four points that must be pressed at the same time—two on the wall, and two embedded in the floor. Let me think…"

The crafter got down on his hands and knees and searched until he found one of the release points in the floor. He felt around the edges of it and then asked for one of the Tular Tevoil to bring a torch closer, as well as bring him his bag.

In the dust on the floor, Bearach drew a few lines and arrows. After several moments, he reached into his bag and brought out a few metal spikes of different sizes and a small hammer. After motioning for the Tular Tevoil man to get closer, Bearach slowly tapped in a few spikes around a brick in the floor. He stood, then did the same with one of the release points in the wall. He stepped back and double-checked the lines and arrows he had drawn. "Try it now," he said.

Snapdragon went to the other side of the passageway and found the other two release points. He pushed against the wall first, and after waiting for the sound he had heard when Sverre had done it, he stepped down hard on the floor release point. The stairs that led to Itamunno Kael closed with the sound of heavy rock moving against heavy rock.

"Amazing," Snapdragon said.

Bearach grunted. "Don't be too sure until you try opening it."

454

Snapdragon repeated his actions, and the stairway dutifully opened again.

"How did you—" Snapdragon started to ask, but Bearach waved the question away with his hand.

"Once you understand the basic concept of how these people thought, it can be applied to any number of things. It's actually not too different from the idea I came up with to close the doors in the main hall from the throne room, though these people took it a few steps further. But tell me, why don't you want the stairway left open?"

Snapdragon shook his head. "As I told you, I alone must remain behind. In case I fail, I want to ensure that the Rifna Erd will not find their way to Itamunno Kael. I'll close the stairway after you leave. If things do go according to plan, I'll need to make a hasty escape. Before you go, we'll need to make sure I can close the stairs from the tunnel."

"Ah, that is a separate part and shouldn't be changed from what I did here, but aye, we'll check."

Then Snapdragon addressed the rest of the Tular Tevoil as well as Bearach. "Gather your items. Prepare to leave soon. Take the wagon with you, but leave the horse, one of the white robes Sverre sent along for you to change into, and several torches."

As the men set about to do just that, Snapdragon grabbed Bearach by the arm. "Merton needs the final door working and expects you to repair it upon your return. *Fix* it as soon as you can, and then get some rest."

From the expression on Bearach's face, Snapdragon knew the crafter had heard the emphasis on the word "fix."

Snapdragon removed a small object from under his belt and passed it to Bearach when they shook hands. "See if you can find a way to incorporate this in your repairs."

Bearach looked quizzically at what Snapdragon had given him, but then nodded.

"Lastly, don't let them leave for Bariwon until I return. Explain that we have to be sure that the Rifna Erd are properly distracted."

"And what if you don't return?"

"Then Merton will have to find someone else to be his puppet, because I'll be quite dead."

Bearach made sure the stairs could still be opened and closed from the tunnel below before he left. After saying his goodbyes, Snapdragon closed the stairway, leaving just him and his horse behind.

It was well past midnight now, and for the first time all day, Snapdragon started to feel fatigued. He shook his head and set about his next task.

Exiting the temple, he could still see the campfires on the horizon, and though it may have been his imagination, he thought even more fires had been added since the last time he looked. Just how many Rifna Erd were there?

Walking to the signal fires used to summon the Rifna Erd, Snapdragon saw a neatly stacked pile of wood next to each fire. He added more fuel to the fires so they would continue to blaze for the next several hours.

Next, he went back into the temple, and after checking on the horse, took a lit torch and started climbing the stairs of the temple. For the next few hours, he explored and put to memory the layout as much as possible, trying to stay calm despite the fact that so much depended on what happened here. He found a couple of different ways to reach the spot where they had hung the bodies. Then he returned to the antechamber.

Now he could do nothing but wait. He sat down and leaned against the frame of the entrance to the temple. Looking out into the evening sky, he tried to clear his head. It was comforting to recognize the star patterns he could see from Bariwon.

His eyes rested on the waxing moon. Waylon had said it was a symbol of change and growing strength. That conversation in the tavern seemed so long ago, though it had only been a few days. So much had happened since then. In a moment of clarity, Snapdragon realized that his outlook had changed. Just a few days ago he had been angry when Fallon assigned him a lesser task than he thought he deserved. He had been looking only inside himself. Now he knew there was a bigger picture. In the last few days he had forgotten about himself and tried to help those around him. It was like he was a new moon, and his actions and attitude filled up the void over time—much like how a waxing moon filled the new moon with light. It was Snapdragon's choice how he filled the void.

⇥✦⇤

The sun breaking over the far eastern mountains jerked Snapdragon awake. He didn't recall falling asleep. In a moment of panic, he looked across the river. The Rifna Erd were still encamped and hadn't approached the temple. It hadn't been his imagination last night when he thought more campfires had been added. He now saw what must be thousands upon thousands of Rifna Erd gathering. He was alone against all of them.

At this distance he couldn't make out individual people, just groups of them gathered around fires, as well as horses and what he imagined to be the odd shelters he had seen before. He realized that if he couldn't make them out, then they couldn't see him, either.

Standing and stretching, Snapdragon looked up and down the river and didn't see anything to cause alarm. Then a frightening thought occurred to him: What if they approached from a direction besides east? He hadn't considered that. He went back into the temple and hurried up the stairs, double-checking his memory of the place from the night before. After reaching the top, he carefully moved out on the platform just far enough to get a full view.

He let out a breath of relief when he saw the Rifna Erd were only gathering from one side—the area from which Snapdragon and his companions had escaped. While that was good news, it also meant it was impossible to get back to Bariwon that way. From the west side, there was nothing but open plain, though Snapdragon saw storm clouds beginning to gather. He remembered how fierce the storm in Procep had been and how hard the rain had fallen. If the same thing happened here, it would most likely ruin all his plans.

Frustrated by this latest complication, Snapdragon went down to the antechamber to prepare everything he needed for later. He set out a few unlit torches and laid them side by side next to the entrance. Next to those he put the white robe he had requested to be left for him. Suddenly, he realized he needed a way to light the torches when the time arrived. He couldn't light them from the bonfires—he couldn't let the Rifna Erd see him so early. If he built a fire in the antechamber, it would fill up with smoke. Or would it? He looked up and saw the holes in the ceiling that let in light. They should act as a chimney of sorts to keep the smoke from filling up the area.

Then there was the horse. At the right time, Snapdragon would need to hurry back to Itamunno Kael, but the horse couldn't be left in the antechamber. Snapdragon had to be ready for the quick trip back, provided everything in his plan worked to that point. He opened the stairs to the tunnel and then guided the chestnut mare down. He gave her most of the food that had been left behind, reserving only some sort of tuber for himself for a mid-day meal.

There wasn't a place to tie up the horse in the tunnel below, so Snapdragon took the reins and jammed them into a crack between two large rocks. He climbed back up the stairs and closed them from the antechamber. Peeking back outside to make sure the Rifna Erd were still far away, he set about making a fire with the remaining supplies. Soon, the fire came to life and chased away the shadows in the room.

Snapdragon wasn't sure how long the Rifna Erd would hold back or even if they would approach the temple. Merton had been a bit vague about what had happened the last time such a meeting happened, but Snapdragon hoped the Rifna Erd would stay on the other side of the river. The Tular Tevoil needed time to finish their preparations to leave, and Bearach needed time to finish his work. Plus, the plan would be much more effective at night, meaning Snapdragon needed the Rifna Erd to stay where they were for at least one more day.

Convinced he needed to do something to keep himself awake and alert, Snapdragon again looked at the pictures drawn on the walls—the history Sverre had recounted for them of the Rifna Erd and Tular Tevoil. Snapdragon was roughly halfway through the tale when he heard a low rumbling sound. Looking around the room, he noticed it was a bit dimmer than it had been a few moments before. It seemed the storm was developing after all.

After lighting a torch, he went up the stairs to the top of the temple to check the progress of the storm. From the platform, he looked to the west and saw massive, roiling clouds moving towards the temple. Snapdragon's heart sank, and the sheer power on display made him shudder and take a step back.

The deep rumbling continued to get louder, and he finally realized the sound wasn't coming from the storm he was facing, but rather from behind him. He turned.

The Rifna Erd were on the move. All of them.

A few were on horseback, though the vast majority were not. Glancing back and forth between the horde of people and the heavy, swollen clouds, Snapdragon estimated the Rifna Erd would arrive before the storm.

Deciding he was at the best vantage point possible, Snapdragon sat down. Over time, he thought he could make out the broad-shouldered Rifna Erd who had the three stripes in his beard, and rocks pierced through both the lower lobes and upper parts of his ear. Astride a horse, he was leading the people to the temple.

The sky continued to dim as the Rifna Erd approached. Soon, they arrived at the stone bridge that spanned the river. This was what had stopped them before, and Snapdragon felt his heart quicken as he watched to see what would happen.

The leader of the Rifna Erd barked out orders Snapdragon could not make out from this distance. Several men stepped forward and approached the bridge, appearing reluctant to do so. Their leader continued to scream and point, waving a jagged sword over his head, forcing the men forward. Squinting, Snapdragon recognized the men with blue stripes in their beards. Just then, he recalled something Sverre had said when they had first met. He said the Rifna Erd did not cross the bridge because they didn't have any ... what was the word? Mylnohe? Perhaps the men with the blue-striped beards were these mylnohe. Hadn't Alethea said that the mylnohe would cross the white circle when "properly motivated?" This didn't bode well.

Snapdragon's conclusion was confirmed when the men ascended the bridge and then proceeded to form a circle around the white stones, with their backs facing each other. When the last man got into place, the leader of the Rifna Erd barked something else. For a moment nothing happened. Turning his horse to another group of Rifna Erd, their leader again shouted and motioned to the temple. Still not getting the response he wanted, he brought his horse forward and cut down one of the men closest to him. Snapdragon gasped.

It seemed enough motivation for those standing close by. Three men, armed with nasty-looking weapons and wearing red-striped beards, raced from the crowd and over the bridge, skirting around the mylnohe, then entered the temple, screaming battle cries.

Instinctively reaching for his sword, Snapdragon leapt to his feet. It took him the briefest of moments to remember that Sverre and Merton had not allowed him to bring any weapons with him. Instead, he grabbed the torch and raced back into the temple.

He ran down a flight of stairs, then stopped and listened for the men who had entered. They must be moving quietly now as they searched the temple. Snapdragon hurried down another set of stairs, and just as he reached the bottom, he realized his torch would act like a beacon. He turned the corner and froze in his tracks. On the far end of the hallway were two of the three men. They spun around, and Snapdragon knew they had seen him when they yelled and raced toward him, weapons at the ready.

Leaping back up the stairs two and three steps at a time, Snapdragon quickly devised a plan. He reached the top and stopped, then flipped around and faced the Rifna Erd.

"Stop!" he shouted, holding the torch out in front of him like a shield.

The lead Rifna Erd did just that, causing the one behind him to stop as well.

"Go back!" Snapdragon shouted, hoping these men would understand him well enough.

The lead man apparently did when he grinned and said, "You are nothing." He spit on the ground. "This place is nothing. Old stories to scare younglings. I do not fear you."

Snapdragon said gravely, "Your mistake."

Quickly side-stepping, he grabbed the lever at the top of the stairs and shoved it down. The Rifna Erd looked puzzled until the stairs beneath them angled down and Snapdragon heard the spikes at the bottom click into place.

The lead Rifna Erd lost his balance right away and, with arms pinwheeling, fell backwards into his companion, causing them both to tumble. Their screams ended abruptly when the men hit the spikes.

Shuddering, Snapdragon wondered where the third man was. He turned to go down the hallway, then saw the last man standing between him and the next set of stairs. The man was bigger than the other two, his muscles rippling as he moved forward with his weapon drawn.

There was simply no place for Snapdragon to go. Acting on instinct, he threw the torch at the man. It spun end over end with such speed that the Rifna Erd couldn't dodge it. The torch hit him squarely in the chest. The blow startled him enough that he didn't notice Snapdragon charging him until the last moment.

The guardian from Bariwon crashed into the bald man, and the two fell to the floor. Both men got up quickly. The Rifna Erd must have noticed Snapdragon was without a weapon, for the armed man grinned and moved forward.

Now on the opposite site of the hallway, Snapdragon raced back up the stairs. Within seconds he heard the man in close pursuit. There was no way Snapdragon would be able to lose him, so the guardian continued upward.

He reached the platform and felt the wind of the oncoming storm. He tried to keep out of sight of the rest of the Rifna Erd, who waited below.

The remaining attacker emerged from the temple onto the platform and followed Snapdragon for a moment before turning to look at the bodies that had been hung with the white canvases as a background.

The man was obviously shaken by the sight, and he paused for a moment. That was all the time Snapdragon needed. In two quick steps, he reached the man and grabbed him by the arm. The Rifna Erd turned to react, but not before Snapdragon set himself and, using his weight and momentum, spun the man off the edge of the platform. Snapdragon watched him fall end over end off the west side of the temple—opposite where the Rifna Erd were waiting—before landing on the plain below, his body twisted unnaturally.

Though it was only mid-day, the sky was as dark as at sunset, and the wind continued to pick up.

Snapdragon looked back toward the east and saw that the mylnohe had stepped off the bridge and entered the crowd again. It seemed as if all the Rifna Erd were holding their breath while waiting for their men to return. How long would they wait?

Snapdragon went back down to where he had left his torch and found it barely burning. After quickly locating a room he remembered from his explorations, he set down his torch and went to the stone apparatus he, Sverre, and Bearach had looked at earlier. Recalling what the crafter had done, Snapdragon released the stone that held back the flammable liquid and closed off the other side that acted as a drain. Bearach had indeed made some alterations, as the liquid went off into four different troughs. Snapdragon watched long enough to know the liquid would keep flowing. Then he left the room, taking the nearly burnt out torch with him.

As Snapdragon hurried back to the top of the temple, the torch burned out, and he had to use his memory and hands to find his way. By now the sky was almost completely dark. Though it had not started to rain, Snapdragon could feel the air become heavier. He was rapidly running out of time.

Looking down, he could see that the Rifna Erd were still waiting and the bonfires were all but out, only giving off enough light to allow him to see the first few rows of the people.

Bracing himself, Snapdragon stepped out onto the platform and then went to each of the bodies that were tied to the poles with canvas backings. One by one, he turned them so the bodies were now facing east, toward the crowd. He knew it was too dark for the Rifna Erd to see any change at the moment, but that actually worked in his favor.

After spinning the last body into place, Snapdragon verified that the troughs Bearach had constructed along the edge of the platform were filled with the strong-smelling liquid Snapdragon had just released.

Snapdragon took a different path down to the antechamber to avoid the impaled Rifna Erd. He saw that the fire he had lit in the main chamber was almost out, but still ablaze enough to light the two remaining torches. He could hear the rain just starting to fall outside. It was now or never.

Before lighting the torches, he quickly donned the white robe, thankful that this one included a hood, which he drew over his head. If he kept his head bowed, the Rifna Erd wouldn't be able to see his face.

Fighting off his nervousness, Snapdragon lit the torches and then walked out of the temple toward the Rifna Erd. He held the torches low and away from his body. A collective gasp came from the crowd when he appeared. The rain was starting to fall harder now.

Snapdragon's plan from the beginning was to play off the deeply seeded fears of these people—to stir them into a frenzy long enough to distract them. The image of a person dressed in white had spooked the Rifna Erd when Seraphina had saved Snapdragon and his companions earlier, and he hoped his appearance would have the same effect.

The broad-shouldered leader of the Rifna Erd was shouting at his people to be quiet and calm down—at least that was what Snapdragon could gather from the man's speech. Apparently seeing that his words were having little effect, the leader urged his horse forward and started up the bridge, regardless of the fact that there were no mylnohe around the circle.

In the most forceful voice Snapdragon could muster, he shouted, "Nie syll esse! Nie syll esse!" He knew he probably didn't have the pronunciation correct, so he was relieved when the leader of the Rifna Erd stopped on the bridge. The man's hesitation was all Snapdragon needed as he took a step forward and used the torches to ignite the troughs, which by now had filled with liquid.

The fire raced along the troughs that were set in a circular pattern along the east side of the temple. A giant, flaming white circle blazed into the symbol of the new moon. From there, the fire lit up the troughs on the upper platform, giving off an eerie glow that illuminated the eight dead bodies backed by white canvas.

The crowd of Rifna Erd exploded in panic. Even the leader was stunned into inaction.

Snapdragon raced back inside and opened the stairs to the passageway below. Then he removed the white robe, retrieved one of the torches, and sped down the stairs.

The horse was not there.

Had the Rifna Erd sent in more men and found a way into the tunnel? Hearing shouts from above, Snapdragon hit the rock at the bottom of the stairs, causing them to go back into place. He started to race down the passageway.

He knew the trip back to Itamunno Kael would take several hours, and he doubted he could run the whole way, already fighting off fatigue and hunger. Although it hadn't been a full day, the Tular Tevoil needed to be ready. The Rifna Erd were distracted, but Snapdragon wasn't sure for how long. He pushed back the thought of coming this far just to fail now. If he didn't succeed, what would become of Seraphina? Of Bearach? Of Alethea and the rest of the people of Eddinh? Of Creighton and the people of Procep? No, too much was depending on Snapdragon. Horse or not, Rifna Erd or not, he had to make it back.

After sprinting for just a few moments, he saw something ahead. He slowed down as he realized it could be the Rifna Erd who had found their way down to the passage from the temple to Itamunno Kael. Relief washed over him as he realized it was his horse. She must have pulled free from the wall and started to wander.

Keeping the torch as far away from her as possible, Snapdragon jumped on the mare. He kept his head low, then urged her forward.

Just as they started moving, a booming noise from above was followed by the earth shaking. Behind them, Snapdragon could hear the tunnel starting to collapse. Kicking his skittish mount in the sides, he tried to convince her to gallop in an all-but-dark tunnel with a single torch as a light source. The world was falling in on top of them.

CHAPTER 49

The dust from the collapsing tunnel swirled around Snapdragon as he raced on, making it even harder to see. What had happened? Could the Rifna Erd have a powerful weapon that would cause such destruction? Perhaps Snapdragon had underestimated them. But it didn't change what he had to do next.

Thankfully the shaking of the earth had stopped, but the tunnel still continued to crumble, though the more distance Snapdragon put between him and the temple, the less the tunnel was collapsing.

After several more intense moments of riding a galloping horse through a nearly dark tunnel, Snapdragon noticed the destruction was waning. When there no longer appeared to be a threat, he slowed the mare to a walk.

He glanced back and saw the tunnel was still filled with dust. From what he had seen of the collapse, he was confident the Rifna Erd could not follow him through the passageway. Of course, that also meant there was no returning to the temple.

Urging the mare forward, Snapdragon kept the torch in front of him, looking for the exit back to Itamunno Kael. He had gotten Merton to agree to keep it open for his return, promising that the Rifna Erd would not be following him. Snapdragon needed to get back to the Tular Tevoil, report his success, and tell them they could finish preparing for their exodus.

Although things had not gone exactly according to plan thus far, the end result was the same. Snapdragon just hoped and prayed that the rest of the plan went as well.

After a time, he found the stairway up to Itamunno Kael. He got off the horse and led her up the steps. The passage wasn't tall enough for him to ride, plus it would be precarious to climb the stairs on horseback.

464

Snapdragon's legs ached, and he fought off the urge to rest and continued climbing. He looked for the light that would indicate he was near the top, but only saw darkness. Had they closed off the top entrance to the passage? He didn't recall seeing the Tular Tevoil open or close it before, and he had no idea if there was a release point from inside.

Lacking any other real options, Snapdragon continued up the stairs, focusing on putting one foot in front of the other. For the longest time, the only sounds were those of him and his horse breathing and their footsteps. But then there was another sound, a soft, constant tapping. Continuing up, Snapdragon finally realized it was the sound of rain falling. Soon after, the air in the tunnel became humid, and at last he could make out the shape of the exit ahead, though the light coming through was very dim.

"Hello!" he cried out.

A moment later, two pinpoints of light were visible in the doorway—torches from the protectors who must have been awaiting his return.

"Who are you?" a voice called back in a Tular Tevoil accent.

"Snapdragon!" he shouted, still climbing the stairs.

There was no response, but the torches stayed in place.

When he was only a few steps from the top, he called out again, "It's Snapdragon. I've returned."

Exiting the tunnel with the mare still in tow, he felt light raindrops fall on him. Two protectors with long spears held the torches, and Sverre stood several paces back.

"It appears you were successful," Sverre said. "Although you are back before we expected."

Snapdragon looked up at the sky and let the rain fall on his face. "It couldn't be helped. The Rifna Erd forced my hand a bit earlier than planned. But you can trust me when I say that they are distracted."

Frowning, Sverre said, "I heard the noise. I thought it was the storm, but a bright light, brighter than lightning, appeared in the sky. What did you do?"

Snapdragon smiled mysteriously. "I did as promised. I distracted them. The way back to Bariwon will be safe now, though we need to move sooner rather than later."

Sverre folded his arms, peered at Snapdragon for a moment, and then said, "Follow me."

The protectors followed behind Snapdragon and Sverre, but not before one of them closed the passageway behind them. One of the Tular Tevoil took the horse away, but not before Snapdragon patted her on the neck and whispered, "Thank you for saving my life."

Sverre led Snapdragon through the nearly deserted town. He could hear a crowd ahead, and from what he remembered of the layout of the area, they were gathered by the exit Bearach needed to fix.

As they turned a corner, Snapdragon saw the crowd, all with carts and packs of their possessions, ready to leave. On the far side of the crowd was a sight that made him stop in his tracks.

The door to the passage that led to the tunnel back to Bariwon was wide open.

No! Snapdragon thought. *Bearach shouldn't have let this happen.*

At the wide-open door a number of large fires burned, illuminating the area around the exit. The rain had all but stopped now, and Snapdragon scanned over the crowd for Seraphina or Bearach or Darius. He didn't see them.

The crowd opened a pathway wide enough for Sverre, Snapdragon, and the two protectors to pass through to the door to the passage. Sverre called ahead, saying something in the Tular Tevoil language that started a stir of motion near the front of the group.

From a small building just off to the side of the open door, Merton emerged, flanked by several others, including Bearach and Seraphina. Snapdragon let out a sigh of relief. Also among the group was Waylon, still dressed like a Tular Tevoil.

Sverre continued forward, with Snapdragon not far behind. Suddenly, a large man stepped in the path and snarled something at Snapdragon he didn't understand. Looking up at the man, Snapdragon realized it was Darius. Alethea's cousin took a step forward and, while still scowling at the guardian, whispered, "Third building on your right."

Sverre ordered the protector to get away from Snapdragon. The protector barked back a reply, to which Sverre responded even more forcefully. Darius scowled harder and backed away. Sverre came back to Snapdragon and said, "It appears that there are those among us who still do not trust you."

Snapdragon just stared back at Sverre stoically. Sverre started back toward the front of the crowd.

The door Bearach had fixed was quite large. It was a good fifteen paces across and about the height of three tall men. Like several of the other doors in the town, it opened on a center pivot point and was perfectly balanced so that when triggered by the release mechanism, it would open or close.

Merton took a place in front of the doors and, with a pompous look on his face, acknowledged Sverre and Snapdragon. "Report," Merton said in way of greeting.

Snapdragon glanced over at Bearach and Seraphina. The beautiful nursemaid appeared to be on the verge of tears. Bearach looked confident, which was strange, since his task had been to make sure that the door would not allow the Tular Tevoil to leave, yet here it was—wide open.

Snapdragon took a step forward. "I've done what was asked. The Rifna Erd are distracted and won't stop us from returning to Bariwon."

"You have done what was expected," Merton said.

"Then you're ready to leave?" Snapdragon asked carefully.

Smiling in a self-important manner, Merton said, "We were ready early, just in case. Yet, this is something that will be spoken of for generations. It is not to be taken quickly or lightly. I will speak to my people before we go."

Snapdragon made a dramatic gesture of looking around. "I don't see my possessions, or those of my companions. We'll need those for the return trip."

Waving a hand as if swatting away an insect, Merton said, "You may gather your things during my speech. It will not be for you to understand anyway."

Snapdragon eyed the open door and started to say something, but Bearach stepped beside him and said, "You heard the man—let's go get our stuff so we can leave."

He looked into Bearach's eyes and then back at the opening. Had Snapdragon not been clear enough on this point? Had something happened while he was gone?

Bearach seemed not to notice Snapdragon's hesitation. Instead, he started working his way through the crowd. Seraphina came up next and moved close enough to Snapdragon to whisper, "I'm glad you aren't dead."

Looking down into her stunning green eyes, he whispered back, "The day isn't over yet."

He followed Bearach through the crowd of Tular Tevoil while Merton announced something to the people, to which they all cheered.

When Snapdragon caught up to Bearach on the edge of the crowd, he grabbed the man's elbow and said quietly but fiercely, "The door is open! Didn't you understand what needed to be done?"

Bearach held up a hand and smiled. "Have a little faith, will you?" Motioning to the front of the crowd, he said, "Watch."

Snapdragon turned and looked at Merton, who was speaking adamantly to the crowd and walking back and forth. In a dramatic gesture, the leader went to the release lever, a square rock built into the doorframe. He pushed it, using some effort, and the door closed.

"Now we have to move quickly," Bearach said, turning and walking briskly back toward their old quarters.

When they were out of earshot of the crowd, Snapdragon asked, "How did you know…?"

"Ah," Bearach said. "That Merton is a showman. He wanted to make sure he could close the door as part of the speech as a dramatic example of their captivity. He'll open it again when he finishes. Or at least he will try to."

Bearach grinned again and led them back to their room, where he quickly gathered up his items and placed them in his pack. Seraphina had retrieved her belongings and handed Snapdragon his sword.

"How soon before he finishes his speech?" Snapdragon asked while placing his sword in the scabbard that hung from his waist.

"I heard him practice it several times," Seraphina said. "We don't have a lot of time."

Snapdragon looked around to make sure he had everything, and the three friends headed out the door.

"Darius said it was the third building to my right when he stopped me in the crowd," Snapdragon said. "We better hurry."

They worked their way through the crowd as quickly as possible without drawing attention to themselves. Merton was all but screaming now in his speech, and it was apparent that he had the people's full attention. Several times it appeared the speech had come to an end, as indicated by the reaction from the crowd, but then Merton would start up again, whipping them into even more of a frenzy.

At last the three survivors reached their destination, and Snapdragon saw Darius standing just inside the building, motioning for them to hurry. The crowd was thicker here, and getting through the last few paces proved to be more challenging, especially with the furor of the crowd.

Seraphina got inside the building first, followed shortly by Bearach. Snapdragon had almost made it to the entrance when the crowd erupted again at something Merton had said, but this time, they didn't stop cheering. Looking up at where Merton had been speaking, Snapdragon saw the leader of the Tular Tevoil approach the release lever. Not caring if he created a scene or not, Snapdragon tried to force his way to the building.

468

The crowd suddenly became quiet. Unable to help himself, Snapdragon watched as Merton pressed on the release. The rock slid into the frame.

The door did not open.

Merton pressed again, and this time Snapdragon saw the man bend down and pick up an object that appeared to have fallen when the rock had been pushed in. Merton held it up to the light, and Snapdragon smiled when he realized it was a coin—the same coin he had used to demonstrate the point of distraction, and the same coin Snapdragon had given Bearach to incorporate in "fixing" the door.

Snapdragon saw the realization on Merton's and Waylon's faces just before he made it into the building.

⇥⇤

"This way! Quickly!" Darius said as he made his way further into the building.

Snapdragon looked back over his shoulder and heard Merton shouting something and the crowd reacting loudly. No doubt the leader of the Tular Tevoil was telling them to search out Snapdragon and his companions.

Darius entered a room and ushered them inside. To Snapdragon's surprise, Alethea and Creighton stood waiting for them.

Holding out the tool Snapdragon had given him earlier, Darius said, "I could not get the door open, and they had Bearach locked up until your return."

Bearach reached out and grabbed the tool from Darius. "Where is the access here? I don't recall."

While Darius showed him, Snapdragon closed the door to the room as quietly as he could, fearing that people might already be in the building looking for them. Just before the door closed completely, he heard frantic voices down the hallway.

"They're on their way!" Snapdragon hissed to Bearach, who was putting his full attention on the door.

Darius looked at Snapdragon and the rest of them apologetically. "This is the only room that leads to Eddinh that I could safely get Alethea and Creighton to. I've been trying all day to get this open."

"We all gave it our best effort," Creighton said.

Snapdragon frowned. "Alethea, you'll have to convince the people of Eddinh to get ready to leave as fast as possible. The Rifna Erd are scattered now, but I've found their leader to be quite unpredictable. We'll need to—"

"Got it!" Bearach exclaimed.

The loud sound of the hidden door opening made Snapdragon cringe. "Everyone in! Alethea and Darius, take the lead!" he commanded.

After everyone had entered the passage that led to Eddinh, Bearach hit the release lever and the door began to close just as one of the Tular Tevoil entered the room. The person's shout of surprise was cut off as the door came to a close. It was pitch-black in the passageway now, and Snapdragon heard Bearach grunt.

"It would be easier to disable this with some light," the crafter mumbled.

Snapdragon reached out a hand and found the door. "Can I help?"

"Just keep it closed until I... wait, maybe—"

There was a drawn-out moment of silence.

"Well?" Seraphina asked.

Snapdragon thought he felt pounding on the door behind him.

"Whew!" Bearach said. "I think that should do it."

"Let us be on the way then," Alethea said. "There is much yet to do."

Taking a step forward with his hands out, Snapdragon bumped into something soft.

"Pardon me," Seraphina said teasingly.

Snapdragon was glad the darkness hid his red face. "I didn't mean to, uh—"

"Grab my arm like that?" Seraphina asked. "It's all right. I think I would prefer if you held on to me as we walked."

Snapdragon ignored Bearach's chuckle, and after a few awkward moments, the guardian and Seraphina held hands as they made their way down the dark passage.

After they had walked for a few minutes, Bearach said, "We were locked up during the storm. Did your plans at the temple work out?"

"Well, it didn't quite go as expected, but I think it will do the trick," Snapdragon responded. He thought about mentioning the tunnel collapsing, but he didn't want to frighten his friends. If the Rifna Erd had a weapon powerful enough to cause that much destruction, would any of them be safe—even if they did get back to Bariwon?

Flickering lights from fires were the first indication that they were close to their destination. Snapdragon heard a startled cry when Alethea and Darius exited the passageway and entered Eddinh.

470

Creighton was next, followed by Bearach and then Snapdragon and Seraphina. Word spread quickly through the secret town, and soon people came running. Alethea started speaking in her native tongue to people she knew, which caused them to run off in different directions.

Pushing his way to the front of the crowd was a man who resembled Creighton.

"Kerr!" shouted the man from Procep as he ran and embraced him.

"Yeah, Brother," Kerr grinned. "I thought you had gone and got lost again."

Creighton laughed. "Ah, not a chance. I would've just tunneled my way back to Bariwon if I'd needed to."

Snapdragon noticed several of the people of Eddinh eyeing him and Bearach warily—and for good cause. Last time they had been here, they had blocked off these people from any escape. Snapdragon imagined Alethea was explaining what happened, which kept them at bay, thankfully.

"Tell me, Brother," Kerr said, "do you know what happened to the pyramid down there?"

Snapdragon's eyebrows shot up.

"What do you mean?" Snapdragon interrupted, trying to sound calm.

Kerr blinked at him a couple of times. "Didn't you hear or see it?"

"What are you talking about?" Bearach asked.

"Come, come. Take a look!" Kerr headed to the large opening in the cave that overlooked the plain below.

Alethea and Darius were still giving instructions to their people, so Snapdragon, Seraphina, Bearach, and Creighton all followed Kerr.

The storm had passed and the setting sun provided sufficient light to see the area below. Snapdragon took several steps forward and shook his head in disbelief.

The entire top of the temple was gone.

CHAPTER 50

Oakleaf found his father exactly where he thought he would be—in the royal gardens. After Garth had turned down the offer to be a councilor, King Rayne had offered him the position of head gardener at the castle. Oakleaf didn't think his father really cared where he worked, as long as he got to work outdoors with plants.

"It's looking good, Dad," Oakleaf said as he hobbled toward his father.

Garth was on his knees, meticulously weeding around some blue-petaled flowers that lined the walkway. He nodded at his son.

"I've heard from those who have spent their lives in the castle that the gardens have never looked so good," Oakleaf continued.

"We've had good rain during Rayne's reign." Garth stopped working and stood up to face his son. "But you aren't here about that."

"You know me too well, Dad." Oakleaf smiled. "I guess I need some advice."

Garth harrumphed. "Free advice is usually worth what you pay for it." He motioned to the next section of flowers that needed weeding.

Oakleaf took the hint. He and his father both went to their knees, though Oakleaf had to take it a bit slower due to his injured hip.

"So, Dad..." he started.

Garth looked at him and then nodded his head toward the flower bed. Oakleaf rolled his eyes and started pulling some weeds.

"So you want to know what to do next, correct?" Garth asked.

"Right as always, Dad." He pulled out a few more weeds. "I feel like something is about to happen, but I don't know what. It's as if there are things hiding, just below the surface, waiting to emerge—I'm just not sure when or where."

"And if you start digging in the wrong place, you may not be ready for when they do emerge, right, Son?" Garth asked.

"Something like that."

Garth didn't say anything; he just kept pulling weeds. Oakleaf did the same, waiting for his father to respond. Several minutes passed.

"Dad?" Oakleaf finally said.

Pointing back toward the garden entrance, Garth said, "You can stand back there and wait for these weeds to grow back."

"Why would I—"

"Or," Garth interrupted, "you can walk around the garden, looking for another spot to wait."

"But there are weeds right here in front of me. Why would I sit and wait while there are things to be done?"

Garth merely chuckled.

⇥‡⇤

"Let's review again what you would do in the event of an attack," Oakleaf said to the men guarding the front gate. Since talking with his father, he had decided there *were* things he could do at the moment, and this was one of them.

One of the more experienced royal guardians, Duncan, appeared to fight off a sigh at the question. His skin was a dark brown from time spent in the sun, matching his hair and eye color. He pointed to the lever on the wall and repeated the instructions. "We would hit the lever to release the portcullis. The lever there, the one that Bearach made, is very touchy. It doesn't take much force to trigger it. When someone hits the trigger, the portcullis comes down with a lot of force, so you'd best be out of the way. It will keep anyone from entering the castle. At that point, if we are rushed by an attacking force, the portcullis will keep them out, while the archers above will shoot down on them."

Oakleaf nodded. "Very good. Shall we go over it once again?"

"With all due respect," Duncan said, "we've been over it several times. And honestly, I don't see how an attacking force could even get close to the castle without us knowing about it. As soon as the spotters in the watchtowers sound the alarm, we'll close the portcullis."

Oakleaf looked over the four men standing in front of him. These were good men—he had handpicked them when he had been left in charge of the defenses. Still, something inside told him to be alert and ready.

"I know I can trust you men. I just want to be as ready as possible. Yes, let's review again—this time, slow it down and take me through it step by step."

⇥‡⇤

The destruction to the temple was greater than Snapdragon had thought possible. Lightning couldn't have done it. Neither could a strong wind. And it would've taken time for the Rifna Erd to use their manpower to cause such damage. No, it had happened quickly, and it was immense.

"What in the world?" Bearach said.

Seraphina gripped Snapdragon's arm and leaned in close to him. "What happened? We didn't see or hear. We were locked up until Snapdragon returned," she said in an awed whisper.

Pointing, Kerr said, "We saw the Rifna Erd gathering on the far side of the plain. It was a fearsome sight. There were so many of them. Then, just before mid-day, they started toward the pyramid. We could hear the rumbling, even from up here."

"So the Rifna Erd did that?" Seraphina asked.

Kerr shrugged. "We don't know what happened. The sky got very dark, the storm was raging pretty hard, and we couldn't see much. Then the pyramid lit up. On one side there was a bright white circle, and along the top were two white lines. After a few moments, there was a tremendous light, followed by a loud boom that nearly knocked me off my feet. It wasn't until the storm started to pass that we noticed what you see now."

Seraphina crinkled her nose. "Come to think of it, Bearach and I heard a loud sound, but we just thought it was thunder. Snapdragon, you were down there—what did you see?"

Before he could answer, Bearach hooted loudly. Then he doubled over and started laughing uncontrollably. "Snapdragon," he said through fits of laughter, "before you lit the liquid on fire, what did you do?"

Snapdragon frowned as he thought back. "I did as you showed me. I opened the stop to let the troughs fill, and I closed off the drain."

Looking back down to the temple, Bearach laughed even louder, causing the people from Procep and Eddinh to start to gather around. "And then what?" the crafter asked.

"I was in a hurry," Snapdragon said. "I ran down to the ante-chamber, got dressed in the robe that was left for me, and then, well, let us just say I put on a show."

"That you did," Bearach said, starting to regain his composure. "But let me ask you this, after you filled the troughs, did you put the stop back into place and open the drain again?"

Snapdragon shook his head. "Like I said, I was in a hurry."

"*You* destroyed the temple," Bearach said, poking the guardian in the chest. "When you lit the liquid on fire, it went up around the side in a circle, right? And then it lit the top troughs, right? Well, where do you think the fire went next? Back to the source!" Making a dramatic gesture with his hands, Bearach said, "Boom!"

Everyone looked at Snapdragon. He said sheepishly, "Well, I dare say I did what I set out to do and scared the Rifna Erd to distraction."

Alethea came over and stood by Bearach. "We will be ready to leave soon."

"What can I do to help?" Snapdragon asked.

Before Alethea could answer, Seraphina said, "I think Snapdragon's done enough for now. He should get some rest before we go."

The dark-haired woman considered Seraphina a moment before saying, "Agreed. He can rest in my room."

"Your room?" Seraphina echoed. "Only if I accompany him."

Alethea shrugged. "If that is what he wants."

Kerr, Creighton, and Bearach looked at Snapdragon as if awaiting his reaction.

"Uh... yes. Seraphina's a nursemaid," he said. "It may be best if she were to make sure I'm as ready as possible for the trip home."

Bearach harrumphed and shook his head.

"It is settled then," Alethea said. "Follow me." She faced Bearach. "When I return, I will need your help to fix the door you broke."

He nodded, looking ashamed at what he'd been forced to do before when he trapped all the people in the cavern.

Snapdragon and Seraphina followed Alethea to one of the buildings. As with everything else in the secret town of Eddinh, the walls were all made from rock, and the floor was compacted dirt. Nevertheless, the room they entered was remarkably clean. The furnishings were simple, and Snapdragon was drawn immediately to the bed. Though the frame was of stone, Alethea had explained that the mattress was a soft cloth stuffed with wool from sheep raised in Itamunno Kael and smuggled here over time.

"I will have food and drink brought to you," Alethea said before she left.

Snapdragon couldn't imagine anything softer than the mattress, and he leaned back, both hands on the bed, and exhaled deeply.

Seraphina sat near a small table that held a stone washbasin. "Are you hurt?" she asked, reaching for a cloth next to the basin.

Thinking back over the last few days, Snapdragon realized he had been knocked unconscious, been in combat several times, and, more than once, been at risk of losing his life. There wasn't one part of him that hurt more than any other, though he felt like he had been sparring for two days straight.

"I'm just tired and sore all over," he said. Then he looked Seraphina in the eyes. "But what if I had something that was in need of attention?"

Seraphina took the cloth, dampened it in the basin, and moved to sit by Snapdragon. "Well then," she said softly, "I'd need to attend to it, now wouldn't I?"

He looked at her carefully. From the moment he had first seen her, she had enthralled him. Even though he knew he was a royal guardian and forbidden to marry until after he retired, that all seemed so far away now. After facing life and death with this beautiful young woman, it hurt him to think anything could happen to her. He knew he would lay down his life to save her, though he'd rather be alive to spend more time with her.

"Actually, I did get hit on the head pretty hard by the Rifna Erd at the river before you saved us," he said, pointing to where he had taken a rock just above his left temple. "It was bleeding pretty badly."

Sliding in closer, Seraphina focused on the spot he had indicated with just the smallest hint of a smile on her lips. "A blow to the head can be nasty. I'd better make sure it is clean."

She dabbed his head lightly with the cloth, running her fingers through his dark hair carefully for further inspection. While she was focused on his wound, Snapdragon focused on her. The splash of freckles on her nose played against her sparkling green eyes.

After a moment, she appeared to sense his gaze. She met his eyes, then ran her hand down his cheek and his jawline, across a few days' worth of stubble. He felt a strong urge to kiss her. He was a royal guardian, but would it really matter if he tried to kiss her, here and now, away from their lives in Bariwon? Would she even let him? His head spun from lack of sleep.

"Seraphina…" he said softly.

She put a finger to his lips. "You need your rest. You'll need it to get us home."

"But—"

"Shhh now." Seraphina smiled warmly. "I won't leave without you."

❖

Eadward felt like jumping out of his skin. Tomorrow would be the day. Watching the sun set from his room at The Bull's Horns, he smiled. The land was covered in a reddish glow. A good sign. That usually meant the morning would be clear—a bright morning to mark the start of a bright new future for Bariwon.

The men he had trained were ready. They all had light brown cloaks, the kind normal townspeople wore. However, his men had armor and weapons hidden under their cloaks.

After getting confirmation from Ciar, Eadward had spread word to his men to gather at the castle gates just before dawn. Abrecan and his men would be freed from the dungeon, and once they were safely out of the castle, his men would attack. Ciar had insisted that the guardians at the gate would be taken care of.

Yes, everything was falling into place.

A strong hand grabbed Snapdragon by the shoulder and shook him awake. He didn't recall Seraphina having such a grip, but he soon realized it was Darius standing over him.

"We are almost ready," the former protector of the Tular Tevoil said. "Did you rest well?"

Looking around the room, Snapdragon saw that Seraphina was gone. They had shared a wonderful moment, and not long after, his meal had been delivered, and despite himself, Snapdragon had wolfed it down. Seraphina had insisted he rest before they left, and though he had wanted to stay awake and be with her, his body had other ideas.

"How long—" Snapdragon started to ask.

"I fear you have not slept long, but you said we needed to go quickly, and that time is almost here," Darius interrupted.

Snapdragon managed to sit up. "Yes, we need to be off as soon as possible. Was Bearach able to open the exit?"

"It is ready."

Snapdragon swung his legs over the side of the bed. "We'd better be off then."

The tower guardian smiled. "Eggnog? What's the occasion?"

Ciar simply shrugged. "Can't say for sure. I'm just following orders. Maybe Oakleaf is showing his appreciation for all the hard work you've been doing."

"That would make sense. He's been driving us pretty hard the last few days," the guardian responded.

Ciar passed tankards of eggnog to the rest of the archers. "I wouldn't wait to drink these. I hurried up here so the eggnog would be as fresh as possible, and I still need to give some to the guardians at the gate."

The guardians smiled as they took the drinks. "You need not worry about that. We'll have these finished in no time."

⊰⧉⊱

Melanie smiled sweetly at Guardians Asher and Stuart. "You two get the night shift again?"

Stuart sat on his chair next to the dungeon entrance. He mumbled a complaint under his breath.

Asher said, "Never mind him—he just hates being assigned dungeon duty, no matter what time of day it is."

"Well, I have something that will hopefully cheer you up," Melanie said lightly, handing both men tankards.

"It's not ale, is it?" Asher asked. "You know we aren't supposed to have ale while on duty."

Stuart grumbled something about wishing it was ale.

"It's eggnog!" Melanie said brightly. "Though I'm afraid there is no ale in it."

Stuart's eyes widened. "Eggnog, you say? Well, that's the next best thing to ale!" He reached out for his tankard.

"Wait a moment," Asher said, stopping Melanie from giving Stuart the drink. "Why are we getting eggnog?" he asked suspiciously.

"Well, I can't say for sure. I was just told to bring this to you men. I thought I heard something about Queen Sunshine getting after Oakleaf for being so tough on the guardians the last few days. I'll bet she was just trying to do something nice in appreciation for all your hard work."

"That sounds like something Queen Sunshine would do," Stuart said, still holding his hands out for the drink.

Asher sighed. "You're right—that does sound like her."

"I'd suggest you drink it right away. It's fresh right now," Melanie said. "And I'm sure the queen will be happy to know when I report that the men were grateful for her kindness."

At that, Asher conceded, and both men were soon gulping down the spiced drink as Melanie watched.

⊰⧉⊱

"I'm having second thoughts," Bearach said to Snapdragon under his breath.

"Oh? Why's that?"

They stood just off from the group that was gathering to leave.

"We've had nothing but trouble since we came here," Bearach said. "Things were so much simpler in Bariwon—at least it seems that way to me. And now we are bringing these people, and everything we have learned, from Eddinh back with us. I want things to be the way they were. But nothing will be the same after this, will it?"

Snapdragon knew the crafter had a point. The people of Bariwon had been isolated for generations. Things would most certainly change with what had been discovered here, and with the advent of the people from Eddinh. But as Snapdragon looked over the crowd that had gathered, he smiled. "See the people getting ready to leave?" he asked.

Bearach looked around and grunted, "Yeah."

"Notice anything interesting?"

"No, not especially."

"There are people from both Eddinh and Procep here. But they are not off in their own little groups," Snapdragon pointed out. "In just a few short days, they have already started to become friends—to become one people. Are the people from Procep the same as the people from Eddinh? No. But different doesn't mean bad. Who knows what wonderful things we may learn from them, and vice-versa?"

Bearach grunted again. "That's only part of my concern. What about the Rifna Erd? They know we came through the tunnel. They know there are people on the other side. Don't tell me you haven't thought about that. Even with all the guardians in the land, we would be overrun if they invaded. What are we going to do about that?"

"I think we have scared them off for a time with our demonstration at the temple. I seriously doubt they'll cross over the white circle in front of the tunnel or pass under the warning sign written above."

"Are you certain?"

Snapdragon sighed. "No, I'm not certain about anything with the Rifna Erd. Though if you had seen what I saw at the temple, you'd be more confident that we'll be safe until we can get back to King Rayne and report. He'll know what to do."

There were no big speeches or dramatics when they departed. The people from Procep were ready to go home, and the people of Eddinh were excited to go to Bariwon—away from the Rifna Erd and the Tular Tevoil.

Snapdragon had slept very little, as it was the middle of the night when they started traveling. They had fashioned many torches, which were lit and carried by most of the people. He guessed there were roughly five hundred people on the move, the vast majority of them from Eddinh.

He was amazed at how readily they gave up most of their possessions to be free. They brought records of their history and a few artifacts, but anything else not essential to survival was left behind.

A few of the more able Eddinh men led the way, moving the people quickly through the exit and down a narrow canyon that exited near the tunnel.

Snapdragon walked alongside Seraphina and Bearach, with Creighton and Kerr just ahead. Kerr was with a lovely young woman dressed in a robe common to Eddinh. Interestingly, Alethea walked side by side with Creighton and seemed to be quite enamored with him, much to Seraphina's obvious delight.

"How long do you think it'll take us to get back to Bariwon?" the nursemaid asked Snapdragon.

"I'm not sure how long it will take us to get to the tunnel, but once we enter, I suspect it will take the better part of the night to get all of us through. When we came through the first time, we didn't move much faster than this group is moving now. I wouldn't be surprised if we arrive in Bariwon around sunrise."

Seraphina hooked her arm around his. "The sun rising on a new day for Bariwon. Seems fitting, doesn't it?"

"It does. Let's just hope it's a bright, clear morning."

Thankfully, the storm had blown through and the night sky was ablaze with stars. Even with only a waxing moon for light, it was clear enough that traveling wasn't difficult. Along the way, Alethea pointed to one particularly bright star. Though she was ahead of him and talking to Creighton, Snapdragon heard her refer to it as the Zealous Star and explain that it had special meaning for her people.

Snapdragon tensed up when they arrived at the hidden passage that exited not far from the tunnel. The group came to a stop and waited for the scouts to search ahead. There was no guarantee all the Rifna Erd had gathered at the temple, or that they would not return to this area where they had all but slaughtered Snapdragon's companions. The plan from the start had been to rattle the Rifna Erd enough that the people from Procep and Eddinh could escape. They would find out soon enough if it had worked.

Moving to the front of the crowd, Snapdragon heard the scouts talking among themselves. Darius was with them and noticed Snapdragon approach.

"There seems to be no one close by, from what they can tell," the former protector said. "At least not from here to the Pendeltune."

"Well, that's a good sign," Snapdragon replied. "But tell me, what's the delay?"

Darius grimaced. "The Rifna Erd have been busy at the Pendeltune entrance."

⊰‡⊱

Gone were the words above the tunnel entrance. It appeared they had been chiseled away. But even more disturbing was what was on the ground—or rather, what was no longer there.

Where the white circle of stone had been inlaid in the ground, there was now a large hole. Next to the tunnel entrance sat the wooden wagon Bearach and Grant had brought. It was loaded with large pieces of white rock that had obviously been removed from the ground.

"Do you think they have already gone through?" Darius asked, standing next to Snapdragon.

The guardian took a torch, walked to the tunnel entrance, and crouched down to study the ground. "I can't tell. The storm washed away any tracks." He stood back up and looked at Darius. "But I don't see much of a choice except to keep everyone moving. We'll send everyone through, and I'll get Bearach to help me get these rocks back into place to form a circle."

Darius shook his head. "No, I will remain behind to help you. Bearach is needed in Bariwon more than I am. He is a man of special talents. But would it not be best if we had all of the other men help us?"

"Like you said, the Rifna Erd may have already sent people through. I think the people need to go through as quickly as they can, and with as many of the men as possible."

Darius appeared to agree with Snapdragon's logic.

⊰‡⊱

"Not again." Seraphina appeared to be fighting to keep her emotions in check. "Why do you have to play the hero? There are any number of men who can stay behind and do this."

Snapdragon looked beyond her to the people moving to the tunnel entrance. "Because I have to know this is done so I can report it." He felt responsible for getting these people to safety. He couldn't do that if he wasn't certain the circle was rebuilt and he was the last one through the tunnel.

Seraphina blinked away her tears and, on her tiptoes, leaned up and kissed Snapdragon on the cheek.

After seeing her off and watching the last of the people enter the tunnel, Snapdragon turned to Darius. "We'd better get to work."

⊰✢⊱

It seemed darker now than it had all night. Ciar had worked enough night shifts to know dawn was near. He stood in the shadows, just over the bridge and beyond the moat. He wanted to be here when Abrecan was freed. He wanted to see Bariwon's true leader return triumphantly in all its glory. Ciar could see that all the guardians at the gate were slumped over. The plyese had worked as well on them as it had on him.

Before crossing the bridge, he had checked on the tower guardians. They, too, had fallen victim to the drug and were in a deep sleep.

Men in cloaks started gathering by the bridge. Ciar recognized some of them as Eadward's men. There were others Ciar couldn't see clearly, but they had to be Eadward's men as well. The gathering group was larger than Ciar had expected. This was going to be a historic moment, and he would be there to witness it all.

⊰✢⊱

Melanie struggled to turn the key to Abrecan's cell in the dungeon. Guardians Stuart and Asher were fast asleep at the dungeon entrance. It had been easy enough to get the keys away from them.

"Hurry up!" Abrecan said tersely.

He had never spoken so harshly to her. It was understandable, though. He had been locked up a long time. She was just as anxious to see him as he was to be freed.

Putting all her strength into twisting the key, she finally managed to twist it and release the lock. With shaking hands, she released the lever and pulled the door open.

In the light from her torch, she saw Abrecan for the first time since his imprisonment. She put a hand to her mouth in shock. He had lost so much weight. His face was gaunt, though his eyes still burned with sharp intelligence.

She went to embrace him, but he brushed her aside and started heading down the hallway.

"Abrecan—" Melanie said, reaching for him again. He ignored her. "But what about the other men?" she asked. "Ivor, Sullivan, Cameron, and Caldre—they are all close by. It won't take long to free them."

Abrecan glared at her. "They stay. They failed me. They're paying the price. Now get me out of here, unless you want to join them."

Melanie choked back a sob. She headed out of the dungeon, holding the torch in front of her. She was able to find her voice to explain that they needed to take less traveled hallways, even though it was still night and no one should be awake.

She tried to move as quickly as she could, but Abrecan kept telling her to hurry up. She was so distracted trying to keep him happy that she didn't notice the figure standing against the wall of one of the hallways they passed.

❖❖❖

Even with the starlight and moonlight, Snapdragon had requested that a dozen or so torches be left behind so Darius and he could have better light. After setting up the torches around the perimeter of the hole caused by the removal of the stones, Snapdragon and Darius began putting the superstitious barrier back together.

Without tools to clean out the hole where the sides had collapsed, the work was slow going. They would remove a rock section from the wagon, carry it over to the hole, dig out the sides so it would fit, and then put it into place. They also discovered that if they didn't put the stones back the way they had been before, it would not be a perfect circle.

"Do you think they are through yet?" Darius asked as he patted down the soil next to the rock they had just put into place.

Snapdragon tried to estimate the time. "I wouldn't be surprised. They started moving quicker once they got into the tunnel."

"Have you noticed some of these stones are stained? What do you make of that?"

"It's best we not think about it," Snapdragon said, moving back to the wagon to get the next stone.

Darius nodded and started walking to the wagon as well. Two steps from the circle, however, he jerked suddenly to his left, nearly falling to the ground. He regained his balance and looked at Snapdragon quizzically before looking down at the object protruding from the right side of his ribcage.

Before Snapdragon could register what had happened, he was slammed back against the wagon. Stunned, he tried to move forward but found himself pinned in place.

By this time, Darius had fallen to his knees, staring at Snapdragon and trying to say something, though no words came from his bloody lips.

Again Snapdragon tried in vain to move to help his companion. He didn't understand why he wasn't able to move away from the wagon until he saw that an arrow, about the thickness of his thumb, had impaled him through the right shoulder. It had exited out his back and pegged one of the wooden slats on the wagon, holding him in place. From the shadows emerged a figure on horseback. He had broad shoulders, a beard with three stripes, and a wicked grin.

CHAPTER 51

There wasn't much pain at first, but as Snapdragon came to comprehend that he had been shot, the pain started to increase.

The broad-shouldered man urged his horse forward slowly, as if enjoying the moment of Snapdragon's demise. From behind the leader of the Rifna Erd came more men, several holding long bows with arrows at the ready.

Snapdragon noticed Darius lay motionless, facedown by the hole they had been filling. The leader of the Rifna Erd ignored the fallen man while moving his horse forward.

Looking down at his shoulder, Snapdragon noticed that the arrow had been fitted with sharp barbs near the feathered end so it couldn't easily be pulled out in that direction. The arrowhead must have been broad and flat to have stuck so solidly into the cart behind him. He tried moving forward again but could barely budge.

The broad-shouldered man looked back at his men and shouted, "This one is mine to kill."

From his time with the Tular Tevoil, Snapdragon now had enough practice with the Rifna Erd language to understand it better, though the leader spoke with a unique accent.

Snapdragon watched as the leader walked his horse around the area, inspecting the work he and Darius had been doing. The leader said angrily, "You think by putting rocks in the ground you would stop me?"

Pausing at the entrance to the tunnel, he looked up to where the words had been scraped away. "What was next? More warnings written in stone? I will not be denied what is rightfully mine!"

He dismounted his horse, grabbed his sword, and approached Snapdragon, seeming to take his time as if he savored the moment.

Though Snapdragon was armed, he knew he couldn't defend himself while stuck to the cart. He wondered if it was best to just stand there and take it without flinching—to show these Rifna Erd that even with the odds so far against his favor, he would not cower. Perhaps the leader would make it quick, but Snapdragon realized that wasn't likely to be the case.

Had the people from Procep and Eddinh made it through yet? Even if they had, there was no place for them to go or hide if the Rifna Erd came through the tunnel. Once again, Snapdragon felt the possibility of failure press on him. But he had come so far, done so much, lost so much, and he would not give up. He would use his last breath to fight.

With the leader of the Rifna Erd only several paces away from Snapdragon, a royal guardian of Bariwon *acted*. Reaching up with his left hand, Snapdragon grabbed the arrow where it had entered his shoulder and broke the shaft in half. Not stopping to think, he pushed himself forward, feeling the remaining part of the arrow rip through his body with a jolt of pain. Stars danced in front of his eyes, and he fell to one knee. Gritting his teeth, he rose to his feet, then drew his sword and pointed it at the leader of the Rifna Erd.

The men behind the leader cried out. Several of the bowmen pulled back on their strings, preparing to let loose more arrows.

"No!" screamed the Rifna Erd leader. "He is mine! See how he uses his off hand to fight? What other proof do you need that these people must be destroyed?"

Quickly taking the last few steps toward Snapdragon, the leader brought his weapon up to strike. Snapdragon stepped in, raised his own weapon, and blocked the attack. Again the Rifna Erd man struck, and again Snapdragon fought off the blow. The two men danced in a circle, each taking turns going on the offensive. Snapdragon realized the other man was not accustomed to fighting a left-handed opponent, and perhaps that was something on which he could capitalize. Soon, the leader of the Rifna Erd switched to holding his sword with both hands.

Clenching his right fist, Snapdragon waited for an opening where he could use his seemingly useless arm to strike. The leader was paying no attention to Snapdragon's right side, which meant the guardian had surprise to his advantage.

After a particularly hard strike that left both men off balance, Snapdragon decided it was time. A strong blow to the other man's face or throat would stun him long enough that Snapdragon could finish him with his blade. Or at least that was the plan.

In reality, when Snapdragon went to lift his right arm, he found it didn't respond the way it should. In fact, the pain left him momentarily dazed. The leader of the Rifna Erd took advantage of the moment and, swinging hard, knocked Snapdragon's weapon out of his hand and beyond his reach.

Snapdragon fell to his knees, dizzy from the pain. The leader smiled in triumph and raised his sword high above his head. As the sword started to come down, a large shape crashed into the broad-shouldered man, knocking him off his feet. It was Darius.

The protector from the Tular Tevoil looked back at Snapdragon and shouted hoarsely, "Go!" and then motioned to something.

Looking over his shoulder, Snapdragon saw the leader's horse still stood near the tunnel entrance. In a moment of clarity, the guardian understood Darius's sacrifice. Snapdragon could still warn the others to scatter, and with a horse, he could send for help. With renewed resolve, he sprang to his feet, ran to the horse, and mounted it as quickly as he could with only one working arm. Pinning his legs against the horse, he reached down and grabbed one of the torches, then kicked the horse into a gallop toward the tunnel. Arrows flew through the air around him. One nicked his right ear, while another slashed across his right leg, leaving a gash. Snapdragon entered the tunnel, and shortly the descending angle of the ground protected him from any further attempts by the archers.

Snapdragon had seen the broad-shouldered man ride this horse while holding weapons in both hands, so it was logical that the horse had been trained to be guided without reins. This proved to be true as the guardian's ruined right arm dangled helplessly at his side and his left hand held the torch, yet he was still able to steer the horse using his body weight and legs.

With the light from the torch, Snapdragon quickly examined the horse. The saddle was a thick cloth of some kind with ropes dangling off each side, tied into loops where the rider could place his feet. The saddle was also tied around the horse to keep it firmly in place.

After a few moments of racing through the tunnel, Snapdragon noticed the torch was dimming. Soon he realized it was as ablaze as before, but his eyesight was failing. Lifting the light closer to his right shoulder, he could see his wound was still bleeding quite badly—at least from the front.

He still had quite a distance to go, and he doubted he would make it unless he could stop the bleeding somehow. He only had the one free hand, and that one was needed to hold the torch.

At first he dismissed the idea that entered his mind, but he soon decided it was his only viable option. Twisting his ankles around the ropes that hung below, he secured himself to the saddle as best he could. The horse continued to gallop onward, and they had just passed the tunnel's only turn—they were headed due south now toward Bariwon.

Bracing himself, Snapdragon took a deep breath and then shoved the torch up against his ruined right shoulder. Somewhat detached from the process, Snapdragon couldn't decide which was worse, the sound of sizzling flesh or the smell that accompanied it.

Using every bit of willpower he had, he fought to hold on to the torch, even after he removed it from sealing up his wound. He felt himself start to fade, but his feet were still attached to the saddle, so he didn't fall from the horse.

Off the flat tunnel walls, Snapdragon could hear the Rifna Erd shouting war cries as they pursued him. Snapdragon prayed he would make it to Procep in time.

⊰⧉⊱

Bertram, head of the Hierarchy of Magistrates, normally enjoyed his walks. He often woke in the middle of the night and, especially lately, had a hard time falling back to sleep. He had consulted with Nursemaid Ophelia before she left on the trip with Captain Fallon. She had suggested Bertram get up and walk around—it would help clear his mind and make him tired enough that he could go back to sleep.

As he got older, he found himself wanting to go to bed earlier, which, of course, meant that he would wake up early. Not that waking up early was a bad thing. How did that old saying go? *"Late to bed and late to rise, makes a man tired, wired and despised."*

It was usually quiet this time of night when he walked, but tonight he heard voices. As they became clearer, he thought he recognized one of them—but that was impossible. His mind must be playing tricks on him.

He heard the voice again, and this time, there was no mistaking it. Bertram knew that voice all too well.

It was Abrecan.

Bertram pressed up against the wall, realizing the voices were coming from a hallway that ran perpendicular to his. *Don't turn down this hallway,* he prayed as the voices grew closer.

He held his breath as they walked past. Fortunately, they didn't look down the hallway where he stood. There were two people—Abrecan and a female servant. How could he be free, and where would she be taking him?

Bertram turned and went as quickly as he could to find Oakleaf.

◆╬◆

Pounding on the door woke Oakleaf. It had been his night to get up with his son Rowan—Oakleaf and his wife Arlie took turns—and so far it had been peaceful. The pounding hadn't woken the infant, but Oakleaf knew he'd better hurry before it did. He quickly put on a pair of trousers and grabbed his walking stick before heading for the door.

The pounding continued, becoming more frantic. Oakleaf undid the lock and opened the door. Standing there was Magistrate Bertram, pale and out of breath.

"We must hurry!" the magistrate said. "Abrecan is free!"

"What do you mean free?" Half asleep, Oakleaf wondered if he was hearing things correctly.

Bertram pointed down the hallway. "I saw him! He was following a servant. It looked like they were headed for the castle entrance. There was no mistake him—it was him!"

But how? Oakleaf thought. There were guardians at the entrance of the dungeon, as well as at the front gate. Abrecan couldn't have just walked by them—unless the guardians were dead.

Now fully awake, Oakleaf said, "Go to the tower and ring the alarm bell."

"And what are you going to do?" Bertram asked.

Reaching for the bow and quiver of arrows he kept by the door, Oakleaf said, "I'm going to stop Abrecan."

◆╬◆

At last, Snapdragon could make out the wall that had been built to block off the tunnel. Dawn was breaking in Bariwon, and he could make out the far exit. With renewed strength, he lowered himself closer to the horse and unwound his feet from the ropes. He would ask Bearach to take the horse to the closest town to ask for help, and then he would scatter the rest of the group. He realized now that the group had made it through, and he hoped they were still prepared to move quickly.

Ducking low as he passed the torn-down wall and entered the mine shaft, Snapdragon felt his heart pound even faster as he approached the large group of people. "Hey!" he shouted several times, trying to get their attention.

When he reached the exit, he stopped in his tracks. The people from Procep and Eddinh were not the only ones there. With the sun rising, Snapdragon could make out the silhouettes of dozens upon dozens of armed men on horseback. Several of their bows and arrows were drawn and trained on the mine entrance.

Snapdragon's heart sank. Of course there would be Rifna Erd here. There had been nothing to stop them from coming through the tunnel once the symbol was removed. He had taken the people of Procep and Eddinh from a relatively safe place and put them in the middle of a trap.

-⇒✦⇐-

Melanie saw the entrance to the castle just as the first rays of dawn broke over the horizon. The guardians at the gate were all slumped on the ground, still in a deep sleep from the plyese she had put in the eggnog. Beyond the gate and over the bridge, two large groups of men had gathered, one behind the other.

When Abrecan saw the entrance, he practically ran toward it. Spending years in the dungeon seemed to have slowed him down some, but even then, Melanie struggled to keep up.

The men across the bridge noticed Abrecan when he was a dozen or so paces from the gate. Melanie recognized Eadward, front and center with a wide grin on his face.

They had made it! Abrecan was free, and Eadward's men could easily take the castle.

"Abrecan, stop!" shouted someone behind them.

Both Melanie and Abrecan spun around to see Oakleaf, barefooted and shirtless, holding his walking stick in one hand and a bow in the other. On one of his shoulders hung a quiver of arrows.

"Not this time!" Abrecan shouted back. "You've lost and you don't even realize it. Now, no more wasting my time, cripple. Put down your weapon and maybe, just maybe, I'll spare the life of your family. But don't test my patience."

"You will surrender and return to the dungeon before it's too late," Oakleaf said. "You can avoid a lot of bloodshed today if you do as you are told."

Abrecan sneered. "As I am told? *I* am the one destined to rule. Not you, not your fool of a king. Me!" He pointed to the men waiting on the other side of the bridge. "These men are loyal to the true ruler of Bariwon. You're outnumbered and have been outwitted. I'll waste no more time talking to the likes of you. Take your best shot—nothing you can do will stop me!"

Abrecan grabbed Melanie by the shoulders and positioned her between himself and Oakleaf. She was too shocked to react.

Oakleaf quickly dropped his walking stick and, in one fluid motion, drew an arrow and shot it as Abrecan raced for the gate.

Melanie recalled that Oakleaf was renowned for his skill with a bow and arrow. So when his shot went wide, she thought perhaps Abrecan had been right and he was destined to escape.

⭄⧧⭅

Pulling up his horse sharply, Snapdragon expected to be peppered with arrows at any moment. But then, as he could make out the details of the forms in front of him, he realized there was something odd about how these Rifna Erd were dressed. They wore armor with helmets and...

These were not Rifna Erd.

Sitting on a horse at the forefront was the last person Snapdragon had expected to see. It was King Rayne.

Beside him was Grant. The crafter was bandaged quite heavily, but he sat on a horse, large hammer at the ready.

Snapdragon sighed in relief. The other armed members of the group were guardians, both royal and district. How they had gotten there and how Grant had survived were questions that would have to be answered later.

"Snapdragon!" King Rayne cried, moving toward him.

Snapdragon threw the torch off to the side of the entrance and said, "Your Majesty, there isn't much time. The horde of Rifna Erd is right behind me!"

The sounds from the tunnel reaffirmed Snapdragon's statement. King Rayne sat up tall in his saddle and said, "Snapdragon, get behind the line. Quickly!"

He did as the king commanded and nearly fell off his horse when he was safely behind the line. He saw that the people of Procep and Eddinh had moved to the village, and he wondered where Seraphina was.

From the tunnel came the broad-shouldered leader of the Rifna Erd, looking furious. He held something in one hand, and Snapdragon realized with horror that it was Darius's head.

About two dozen more of the Rifna Erd emerged from the tunnel. The leader stopped just past the entrance and ordered the rest of his men to stay where they were until he called for them. He then moved his horse a few steps forward. Eyeing the line of guardians that surrounded him, he said loudly, "Is this all? This is what you send to stop me?"

He laughed and threw Darius's head so that it bounced and landed in front of King Rayne.

The king pointed his sword at the leader of the Rifna Erd and said, "Go back to your lands and never return."

Furrowing his brow and tilting his head to one side, the Rifna Erd leader said in his thick accent, "Go back to my lands?" He swept his hands majestically around him. "But these are my lands! You will kneel before me!"

To King Rayne's credit, he seemed to get the point of what the leader said, even if he didn't understand every word. "I'll give you one more chance to leave peacefully. I suggest you take it," the king said forcefully.

Looking up and down the line of guardians once again, the broad-shouldered leader laughed, then folded his arms and said smugly, "Do your worst."

⇥⚔⇤

Abrecan smiled when he realized Oakleaf's shot had missed him and Melanie. This was *his* moment—his triumphant return. Nothing would stop him from getting his revenge and reclaiming the kingdom.

The arrow Oakleaf shot bounced off the wall. No, not the wall—off a lever. Suddenly, Abrecan remembered what the lever did—it lowered the portcullis, the spiked metal grating used to block the gateway. He ran toward the gate. He was within a few feet of freedom, and at his present speed, he would make it under the portcullis in time. Oakleaf had failed again.

At least, that was what Abrecan thought until he felt something hit the bottom of his left calf. The impact caused him to stumble and then fall face first. Spinning onto his back, he looked down to see an arrow protruding from his leg.

He heard Melanie shout something in warning. Bah! He didn't need the help of a woman. Then he realized he lay directly below the rapidly closing portcullis. He tried to push himself out of the way, but wasn't quick enough. A sharp metal spike from the bottom of the portcullis piercing his chest was the last thing Abrecan saw.

492

-}‡{-

King Rayne nodded to Grant, and the crafter yelled, "Now!"

Several of the men on horseback started racing away from the Rifna Erd leader, appearing to be running from him. Snapdragon wondered if the king was sending the men to get reinforcements. Rayne had about a hundred and fifty men with him. Though roughly twenty Rifna Erd had exited the tunnel with their leader, Snapdragon guessed there were hundreds more behind them in the tunnel. Then he noticed a rope attached to each galloping horse—a rope that led to the mine shaft.

Several of the ropes became taut, rapidly followed by the rest. The leader of the Rifna Erd had also noticed the ropes and looked confused—until the support beams at the entrance of the mine began to fall.

"No!" screamed the leader. He turned his horse around to go back into the mine, but it was too late. A great cloud of dust came from the entrance, now completely collapsed.

The broad-shouldered man drew his weapon, shouted an order to his men, and then charged the king and the guardians.

Arrows took out a few of the charging attackers, but still a dozen or so collided with Rayne's men. Snapdragon, several paces behind the line, willed his body into action, but it didn't respond. He watched helplessly as the battle was engaged.

-}‡{-

Rayne drew his sword and prepared to engage the leader of the Rifna Erd, who seemed focused on the king. Time seemed to slow down, as often happened in combat. From the corner of his eye, Rayne saw a rider coming in fast at an angle. For a moment, the king feared another of the enemy had broken through and he would have to fend off two attackers. It was then Rayne noticed the other rider was wearing a thick bandage on his thigh and wielding a large hammer. It was Grant.

The leader of the Rifna Erd turned toward Grant a moment too late. The large crafter swung his heavy weapon at the perfect time to connect with the leader's head, intercepting him before he could reach the king.

After seeing the damage the blow did to the man's skull, Rayne knew the leader of the Rifna Erd was no longer among the living.

-}‡{-

The battle soon ended. The guardians from Bariwon were simply too many in number, and though the Rifna Erd did inflict some damage, Rayne's men won handily.

Snapdragon looked again at the mine and noticed part of the mountain above it had collapsed. King Rayne started issuing orders, but Snapdragon had a hard time understanding them. The world started spinning around him, and the next thing he knew, he felt the prairie grass next to his face. He found that odd since he was on the horse, but then he noticed the horse standing next to him.

He took in a deep breath, and somewhere in his mind, he realized he was safe. The people of Procep were safe. The people of Eddinh were safe. He took another deep breath that he held for a moment, then released. He had completed his duty.

Closing his eyes, he surrendered to the darkness that beckoned.

⊰‡⊱

The peal of a warning bell sounded from one of the towers. The sound snapped Eadward out of his shock at seeing Abrecan impaled. How could the alarm be sounded? Ciar had assured him the archers had been drugged. Eadward should have known he couldn't trust his cousin with such an important task.

Still, the former governor of Erd knew he had more than enough men to tear down the portcullis. They would still attack the castle, and then Eadward himself would take the throne.

He turned to face his men. They were even greater in number than he had expected. Had his men recruited more followers over the last few days? They must have. Even better.

Removing his cloak, Eadward revealed that he was wearing the colors of Erd—dark crimson with silver trim. In a loud voice, he shouted, "Storm the castle!"

⊰‡⊱

Oakleaf picked up his walking stick and went as quickly as he could to the front gate. The servant who had helped Abrecan escape was curled up in a ball, leaning against one of the walls and sobbing.

Oakleaf heard the sound of running feet behind him as guardians who had been alerted by the warning bell raced to their battle positions. Most of them were archers and headed toward the towers, though some had swords and shields with them and came to back up Oakleaf.

A man he recognized as Eadward was calling his men to action. They were all removing their cloaks, revealing that they were also dressed in Erd's colors and armed for battle.

Actually, not all of them were dressed in crimson and silver. There was a large group in the back, a hundred and fifty or so men, who were also removing their cloaks. However, these men were dressed in royal blue and gold—the king's colors.

Oakleaf realized the king's plan would work. Rayne's plan all along was to send half of his force back to town to lie in wait. Rayne wanted Abrecan's supporters to believe taking the castle would be easy—that is why he had left the castle so poorly defended. Many had been critical of the king when he elected to put Abrecan in the dungeon instead of having him killed. But Rayne knew the man still had many followers, and the king wanted them to reveal themselves. And they had.

Oakleaf saw Eadward pause when he noticed the king's guardians behind his men. With the castle gates secure, more and more archers lining the wall, and Eadward's men blocked from retreat, Oakleaf hoped Eadward would surrender.

Before Oakleaf could offer him the chance, Eadward shouted to his men once again to attack. The men from Erd responded immediately. All Oakleaf could do was to take a step back and watch as they were slaughtered.

⇥✦⇤

Why? Why would Abrecan do that? Melanie thought as she climbed the steps. Every time she closed her eyes, all she could see was him pushing her into harm's way, or the look of annoyance he gave her when she tried to warn him about the portcullis. Then the image of his horrific death flashed through her mind, and she cringed.

Fortunately, Oakleaf was so distracted by the battle that she was able to sneak away. However, she knew her role in Abrecan's escape would soon be revealed. Someone must have seen her leave with him and warned Oakleaf.

She reached the top of the stairs to the archer's tower. The wind was blowing strongly enough that she could smell the death that littered the street below. She numbly walked to the edge and looked down. It appeared none of Eadward's men survived the attack.

For the last few years, Melanie had waited for and dreamed of the day Abrecan would be freed and they could be together. That dream had turned into a nightmare. There was no hope. Certainly she would be executed for treason against the crown.

She refused to let that happen. Instead, she climbed on top of the tower wall and without another thought, jumped to join the dead.

⊰✠⊱

Ciar looked at Selene expectantly. While he had received communications from her, he had never met the magistrate until today.

It wasn't easy escaping to Erd. He had no money when he fled. He ended up walking most of the way, begging for food and shelter, and stealing provisions when no one would help him.

But now that he was here, she would know what to do. Certainly she couldn't blame him for what happened. He had done all he was asked to do and more.

"We must take you somewhere isolated—somewhere people won't look for you. You know too much," Selene said, staring at Ciar.

"Thank you, Magistrate. Thank you. I'll be of good service to you. Just tell me what to do."

Selene's face was impassive. "Crescens will escort you. He'll make sure you are taken care of."

⊰✠⊱

It was near dawn, and the small, flat-bottomed ferryboat glided across the lake known as Dylobo. A light mist rose from the water, giving an almost ethereal quality to the scene.

Ciar had volunteered to pull the ferryboat across the lake by the long rope attached to the opposite shore. It was the least he could do to help Crescens as they headed to what Selene referred to as Ciar's new home. He'd never been here before, but as they left the shore, he spotted dwellings here and there by the lakeside, so he assumed he would be staying in something similar.

"I can't thank you and the magistrate enough," Ciar said.

Crescens didn't look at Ciar when he answered. "Magistrate Selene wanted to make sure you were taken care of, based on your actions at the castle."

"Do you know what she will have me do to help her?"

"Yes, she told me," Crescens said distantly.

"When will I find out?"

"Soon enough."

After a few more moments, Crescens said, "Stop here."

Ciar did as directed, though he wondered why they should stop when they were still some distance from the shore.

"Look out there," Crescens said, pointing at something to the starboard of the boat.

Ciar did as he was told, careful to stay away from the edge of the ferryboat. The last thing he wanted was to fall into the water. He'd never been much of a swimmer.

He squinted but didn't see anything in particular. He sensed Crescens move in behind him. Perhaps the assistant magistrate would point out what he was looking for.

"What, exactly, am I supposed to see?" Ciar asked.

His answer was a sharp blow to his back that nearly knocked him overboard. Ciar was confused until he looked down and saw the tip of a short sword sticking through his chest.

"You are seeing what happens to those who fail Selene," Crescens said tightly.

Ciar tried to respond, but before he could, Crescens pushed him over the edge. The cold water was a shock, but not nearly as great of a shock as realizing he was a dead man.

❧❦❧

Selene stared into the fire roaring in the hearth. It had been three weeks since the disaster at the castle—three weeks for her to contemplate her next move. She had, of course, denied any foreknowledge of Eadward's attack. Crescens had also sworn to the governor, as well as to the king's men who had been sent to look into the matter, that they knew nothing about any planned attack. Yes, they had known Eadward was training men, but they thought it was for the next Mortentaun. For now, the king's men appeared to believe the story.

Selene doubted the truth could be hidden forever. She heard Melanie had taken her own life, which was a shame. She would have rather had the servant woman suffer.

Ciar had actually helped Selene by coming to Erd. Crescens had taken care of that loose end. He returned from the deed a bit shaken, but he was proving to be a valuable asset.

Her last worry was what to do about the people from Eddinh, the outcasts from the Tular Tevoil. At first, Selene feared they would reveal her bloodline, but they seemed to have no interest in doing more than living peacefully. Perhaps she could use this to her advantage. Apparently, the Rifna Erd would make a powerful ally. For the moment, though, they were cut off from Bariwon.

Selene sat down in her room and sighed. There were so many plans to put into motion—all of which would take years to come to fruition. But she was nothing if not patient.

CHAPTER 52

A cool breeze caused the curtains to dance to an unheard rhythm. Shafts of soft blue light shone through the open window, illuminating dust particles in the air.

The smell of bread teased Snapdragon's nostrils, and he felt his mouth watering. Blinking again, he realized he was in the castle, though he wasn't sure exactly where. He idly wondered why he had fallen asleep here and not in his own quarters.

What day was it? What were his duties for the day? He couldn't seem to recall. Regardless, he needed to get up and prepare for the day.

He went to sit up but found it rather difficult to do so. His right arm didn't seem to respond. That was odd.

Using his left arm, he propped himself up. Even that arm felt weak. What was wrong with him? Looking down to inspect his body, he was startled. This was *not* his body.

Gone were the well-toned muscles and bulk. In their place was a sickly, thin frame. There was an ugly scar on his right shoulder—a center scar surrounded by what appeared to be healed burnt tissue.

At that moment it all came back to him. The trip to Procep. The attack on his companions. The escape to and from Itamunno Kael. All of it.

But what had happened since?

He pushed himself further, causing the bed to creak. While he was still trying to force his body into a sitting position, the door to the room opened and a nursemaid whom Snapdragon didn't recognize entered.

"Thank the Zealous Star you are awake," the lady said with a strange accent. Snapdragon realized with a start that she spoke like someone from Eddinh, though much more clearly. "We were not sure you ever would."

"What happened?" Snapdragon's voice cracked.

The nursemaid smiled. "All in due time. There are people who want to be informed that you are awake. Please remain here."

She left the room, leaving the door slightly ajar. Snapdragon managed to sit up a little with his back resting against the headboard.

Looking out the window, he noticed the trees were ablaze with red, orange, and gold leaves. Had he been asleep for that long?

The door opened swiftly, and in entered a vision of beauty. Seraphina's freckles had deepened some, and her hair was a touch lighter, no doubt due to the summer sun. She wore a nursemaid outfit that flattered her figure—though just about anything she wore did that.

She rushed to Snapdragon's bedside and put her arms around him. He did his best to return the embrace.

"Seraphina," he breathed. "You're safe."

She looked at him through tearful eyes. "Aye, I am, thanks to you. I'm so glad you woke up."

"Me too," Snapdragon said. "What's happened? I don't quite remember…"

She put a finger to his lips. "Shhh. There will be time for that."

Her closeness made him feel uneasy when he knew he should be enjoying it. Then he remembered. "Seraphina, we can't be doing this. As a royal guardian, I can't court anyone."

"You need not worry about that," King Rayne's voice came from behind Seraphina. He came to Snapdragon's bedside and laid a hand on his shoulder. "You are no longer a royal guardian."

Was this some sort of punishment? Surely Seraphina had told the king everything that had happened. Snapdragon had been put into an impossible situation—there was no way he could have saved everyone he had been charged to protect. "I… I don't understand," he managed to say after a moment.

The king nodded and then said to Seraphina, "Will you please give us some time alone?"

She hesitated briefly before saying, "Of course, Your Majesty." Putting her hands on her hips and addressing Snapdragon, she said firmly, "And don't you go falling asleep again while I'm gone."

Snapdragon mustered a smile. "I'll do my best."

She looked at him for a long moment and then left the room.

The king took in a deep breath. "I know you have a lot of questions. Are you strong enough now to hear the answers, or do you need more time to rest?"

"I'll be fine, Your Majesty."

"For now, let's keep titles out of it. Yes, I'm your king, but I'm also your sister's husband. We've known each other for a long time. I want to have a forthright discussion, and that means I want you to tell me your thoughts as they come. Will you do that?"

"Yes."

"First of all, let me explain why you are no longer a royal guardian. After you collapsed in Procep, we got you back to the castle, where you were treated by the best healers in all of Bariwon. They came to two conclusions. Number one, the arrowhead that pierced you had been treated with a slow-acting poison. You should've died, but the healers guessed that because the arrow went all the way through your shoulder, only a small amount of poison entered your body. Because of that, and because you are young and in good health, you survived. However, your body needed time to recover, so you've been in a deep sleep for quite a while. The healers thought you might wake up one day, but they weren't certain."

"And what was the healers' second conclusion?"

Rayne shook his head slightly. "They all agree that your right arm will never be fully functional again. The Tome of Laws states that in cases like this, the guardian is to retire—honorably, but retire nonetheless."

"But I use my left hand! I'm not worthless!"

Rayne arched an eyebrow. "Why, of course you aren't worthless. Just because you aren't a royal guardian doesn't mean you can't serve the kingdom. There's much to be done, and I need men like you."

Snapdragon was still trying to accept the fact that he was no longer a royal guardian. It was something he had wanted to be his whole life. He hadn't even thought about what he would do once he retired.

"Need me how?" he asked wearily. He motioned to his body. "I can hardly sit up on my own. It'll be some time before I can even walk again, I fear."

Rayne sat back and folded his arms. "I've heard from Seraphina and Bearach, as well as others, what you accomplished north of the mountains. It wasn't just your body that achieved what you did. It was your *mind*. You haven't given yourself enough credit for how intelligent you are. Remember, I'm married to your sister, and she is brilliant. It runs in your family. We are at a crossroads of sorts in Bariwon, and nothing will ever be the same. I need your assistance to make certain we handle these changes in the best way possible."

"You mean because the people from Eddinh are here, or because we now know of the Rifna Erd and the Tular Tevoil?" Snapdragon asked. "Are these the changes you are talking about?"

"In part, yes to both. But there is more to it than that."

Slumping down in his bed, Snapdragon said, "There is still so much I don't understand. For example, how did you end up in Procep? How did Grant survive? What happened to—?"

Rayne held up his hand and shook his head. "Let me explain much of what you don't know. Things will be clearer after that."

The king summarized what had transpired. "So you see, Snapdragon," he said, "we were still gathering men to go into the tunnel when the people of Procep and Eddinh emerged. At first we thought it was the invading force, until Grant recognized Bearach leading them. Their story was almost unbelievable, but I can't tell you how happy I was to hear that you were alive."

"But didn't you tell me the Rifna Erd were following Grant in the tunnel? Why didn't you see them, or for that matter, why didn't the people from Eddinh and Procep run into them?"

Rayne rubbed his chin. "From what we've been able to piece together, the Rifna Erd *were* following Grant through the tunnel. However, something made them turn back. If we have the timeline right, it appears they turned around when the fires were set at the Temple of the New Moon. Apparently all the Rifna Erd went to the temple—even the ones following Grant."

Snapdragon grimaced as he sat up a bit straighter in the bed. "If you were going to go in with the men you were gathering, then why did you make it so the tunnel would collapse?"

"It was actually Grant's idea," said Rayne. "That man is remarkable. Even with his injuries, nothing could keep him from the final battle. It was a good thing, too. He probably saved my life. But back to your question, Grant recalled how easy it would be to cause the tunnel to cave in if we took out the buttresses. It was a great plan to reinforce our initial strategy, and as things worked out, it saved a great deal of bloodshed that day."

Snapdragon frowned. "It's a shame the same couldn't be said about Eadward's attack. How many men did we lose again?"

Rayne rubbed his hand over his eyes. "We lost twenty-seven good men, but it could have been worse. Much worse. Over three hundred men from Erd died that day, including Abrecan and Eadward."

"So it seems the kingdom is safe. Abrecan is dead, his followers are dead or scattered, and the Rifna Erd were stopped."

Frowning, Rayne said, "The Rifna Erd were stopped? I don't think so. 'Delayed' is more accurate. And that is why I need men like you, Snapdragon."

⊰✦⊱

"You need to take it slowly," Seraphina said, watching Snapdragon as he prepared to eat. "You've had only porridge and water for months. You can't just go back to eating like you did before."

Snapdragon was sitting up in his bed, holding a large plate covered with a thick steak, lightly seasoned potatoes, and breaded green beans. A tankard of water sat on the table next to him.

"But didn't you tell me that the first step to getting strong again was to eat better?" Snapdragon countered playfully.

Seraphina sighed. "You aren't going to use my words against me. I'm to help you get better, and you *will* do what I say. Unless, of course, you'd rather have one of the older, sterner nursemaids assigned to you."

Thinking of one rather unpleasant nursemaid who gotten after him over the years, Snapdragon shuddered involuntarily. He wasn't sure how Seraphina had managed to get this assignment, but knowing her strong will, he doubted she would have let anyone else do it. Yes, he should be very thankful to have her so close.

"All right! All right! I surrender," he said. "What am I allowed to eat today?"

"Let's start with half of what was prepared for you. After that, we're going to get you out of this bed and see what shape your legs are in."

Over the last couple of days he had gained enough strength to sit up and roll over onto his stomach, but he still hadn't tried to stand or walk. He was mortified to have Seraphina see how broken down his body was, but if it bothered her, she didn't let it show.

He let out a heavy sigh. "I'm afraid of what we'll discover if I try to walk."

She looked at him and responded softly, "Snapdragon, I'm here to help you get better. We'll get through this, no matter what. As far as we can tell, the poison hasn't damaged the muscles in your body—they have only gotten soft from not being used. We just need to teach them how to work again."

⊰✦⊱

Three days later, Snapdragon walked out of his room by himself. Seraphina looked on, the pride on her face unmistakable. He turned around and walked back into the room, but instead of going back to his bed, he went to Seraphina and embraced her with his one good arm.

"See?" she said, her voice quaking. "I told you that you could do it."

"Excellent! Now tell me some more things I can do so we can get working on those as well."

❖

"So, do I have your permission?" the king asked the nursemaid.

Seraphina arched an eyebrow. "I'm enjoying having a king ask me for permission. I could get used to this."

Snapdragon and Rayne shared an amused look. "She's something else, isn't she?" Rayne said.

"Aye, that she is. Putting her in charge of my recovery has given her quite the illusion of power. Now to have you ask if I can attend the next court, well, I think you have just pushed her over the edge." Snapdragon laughed.

Playfully punching Snapdragon in his left shoulder, Seraphina said, "Actually, Your Majesty, I think having him attend court would do wonders not only for him, but for those in attendance. It's only been through my insistence that he not have visitors, aside from immediate family, that he has not been overwhelmed with well-wishers."

Snapdragon took a step back. "What do you mean?"

King Rayne smiled. "Snap, word has spread of your heroic deeds. I've already heard of a bard or two singing songs about what you did. The people from both Procep and Eddinh, and countless others, owe their lives to you. Had the Rifna Erd come through the tunnel, who knows how many lives would have been lost? You, Snap, are Bariwon's hero."

"But... I didn't do it for those reasons. I was just trying to do what was right."

"Perhaps talking with Oakleaf will give you some perspective on that," Rayne said. "For now, rest up for court tomorrow. Some matters will be discussed that will affect generations to come."

❖

Snapdragon entered the main hall from the side entrance usually reserved for royalty. He felt odd doing so, but Rayne had insisted it would be better that way.

When he came into view of those in attendance, they all stood and clapped. There were shouts of praise and even one proposal from one of the young female servants.

Embarrassed, Snapdragon waved to the crowd with his left hand and put on his most gracious smile. Walking as quickly as he could to the front bench reserved for him, he noticed that King Rayne and Queen Sunshine were also standing and clapping.

He waved again to the crowd before sitting down next to his father and mother. Iolanthe grabbed her son by the arm and squeezed it tightly, whispering to him how proud she was. Garth clapped Snapdragon on the knee and said, "You look good, Son."

"I welcome you all to court," King Rayne said loudly, quieting the crowd. "Please be seated."

The hall was full to bursting, which made Snapdragon a bit curious. From what he had heard when Daimh was king, very few people attended court, and even then, it was only those absolutely required to be there. Today, all the district governors were in attendance. This must be a special court indeed.

"Thank you all for coming," the king began. "I would like to acknowledge the presence of my wife's brother, Snapdragon. As you all can see, he is feeling quite well. I want to officially thank him for his service to Bariwon."

More applause.

"In addition, I'd like to recognize Alethea from the people of Eddinh. We will hear from her shortly."

Snapdragon looked back into the crowd and spotted the raven-haired woman he had helped save. She sat next to a man whom he recognized as Creighton of Procep. They both caught Snapdragon's eye and smiled.

"After presenting our mutual problems to the leaders of Bariwon and then considering their responses, we have decided how to proceed," announced the king. "To that end, I've asked Magistrate Bertram to explain further."

King Rayne sat down and the tall, thin leader of the Hierarchy of Magistrates stood and made his way to the center of the dais.

To Snapdragon, he appeared nervous, but after receiving a smile from Queen Sunshine, Bertram confidently addressed the court.

"Over the last two months, an inventory of the items in the castle was completed. The amount of treasures and riches is quite substantial. The vast majority of these will be used to fund the organization and ongoing costs of creating a kingdom-wide militia."

The announcement brought a ripple of noise from the crowd, and to Snapdragon, the response seemed favorable.

"We will ask for volunteers," Bertram continued. "From what we are asking of militia members, I believe everyone will be fairly compensated, so I doubt we'll have an issue getting the numbers we need.

"The savants are drafting notices to be sent throughout the kingdom, outlining the qualities we are looking for and the details of the plan. To sum it up, members will be provided with weapons and armor as well as a monthly stipend for their service. They'll also be expected to give two days a month for training with the guardians in battle techniques."

Again, the crowd responded favorably. During the pause, Snapdragon couldn't help wondering, was King Rayne so fearful of the Rifna Erd's return that he was willing to form an army of sorts? Or was there something else he feared?

"These notices will be ready by tomorrow for the representatives of each district to take back with them," Bertram concluded, then turned and sat down by the rest of the Hierarchy of Magistrates.

King Rayne stood. "I know many of you have questions about the details, but please wait until you receive the notices—they should answer most, if not all, of your questions. And now, I've asked Alethea to give us a report."

Snapdragon watched as she walked up to the dais and turned to the crowd. She possessed an air of confidence and looked directly at the crowd before she started to speak.

"I apologize if I am unclear to some of you," she said, her accent still strong. She looked at Creighton. "First, I would like to announce that I have accepted Creighton's proposal of marriage."

Thunderous applause echoed through the hall, which Snapdragon found somewhat odd for two people in the kingdom that most of the court didn't know. But clearly they were better known than he supposed.

"Our union is not only the first marriage between our two peoples, but it will also mark the joining of the people of Eddinh with the kingdom of Bariwon. We have agreed to accept the king's offer. Work will commence shortly. Thank you all for your time." Applause followed Alethea back to her seat.

What offer? Snapdragon thought.

Once again King Rayne stood. "For those of you who haven't heard, the people of Eddinh have agreed to join the district of Erd. In exchange for the good people of Erd opening their lands for settlement, the people of Eddinh will help construct a wall along the mountain range with watchtowers set up within sight of each other to help protect our kingdom."

Suddenly, things clicked in Snapdragon's mind. The first line of defense would be the wall. The second line would be the militia, in case the watchtowers failed. This would certainly bring more people and resources to Erd, which would bring in more trade and help the district. No wonder they would be willing to share their lands with the people of Eddinh.

"We will need strong leadership to see these mighty tasks completed," King Rayne went on. "Oakleaf has agreed to lead the formation of the militia. He has been an invaluable advisor to me, and I know he will do an outstanding job."

The crowd showed their approval of the choice by cheering loudly. Following the eyes of the crowd, Snapdragon turned and saw his brother stand up. He hadn't noticed him sitting behind him and to the left with his wife Arlie.

After the crowd settled down, King Rayne said, "That means I need to choose someone with equal leadership ability to oversee the defenses of the northern mountains. He must be a man who has the respect of the people he will lead, as well as the ability to assume what is sure to be a challenging task.

Rayne's eyes shifted from the crowd to Snapdragon. "Fortunately, I have the perfect person in mind."

⟢⟡⟣

Snapdragon ran. He ran and he didn't look back. It wasn't that he was afraid of what was behind him. He didn't look back because he would have to take his eyes off his goal, a large tree on top of a slightly sloping hill not far from the castle. His legs felt as if they might collapse underneath him at any time, but still he ran. And he was happy he *could* run.

He had been walking for a couple of weeks now, and he was getting stronger, but he hadn't had a full run until today. Seraphina wasn't sure he was ready and had said as much. He knew she was watching him from one of the towers, probably as anxious as could be. If he didn't show her—and himself, for that matter—that he was regaining his strength, what chance did he have of fulfilling the king's assignment?

As he reached the hill, it became more difficult, as he now was not only running, but climbing as well. His body was screaming for him to stop, but his mind wouldn't let him. He was too close now.

With a final burst of energy, he reached the tree and slowed down to a walk as he circled it. Coming around the far side so he faced the castle, he waved, doubting they could see that much detail, but knowing they could at least see he was still standing.

With a renewed sense of confidence, Snapdragon started walking back to the castle. He wouldn't go see Seraphina right away. There was someone else he needed to see first.

Bearach smiled. "Of course! It would be an honor!"

Snapdragon shook the crafter's hand. "Are you sure you don't want more time to think about it? This isn't a quick or easy assignment, Bearach. We're basically doing something that has never been done before. I mean, I'm not even sure how we are going to start."

"Funny you should mention that," Bearach said, walking to a shelf and removing a long parchment. "I've actually started sketching out some rough ideas to give to whomever was assigned the task."

After setting the drawings on a workbench and spreading them out, Bearach beamed, "But I guess the person I'll give these to is me!"

Snapdragon looked over what the man had drawn, and though a lot of it was complex, he understood the basic idea.

"See?" Bearach pointed to something on the page. "I used the basic concepts of how the castle was built and incorporated things I discovered with the Tular Tevoil."

Snapdragon laughed. "To be honest, I don't really see it at all, but I believe you. I trust you have come up with something that will work."

"Of course it'll take a lot of men and quite a bit of time to make this happen," Bearach said.

"As for the manpower, I was assured we'd have all we would need between the people of Eddinh and Erd. As for time… who knows? I am going to be meeting with Alethea tomorrow to get any insight she may have on the matter."

Bearach rubbed his hands together. "Very well. When do we leave?"

"Within a couple of weeks, I suppose. Seraphina is still being overly protective of me. She tells me I still need to regain more strength before I can go."

"Are you sure that she isn't trying to keep you here longer for other reasons?"

Snapdragon felt his face turn red. "That thought had crossed my mind."

"Well, let me help you. I've been working on something special for a while, and I think now is as good a time as ever for you to have it." Bearach went back to the shelf and almost lovingly removed a pouch of fine etched leather. It was tied with an exquisite silver chain. Handing it to Snapdragon, he said, "Please take this."

"What is it?" Snapdragon asked.

"You'll see."

CHAPTER 53

The evening was crisp, and the smell of roasting apples spiced with cinnamon filled the autumn air. Snapdragon stood next to Seraphina overlooking the land around the castle. A few wispy clouds floated in the night sky, doing little to dim the blazing stars and waxing moon that illuminated the scene.

This was one of Snapdragon's favorite places. Technically it was a guard tower, but to him, it was a quiet place to reflect, especially at this time of the evening.

Motioning to the moon that sat heavily in the sky, Snapdragon said, "Did I ever tell you about the night I spent alone at the Temple of the New Moon before the Rifna Erd attacked?"

Seraphina, wrapped in a grey-hooded cloak, simply shook her head.

"The moon that night was very much like the moon tonight," he said. "Waylon had taught me how the Rifna Erd had superstitions based on the phases of the moon. The waxing moon meant a time of change and growing strength, as I recall."

The nursemaid looked at the moon, and Snapdragon thought he saw tears form in her eyes.

"I don't really believe in such things, but this *is* a time of change," Snapdragon said. "So at least in that, the moon is right."

Seraphina said softly, "Change can be difficult. It can mean giving up something you love."

"It can," Snapdragon conceded. "But it can also be wonderful. It can be a good thing."

She flashed her eyes at Snapdragon. "How can you be so ready to leave? To leave all this behind? To leave..."

"You?" Snapdragon prompted when she didn't continue.

Her response was simply to nod.

"Actually, I have something I hope will help bring about one of those good changes."

He pulled out the pouch Bearach had given him earlier that day and handed it to her.

"What's this?" Seraphina asked, staring at the bag.

"Open it."

After pausing for only a moment, she slowly unfastened the silver chain and opened the pouch. Inside was a ring of amazing workmanship. It was gold, with a sparkling sapphire set on top.

She stood there for a long moment before she said, "Snap… does this mean…?"

"I'm going to be in Erd for a long time. Probably years. The thought of not having you with me is, well, unbearable. I can only use the excuse that I need a nursemaid for so long. However, if you would be willing to go with me as my wife, well, then I wouldn't have to make up excuses to have you stay close."

Looking him straight in the eye with a serious expression, she said, "I don't know."

Snapdragon's heart lurched in his chest. He had been so sure she would accept his offer of marriage. In his mind, he struggled to find the words that would convince her.

But before he could speak, Seraphina smiled and said, "I want you to find excuses for me to stay close, even after we are married."

Part 3

THE ZEALOUS STAR

CHAPTER 54

Slowly starving to death in a pit with rotting corpses was not a good way to die. Waylon knew that if his idea didn't work, that would be his fate. He tried not to dwell on such thoughts—he needed to focus on the here and now. Only then would he regain Merton's trust; only then would the leader of the Tular Tevoil let him live.

"How much longer?" Merton asked. He spoke in Waylon's language.

Waylon wiped nervous sweat from his brow. "It won't be long now, they are making excellent progress."

Both Waylon and Merton watched several of the larger men from Itamunno Kael, the town where they were trapped, use a heavy stone battering ram to pound a large door—a door that would lead them to freedom. The door shuttered with each hit, and it appeared ready to break open at any time.

Bearach, one of Waylon's former companions, had sabotaged all the stone door exits from Itamunno Kael. That prevented the Tular Tevoil's return to Bariwon, or the "land of the first temple" as they called it.

They had first tried to open the main exit, but it was far too large. When it became obvious to Waylon that he would be blamed for this disaster, even though he had turned against his companions to join the Tular Tevoil, he quickly thought of an alternate plan.

That was three days ago. It had taken that long to get the men to create a battering ram, and then find a door they believed could be opened. None of the Tular Tevoil had kept up with the old traditions of how the doors functioned, so they had no idea how to fix the damage Bearach had caused before he had escaped.

Another blow to the door caused the men to redouble their efforts. It was about to break open. Waylon glanced at Merton and was pleased to see him smiling.

Merton said something to one of his aides, a man by the name of Sverre. From Merton's hand motions, Waylon guessed it was instructions to get the people ready to move. Waylon had picked up a few words here and there of the Tular Tevoil's primary language, but not enough to understand it fully.

One last hit from the battering ram and the door collapsed. The men cheered. Waylon felt a huge sense of relief. It had worked. There was now a path clear from Itamunno Kael to the tunnel under the mountains that led to Bariwon.

"As you can see, I am still of use to you," Waylon said.

Merton looked at the stout savant and responded in Waylon's language, "Be happy your idea was successful, for your sake. Now, tell me, how soon after we arrive in the land of the first temple will their ruler come to greet me? I will be very disappointed if—"

The leader of the Tular Tevoil stopped speaking. There was sound coming from the passageway they had just opened. Waylon squinted into the darkness.

His earlier excitement diminished when the sounds from the tunnel became louder, and from their tone, hostile. Waylon took several steps away from the recently opened door. He noticed Merton and the rest of the men doing the same.

The noise increased. It sounded like many men were coming through the passageway. Waylon turned to run when he saw a man emerge from the tunnel. He was bald and had a long, pointed beard with a red stripe running its length. He was wielding a jagged sword.

It was a Rifna Erd—barbarians that were the sworn enemy of the Tular Tevoil. As more bald men poured out of the passageway, Waylon realized that dying in the pit would be better than what these men were going to do to him.

⊰⧈⊱

Snapdragon was outmatched, and he knew it. The man in front of him had been well trained in the art of swordplay. He was also strong and quick. And unlike Snapdragon, the man hadn't spent several months in bed recovering from a life threatening wound.

"Are you waiting for the stars to come out, or are you going to attack?" the man taunted.

Snapdragon gripped the hilt of his sword tightly in his left hand. While most of the people in the kingdom of Bariwon primarily used their right hand, he was one of the few who naturally used his left. Snapdragon had found that gave him an advantage most of the time because his opponents weren't used to facing a left-handed fighter. Snapdragon's right arm hung practically useless at his side. He had taken a poisoned arrow in his right shoulder, which not only severely limited the use of his arm, but had also put him into a coma.

"You're waiting for me to strike first?" Snapdragon asked. "Afraid to see what happens if you make the first move?"

The man smiled and then nodded. He took a step forward and swung his sword. Snapdragon batted away the attack, and then shifted a few steps to his left. Out of the corner of his eye, he noticed his fiancée, Seraphina, watching among the crowd with a worried look on her face.

When Snapdragon had competed in the weekly sparring contests before he was injured, he was able to block out everything around him. The fact that he was aware of Seraphina watching him now gave him some concern. Perhaps she was right. Perhaps he wasn't ready to compete again.

Another strike came from his opponent, this one toward his legs. The swords were made of wood, but still, they could break bones if they hit solidly enough. Snapdragon jumped over the blow, allowing the sword to swish harmlessly below him.

After landing on his feet, he recited a mantra in his head to keep him focused. *Knock down, knock out, or knock around.* He would win the contest if he could knock the man to the ground or get him to yield. The contests were held in the main hall of the castle, so there wasn't a circle for them to stay within.

It became clear to Snapdragon that he was not going to out-muscle this man. No, another tactic would have to be used. Snapdragon took several steps back and analyzed his fellow competitor. He wore a padded cloth tunic that was tucked into his durable, but simple, cloth leggings which were cinched at the waist with a thin rope belt. His boots were fine leather, as was his cap.

An idea popped into Snapdragon's head and he decided to act on it before he could convince himself that it was foolishness.

He raised his sword high and charged. The other man seemed shocked by the sudden change of attack and raised his sword to block. This allowed Snapdragon to be almost chest to chest with his opponent. Although he couldn't move his right shoulder, he could still bend his arm at the elbow.

With his opponent distracted by the swords locked together, Snapdragon reached up with his right hand and grabbed the man's skinny belt. After making sure he had a firm grip on it, he then backed away and yanked hard on the thin rope. The belt broke and slid from around the man's waist while Snapdragon continued his retreat.

For a moment, the man looked confused until his cloth pants slid down his legs and pooled around his ankles. Fortunately, his shirt hung down to his mid-thighs. At least he wasn't naked in front of the crowd.

"Do you yield?" Snapdragon asked.

The man looked down, and then back up again; his face crimson. He tossed his sword to the ground and then reached down to pull up his pants. "I most certainly do!" he cried out.

The hall filled with the spectators' laughter.

→⇟⇞←

"Are you quite done?" Seraphina asked.

Snapdragon checked his reflection one last time. "Just about."

"I'm not talking about getting ready to meet with Alethea and Creighton," she said.

He recognized that tone in her voice. She wasn't happy with him. He faced his wife-to-be and saw her glaring at him with arms folded. They were inside his room in the castle, not long after the sparring contest had ended.

Instead of guessing what she meant and getting himself into even deeper trouble, he asked, "Am I done with what?"

"Snapdragon," she said, nostrils flaring, "you know quite well what I mean."

He thought for a moment. It had been two days since he had asked for her hand in marriage. Since that time, things had been wonderful—until now. They had met for breakfast in the eastern courtyard, one of her favorite places. They had talked about the day's events. There was a meeting with Alethea and Creighton in the afternoon. But she wouldn't be upset about that. He had planned on practicing swordplay with some of the guardians that morning—she didn't argue with him. She had said it was good for him to keep moving and gaining strength. While working with the guardians, one of them suggested he compete in the weekly sparring contest. He jumped at the idea. Oh…

"Are you referring to the contest today?" he asked.

"What else would I be referring to?"

He smiled at her. She continued to glare at him.

"I was in no real danger during the contest, sweetheart," he said, trying to convince her as much as himself.

"I don't know what it is with men and your need to prove your manliness." She sighed. "I only agreed to let you spar this morning so you could continue on your road to recovery."

Snapdragon gave her his warmest smile in an attempt to calm her down. "Thanks to your skills as a nursemaid, I feel as good as I have in a long time. I thought you'd appreciate a demonstration of how well I've healed."

Her response was to unfold her arms and approach him. At first he wasn't sure what she was going to do until she gave him a big hug. "You wooden head, you have nothing to prove to me. I just want you safe. Can you understand that?"

He kissed her on the forehead. "I'm sorry, sweetheart. I'll talk with you before I do anything else manly. All right?"

Seraphina looked up at him. "You'd better."

⇥✦⇤

"Congratulations!" Alethea said to Snapdragon when he entered the room.

Creighton, a well-built miner from Procep, was there as well. He echoed his fiancées statement. "Must be something in the air. Don't you think? All these women are finding ways to get us men married." He was referring to Snapdragon's recent engagement to Seraphina.

Snapdragon smiled. "If it's something in the air, I'm sure more women would wish it could be bottled."

Alethea, one of the people who he had rescued from beyond the northern mountains, looked blankly at her husband-to-be briefly and then at Snapdragon before moving on, obviously ignoring their comments.

"So, you have agreed to move to Erd and oversee the building of the defenses, correct?" she asked. Her accent was still fairly thick, but she was getting easier to understand.

Snapdragon nodded.

"Please, have a seat so we can talk."

Alethea's room in the castle was simple, but elegantly decorated. Snapdragon noticed his sister's taste in the furniture and was pleased to see that the castle's redecorating had reached as far as the visitors' rooms.

Snapdragon sat. "Thank you. There's much to discuss, but I need to know something first."

"Which is?" Alethea asked.

"How much time do we have before we can expect the Rifna Erd to come back?"

Alethea and Creighton shared a look before she responded. "It is hard to say," she said. "The leader of the Rifna Erd was not a holder of the old traditions. Now that the Rifna Erd are without a leader, there will be a bloody battle for the right to rule. A competition will be held. The fights will be to the death and the strongest man to survive, wins."

Snapdragon couldn't help but wonder if the competition she spoke of was some sort of perverted version of the Mortentaun, the event where young men from all over Bariwon competed to become guardians. It sounded too similar to be a coincidence.

Creighton said, "There's a chance they might not come at all. With the destruction of the Temple of the New Moon, and then later, collapsing the tunnel that connected our lands, this might feed the fears and superstitions of the Rifna Erd."

Snapdragon nodded. "That was my intention with the Temple of the New Moon—to frighten the people of the Rifna Erd."

"It may have worked," Alethea said. "Then again, it may have made things worse. The Temple of the New Moon stood as a symbol to the Rifna Erd. It was something they feared. Now that it is gone…"

Creighton patted Alethea on the knee. "Don't you worry about that now, Snapdragon. Your actions were amazing. But still, we need a plan."

"Agreed," Alethea said. "I believe we will have several years before we have to deal with the Rifna Erd. But we must prepare. This is very important."

Snapdragon tried to fold his arms, but his ruined right arm wouldn't cooperate. He still hadn't adjusted completely that his right arm would no longer work properly. He brushed that aside for now and addressed the situation at hand. "I agree it's important, but it seems like there's something you aren't telling me."

Alethea sat up straight. "It is important because when they do come, they will come with only one goal in mind: the complete domination of everyone in this land."

⭒⚜⭒

Snapdragon had never been to Erd proper before, and so far, he wasn't impressed. The capital town of Erd felt uninviting. He didn't think it was because the buildings were tall and narrow, sometimes with little or no room between them. Nor was it because they were made of dark stone accented with black iron fixtures. It was something different, something he couldn't put a finger on.

And then there were the residents. The faces of the people in the town that watched him and his companions ride toward the palace weren't hostile, per se. He would describe them as guarded, suspicious even.

Riding next to him, his beautiful wife Seraphina was frowning slightly. It seemed that she, too, felt something was off about this place.

They had been married just five days ago. While there were those in the castle that protested about not having time to put on an elaborate wedding, the fairly simple ceremony with close family and a few guests was just fine with Seraphina—and as long as she was happy about it, so was Snapdragon.

Finding time to be alone proved to be the biggest challenge, as there was much to do in preparation for the move to Erd. Still, the king made it a point that there were times when Snapdragon and Seraphina were not to be disturbed for any reason. He felt himself blush slightly when he thought back to those times, and he felt his heart quicken when he found himself looking forward to another one of these "declarations from the king."

They had left the day after the wedding to go to Erd. While Alethea, Creighton, and Bearach had left for Procep, Snapdragon and Seraphina, along with an armored escort, had been asked to go to Erd proper to meet with the governor of the district.

They had entered the large town near midday, and had thought to stop at one of the local taverns to eat, but elected not to after the cool reception they had gotten from the general populous. Instead, they decided to press on to the palace. Snapdragon sincerely hoped they would be better received there.

"I think we stand out too much," Seraphina said as they continued through the town. "Maybe we shouldn't have come dressed as we are."

Everyone in the entourage wore the blue and gold standard of Bariwon, and even the horses were adorned in the kingdom's colors. It took Seraphina's comment to help Snapdragon realize just how much they stood out among the red and silver of Erd's townsfolk.

"There's not much we can do about that now, unless you want to disrobe here in front of all these people." Snapdragon winked.

It was Seraphina's turn to blush. With her eyes twinkling slightly, she said, "I think I'll wait for later."

A rider wearing a red cape and the standard of Erd embroidered on his tunic approached them from ahead—fast enough to show his urgency, but not so much as to be threatening.

"Hail there!" the man said, raising a hand in greeting.

Snapdragon responded in kind, and then stopped his horse, allowing the man to approach.

"My apologies!" he said. "We just got word of your arrival. Had we known you were coming, we would have had a more formal reception prepared." He was middle-aged, slight of build, and wore the neatly trimmed mustache and goatee which seemed to be the style in Erd. "My name is Crescens, assistant magistrate of Erd," he said by way of introduction.

Snapdragon nodded. "Well met, Crescens. I'm Snapdragon, and this is my wife Seraphina. We've been sent by the king to meet with the governor."

Crescens' eyes grew wide. "Snapdragon? Well, this is indeed an honor! And Seraphina, it appears that word of your beauty does not do you justice. If you will please follow me, the palace staff is preparing for you. I hope you have not eaten yet—it would be our pleasure to entertain you."

The palace itself was the second largest structure in all of the kingdom, with only the castle in Bariwon being larger. In fact, it did look very much like the castle in many ways, only with more gargoyles and arrow towers around the rim. Large iron spikes surrounded the moat, making the palace feel rather unwelcoming. Governor Wardell met them as soon as they crossed over the drawbridge. He was a fairly tall man, getting on in age, as indicated by his gray hair that was balding on top, but long on the sides and back. His mustache and goatee were also gray, but it was his kind blue eyes that caught Snapdragon's attention. They held a sincerity that couldn't be faked.

"Ah, Snapdragon, what a surprise!" he said, offering a hand to help him down from his mount.

Snapdragon allowed the man to help him.

"Allow me to introduce my wife, Seraphina," Snapdragon said. He helped her down.

Wardell bowed. "It's my pleasure, Seraphina."

The armed escorts dismounted next, allowing the servants to take their horses.

Seraphina looked at the governor for a moment before she asked, "We've met before, haven't we?"

The governor smiled shyly. "You honor me with your comment. Yes, we have. And I've also met you before, Snapdragon, though that was several years ago."

"I apologize that I don't recall, Governor," Snapdragon said.

"Not to worry," Wardell said. "I was a savant in the castle for years before your brother-in-law became king. You were young back then, and we only met in passing. But I was there for a time when Seraphina was younger. She's one that is hard not to notice."

Snapdragon said, "Aye, I must agree on that."

"Forgive me, I'm being rude, please, come, come! We have a meal being prepared for you," the governor said, motioning for them to follow.

⊹

"And so after Rayne became king, many of the people from Erd who lived in the castle felt it would be better if they left, fearing their association with Abrecan would be, well, let's say, a disadvantage to them," Governor Wardell said, just before taking another drink.

The meal was delicious, and Snapdragon was glad they had waited. The welcoming party wasn't large, just Wardell, his wife Samara, and Crescens, the assistant magistrate. He had asked the governor about how he had gotten his position, and that was the topic of conversation at the moment.

"I didn't really know King Rayne then, or how good of a king he would be—I guess my fear of living under Abrecan's rule—and let's not kid ourselves, it was Abrecan's and not Daimh's rule—that made me leave," Wardell continued.

Snapdragon took another bite of venison, which had been richly spiced to perfection. "I heard a great number of the royal guardians from Erd also left at that time. Were these the ones that joined Eadward?"

Nodding, Wardell said, "Aye, it appears so. There was a lot of rotten fruit in that basket—I can't begin to tell you how badly we felt over what happened. But back to your original question, when Eadward was removed as governor of Erd, King Rayne needed to fill the spot, and wanted to do so with a person from Erd. Even though I grew up on the Erd-Lewyol border, I was technically from Erd. I apparently had made a good impression on several people in the castle from my time as a savant there, so the king asked me. And who am I to refuse the king?"

Seraphina spoke next. "When we came into town, I didn't feel like we were very welcomed. Why would that be? I thought the people of Erd were miserable under Abrecan's rule?"

"Oh, the majority of the people were unhappy, to be sure," Wardell said. "Unless you were thick as thieves with Abrecan or his men, you were taxed heavily and taught to fear authority. But that isn't why you received such a cool reception."

Snapdragon leaned forward in his chair. "Then why?"

"Reverse prejudice," Wardell said flatly.

That caught Snapdragon off guard. "How's that again?"

"The people of Erd feel, well, like a lower class than the rest of the kingdom. It was one of their own that tried to trick the Hierarchy of Magistrates in the last Shoginoc. Then there was the unpleasantness with Eadward attacking the castle and trying to free Abrecan. If that wasn't bad enough, word is now spreading how our distant cousins, the Rifna Erd, are coming to destroy us all."

Snapdragon felt shocked. "I've never blamed the people of Erd for what the Rifna Erd have done. You may have a common ancestry, but why would people make that connection?"

"It isn't just that," Wardell said. "Remember that it was people from Procep, which are people from Erd, who uncovered the tunnel that led to the Rifna Erd threat. It also led to the death of many good people, and brought us to where we are today."

Seraphina shook her head in disbelief. "I still don't understand. Like my husband said, that isn't how we feel about the situation. I'm certain the king doesn't feel that way, either."

"Oh, you don't need to convince me," Wardell said, spreading his hands. "I'm not the one feeding the fires of discontent."

Snapdragon frowned. "Well, who is then?"

"I can't say for sure," Wardell said, this time his voice sounding troubled. "There are reports of secret meetings—even after the death of Abrecan, Eadward and his men. There's even stories of people wanting the Rifna Erd to return so that the Erd and Rifna Erd can rule Bariwon."

Crescens politely interrupted. "But as the governor has said, these are just stories and rumors. I think King Rayne sees this situation as a chance to bring us all together and put the issues of the past behind us. Working toward a common goal—the building of the defenses at the mountains—can reunite us as a people."

"Well said," Samara said. She then turned to Wardell. "Husband, you really shouldn't worry so much about these rumors. Plus, we have guests. We should be entertaining them, not scaring them."

Wardell patted his wife's hand. "Yes, you're right. Forgive me."

The conversation then took on a happier note for the next several moments, talking about Seraphina and Snapdragon's wedding and such until one of the doors to the hall opened.

In strode a sleekly built woman, her hair as dark as night on a new moon. She had a sharp nose and high, firm cheekbones. Her skin was quite pale, and she was dressed in a fairly tight and low-cut crimson dress.

"My sincere apologies for being late," the woman said, though her tone sounded anything but sincere to Snapdragon.

Wardell stood, as did Crescens and Snapdragon when she entered.

"Ah, there you are," Wardell said. "Let me introduce you. Snapdragon, Seraphina, this is Selene, magistrate of Erd."

⊰✦⊱

Snapdragon looked back over his shoulder, happy to be leaving Erd proper behind. The visit had been successful with the pledge of one thousand men and their families to be dedicated to the building of the northern defenses. They would be coming over the next few months, with everyone in place by the following spring. It was all that Snapdragon could have hoped for, yet still he felt uneasy.

"I'll say this much," Seraphina stated as they rode off. "The magistrate of Erd is someone I'd rather not have to meet with again."

"Selene? Yes, she is rather…intense. Did you see her smile?" Snapdragon asked.

Seraphina seemed to think a moment before she responded. "What about her smile? I don't recall anything strange about it."

"You misunderstand my question," Snapdragon said. "I wasn't asking if there was anything about her smile, I was asking if you had seen her smile at all."

Seraphina shook her head. "Come to think of it, no, I don't recall her smiling."

"As I said before, a very intense person. To her credit, things seem to be running well in the town. I thought it would be more rowdy, but it was rather subdued, if that is the word I'm looking for."

Seraphina bit off a harsh laugh. "I think subdued is as good a word as any. The people in town were acting like a dog that is trying to avoid the attention of its master for fear it would get a beating."

They traveled to the village of Stur, which they were told was a day's ride from Procep. Though not more than three hundred or so people lived in Stur, it had a tavern with several rooms to rent for the night. There were also indications that of the three hundred people, several were new families who had moved there, no doubt after they had heard of the new opportunities that would soon be available in the area.

In fact, as they traveled from Stur to Procep the next day, there were several groups setting up homes along where the wall would be built. Snapdragon greeted as many of these people as possible, promising them that there would be work enough for everyone to do soon, and fair pay to go with it.

Near sundown, they arrived at Procep. Snapdragon had to simply stop and stare when he arrived. The once tiny village had exploded into a booming town over the course of just a few months. All along the outskirts were neatly plowed fields, some already harvested.

The people of Eddinh had been busy. There were well-marked roads and strong-looking stone buildings that resembled those in the cave where they had come from. The old village of Procep was now the town center, with many of the houses built up and expanded.

They found Bearach covered in sweat and soot at a blacksmith shop, looking as happy as they had ever seen him.

"Snapdragon! Seraphina!" the crafter shouted upon seeing them arrive. He took off his apron and after waiting for them to dismount, gave them each a giant hug.

"It looks like you have already been busy," Snapdragon said, motioning around him.

Bearach looked surprised. "Me? I got here just a couple of days ago. They had already gotten the smith set up. These people from Eddinh are very industrious. And the people from Procep are hard workers. We've just been waiting for you to give us some direction on what to do."

Snapdragon took a deep breath. "Well then, let's get to work."

CHAPTER 55

Seven Years Later

"Dad," Reed complained, "that's not fair!"

"Yeah, Daddy, dat's not fair!" Diantha echoed.

Snapdragon eyed his two young children. "Fair or not, that's the way it is."

"But Dad, I'm almost six now. You said I could go with you when I'm six!" the little red headed boy said. He was tall for his age, and looking at him, you would guess he had seen at least eight winters.

Diantha chimed in again as well. "Yeah, Daddy, and I'm almost..." she stopped and whispered to her older brother, "How old am I again?"

"Three," Reed whispered back.

"Yeah! I'm three! And dat's almost six!"

Where Reed took after his father, Diantha was a miniature of her mother. She, too, had red hair. Despite neither Snapdragon nor Seraphina promoting the notion, Diantha knew she was cute and that she could often get her way with people if she played upon that trait.

"Well, last time I checked, being *almost* six is not the same as *being* six," Snapdragon said. "I won't be gone long. I just need to go to Stur for a couple of days and I'll be back."

Sticking out her lower lip, Diantha said, "You always have to go places."

Snapdragon lowered himself down to her eye level. "When I get back, we'll play with the wooden sword your Uncle Bearach made for you, all right?"

"Aw right, Daddy," Diantha said, sounding defeated.

"I don't want to play swords. Will you at least let grandpa show me how to trim the bushes?" Reed asked, sounding like he was trying to win something from the loss.

Snapdragon's parents had been visiting for the last several weeks. They had come up "just to see their grandchildren," but Snapdragon knew better. His wife was due to have their third child soon, and despite Seraphina's insistence that she didn't need help, it was nice to have his mother along to help—especially now that he and his wife would soon be out numbered.

Reed had taken quite the interest in his grandfather's activities. Snapdragon's father, Garth, was the castle gardener, and had an amazing ability to work with plant life. Though Snapdragon wished his son took an interest in becoming a guardian, it was becoming more apparent that he had no interest in doing so. Diantha, on the other hand...

"Sure," Snapdragon said to his son. "In fact, why don't you make sure to stay close to grandpa and keep him out of trouble."

Reed beamed. "I can do that! Thank you, Daddy!"

⋙✠⋘

Snapdragon hugged his wife as well as he could, which wasn't easy due to the size of her ever expanding belly.

"This is the last trip you will take before the baby comes," Seraphina stated.

Snapdragon smiled. "That didn't sound like a question."

"It wasn't one. And it wasn't a request. It is a fact," she said.

After all these years, Snapdragon knew better than to disagree with his wife when she had taken on that tone.

"All right," Snapdragon conceded. "This is the last trip. I just need to see Bearach before I go, and then I'll be leaving. The sooner I go, the sooner I can return."

Seraphina said, "Then you better leave now."

He brought her close, hugged her with his left arm and gave her a long kiss. "If you do give birth while I'm gone, just don't let my father name our next child. I don't think I could handle a daughter named Mistletoe or a son named Stinkweed."

⋙✠⋘

Enoch slowly opened his eyes. The light was just bright enough in his room that he knew he had to get up. He had to rise with the sun if he were to get his morning chores done before going to train with the militia.

Climbing out of his bed of hay, he dusted off the stray strands that stuck to his rough woolen sleeping tunic. It had been another rough night. He had woken twice with sharp pains in his legs, like someone had tied his muscles into knots. He had had to massage them for a good long while just to be able to lie down and try to get some more sleep.

He had asked one of the nursemaids in Stur about what could be causing them. She reassured him that it was normal for boys to get those during their growing years. And growing, he had been. Putting on his breeches, he noticed they were a good hand span above his ankles now. Kerr had told him he'd get him more clothes, but Enoch didn't want to be a bother.

Although when he looked at his boots, he thought he should reconsider. They were so small now, his toes were pinched up and he could barely get them on.

Enoch was grateful for the mayor taking him in and giving him food, clothing and shelter. While Kerr was a father figure of sorts to him, Kerr insisted that Enoch call him by his first name. The mayor had married a few years after taking over Stur. They had had children of their own. Enoch was older and larger than all of them, and he certainly didn't look like the rest of the family. While they included him in all the family activities, he still felt like an outsider.

He knew that being an orphan was something people in Erd frowned upon, though he wasn't sure why. From what he understood, it wasn't always that way. It wasn't his fault his parents had died. He didn't even remember them. When he asked about them, all that Kerr would say was, "They would have raised you if they had a chance—but sometimes fate has different plans for us."

Enoch didn't believe much in fate or chance. Even from a young age he believed there was a reason for everything that happened. He was sure that was due to the influence of the people from Eddinh. One of the things they brought with them from beyond the mountains was the concept that people were responsible for their own actions.

He replaced his sleeping tunic with his work tunic and then forced on his boots. He squinted a little at the rising sun as he walked to where the cows were waiting to be milked. He enjoyed the activity because it gave him time to think.

⊰✦⊱

"Enoch!" Kerr called.

He looked up from milking the cow before he responded, "Yes, sir?"

"I need you to go to Scimron to check on their progress. Come see me when you finish."

"As you say."

This wasn't the first time Enoch had been sent as a messenger, and he didn't mind it. In fact, anything he could do to help, he was more than willing to do. Scimron was a third of a day's walk toward the west. It was right up against the wall, as were most of the settlements in the area.

Enoch finished his chores and then after cleaning up his appearance, went to see Kerr. He found the man that raised him standing outside what had become the village center. There were several people vying for the mayor's attention. Enoch knew Kerr well enough that the more the people pressed him, the harder he would press back.

"I understand! Really I do!" Kerr shouted to the people. "But you must give me time. I've sent a messenger to Procep and expect to hear word as soon as possible. Please, go about your business. I will inform everyone once I've heard."

Though many of the people didn't seem completely satisfied, the group did disperse. Kerr noticed Enoch standing on the edge of the group and motioned him to come over.

Kerr took Enoch by the shoulders. "Before you go, I have a few things for you."

"Oh?"

"Now don't you be thinking I've not noticed how fast you've grown. I'm sure those boots you're wearing are too small now. And I know you well enough were you wouldn't ask for new clothes or complain about what you have." He motioned to the building behind him—the village office. "There's a new outfit for you in there. Get changed before you go."

Enoch felt tears well up in the corner of his eyes. "Thank you."

"It's the least I can do, Enoch. You've been a huge help to me." The older man looked like he was going to say more, but then just grinned. "Off with you now."

"I'll be back before dark."

⁂

The news from Scimron was promising. The wall was almost completed.

Enoch stayed long enough to talk to several of the merchants, who, he found, tended to be a great source of information. This was no doubt due to the number of people they helped and the traders that brought in goods from other areas.

Convinced he got the information he was sent for, Enoch headed back towards Stur.

On the edge of the village, he noticed a young boy cringing at the sight of two larger boys walking toward him. The smaller boy crossed to the other side of the road, but when he crossed, so did the other two.

Enoch was following behind the two larger boys, who he guessed were about his same age. While Enoch wouldn't turn fourteen for a few more months, he looked several years older than that. He'd been training with the young men preparing for the Mortentaun, and those who were in the militia, and was able to hold his own, despite his young age.

The two older boys shouted something to the young boy, something Enoch didn't quite hear. Whatever it was, it seemed to frighten the young boy even more. That wasn't fair. The little boy hadn't done anything wrong that he could tell—why would the bigger boys be picking on him? Enoch increased his pace to close the gap.

When the bigger boys reached the younger one, they started shoving him around and calling him names. Enoch was not a violent person. At the same time, he didn't like it when things weren't fair.

He came up from behind the older boys, and placed his hands on their shoulders. "That's enough."

The bullies spun around to face him and one of them started to say, "Yeah, what are you gonna…" He stopped when he looked up, and then up some more at Enoch.

"Just go home and let him go on his way," Enoch said in a deep, but soft voice.

They glanced at each other, then nodding, turned and walked away.

Enoch approached the young boy who was looking at him in awe.

"Are you alright?" Enoch asked.

The boy simply nodded yes.

"What's your name?"

"Giles," the boy responded.

Enoch offered him his hand. "My name is Enoch."

"Enoch? Aren't you the *orphan* who lives with the mayor of Kerr?" Giles asked.

The way Giles said "orphan" made it sound like it was a disease. However, Enoch had grown accustomed to it and pressed on. "Aye, that be me. But let me ask you, where are your parents, Giles?"

Biting his lower lip, Giles responded, "My Mum and Dad are goat herders. They sent me into town to tell Cordell we'll need seven less ropes taken from our order. Cordell gets mad when he makes things for us and then we don't end up needing them. It's been a rough year for our herd…"

"I see," Enoch said thoughtfully. "Will you be all right getting back to your parents?"

Giles nodded his head. "I will be now, thank you. Those boys are mean. When I get to be your size, I'll show them."

Shaking his head slightly, Enoch asked, "What good would that do? You can be better than that. You can *show* them by acting better than that. Just because they were bigger than you, it didn't give them the right to bully you around—anymore than it gives me the right to bully them around. Don't you see? It takes more courage to *not* be like them."

Giles looked at Enoch skeptically before responding, "I don't know…"

"Promise me you'll think about it, alright?" Enoch asked, smiling encouragingly.

Biting his lower lip again, Giles looked down and didn't respond.

"Giles?"

"All right, I promise," Giles conceded.

⊰⧉⊱

Enoch sat on top of a watchtower and looked out into the evening sky. It was a clear night, with the stars filling the heavens with countless points of twinkling lights. Kerr sat next to him, as they often did to wrap of the events of the day.

"Thank you again, Enoch, for going to Scimron."

"You're welcome."

"Did you run into any trouble?"

Enoch shrugged. "Not really."

"What do you mean by 'not really'?" Kerr faced Enoch.

Continuing to look at the sky, Enoch responded, "There were just a couple of boys who were picking on a younger lad. I told them to stop."

"And did they? Stop, that is."

"Yeah," Enoch said, "but I didn't hurt them. I guess they were just scared of me."

For a moment neither one of them spoke. Then quietly, Enoch said, "A lot of people are scared of me."

He felt Kerr place a hand on his back, as a way to comfort him. "These are strange times, Enoch. People are afraid of a lot of things. Even though the people of Eddinh have been nothing but helpful, there are those that are leery of them. Both Creighton and I have been treated differently since we married women that came from beyond the mountains—which is too bad, because our wives are wonderful."

"It also doesn't help than I'm an orphan," Enoch lamented.

Kerr reached up and clasped Enoch on the shoulder, then turned the younger man to face him. "You have no reason to feel like a lesser person. In fact, you have shown me you are quite wise for your years. Other young men your size would use that to their advantage, especially if they had been teased for being an orphan. But not you. You've always tried to be a good lad, haven't you?"

"I don't like it when people are upset at me. It seems that if I do what I'm supposed to do, then people don't get mad as often."

"And is that the only reason you try to be good?" Kerr asked.

Enoch thought for a moment before he responded. "I guess also because I feel better inside when I'm good."

"As well you should," Kerr said. He then pointed to a bright star in the sky. "Do you remember what the people of Eddinh call that star?"

Confused by the sudden change of subject, Kerr answered, "I don't think so."

"They call it the 'Zealous Star'. Unlike the other stars in the sky, it doesn't move with the seasons. It stays constant, regardless of what else may be going on around it."

"The Zealous Star?" Enoch asked. "I don't understand. What does this have to do with people being afraid of me? Are you saying people are afraid of a bright star in the sky as well?"

"Afraid? No. As for why I pointed it out to you, I want you to give it some thought. You're a smart lad. Very smart, in fact." Kerr patted him on the back. "Let's get home, shall we?"

Enoch didn't move. "If it's all right with you, I want to stay up here a bit longer."

"Sure," Kerr said. "Just don't be up too late. We have another big day ahead of us tomorrow."

He watched as Kerr descended the steps of the watchtower. Enoch then turned back toward the star Kerr had pointed out, or the Zealous Star, as it had been called. He stared at it for a long time, pondering what Kerr has said.

CHAPTER 56
Thirteen Years Later

Diantha looked into the full length mirror and frowned. Her hair was glistening like spun copper in the sunlight. Her dress was a deep blue with intricate yellow trim which was tailored specifically for her sixteen year old body. The emerald earrings and necklace she wore matched the sparkling of her eyes. As her father would say, she was a "vision of beauty."

She hated it.

Spinning away from the mirror, Diantha picked up her practice wooden sword and swung it around a few times. The dress confined her movements, which added to her frustration. She swung harder, moving into one of the many fighting stances she had been learning.

She switched forms and swung again, this time with more force. That's when she felt the dress rip. Apparently, the sound was loud enough to get her younger sister's attention.

"What are you doing?" asked the thirteen-year-old Winter upon entering Diantha's chambers.

Diantha quickly hid the sword behind her back. "Nothing, Winter, go away."

Winter's brown eyes grew wide. Pointing, she said, "You've ripped your dress! Oh, Mom is going to kill you."

Diantha walked over and grabbed her little sister by the arm. "Not if she doesn't find out. Quickly, go get a seamstress!"

"Just because you're three years older than me doesn't mean you can boss me around," Winter said, shaking away Diantha's grip and then putting her hands on her hips.

Diantha winced. She knew better than to argue with Winter when her sister took that stance. "What do you want?"

"Promise me we'll play dolls tomorrow—all afternoon, and I'll go get a seamstress," Winter bargained.

Diantha sighed. "You know I hate playing dolls."

"All right, I'll go tell Mom about how you ripped your dress and—"

"Fine! We'll play dolls tomorrow. Just hurry and go get a seamstress. Princess Rainbow's wedding is at nightfall. I need to get my dress fixed by then."

"Shake on it." Winter extended a hand.

Diantha gritted her teeth, brought her right hand from behind her back, took her sister's hand and then shook it forcefully.

"Ow! Not so hard!" Winter said, pulling her hand away and nursing it. "I'm not one of those boys you play swords with."

Diantha gave up and tossed her sword from behind her back to her bed. "All right, I'm sorry," the redhead said, sounding anything *but* sorry. "Just go get the seamstress."

"Say please."

It was Diantha's turn to have her eyes grow wide, but it was from her temper and not from surprise.

"Please."

"Say pretty please with strawberries on top."

Diantha said through a clenched jaw, "Pretty please with strawberries on top."

"See? All you had to do was ask nicely… and agree to play dolls with me." Winter smirked before leaving the room.

⊰⧊⊱

King Rayne reached down and took his wife by the hand. He squeezed it gently. Queen Sunshine looked at her husband and smiled.

"Isn't she lovely?" Rayne asked, watching his daughter dance with her new husband.

Sunshine could see tears forming in her husband's eyes. "Are you crying?" she asked playfully.

Wiping away the moisture from his eyes, Rayne said, "Not at all. It must be all the perfume in the air."

The castle's main hall was filled for the wedding reception for Princess Rainbow and her husband Elisedd. The young couple was in the middle of the hall, having the traditional first dance of the evening. Rainbow's dark hair shimmered against her white dress, and she smiled when she saw her parents watching.

"It's almost your turn," Sunshine reminded her husband. "Just try not to trip."

Rayne grimaced. "You know I don't like to dance. I'm nervous about it as it is. Saying things like that isn't helping."

"Perhaps you should let Rainbow lead," the queen suggested. "She's an excellent dancer."

Before Rayne could retort, the music ended and everyone clapped politely. Rayne glanced back at his wife while making his way to dance with his daughter. Sunshine was motioning again for him to let his daughter lead, a teasing smile on her lips.

Elisedd bowed to Rayne upon his arrival. Rayne nodded and then let Elisedd give his new bride over to the king for the next dance.

Rainbow smiled up at her father, waiting for the music to start.

"Would you like me to lead?" she asked, grinning.

Rayne rolled his eyes. "Not you too."

The music started, a traditional waltz with which Rayne was familiar. He tried to focus on his footwork, and resisted the urge to look down to watch his feet. Rainbow glided from step to step, swept up in the music. Her blue eyes twinkled as she watched her father concentrate.

"Have I told you how happy I am for you?" he asked.

"Only about one hundred and thirty eight times," Rainbow replied lightly.

Rayne paused a moment, thinking forward to the next set of steps before he spoke again.

"Elisedd is a wonderful young man, and will make an excellent king. He's got a good head on his shoulders and is very genuine in his actions."

Rainbow spared a quick glance to her husband. "Aye, he reminds me of someone else I know very well." She squeezed her father's hand in emphasis to make her meaning clear. "I'm glad I was allowed to choose my own husband instead of having one arranged for me."

"We can thank your mother and Magistrate Bertram for that," Rayne responded. "Had they not discovered the error in The Tome of Laws, you could have easily been married to Goran."

Rainbow shuddered. "Thank goodness I wasn't forced to. I wonder if that man has taken a bath in his life—plus all he wanted to talk about was hunting for wild game. He fancied himself quite the mountain man."

The music picked up tempo slightly, indicating the dance was coming to an end. "Shush now, I need to focus on these last few steps," Rayne said, perking his ears up to the music.

Father and daughter danced around the middle of the hall to the completion of the music. Rayne, to his credit, didn't step on his daughter's toes. As the music ended, Rainbow gave her father a big hug and whispered, "I love you, Daddy."

⊰⧉⊱

Prochorus bowed deeply before Diantha and asked, "May I have this dance?"

He was a couple of years older than her, and the son of a wealthy merchant. He wore a heavily embroidered deep blue coat over his white ruffled shirt. The coat was cinched at the waist, but ran down to his knees. His bright yellow stockings were tucked into blue velvet shoes. Diantha thought he looked ridiculous.

"You certainly may," Diantha said, her voice flat. "Just with someone else."

The young man blinked, and then turned somewhat red in the cheeks before backing away.

"That wasn't very nice," Winter said to her older sister.

Diantha responded, "Did you see how he was dressed? That poor boy would probably faint if he chipped a fingernail."

Winter giggled. "You're probably right, but that still wasn't nice."

"Then why don't *you* go dance with him?" Diantha countered.

"I'm only thirteen! I don't want to dance yet."

Diantha folded her arms, and stuck out her lower lip. "Well, I'm sixteen and I don't want to dance yet either."

"But you dance with boys all the time!" Winter pointed out.

Diantha raised an eyebrow. "I do not."

"Sure you do—you just do it with a practice sword in your hand."

"That's different," Diantha said, defensively. "That's not dancing— that's fighting."

Winter harrumphed. "Well, it looks like a dance to me when you are doing it."

⊰⧉⊱

Garth padded his grandson Reed on the shoulder. "That's it. Perfect."

"What's it, Grandfather?" Reed asked, standing up and wiping away the dirt from his hands on his apron.

The men stood in the middle of the royal gardens of Bariwon. Garth had accepted the position of castle gardener when his daughter Sunshine became queen. By right, he could have taken on the title of councilor and aided in the running of the kingdom. But as he told her at the time, "The flowers and trees would miss me." And he meant it. Though both of his sons, Oakleaf and Snapdragon, had become royal guardians and his daughter, Sunshine, became a savant before she married Rayne and was crowned queen, Garth never had the desire to do anything more than be a gardener. It appeared that this trait skipped a generation as Reed had followed in his footsteps.

"You've made the flora happy," Garth said. He motioned to the flowerbed in front of them.

Reed crinkled up his nose while he looked over his work. "They do seem to be smiling more, don't they?"

The elderly gardener nodded. "That they are."

"Thank you, Grandfather," Reed said.

"You are thanking me because you made the flowers happy?" Garth asked.

"They are smiling because you showed me how to help them do so."

Tearing up slightly, Garth said, "You should thank your father and mother as well. I'm sure there is a lot of pressure for you to become a guardian. They have let you follow your heart."

"I still have two more winters before I would compete in the Mortentaun," Reed reminded his grandfather. "But I've made it clear so far that I have no interest in competing. They've respected that."

"As well they should," Garth said.

"I was thinking, Grandfather," Reed said.

"Thinking is good, it is better than the alternative."

Reed continued, "Perhaps I could move here to the castle and stay with you. Mom and Dad say that since grandmother passed away you hardly speak to anyone. You just stay in the gardens. I believe there is a lot I can learn from you. Even more than gardening."

The older man's eyes were now full of tears, streaming down his cheeks. "I talk to her, still, here among the trees, bushes and flowers."

"But does she answer?"

Garth reached up and caressed the pink blossoms of a nearby tree. "In her own way." Without taking his eyes off the blossoms, Garth said, "I would be honored if my grandson would stay with me and become my apprentice."

"Wonderful!" Reed said. "I'll tell my folks over dinner."

"Yes, that will do." Garth turned and faced Reed. He placed his hand on his grandson's shoulder. "Now, let's go see what we can do about those two dogwood trees in the front courtyard. They seem to have taken on a different life recently."

⋰⧓⋱

Seraphina snuggled up close to her husband. Snapdragon was sitting on the floor in front of their castle room's fireplace, reading what looked to be a copy of The Tome of Laws. It had been nice to get away from Procep for a few weeks. While they had built a fine home for themselves there, part of her really missed the castle.

Rubbing a hand along his back, she peered down at the book. Yes, it was The Tome of Laws.

"Thinking about becoming a savant, sweetheart?" she asked.

Not taking his eyes off the book, Snapdragon said, "I don't think they would take me. I'm not sure I have the patience to copy books and teach children."

"Well," Seraphina said, "you are wrong about the last part. You are actually very good at teaching children. After all, wasn't it just yesterday you were with the thirteen and fourteen year-olds in guardian training?"

Snapdragon nodded, still focused on the book.

Whatever it was that he was looking for, Seraphina knew her husband well enough that he would become frustrated soon if he didn't find it.

"So, what is it then?" she asked.

"Diantha."

She moved behind him and got on her knees, then rested her chin on his shoulder while looking down into the book. "I'm pretty sure our daughter isn't hiding in The Tome of Laws," she teased.

Snapdragon didn't say anything.

She leaned over and kissed her husband on the earlobe. "Maybe if you tell me what you are looking for, I can help you," she whispered in his ear.

The whisper and the kiss was enough to get his attention. He closed the book and set it down.

"Diantha told me today that she wants to become a royal guardian," Snapdragon stated.

Seraphina stiffened up in surprise. She moved to his side and asked, "She really said that?"

"Yes." Snapdragon frowned. "She said if Queen Sunshine could become the first female savant, then she could become the first female royal guardian."

Seraphina thought a moment. "At least it wasn't Reed telling you he wanted to become the first male nursemaid."

"The thing is he could if he wanted to. In The Tome of Laws, it never states that you have to be male to be a savant or female to be a nursemaid—it has just been traditionally so. However, when it mentions about becoming a royal guardian…" Snapdragon let his voice trail off.

"It's quite clear it's a men's only club, right?" Seraphina asked, starting to get upset.

Snapdragon sighed. "Not you as well. I was honestly looking for a way that she could become one if she wanted to. But The Tome of Laws is quite clear about it. And by the way, it isn't a 'men's only club' as you said."

Seraphina bit back her reply. There was no use getting mad at her husband. It wasn't his fault. "So, what are you going to tell her?"

Gazing into the fire, Snapdragon said, "The truth."

⇥╪⇤

"But that's not fair!" Diantha shouted at her father.

"Diantha…"

The sixteen year old was looking more and more like her mother every day, though it did appear that she was going to be taller and more muscular. His daughter was usually very respectful, but like her mother, and for that matter most of the redheads he knew, she had a quick and passionate temper.

"Well, it's not!"

"I've gone to your Aunt Sunshine and had her double check with the Hierarchy of Magistrates, and the law is quite clear that only men can become guardians, royal or otherwise."

Diantha looked at her father and he saw tears start to form in her green eyes. "But Dad, I just can't… I mean I don't want to…"

"Can't or don't want to do what, sweetheart?" Snapdragon asked, beckoning her to come closer.

It appeared as if she fought the idea, but then acquiesced and came to where her father could give her a comforting hug. "I don't want to dress up like a doll when I grow up. I don't want to have to go to parties and balls and be expected to entertain boys who just want to kiss me. I'm sure that Winter will be good at that, but I don't want to."

"Well then, what do you want to do?" asked Snapdragon.

Diantha sniffled and then said, "I want to do what you told me I can't."

⇥╪⇤

Governor Wardell of Erd lay on what he knew was going to be his deathbed. It had happened so suddenly. Just last week he had been feeling fine, but then two days ago, he'd started to feel queasy. The nursemaids were not sure what to do for him. By yesterday, he couldn't even stand on his own two feet, and today he lacked the strength to lift his head off his pillow. He had heard of such illnesses happening to others; he'd never thought it would happen to him. His wife, Samara, was by his side, and had been since yesterday.

The nursemaids said the best they could do was to make him comfortable. It was getting harder to breathe. He looked to his wife and saw that she was holding his hand, though he couldn't feel it.

At least the district would be in good hands when he left. Yesterday, while he'd still had the ability to do so, he had signed the documents declaring that Magistrate Selene would be his successor. She had been good at keeping the peace in the district over the years. It was good of her to suggest that she be allowed to continue to help Erd as its governor.

Was it getting darker in the room? My, the day went by quickly. Wardell labored through another breath. He smiled at his wife, or at least he tried to. He wasn't sure if his body was even being responsive enough to smile. It was getting darker still. The sun was in a hurry to set today. Maybe it wasn't night after all. Perhaps the sun was being hidden by a storm.

Those were the last thoughts Wardell had before he took his last breath.

※

Selene smiled.

If she got nothing else from her ancestors, Selene had inherited the ability to be patient. For generations her family had kept the secret of the Rifna Erd. It was a shame that it had to be a secret; a shame that people blamed the noble Rifna Erd for the nislles—a plague that had swept over Bariwon. Even worse was when word came that the Rifna Erd had been found, living north of what were thought to be impassible mountains, and the reports were that they were savages. It could not be true! Passionate in their beliefs, most certainly. But savages? It just showed the ignorance of the people of Bariwon.

Then, at the time of what should have been their glorious return, they had been stopped. Stopped by King Rayne and his men. Soon after, former Councilor Abrecan had been killed at the castle when he was trying to escape.

And it was time she needed for her to gather enough supporters for her next plan. Most of her former supporters had been killed trying to free Abrecan. It had taken over a decade and a half, but she would be able to move soon. The first step was to rid the district of Rayne's puppet, Governor Wardell. The poison he had been given had worked as promised, and he'd stayed alive long enough to sign the documents making her the next governor of Erd.

As for the next step, that was something that would take a few more years. But again, she was patient, and it would be worth the wait.

CHAPTER 57

Two Years Later

Amon fell to the ground, gasping for breath. He had taken a hard blow to his chest—harder than he thought possible from his opponent. Amon's two friends kept up the attack, but seemed to be losing ground to their solitary foe. They were all dressed in leather armor, including gloves and caps to help protect them in battle. Even with that protection, Amon knew he would be bruised in several places after the fight.

"Go behind!" one of his friends shouted to the other.

Their foe side-stepped quickly, preventing the move. Appearing frustrated, one of Amon's friends lunged in, only to have his sword not only blocked, but twisted out of his hand and sent flying out of reach.

The remaining armed man, who stood a good head taller than his foe, licked his lips, seeming nervous. Amon tried to stand, but still hadn't caught his breath. He knew that without his help, his friend was doomed—even though he had a longer reach and weighed more. Their opponent was too quick and accurate. One of them by themselves didn't stand a chance.

As if reading Amon's mind, the tall fighter tossed his sword away and shouted, "I yield!"

For a moment, Amon thought their foe was still going to press the attack. Instead, the talented fighter removed her leather cap. Red hair flowed down and cascaded over her shoulders.

"You yielded too quickly!" She sounded angry. "How am I supposed to get better if you quit on me just when it's getting good?"

Finally finding his breath, Amon answered, "I don't see why you are trying so hard, Diantha. You can't become a guardian. We're just being nice by letting you practice with us."

"Nice?" she asked, her nostrils flaring. She took two steps towards Amon, who was still on his back. She thrust her sword in his face, a hand span away from his nose. "When the Rifna Erd come back, do you think *they* will be nice? Do you think they will care if I have a title or not when they attack? I'm not going to be one of those damsels in distress waiting to be saved when we get attacked. I intend to have them regret coming to Bariwon."

Amon put his hands up. "I know your father is in charge of the defenses, and it's his job to believe that the Rifna Erd will return, but it's been over twenty-two years since they came through the tunnel. And if I'm not mistaken, it's been at least two years since Commander Snapdragon told you that the Tome of Laws doesn't allow women to be guardians. I honestly can't see why you are pushing yourself so hard. I think you're wasting your time."

His commander's red haired daughter stared at him for a moment. He thought he saw an instant where she looked like she might cry, but that was fleeting as a stone faced expression replaced any sign of weakness.

"Then I feel sorry for you," she said. "Mark my words, when the Rifna Erd return—and they will—you'll wish you had trained harder."

⋗⊰⊱⋖

"I'll be leaving soon," Snapdragon said to Bearach.

Both men were standing on a tower, three stories high, that overlooked the section where the tunnel had been collapsed. A containment area surrounded the old mineshaft. It was a stone wall, four paces thick and two stories high. If the Rifna Erd were to come through the same way they had before, they would be trapped.

Fortunately, the mountains contained an excellent supply of stone for the structures they were building. Bearach had insisted they dig further up the mountain, above and to the right of the containment area. It made sense, because once stone was removed from the quarry, Bearach let the slope of the mountain be the primary force to bring the stones down to the wagons that would carry it off to their destinations. A large section of the quarry had been sectioned off to make a man-made lake. Aqueducts had been built from the lake, bringing water to the people of Procep.

Outward from the main tower was a stone wall that went as far as they could see in either direction. It, too, was two stories high and thick enough that it would be easier to climb over than knock down. All in all, it was an amazing achievement.

"So, off to Stur then?" Bearach said.

"Yeah. It's been awhile since I've visited them. Kerr has done a great job as mayor, and he sent me a note that he'd like to talk with me when I was free."

"Hmm. Any idea what about?"

Snapdragon shrugged. "Nope. It's been quiet—aside from the usual disagreements that happen between people. Last time I was in Stur, I was asked to mediate between—"

"Father!" Diantha's angry voice came from the stairway.

"Uh oh," Bearach said under his breath.

Snapdragon looked at his old friend and rolled his eyes.

"Yes?" he called.

He heard her stomping her feet as she came up the stairs. When she came into view, she was wearing leather armor, the kind used in sparring.

"Father, you need to talk to Amon. He's being difficult."

"The captain of Procep's militia is being difficult?" Snapdragon sounded incredulous.

"Yes! He's holding back when I practice with them. And then today, he told me I was wasting my time!"

"Sweetheart, we've talked about this."

"No we haven't."

"Diantha, yes we have."

She folded her arms. "Fine. Yes, you've told me I couldn't be a guardian. But, you didn't say anything about not being able to join the militia."

Snapdragon spared a glance at Bearach. His friend held up his hands in a gesture that told Snapdragon he was on his own.

"Diantha, sweetheart, it's a moot point to discuss right now. You have to be twenty-one to be in the militia. You still have three years before you'd be eligible."

"So? Are you saying everyone should wait until they are twenty-one before they start to train?"

He knew that when she was in her current mood there would be no reasoning with her.

"Listen, I'm headed to Stur right now. I'll be back in a few days. I promise you we'll discuss it when I get back, all right?"

"If by 'discuss' you mean you'll agree to let me train with them, then fine."

"That's not what I meant. And until I get back, stay away from the militia. Do you understand?"

Her response was to glare at him and then walk back down the stairs.

-»⁑«-

Diantha was too upset to go home. There was no use talking with her mother. She wouldn't understand. Both of her parents had agreed to let her learn some basic combat skills, but Diantha enjoyed it and realized she was good. She had practiced every free moment while growing up. And now, she was better than anyone in the militia. They knew it. She knew it. Why didn't her parents see it?

When she stated she wanted to compete in the Shoginoc to become a royal guardian, she'd been told that wasn't possible. The Tome of Laws, the book the rulers of Bariwon followed, stated that only young men could compete. Diantha had been angry, and even petitioned her cousin, Queen Rainbow, but to no avail.

Instead of going home, Diantha went to Bearach's house. Though they weren't related by blood, she'd called him Uncle Bearach her whole life. And Bearach's daughter, Rosalind, was like a cousin to her.

Bearach's house was like many of the newer buildings. The old village of Procep was now the town center, with many of the houses built up and expanded. The newer buildings were made from stone and were fashioned after the buildings in Eddinh—a village north of the mountains that had been liberated by her father.

Diantha paused a moment and then knocked on the front door. Rosalind answered.

"Hello, Di." She noticed the leather armor. "It looks like you've been playing with the boys again."

"Jealous?" Diantha was still seething and not in the mood for levity.

"Me? Jealous?" Rosalind answered, ignoring Diantha's harsh reply. "I can think of many different things I'd rather do with boys than play swords with them. Anyway, come in, come in."

"Thanks," Diantha said.

They sat down on a padded bench by the front window.

"You're not working with my dad at the smithy today?"

"Not today. He's overseeing some work on the wall. It gave me a chance to spar with the militia."

"So, even when you're not working in a sooty building, you're finding a way to keep your strength up, eh?" Rosalind teased her.

"Your dad is one of the few that takes me seriously," Diantha responded between gritted teeth.

"Relax, Di, relax. I take you seriously, even if I don't understand it."

Diantha let out a frustrated breath. "You don't understand because you're like my little sister—all pretty dresses and having your hair just so."

"Yes, Winter is a very girly girl. You know, it wouldn't hurt you to get dolled up once in a while. There are plenty of available men with a militia unit stationed here. We could go tonight to one of the taverns. I know a good one that—"

"I'm not in the mood."

Rosalind chuckled. "Obviously."

"What do you mean by that?"

"I know you. You're spoiling for a fight—but you've already had one. That's why you came here instead of going home. You knew you'd get into a fight with your mom. Am I right?"

Diantha hesitated. "Maybe."

"You need to calm down. Relax. Do something fun."

Maybe Rosalind was right. Maybe she needed to find another way to blow off steam.

"All right, fine. Let's go."

"Oh no, no. You can't go looking like that."

"How am I supposed to look then?"

Rosalind smiled.

⇥❋⇤

The tavern was full—the work was done for the day, at least for everyone but the barmaids and tavern owner.

Heads turned when Diantha and Rosalind entered. Several of the men looked at Diantha appreciatively until they recognized her; then they found a sudden interest in their drinks.

"Isn't this better than fighting?" Rosalind asked.

"Not yet."

Diantha felt uncomfortable. It wasn't from the attention—she was used to that. Not only was she the commander's daughter, but she heard time and again how much she looked like her mother—a woman considered to be the most beautiful in town. Her clothes caused the discomfort.

"You look so pretty in that dress," Rosalind said. "I should have lent it to you sooner."

Aside from the tightly fitted dress, Rosalind had insisted on adding more touches, like multicolored beads run through a few strands of her hair. The other woman also insisted on matching earrings with a silver, teardrop shaped disc at the bottom. The last accessory was a silver bracelet on her left wrist—a hand-span wide with shimmering green stripes near each end.

"I feel like an animal on display."

"Nonsense. Come on. Let's get a drink. The spiced cider here is delicious and it doesn't make you go all funny in the head."

Before Diantha could protest, Rosalind waded into the crowd.

Men made room for Diantha as she followed, as if they were afraid to touch her. *Good*, she thought. *They* should *be afraid.*

Rosalind was at the bar and talking to one of the barmaids when Diantha arrived. The barmaid looked up at Diantha and then said, "They'll be on the house."

"Why, thank you!" Rosalind said.

The barmaid nodded to them and went to fetch the drinks.

"You knew they wouldn't charge us if I came, didn't you?" Diantha asked.

Rosalind blinked at her innocently. "Being the commander's daughter has its benefits."

"Your father is just as important," Diantha said. "He designed the northern wall, after all."

Her friend shook her head. "People appreciate might over mind, it seems."

The barmaid returned with the ceramic mugs. "There you go. Anything else?"

"Not at the moment," Rosalind said.

Diantha took a sip of the spiced cider. It was warm, but not scalding. Rosalind was right; it was delicious—and soothing.

"Hello, ladies," a voice said behind Diantha. "Wonderful to see you as always, Rosalind. Who's your friend?"

Diantha recognized the voice, though she couldn't see his face.

"I believe you've met." Rosalind smiled.

"Oh? I think I would have remembered someone as—"

He stopped talking when Diantha turned around. "Hello, Amon."

"Diantha?" He looked stunned.

"Perhaps I hit you too hard today if you can't remember me."

"I—I—I've just never seen you dressed as a..."

"Lady?" Rosalind prompted when Amon stopped talking.

Amon looked at the two women then backed away into the crowd without saying anything else.

"Why are you smiling?" Rosalind asked. "You chased him away."

"I have my reasons," Diantha replied.

The two of them spoke for a while more. The Festival of Gratitude was in a few months and people were already planning on what to give their loved ones.

"What about your brother?" Rosalind asked. "What'll give him?"

"Reed? Oh, I don't know. He's a bit strange."

"Strange? And this is coming from a woman who wants to be a guardian?"

Diantha scowled. "*He* should be the guardian. He's big and strong enough."

"His heart was never in it. I knew that from when we were kids. He's too gentle."

"Still, he was born with the ability to defend Bariwon. Instead he's off pulling weeds with his grandfather."

Diantha finished the last of her cider. The barmaid offered another, but she declined.

"But he's happy, from what I hear," Rosalind said.

"I guess. I still think—"

She was interrupted when someone pinched her behind.

Diantha spun around to face an older man that reeked of ale.

"Hey, purty thing," he slurred. "I've not seen you here before."

"How dare you!" Diantha shouted.

"Now, now, sweet thing," he said, eyeing her from head to toe. "Don't be that way."

"Diantha…" Rosalind warned.

There was a drawn out moment, then Diantha asked, "Would you like to dance?"

He didn't seem to pick up on her angry tone. "But there isn't any music," he said.

"It's not that kind of dance."

⋙※⋘

Seraphina folded her arms and frowned at her oldest daughter. Diantha sat at the family table, back straight with her hands clasped tightly in front of her.

"Mom, before you say anything, let me explain," Diantha said.

There was a drawn out moment of uncomfortable silence as Seraphina considered the young woman before her. She was such a stubborn young woman. Whenever she mentioned that to her husband, he would just smile and say, "I wonder where she gets that from?"

"Fine, explain yourself," Seraphina said.

Diantha looked straight ahead when she spoke. "After Amon told me I wouldn't be allowed to train with his men anymore, I complained to dad. And you know what dad said? He agreed with Amon! How am I supposed to get better with no one to fight? I was upset so I went with Rosalind to a tavern to clear my head."

"And so that justifies picking a fight?" Seraphina asked.

This time, Diantha did look at her mother. "I didn't pick the fight. He started it. I just… ended it."

"As I hear it told, you walked into the tavern wearing a frilly dress you borrowed from Rosalind. One of the men was drunk enough that he didn't recognize you as the commander's daughter and took it upon himself to pinch you. Am I right so far?"

"It was Rosalind's idea to dress up. And yes, he pinched me."

Seraphina sighed. "And when he did, you took it upon yourself to knock him senseless."

"He deserved it!"

"Diantha, sweetheart, it's time to face the fact that you can't be what you want to be. You need to consider making yourself available for the men here to court you. As of right now, they're all scared of you."

Her daughter smiled. "Good."

"This is serious!" Seraphina said, trying her best to stay calm. "What are your father and I going to do with you?"

Diantha slowly stood and faced her mom. "I'm old enough now that you and dad don't have to do anything with me."

"Sweetheart…" Seraphina said, realizing what her daughter said was true. Reed had moved out at her same age to live at the castle as his grandfather's apprentice. But the only thing Diantha knew how to do was fight, well, that and work at the smithy with Bearach—neither of which were suitable skills for a young lady. "Let's talk about this more when your father returns from Stur in a couple of days."

The eighteen year old in front of her didn't nod or say anything. She simply turned and went to her room.

CHAPTER 58

The trip between Procep and Stur was one that Snapdragon had made numerous times over the last twenty two years. It was one of the first sections of the defenses that were built. The wall was three times a man's height, and wide enough for a walkway that linked the watchtowers—lookout points spaced within sight of each other.

Snapdragon was amazed by how well people worked when given clear instructions and an explanation of what was expected. From there, each of the foremen took pride in their section of the wall. Any conflicts over resources or work schedules were to be sorted out on the local level with Snapdragon only getting involved if an agreement couldn't be reached.

Despite his wife's misgivings, Snapdragon often made these trips alone. All along the wall were farms, small villages and militia checkpoints. The people that helped build the wall were given land grants as part of their payments, so rarely was Snapdragon out of sight from at least one of these dwellings.

His argument for traveling alone was that he was always needing to deal with *this* visitor, or *that* supervisor, or Mayor Whomever from Such-and-Such a place—trips like this gave him a chance to be alone, a rarity, while still performing his duties.

For twenty two years there had been no sign of the Rifna Erd. However, Alethea was convinced that they had to remain vigilant. Her conviction was strong enough to keep Snapdragon believing it wasn't a matter of *if*, but rather *when*, they would be attacked.

He shook his head and tried to think of more pleasant thoughts. He started to ponder on the upcoming Festival of Gratitude and what gifts he would like to give when he saw several riders approaching from the south.

Snapdragon glanced along the wall and noticed he was in-between villages. A hard ride would get him to a farm about the same time the riders would, but he had no reason to think the riders meant him any harm. Still, it was strange to have the riders charging so hard at him from the south—the opposite direction of the wall.

Sighing, Snapdragon armed himself with his sword, though he left it resting flat against his legs. He didn't have a bow and arrow—he simply couldn't use one with his ruined right shoulder. While he could bend his elbow and move his right hand, he couldn't move his shoulder—which effectively prevented him from using a shield. He did keep a belt knife on his right hip, just in case he lost his sword in battle.

He didn't know who was coming at him, or what their intentions were, but he was going to err on the side of caution and thus kept his sword at the ready.

There were four riders in all, mounted on dark stallions and dressed in loose fitted chain mail armor and leather caps on their heads. They wore no standard that Snapdragon could see—not a good sign. Whoever they were, they didn't want to be identified on sight.

They slowed down when they noticed that Snapdragon was waiting for them.

"Hello there!" Snapdragon shouted when they came into range.

One of the men to the right of the lead rider asked something that Snapdragon thought was "Why ain't he runnin'?"

The lead rider told the other man to shut up as he slowed.

It seemed to Snapdragon that only the lead rider was comfortable on a horse—the other three were much less practiced.

"Are you Snapdragon?" the lead rider called.

Snapdragon watched the men slow to a stop a dozen or so paces away. "Aye, and who might you be?"

"I'm the man who's gonna place your head on top of a pike for the Rifna Erd to see when they return," the man responded gruffly.

Snapdragon felt the familiar fire roil inside of him before he was about to go into battle. Despite his wife's objections, he had kept up with his guardian training over the years.

This man was not only clear in his intent, but it was alarming that he knew Snapdragon was going to be here—at this place and at this time. Whoever he was, Snapdragon didn't believe he was acting of his own accord. Someone had put him and his lackeys up to this. But who? And why? Whatever the reason, Snapdragon was out here on his own against four armed men.

Snapdragon made it obvious that he looked at each of the four riders in turn before saying, "Who sent you? They've gotta be pretty wooden headed to send only four of you."

Two of the men shifted uneasily in their saddles. The one who spoke before said, "I thought he's supposed to be a cripple."

"I told you to *shut up*!" the lead rider shouted at his companion.

Then turning to Snapdragon, he said, "Death is near."

Snapdragon tightened his grip on his sword. "Well, make sure to tell 'Death' I said hello."

With that, Snapdragon kicked his horse in the flanks and charged directly toward the lead rider. The rest of the men were stunned into inaction while Snapdragon approached. The lead rider, to his credit, didn't panic but set himself for the oncoming attack.

However, at the last moment, Snapdragon cut to the right. The rider that was now the focus of Snapdragon's attack tried to turn his horse to defend, but suddenly found himself headless.

The lead rider barked orders, but the other men kept getting in the way of each other until another one fell when Snapdragon impaled his leg, just below his shirt of chainmail. The strike caused a wound that bled so profusely that Snapdragon knew the man wasn't long for this earth. The third one, the talkative one, fell to the ground on his own and howled in pain when he was stamped on by his own horse. Two more stomps and the man was deadly quiet.

Now, with just one opponent remaining, Snapdragon used a bit more caution. The lead rider kicked his horse into motion. The other man was right handed, so Snapdragon positioned his horse so the other man would have to attack from across his body.

Even with Snapdragon having the advantage, when they met, they did so with such force that both men were knocked to the ground.

They stood and faced each other. Snapdragon held his sword in his left hand, while the other man used both hands on the hilt to attack.

The man knew how to fight—and well. He must have had guardian training. Snapdragon's right arm hung limply at his side, and that was something his opponent noticed and started to exploit. Using his sword primarily as defense, Snapdragon fought on, waiting for the other man to make a mistake.

One set of blows ended up with the swords being above their heads, hilts close together. The lead rider reached out with his right hand and grabbed a hold of the base of Snapdragon's sword.

The man was strong, and he held the swords firmly in place. He glared into Snapdragon's eyes and said, "I almost feel bad for killing a cripple."

Snapdragon's response was to remove the belt knife from his right hip and then bending his right arm at the elbow, he slid the knife up under the man's loosely fitted chain mail and stabbed him just below the ribcage.

The glare in the man's eyes turned to shock and then lost any light of life at all.

Watching the man fall to the ground, Snapdragon said, "Remember to tell 'Death' hello."

Snapdragon looked around. All of the attackers were dead except the one he had wounded in the leg. He approached the injured man and knelt beside him.

"Who sent you?" Snapdragon asked.

"No! I won't tell you!" said the last of the riders.

Snapdragon pressed his knee against the man's ruined leg, causing him to scream in pain. "You're bleeding very badly. You won't last long unless you're treated. Tell me who is behind this attack and what their plans are."

The man started to lose focus in his eyes. Snapdragon cuffed him across the cheek. "Tell me and I'll help you live."

"No chance," the man said through bloodied lips.

Snapdragon brought his face close to the man. "You don't have to die like this. Do something right, something noble, in your last moments."

The man looked at Snapdragon and for a moment seemed to consider the offer. But before he could say anything, his eyes glazed over with a look that Snapdragon knew all too well.

Snapdragon stood and sighed. All the horses had scattered. It would take him quite a while to get to the nearest farm, and then longer to get to Stur. He'd have to warn them about the attack, set up plans and then head back to Procep. He was going to be gone longer than expected. Seraphina wasn't going to be happy.

It was nearly dark when Snapdragon arrived in Stur. The scout from the watchtower had spotted him approaching and had sent several men to meet him.

"Commander Snapdragon," one of the men said. "What are you doing here? Why are you riding *that* horse?"

"What am I doing here? Mayor Kerr sent for me," Snapdragon said.

The one who spoke looked at the other men. "We were not made aware of that."

Snapdragon considered them a moment. He sensed no deceit. "Well, perhaps that's the reason I don't have my normal horse. I had to borrow one from a farmer down the way."

"I don't understand," the man said.

"Take me to the mayor and I'll explain everything."

Before long, Snapdragon was escorted to the building that acted as the town center. Like Procep, Stur had been a small mining village before the northern wall was built. It was now a town of decent size.

"Snapdragon!" Kerr said when he entered the hall. "This is a surprise. What brings you—wait, is that blood on your clothes?"

"Yes."

"From the looks of you, it's not yours."

"No. It's not."

Kerr's face paled. "Was it the Rifna Erd?"

"It wasn't. Thank the Zealous Star," Snapdragon responded.

"Then what happened? No, wait. Let me get Stur's new militia captain. You can tell us together."

Kerr stepped outside and returned a moment later with a young man who was well built and looked sure of himself.

"Commander Snapdragon, this is Captain Mason," Kerr introduced.

Mason saluted. "Pleasure to meet you, Commander."

Snapdragon returned the salute with his left hand. "Likewise."

After sitting down around a stone table, Snapdragon explained what happened. Both Mason and Kerr looked genuinely surprised, especially when he told them the reference one of the men made about the Rifna Erd.

"I don't understand," Kerr said. "It doesn't make any sense. Why would anyone *want* the Rifna Erd to return?"

"No idea," Snapdragon said. He paused and looked at the new leader of the local militia. "Where were you sent from, Captain Mason?"

"Me? Oh, I come from the Donigi district. Why?"

"Have you heard any talk about people wanting the Rifna Erd to return?"

"No, I haven't, Commander."

Snapdragon wondered if it was a coincidence that he had been attacked at the same time that Mason was assigned to the town. As if the younger man read his mind, Mason said, "Be assured, Commander, I knew nothing of this. I was assigned to this post by your brother, Commander Oakleaf. You can check with him if you doubt my story."

"I get a report from Oakleaf every week with any changes he's made with the militia captains," Snapdragon responded. "If you're on the list, you have nothing to fear."

Mason looked relieved. "Then I have nothing to fear, well, at least about my presence here. I guess we now need to be vigilant of possible attacks from the Rifna Erd *and* from inside our own boundaries."

"That we do," Snapdragon said.

The three men didn't speak for a moment while they let that realization sink in.

A knock sounded at the door. "Come in," Kerr said.

A large young man, so tall he had to stoop, entered.

"Ah, Enoch," Kerr said. "What can we do for you?"

"Enoch?" Snapdragon said. "My word! You've grown even taller since I saw you last."

"Greetings, Commander." Enoch's voice was deep. "I apologize for the interruption. I came to report that your horse was just brought in by a patrol."

"Is he injured?" Snapdragon asked.

Enoch looked surprised. "Not that I was told, Commander."

"Thank you, Son," Kerr said. "Please make sure the commander's horse is taken care of."

"It will be as you say," Enoch said, and then left.

"May I ask you a question?" Mason said to Kerr.

"By all means."

"That was *your* son?"

Snapdragon and Kerr exchanged an amused look.

"After a fashion, yes."

"After a—"

"I raised him as if he was my own son," Kerr interrupted. "His mother was pregnant with him when we escaped from Eddinh. She died giving birth and I promised to raise him."

"I don't know that I've seen anyone so—so—"

"Big?" Snapdragon said.

"I was trying to think of a better word," Mason said. "He's not fat. Aside from being tall, he's quite muscular."

"I'm glad you met him here. Let me explain a few things about him," Kerr said. "He's a member of the militia, though he was off duty when you arrived—that's why you haven't met him yet. He's a good boy, always trying to do what's right. He's strong, but not very agile. People mistake his slow movements as being slow in the mind as well, but that's not true. Despite my relation to him, I want you to treat him like any other of the men, am I clear?"

"Yes."

"All right then, gentlemen," Snapdragon said. "What are we going to do about our new threat?"

※

Seraphina was visibly upset, and didn't appear to be afraid to let Snapdragon hear about it, despite the fact he had just returned safely. Her green eyes flashed with anger as she addressed him.

"So, perhaps traveling by yourself wasn't such a good idea after all, was it?" she said. Before he could respond, she continued, "Yes, the messenger you sent back told us all about what had happened."

Snapdragon knew this was an argument that he had no hope of winning—but he was fine with that. Years ago, he'd gone on a trip while his wife was pregnant with their third child. He'd gotten delayed, and since he wasn't there to name his new daughter, his father, Garth, had picked one. Winter was an odd name for a child, but no more so than Snapdragon or Oakleaf.

"You're right, sweetheart," Snapdragon said. "I'm sorry. I will never travel alone again."

She looked like she wanted to tell him off some more, but it seemed his apology and tone calmed her down.

"Fine, now that is settled, we need to talk about your daughter."

"Which one?"

Seraphina gave him an exasperated look.

"Oh, you must mean Diantha. What did she do now?"

His wife told him about the events at the tavern. Snapdragon shook his head.

"Where is she?" Snapdragon asked.

"In her room. Do you want to talk to her now, or *now?*"

Snapdragon thought it best not to give his wife more reasons to be upset. "Now would work."

"Good choice."

Seraphina left the sitting room and returned a moment later with a very defiant looking Diantha.

"Mom said she already told you what happened," Diantha said in greeting.

"And?" Snapdragon prompted.

"And what? What he did was inappropriate! He needed to be taught a lesson."

Snapdragon sighed. "That's not how we enforce the law."

"Well, maybe it should be."

"Diantha, you need to think about more than yourself. I'm the commander of the northern defenses." Snapdragon stood. "How can I keep the men's respect if I can't control my own daughter?"

"You shouldn't be trying to control me. I'm an adult now."

"Then it's time for you to act like one."

She glared at him. "You want me to be an adult? Fine! I'm moving out. I expect the same treatment Reed was given—or is that also against the Tome of Laws?"

CHAPTER 59

Crescens felt the familiar knot in his stomach when he knew he would have to go see the governor of Erd. For years he hid his feelings toward her. He didn't dare express them. No, that would never do. She had made him magistrate over the district when she had become governor several years ago. He was also the only one who knew that she was a direct descendant of the Rifna Erd—left behind to help prepare for their return from beyond the northern mountains one day.

If he was to declare his love for her, and she rejected it, she would most likely see him as a liability. That meant at the very least his title would be stripped away and he'd be banished. At the very worst, she would—no, he didn't want to think about that. It was better that he kept his feelings hidden. This way, he'd still get to be close to her, though not as close as he would like.

Even after all these years, he became nervous when he knew he was going to speak to her. But today, he truly had a reason to be worried. Selene had set her plan in motion—a plan that had been years in the making, and one he knew little about. The parchment he'd just received held the news of how part of her plan, a key part according to her, had worked out.

He screwed up his courage and knocked on her door—the door that led to her office in the palace.

"Come."

Crescens did as instructed. Selene was sitting behind her desk.

Her long, dark hair cascaded over her shoulders and down her back. She was simply the most beautiful woman Crescens had ever met.

"Yes, Crescens?" she asked, not looking up from the scroll she was reading.

"We have received word from the north, Governor."

"Bring it here," she commanded.

Crescens walked to her desk and handed the rolled up parchment to Selene. It had the wax seal from the mayor of Stur, which Crescens had double checked to make sure was authentic.

He watched as she used a long, silver knife to break the seal and then unfurl the parchment. Her face gave nothing away as she read the document, at least not until the very end when he noticed her lips curve up just slightly.

"Snapdragon killed the men we sent," she said.

"What? How—how could they fail?"

"Fail?" Selene asked.

"Well, yes. Snapdragon is alive and the men we sent are dead."

"They didn't fail," Selene said.

Crescens was confused. His expression must have shown it.

Selene sat back in her chair and pointed to the seat next to her desk, indicating for Crescens to sit.

Once he sat, she said, "Snapdragon will now need to be focused on attacks from both inside and outside of Bariwon. It will split his attention and let the next part of the plan work."

Crescens again felt frustrated because Selene kept her whole plan from him. "All right, then. What do we do now?"

She referenced the parchment. "Mayor Kerr is asking for more men to help guard the outer settlements. It seems Commander Snapdragon was there recently and wants to be prepared against future attacks."

Crescens understood. "Oh, I see now."

"Good. I want you to arrange for the next raid."

"Did you have a certain place in mind?"

Setting the parchment aside, Selene pulled out a map from her top drawer. She unfolded it on the desk in front of her. It showed the wall from Procep to Stur to the coastal town of Mocnirs. Pointing to an area roughly two-thirds away from Stur toward Mocnirs, she said, "Send ten raiders here. Have them kill any livestock they find in the area. As for the reinforcements, send fifty more men to Stur, making sure the specially trained ones are sent *here*." She pointed to an area fairly close to Procep— an area they had been sending these specially trained men for several years.

"It will be done, Governor."

⊹⊱✦⊰⊹

"I'm not moving, Aaron," Diantha said. She was sitting on the ground, next to her horse. The sun was just beginning to rise. They had finished their morning meal and completed cleaning up their campsite.

The grizzled guardian looked at Diantha with a bewildered expression. "How's that again, Diantha?"

"You heard me," she said while glaring at him, "I'm not moving until you leave."

"Your father's orders—"

"My father's orders were for you to make sure I was safe," Diantha said, cutting him off. "We're on the main road between Procep and Erd Proper. There are plenty of farms and small villages between here and there. By nightfall, I'll be in Erd Proper and then from there, I'll be on my way to the castle. In my opinion, I'm as safe as I can be."

Aaron didn't speak. Instead he folded his arms and continued to stare at her.

In return, Diantha stared right back at him, refusing to wither under his gaze. She knew he was testing her.

For several moments they stayed like that. Finally, Aaron rolled his eyes and said, "You would sit here all day, wouldn't you?"

"Try me."

"No need," he said. "I've watched you grow up. I know how stubborn you are." He then gave her a smile. "I also know you're an excellent fighter. Personally, I think it's a shame you aren't allowed to compete to be a guardian. And you're right, this part of the land is fairly safe. Still, there are bandits and ruffians who are about. Promise me you'll go directly to Erd Proper—and you'll be cautious in doing so."

Diantha stood. "You know that's a promise I'll keep," she said.

"But I want to hear it."

"Fine, I promise."

Aaron nodded, and then mounted his horse. "I understand everyone needs to find their own path," he said. "But I also want to remind you that your father is a good man. You may not see that now, but I know he still loves you."

"Did he tell you to say that?" Diantha asked.

Aaron shook his head. "Best of success on your path, Diantha." With those final words, he left.

Diantha watched as he rode back the way they'd come, if nothing else, to make sure he wouldn't change his mind. Convinced he was truly leaving, she got back on her horse—an older, light brown mare. She wasn't Diantha's personal horse, she didn't own one, the horse belonged to the kingdom and was used to carry messengers back and forth to the different parts of the land.

The saddle bags were filled with Diantha's belongings: a change of clothing, a couple of books, rations and some money she had saved up from working at the smithy. Also, she brought along her sword—one she made with Bearach. It was a fine sword, and one designed especially for her. It was lighter than most weapons, but perfectly balanced and made of the finest, and hardest, metals found in the land.

Her Uncle Bearach was one of the few that didn't think she was wasting her time learning the art of combat. Maybe it was because he had been north of the mountains with her father and seen what the Rifna Erd were like. He had even let her work in the smithy with her on a regular basis. Diantha first did it out of spite because it was another thing that wasn't ladylike, but she found that she actually enjoyed working with metal. In addition, the hard work made her stronger.

She looked back at the saddlebags. It was somewhat humbling to realize she had with her the sum total of what she owned. At the same time, it was liberating.

Her parents weren't happy to see her go, but neither could they stop her. Still, her father had insisted that she take a messenger's horse to travel to the castle—and Aaron, one of the guardians assigned to Procep, was to accompany her.

When her parents asked what she planned on doing after she left, she told them she would stay with her grandfather in the castle until she could decide what to do next.

Her mother was in tears when she left. Her father kept his emotions in check. When he went to give her a good-bye hug, she shrugged it off. Maybe one day he would see the error of his ways. Until then, she would show him—she wouldn't have anything to do with him until he apologized.

After traveling toward Erd Proper for a few hours, Diantha calmed down quite a bit. Perhaps what her mother said was true—perhaps she let her emotions dictate her actions too quickly. Then again, it seemed to be a trait that she had gotten *from* her mother. Maybe it was something about having red hair.

The first night she and Aaron had slept under the stars. But for tonight, she looked forward to sleeping at an inn with a meal that consisted of more than hard cheese, dried meat, and water.

The sun had just dipped below the horizon when she saw the outskirts of Erd Proper on the horizon. The outline of the palace was the most prominent feature on the city skyline, though there were several other buildings that were a couple of stories high.

Farms dotted the land around her, though most were built a good distance from the road—as if the farmers were leery of getting too close to other people. Though the district of Erd was rocky, there were clumps of trees here and there.

She was approaching one of these small groves when she noticed a form hunched over near the side of the road. In the fading light, she couldn't quite make out all the details, though he appeared to be a person, and not some animal.

"Hello there!" Diantha called out.

The response was a low groan, as if the person was injured.

At first, Diantha felt a sense of apprehension. She shook the feeling off, sure she could handle any threat the person may pose. Still, it would be foolish not to be a little cautious.

"Are you hurt?" she called out as she drew nearer.

Again the response was a non-committal groan.

When she was within ten or so paces, she stopped her horse on the other side of the road and slowly dismounted, trying to sense if anyone was hiding in the trees close by.

Instead of wearing her sword on her hip, as was customary, she wore it on her back, with the strap of the sheath running over one shoulder and down her chest. She felt it gave her more freedom when she ran while armed.

She thought to draw her sword, but decided against it. If the person was indeed hurt, the sight of someone approaching with a sword could only make things worse. They may try to run, and in the process, become more injured.

Diantha approached the person, who was bent over with their knees tucked in and their head touching the ground.

"Are you in need of help?" she asked, now only a few steps away.

The person groaned again, at first, but then the sound turned into a deep, throaty chuckle.

"No," the person said, "but *you* are."

The figure sprang to his feet. He wore a tattered cape, but underneath was metal studded leather armor—the type preferred by highway men and bandits. He held a long knife in one hand that curved slightly at the tip.

"A pretty thing like you should know better than to ride alone this close to dark," he said. He then gave a low whistle. From behind her, Diantha could hear sounds coming from the trees. She turned her head to one side, able to keep an eye on the man before her as well as to see what made the noise. Three more men came from out of the trees—each dressed in similar armor as the first man.

"Looks like we got lucky tonight, eh boys?" the first man said. "Not only did we get ourselves a horse, but a pretty young thing too."

The men behind her laughed. It was not a joyful sound.

"What's the matter, little lady? Didn't your daddy teach you not to go riding alone at night?" one of the men taunted.

Diantha took in a deep breath. This wasn't like sparring. They were not using wooden weapons. These men intended her harm.

"This is a mistake," she said firmly.

"Mistake?" the man in front of her echoed. "You got that right."

"No," Diantha said. "*Your* mistake."

With that, she reached over her shoulder and drew her sword. The first man didn't wait for her to get set before he lunged at her. In one fluid motion, she side-stepped and brought her weapon down.

The man's hand still clutched the curved knife, only now it was on the ground, separated from his body. For a moment, her attacker looked at the stump of what was once his right hand, as if he didn't believe what he saw. Shock turned to realization as he tucked his ruined arm against his body and ran off howling in the night.

The action didn't scare away the other three men. If anything, it seemed to firm their resolve. Diantha's horse had been spooked by the first man's cries and bolted down the road, leaving just her and her assailants.

They were all roughly the same size. One was hefting a large mace, while the other two had curved daggers. The men with the short blades spread out and flanked her on either side, while the man with the mace faced her straight on.

Diantha had practiced often against several opponents and let them take their positions while she formulated a plan. As soon as the men with knives were set, Diantha made to dash between one of them and the man with the mace. Both men closed in to cut her off. Once she got between them, she stopped and faced the man wielding the large weapon made from a long rod of wood attached to a big block of metal. He set his feet and swung the mace at her. Diantha dropped to her stomach, and in the process, kicked the legs of the man approaching behind her. He tripped and would have fallen on top of her, but Diantha timed it perfectly so that as the man fell, he was hit solidly by his companion swinging the mace. The force knocked him off to the side, so that he landed beside her. The sickening sound of crunched bone let her know he was out of this fight.

She sprang to her feet and brought her weapon up to attack. Diantha feigned a swing at the man who had just crushed his partner, but at the last moment, twirled and went to one knee, extending her sword toward the other man who was armed with a knife. Again, her timing was ideal as the tip of her blade pierced the man in the stomach. With his momentum, and with Diantha being set firmly on the ground, her sword tore through his leather armor and into his soft middle.

Swiftly, she pulled out her sword, and while still crouched, sliced toward the man with the mace who was still trying to right himself after his first swing. Diantha's blade caught him just below the left knee, doing enough damage that he shouldn't be able to put any weight on it. This turned out to be true and he crumpled to the ground, dropping the mace and reaching down to clutch his ruined leg.

Diantha stepped back and then spun around, looking to see if there was any more attackers. She didn't see any. Maybe if there were, they were scared away by what they just witnessed.

The man with the wound to his belly and the man with the nearly severed leg cried out in pain, while the third man remained motionless on the ground. With the threat of attack no longer present, Diantha was able to consider the scene.

She had just cut off a man's hand. And while she hadn't killed him directly, her actions led to the death of the man whose skull had been crushed. Rationally, she thought she should feel remorse. But she didn't. Instead, she felt resolved. This proved to her that it was a mistake not to let women become guardians. Though attacks like the one she just experienced weren't common, they still took place. She shuttered to think what would have happened to her had she not been able to defend herself.

There was a lesson to be learned here. One that she should teach to others. One that would let people know that criminal acts would not be tolerated.

But how? As she pondered the question, Diantha noticed the bloody, severed hand lying on the ground. It reminded her of a story she had heard when she was younger.

It gave her an idea.

⇥⧏⧐⇤

It took Diantha a while before she was able to find her horse. Thankfully, most of the farms had fences built up near the roadside which meant the horse would have to stay on the main road. The going was even slower, because not only was she looking for her ride, but she also was keeping an eye open for anyone one else that might think she would be an easy target.

She had gotten blood all over her riding outfit. Showing up at an inn in such a manner would only raise questions she didn't want to answer—she didn't want word to get back to her father she had been attacked. She was sure he was furious that she'd sent Aaron back, and she didn't want to make him even more upset.

Once she found her horse, she changed into her spare set of clothes. Thankfully the road was quiet this time of night so she was able to switch clothing without being watched.

It was near the middle of the night when she pulled into Erd Proper. One thing she learned from her father was never to stay at the first inns you came across. The inns on the outskirts of town tended to be overpriced, or shady, or in some cases, both.

She kept heading toward the palace, looking at the tall, thin buildings that lined the cobblestoned road. A lot could be said about an establishment by its name. There was "The Inn and Out Inn" which most likely appealed to people not planning on spending the whole night at said place. Other names she saw were "The Moldy Eye," "The Unempty Mug," and "The Come On Inn." Finally, she spotted an inn that looked somewhat respectable—at least the name didn't cause her to cringe. "The Bard's Tale Tavern" was well lit even at this time of night. A stable hand waited outside and stood up straight when he saw her approach.

"Lookin' for a place to rest your head, ma'am?" he asked.

"Yes, that I am," Diantha responded.

He cleared his throat. "You won't be findin' a finer place than The Bard's Tale Tavern. The food is good, the beds are bug free, and there is live music every night."

Diantha got off her horse. "Sounds wonderful."

She went to remove the saddlebags from her horse when the young man ran over to help her. "Allow me, ma'am."

Though she was only eighteen years old, she found that she enjoyed being called "ma'am." It was a sign of respect—something she wasn't getting at home.

In short order she had acquired a room and paid the stable hand a tip for his help. Her room was on the second floor and was clean, if somewhat small. She placed her belongings into the room's modest wardrobe and then washed her face using the bowl of water that had been set next to her bed on a small table.

She was bone weary; yet, her body was still tense from her attack not long ago. She started to wonder if she did the right thing before leaving the men on the road. Those were the thoughts she pondered as sleep finally claimed her.

CHAPTER 60

Queen Rainbow arched an eyebrow at the man standing before her. "What did you say?" she asked, knowing full well what had been spoken, but she wanted to see if the man before her had the nerve to repeat it.

The governor of Regne was a small man, with pale skin. Despite his lack of physical prowess, he stood confidently, and didn't appear to be intimidated even though he was standing in front of the queen and king.

"I said the district of Regne is filing a formal complaint against the crown for misuse of the kingdom's resources," he repeated, not looking the least distraught that he was asked to repeat himself.

Rainbow turned to her husband, King Elisedd, and then to her parents, Councilors Rayne and Sunshine to see if they had the same reaction she had to this statement. Whereas Elisedd looked bewildered, her father kept his face expressionless.

Holding the weekly courts was one of Rainbow's favorite duties. As the blood heir to the throne, she had the final say if there was ever a disagreement between her and her husband, which had happened just once in the few years they had been the rulers over Bariwon. Even then, it was a simple matter over what to serve on the first night of the Mortentaun—Elisedd preferred pork, whereas Rainbow wanted to forgo any meat at all. They playfully debated the matter, neither giving up, until Rainbow used the "blood heir" card.

One thing she loved about Elisedd was while he had very firm beliefs in doing what was right, he wasn't afraid to let her take the lead in court. Rainbow would have to admit she was good at holding them—no doubt due to the training and guidance of her father and mother, who had been king and queen before her.

This was the first time since she had become queen that a statement said in court truly baffled her. A formal complaint? Misusing the kingdom's resources? What had gotten into this man?

"Governor, the district governors enjoy quite a bit of latitude on how they run their respective lands, as long as they abide by The Tome of Laws. Taxes have been nearly cut in half since Daimh was king, and so I can't possibly see the logic of your statement. As you see by your tour the castle, we have kept things simple, but elegant. Gone are the gaudy, imposing features prominent just a few decades ago. Will you please elaborate on why you believe the kingdom's resources are being misused?"

The little man pointed north, as if all could see what he was talking about from the main hall. "How much time and money has been spent in building a wall in front of an already impassable mountain? Wagonload after wagonload of timber has left Regne to support this foolish venture."

Rainbow had prided herself on remaining calm, even during the most intense arguments, but she found herself struggling to keep her cool after this last statement. She took a deep breath, leaned back in her throne and drummed her fingers on the armrest. For several heartbeats, she didn't say anything. She spared a quick glance at her husband, and noticed that his ears were turning red—a sign he was getting upset, and for good cause.

"I think, perhaps," Rainbow started, and then paused for a moment before continuing, "you should rephrase how you refer to the northern defenses." She stared at the man, unblinking. For the first time, she saw his bravado waver.

"I am simply repeating what others are calling it," the governor said. "Unlike them, I'm not afraid to speak up for the people of the kingdom."

This time, Rainbow couldn't help herself as yet another ridiculous statement came from this man's mouth. "So, you are speaking for the people of the kingdom, are you?" Rainbow asked, her voice rising. "Or could it be you are speaking only for those in your district that are seeing the timber smiths profit while they, themselves, have had nothing to gain from this 'foolish venture' as you call it? I believe that it's the latter of the two. I've spoken to my uncle, Commander Snapdragon. I've heard what he experienced, and the threat it poses to Bariwon. I've spent time among the people of Eddinh—those people from beyond the mountains that were fortunate to escape. I've heard horror stories of what these Rifna Erd are capable of doing. I've also heard from others, like those that sent you, about how unfair it is that only those who can help the cause are benefiting from it."

Rainbow stood, causing the little governor from Regne to jump back. Motioning to everyone in the hall, she said, "*All* of the people in Bariwon are benefiting from the protection the northern defenses provide. If you have any doubt of that, I will commission that the tunnel be reopened, and you can lead those who sent you on an expedition to discover whether or not the defenses are worth it."

Though she didn't think it was possible, the governor of Regne turned even paler than before. "That won't be necessary, Your Highness. Regne officially withdraws its formal complaint."

Diantha looked at her blood-stained clothes and frowned. Had she cleaned them right away, perhaps she could have avoided them from being stained. Now, she feared, nothing would get them clean. She'd only brought one extra change of clothing, and she didn't fancy the idea of having to wear the same thing every day until she reached the castle.

Perhaps she could find a stream once she left Erd Proper. For the moment, she put the clothes back into her wardrobe and headed for the common room for breakfast. The smell of freshly baked bread, along with cooked meat, made her mouth water.

She took a table against one of the walls, making sure she was facing the crowd. The room was about three quarters full. There was something odd about how the people were acting. Many were huddled together and would occasionally look over their shoulders.

A barmaid of middle age approached Diantha, rubbing her hands on her apron. "What'll it be then, miss?" she asked. Her eyes darted back and forth as she spoke.

"What do you suggest?" Diantha responded.

"Our standard breakfast is two eggs, a chunk of bread and sliced pork."

Diantha's stomach growled as if to answer for her. "Sounds wonderful."

The barmaid turned to go, but before she did, Diantha asked, "Tell me, is it always like this here?"

"Always like what?" The barmaid sounded nervous.

Diantha motioned for the server to come closer. It a quiet voice, she said, "Everyone seems on edge—anxious even. I didn't sense that when I came in last night."

"You've not heard?" the barmaid asked.

Diantha gave her a look that told her she hadn't.

Speaking in just above a whisper, the woman said, "Dark times, these are. Strange things are happening—things that shouldn't be, but are."

"Are you talking about the raid by the northern walls?"

The barmaid shook her head. "So you've not heard." She looked around before she spoke again. "One of the men that came in early this morning reported seeing something very disturbing on his way into town. Torn and bloody cloth."

Diantha tried to keep her face from showing emotion. "Torn and bloody cloth?"

"Aye, he said there was a cloth—looked to have been an undershirt at one point—that was torn nearly in two, and dripping with blood. It was hanging from a tree near one of the roads close by. When he looked around, he found a severed hand. It reminded him of the old legend."

A shout from the back room caused the barmaid to straighten up. "I must get back to serving. Just you be careful, young lady." With that, she spun and headed to the kitchen.

Diantha leaned her back against the wall and thought. Last night, after the battle, she had taken off the dead man's shirt to clean her sword. She ripped it, not quite in two and then tied it to a tree branch which hung over the road. She had assumed the men she'd injured, but not killed, would have taken the hand she'd cut off, but it appears they hadn't.

Her actions were based on the story of the Noble Trod—the legend told of a man who lived during the bloody battle for power when the terrible sickness, the nislles, killed off the rightful heirs to the throne. From the stories, after a mêlée he would hang ripped, bloody cloth around the battlefield in an attempt to stop the people from civil war. Why he did it, Diantha didn't know, but she hoped the symbolism wouldn't be lost on the people who found the cloth.

She also wanted to teach the attackers a lesson. By hanging the cloth, she hoped to invoke the memories of the Noble Trod. It wasn't very ladylike, she thought, but not much about her was; although she still wore the beads in her hair, the earrings and bracelet Rosalind had given her. She liked the way they looked on her—giving her distinction without being too feminine.

Soon, her breakfast arrived and she paid the barmaid. While eating, a man in a guardian uniform stepped into the common room from the street outside.

"May I please have your attention!" he called out.

Everyone in the room fell quiet and looked toward the man.

"Due to recent events, each road leading out of Erd Proper will have guardians stationed there until further notice. We will be inspecting what people are bringing in and out of the area. Be advised, this is for your protection."

Several people spoke up to ask questions, but the guardian left, ignoring them.

This was a problem for Diantha. If they searched her bags, they would find the bloody clothes—if she took them with her. She could leave them behind, but she'd have to find a place to get rid of them that couldn't be traced back to her.

Perhaps it would be best if she waited a few days. She was sure things would settle down by then. She had earned enough money over the last several years working in the blacksmith shop with Bearach that she could stay in Erd Proper for quite a while. She was anxious to get to the castle, but her actions last night were going to delay that. No, not *her* actions— the actions of the men who attacked her. They got what they deserved.

After eating breakfast, Diantha made sure her clothes and sword were hidden well in her room. She didn't know anyone in the town, and wasn't sure what Erd Proper had to offer. She decided to walk around. Her primary goal was to find a place to get rid of her clothes.

She noticed that her room had a window right above the roof over the stables. That meant if she opened her window, the smells would be less than pleasant. Still, she could sneak out her window at night and not worry about dropping down a couple of stories.

The palace in Erd was the center point of the town—even though it was right up against a fairly large lake. It reminded Diantha of the castle, though it was smaller, and somehow, sinister. Maybe it was the dark stone, intermixed with red, marbled columns or the iron spikes that lined the walls—or maybe it was something she couldn't place her finger on.

Everywhere she walked, she noticed peoples' stares. She had been told she was very pretty, though she believed it had more to do with her red hair—something not usually found in this part of Bariwon.

Once she had walked several blocks, she came across a grate in the ground. She bent down and looked in it. There was water running beneath it, seemingly going under the road. Diantha had no idea its purpose, but it gave her an idea.

Diantha walked around the town for most of the day, getting a feel for its layout. Once she went back to her room, she made sure the window was open enough that she could slip through it. The window was old and it made a harsh noise lifting it up, even half way. The sun was just starting to set and people were downstairs eating and listening to the bard who was performing. She doubted anyone heard her opening the window. Just as she predicted, the smell of horse droppings came from the stables below, but it wasn't overbearing.

She planned on slipping out in the middle of the night, going to the grate and prying it open with her sword. She'd then put her bloodied clothes down into the water which should wash it away to someplace that couldn't be traced back to her. After she'd put the grate back in place, she'd return to her rented room and then leave the next morning. She just needed to wait long enough for everyone to be asleep.

Not having anything else to do for the moment, she made her way to the common room. She noticed the room was fairly full, and they all had their attention fixed on the bard who sat by the room's large hearth.

She thought she recognized him from the Mortentaun. Then again, a lot of bards came to the biggest event of the year where young men competed to become guardians. The reminder of the event she wouldn't be allowed to participate in quickly turned her mood sour.

The bard was dressed in a long robe made up of many colors—so varied and bright it almost gave her a headache to look at him. She was able to get a small table against the wall, in a slightly different spot from where she had sat before. The barmaid noticed her and motioned that it would be a moment before she would be served.

"Thank you, thank you for your kind applause," the bard said, after he finished his song. "And now, by popular request, I present to you a story of adventure, romance, action, and heroics!"

Diantha noticed that everyone appeared anxious. While the bard paused for dramatic effect, she wondered which song it would be.

"Ladies and Gentleman, *The Ballad of Snapdragon the Brave*!"

As the bard started playing the first notes on his lute, Diantha sat there in shock. Snapdragon? As in *her* father?

In a village far north
A long way from here
One day all the people
Vanished—disappeared!

We didn't know, where they would go
Mountains TOO high to climb
When they all vanished, it put a panic
Into YOUR hearts and mine

The King sent his best men
Up north to discover
Where the people had gone
A mystery to uncover

Not one person in Procep, was found on a doorstep
But THERE they found a cave
To see where it led, starts this Ballad
The BALLAD of Snapdragon the Brave!

Despite herself, Diantha listened to the bard. His song told of the tragedy of what happened once the scouting party had gone through the tunnel. He sang of the love that blossomed between her mother and father, and of all the heroic deeds her father did to save the people of Eddinh.

She had heard stories growing up of what happened, but mostly from other people aside from her parents. While her father made sure she was taught the seriousness of building the northern defenses—and how big of a threat the Rifna Erd were—he never went into details of the actual events.

Granted, Diantha knew that bards tended to exaggerate in their stories. However, as he continued singing, she was able to put together the various events she heard from others as she grew up. If even half of what the bard sang was true, she was stunned by what both her mother and father did to survive.

Though it gave her a new appreciation for her father, it also made her more upset. Why hadn't he told her? Did he think she was weak and couldn't handle it?

When her dinner arrived, she found herself too frustrated to eat. However, Diantha forced down the food, knowing she would need her strength for later. After listening to the bard sing a few more songs, she went right back to her room. It was early yet, so she decided to take a nap.

When she awoke, it was to the sound of two men arguing. Her mind was muddled because she was still waking, and she wondered why she could hear them so clearly. Coming more to her senses, she realized that their voices were coming through her window. Apparently the men were in the next room and had their window open.

"And I tells you this is the perfect time!" one man shouted. His voice sounded as if he had gargled rocks.

The other man spoke, his voice deep. "Quiet down. You're gonna wake the whole tavern."

"Look," the first man said, this time his voice quieter. "All the guardians are stationed on the roads in and out of Erd. Not a one of 'em is in town. We slip into Sterling's place, you give him a beatin' for cheatin' us at cards, we take our money he stole and we head back here. No one will know! Especially after we tell Sterling that we'll kill him if he tells anyone."

Diantha sat up on her bed, trying not to make any noise. There was no sound from the men for a moment—maybe they had heard her.

"Aw right," the deeper voiced man said.

"Good!" his companion replied. "You head out like you need to drop a load. I'll follow you in a few moments. We'll meet up in front of the bakery just down the street. Got it?"

"Yeah."

Diantha felt sick to her stomach. Because of what she had done to her attackers, there were no guardians in town—which meant that men like the ones she heard would be free to do as they pleased. She couldn't help but feel responsible. Even if what these men said was true about being cheated at cards, it didn't give them the right to inflict harm on another. She doubted she could get to the edge of town to get a guardian to help in time. Fully awake now, her mind raced.

Her eyes fell upon the wardrobe where her bloodied clothes and sword were hidden. It took little time for her to decide what to do.

⇥✦⇤

Sterling was awakened by the sound of his back door being kicked in. He lived on the first floor of a two storied building—the top floor belonging to old man Wyot. He sat up in his bed, trying to blink away the darkness. Heavy footsteps came from the hallway, approaching his room. For a moment, he thought about trying to escape through his window, but it was old and difficult to open.

He cursed for not keeping a weapon in his room—he felt he hadn't needed one since Rayne had become king and guardians kept the peace.

The footsteps stopped on the other side of his door. Sterling pulled the covers up to his chin—unable to force his frightened body to put up more of a fight.

The door to his room burst open and he could see the silhouette of two men fill the door frame. A small cry escaped his lips and he felt his knees knocking together.

But his probable attackers didn't come into the room. He didn't know why. Then he saw the men turn as if to look behind him. A scream cut through the night—but even that wouldn't be enough to wake his deaf neighbor who lived above him.

"No! Wait!" a deep voice called out, but was followed by a man crying out in pain.

He saw the shadowed forms fall to their knees. Sterling's eyes adjusted enough to the dim light to make out another form in the hallway. This one was slim and much shorter—but the person was wielding a blade. Sterling wasn't sure which frightened him more, the large men or the person with the sword.

The thinner figure bent down for a moment and appeared to rip one of the men's shirts. Then smoothly, almost as if it was a dance, the armed person went down the hallway and out the back door.

⇥‡⇤

Diantha looked back over her shoulder as she moved stealthily down the road. She had gotten more blood on her already blood stained clothes. She glanced at her sword—she'd been able to clean it using one of the men's shirts.

What had gotten into her? It was as if she was watching someone else tie the bloodied, torn cloth used to clean her sword to the porch's rafter where she had attacked the men. Still, she had stopped them from harming another human being—hopefully, ever again. She'd given them surface wounds, bad enough that they would bleed and leave a scar but not enough to do permanent damage. Just like those who attacked her on the road, she doubted they would come forward to admit they were wounded by a woman they attacked.

She saw the stables ahead, and then taking a quick glance around, she approached them. Before, it wasn't hard to climb out of her window and onto the roof over the stables. From there, it was an easy jump to the ground below. Now that she was back, she needed to figure out a way to climb back onto the stable roof.

A water barrel was placed at one of the corners to catch the runoff from rain storms. Even though its top was open, she was able to get on it and stand on the edges. From there, she could reach the roof. After setting her sword on the wooden shingled covering, she pulled herself up and climbed back through her window into her room.

Getting rid of her stained clothes would have to wait for another night. She couldn't risk trying it after the men had let out such cries.

Diantha stood in the middle of her room, looking at her recently used sword and dirtied clothes. She couldn't explain why, but she felt good—and *right*.

CHAPTER 61

E noch's punch knocked several of his foe's teeth flying. The man before him stumbled back a few steps from the blow. He wiped the blood from his mouth then went to reach for a knife he had stashed in his boot, but Enoch noticed the movement and advanced. Enoch clenched his hands together, effectively making them into a big weapon and swung at the man's head as he was straightening up with the knife in his hand. The blow knocked Enoch's enemy backwards and off his feet— his knife flying out of his hand when he hit the ground.

The sounds of the continuing raid surrounded Enoch, but at the moment, no one else was within reach. He went to one knee by his fallen foe, keeping a watchful eye on him. The man had been decent with a sword, enough so that he was able to break Enoch's pike—a long staff of wood with a sharp metal head placed on one end. But in doing so, the sword had been batted from his grip. That's when the hand-to-hand fighting had begun, something Enoch was good at. It had only taken a few blows to knock the man down.

Dressed in non-descript armor, bearing no colors or standard—the same way the other attackers were dressed when they attacked Commander Snapdragon a week ago—his fallen opponent seemed to be out cold. However, Enoch knew to be careful. He went to touch the man over when the raider's eyes snapped open and he began to sit up. Enoch had prepared for such a tactic, and planted a blow into the man's chest, knocking the air from his lungs.

With the raider struggling to catch his breath, Enoch flipped the man onto his chest. He then grabbed the man's wrists and using rope each of the militia was supplied as standard equipment, tied the man's hands then feet together.

After making sure the ropes were tight, Enoch picked up the man with one hand by grabbing a hold of his tunic. The man was of a decent build, but Enoch was strong enough to lift him.

Enoch backed up toward the wall, carrying his prisoner. He was glad that the order was to capture, and not kill, any raiders if at all possible. He set the man down next to his previous captive, but far enough away to keep them from helping each other get free.

Next, Enoch left to get another pike so he could head back into battle.

⊰⧻⊱

Captain Mason looked at the five men Enoch had captured and shook his head in disbelief. "You got all these yourself there, big guy?"

"Yes, sir."

"How in the name of the Zealous Star did you capture all of them?" Mason asked.

"Actually, they helped me," Enoch said, motioning to the bound and gagged prisoners.

Mason looked at Enoch dubiously. "They helped you?"

"After I had the first two tied up, I went to get another weapon—you know, from the cart we brought? Once I was out of sight, they started yelling for help," Enoch explained. "I noticed that they got the attention of some of the other raiders, so I stayed hidden behind the cart over there and waited for them to come to me. I snuck up behind them as they were trying to free their companions and took them by surprise."

His captain grinned and shook his head. "Ah Enoch, you're always doing the unexpected."

The statement took him a bit off guard. "Unexpected?"

Pointing to the prisoners, Mason said, "It would have been much easier to kill these men than to capture them. The rest of the raiders were killed in battle, while only one of our militia was injured."

"But weren't we supposed to capture, and not kill them?" Enoch countered.

"Yes..." Mason said slowly. "But, to be honest, I'm not sure why. From what they told us, these captives are no more than street thugs hired by someone they didn't know. And, I doubt anyone will step forward to try to barter for the raiders we have captured."

"Maybe one of these men will know something else when we question them more," Enoch pointed out.

"Maybe," Mason agreed, if somewhat reluctantly. "In the meantime, get them loaded into the wagon while I check on the rest of my men."

⊰⊱

The bald man had a long, pointed beard, with a green stripe running its length. He was bare-chested and wore simple, but durable breeches and boots made of animal skin. At least, Crescens hoped it was animal skin—it looked like something he'd not seen before. Maybe there were hairless animals north of the mountains, where this man, this Rifna Erd, came from. His teeth were rotting in his mouth and he smelled as if he'd bathed in sewage. Indeed, he was an imposing, and somewhat disturbing, figure of a man.

He was perfect.

"How much more do I have to wait?" the man asked. His accent was thick and he pronounced some words differently, but if Crescens tried hard enough, and also included the man's body language, he could figure out what the man was saying.

"She'll be along shortly," Crescens said.

They sat in a small hut on the edge of Lake Dylobo—almost directly across from where Erd Palace stood on the far side. The night was dark, with clouds canopying the sky. It had only taken twenty-two years to get this man here—a very long time indeed to wait. Crescens was amazed at Selene's patience.

"I don't like it here," the man said. He sniffed the air and then looked around. "It is too quiet. I smell no meat cooking." He looked up at the hut's ceiling. "And I cannot see the stars."

"Are you hungry?" Crescens asked, trying to glean the meaning of what the Rifna Erd was saying.

"No. I was fed by those that brought me here."

Unsure what to say next, Crescens studied the note he held. It had been written in code in case it got intercepted. The message stated that this Rifna Erd man was being brought to this hut tonight—that the raid had caused enough of a diversion to insure he could arrive undetected. Selene had sent Crescens ahead, and said she would join him after the evening meal so as not to raise suspicion.

Crescens could see from the corner of his eye the Rifna Erd was staring at him. It made him feel very uncomfortable. Not for the first time, Crescens wondered if it was such a good idea to come alone. This man from beyond the northern mountains looked like he could kill Crescens with his bare hands, and not break a sweat doing it.

For several, long moments, they sat there. At last, Crescens heard the sound of the ferry approaching. The rope on this end of the lake made a distinct creaking noise when the ferry was close.

"Wait here. I will go get her." He stood to leave.

The man continued to stare at Crescens with an expression that was difficult to read. It wasn't hostile, but neither was it pleasant.

Torn between turning his back on this strange man and leaving, Crescens picked the latter, trying to convince himself he wasn't fleeing.

Upon exiting the hut, Crescens could make out the ferry pulling up to the dock. The ferryman was a large fellow that preferred shirts with no sleeves. This was no doubt to show off his well-muscled arms. Selene trusted the ferryman for the simple reason that he was born a deaf mute—he could not tell anyone of their coming and goings. Crescens was glad she had found this man—before, Crescens, himself, would have to pull the ferry along. He was getting too old to do that.

The ferryman helped Selene onto the dock. She gave him two coins and then motioned for him to stay there.

Selene was dressed in a hooded robe, but one that had been tailor fit. Even though she was getting on in age, she was still quite curvaceous.

"Crescens," she said in greeting. The tone of her voice matched the chill in the evening air.

He bowed. "Governor."

"Is he here?"

"Aye."

Without saying another word, Selene strode purposefully toward the hut. Crescens hurried to keep up. He beat her to the door and opened it. Selene walked in. The Rifna Erd man remained seated, showing no reaction to her entrance. Crescens knew Selene well enough that she was bothered by the man's lack of respect, though she remained calm.

"I am Selene, Governor of Erd," she said.

The Rifna Erd continued to stare at her.

"Governor Selene," she said again, pointing to herself.

"Serkan." The bald man pointed to his chest.

"Serkan," she repeated.

She sat down across from him, taking the only other chair in the hut. Crescens would have to stand, but at least he would be close to her.

Selene pulled down her hood to reveal her flowing, dark hair. "Well, Serkan, we have much to discuss."

⊰⧉⊱

The winter had been a wet one. Spring was in full bloom in the valleys, and it was a stark contrast to see flowers growing while the mountains were still half white with snow.

Snapdragon took in a deep breath of the early morning spring air. The last several days had been difficult. Diantha had basically stormed out of the house, vowing never to return. His wife, Seraphina, had cried most of the night his oldest daughter left. Snapdragon had cried a little as well, though in his heart, he knew Diantha had to find her own way.

While she was certainly her own person, Snapdragon saw a stubborn streak in her that he recognized in himself—or at least one he had learned to control over the years. How could he be angry with her if he would have probably acted the same way in her shoes? Hopefully she would find what she was looking for at the castle. He wasn't happy with Aaron who was supposed to escort her. Still, he understood Aaron's predicament. Still, he'd feel better when he knew she was safe in the castle.

A different type of safety was the reason Snapdragon was headed to the main tower. He took in one more deep breath before heading up the stairs. At three stories high, it was the tallest structure in the area—and one of Snapdragon's favorite places to visit.

From the top of the tower, he could see many things. For one, there was the town of Procep—really more of a city now. It had grown to be quite large over the last couple of decades. Also, he could view the semi-circular wall that surrounded the collapsed tunnel entrance which had led to the land beyond the northern mountains. It was separate from the wall that ran the length of the mountain range.

It didn't seem possible to Snapdragon at first to build a wall that would run from the steep cliffs of the western sea to the far marshes of the east. Granted, they were still working on the end by the marshes—it was slow going due to the nature of the ground and the distance from a decent quarry.

A quarry was why Snapdragon was headed to the top of the tower. He was asked to meet Bearach to discuss a potential issue. He climbed the stairs, taking two at a time. Upon reaching the top, he saw Bearach was already there.

"Thanks for joining me, Snap," Bearach said in greeting.

"Anytime, old friend. I heard you wanted to discuss something about a quarry?"

Bearach nodded. "Not just any quarry, that one." He pointed to the one that had been converted into a lake which provided Procep with water via aqueducts.

"Is there something wrong with it?" Snapdragon asked.

"Not yet."

Snapdragon looked intently at the man he had known for many years. Bearach had an uncanny knack with mechanics—a skill that ended up saving their lives when they were younger. His friend was very pragmatic, so for him to make this statement gave Snapdragon reason to pause. "What exactly do you mean by 'not yet'?"

Motioning at the mountains, Bearach said, "We've not had this much snow since we've lived here. In the past, the aqueducts have always been enough to handle any runoff."

"But you're concerned that won't be enough this year, right?" Snapdragon asked.

"Exactly."

Snapdragon raked his hand through his hair. "What's the worst that would happen?"

"Well," Bearach said, "the water would overflow the banks of the lake and flood Procep. Most of the buildings are made from stone, but still, it would make a huge mess."

"All right, Bearach, out with it," Snapdragon said. "It isn't like you to not have a back-up plan."

The crafter smiled. "Ah, you know me too well." He then walked to the other side of the tower. "Let me show you something."

Snapdragon followed him.

Bearach stopped in front of a half wall, built out from the main one. Placed into it were several stones with different types of markings on them.

"I learned quite a bit when we were trapped on the other side of the mountains. The people that built the tunnel were masters in the art of mechanics. Remember how they designed rocks to move using pressure points?"

"Aye, that I do."

"Well, the stones marked with symbols are designed the same way—though you have to push them in a certain order," Bearach said.

Snapdragon looked at the stones and for the life of him couldn't see a rhyme or reason to the symbols. "And what happens when you press them in a certain order?"

"Want to see?" Bearach looked at him excitedly.

"Absolutely."

Bearach first pushed on a stone that had wavy, horizontal lines. He then pushed one with three dots, followed by one with an arrow pointing down. After pressing in the last one, there was an audible *click*.

Trying to act casually, but not being very convincing, Bearach walked back to the other side of the tower. Once again Snapdragon followed him.

Peering up at the lake, Snapdragon tried to see what Bearach had done. At first, he didn't notice a difference. Then, on the far side of the lake, just within sight, he saw water streaming out of what appeared to be the side of the mountain. It caused a small waterfall, of sorts, to flow away from Procep.

"Amazing. Simply amazing," Snapdragon said. "You made that waterfall by pushing rocks on the panel? I can't even begin to imagine how you did that."

"It took me some time to figure out how to do it, but as you can see, it worked." Bearach was beaming with pride.

"All these years, and you never told me?" Snapdragon asked.

Bearach shrugged. "I showed it to you when we got started—it was part of the original plans."

"The plans you showed me over twenty years ago?" Snapdragon laughed. "I barely understood the basics of those. But, you're right. I'm sure you told me. There was much going on those days."

"Not to mention you were newly married and all goofy eyed toward Seraphina most of the time," Bearach teased.

"Fine, fine. I get your point." Snapdragon motioned over to the shelf with the stones Bearach had pushed. "What else does that do?"

Pointing to the aqueducts, Bearach said, "They allow me to open and close the water supply to Procep. You know, in case something happens to the water."

"Anything else?"

Bearach smiled. "As you said before, I always have a back-up plan."

CHAPTER 62

"Bloodied cloth?" Selene asked.

Crescens nodded. "Yes, Governor. Another ripped cloth, soaked through with blood, was found this morning. This time, inside the town."

The shapely governor leaned back in her chair and tapped her lips with her finger. Crescens wasn't sure how she would take the news. He was starting to put together bits and pieces of her plan, though she had not revealed everything to him.

"And how are the people reacting to the discovery of these symbols?" she asked.

"They're frightened," Crescens responded. "I've heard rumors of ghosts or other evils from beyond the grave roaming the area. Many have claimed to have seen certain things, though none of their stories match. The only constant is the torn, bloodied cloth hanging by places where people have been attacked."

For a moment Selene seemed to be deep in thought. She then asked, "And have the people who have been attacked come forth?"

"We've only found one—identified as a local cutpurse. He was on the side of the road where the first cloth was found. He was dead. His skull had been crushed. That news has also spread and has added to the peoples' fears."

Selene's expression changed into one that Crescens rarely witnessed. She smiled.

"Go to your contacts," she commanded. "Make sure they spread the word that people *need* to be afraid."

Once again, Crescens didn't fully understand what she was planning. It was yet another strange reaction from her. "It will be as you say," Crescens said. He turned to leave.

"One last thing," Selene said.

He faced her.

"Your beard is coming in quite nicely, Crescens. It makes you look distinguished. You should have grown it out years ago."

He felt his face redden at the compliment received from the woman he desired for all these years. She was stingy with praise, so Crescens relished the moment.

"Thank you, Governor," he said, bowing.

With that, she dismissed him with a wave of her hand. As soon as Crescens was out of her sight, he found that he couldn't stop grinning.

⊰✠⊱

Enoch gaped at Mason. His friend, the captain of the militia, had been gone to Erd Proper for a few days and was now just returning. It wasn't the sight of Mason on horseback, or that he had someone with him, but rather what was on his friend's face. It was a beard—and fairly thick as well.

"Enoch!" Mason called out when they made eye contact.

Assigned to gate duty that day, Enoch was the first to see his captain return. He saluted him in greeting. Mason saluted back.

"Report," Mason said when he was almost to the gate.

On a horse next to the captain was a woman with gray, wavy hair. Enoch had never met her before, so he wasn't sure what he should say in front of her. Mason picked up on his hesitation and said, "It's all right to speak in front of Magistrate Larissa."

"As you say, Captain," Enoch replied. "There have been no raids reported while you were gone. There have been no disturbances in the town. We did receive some strange news about events in Erd Proper, but since you were just there, I'm sure you know more than I do."

The woman leaned forward in her saddle. "What have you heard?" Her voice was hard and it matched her expression.

"Not much, really. Mostly rumors of the Noble Trod coming back to life, hanging bloody clothes around town, and even one person said they swore that they saw the Devil's daughter roaming the street."

She continued to stare at him with unblinking eyes. "And what do you think of all this?"

"Well, Magistrate Larissa—"

"No!" she shouted. "It's pronounced Lar-eye-saw!"

586

Enoch was stunned by her reaction. He had never heard that name said with that pronunciation. Even though Mason had pronounced it the way she preferred, he had thought it was just his friend's odd accent.

"Magistrate Lar*i*ssa," Enoch corrected, this time putting the proper emphasis on the middle vowel. "I don't believe much of what they say. Often these things are easily explained and people let their imaginations get the best of them."

"Oh? So you don't believe in things you can't see, is that it?" She mocked.

Instead of answering her, Enoch looked to Mason. "Captain, I don't understand why a magistrate would speak to me, or anyone, in this manner. You said she is a magistrate, but from where?"

Mason's face turned red—something Enoch knew was not from embarrassment, but rather, from anger. "She's been assigned to oversee the militia across the entire northern wall."

Larissa smirked at him. "That's right. I oversaw the militia in Erd Proper and we always scored the highest rankings. I've been rated number one for the last five years. I've been sent up here to make sure these raids are stopped and that the militia is performing at its best. I will not accept anything less than perfect."

"She's been promoted to magistrate and I now answer to her," Mason said. He glared at Enoch.

Rankings among the different militias was something Enoch knew about, but didn't give much thought. Every season, or four times a year, each militia unit was inspected to make sure they were staffed properly, had the right equipment, and were doing the needed training. Several years back, a few of the militia from Erd asked that the findings be made public. After that, someone from Erd then sorted through the information and ranked everyone. Before Mason, the militia of Stur had always done very well, even making it to number three in the rankings a few times. Things had even gotten better once Mason arrived. Certainly the raids weren't Mason's fault—he done well in fighting off the attack.

"I understand, Captain," Enoch said respectfully. He then faced Larissa. "To answer your previous question, no, I don't believe only in the things I can see. However, fear of the unknown can cause people to make questionable choices."

The magistrate looked him over once, and then again. She sat up in her saddle, and then said, "Enough. Let us in. I'm bored with this conversation."

⋙✦⋘

Mason ran his fingers through his beard. Enoch was amazed at what Mason had been able to grow in a just a few days. They had sat down for dinner at the Silver Vein Tavern moments ago, and it was Enoch's first chance to speak to his friend, and captain, alone without Larissa around.

"So, why the chin warmer?" Enoch asked.

Mason beamed with pride. "Everyone is growing them in Erd Proper these days. Many have them grown all the way to their mid-chest."

Rubbing his hand over his cleanly shaven face, Enoch said, "This may be a problem."

"Oh?"

Enoch shook his head a little and rolled his eyes. "Do you know why I shave every day?"

"I hadn't really thought about it, but now that you mention it, I don't think I've ever seen you with facial hair."

"I tried once to grow a beard and mustache. It was just before you arrived. Let's just say I was... unsuccessful."

"Meaning?" Mason asked.

"It looked terrible! It took forever for it to be noticeable, and even then, the beard grew only in patches here and there." Enoch shrugged and gave a little smile. He was big and strong, so he thought growing facial hair would have been easy.

Mason laughed. "I didn't know! Imagine, you, of all people, not being able to..." He couldn't continue because he was laughing so hard.

"All right, all right," Enoch said. "So, tell me, what's it been like spending the day with Magistrate Larissa." He once again emphasized the way she demanded it be pronounced.

His friend looked around to make sure he couldn't be heard. "It's been a nightmare. She's so picky about everything. She'll find something she says we're doing wrong. I'll explain that's how we were told to do it, to which she'll respond, 'You should know better.' And she can't go more than a few sentences without mentioning she's been ranked number one for the last five years."

"I don't get it," Enoch said.

Mason took a drink from his mug, and then asked, "Don't get what?"

"I mean, who cares that she's been number one? This militia has always done very well on the reviews—doing better in every category than what is expected. Plus, things are different in running a militia in a town compared to up here against the wall. We can't control what happens elsewhere—just here. Shouldn't we be happy they are doing well? After all, we're all on the same side."

Taking another drink before responding, Mason said, "I'd never really thought about it that way. But for whatever reason, it means the world to Larissa."

"Is she married?" Enoch asked.

Mason looked at him for a moment, and then burst into laughter. "No, she's not. As far as I know, her whole life is focused on the militia. Why? Are you interested in her?"

Unable to hide the distain he knew was on his face, Enoch said, "No, I'm not. I was just thinking that maybe she's confused her job with her life. Maybe she thinks that being rated number one makes her a better person or something."

Mason stared at Enoch and didn't say anything. After a moment, Enoch became so uncomfortable that he asked, "Mason, are you all right?"

His friend nodded his head. "Enoch, every once in a while you will say things that catch me by surprise. You're very insightful. Tell me more on your thoughts about Larissa."

Enoch shrugged. "Well, it's not just about her. I've noticed that there are those that seem to think the only way they can feel good about themselves is by pointing out the flaws in others. It sounds like she fits into that mold. It's sad, really."

"So, what do you do to feel good about yourself then, eh?"

Enoch took a sip of his drink and thought about the question before answering. "I guess I've made decisions on what's right and what's wrong and try to stay true to those. I get sad when I've not remained true to what I know to be right."

Mason sighed. "Well, in the case of Larissa, she's making a big deal out of things that aren't 'right,' as you call it. For example, she said we needed to have the weapons in the armory lined up in alphabetical order, which I'd never heard before, and frankly doesn't make a lot of sense. But she's my superior and even though I think she's making a mistake, I have to do what she says. So which is more wrong? Doing what I know is right—or at least think is right—and in the process, disobeying my superior or just doing what I'm told so I don't get in trouble."

It was odd for Mason, his captain, to be asking such deep questions to Enoch. For the most part, their friendship was based on Enoch being responsible and a hard worker, and thereby being respected by his captain. Perhaps Mason was testing him. He decided to answer as if the latter was true.

"With all due respect, Captain, you've not asked me to do anything wrong."

Mason's eyebrows rose. "Do you think that's what this is about? Well, no matter, it will still give me my answer. What if I ordered you to do something you thought was wrong, not an incorrect action as much as a morally wrong choice?"

The question was troubling simply because he didn't want to upset the other man. Yet, Enoch knew the answer without having to think about it. "I'd do what I thought was right."

"Even if you got in trouble?"

"In trouble from who? You? Larissa? If that's all I was concerned about, than I'm sure I'd act much like your new leader. In the end, I need to be true to me."

Mason eyed him. "You are a wholly unique person, my friend."

The next morning Enoch, along with the rest of the local militia, were told to get into formation as the first rays of dawn shone from the east. Enoch had been fortunate that he'd not had one of the night shifts—some of his fellow militiamen looked rather haggard from lack of sleep.

They stood in two rows of ten men each. They were all dressed appropriately and were standing at attention. Not long after they were in position, Magistrate Larissa rode her horse from the stables and stopped in front of the men. It didn't make any sense to Enoch for her to be mounted, aside from perhaps giving her the ability to look down at them.

"By a raise of hands, who here has joined the militia since the last reviews were completed?" She didn't bother greeting them first.

A couple of the younger men lifted their hands.

Larissa sniffed and then peered down her nose at them. "You poor, poor boys. You have no clue on what to expect. I have no doubt you'll freeze when faced with some of the trials. Actually, I wouldn't be surprised if you didn't start crying like little girls."

Enoch knew the men she was talking to. These were good soldiers who had trained to become guardians but fell a little short at the Mortentaun. They had been a part of fighting off the last raid, and had done very well. It bothered him that Larissa would speak to them in such a manner without really knowing them. He glanced down the row where Mason was, but his captain simply stood at attention and focused his attention at Larissa.

Well, if Mason wouldn't speak up for his men, Enoch would.

"Magistrate," Enoch said before she could continue, "I can vouch for the men you are addressing. They are not weak. Give them a chance."

Larissa looked as if she had been slapped. "Wha—what did you say?" Spit flew from her mouth as she spoke.

"I said that you don't need to speak to them that way. It isn't helping anything. It's not going to motivate them—it's just going to make them become defensive and not hear you when instructions they do need are given," Enoch said.

"Who do you think you are?" Larissa roared. "I have been rated number one for five years! I know what I'm doing. How dare you speak to me that way! What was your name again?"

He didn't flinch at her outburst. "Enoch."

"No, I don't think so. From now on, you'll be known as Eunuch," she said, smirking.

Enoch shook his head. "But that's not my name, Magistrate Larissa." Again, he put a strong emphasis on the middle part of her name. "And Magistrate or not, and being ranked whatever number for however long doesn't give you the right to speak to me and these other men this way."

For the first time since he'd met her, Larissa seemed to be at a loss for words. She just gave him a crazed look. He'd seen that look before—it was one of a person who was used to getting there way and told for the first time they couldn't.

Turning to Captain Mason, Larissa screamed, "I want this man out of service! Now!" She pointed to Enoch.

"You are dismissed, Enoch!" Mason said.

Despite the command being unfair and the whole situation being ridiculous, Enoch nodded and left the group.

He went back to his room and waited. While he sat on his bed with his hands resting on his chin, Enoch thought back over what had just happened. It seemed like a coincidence that Mason would ask him about standing up for what he believed in and then the very next morning, he was faced with such a challenge. Did his captain know this was going to happen? If so, why didn't he warn Enoch? Actually, perhaps it was *because* of the conversation that gave him the prompting to stand up to Larissa. It was all very troublesome.

Yet Enoch was certain he was right for speaking up. Mason had worked hard to get the men under his command to trust each other and work together as a unit. He wasn't sure what Larissa was trying to accomplish aside from perhaps establishing her authority. In his opinion, she was going about it all wrong.

Several moments later, there was a knock on his door. It was Mason, and he was looking none-too-pleased. But he knew his captain well enough now that it wasn't an expression of anger, either.

"Captain," Enoch said in greeting. "Come on in."

Mason nodded in appreciation and entered Enoch's humble hut. "Enoch, we need to talk about what happened this morning."

Motioning to the hut's only chair, Enoch said, "Please sit down."

His captain did so while Enoch sat down on the edge of his bed.

"Captain," Enoch said, "I'm sorry if I got you in trouble, but I'm not sorry for what I said."

"I understand, yet that's the problem."

Enoch frowned. "I don't understand."

"Larissa, is, well, very particular on the way she wants things done. She's convinced if it isn't her way, it's wrong," Mason shook his head and sighed.

"But don't you see she was destroying everything you have built here among the men?" Enoch asked.

"She's in charge now," Mason said.

Enoch didn't get upset often—he found it rarely helped things and clouded his judgment. However, it felt like a fire was starting to build inside his chest. "I can't imagine Queen Rainbow or Commanders Oakleaf and Snapdragon assigning someone like Larissa. The royalty and other leaders have always been supportive and positive—the exact opposite of everything Larissa represents."

"She wasn't assigned by them," Mason said.

"Then who sent her?"

Mason didn't look him in the eye when he responded, "Someone you'll be meeting soon."

CHAPTER 63

Queen Rainbow sat across the table from her father. Her elbows were on the flat surface between them with her chin resting in her hands. They were playing a game that consisted of a board separated into seven sections. Each player had twenty-four tokens of various shapes. The goal was to gain control of at least four of the sections by taking turns in moving their tokens. Each of the tokens had a special ability which added to the depth of the game. Rainbow had been told the game was easy to learn, but difficult to master. She noted how the same thing could be said about being queen.

Her father, Councilor Rayne, had just gained control of his second section and was on his way to capturing his third. She'd never beaten him in this game, though she had gotten close several times. Today he was using a strategy she hadn't seen him use before and it had her befuddled.

"Just when I think I have you figured out, you change tactics," Rainbow said, puzzling over her next move.

Rayne leaned back in his chair and smiled. "Would it be any fun if I made the same moves each time?"

"No," Rainbow answered as she moved one of her tokens, "but it would make my life easier."

"So, you're saying that it's more fun to have a harder life?"

She looked up at him. "Now you're sounding like mom or Grandpa Garth."

"That is something they would say, isn't it?" He laughed. "I guess they've rubbed off on me."

Rayne leaned back toward the table and made another move. With it, he captured his third section.

"Well, the change of tactics reminds me of the raids on the northern wall," Rainbow said. "The attacks don't make any sense."

"What do you think are the reasons behind the raids?" Rayne asked.

Rainbow shrugged. "It could be any number of things. Disgruntled people like the governor of Regne who think they aren't getting their fair share. Or people still loyal to Abrecan's memory and are lashing out. Whatever it is, I don't believe it's random or chance."

"And that's what's the most frustrating, isn't it?" Rayne said. "Nothing seems to have been gained from the attacks, aside from keeping the militia in practice."

Rainbow looked up at her father. "Do you think that has anything to do with it?"

"Which part?"

"About keeping the militia trained."

Rayne rubbed his chin. "It's possible, but to what end? Who would spend their money to send men—who are no more than thugs—to attack Snapdragon and then another village by the wall? Oakleaf wouldn't do it—people have died in these attacks. No one here at the castle has arranged them, or we'd see unaccounted funds leaving the treasury. And, there are better ways to train the militia than attacks."

"Basically what you're saying is that we still have no idea about the motivation for the attacks," Rainbow said.

"No, we don't." Rayne shook his head. "Back to the game. It's your turn."

Analyzing the pieces in front of her, Rainbow realized she had been using many of the same tactics in previous games where she had almost won. She had become predictable. That's why she hadn't beaten her father. *Almost* winning wasn't the goal. She examined the board and decided to make a nonconventional move. After doing so, she noticed her father smile and nod his head in approval.

⇥✦⇤

Court that afternoon was fairly straight-forward. There were the usual reports from the various districts, none of which were out of the ordinary until the representative from Erd spoke. He had been the liaison from the northern most district since Rainbow was crowned as queen. The man was very no-nonsense, and until recently, clean shaven. As with just about every man from Erd she met recently, he was growing out his beard.

"Someone is attacking people in Erd Proper and then hanging bloodied, torn cloth on display?" King Elisedd asked.

Rainbow was glad he was asking for clarification. She, too, thought the man from Erd must have misspoken.

"Yes, Your Majesty," the liaison replied.

"Very odd," Elisedd said. "It reminds me of the story of... oh, what was his name?"

"The Noble Trod?" Rainbow prompted.

Elisedd snapped his fingers. "Yes! That's the one."

"Do you believe that whoever is doing this is linked to the attacks by the wall?" Rainbow asked the man from Erd.

He shook his head. "There's no evidence to support it."

"Why would anyone do such things?" Elisedd asked.

"That's where the reports become the most interesting. It seems the common thread is that all the people attacked have been breaking the law or threating others. In every case, any money or possessions were returned to the proper owners. Also, though some of the reports contradict each other, we've gathered that it's the same person, but we haven't been able to get an accurate description."

Rainbow strummed her fingers on the armrest of her throne. "We can't have someone running around taking the law into their own hands. The Tome of Laws is quite clear on this point."

"I don't know, dear," Elisedd said. "It seems to me that this person is actually helping. Maybe not in the way the Tome of Laws states, but assisting the guardians none-the-less."

The crowd in the main hall attending court became very quiet. This wasn't the first time the king brought up a different point of view. It was actually something Rainbow appreciated. Elisedd wasn't afraid to look at things from a different perspective. This trait had helped on more than one occasion. In the end, he would support whatever Rainbow decided, and not just because she was the blood heir to the throne and would have the final say. He had explained to her that while she had studied The Tome of Laws all her life and had trained to rule Bariwon, he still had much to learn. Admitting that is just one more thing she loved about him.

"One concept I was taught time and again was that I should always strive to do the right thing and for the right reason," Rainbow responded. "The Tome of Laws was written to not only keep the peace, but to protect the innocent. What if the person who is doing this makes a mistake and attacks a guiltless person? That's why we require at least two witnesses before punishment is handed out."

Elisedd nodded his head. "Of course. I see your point and do not disagree."

Rainbow turned her attention to address the man from Erd. "Please tell Governor Selene that if she requires any help from us, it will be granted. But one way or another, these attacks must end."

"It will be as you say." He bowed and backed away.

The head of the Hierarchy of Magistrates stood. Rainbow liked him. Bertram had faithfully served the kingdom for many years and was a close personal friend to her parents.

"We have just one more item for today's court," Bertram said. "The governors of Donigi and Regne have asked that we hear a dispute they have been unable to resolve."

"The people involved may approach," Elisedd stated.

Two men from the crowd moved to the front of the dais. While they were both dressed nicely, Rainbow could tell they had experienced hard labor most of their lives. They were both older—one with nearly white hair and the other bald. While they stood side-by-side, they appeared uncomfortable being so close together.

"You will both be allowed to tell your side of the story," Elisedd said, "and we ask that you not interrupt the other person."

Both men nodded. Indicating to the man with white hair, the king said, "You may go first."

"Thank you, Your Majesty." He bowed. "My name is Alton. I own a farm that spans between the districts of Donigi and Regne. It has been owned by my family for generations. It was once part of a larger farm that was split into two and given to the sons of the original owner—my ancestor.

"Next to my land is Elwood's farm. When the contract was written up to divide the land, it stated my part went from the river Dremeal to a large oak tree which grew roughly halfway in the middle of the original farm. Recently, Elwood has been letting his herds graze on my land which is destroying many of my crops. All I ask is that you enforce the contract."

Alton held out an old parchment that had been rolled into a scroll. Elisedd motioned for a guardian to take it to the Hierarchy of Magistrates.

"While the magistrates review the contract, Elwood, you may address us," Rainbow said.

The bald man bowed even deeper than Alton had. He then straightened up and smiled at them. To Rainbow, the smile looked insincere.

"Let me first state that I have every intention of supporting the contract," Elwood said. "To that point, the exact wording is, 'One section will run from the shores of Zuera Lake to the giant oak tree that stands alone in the field between the lake and the river Dremeal.' I have brought witnesses to verify that I've not broken the contract."

Rainbow looked at Alton. "And I suppose that you have witnesses stating that Elwood *has* broken the contract, am I correct?"

The white haired man nodded.

"Well, you both can't be right, and the penalty for lying in court is quite severe," Elisedd said. "Do either of you wish to recant your story before we find you guilty of providing false witness?"

"If I may, Your Majesty," Alton said, "there is part of the story you've not heard yet."

"Then enlighten us."

Pointing a finger accusingly at his neighbor, Alton said, "A few years ago, Elwood planted several trees next to the large oak. They were on his side of the land, so I gave it no mind. When I found his animals on my land, I confronted him. His claim was that the giant oak tree no longer stood alone, as written in the contract, and therefore he had legal claim to any land up to where a lone oak tree grew."

Before Rainbow could say anything, Elisedd asked the other man, "Is this true?"

Elwood shrugged and gave them a crooked smile. "I have a right to plant whatever I want on my land. Anyone that visits the area can clearly see that the oak tree does not stand alone as stated in the contract. I've done nothing to break the law."

Elisedd looked at his wife after the statement. She knew him well enough to know that meant he would support her in whatever she decided. Rainbow also knew that her husband understood that she fully intended to render a judgment.

"Magistrates, have you reviewed the contract?" Rainbow asked.

"Yes, Your Highness," Bertram answered.

"And what have you found?"

The head magistrate cleared his throat. "The way the contract is written, Elwood has followed the letter of the law."

Elwood beamed with self-satisfaction. Alton's face showed his feelings of disappointment and frustration.

Earlier in the day, Rainbow had lost the board game for the countless time against her father. But after she switched her tactics, he found it very difficult to capture the final section. When hearing all the information, Rainbow's initial response was to state how the laws of the land were just words and it was the meaning behind them which made the difference.

The most significant example of that principle was when her father had been chosen as king of Bariwon.

However, if she found in favor of Alton, Elwood could stir up trouble, stating the queen ignored the binding contract. And if she upheld Elwood's claim, that could open the door for more people to find ways they could exploit various laws and contracts.

For a moment she pondered while everyone in the main hall watched her. This situation seemed so small and ridiculous compared to the threat of the Rifna Erd—yet to each of these men it was very significant in their lives. She felt angry at Elwood for his actions, no matter how he justified them. Everyone should be helping each other in the kingdom, not looking for ways to exploit his fellow man. And with that thought, the answer came to her.

"Magistrate Bertram, will you please open The Tome of Laws to chapter seventeen. The passage I'm looking for is roughly a third of the way into the chapter. It starts with 'The greater good of the kingdom.'"

The magistrate thumbed through the pages. It was times like these that Rainbow was grateful for all the hours she had spent reading and studying the Tome of Laws.

"I have found it, Your Highness," Bertram said.

"Please read it for all to hear. I'll stop you when we've heard enough."

Rainbow noticed that both farmers looked confused at her actions. They wouldn't be confused for long.

"The greater good of the kingdom may require sacrifices of the people when the kingdom in general is at risk. During such times, the rulers may annex resources, including land, for support of the kingdom. Once the threat has passed, the kingdom will return such items, as possible, to their respective owners. Examples of how such situations follows—"

"Thank you, Magistrate," Rainbow interrupted.

Bertram nodded and sat down.

Facing Elwood, Rainbow said, "It is my opinion that the kingdom is at risk from the threat of the Rifna Erd. The northern defenses and the militia are more than enough to support this claim. The land by the mountains could have been annexed, but it was given freely by the district of Erd."

The bald farmer was no longer smiling. He seemed to understand her reasoning.

"By the authority of my title as queen, I officially annex your land, Elwood, for the good of the kingdom. The first thing you will do is to remove any trees by the oak tree mentioned in the contract. You will continue to live on the land and work the fields. However, one-fifth of your crops and animals will be donated to the general supplies of the kingdom. If at any time you fail to meet any of these requirements, I will have you removed from the land and will allow Alton to take over both farms. Are you clear on these points?"

Elwood looked like he was trying to form words with his mouth, yet nothing was said. In the end, he simply nodded.

"Then before I declare this court to be completed, I want everyone to know that as a kingdom we need to stay strong. There are troubles enough as it is without us inventing new ones. To peace in our kingdom!"

"To peace in our kingdom!" the people echoed.

⋙⊹⋘

Diantha held the coin pouch in her hand. It was heavy.

The man on the ground before her had his right arm tucked against his body. She'd stabbed him in the hand, not too deep, but it would leave a scar.

With her back to the moon in the darkened alleyway, she doubted he could see her clearly. It didn't really matter if he could. She had pulled her hair up into a cap she had purchased recently. From her last few outings, she had made sure her clothes were stained blood red. In addition, she wore a red scarf that covered her nose and mouth.

"Take it! Take it all!" he pleaded. "Just don't kill me!"

"Where did you get this money from?" she asked.

"Here and there," he said. "I'm just a poor cutpurse. It's mostly coin I stole at the Mortentaun."

She pointed her sword at his face. "Keep pressure on your bleeding hand—that is if you want to live. After that, leave here and stop your thieving ways. There is plenty of honest work to do."

"I will! I promise!"

Diantha moved away from the man and looked down the street. The patrols increased over the last couple of days. Fortunately, she had avoided them thus far. She spotted a lamppost just down the street a ways—it would be a good place to hang bloodied cloth she'd ripped from his shirt.

After making sure the cloth was attached securely, she moved stealthily down the street and into the shadows of a narrow passage between two of the buildings. She tied the coin purse to her belt and started to scale the walls using the rough stone from which they were constructed for hand and footholds. It was simple enough to climb the two story buildings. They were built so closely together it was easy for her to get around Erd Proper without being noticed. She could jump the gap between them without much effort and in her soft leather shoes, without making much noise.

Diantha crossed over half a dozen buildings before she stopped and considered her latest dilemma. She wasn't a thief. Any money she had taken from the others had been returned to their owners. It simply wasn't possible for her to do it with this coin pouch. She sat down on the flat roof and crossed her legs.

What am I doing? She asked herself, and not for the first time.

She had sent word to the castle that she was going to stay in Erd Proper for a while so that her parents didn't worry about her. But stay here and do what? Keep roaming the streets at night and looking for those intent on doing evil? She heard people refer to her as the Noble Trod—based on the old stories. Granted, that is where she got the idea to hang the ripped and bloodstained cloth.

Maybe her actions was a way of releasing frustration and showing everyone, including herself, that she was just as good as any guardian.

Her own money was starting to run out—she couldn't stay at the Bard's Tale Tavern indefinitely. She had learned a lot from Bearach about being a blacksmith—perhaps she could get a job at one of the smithies here in town. She could earn enough money to rent a place of her own. Diantha laughed. A woman blacksmith—would anyone take her seriously? However, they hadn't taken her seriously about becoming a guardian and she proved she had the skills.

As for what to do with the coin she acquired, what could she do with it? The answer came to her as she spotted a church steeple several blocks away.

⊹⧊⊰

The next morning while Diantha was eating breakfast, she noticed the crowd in the common room seemed anxious. She sat at what had become her regular table. Though a few times in the evening she'd been approached by men looking to win her attention, for the most part she had been left alone. This was especially true when the men who she had turned away had told the others how cold and disinterested she had treated them. Once the barmaid had brought her breakfast, Diantha strained to hear the conversations.

"Aye, hanging from a lamppost this time!" she heard from one man.

"I don't dare walk the streets at night anymore," a worried woman said.

"The priest told me himself—a whole bag of coins was put in the poor box!" another man exclaimed.

Diantha smiled as she sipped her drink. She was making a difference in these people's lives—and she liked the way it felt. Sure, one of the women said she was afraid to be out at night, but from what Diantha had seen, it was best if all the women stayed inside after dark.

She knew the day wasn't going to be easy as she sought employment with a blacksmith. Yet, the conversations around her buoyed her spirits. She had just completed her meal when a huge man entered the tavern. There were two things about him that she noticed right away. First was just how big he was. He had to duck to enter, as well as turn his shoulders to squeeze through. His bulk wasn't due to fat—he was just *large*.

The second thing she noticed was that he was clean shaven. That meant he was either not from here, or he refused to follow the trend of growing a beard.

He looked around the common room and blinked a few times, no doubt letting his eyes adjust to the dimmer light inside the building. The barmaid approached him. She wasn't tall in the first place, but next to him, she looked like a child.

Diantha couldn't hear the discussion, but from the body language, it seemed that he was asking for directions. After a moment, he smiled and nodded to the barmaid and handed her a coin. The large man then left the tavern. Diantha watched him go, and then realized that everyone else in the common room was doing the same.

"I'll bet he's the one!" someone said a few tables over. "You know, the one who's been attacking people at night. It would have to be someone that big to be able to do it."

With that one statement, Diantha's earlier happiness vanished.

CHAPTER 64

Enoch stepped back into the sunlight and sighed. Magistrate Larissa told him to find the head of the militia in Erd Proper as that was his new assignment. Once he had arrived in the town, he'd thought to ask for directions at the first tavern he encountered. However, the guardians watching the gate advised him to go further into town to ask for information—they didn't say more than that. He continued into town until he spotted The Bard's Tale Tavern. The nice barmaid wasn't sure who was in charge now that Larissa had left, but she directed him to a merchant down the street who apparently was in the know about such things.

The shop was a couple of roads over. He hadn't been given a horse when he was reassigned—he had been told to walk. He didn't mind walking, but he felt it was just another slight against him from Larissa. He had visited Procep once with Kerr, the man who had raised him, but found he liked the simpler life in his village of Stur. Being in a big town, like here in Erd Proper, was unsettling.

People stared at him as he walked by. He wasn't sure if it was because he was so tall, or if it was because he didn't have a beard. Enoch found it odd that every man he saw was growing facial hair.

The shop was called "The Peculiar Bazaar" and was sandwiched between a cobbler and a butcher shop. From the looks of it, the two storied buildings had the shop below with the living quarters above. While that would work well for the cobbler, Enoch doubted the smells wafting up from the butcher shop would be pleasant at night.

Enoch opened the door and stooped as he walked in. The shop was full of the strangest collection of items he'd ever seen. There was a section of tools, one for cooking supplies and a whole table of what looked to be used clothing. Other than that, various items were placed all over without any sort of rhyme or reason—at least none that Enoch could decipher.

"Aren't you a big one, eh?" said an old man sitting behind a counter. He had a thick forehead and his eyes were sunken. Though he was mostly bald, tufts of white hairs stuck out over his large ears. It gave him the appearance of an animal peeking through a thicket of bushes.

Enoch closed the door behind him. "Are you Shaw?"

"That be me," the man said. He remained seated.

"Can you tell me where to find the leader of the militia?" Enoch asked.

"And why would you be looking for such a man, eh?"

Enoch stepped up to the counter. "I was sent here by Larissa. I'm supposed to join the militia here in Erd Proper."

The old man looked him up and down before responding. "Now why would Larissa send away someone as big as you? Are you stupid or something?"

"I don't think of myself as stupid. Then again, if I was, would I know it?" Enoch replied.

Shaw laughed. "I guess you got a point there. You don't seem stupid to me. I'm not stupid either, though the older I get the harder it is for me to remember things—like who is in charge of the militia."

The shop owner looked away. Enoch rolled his eyes and reached for his coin purse. He opened it, removed a coin and placed it on the counter. Shaw's eyes lingered on Enoch's coin purse for a moment before he smiled and retrieved the coin.

"Ah, yeah, I remember now. His name is Terence. He and his men are out in the southern fields training today, that's why you ain't seen them on your way in. They usually get back after dark. I got a map of the town I'd be happy to sell you. It'd be the easiest way to show you where to meet up with him."

Shaw pulled out a parchment. The map, if it could truly be called that, looked to have been drawn by someone's toes.

Pointing to a corner on the western edge of town, Shaw said, "This where they'll be. Make sure you show up unarmed. They get all twitchy around here with the Noble Trod roaming around an all."

"The Noble Trod?"

"Ain'tcha heard of the Noble Trod? He roams the street at night, attacking people at random. He cuts off their clothes, cleans his bloodied sword on it, rips it, and hangs it for all to see. It's got the whole town spooked."

"Why is he called the Noble Trod?"

The store owner looked around and then spoke in hushed tones. "I'm sure you've heard of the nislles, that awful plague, and how it killed off a good number of people in Bariwon, including all the royalty."

"Aye, I've heard the stories."

"During the bloody time afterwards when men were fighting for power over the land, there was a man, some who claimed to be a relative of the royalty, therefore a noble but no claim to the throne, who would trod about after a battle, hanging ripped and bloodied cloth for all to see. The story goes that he was trying to show people how foolish they were in fighting against each other—the ripped cloth was symbolic of how the kingdom had been divided and the blood represented the loss of life. He was eventually caught and publicly killed by Kettil, the primary foe of Roderick.

"Before he died, the Noble Trod yelled out that his sacrifice was worth it if it would help stop the war. He swore an oath that if war again came to Bariwon, others like him would rise again. It's said his words reached Roderick who used them to inspire his men to win the war."

Enoch tried not to frown. He had heard similar stories growing up, and he was sure most of them had been exaggerated over time. "So you believe someone else has taken up the Noble Trod's cause?"

"Yes!" Shaw again looked around. "It all makes sense! The signs are all around us. The threat from the Rifna Erd. The attacks near the northern wall. It couldn't be more clear!"

"Maybe that's something I can help with here—capturing this Noble Trod."

Shaw barked out a laugh. "Yeah, you do that. In the meantime, I'd suggest you get yourself something to eat at The Bard's Tale Tavern. No better food in town."

When Enoch returned to the tavern, the barmaid didn't look the least surprised to see him. No doubt she had some sort of agreement with Shaw. Enoch assumed she sent people to Shaw, and vice-versa. No matter—Enoch got what he needed.

After the trip from Stur, it felt good to sit and rest a bit. As the day passed, Enoch watched people come and go. One young woman he noticed was a stunning redhead. She left about the time he had come from Shaw's shop. She returned a while later, looking upset. After she got something to eat, she left again. She didn't return until the sun was setting and Enoch was preparing to leave. She was covered in sweat and soot, but this time, she appeared rather pleased with herself.

He caught her eye when she came in. For whatever reason, she gave him quite the icy glare. Enoch guessed she was just like most people in this town—untrusting and only out to help themselves. It was a shame. She was rather pretty.

Enoch finished his dinner, and after giving the barmaid an extra coin for letting him sit there all day, went to leave.

When he was told to go to Erd Proper, he was only allowed to bring a sword, some food for the trip, and any coin he had. Since his basic needs were taken care of from his work in Stur and the militia, he had been able to save up a decent amount of coin, which he carried with him. He was about to leave when he remembered what Shaw said about being armed when he went to see the militia. He went back to the barmaid who gave him a warm smile.

"Would you be willing to hold onto my sword until I can get it back from you?" he asked.

"Now why would you be going off into the night without a sword? Haven't you heard of the Noble Trod?" she asked.

Enoch forced himself not to roll his eyes. "Shaw told me I shouldn't show up at the militia with my sword. It might give them the wrong idea."

"Ah, well if Shaw told you that, then it must be good advice. Yes, I'll keep your sword safe here in the tavern." She looked at him expectantly.

Enoch undid the scabbard which held his sword. He handed it to her, along with another coin.

"Be safe now, you hear me?" she said. "If you see or hear anything that spooks you, you just go running."

"I don't spook easily," Enoch said, and then became embarrassed because it sounded like he was boasting.

The first thing Enoch noted when he left was how quiet the streets had become after dark. It had been bustling with activity during the day, but now he didn't see a soul. He reconsidered taking his sword along, though he was far from defenseless without one—he actually preferred to fight with his hands.

He pulled out the crudely drawn map. Looking up at the sky, he located the Zealous Star which gave him his bearings. Enoch set off down the street toward the location indicated on the map.

Time and again, he would see people looking out their windows, but they would hide as soon as he looked in their direction. This Noble Trod seemed to have quite the influence on the people.

The town was laid out haphazardly. There were quite a few dead ends and rarely did any of the streets run for very long. It was like walking through a maze. At one point, he stopped to look at the Zealous Star again to make sure he was still headed the right direction. From the corner of his eye, he thought he saw something move on top of one of the buildings. It must have been a cat, though he thought it was too big to have been one. Most likely, it was his imagination playing tricks on him, no doubt fueled by the stories of the Noble Trod.

At last, he approached his destination. It was just ahead and to the left. When Enoch turned the corner, he frowned. It appeared to be another dead end. He took several steps down the blocked off road before stopping to double check the map. He was certain this was the right place—or at least the place Shaw had told him to go to. Enoch surveyed the area. Maybe there was a door at the end of the street before it ended. However, all he found was a barrel used to catch rainwater.

Either the map was wrong, which was entirely possible, or Shaw had made a mistake. Sounds from behind Enoch made him realize that there was a third option. He turned around slowly and saw ten or so men standing in the street. In the light given off from the moon and the stars, he could see they were all armed. Perhaps they were the militia.

"See, I told you old Shaw would come through for us," one of the men said. Though he wasn't the tallest, he stood in the middle and the rest of the mob appeared to follow his lead. "The fool didn't even bring a sword. He made it all too easy for us."

Enoch realized he had been set up. While he could take on more than one man at a time, the number here was simply too many.

"If you want my coin purse, you can have it," Enoch called out to the men. "Just let me pass."

The man who spoke before laughed. "Let you pass? And do what? Go running off to tell the militia? I don't think so. They're so busy chasing ghosts that it allows me and my men to profit like never before. But, I tell you what. I'll make it as painless as possible if you don't make a fuss."

Enoch knew he had no chance of defeating all the men. But then again, he didn't have to. He just needed to get by them. Glancing around, he noticed he could probably climb the walls, but not before they could get to him. The only way out was the way he came in—the same place where the men stood. However, he did see something that he could use.

Taking two quick steps back, Enoch was now by the rain barrel. It was about half full, which would make it heavy—but all the better. With the men still ten or so paces away, Enoch lifted the barrel and threw it at them.

Several of the men shouted in surprise and scattered while the ones up front were too slow to react. The barrel hit a man off to the left of the leader and knocked him down, and in the process, flattened several of the men by him. This was the opening Enoch was looking for. He rushed toward the gap and just as he was about to jump through, it closed up with men brandishing weapons.

Enoch stopped before getting skewered. He then jumped back several times to avoid the weapons slashed at him.

"That was stupid," the leader said. "Men, take your time killing him."

Still backing up, Enoch looked around for something he could use as a weapon. There wasn't anything. He set his feet and prepared to rush the first man that got close. All he had to do was get passed the point of the man's sword and he could perhaps wrestle it free. From there, he had a chance. It would be slim, but a chance none-the-less.

He was just about to spring toward the first attacker when a cry came from the back of the group. It was followed by another, and then yet another. The sound of men screaming in pain was enough to stop Enoch's attackers from advancing. Perhaps the militia had found him after all.

"It's the Noble Trod!" someone shouted. At that, several of the men went running off in different directions.

Metal swords clanging in battle were intermixed with more men howling in agony. By this time, the attackers completely ignored Enoch and turned to face their new enemy.

Enoch tried to look through the crowd to see the Noble Trod, but the constantly moving bodies made it impossible. The man who a moment ago was going to attack Enoch headed back to the street entrance. He didn't make it far as a blow to the back of his head from Enoch's fist flattened him. Two more men went down in a similar fashion until they realized they were being attacked from the front and the rear. At that point, the rest of the men ran in different directions, giving Enoch his first good look at the Noble Trod.

He had expected to see a man at least as big as he was, if not bigger. Instead, he saw a lithe form dressed all in red. Though the lighting wasn't the best, he could tell the Noble Trod was a woman. Her hair was pulled up and tucked into a cap and her face was covered with a cloth that covered her nose, cheeks and mouth. She held a sword expertly in one hand.

She pointed the sword at Enoch and said in a raspy voice, "Go!"

Enoch nodded and moved around her, stepping over the men she had defeated. One of the attackers reached up and grabbed his leg, but Enoch was able to swat it away. Once he was clear, he ran half a block before looking back. The woman who had saved him was on one knee, and seemed to be cutting something. Enoch didn't consider himself a coward, but he knew when he was out matched.

As he ran down the street a bit more, he realized he had no idea where he was, or where he was going. He pulled out the map and decided he would return to the tavern. He still didn't know where to find the militia. But he knew where his sword was.

After figuring out which way to go, he ran. While he navigated the streets, he tried to figure out his next move. Shaw was in on this attack. Was the barmaid as well? Either way, he would confront them both soon and get some answers.

Enoch found the tavern after a time. He hadn't seen anyone else walking in the streets after dark; it appears Shaw was right—people were spooked by the Noble Trod. He heard someone singing from the tavern, which made sense because earlier in the day people had mentioned one of their favorite bards would be singing that night.

If the barmaid was working with Shaw, what would Enoch say to her? "Guess what? I'm not dead!" How would she react? He realized she had his sword. Maybe he could pretend he decided to come back for his sword—that way she wouldn't know he'd been attacked.

Just before he entered the tavern, he heard someone far down the road cry out, "There he is! There's the Noble Trod!" Enoch looked down the road in each direction, but didn't see anyone. He thought it best to get inside quickly.

He entered the tavern and noticed how all eyes were watching an older man who was singing and gesturing majestically. Enoch scanned the common room for the barmaid and spotted her placing a couple of mugs on a table near the far left of the room. The bar itself was on the right side, and Enoch knew she'd have to return there sooner or later.

No one looked at him as he approached the bar—they were all too captivated with the performance. When he got to his destination, he leaned against the bar and watched as the barmaid weaved her way through the crowd back toward him. He caught her eye and she smiled at him. She didn't seem to be distraught by his return. Maybe she hadn't been in on the attack.

But then, her eyes grew wide and she dropped one of the empty mugs to the floor. It broke into pieces and was loud enough that it caused several of the patrons to look at her. By her response, maybe she had been working with Shaw and just now realized what his return meant. But her reaction was much different than what he expected. She turned pale and covered her mouth with one hand. The people who had been distracted by the mug breaking turned to see what caused her reaction. In turn, they looked at Enoch. As they did, they each reacted a little differently, though the common reaction was fear.

It didn't make any sense. Enoch hadn't done anything to scare these people. At that moment a man in his middle years burst through the front door. "The Noble Trod has attacked again!" he cried.

Enoch felt his back stiffen. Word had spread fast considering the streets seemed to be empty. Before he could give anymore thought to the matter, the man who had just entered pointed to Enoch. "There he is!"

What? Him? No, why would people think that? Was it because of his size? He noticed everyone was looking at him now. Even the bard had stopped singing. It didn't make any sense. The patrons closest to him were backing away. One of them pointed at him. Wait, not really at him as much as at his legs.

Once Enoch looked down, he understood their reaction. One of his pant legs was smeared with blood.

CHAPTER 65

When Diantha returned to the tavern, she heard quite the disturbance coming from the common room. She was both tired and exhilarated at the same time—it was a curious sensation. She had gotten work at a blacksmith shop, but only after she agreed to work the day without payment to show her employer what she could do. At the end of the work day, she had impressed him enough that he agreed to take her on.

Working in the blacksmith shop was tiring labor, but it also helped her remain strong. Even though she wanted to do nothing more than sleep when she got back from the smithy, the urge to put on her red clothes and roam the streets to defend the innocent had too much pull. She hadn't been out long when she saw the big man she'd seen earlier—the man others thought could be the Noble Trod.

Sure enough, he got himself in trouble, as many did who walked the streets alone at night. Never had she taken on so many attackers, but she had surprise and their fear on her side. It helped that the large man she was trying to save injured a couple of them when he threw the rain barrel.

Diantha returned to her room after tying bloody, torn cloth near the attack. She changed into some new clothes purchased recently and thought to get a quick bite to eat before bed when she entered the common room. What she saw changed those plans quickly.

The large man she had saved earlier was surrounded by dozens of people, all of them pointing and shouting at him. To his credit, the man had his hands raised in a sign of peace and seemed to be trying to calm them down.

"Guardians from the palace are coming!" she heard someone shout.

"Don't let him escape!" another shouted.

"I saw him first and deserve the reward!" yet another man yelled.

From the top of the stairs on the second floor, Diantha could see over the heads of the crowd enough to get a good look at the accused. One of his pant legs was covered in blood. She realized an attacker must have grabbed him while he escaped. The sight of his bloody clothes was enough to assure people he was the Noble Trod.

Once again, Diantha became very upset. Why did people assume the Noble Trod had to be a man? It was the same prejudice she was trying to fight by assuming the role of the legendary character.

"It wasn't me." she heard the man say. "Let me explain."

"No! Keep your mouth shut!" someone in the crowd called back.

The banter went on for a few more moments. Diantha didn't want to go down to the common room with the patrons so worked up. She was about to head back to her room when the tavern door opened and several guardians dressed in silver and crimson entered. The large man didn't put up a fight when they arrested him and took him away. The people cheered once he had left.

Diantha felt like she had taken a blow to the stomach. These people were happy to see the arrest of who they thought was the Noble Trod. These were the same people she was trying to protect. She thought she had been making a difference—in her own way—but once again, her actions were not only unappreciated, but were frowned upon.

She fought the urge to cry as she turned to her room—no longer hungry and with an intense desire to be alone.

⊹⋇⊱

"Try this," Selene said. She handed a mug to Crescens.

He smelled it. It had an odd scent to it. "What is it?"

"Just try it."

He had never been able to say no to her. The mug contained a liquid that was mostly clear with just a slight green tint to it. He placed the rim to his lips and sensed it was warm, but not so hot that it would burn him. After taking a small sip, and not gagging, he quaffed the rest.

"And?" Selene said.

"It has a bit of a woody aftertaste, but it wasn't unpleasant. What is it?"

"Serkan called it viceditad. It's made from some sort of plant that grows only north of the mountains."

Serkan? As in the Rifna Erd they had smuggled into Bariwon? "What does it do?" Crescens asked.

"He said it helps the people be loyal."

Crescens blinked a few times as he thought about what she said. "Loyal? It makes people loyal? But how?"

"I don't know," Selene said. "I tried to get him to tell me, but I couldn't understand his explanation. He finally told me to try it out on someone."

"But—but—I've always been loyal to you," Crescens said. "I didn't have to drink something to make me loyal."

Selene walked behind her desk and sat. "I made that same point to Serkan. He told me to try it on someone I trusted. He said it would take a couple of days for it to take full effect."

Whether from the drink or because he was being used as an experiment, Crescens felt lightheaded. He placed a hand on her desk to steady himself. "How do we know if it works?"

"Simple," Selene said. "Tell me everything you are feeling—starting tomorrow."

⋰⊹⋱

Enoch sat on a stone bench in a windowless room. A thick, wooden door was the only way in or out. He'd been there for quite some time. He imagined it must be morning by now. The guardians who put him in this cell informed him he could tell his story to the magistrate in the morning. He had tried to explain what happened to the men who arrested him, but they had told him to shut up.

He reviewed the events from the night before in his head. He wanted to make sure he had all his facts straight when he finally got to speak to the magistrate.

Enoch stood and stretched. He was tired, but not sleepy. The events from fighting off the mob in the alley, coming face-to-face with the Noble Trod, and then being arrested had left him quite wound up.

Eventually the door opened and in walked a man in his middle years. He was followed by two guardians who had their weapons drawn.

"So, you are this Noble Trod that has everyone spooked, eh? Big spooky man, are you?" the man said.

Enoch noticed the man's eyes were flitting back and forth and he seemed to have a hard time standing still.

"My name is Enoch. I'm from the town of Stur. I was sent to Erd Proper by Larissa to join the militia here. You can verify my story with the people in Stur."

"Oh, we will. We will." The man was wringing his hands now, quickly. "I'm Magistrate Crescens. Yes, that's me. Me. Me. Me."

Something was off with this man. He was acting very oddly. "Magistrate Crescens, I'm not the Noble Trod. But I did see her last night."

"Her? Did you say *her*? As in a woman? You are saying the Noble Trod is a woman, is that it?"

"Yes, that's exactly what I'm saying."

"No. No. Can't be. No. A woman couldn't do what's been done. No. It must be someone big and strong—like you. See. There is blood on your leggings. See? Right there." Crescens pointed. "See? You have blood on you. You must be him. Blood right there on your leggings."

Enoch noticed the two guardians exchange confused expressions. It seemed they noticed something odd about Crescens's behavior as well.

"I'm telling you, I was attacked by a group of men. The Noble Trod saved me. One of them reached up and touched me with their bloody hand. That's why I have blood on me."

Crescens laughed hysterically. "You're saying you were saved by a woman? A woman!" He laughed some more. He smacked one of the guardians in the chest. "A woman! He was saved by a woman!"

"It's true," Enoch said, though it appeared Crescens was no longer listening to him.

"You'll hang," Crescens said. He made a gesture of a noose being put around his neck and it getting pulled. "You'll hang. Get it? You'll hang like the cloth you hang. But not just your head, all of you. Including all of your fingers." Crescens wiggled his fingers in Enoch's face.

"But—"

Crescens turned and left before Enoch could say anything else.

⋅❖⋅

Sparks flew as Diantha hit the metal with her smithy hammer. It felt good to take out her frustrations.

"Easy there, darlin'" her boss said. He was a good head shorter than her, but made up what he lost in height with bulk. "The metal didn't do nothin' to ya."

"Sorry, Goban," she said. She held up the glowing metal to inspect it.

"What's got ya so riled up, eh?" Goban said.

"It's nothing."

"Nothing?"

She spoke without really thinking ahead. "This whole Noble Trod business bothers me."

"I'd think ya'd be happy they finally caught him. I heard during our mid-day meal that they're going to hang him tomorrow."

Diantha nearly dropped the red-hot metal. "How can they do that? Don't they need two witnesses to prove his guilt?"

"Two witnesses?" Goban laughed. "Darlin', they got a whole tavern full of witnesses."

She looked at him. "Do you think he did it?"

"It don't matter what I think. I'm just glad it will be over. I've seen one of those bloody cloths hanging from a doorframe. It gave me the creeps."

Diantha wanted to argue with him, but instead turned her attention on her work. She started pounding the metal into shape, each blow coming as hard as the one before.

She confronted her feelings as she worked. Why was she so angry? She was upset because people didn't appreciate what she was doing—they saw her as some sort of threat that needed to be stopped. But there was something more. It was that big man's fault. Everyone assumed it was him. All they needed was any sort of proof; or at least proof they could twist into convincing the magistrate. And now, he was going to die—because of her. She couldn't let that happen. Maybe she should turn herself in. No, that wouldn't work. No one would believe her. Sometimes it was easier to believe what seemed likely than the truth. Still, she needed to do something—but what?

After a few more hits with her hammer, an idea came to her. She thought it out and believed it could work.

She moved the metal into the cooling solution creating a loud hiss accompanied with a plume of steam.

"When are they going to hang the Noble Trod tomorrow?"

"They said at dusk," he said. "Why?"

"Could I leave work after mid-day tomorrow?"

"Wanna see the hanging up close, do ya?" he asked.

"Yes. Yes, I do."

⇥❈⇤

It was a day before the hanging. The sun had gone down and stars dotted the sky. Normally by this time of night everyone in Erd Proper remained inside. But not tonight. If anything, there were as many people out tonight as during mid-day.

Diantha crouched on top of a building overlooking the main square where the gallows were being erected. Residents of the town stood and watched as they were being put together. Each blow of the hammer she heard felt like a punch to her stomach. She couldn't let the big man die for things she had done.

The main square was in front of the palace. From her vantage point, she could see Lake Dylobo just beyond it. It seemed so peaceful compared to the noise and impending violence in the square.

She had come up with a basic plan, but was missing one key element. She hoped she would be able to find it tonight.

In the past, the preferred method of execution was beheading. For some reason, she wasn't sure why, it had been changed to hanging. Maybe hanging was less gruesome—after all, there wasn't any blood with hangings.

She had been to one hanging before. It had been a few years back while she was living in Procep. A man had too much to drink, got into a fight, and beat up another man. He was captured, but while he was in prison awaiting his chance to defend his actions in court, he had tried to escape and in the process, killed two of the militia. The punishment for that was death. She hadn't wanted to watch, but her father thought it was important that she understood the price people paid for murder.

Diantha was still reflecting on that event when she noticed a man dressed all in black, including a hood over his head, climbing upon the nearly completed gallows. He was the executioner. The executioner in Procep had been a big, imposing figure, but this one was much smaller in stature. A tall guardian dressed in red and silver motioned to where the rope was attached to a beam over the wooden platform. The guardian then demonstrated the lever which opened the door below the rope.

After the demonstration was completed, Diantha knew she had found the missing piece she was looking for.

-»§§«-

"Did you contact Stur?" Enoch asked. It had been nearly two days since his arrest.

The magistrate shook his head violently, almost like a dog shaking off water after getting wet. "No, no need. You're guilty. The gallows are built. People are excited, you see? They're excited to see a hanging. You're guilty so there was no need to contact Stur."

"But the mayor—"

"Guilty. Guilty. Guilty. You're going to hang."

Enoch looked at the eight or so guardians that had accompanied Magistrate Crescens to his cell. They were all well-armed and in a fighting stance. Even if he tried to escape, he wouldn't make it far.

This wasn't right. He'd done nothing wrong, yet he was being punished. It reminded him of his feelings when he was younger. It was unfair that he was treated differently because he was bigger than everyone else. It wasn't his fault. But if he had learned nothing else, it was that life wasn't fair.

He held his hands out toward the magistrate. "Just bind my hands so we can get this over with."

A couple of guardians came forward with a thick rope and tied his hands together. Enoch noticed one of the other guardians had drawn his bow and had pointed it at Enoch's head.

Once they double checked the rope, one of the guardians said, "He's ready."

"Excellent! Ropes on your hands and soon a rope around your neck. It will be a matching pair!" Crescens laughed loudly at his own joke.

Enoch was escorted out of the cell and into the main square. It was full of people, packed arm to arm. Some men even had children sitting on their shoulders to get a good view.

The sun had set recently as the sky was just starting to darken.

"There he is!" someone shouted when they spotted him. "It's the Noble Trod!"

Jeers and catcalls followed. Enoch fought the urge to hang his head. He recognized the irony of the action and gave a mirthless chuckle. He'd done nothing wrong, and he wouldn't be ashamed in front of these people.

The guardians skirted around the edge of the crowd until they got to the gallows. There were guardians standing in front of the platform, preventing anyone from getting too close or behind it.

Enoch was let through and then directed to go to the stairs that ran up the backside of the gallows. Two guardians went up first. While waiting for them to climb the stairs, Enoch noticed Magistrate Crescens watching from one of the archer towers in the palace. Next to him was a woman with long, straight black hair and nearly white skin. She held an air of malice about her.

"Move along now," one of the guardians said, trying to push Enoch forward.

Someone in the crowd was beating a drum in a slow but steady rhythm. The crowd seemed to sway with the pounding. Enoch climbed the stairs and felt them creak under his weight.

There was a large red X painted on the trap door of the gallows. Enoch looked up and examined the rope. The noose was ready, waiting for him. There was a stepping stool next to the trapdoor.

A jab in his back from one of the guardian's swords spurred him forward to stand on the red X.

Then at once, the crowd quieted. Even the drummer had stopped. Enoch wasn't sure why until he turned his head.

A man dressed in an oversized black robe came up the stairs. His head was covered by a black hood that only had the smallest of slits for eyeholes. Enoch wondered what kind of man would willingly be an executioner.

The guardians backed away as the executioner approached. He was shorter than Enoch by quite a bit, but then again, most people were.

Enoch looked up into the sky. He thought he saw movement on top of one of the buildings. He squinted but couldn't be sure. It looked like a person. Most likely they had gone up there to get a better view of the hanging.

Only one star was visible at the moment. It was the Zealous Star—the brightest star in the night sky. Enoch remembered Kerr pointing out that star to him when he was younger. Though he had always called him Kerr, Enoch considered the man to be his father. He wondered what Kerr would say if he was here.

The executioner climbed to the top of the stool and reached up for the rope. Enoch didn't flinch when it was looped around his neck. He felt the noose tighten, but he also felt something else, a back and forth motion on the rope. It must have been the executioner pulling on it to make it tighter.

The noose was tight enough now that he struggled to breathe. He felt the executioner lean in next to him.

"Look for me after you fall," said the husky voice.

So even at the end, Enoch was being taunted.

As the executioner climbed down from the stool and moved to the lever that would open the trap door, the drummer started up again and the people started crying out for him to hang.

Instead of looking at their faces, or the executioner, Enoch focused his attention on the Zealous Star. He wanted his last sight in this life to be something good.

The executioner pulled back on the lever. The trapdoor opened. Enoch felt himself falling and prepared to feel the noose break his neck.

CHAPTER 66

Once the rope became taut, it broke. Enoch tumbled to the ground under the gallows. He heard gasps from the crowd. The guardians in front of the platform turned to face him.

"This way!"

Enoch swung around and looked for the source of the voice. It was the executioner. He was waving his hand frantically for Enoch to follow.

Not stopping to wonder what was happening and why, Enoch crawled on his hands and knees toward the back of the gallows.

A couple of guardians came off the platform toward the executioner. The man in black pulled out a sword from under his robe and stabbed the oncoming guardians in the legs before they could react.

Once Enoch was clear of the gallows, the executioner took off at a dead run toward the palace. Enoch followed him. Instead of going over the drawbridge, the executioner turned to the right and ran along the edge of the moat.

Enoch spared a glance over his shoulder and saw dozens of guardians in pursuit. They had had to come around the gallows which gave Enoch a decent head start. Where was the executioner running to? Going around the moat would only lead them to the lake. His hands were still bound and so he wouldn't be able to swim—not that he was much of a swimmer anyway.

Still, something inside him drove him onward. The executioner was fast. Enoch had never been much of a quick runner and a gap was starting to widen between him and the man sent to kill him, while the guardians were gaining ground. It made no sense. Why would the executioner do what he was doing? Did he know the rope would break?

Angry shouts and threats came from their pursuers. Instead of intimidating Enoch, he used it as motivation to keep running. Once around the moat, the executioner ran toward the lake. And then Enoch saw it. A ferry. It was the kind that was flat and square with a rope running through some metal hoops on top of beams attached to the floating platform. The rope was attached to the dock on this side and then went off across the lake and out of sight. Enoch guessed it was attached to the shore on the opposite side of the lake.

The executioner hopped onto the ferry and then started pulling on the rope, separating the floating platform from the dock. He hadn't made much progress when Enoch arrived and was easily able to jump the gap. The ferry wobbled a little once he landed on it, but it didn't capsize.

"Pull the rope!" the executioner shouted. There was something odd about his voice.

Even with his hands tied together, Enoch was able to grab the rope between the metal hoops and pull hard. The gap widened between the dock and the ferry, but not enough to stop the first two guardians who gave chase to leap onto the ferry.

"Keep pulling!" The executioner faced the two men with his sword drawn.

Enoch glanced at the guardians. He watched as one began to step forward. At the same moment, Enoch pulled the rope as hard and fast as he could. The timing was just right and the guardian was thrown off balance. He tumbled backwards and into the lake.

The second guardian was more cautious. He watched Enoch carefully before he advanced. However, in doing so, he took his attention off the executioner. Quicker than Enoch thought was possible the executioner lunged forward and stabbed the guardian through the wrist, causing him to drop his sword.

The guardian fell to his knees and clutched his wound to his chest. "Why?" he asked.

And then the executioner did something odd. He took off his robe and hood. And when he did, both Enoch and the guardian could only stare. The executioner was a woman dressed all in red, including a cap and a scarf over her face. It was the same woman that had saved him before: the Noble Trod.

"Because you were about to kill an innocent man," she said, this time no longer speaking in a husky voice.

Before the guardian could say anything else, she stepped forward and kicked him hard in the shoulder, spinning him enough that he fell off the ferry.

She turned to Enoch and said, "Keep pulling!"

⟨⁂⟩

Selene stared at Crescens in bewilderment. He'd been acting, well, almost hysterically ever since she had given him the viceditad to drink. If this was the Rifna Erd's idea of being loyal, she wondered if they were really the allies she needed.

Still, she expected Crescens to do his job as magistrate. "What happened down there?" she said. She pointed at the gallows.

"Exciting! Wasn't it? Exciting! The rope broke. Snap! Broke instead of his neck. And then he ran. Shoo! Shoo! Run!"

She faced Crescens and grabbed him by the shoulders. "Crescens! Answer me! Why did the executioner help him escape?"

Instead of answering her, Crescens leaned in to kiss her. She slapped him. He didn't seem to notice and tried to kiss her again. This time, she shoved him backwards.

"What are you doing?" she asked.

"I've been in love with you forever," he said. He took a step toward her. "I can't believe I've waited all this time to tell you."

"Crescens!" she shouted and then slapped him again.

Still, he advanced on her with a dreamy look in his eyes. She backed up and then saw a guardian from the far tower running their direction. He had his hand on the sword's hilt, but hadn't drawn it.

"Is something the matter?" the guardian called out.

"Aside from the man who was supposed to be hung escaping and Crescens acting crazy, everything is fine!"

Crescens still walked toward her, arms out, lips puckered and making kissing noises.

The guardian pulled his sword out of its scabbard and approached Crescens from behind. "What do you want me to do, Governor?"

She was still backing up. "Stop him!"

For a moment she thought the guardian may stab Crescens, but instead, he hit the magistrate hard against the back of his head with the pummel of his sword.

After watching Crescens slump to the ground, the guardian asked, "Did he hurt you, Governor?"

"Worse!" she said. "He tried to kiss me!"

⟨⁂⟩

Diantha watched the large man as he pulled on the rope, moving them toward the middle of the lake. He was big and strong, yet seemed gentle. It was an odd combination.

"Here, let me free your hands," she said.

He stopped pulling and faced her. He gave her a wary look.

"You don't have to fear me," she said.

He looked to be thinking how to respond. His eyes seemed focused on her sword.

I promise," she said. The big man still didn't look convinced. She sighed and then took off her cap and scarf.

His expression changed from one of distrust to recognition. "I saw you at The Bard's Tale Tavern," he said.

"And I saw you," she said. "You're hard not to notice."

"I could say the same thing about you," he said. His eyes grew wide and he quickly looked down, appearing embarrassed by what he had admitted.

"Are you going to let me free your hands or not?"

He paused only a moment before holding his hands out toward her. With her sword, she cut through the bindings. Once his hands were free, he reached up and removed the noose. He looked at it carefully once it was in his hands.

"You cut the rope nearly all the way when you placed it around my neck, didn't you?"

"That I did. It was tricky with so many people watching, but I made it look like I was tightening it."

He tossed the noose into the lake. He then faced her. "Why?"

"Because you're innocent."

"No, why are you dressed up like that?"

The way he asked the question wasn't accusatory or demeaning. It sounded like he genuinely wanted to know.

"It's a bit hard to explain," she said. "And we still have work to do before we're free."

The man looked down both lengths of the rope he'd used to pull the ferry along. "I can't see either shore from here."

"Good."

Diantha lifted her sword over her head and stepped toward the man she had saved. He looked surprised and lifted his hands to defend himself. However, her target wasn't him, but rather the rope attached to the ferry. It took a few hacks, but she was able to cut it. He watched on, looking confused.

"I don't understand," he said.

She pointed in the direction of the shore opposite of the palace. "The guardians know where this ferry goes. They are most likely racing there on horses as we speak. They're also probably putting small rafts together by the palace to pursue us."

"What's your plan?" he asked.

"First things first," she said. She put her sword into the scabbard she wore on her back. "My name is Diantha." She stuck out her hand.

He stared at her a moment before taking her hand and shaking it. "I'm Enoch."

"Enoch?" she said. "Were you raised by Mayor Kerr?"

He nodded. "How did you know?"

"My father and your father are friends."

"Diantha... Aren't you Commander Snapdragon's daughter?"

She grimaced. "Yes."

"This makes even less sense. I don't understand why you're in Erd Proper and dressed like the Noble Trod."

"I'll make you a deal, Enoch," she said. "If we survive until morning, I'll tell you the whole story."

Enoch's forehead scrunched up. "Fine. It's a deal. Now, what's your plan?"

"We need to land the ferry along a point of the shore they don't expect. From there, we'll find a place to hide until we can decide what to do next."

"All right," Enoch said. "How are we going to paddle?"

Diantha looked around the raft. There was nothing on it. "Uh..."

"I have an idea." Enoch grabbed one of the wooden beams that pointed up from the ferry—the beam that had the metal hoop where the rope had gone through. He got a firm grip on the beam and then tore it off. He did the same thing to the other one.

"We can use these for paddles," he said, handing one to her.

She took it from him and nearly dropped it. It was heavy.

"Enoch, I'm not sure I can use this."

"Oh, I'm sorry. I didn't think... anyway, which way should we go? I'll paddle."

Diantha set down the beam and then put her hands on her hips. She looked around.

"I'm not sure. We don't want to end up by either of the docks."

"How about that way?" Enoch pointed.

"Yeah, that should work. But in the dark, how are you going to keep your bearings?"

Enoch looked up into the night sky. He seemed to be gazing at a particularly bright star.

"I have a way."

⭄⧻⧼

Crescens had a hard time opening his eyes. The back of his head throbbed in pain, but there was something else. He felt feverish. His body was shaking as if he was cold. It didn't make any sense. He let out a low moan.

"Magistrate?" a female voice asked. He thought he recognized it, but it wasn't Selene. "Are you awake, Magistrate?" the voice asked again.

He forced his eyes open. Light shone through the window of his room. From its angle, he knew it was morning time. He didn't remember how he got to his room or what happened the night before.

"I'm awake." His voice croaked when he spoke. The woman sitting next to him was one of the nursemaids in the palace.

"How do you feel?" she asked.

Crescens looked at her. She wore the standard gray-hooded cloak of a nursemaid. "Terrible."

"You look the way you feel," she said. There was no humor in her voice.

"What happened?" he asked.

"You don't remember?"

"No."

The nursemaid pursed her lips. "What's the last thing you do remember?"

Crescens tried to think, but his pounding headache made it challenging. "I remember drinking something the governor gave me and then going to bed. I had some strange dreams about us catching the Noble Trod and him escaping when we tried to hang him." He remembered something else he had dreamed about, but he didn't share that with the nursemaid.

"Anything else?" she asked.

"No. Just those strange dreams."

"They weren't dreams."

He stared at the nursemaid. "Wha—What did you say?"

"They weren't dreams," she repeated. "You've been acting very strangely the last couple of days."

Crescens started to panic. Had he really acted that way? Had he thrown himself at Selene? What did that drink do to him?

"It must have been the drink," he said. "I wasn't myself."

She nodded. "Can you stay awake?"

His body hurt all over. Even if he wanted to, he didn't think he could fall back asleep. "Yes."

"I'll be right back." She stood and left.

A moment later, Selene walked into the room. He couldn't tell if she was upset. In fact, she wore a cold, calculating expression.

"Crescens," she said. There was no emotion in her voice.

"Governor," he responded. "Forgive me for not standing when you came in. I'm very sick."

She walked to his bed and sat on a chair next to it. "I spoke to Serkan. It took some time, but I was able to deduce from him that your actions over the last couple of days were a normal response to the viceditad. The first time anyone drinks it, they go... oh how did he phrase it, 'wrong in the head' for a couple of days."

"I'm so sorry for anything I did or the way I acted," he said.

"Then you remember what you tried to do to me after the hanging went awry?" she asked.

"It seems like a bad dream," Crescens said. "I wasn't in control."

"I understand. After all, if you truly had romantic feelings toward me I would've expected you to make that clear years ago."

Crescens wasn't sure how to respond. Did that mean she would have been receptive to him if he'd told her nearly twenty years ago? It was all so confusing. He decided to change the subject.

"Is the viceditad supposed to make me ill? I feel as sick as I've ever been."

She tapped a finger against her lips. "Serkan said you would be submissive after a couple of days. Maybe that is what he meant. He said that if I gave you more viceditad it would calm you."

Crescens shook his head. "No. Not if it makes me act crazy."

"Did you think you had a say in this matter?" Selene said.

He knew he didn't. He was being used to test the viceditad. "Forgive me, Governor. Of course I'll do what you say."

"Bring it in!" Selene called over her shoulder.

The nursemaid who had been there before entered holding a cup. She helped Crescens sit up enough to sip the drink. Perhaps it was his imagination, but it seemed that after his first sip, he started to feel better. He quickly gulped down the rest of it. Within several moments, not only were the shakes and pain gone, but he felt energized.

He sat up and swung his legs off the side of the bed. Both of the women in the room looked surprised.

"It seems to have worked! I feel wonderful!"

❖❖❖

Enoch peered around the tree. He didn't see anyone following them. They had been able to land the ferry undetected and made it to a wooded area north of the lake. From there, they had doubled back a few times, climbed trees and dropped to the other side and even splashed through a small stream in an attempt to confuse any trackers.

"I think we're safe," he said.

For now," Diantha answered.

She was sitting cross-legged on the ground with her hands resting on her knees. Even then, it looked to Enoch that she could spring into action at any moment.

"I think we're safe enough to rest a bit," he clarified.

Aside from drinking from the stream, they hadn't had anything else to eat or drink since the day before. "Are you hungry?" he asked.

"Yes, but I don't have any food and I don't think it's safe to build a fire."

Enoch scanned around the area. "Let me take care of that."

She didn't say anything. Instead, she just watched him intently.

There were several edible plants and tubers that grew in the area. Within a short amount of time, Enoch was able to collect some leafy plants, a couple of tubers and a few berries. He brought them back to Diantha. She was still sitting in the same position.

"Breakfast is served," he said.

She arched an eyebrow at the food he presented. "You're sure this is safe to eat?"

"Yes. Kerr taught me how to identify which plants were safe to eat and which ones weren't." He gave her several of the items and then sat down across from her.

When he first saw her, he thought she was very pretty. When he looked at her now, she was still pretty, but he also saw her as being dangerous.

"You promised to tell me your story," he said. He bit into one of the tubers.

She narrowed her eyes while looking at him. "I guess I do owe you that much." After popping a few of the berries in her mouth and swallowing them, she said, "My father wouldn't let me enter the Mortentaun."

This took Enoch by surprise. "You want to be a guardian?"

"Yes, but I was told I couldn't be one."

From there, Diantha explained the sequence of events that led her to last night's actions. "I couldn't let them kill you. You didn't do anything wrong."

"And for that, I thank you," Enoch said. "Yet…"

"Yet, you've still been convicted of being the Noble Trod, haven't you?" she said.

"Yes. But you showed yourself to the guardians that jumped on the ferry."

She laughed. It wasn't joyful. "They won't tell anyone. They're too proud to admit they were beaten by a woman."

"It sounds like you're fighting several battles at once," Enoch said.

Her expression changed. "I have to admit I've misjudged you."

"How so?"

"I assumed you were a big, dumb brute. But that's not it at all, is it?"

Enoch didn't say anything. Instead, he took another bite of his meal.

"And now I've offended you," she said. She reached over and put a hand on his knee. "I'm sorry."

Why did he care so much about what she thought? He'd been treated that way his whole life. Yet, it seemed to sting more coming from her.

He shrugged. "I'm used to it."

"Do you accept my apology?"

She looked directly into his eyes. Even if she wasn't pretty, he would have had a hard time holding a grudge against her. "Yes, I accept it."

"Good." She ate a few more berries. "Now, what are we going to do?"

"Uh, I'm not sure. I can't go back to Erd Proper," Enoch said. "But I'm also not allowed in Stur—or by any of the northern towns by the wall."

"Why not?"

"I made an enemy of Larissa, the new magistrate assigned to the northern defenses."

"What did you do?"

He told her.

"Because you stood up to a bully, you were exiled?" Diantha asked. "Does my father know this?"

"Not that I'm aware of."

"He'd never permit such things."

"I thought you said you and Commander Snapdragon didn't get along," Enoch pointed out.

She frowned. "Just because he and I had a fight and he's wrong about not letting me become a guardian doesn't mean he's a bad person. Getting some time and distance from him has made me appreciate that he is a very good leader."

"So, are you suggesting I go to Procep and talk to your father?" he asked. "If so, what am I supposed to tell him about this whole Noble Trod business?"

"That could pose a problem, yes." She looked troubled.

"Maybe we could start to head back to Procep," Enoch suggested. "We can figure what we're going to do on the way."

"That's a good idea. We need to get more distance from Erd Proper."

After finishing their modest meal, they continued to head north, toward the mountains and the defenses built against the Rifna Erd.

The first village they came across was named Joro. It had only a few buildings, one of which was a tavern, inn and market all-in-one.

"Let me check out the village first," Diantha said.

Enoch looked her over. "You realize you're still dressed like the Noble Trod, right?"

She examined her outfit and frowned. "Well, it's either I head into town wearing this or going naked. I think this way I'll attract less attention."

Enoch felt himself blush. "I could go instead."

"No. There's a chance that word has already spread that you're on the run. You'd attract more attention than I would."

It was true. Even though Diantha was pretty and wearing all red, she wouldn't be as noticeable as he would be.

"At least take my shirt to cover your outfit—at least some of it."

She seemed to consider it for a moment and then nodded.

Enoch took off his shirt and handed it to her. "I'm sorry. It probably doesn't smell very nice from me being locked up and then us running."

"It'll be fine." He noticed her eye his muscular chest for a moment before she slid the shirt over her head. It almost looked like a nightdress on her as it went below her knees.

"How do I look?" she asked.

He was about to say "beautiful" but instead caught himself and said, "A bit odd, but not as strange as wearing all red. By the way, how did you dye your clothes red?"

"It's blood." She said matter-of-factly. "Now stay here and out of sight until I return."

Enoch watched her head toward the village.

Blood? And the way she said it was so nonchalant. The more he learned about Diantha, the more complex she became. Then again, Enoch had never been one to understand women. He had mentioned that to Kerr once. The response Kerr gave was just as confusing.

Enoch had asked, "Why do women do the things they do?"

Kerr's response was to point to the night sky and say, "How many stars are there?"

"Too many to count."

"You have a better chance counting all the stars than understanding women."

Enoch was still contemplating that when he saw Diantha return. She appeared to be walking as if she didn't have a care in the world. However, once in a while, she'd look over her shoulder, as if she was checking to see if she was followed.

Upon returning to where Enoch was hiding, she said, "It was as we feared. The guardians from Erd Proper have already been here. There is a price on your head."

He felt his shoulders sag. "It's only a matter of time before Kerr finds out about this. What will he think?"

"There are other things you should be more concerned about."

"Oh?"

Diantha grimaced. "The reward for you is the same dead or alive."

"I see."

"We'll need to find somewhere to lay low for a while," she said.

"We?"

"Yes, we. It's my fault you are a wanted man."

"But… I don't know where we could go. I've lived my whole life along the northern mountains."

Diantha looked thoughtful for a moment. "I remember a story my Uncle Rayne told me once about where he had grown up."

"As in King Rayne?"

"Well, he's a councilor now, but yes, him. Anyway, I think I know where we can go."

"Where's that?"

She looked up at him and then pointed south. "We're going to Tevoil."

CHAPTER 67

C rescens's beard was itchy. And hot. Over the last several weeks, the days had been getting longer and warmer. However, Selene had said she liked his beard—one of the few compliments she'd given him about his appearance. It was worth the discomfort if she liked it. Granted, every man in Erd Proper was growing a beard. The people here tended to follow fads, something Selene must have known when she instructed the men in the palace to grow out their facial hair. It was all part of her overall plan.

He gave his beard one last scratch before he entered Selene's office. For once, she wasn't sitting at her desk. Instead, she was sitting on a padded bench and reading a book. She had many books in her office, but he'd not seen her read before. He wondered what kind of books she liked. Maybe if he found that out, he could read some of the same books so he would have more to talk with her about.

"Yes, Crescens?" she asked without looking up.

"You instructed me to come here after lunch," he said.

She appeared confused. "Lunch already?" She peered out the window and seemed to notice the sun's position. "Time got away from me," she said.

"Would you like to have something brought to you?" Crescens asked.

"No. I'm not hungry," she said. "Come in and sit down."

Though there was room on the bench next to her, he decided not to be so forward. Drinking the viceditad gave him confidence and energy he'd not felt before, but with Selene his sense of caution overrode those feelings—especially after he had tried to kiss her while he was adjusting to the drink. He sat on a chair next to her.

"What are you reading?" he asked.

She looked at the book, then back at him. "It's a book of children stories, of all things."

"Oh?" *Children stories?* It didn't make any sense.

"I was reading up on the Noble Trod, and I discovered this book. It's full of interesting stories based on events before the Tome of Laws was written. These stories are giving me great insight to what life was like when the Rifna Erd still lived in the land. It was a wondrous time. It confirms that bringing them back here is the right thing to do."

"Ah, I see," Crescens said. "And were you able to find out anything about the Noble Trod in the book?"

"Nothing that would explain why he would appear after so many years, escape capture and then… nothing. How long has it been since he escaped? A month? More?"

Crescens reached up to scratch his beard, but stopped himself. "It's been just over a month."

"Very strange. He was a good distraction while he was here. But enough about him. Do you have the latest report?"

"Yes, I do." Crescens unrolled a parchment he had completed that morning. "Would you like to hear it?"

"Why else would you be here?" she asked.

Why else indeed? He thought. *If only… but no.* "As you command. Let's see. The viceditad shipments are coming in regularly. We've been filtering distribution through the local merchants. It's spreading throughout the kingdom—aside from Procep, per your orders. The guardians and militia have especially been targeted. My sources tell me it's even reached the royal court."

"Excellent."

"If I may ask, why has Procep been excluded?"

Selene gave him a little smile. "They will have their turn—in time."

Again, this seemed like something part of her plan that she didn't want to share for whatever reason. Maybe she didn't know herself? No, that couldn't be it. He decided not to press it and continued with the report. "The only concern is that the demand is beginning to be larger than the supply. I spoke to Serkan and he insists that we'll have enough," Crescens said.

Selene frowned. "If we end up running low, make sure the castle, militia and guardians get first priority."

"It will be as you say," Crescens said.

⊹⊱⊰⊹

"I have a problem," Queen Rainbow said.

Her mother, Sunshine, looked at her. "What's the matter, dear?"

Rainbow reached out and touched the leaves of a nearby tree. They were walking in the castle's garden—a place she often came when she was troubled and needed to think. She had invited her mother to join her.

"My dresses. Well, they seem to be shrinking," Rainbow said.

"Shrinking?"

"Yes. They are getting quite tight in certain places, especially around my waist."

Sunshine smiled. "Oh, and do you think someone is sneaking into your wardrobe and altering them while you're not looking?"

"I would like to think so," Rainbow admitted.

"But you and I both know that isn't true, don't we?"

Rainbow placed a hand on her stomach. "Yes."

"It sounds like the solution to your problem is to get the seamstresses to make you some new dresses. After all, it will only get worse."

"How much worse?"

"Let's see." Sunshine faced her daughter. She reached out about a hand-width's space away from her stomach. "At least to here."

Rainbow's eyes grew wide. "That far?"

"At least."

"How did you manage?" Rainbow asked.

"Easy. Every time I look at you I know that it was worth it."

Rainbow started to cry. Her mom hugged her.

"What's even worse is that my emotions are a mess," Rainbow said through her tears. "I cry over the littlest things. Or there are times I get really upset, and I don't know why. Elisedd says living with me is like trying to stand still in a raging storm. He's never sure which way the wind will blow him."

"You know he's joking with you, right?" Sunshine asked.

"Yes, but I know he's correct." Rainbow pulled back from her mom and blinked away her tears. "And there's one other issue with my current state."

"Oh?"

"The nursemaids have been very careful to watch over what I eat and drink. I've been very curious to try this new viceditad drink that everyone has been raving about—but the nursemaids won't let me."

Rainbow noticed her mother's expression change. "Sweetheart, I have some concerns about that."

"About what? The viceditad? Elisedd has tried it. Sure, he was a bit strange for the first couple of days—which people say is normal—but after that, he's been like a new man. He's full of energy. He said he's never felt so good in his life."

"That's my point," Sunshine said. "Doesn't it seem strange to you that people enjoy it so much?"

"Not really," Rainbow said. "After all, we use plyese to help us sleep and rest. It's just another plant someone has discovered that has benefits. Haven't you or dad tried it yet?"

"No." Sunshine shook her head for emphasis. "Magistrate Bertram advised us against doing so. He finds it troubling as well."

"I know Bertram is a good friend of yours, and as the leader of the Hierarchy of Magistrates it's his job to be cautious. But, many people have been drinking it for a while now and nothing bad has happened."

"At least, not yet," Sunshine pointed out.

Rainbow tilted her chin up a little. "Well, as queen, I officially proclaim it to be safe."

"Well, as your mother, I proclaim you to be with child and not allowed to have any of it."

※

"Commander Snapdragon!" Kerr said, offering his hand. "Thank you so much for coming!"

Snapdragon took Kerr's hand and shook it. He looked around the room. A couple of tapestries hung from the walls. They looked to be fairly new. "It's seems you've spruced up your office some."

Kerr shrugged. "Ah, you can thank my wife for that. She said it was too sparse to be receiving visitors. Have a seat, please."

Snapdragon sat in a padded chair that faced the mayor's desk. Kerr sat behind the desk.

"Well, old friend, I got your message—and that you needed to discuss it in person. And it needed to be here in Stur," Snapdragon said. "What's going on?"

"My son, well, he's not really my son… Anyway, did you hear about Enoch?" Kerr asked.

"Just that he'd been transferred to Erd Proper. I didn't hear why."

"I'll explain why in a moment. Now, let me ask you something else. What have you heard about the Noble Trod?"

Snapdragon scratched his chin. "Aside from the stories we were told growing up? There were rumors he was spotted in Erd Proper recently.

And then there was something about him being caught and escaping. There are wanted posters hung around Procep. Yet, the stories conflict. It's all rather confusing. Why do you ask?"

"Well, here's the thing," Kerr said. He looked troubled. "The witnesses describe the Noble Trod in a way that it could only be Enoch. There's a bounty on his head."

"Enoch? I guess the man on the posters looks like him. But I don't see how that's possible. Every time I've met him, he's been kind and gentle," Snapdragon said.

"Exactly! Also, from what information I've been able to gather, the Noble Trod appeared in Erd Proper before Enoch was sent there."

"So, where is Enoch now?" Snapdragon asked.

"I don't know," Kerr said. "I was hoping you could ask around—perhaps send word to the king and queen, and to Governor Selene—to offer him a fair trial and remove the dead portion of the bounty."

"Certainly," Snapdragon said. "I was considering taking a trip to the castle soon. I needed to stop in Erd Proper anyway."

"Something the matter?" Kerr asked.

"You aren't the only one dealing with children issues. Diantha was supposed to go to the castle but decided to stay in Erd Proper instead. The last thing we heard from her was that she became an apprentice blacksmith, but we've not heard anything from her in several weeks. By going to the castle I can go to Erd Proper along the way. I'll talk to Governor Selene about the bounty on Enoch while I'm there."

Kerr looked relieved. "Thank you so much. I can't tell you how worried I've been."

"Believe me, I understand. It seems no matter how old your children get, you never stop worrying about them."

"There's one more thing while you're here," Kerr said.

"What's that?"

"We've had a number of complaints from the men about the new magistrate. I've done what I can, but it keeps getting worse."

"What seems to be the problem?"

Kerr shook his head. "I think you'll figure it out once you meet her." He got up and told one of the guardians at the door to get the magistrate.

"I think it would be best if I wasn't here when you spoke to her," Kerr said.

"Oh?"

"Like I said before, you'll see why."

Moments later, a woman with curly grey and black hair walked into the room without knocking.

"I'll leave you two to speak," Kerr said, not meeting her eyes as he left.

Snapdragon stood. "I don't believe we've met," he said.

"And whose fault is that?" she said. "I've been ranked number one for five years in a row. I've been expecting you to come to me before now."

Snapdragon was surprised by how much this woman thought of herself. "Ranked? Ranked how Larissa?"

"It's *Magistrate* Larissa," she corrected, putting the emphasis on her title and the middle vowel of her name. She scowled at him.

"Ranked how, Magistrate Larissa?"

"How can you not know, Snapdragon?" She looked bewildered.

"It's *Commander* Snapdragon." Though his tone was firm, he didn't let his frustration show.

"Fine—*Commander*. Each division of the militia is ranked every quarter in several categories to ensure its readiness and effectiveness. My division in Erd Proper has been number one for the last five years." She folded her arms and smiled at him triumphantly.

Snapdragon was so tired of self-important people. Larissa wasn't the first person to let her title and perceived prominence affect her behavior. And sadly, Snapdragon didn't think she would be the last.

There hadn't been the need for a magistrate in this part of Erd before because it had been too sparsely populated. However, since the building of the northern wall, apparently Governor Selene thought enough people resided in the area to warrant one.

"I'm aware of the inspections. After all, it was my brother Oakleaf who put the system into place. I'd heard that people wanted the findings to be made public. Oakleaf only agreed in order for divisions that were lacking in an area could learn from divisions that were doing well. It was never intended to be regarded as an award. But that's not why I'm here. Mayor Kerr tells me there have been a number of complaints against you. What do you know about these?"

"Let me say this again. I have been ranked number one for over five years."

"So?"

"That is my answer to any complaints."

Snapdragon shook his head. "Being highly ranked isn't a reasonable answer."

She looked at him a moment, seething. "It's true what I've heard about you," she said.

"Oh?"

"You're too soft. You've been too lax in your duties. Since I've taken over the militia, there have been no successful attacks against the northern walls. The men are complaining because they're not used to real discipline. Any complaints against me are *your* fault." She pointed at him.

Snapdragon rubbed his eyes. This woman was giving him a headache. He didn't say anything for a moment. He wanted his response not to be said out of anger—but she was making it difficult.

"Magistrate Larissa," he said. "There have been no successful attacks since you took over because there have been no attacks at all."

"Ha! You're only proving my point! Whoever is behind the attacks must have heard I was in charge and knew it would be foolish to try."

Snapdragon could only stare at her. She was so convinced she was right. Anything he said, she would find a way to twist it to make it about her. "Remarkable," he finally said.

"Yes, I know," she said, gloating. "So, you've wasted your time coming out here. However, I will be visiting Procep in the next few weeks to undo the lack of discipline you've fostered."

This had gone far enough. "May I ask you a question, Magistrate Larissa?"

"Yes. It's the only way you'll learn."

"Why is there a militia?"

She responded like it was the dumbest thing she'd heard. "To make sure the people are safe."

"Safe from whom?"

"Raiders, bandits, robbers and most of all, themselves."

"And why was the northern wall built?"

"Because you were so scared from a run-in with some wild men north of the mountains that you convinced the king to build it. I know it's not what you want to hear, but it's about time someone told you."

"And what's your role in all this?" he asked.

"To do what you won't, or most likely *can't*, do."

Snapdragon gave her a thoughtful look and nodded his head.

"Larissa—" he said.

"It's *Magistrate* Larissa."

"Not anymore," he said. She was about to say something but he kept talking. "Based on our conversation and the complaints, I am exercising the power granted to me by King Rayne and later endorsed by Queen Rainbow to ensure the peace and safety of the people of Bariwon. It is my opinion you are delusional and power hungry. Your methods are causing more problems than they are solving. You will return to Erd Proper where Governor Selene can do with you what she will. However, you are not allowed to come within a day's journey of the northern defenses. You have until mid-day tomorrow to leave."

"Now you listen here—" she spat.

Snapdragon leaned in toward her and put his face close to hers. "If you want to test your theory that I'm a soft leader, say one more word and you'll discover exactly what I'm willing to do to protect the people of Bariwon."

Her eyes grew wide and for the first time since the meeting began, her boldness faded. She nodded her head in understanding.

⇥⧘⇤

Crescens doubled over in pain. "What do you mean we're out of viceditad?"

The guardian before him shrugged. "We've not received the next shipment."

"Go, double check. If you need to, go out to the town and buy some," Crescens instructed. He handed the guardian a pouch full of money. "Hurry! Also, fetch me a nursemaid."

"As you say." The guardian left the room.

Crescens somehow made it over to his bed and fell on top of it. He remembered how he felt the first time he'd gone without viceditad. That was like a restful nap compared to how he was feeling now.

What seemed like an eternity later, a nursemaid entered his room.

"Magistrate?"

"I need more viceditad," he said.

"We've run out," she said. "We're supposed to get some soon."

"I need something!"

The nursemaid placed the back of her hand on his forehead. "I'll see what I can find, but you need to rest. I'll return shortly."

Crescens watched her leave. He rolled on his back and stared at the stone ceiling. He had never felt so wonderful as when he had been drinking viceditad. And he'd never felt so awful as when he went without it.

Moments dragged out until the nursemaid returned.

"I've double checked," she said. "I'm sorry. We are completely out of viceditad in the palace. Our next shipment is scheduled for tomorrow. But I brought some plyese tea to help you relax and sleep."

"Fine, anything to help me feel better," he said.

She came to his side and helped him sip the tea. After finishing it, he felt no different. He said so.

"Unlike the viceditad, plyese takes time," she said. "I'll check back on you in a little while and make sure that you're not disturbed."

Crescens nodded and she left.

He focused on breathing slowly, but struggled to do so. His heart was pounding heavily in his chest and beads of sweat formed on his brow.

He lost track of time. The pain was so intense he could focus on nothing else. His stomach roiled. Using what energy he had left, he reached under his bed and removed the chamber pot. His stomach lurched and he vomited. Though his vision was blurry, he thought he saw blood mixed in with what he had thrown up. That had never happened before. Again and again he retched. Finally there was nothing left in him.

Crescens wasn't sure when the nursemaid returned. He had become delusional—maybe he was imagining her. She had a look of horror on her face.

✤

Selene stood at the window and looked out at the northern mountains. She had requested to be left alone. The main hall usually brought her peace. But not today.

She had been summoned to Crescens's room a couple of days ago. He looked terrible. His body was shaking and he was soaked in his own sweat and vomit. For two days the nursemaids did all they could. They were even able to get a hold of some viceditad a day after he became ill, but he threw it up as soon as he drank it.

In the end, Crescens died a horrible death.

He had done his job well, doing what he was told, even if he didn't appear to agree with it. That, in and of itself, is what she'd miss the most. She needed to replace him—but she wasn't sure who she could trust. The only person that came to mind was Larissa. Selene had sent her to be the magistrate along the northern wall, though her job was more involved than just that.

For some reason, Snapdragon had dismissed her and sent her back to Erd Proper. Perhaps it was for the best. Things were going according to plan and Larissa was trustworthy. A knock on the door interrupted her thoughts.

Annoyed, she shouted, "I said I did not want to be disturbed!"

The door opened and a nursemaid stepped in. Selene couldn't believe the gall this woman had. No one dared show this level of disobedience.

"Governor—" the nursemaid started to say.

"Leave before I have you executed."

"Begging your pardon, but I need to tell you this. It's of the utmost urgency."

Selene folded her arms and glared. "What is it?"

"We have examined Crescens's body and reviewed our books on what could have killed him."

"This is the news that couldn't wait? Perhaps we'll get to use the gallows again sooner than we thought."

The nursemaid held her hands up. "Please, wait! You don't understand!"

"Then tell me."

"We've determined that based on the way Crescens died, it could only be one thing."

"Which is?"

The woman before her gulped and then said just above a whisper, "The nislles."

CHAPTER 68

Diantha dove to her left, just barely in time to avoid getting hit. She rolled onto her feet, but stayed in a crouching position. Her opponent had lost his balance after his latest attack and had his back to her. Diantha took advantage of it by leaping forward and kicking him behind his right knee. It worked as his leg buckled and he had to reach out with his hands to stop his fall. In the process, he dropped his sword.

Seeing this as an opportunity to finish him off, Diantha swung her sword toward his back. However, he then did something unexpected. He rolled onto his back and reached up to stop the sword with his bare hand. His timing was perfect as he grabbed it by the hilt. His hand surrounded hers. His grip was so strong Diantha couldn't shake free. He then swept his legs toward her. She tried to jump, but couldn't do so effectively because she was being held into place. Their legs collided and she fell down on top of him, her face just inches away from his. For a moment the two opponents stared at each other. She could press the attack, but this had gone on long enough.

"Let's call it a draw," she said.

Enoch laughed. "A draw? Just when I'm about to beat you?"

"You're not about to beat me. I could hit you with my head and daze you enough to get free."

"And you didn't think I'd be ready for that?" he asked.

"What would you do?"

"This!" He leaned up and pretended he was going to bite her nose.

She laughed. "You would really bite me?"

His countenance changed—his features softening. "No, I wouldn't want to scar your beautiful face."

At that moment, Diantha realized the position she was in. She was on top of him with their faces close together. For the first time since they had met, she had a strange sensation in her chest. It was unfamiliar, but not unpleasant.

"All right, I'll yield," she said. "If for no other reason than to keep you from biting me."

He let go of her hand and she got to her feet. She offered him a hand to help him up—knowing full well he was too big for her to do any good. Enoch took her hand anyway and stood.

"You're getting better," she said.

"Thanks to your help," he responded.

Diantha looked up. The sun was just passing overhead. "Are you hungry? It's about mid-day."

He nodded. "I'll go gather some more firewood if you want to get the meal started."

"All right."

Enoch picked up both of their wooden practice swords and leaned them against a tree. He then headed into the woods.

In the month she and Enoch had lived in Tevoil, they had grown to be quite comfortable around each other. They'd been able to make it to the farm where her Uncle Rayne was raised. The farmhouse had been burned down years ago, but between Enoch's strength and Diantha's knowledge she got from being a blacksmith, they were able to fashion together a sturdy shelter—incorporating the house's original stone fireplace. They were also able to salvage several cooking items including a pot they used to make soup. Under one of the charred floorboards they found a pouch full of coins, which they held onto in case of an emergency. They were isolated enough that no one bothered them. She knew they couldn't live there indefinitely, but for now, it was a safe place.

She considered her situation while she started to prepare the soup they would have for their meal. When she was younger, men her age saw her as a prize to be won. She had often been told she looked like her mother, who everyone considered to be beautiful. To her, this caused unwanted attention from the wrong sorts of people.

Enoch had been different. He'd been a gentleman ever since she had met him. At first, she considered leaving him behind. He was so strong that he could over power her if she wasn't careful. But he had never tried. Within a shorter period of time than she thought possible, she was very comfortable around him. In many ways, he was the closest thing she had ever had to a best friend.

Yet, just moments ago, he had said she was pretty. It was the first time he'd said anything like that. While she had been told that many times growing up, when he said it, she felt differently. It was an odd emotion.

Soon, the pot was hanging over a crackling fire and the smell of soup filled the air.

"That smells wonderful," Enoch said. He had just come inside with an armful of firewood.

"It does, doesn't it?" she answered.

He set down the wood next to the fireplace and then sat on one of the bigger logs they used for chairs. "I ventured out a bit farther than before," he said.

"Oh?"

"I was careful. No one spotted me," he reassured her. "And I found something interesting."

"What was it?"

Enoch seemed to think about it for a moment. "It's best I show you after we eat."

⊰⊱

"The nislles?" Selene asked.

The nursemaid nodded and wrung her hands together.

Selene considered the situation for a moment. Could Serkan have brought the fatal disease with him from beyond the northern mountains? Was she at risk? But that didn't make any sense. Snapdragon had brought the people from Eddinh with him back to Bariwon over twenty years ago and there hadn't been any sign of the nislles. It had to do something with Serkan.

"Go find Larissa. She's just returned from the northern defenses. Bring her here right away. Also, speak to no one else of the nislles."

The nursemaid said, "Yes, Governor."

Selene watched the nursemaid leave. She then started to pace. A meeting with Serkan was scheduled for that evening where they were going to be discussing the next part of the plan. However, instead of her crossing the lake and meeting with him, she decided to bring him here to the palace. If the nislles had indeed returned, maybe she could use the threat of putting Serkan in the room with Crescens's body to get the Rifna Erd to tell her the truth.

A few moments later, there was a knock on the door. "Enter."

Larissa entered and closed the door behind her.

"Why are you here?" Selene asked.

"You summoned me."

Selene scowled. "No, why are you here and not at the northern mountains where I sent you?"

It was Larissa's turn to make an ugly face. "Because that idiot Snapdragon dismissed me. He saw me as a threat to his authority and sent me away."

"So, you are saying you were dismissed because you were doing your job too well?"

Larissa nodded. "It's the only thing that makes sense." Before Selene could say anything else, Larissa continued, "But don't worry. I have men I trust taking care of the main reasons you sent me. We'll still be able to ship in the viceditad, as well as smuggling in more of Serkan's men."

"Serkan's *men?*" Selene asked.

"Yes. We've snuck in several more of his men over the last few weeks."

"I knew nothing of this," Selene said.

"I don't understand. Why would he keep that secret from you?"

"That's what we're going to find out," Selene said. "After the sun sets, you are to go to Serkan's hut on the edge of the lake and bring him here. Work with guardians you trust. Make sure no one sees him arrive."

"Yes, Governor."

Larissa turned to leave. "One last thing," Selene said. "Crescens is no longer in my service, so as of this moment, you are magistrate over Erd Proper."

"It's about time," Larissa said, then left.

⊷⧉⊷

Beams of light shown through the canopy of leaves. There was a light breeze blowing—just enough to make the warm day comfortable. Enoch led Diantha to the clearing he found. He couldn't explain why, but he felt peaceful here.

"I can't believe we've been here this long and not found this place," Diantha said. She walked into the clearing and twirled around, seeming to take it in.

"Well, we've been careful not to venture too far. We're still wanted people."

Diantha's face fell. "Sometimes I forget that."

"I know," Enoch said. "Sometimes I pretend it isn't true."

"Well, if it wasn't true, then why would we be living out here?"

He kept quiet. He couldn't tell her that sometimes he pretended they were married and living out here by choice. Enoch had never been around a woman his age long enough to become familiar with her. Diantha didn't treat him like a big oaf. She treated him like a friend. Enoch considered his previous leader, Mason, a friend, but with Diantha, it was different. He felt safe and comfortable around her.

"Enoch?" she asked. He realized he'd not answered her.

"Oh, I don't know. We could be living out here for any number of reasons," he said.

She eyed him and tilted her head to one side, as if she was considering his answer. "I guess."

"There's another thing I found here," he said, trying to change the subject.

"Yeah?"

He walked to the far edge of the clearing. Next to one of the larger trees in the area, there was a grave marker. Enoch went to one knee out of respect. He felt Diantha kneel next to him.

"Who is it?" she asked.

"I don't know." He pointed to the marker. It was made out of wood that had aged over time. The only word carved in it was "Father."

"I wonder if my Uncle Rayne knows. Next time I see him, I'll have to ask," she said.

Enoch turned to her. "When do you think that will be?"

She shrugged. "Good question. We've not really talked about it. At some point in time, we'll need to go into a town to get the latest news. Maybe the bounty on you has been dropped."

"Maybe," he said. "But aren't we going to be too noticeable to check? With my stature and your red hair, we don't exactly blend in."

Diantha put a hand up to her hair. "Actually, I think I may know a way around that."

"No!" Enoch said, louder than he intended. "You can't cut your hair."

She looked at him with an amused expression. "I wasn't going to cut it."

"Then what?"

"When I was younger, my family attended a ball where everyone got to dress up as someone else. Using a combination of flowers and roots, we were able to make a paste that changed the color of my hair to black. It lasted about a week and I liked it. It made me look different than my mom. I've seen those same flowers around here, and I'm sure with some trial and error, we could get the mix right."

Enoch reached up and ran his fingers through his hair. "I don't think that will help me."

Diantha laughed. "No, for you we'd need a shrinking potion and I don't know of one that exists."

⇥‡⇤

Selene busied herself with administrative duties until the evening meal. She continued to work in her office late into the night when a knock sounded on her office door.

"Enter."

Larissa came in followed by Serkan and three other Rifna Erd. Serkan was imposing in and of himself, but he was even more so backed up with men like him. There was something different about him tonight, but she couldn't figure out why.

She stood and walked over to the Rifna Erd. Even though he was taller than her, she tried to stare him down.

"What do you know of the nislles returning?" she asked.

Larissa let out a gasp.

"I know nothing of it," he said, his voice matching her tone.

"Crescens, my former magistrate, died a horrible death and my nursemaids are convinced it's the nislles," Selene said. "I find it too big of a coincidence that the one man who had the most contact with you caught that disease. The last time it came to Bariwon was after the tunnel through the mountains was opened generations ago."

Serkan stared at her. "Did he drink the viceditad?"

"Yes, but I'm not sure what that would have to do with it. A lot of people drink it and they have shown no signs of getting sick," she stated.

He leaned in closer to her. "Do you and this other woman drink the viceditad?"

"Larissa?" Selene asked.

"Yes, Governor. I drink it, as do all of your followers per your orders."

Serkan didn't take his eyes off Selene. "Do *you* drink it?" he asked her.

"Why would I drink it?" Selene said. "You told me it creates loyalty. I have no one I need to be loyal to but me."

"Of that, you are wrong," Serkan said. He folded his arms and glared at her.

She took a better look at him and then realized what was different. He now had three colored stripes in his beard: blue, green and red. The men with him only had red stripes. Selene stood up as tall as she could and met his gaze. "Who are you to tell me I am wrong?"

Serkan took a step back. Instead of answering Selene, he looked at Larissa. "You have the respect of the men, even though you are a woman, and you drink the viceditad." It wasn't a question. He then turned and pointed to Selene. "You refuse."

"Serkan, you forget your place," Selene said. "I brought you here. I have spread the viceditad through the land. You are here to help me become the ruler of Bariwon. Once we conquer the land, you and your people will have an honored place among us. But you will do what I say."

The Rifna Erd gave her a dubious look. Selene didn't care for it. Didn't he know that one word from her and guardians would rush in and kill him and his men? Perhaps a show a power is what they needed to see.

"I am going to send all of you to where Crescens's body is rotting. We will discover if you knew about the nislles or not," Selene declared.

Serkan didn't react the way she expected. Instead, he turned to the man on his right and said, "She has fulfilled her purpose."

Selene didn't know what he meant by that, but it soon became clear. Serkan's follower removed a short, jagged sword from his hip and in a swift motion lunged forward and pierced her through her chest.

❄✦❄

Diantha walked into a shop in the town of Lewyol. The first thing she noticed was the smell—wax. She understood why when she saw the shelves lined with all shapes and sizes of candles.

"Hello!" a friendly voice said. It came from a man behind a counter. "Is it still raining outside?"

Diantha shrugged and said, "Hard to say since I'm inside now." It hadn't been raining very hard, but it actually worked in her favor. Townspeople were more focused on watching their step or getting out of the rain than paying attention to a woman in a hooded cloak.

"Uh, yes, well…" the man said. She noticed that he looked puzzled.

"Is something the matter?" Diantha asked. She prepared to bolt if he recognized her, even though the paste had worked and her hair was dark.

"No, nothing's the matter." He smiled. "There was something familiar about what you said, but I can't remember why. Ah, that's what happens when you get old. I'm Chandler. May I help you find something?"

She sensed no deceit from the shopkeeper so she stepped toward him. "I'm just passing through town and headed toward Erd Proper. However, I've been hearing strange stories coming from there. Is there anything I should be worrying about?"

"A month ago, I would have said yes," Chandler said. "There were stories of the Noble Trod coming back to life. I've heard that he was captured but he escaped."

She tried to act concerned. "Do you think it's safe to go there now?"

"I'd be on my guard. The governor has posted a bounty for the Noble Trod, so at least she believes it."

This was not the news Diantha hoped to hear. "That's good advice, thank you."

"Now, what can I get you?" he asked.

She had picked a shop in the middle of town in an attempt to be less conspicuous. She and Enoch could use some candles and she had the coins they found at the farmhouse.

"I'll take four of those." She pointed to a shelf with some medium sized tapers.

Chandler put her purchase in a canvas bag after she completed the transaction.

Diantha stepped out into the street. The rain was just a drizzle now, but she still appreciated the cover it offered. She walked out of town, trying to act casually and not raise suspicions. Once she was clear, she headed to where Enoch was waiting for her in a small grove.

"Are you all right?" he asked when he saw her.

She nodded.

"But the news isn't good, is it?"

"Is it that obvious?" she asked.

"I've gotten use to reading your emotions." He shrugged.

For a moment they didn't say anything. The trees where Enoch was hiding were close enough together that the rain was kept out.

"Where do we go now?" they asked each other at the same time, and then laughed. Enoch motioned for her to speak first.

"We've waited a month and things haven't gotten any better. I'm not sure waiting is going to work."

"I think you're right," Enoch said. "So, what do you suggest?"

Diantha blew out a deep breath. "I don't know."

"Can I make a suggestion?"

"Please."

"Kerr always told me your father was an honorable man and if I ever needed help, I should seek him out."

Diantha shook her head. "I don't think I can face him—at least not yet."

"Why?"

"Because…" and then Diantha realized her reasons didn't compare to the bigger issues.

"Actually, I don't have a good reason."

"Then, we'll go?" he asked.

"Yeah, I guess that's our best option. But we'll need to take less traveled paths."

Enoch chuckled.

"What's so funny?"

"It seems like I've been taking less traveled paths my whole life."

CHAPTER 69

Snapdragon didn't like what he saw. Everywhere he looked in Erd Proper, men had grown long, pointed beards. He knew fashion trends came and went, and for whatever reason, Erd Proper seemed to embrace these changes quicker than the rest of the kingdom. But the beards reminded him too much of the Rifna Erd. There weren't any stripes in their beards and most of the men still had hair on top of their heads, but the visual images brought back terrible memories of Snapdragon's encounters with the Rifna Erd.

"What do you think of their beards?" he asked one of the guardians accompanying him.

"I think they look silly."

The guardian that answered was Aaron. He was older and had been with King Rayne when the Rifna Erd first came out of the tunnel.

"Do they remind you of anything?" Snapdragon asked.

"It's hard not to make the connection," Aaron said.

Three other guardians accompanied them. Snapdragon's wife, Seraphina, wouldn't let Snapdragon go anywhere without at least four guardians. He first fought the idea, but after being attacked near the northern mountains, he knew that she was right.

Snapdragon and his men had arrived in Erd Proper that morning and were headed toward the palace to meet with Governor Selene. He had looked into several recent events and decided he had enough information to confront her.

During the trip, they had come across several smaller settlements. Posted on trees and fences were the wanted posters for the Noble Trod with a sketch of a man that somewhat resembled Enoch. Hopefully Snapdragon could get this sorted out quickly.

Upon approaching the gate to the palace, Snapdragon noticed the guardians on duty seemed nervous—they obviously recognized him, but that didn't explain their reactions. He raised a hand in greeting and said, "Hello! We're here to see Governor Selene."

The men exchanged glances. "One moment please, sir."

One of the guardians went inside. Snapdragon got off his horse as did the rest of his party.

"Something's off," Aaron whispered to Snapdragon after they dismounted.

Snapdragon nodded. "Stay alert," he whispered back, and then took a few steps forward. "Is there a problem?"

"No problem, Commander," one of the Erd guardians said. "We weren't expecting you."

The guardians at the gate looked at each other as if unsure what to do.

At that moment, Snapdragon saw a woman approaching the gate from inside the palace—and it was someone he didn't expect.

"Larissa," he said when she came close enough to hear him. "What are you doing here? Where is Governor Selene or Magistrate Crescens?"

Even stranger than seeing Larissa was the way she responded. In their last encounter, she had been arrogant. This time, she responded in a reserved, humble tone. "Commander Snapdragon, my apologies. We've been meaning to send word, but we've been quite busy."

"Word? Word about what?"

"Magistrate Crescens has passed away. He was crossing the lake on the ferry, slipped, hit his head and fell in. He drowned. Governor Selene is sick with grief and is unable to take visitors at this time. I've been asked to fill Crescens's position. Please, tell me how I may help you?"

Snapdragon was baffled. Something was definitely wrong. Larissa spoke as if she was afraid. He had threatened her, yes, but not to the point where she would be acting this way.

"How soon before the governor will be seeing visitors?" he asked.

He thought he saw her face grow paler. "I cannot say. But as magistrate, I can help you."

"May we come in?" Snapdragon asked.

Larissa licked her lips. "I don't think that would be wise. Please, tell me what I can do to help you."

He knew he could force her to let him in, but he sensed that if he did, it could be dangerous. He wasn't sure why he felt that way, but he couldn't deny the feeling.

"I've come to address the issue of the Noble Trod."

She visibly relaxed. "Yes? What of him?"

"What can you tell me of the situation?"

"Only what I've heard since I've arrived," she said. "He was a large man. At night, he'd go around town and attack people. He'd then hang their bloody clothes from lampposts, trees, doorframes—all sorts of different places. He was captured, but escaped. No one has seen him in over a month."

Snapdragon noticed there was a wanted sign not far from the palace gate. He pointed to it. "Does the man on that poster remind you of anyone?"

"Yes," she said, sounding a bit smug for the first time. "He's Enoch. I dismissed him from the militia along the northern wall and sent him here. He must of gone crazy for being transferred and took on the persona of the Noble Trod."

Snapdragon addressed one of the guardians from Erd. "When was the first attack from the Noble Trod reported?"

The man thought a moment. "It was on a road outside of Erd Proper, oh I'd say about six weeks ago."

"And when did you dismiss Enoch?" Snapdragon asked Larissa.

"It was obviously at the same time."

"No, it wasn't," Snapdragon said. "According to Mason, Enoch's former captain at the northern mountains, Enoch was sent here five weeks ago. We checked with several people and the attacks of the Noble Trod started *before* Enoch was sent here."

"Begging your pardon, Commander," one of the guardians said, "but there were several people who testified it was him."

"Again, you are mistaken." Snapdragon said. "I've read the reports. The people testified that Enoch entered The Bard's Tale Tavern with blood on his clothes. No one said that they saw him attack anyone."

"So, that's why you came?" Larissa asked. "To clear Enoch of the charges?" She sounded relieved.

"Yes, that is exactly the reason." Snapdragon said.

Larissa looked over her shoulder and then back at Snapdragon. "Consider the charges dropped. We will have all the signs removed. We will send out a proclamation that Enoch was wrongly accused and that he is to be left alone if found. Is this permissible?"

It was exactly what Snapdragon wanted, but it was too easy. He had expected to put up a bigger fight. "Yes, that will work."

"Now, Commander, I would invite you in, but I hope you can understand we need to respect Governor Selene's mourning period."

"I do understand. Please give her our condolences."

"I will."

"One last thing," Snapdragon said.

"Yes?" She looked worried again.

"I'm also looking for my daughter, Diantha. She's hard to miss. She has bright red hair. Last I heard she was taken on as a blacksmith's apprentice here in Erd Proper."

"I know nothing of her." She sounded sincere.

"Commander," one of the Erd guardians said. "I believe she was working for Goban, but I don't believe she is anymore."

"Where can I find this Goban?" Snapdragon asked. The guardian gave directions.

"Thank you again for your time, Magistrate," Snapdragon said. He motioned for his men to remount.

They left the palace and headed toward the blacksmith's shop. Aaron leaned over to Snapdragon and said, "That was very strange. She is hiding something."

"I agree." Snapdragon said. "We'll send a report to Queen Rainbow and King Elisedd when we get a chance."

In short order they found Goban's shop.

"Aye, she worked for me—but only for a short bit," Goban said when asked.

"Why did she leave your employment?" Aaron asked. He had not left Snapdragon's side per Seraphina's order.

The blacksmith shrugged. "She didn't say. Last we spoke, she wanted to leave work early to get a good spot to watch the hanging of the Noble Trod. He escaped and I never saw her after that."

Snapdragon sensed no deceit. "Thank you for your time."

He left the smithy and went back to where the rest of his men were waiting.

"Commander," Aaron said quietly once they were clear. "Enoch couldn't have been the Noble Trod because he hadn't arrived here before the attacks started, right?"

"Correct," Snapdragon said. "And I know what you are getting at. It's too big of a coincidence that Diantha arrived here at the same time the attacks started and then she disappeared when the Noble Trod escaped."

❖

Enoch crouched down behind a small hill. Diantha was next to him, her index finger against her lips. He didn't need her to tell him to be quiet. They had been able to avoid being spotted by staying off the main roads and taking back trails. It was Diantha's idea to travel at night, which made it slower going, but safer.

Moments ago they had heard voices and saw pinpoints of light that were most likely torches. The trail Diantha and Enoch had been following was surrounded by rocky hills. They'd been fortunate to find the trail because it would be too difficult and potentially dangerous to cross over the rocky landscape in the dark.

They'd been able to find a small hill they could climb before the approaching people would see them. Enoch watched as Diantha peeked over the top of the hill. He was tempted to look for himself, but with his bulky frame, he was afraid any of his movements would make noise.

Diantha wore her sword on her back and a small knife on her left hip. Enoch's weapon was a pike—a long wooden staff sharpened on one end he'd made while they were in Tevoil.

Voices were heard as the people approached. To Enoch's ear, they were masculine and they spoke with a thick accent.

He felt Diantha tense up next to him. She must have been able to see them. And then she did something completely unexpected: she screamed a battle cry and rushed over the top of the hill toward the trail.

Enoch's first reaction was one of shock, but soon enough he regained his senses and pulled himself up enough that he could see what was going on.

On the trail, there was a large wooden cart being pulled by a horse. Surrounding the cart were six men. Enoch hadn't seen men dressed like them before. They were all bald with pointed beards. None of them wore shirts—they were only dressed in pants and boots. Each of them was armed with a jagged sword. At the front of the line, Diantha was engaged in combat with one of the men.

What had gotten into her? He wasn't sure, but he also couldn't let her take on these men alone. He went to pull himself up more, but a rock under his right foot gave way and he slipped down behind the hill. He could hear the sounds of combat as he regained his footing and climbed back up.

Enoch managed to stand on top of the hill. Roughly twenty paces down and away from him, the battle was fully engaged. Two of the bald men were down and unmoving while Diantha fought off the advances of the others.

One of the men had attacked with a downward swing which Diantha parried by bringing up her sword. This allowed another one of the men to kick one of her legs and cause her to go to a knee. The attacker who had kicked her brought his sword up. Enoch could see that she wouldn't be able to fend off both blows and he was too far away to help. Or was he?

In an act of desperation, Enoch threw his pike like a javelin. It caught her second attacker in the left thigh—enough to knock him off balance and miss her with his attack.

Enoch's action caught the attention of the other two attackers who moved to intercept him.

Unarmed, he thought of how to respond. He shifted to his left and nearly lost his balance again as the large rocks shifted under his weight. It gave him an idea. He made sure he had good footing and then reached down and picked up a large rock—roughly the size of a horse's head. He tossed it at one of the oncoming men. The man tried to dodge, but the rock caught him in the shoulder. When it did, it made a sickening crutch. The man fell to the ground, grabbed his shoulder and wailed in pain.

The second man was more cautious. Enoch searched for another rock. There was one just down the hill from him. He reached for it, but slipped again and tumbled toward his attacker. The bald man had his sword drawn and watched as Enoch came to a stop a few paces from him.

Enoch tried to get to his feet, but he had hit his head during the fall and was dazed. He saw three men with swords approach him, but realized it was only one and his vision was blurry.

A jagged blade raised high against the star filled sky would be the last thing Enoch would see in his lifetime. Or so he thought until the man stopped short and looked down at his stomach. To the left of his bellybutton was the tip of a sword. He looked at Enoch, seemingly confused. There was a sucking sound and the sword tip disappeared. His attacker went to turn around, but only made it part of the way when his head went flying from his shoulders.

When his body crumpled to the ground, Enoch saw Diantha standing there, wielding a bloody sword.

"They're all dead," Diantha said through labored breaths. "Are you all right?"

Enoch put a hand to his head. He only saw two of her, so he was improving.

"I hit my head pretty hard," Enoch said.

She came over to him and knelt. Though all the bald men were down, their torches still burned in several spots on the trail. Diantha ran her fingers through Enoch's hair and examined his head.

"I don't think you cracked your skull, and you're not bleeding. That's good," she said.

"Are you hurt?" he asked.

"A few small cuts and scrapes. It would have been worse if you hadn't hit that one with your pike. Thank you."

Enoch looked at her. She was a bit blurry, but now there was only one of her. "Why?"

"Why what?"

"Why did you attack?" he said.

She bit her lower lip and looked around at the dead men. "Do you not know who these men are?"

Enoch shook his head, and regretted doing so because it ached more when he did.

"These are Rifna Erd. I've heard too many stories from my father, mother and Bearach about these men for them to be anyone else. I guess I just reacted on instinct. It probably wasn't the smartest idea for me to take them on six to one."

"Rifna Erd? That's not possible. They are on the other side of the mountain. How can they be here?" Enoch asked.

Diantha's eyes grew wide. "We've been in hiding for a while. It could be that they've breached the defenses and we don't know about it."

"But then why would they be taking a nearly deserted trail in the middle of the night?"

He could see that she was trying to puzzle it out.

"Let's see what they were hauling. Maybe it will give us an idea." She stood up and walked to the large wooden cart.

Enoch could see it was loaded with dozens of crates. He sat up, though doing so made his head spin. Diantha used her sword to pry open one of the crates, then another, and then yet another.

"Huh," she said.

"What is it?"

She tipped one of the crates over. Out of it spilled some sort of leafy plant.

"What is it?"

Diantha shrugged. "I don't know. But all of the crates are filled with it."

"Why would the Rifna Erd be smuggling in plants?"

"Good question." Diantha walked to the front of the cart and unhitched the horse and then led the mare several paces away. She then picked up a torch and walked back to the cart. "But if the Rifna Erd are smuggling it in, it can't be good."

She threw the torch on the cart. Enoch watched as it caught fire and went up in flames.

⊰❉⊱

Queen Rainbow sat at the head of a long table in the main hall of the castle. King Elisedd was next to her and involved in a conversation with one of the nobles.

"Food is best eaten when it's put in your mouth," her grandfather Garth said.

His comment brought her out of her thoughts. "What's that?"

Garth motioned to her plate. She looked at it and noticed she'd been pushing the food around on the plate and had yet to eat anything.

"I guess I'm not hungry."

"Someone is," he said.

She smiled at him. Most people had a difficult time talking with her grandfather. It was as if he spoke in riddles, but that was just his way. The older she got, the more she appreciated his wisdom.

"You mean my baby, right?" she asked.

"It wouldn't be fair to the little one to starve because you've got something on your mind."

Rainbow noticed her parents were watching the conversation with amusement.

"Fine. I'll eat," she said.

"What's troubling you?" her mom asked. "Are you afraid Grandpa Garth is going to pick a strange name for your child?"

Garth had given his children the non-traditional names of Oakleaf, Sunshine and Snapdragon. He even picked the name Rainbow for her and had a hand in naming her cousins. Reed was a common name, but had a different spelling. Diantha was the name of a flower, but by far, Rainbow's favorite name was that of her cousin Winter.

"I think Grandpa Garth has picked out wonderful names. I did hear someone call them, oh, how did they put it? Ah, yes. 'Groan worthy.' But I don't care. And no, that isn't what's bothering me."

"Then what?" her father asked.

Rainbow leaned toward them and away from her husband. "I'm concerned about this viceditad everyone seems to be drinking."

"Oh?" Sunshine asked. "I thought you said you approved of it."

"I did, at first. But now I'm concerned that people can't seem to go without it for more than a couple of days or they start to get sick."

"They do?" Rayne said. "I hadn't heard that."

Rainbow looked over her shoulder at Elisedd who was still involved in his conversation and not paying any attention to her. She turned back to her parents and grandfather. "Elisedd started getting sick a few days ago. He said he was sure that if he drank some viceditad he'd be fine. I asked him how he knew that. He said he'd heard that from some of the other people in the castle that drink it. Sure enough, as soon as he drank some more viceditad, he was fine."

"Garth," Rayne said, "what do you know about this viceditad?"

"It's a visitor."

"Meaning what, Dad?" Sunshine asked.

"It's not from here."

"We know it comes from Erd," Rainbow said. "Is that what you mean?"

"It won't live here," Garth said. "It dies."

Rainbow noticed her mom's eyes grow wide. "Have you tried to grow it here, Dad?"

"Of course. All living things deserve a place to stay. Even visitors."

"But the viceditad won't grow here?" Rayne asked.

Garth blinked. "As I said."

"Why wouldn't it?" Rainbow asked.

"Why does a fish need water to survive? Why do cows not eat meat? Why can't humans fly?"

"It isn't their nature," Sunshine said.

Garth nodded and resumed eating.

"Have any of you tried it?" Rainbow asked.

"No." Rayne and Sunshine said at the same time. Garth just shook his head.

"Why not?"

Her father said, "Head Magistrate Bertram recommended against it. Years ago, he was looking for an original copy of The Tome of Laws. During his search, he read something about a plant that resembles the viceditad in one of the old texts. It was odd, so he noted it. He searched recently and located the text, but it was very vague—it mentioned a plant that wasn't from here that caused strange behavior. Not long after the entry, the bloody civil war broke out. It may have been a coincidence, but he advised us not to drink it until he could find out more. "

"Why didn't he tell that to everyone?" Rainbow asked.

"Because it was too late. By the time he had located the text once again, a number of people had already started drinking it. He believes that once they start, they can't stop."

"I don't understand. Why can't they stop?"

Rayne looked troubled. "You told us that Elisedd started getting sick when he went without it, right? He only felt better when he drank some more, right?"

"But what if he wasn't able to get more?" Rainbow asked.

"I don't know," Sunshine said. "Do you know, Dad?"

Garth looked at each of the people in the conversation and then said, "If someone thinks they can't live without something, they often find a way to make that come true."

CHAPTER 70

Diantha watched from behind a large rock as the first two Rifna Erd approached. It had been four days since their last encounter. In the meantime, she and Enoch had been busy.

From what they could tell, this trail was the only way through the rocky terrain in the area. That meant that anyone traveling close by would be forced to take the trail, especially if they had a wagon with them.

In the dim light of the moon and stars, she could see Enoch on the other side of the trail, his head peeking over the top of a hill. He'd been able to craft a few more pikes from some of the sporadic trees here and there. Diantha would have preferred to make a bow and some arrows, but the only tools they had were rocks, her sword and the jagged swords she had taken from the dead Rifna Erd they had first encountered.

Diantha's eyes flitted back and forth between the Rifna Erd in the lead and the trail before them. It wouldn't be long now.

Her sword was still in its scabbard on her back and she gripped one of the pikes Enoch had made in her hand. She could hear the Rifna Erd talking. Some of them laughed now and again. That was a good sign. It meant they weren't on alert. Like before, the group consisted of six men and a horse pulling a wagon.

The two Rifna Erd in the lead kept walking forward until the ground fell out beneath them. They let out surprised cries which came to an abrupt end.

Another Rifna Erd rushed forward to investigate. That was her cue. She stood from behind the rock and threw her pike. Enoch did the same. The man didn't have time to react before he was skewered by both pikes.

Enoch then kicked a boulder beside him which caused a mini avalanche to crash into the wagon. A large rock hit one of the wheels and smashed it, causing the cart to tip and crushing one of the bald men.

The remaining Rifna Erd were distracted by the rock slide enough that Diantha was able to descend to the trail, arming herself with her sword in the process. She was to the first man before he could react and a quick thrust to his neck took him out of the fight.

The last Rifna Erd spun and was in the process of setting himself to attack her when he lurched forward. One of Enoch's pikes impaled him in the lower back. The blow didn't kill him instantly, but Diantha remedied that quickly.

Enoch made his way down to the trail from the hilltop while Diantha made sure the Rifna Erd were all dead. She walked to the front of the wagon and looked down at the men they had hit with pikes.

"Good thing we've been practicing with the pikes for the last few days," Enoch said. "I'm not sure we would have been able to hit them if we hadn't."

Diantha nodded. "Digging the pit and putting the jagged swords facing up was also a good idea." She looked over the edge of the pit. They had covered the hole with charred wood from the wagon they burned before and then covered it with dirt to hide it. The two men who had fallen didn't survive the wounds from landing on the swords.

"Let's see what they were smuggling in this time, eh?" Diantha said.

The wagon was loaded once again with dozens of crates. As before, they all seemed to be filled with the same leafy plant. One, however, did have some rations and bladders of water.

"Looks like we won't have to rely on you foraging food for a while," she said to Enoch.

"Are we burning the rest again?" Enoch asked.

Diantha nodded. "And now that we have a second horse, we can be on the move and see where these men are coming from."

⋙✦⋘

"What do you mean we're out of viceditad?" Rainbow asked.

The nursemaid who gave her the news kept her eyes on the floor. "I'm sorry, Your Highness, but the shipments from Erd have stopped. We've sent scouts to find out why."

"Please," Rainbow said, "look again—everywhere. The king is very sick. He's convinced that the only thing that will help is the viceditad."

"I will do as you say. In the meantime, we can provide him with plyese tea to help him rest," the nursemaid suggested.

"Yes, do that. And provide plyese to all those suffering the effects," the queen instructed.

"It will be done." The nursemaid left the room.

Rainbow headed back to where her husband lay sick. She'd never seen him so ill before and it scared her. Upon arriving to her room, she found him tossing and turning on the bed. He looked like he'd lost weight and his face was nearly as white as the sheets around him.

She knelt by the bed. "Elisedd," she said. "You must hang on. We are getting you help."

He looked in her eyes but didn't seem to recognize her. He went to say something, but his voice cracked and he looked away.

Rainbow took him by the hand. It was cold and clammy. She gave it a squeeze. Never had she felt so helpless.

She heard the door open behind her.

"Your Highness," a female voice said, "I've brought the plyese tea."

"Quickly then," Rainbow said.

Together, they were able to get Elisedd to drink it, though it wasn't easy.

"How soon before it will take effect?" Rainbow asked.

The nursemaid shrugged. "We've not seen anything like this before. It's hard to say. Hopefully it will be soon."

⇥‡⇤

Snapdragon spent the next several days looking around the area of Erd Proper for his daughter, but to no avail. He was sure he would have heard something from the castle if she'd arrived, but hadn't. Still, he was close enough to check.

Though he had gone to the castle in Bariwon to look for his daughter, what he found was worse than he could have imagined.

The sounds of people wailing in grief could be heard throughout the town surrounding the castle. People were screaming that the nislles had returned.

Snapdragon didn't pause, but hurried on to the castle where his party was stopped by guardians outside the gates. There were only two of them. Since the attack on the castle over twenty years ago, a minimum of eight were supposed to be stationed there.

"Commander Snapdragon," one of them said. He was a younger man Snapdragon didn't know by name. "You come during sad times, indeed."

"Where are the rest of the guardians?" Snapdragon asked.

"Dead, Commander."

Snapdragon felt panic well up inside him. "And what about the royal family?"

"King Elisedd is dead. Queen Rainbow and her parents are still alive. Your father, Garth, and son, Reed, are alive as well. However, no one can say for sure how long that will be."

"Is it true? Has the nislles returned?"

"It is believed to be so, yes."

"How is it spread?" Snapdragon asked.

One of the guardians shrugged. "We don't know, for sure. Randall and I were on a scouting patrol to the southern wastes and just returned. We've been told that it has something to do with the viceditad. We've not had any, and we've been told by royal proclamation not to. However, it's not been a temptation because there hasn't been any available."

"Viceditad?" Snapdragon asked. "I don't know what that is."

"It's a drink, Commander. Made from a plant that only grows in Erd, or so we've been told."

Snapdragon wondered why he hadn't heard of any such thing, especially since he lived in Erd.

"Please send word to the queen of my arrival," Snapdragon said. "Let's see what we can do to help."

In short order Snapdragon and his men were ushered into the main hall where court was held. The room was deserted.

"Have any of you heard of this viceditad?" Snapdragon asked the guardians that accompanied him while they waited. They all indicated they hadn't.

The door where royalty entered the main hall opened and Sunshine walked in. His sister, the former queen, looked distraught. She rushed over to him and gave him a big hug.

"Oh, Snap. It's terrible. Just so terrible," she said. She started to cry and he continued to hold her.

"Are you all right? I mean, are you sick?" Snapdragon asked.

"No. I'm fine. Has any of your family gotten sick?" she asked through her tears.

"We're all healthy—at least as far as I know."

She stepped back from him. "Not much of a welcome, I'm sorry. Please, sit, all of you."

"If it's the same with you, Councilor Sunshine, you two may sit. We're still on duty," Aaron said.

"Nonsense," Sunshine said.

"With the utmost respect, Councilor, we have direct orders from someone who would be quite upset if we let anything happen to Snapdragon," Aaron responded.

Sunshine looked at Snapdragon, appearing confused.

"Seraphina," was all he said.

"Ah." Sunshine laughed a little as she wiped tears from her eyes. "Yes, I wouldn't want her mad at me either."

"Tell me, what happened?" Snapdragon asked.

Sunshine explained.

"It doesn't make any sense," Snapdragon said after listening to his sister. "We've heard nothing of this viceditad in Procep."

"Sadly, that isn't our only worry," Sunshine said.

"Oh?"

"We're hearing that people in the area are looking to blame someone. Since the viceditad comes from up north, the blame is being placed on the people from Erd. A few of them that have relocated to this area have already been attacked."

Snapdragon rubbed his eyes as he thought. "So, we have hundreds, maybe even thousands, dead or dying. And those that remain are stirring up anger toward the people of Erd."

"And we have so few guardians and militia left. We can't stop the fighting when it breaks out," Sunshine said.

Snapdragon paused and looked at his sister. "Sunshine, this could tear the kingdom apart."

"I know," she whispered.

"What does Oakleaf say about this?"

"I've not heard from our brother in several days," Sunshine said. "Last I heard, he was doing all he could to spread out the remaining militia to deal with the skirmishes."

Snapdragon rubbed his eyes. "Too much—too much."

"Snap?" Sunshine asked.

"I was trying to collect my thoughts," he said. "Tell me, have you heard anything from Diantha?"

"Diantha? No. Why do you ask?"

"She's not been to the castle?"

"We've not seen her. Snap, what's going on?" She took his hand.

"Diantha left to come here—over a month ago. She's disappeared."

"Oh, Snap I'm so sorry. But Reed is here. And he's fine."

At least that bit of news was good. "He's not been giving Dad too much trouble?"

"Quite the opposite. He's really been wonderful. For several years after Mom died, Dad seemed... lost. Even more than normal. Since Reed came here, Dad's been back to his old, odd self."

"That's good. I'd like to see them both before I leave," Snapdragon said. "When will you be leaving?"

Snapdragon looked at his men. He saw the same worry on their faces that he felt about his family. "As soon as possible."

⊹⳾⊱

The sign posted on a tree made both Diantha and Enoch happy, and a bit confused. It stated that Enoch was not the Noble Trod and the bounty on him had been lifted.

"I don't understand what's changed," Enoch said.

Diantha frowned. "Me either. It doesn't make any sense. There are Rifna Erd in the land, and now for some reason, you're no longer a wanted man."

"At least we'll be able to go to the closest village or outpost without fear of being arrested."

"And the sooner we get there, the better," Diantha said. "We need to find out what's going on."

Enoch was relieved when he first spotted the northern wall. While the mountains had been in sight for a while, it wasn't until he saw the wall that he began to calm down.

From what he could see, the wall was intact and there were men in the watchtowers. Yet, it didn't explain why he and Diantha had encountered Rifna Erd in the area. They had followed the tracks from the wagons and it led them to this part of the wall.

"Do you see anything that concerns you?" Diantha asked. She was mounted on a horse next to him.

"No, everything seems to be fine."

"Still, I suggest we be careful."

Enoch nodded in agreement.

They rode closer to the wall, and were soon spotted by the men in the watch towers. Before long, four men on horseback wearing the crimson and silver standard of Erd approached them.

"Hello there!" Enoch called out. He held his hands both up, empty, to show he wasn't armed. Diantha did the same.

"Hello!" the lead rider called back.

Once the four riders got close enough, Enoch noticed that they all had pointed beards, like the men in Erd Proper. The lead rider was tall and thin with sharp angled features and splotches of red on his face.

"Good day to you," Enoch said. "We seemed to have gotten off the main path. Can you tell us where we are?"

The rider in the front leaned forward in his saddle. "Aye. You're about halfway between Procep and Stur. The closest village is a good ways away in either direction. We have a militia station here if you need to rest."

Though the man was nice, there seemed to be something a bit off about him. Maybe that was it—he was being too nice. Shouldn't he be more on guard?

"We'd like that," Diantha said.

Her hair was still dark and so he hoped that if any of these men had met her before, they wouldn't recognize her.

"My name is Hollis. I'm the leader of this section of the militia." He smiled. "Follow me then."

Enoch noticed the militia men at the wall sneaking peeks at him and Diantha, but they would turn away as soon as Enoch looked at them.

Once reaching the militia station, they dismounted and were let inside. It was a decent size room built next to the stone wall. A large table sat in the middle with stone benches along either side.

They were brought some bread, hard cheese and a mug of something to drink.

"What are you doing so far off the main roads?" Hollis asked them.

Diantha spoke up before he could say anything. "My fiancé and I were traveling from Tevoil to visit some family that moved to Procep. I'd never been out of Tevoil before, so I wanted to see more of the land than just the main roads. I convinced him. It probably wasn't the best of ideas."

Fiancé? Enoch thought. Why would she say that?

"And who is your family in Procep?"

"My aunt, Jada. She married Bearach. Surely you've heard of him."

The soldier nodded. "Who hasn't heard of the man who designed the northern defenses?"

"How far is it to Procep from here?" Enoch asked. He was glad Diantha was handling the other questions.

"About half a day's ride." Hollis stood. "If you'll excuse me, I have some things I need to check on. Enjoy the meal." He smiled and then left them alone in the room.

"Fiancé?" Enoch asked when he was sure they were alone.

Diantha shrugged. "Why else would a woman and a man be traveling together? We certainly wouldn't pass as brother and sister. Also, this will keep them from making advances towards me."

Enoch looked at her. She was beautiful. He noticed that right away when he first saw her at the tavern in Erd Proper. He guessed that with her appearance she would get a lot of unwanted attention. He, himself, knew all too well about getting attention he didn't want, though his was due to his size.

"I guess that was a good plan," Enoch said. He took a bite of the bread and then washed it down with the liquid in the mug. It had an odd flavor to it—but not unpleasant. He noticed Diantha had just swallowed some as well.

"Strange drink," she said. "Have you had it before?"

"Can't say that I have."

They continued to eat and talk about what they would do when they got to Procep. The first thing they decided to do was find Commander Snapdragon, though Diantha admitted she wasn't looking forward to seeing him.

Hollis returned a little later. "Are you done eating?" he asked.

"Yes," Diantha said. "Thank you for your hospitality."

"It was my pleasure. If you'll follow me, I've made arrangements for you."

"Ah, that wasn't necessary," Enoch said.

"Believe me, it was. I insist."

Hollis left the room and stepped into the daylight. Enoch and Diantha followed him. Once they exited, they noticed they were surrounded by militia. Many had bows and arrows aimed at them, while the rest had their weapons drawn.

"What—?" Diantha started to say.

"Shut up!" Hollis said. He motioned to one of his men. "Go into the room and check."

Another soldier nodded and did as he was told. A moment later he returned. "It's all gone."

"Gone?" Enoch said. "We didn't take anything."

Hollis laughed. "It wasn't anything you took. It was what you drank." He turned to some other of his men. "Bind them and put them in the holding cell until the madness passes."

"Wait!" Diantha said. "What did you give us to drink?"

"You'll love it," Hollis said, though his tone sent a different message. "It's called viceditad."

Snapdragon knew if he rode his mare too hard, she would die before they could get back to Procep. It took a great amount of patience to let the horses rest. The four guardians with Snapdragon all had families in Procep and he was sure they were anxious to return home.

The mid-afternoon sky was clear on their first day of traveling. At least it hadn't been raining—that would have slowed them down more.

"Commander?" Aaron asked.

Snapdragon looked up from watching his horse drink from a small stream. "Yes?"

"That's too much smoke to be coming from a cooking fire," Aaron said. He pointed to the north and a bit to the east.

Sure enough, a plume of smoke climbed toward the heavens. It was thick and black. Was it a result of one of the skirmishes his sister had mentioned? Investigating would take time—and time was a precious commodity at the moment. Still, he had a responsibility to the people of Bariwon.

"Mount up men," Snapdragon said. "And arm yourselves."

In short order they were on their way. As they got closer to the smoke, Snapdragon could hear screams and cries for help.

The smoke was coming from a wood and stone building—what looked to be the primary dwelling of a farmer. The whole structure was on fire. Around the burning home, chaos reigned. Pigs, cows and chickens were running free. Instead of the farmer and his family trying to put out the fire, they were battling men who were bald, shirtless and had long beards.

They were Rifna Erd.

Snapdragon counted four attackers. Neither the farmers nor the Rifna Erd saw Snapdragon and his men approaching. To his left, Guardian Aaron let an arrow fly. It took down one of the Rifna Erd and got the attention of the rest of them.

"Keep at least one of them alive!" Snapdragon shouted as he headed into the fray.

The Rifna Erd ignored the farmer and his family and faced their new threat. Instead of running away, the bald men raced toward the oncoming horses. Snapdragon thought that odd since they were outnumbered—until he saw five more Rifna Erd come from behind the burning house.

Aaron took out one of the new attackers with another arrow—and after that, Snapdragon entered the battle. As with skirmishes he'd been in before, time seemed to move slower. A particularly large Rifna Erd charged Snapdragon from his right side—the side where he was the most vulnerable due to his disabled arm. The proper response to such an attack would be to turn his horse to face the man on foot. But that would leave Snapdragon's back open to the rest of the battle. Instead, he turned the mare away from the man rushing him—a move that clearly confused the Rifna Erd.

Snapdragon then jabbed the bottom of his sword against the horse's flanks, causing her to kick out her back legs in response. The Rifna Erd couldn't stop in time and was hit hard in the chest by the horse's hoofs—a blow Snapdragon knew was most likely fatal.

The rest of the guardians were still on their horses and dispatching the Rifna Erd without much difficulty. Despite the advantage they had from being mounted, the guardians wore armor and were better trained than the Rifna Erd.

One of the bald men realized he was fighting a losing battle and turned to run. Snapdragon chased after him, thinking of the best way to stop the man without killing him. Information was the most important thing now—information of how the Rifna Erd were getting into Bariwon.

Instead of attacking the man with his sword, Snapdragon pulled up next to the running man and with perfect timing, kicked out his left leg, catching the man in the head. The Rifna Erd crumpled to the ground.

⇥⧺⇤

Enoch pulled on the chains that bound him to the wall. They were secured solidly, but had enough give that he could sit down. Diantha was likewise chained up on the other side of the cell.

His head began to feel light and he had a hard time focusing since he'd been shackled. There was a small, barred window that let in just enough light that he guessed half a day had passed since they were imprisoned. The cell door also had a barred opening where guards could look through.

Neither of them had spoken. Enoch didn't speak because he somehow blamed himself for their capture. He didn't know why she had remained quiet.

He gave a little tug on the chains. He may be able to pull them out of the wall, but it would take time and cause a lot of noise. Even if he got free, then what?

"What do you think they meant by 'madness'?" Diantha asked, finally breaking the silence.

"I don't know about you," Enoch said, "but I'm rather mad about being tied up."

"No. No. That's not madness. That's anger. As in getting upset. Madness is acting odd, strange, crazy."

Enoch looked at her. Why was she babbling? "Diantha? Are you feeling all right?"

"I'm chained to the wall like an animal. If I were an animal, what would I be? A bird—yes, so I could fly. So I could have freedom. Fly! Fly!" She started to flap her arms like wings, causing the chains to rattle. "Not you. No, not you Enoch," she continued. "You'd be an ox. Strong. Powerful. Though you'd need horns. Do you think Bearach can make horns? Maybe he can make me wings."

"Diantha, what's the matter? Why are you talking this way?" Enoch asked.

Laughter from the cell door interrupted any response she could give. "It's the madness," Hollis said. "It's gotten to her first. It takes longer in bigger people. You'll be feeling it soon. It passes in a couple of days."

"Why?" Enoch demanded. "Why do this to us?"

"To gain your loyalty, of course," Hollis said. "The viceditad is very effective that way. You'll see."

"I won't be loyal to you."

Hollis shrugged. "Then you'll die." He turned and left.

Diantha continued to flap her arms as if she was flying.

"Can you hear me?" Enoch said to her.

She stopped moving. "Yes. I have ears. I believe I have two of them. It was wonderful for God to give me a spare."

"Diantha, try to fight it."

She tilted her head to one side. "I'm tired of fighting." She put up her hands like she was about to go into hand-to-hand combat. "I've been fighting for everything since I was little. Fighting to improve my combat skills. Fighting to prove I am more than a pretty face. Fighting to get the respect of my father. Fighting my feelings for you."

"Feelings for me?" Enoch said.

"Big, tall, strong Enoch. Gentle Enoch. Noble Enoch. Creates strange, yet good feelings in my chest. Enoch, the feeling creator." She placed her hands on her heart and blinked at him.

It had to be the viceditad talking. It wasn't possible for someone like her to have romantic feelings for him.

"Diantha, I don't know if you'll remember any of this after the madness passes," Enoch said. "But—"

"Feelings remain," Diantha interrupted. Tears formed in the corners of her eyes. "They remain."

⤐⳨⤏

Snapdragon looked at the three Rifna Erd in front of him. They were on their knees with their hands tied behind their back. They were all that remained alive from the men who had attacked the farm.

"Has any of them spoken yet?" Snapdragon asked Aaron.

"Not yet, Commander."

Of the three, two of them had several wounds—though none was life threatening. The third man, the one who had run, had a nasty goose egg where Snapdragon had kicked him. After the battle was over, Snapdragon and his men did all they could to help the farmer, but his house was beyond saving. One of the guardians had been sent to escort them to a farm close by for safe keeping.

Snapdragon walked up to the three men, sword drawn. He spoke slowly and clearly. "I need to know how the Rifna Erd are entering Bariwon."

Recognition of his words showed on their faces.

"Good," Snapdragon said. "You understand me. Then also understand this. What you've done here is an act of war and is punishable by death. The first man to tell me what I want to know will die quickly and with honor. The other two, well, I'll let you use your imaginations."

The three men looked at each other. The two that had not fled looked defiant. The other man did not. He said, "I can't tell you what I don't know!"

It wasn't what he said that surprised Snapdragon. It was *how* he said it. He didn't speak with the thick accent of a Rifna Erd. Instead, he spoke like someone from Bariwon.

CHAPTER 71

"Over two hundred more died last night."

Rainbow sat on her throne, trying to ignore the empty seat beside her. "Over two hundred more..."

The guardian who gave the report nodded. "Yes. But the number is down from last night, and the night before."

Courts were being held every day to deal with the nislles outbreak. It was draining Rainbow emotionally, especially since she was still mourning the loss of her husband.

"But those numbers are just from the town around the castle, right?" she said. "Have we got a report from the rest of the districts?"

The guardian hesitated.

"Well?"

"Your Highness, the official report is still being formulated. However, I can share what I know."

"Do so."

The guardian gulped. "From what we can tell, the areas south and closest to Erd are the hardest hit—Lewyol especially. We've sent several requests for information from Governor Selene, but we've yet to get a response."

"How many people have lost their lives?" Rainbow asked.

"It's in the thousands, Your Highness. But it's worse than just that."

Rainbow wasn't sure how much more bad news she could take. But it was her responsibility. "What do you mean?"

"We've lost two-thirds of the royal guardians. We've also lost roughly the same percentage of the militia."

"But, we've not lost that many of the general populous, at least not yet," Rainbow said. "Why the discrepancy?"

"I cannot say, Your Highness," the guardian responded.

"If I may," said a voice from the Hierarchy of Magistrates' table.

Rainbow turned to see it was Bertram, the head of the magistrates.

"Please," Rainbow said.

"While studying this issue, I have been able to make several conclusions."

Rainbow looked at her mother and father—councilors who sat on the dais of the main hall with her. They both nodded in indication Bertram should be allowed to continue.

"Enlighten us, Bertram."

The aged magistrate stood, though it appeared to take some effort. "We've suspected for a while that there is a direct correlation between the nislles and viceditad. I wouldn't consider it to be a poison because it doesn't kill the person when it is ingested. They only become sick when they go without it. It's not unlike those who drink ale to excess and then are forced to stop drinking it—though on a much larger scale. Drunkards who are put in the dungeon or in holding cells for long periods of time become ill unless they have more ale to drink. However, they do not die if they are kept from getting any."

"But the same isn't true for the viceditad, is it?" Rainbow asked.

"No, and we are unsure why. But there is something we are certain about."

"Which is?"

"It is too big of a coincidence that the guardians and militia were supplied with the viceditad first. When you consider that it comes from Erd, and we can't get a response from Governor Selene, it seems to lead to one conclusion," Bertram said.

"Which is?" Rainbow asked.

Bertram leaned forward and rested heavily on the table before him. "The kingdom of Bariwon is under attack from the district of Erd."

⋈

Snapdragon took a step back and examined the three men before him. They certainly looked like Rifna Erd. The baldness, the long beard with a red stripe running its length, even their leggings matched his memories of the Rifna Erd.

Still, the man that spoke did so without the almost unintelligible accent of the people north of the mountains.

"You claim you don't know how the Rifna Erd are entering Bariwon, but you look like them. Explain yourself," Snapdragon said to the man who had spoken.

"Don't tell him!" one of his companions said. "They'll kill us!"

"They? They who?" Snapdragon asked. From the way he'd said it, the captured man wasn't referring to Snapdragon and the guardians with him.

"And if we don't tell these guardians, we're dead too," the first man said. He then looked at Snapdragon. "If I tell you what I know, will you spare my life?"

Snapdragon considered the request. "I will make you this bargain. If what you tell me is of worth, and it turns out to be true, I will ask for leniency when your case is brought before the Queen. In the meantime, you will be imprisoned."

"It's a trick! Don't do it!" one of the other men dressed like a Rifna Erd said.

"Shut up! You talked me into doing this in the first place. I'm thinking for myself now." He addressed Snapdragon. "It's a deal."

"No! Don't—"

"Aaron, gag the other men," Snapdragon said, cutting off the protest. "And if they struggle, kill them."

The other men didn't resist as the older guardian did as he was commanded.

"Now, tell me what you know," Snapdragon said.

"For quite a while now, all the men have been growing out their beards. At first it was a fad, but word spread that people who did so would be given free ale to drink. I didn't question it. Free ale is free ale, eh?"

Snapdragon went down to one knee so he could look the man better in the eye. "Keep talking."

"Well, the ale was like nothing we'd had before. It made everyone all goofy for a day or so, but after that, it made me feel like a new man—like I could do anything. Not long after, the rumors started."

"Rumors?"

"Yeah, that Rifna Erd had taken over the palace. I don't know what happened to Governor Selene or Magistrate Crescens, but no one saw them after that. Magistrate Larissa was they only one we saw."

"And no one thought to report this?" Snapdragon asked.

"No! And you know why? Because we were told that if anyone didn't do as they were told, they would be cut off from the free ale—but by now, we knew the name of it. It was called viceditad. It's funny they called it an ale—it changed how we acted, but didn't smell or taste like any other ale I've had."

"But none of this explains why you are dressed like a Rifna Erd, or how they got here, or why you attacked this farm," Snapdragon pointed out.

"I wasn't done! Let me explain!"

"Go on."

"Just in the last couple of days, word came from the palace that every man needed to shave their heads and dye their beard with a red stripe—or again, no more ale. Everyone I know did so. Many did so willingly. They wanted the Rifna Erd to be in power. So, when we found out that there would be payment for men willing to attack outlying settlements, my friends jumped at it and convinced me into helping."

It made sense to Snapdragon. If the Rifna Erd were trying to take over Bariwon, they could weaken the kingdom by causing unrest among the citizens.

"You still haven't answered my main question," Snapdragon said. "*How* did the Rifna Erd get here?"

"I've no idea! You must believe me! I told you everything I know. I promise!"

Snapdragon stood. If the men in Erd Proper had thrown their lot in with the Rifna Erd, and with the death of so many militia and guardians from the nislles, he simply didn't have the resources to fight a war. The most important thing he had to do is find out how the Rifna Erd were getting in and where this viceditad was coming from.

He looked at the other two men. "Is there anything you want to add to what your companion told us?"

Both men shook their heads furiously.

Snapdragon sighed. "Then based on the regulations found in The Tome of Laws for acts of war, I sentence you two to death."

→⚕←

Diantha's head hurt. So did her stomach. Actually, her whole body hurt. The last couple of days had been a bit of a blur. She had been in and out of consciousness. She'd also had some very strange dreams. There was one where she was a bird. There was another in which she had confessed her feelings to Enoch.

The dreams had stopped and only pain remained.

"Enoch?" she said. It hurt to speak.

He looked up at her from the other side of the cell where he was still chained to the wall. "Yes?"

"You don't look good."

"Is that concern or do you think I'm ugly?"

"Enoch?" That response didn't sound like him. "How do you feel?"

"Like I fell from a very tall hill and hit every rock on the way down."

"I underst—"

Diantha was interrupted when the cell door opened. Hollis walked in. He was holding two mugs.

"I imagine you're feeling quite terrible right now," he said. He looked amused by their pain. "But I can help you."

"How?" Diantha asked.

"Simple. Drink these and you'll not only feel better, you'll feel as good as you ever have."

"Forgive us if we have a hard time believing the person who poisoned us," Enoch said.

Hollis took a few steps closer to Enoch and bent his knees so he could look into the bigger man's eyes. "I want you to remember how you feel right now. I've been through it. It's awful. I'd do anything not to feel that way again."

Enoch paused. "What do you want?"

"Drink this." Hollis lifted one of the mugs.

"You misunderstood," Enoch said. "Why do you want us to feel better?"

"I told you before," Hollis answered. "I want your loyalty. As long as you do what I say, you'll be supplied with viceditad. Without it, you'll feel horrible and eventually die. I've heard it's a terrible way to go."

Diantha watched the two men. She would drink it, but only until she was strong enough to find a way to escape and get cured. Certainly the nursemaids in Procep could help.

"No. I won't do it," Enoch said. "I won't betray what I know to be right."

Hollis seemed to consider him a moment. "Fine. I could have used someone as big as you for what is to come, but instead, I'll use you as an example." He stood and faced Diantha. "What about you?"

Diantha could see Enoch staring at her. He seemed to be pleading with his eyes for her to refuse.

"I'll drink it," she said.

✦✦✦

Snapdragon returned back to Procep as quickly as he could after the attack on the farm. He didn't like killing. But the two men executed were done so out of justice—it wasn't murder. And Snapdragon knew one thing for sure: they were at war.

He and his men pushed hard to get back to Procep, though they were slowed down by having to take along a prisoner. The guardians with him didn't complain about the long days of traveling.

Snapdragon and his men would stop time and again at militia checkpoints. The news had not been good. Some of the posts were deserted. Some had men, but they were sick and were begging for either more viceditad to make them better, or plyese to help them rest as they died.

It seemed that the viceditad had been plentiful before, but for some unknown reason, the shipments from Erd had stopped. None of the militia on the main road could recall seeing any shipments, so they weren't sure how they were coming from somewhere in Erd.

On top of all the bad news surrounding the return of the nislles was more bad news, or actually lack of any news, about his daughter. She seemed to have disappeared from Erd Proper without a trace and she never arrived at the castle. He had to face the fact that she was probably dead—something he didn't want to admit, nor tell his wife. Only a few days ago he learned that Diantha might have taken on the persona of the Noble Trod for whatever reason. Now, that was one of the least of his worries. Even if she had done so, he didn't care as long as she was safe.

Procep came into sight just after mid-day. Snapdragon stopped his horse and addressed his men. "We don't know what we'll find here. At the last checkpoint, they'd heard nothing of the nislles nor the Rifna Erd. Don't say anything to the town's people until we can sort things out. I don't want to scare the people. Additionally, we have to consider that there might be someone in town feeding information to our enemies."

"What about him?" Aaron asked. He pointed to their captive.

"You're right. That won't do. If we arrive with a Rifna Erd—or at least a man that looks like one—it will cause a stir." Snapdragon thought a moment. "Cut off his beard, and give him a tunic."

Their prisoner started to protest when Snapdragon shut him up. "So far, you've been allowed to live because you are cooperating. If you stop being helpful, our deal is over."

"I get it," was the response.

"Aaron, make sure when we get back that he's secured in a cell where he can't talk to anyone. After that, check on your family."

As soon as the prisoner was shaved and clothed, they approached Procep. The guardians at the gate acted as if everything was fine—and Snapdragon knew these men well enough not to doubt them.

Trying hard not to seem overly anxious, Snapdragon dismounted and let the men take care of his horse. He then went directly to his home. On the way, people waved to him. No one seemed sick—in fact they all looked healthy. For once, he had some good news—well, not good as much as not bad.

He opened the door to his house without knocking. His wife was sitting at their table and sewing what looked to be a dress.

"Snap!" Seraphina said when he entered. She rushed over and embraced him. "You smell awful."

"It's good to see you too. Are you all right? How's Winter?"

Seraphina looked concerned. "We're all fine. What's the matter?"

"Nothing—and everything." His wife and youngest daughter were safe. It didn't appear the nislles had reached Procep.

"Sit down before you fall down," his wife told him. "Now, what's all this about? Did you find Diantha?" She crossed the room and got a cup and a bowl.

Snapdragon shook his head as he sat down next to their dinner table. "No. She was in Erd Proper but no one seems to know where she went from there."

"She's not at the castle?" Seraphina put some food in the bowl from a pot that was hanging over the fire. She also filled the cup from another pot.

"No, she's not. I went there to be sure. I should tell you that Reed is fine. I saw him while I was there."

"I'm sure Diantha is fine as well. She can take care of herself. She probably just doesn't want to be found—that sounds like her. I'm sure she'll let us know where she is when she's ready." She crossed the room and put the food and drink in front of him. Snapdragon was a bit surprised how well his wife was taking the news about their daughter. Then again, Seraphina didn't know what he knew.

"So, what's troubling you? It's been quiet up here," she said.

The smell of the stew was powerful and Snapdragon couldn't help but eye it. After over twenty years of marriage, his wife had gotten pretty good at reading his mind. "Eat first, then tell me," she instructed.

She was right. He still had much to do that day and he needed energy to do it. He took several bites of the stew and then quickly finished it.

He'd been so focused on his problems, he had put out of his mind any thought of food or sleep. He emptied the cup with several deep gulps.

"Thank you for the meal, sweetheart. I didn't—" There was a weird taste in his mouth. It was something he'd not experienced before. "Did you do something different to the soup?" he asked.

"No, I made it the same way I always do. Why?"

"It tastes different."

"Ah, no. That flavor is from the drink. It's something new. It's called viceditad."

❧❦❧

Diantha couldn't believe how alert she felt. It was a remarkable contrast to how horrible her body ached earlier that day. She tried to put out of her mind Enoch's look of disappointment when she agreed to drink more of the viceditad. It wasn't only to make her feel better, at least that is what she kept telling herself. No, she needed her strength to escape—and to save Enoch.

"I'm surprised your fiancé wouldn't drink the viceditad," Hollis said. The local leader had freed her from the cell and was eating a meal across from her. "You can save him, you know."

She froze in the middle of putting another spoonful of beans in her mouth. Did Hollis suspect her plan? "How so?" she asked.

"Get him to drink the viceditad. Though I've not seen it myself, I've heard that those who refuse to drink die a painful death."

Diantha finished putting the beans in her mouth. She chewed them slowly while she considered her response. After swallowing, she said, "He's very stubborn—no, that's not the right word. Dedicated. That fits better. He's dedicated to what he believes in. I'm not sure he'd change his mind because I asked him to."

Hollis looked surprised. "He doesn't love you enough to do that for you?"

That was a tricky question. She could easily be trapped if she wasn't careful. "His dedication is one reason I fell in love with him," she said. She tried to sound convincing and it was easier than she thought. "Maybe he'll come around. I can only hope. Is there nothing I can do to help him?"

"Yes, there is. Get him to drink the viceditad."

"I don't think he will."

Her captor eyed her and then shrugged. "I'd rather have him alive, but he's of use to me either way. His death will be a powerful example."

"I've not heard of this viceditad before," Diantha said. "If I knew more about it, maybe I could convince him. Where does it come from?"

"You'll see once you earn my trust. For now, I'll—"

A member of the militia burst into the dining area. "Captain Hollis!" He looked pale and out of breath.

Hollis stood. "What is it?"

"We've just gotten word. Our last two shipments never arrived. Our leaders in Erd Proper are furious. And there is something more," the man said.

"More?" Hollis looked anxious as soon as he heard about the missing shipments.

"They say the nislles has returned."

"Wha—? How?"

Diantha tried not to stare, but Hollis was no longer paying attention to her.

"I don't know the details," the messenger said. "I was only told that thousands have died from it. They say even the king is dead."

"Are we in danger?" Hollis asked.

The messenger shook his head. "I was told that viceditad wards off the nislles. That's why they are so angry over the missing shipments."

Diantha made the connection. The missing shipments—they had to be what she and Enoch had destroyed. And without the viceditad, people were dying from the nislles. Her actions directly led to the death of thousands.

"Send word back to Erd Proper that the next shipment will be leaving tomorrow. I personally promise it will arrive safely," Hollis said.

"Yes, sir." The messenger left.

Hollis sat across from Diantha. He looked distraught. "Who would have thought all of this would happen in our lifetimes?"

It was a rhetorical question. Diantha focused on her meal. She recognized she was in shock. The king was dead? What about the rest of her family? Her brother Reed was living at the castle. Was he safe? She realized that regardless of whatever issues she had with her parents, she wanted to be nowhere else but with them right now. But not unless Enoch was with her. It was decided. She would have to escape tonight.

CHAPTER 72

"Viceditad?" Snapdragon said. He stood quickly enough that his chair went flying from behind him and clattered to the floor.

Seraphina looked at him, startled. "Yes. Everyone's been drinking it around here. It makes you act funny for a couple of—"

Before she could finish, Snapdragon ran outside. He heard his wife follow him. "Snap?" she said.

He turned the corner and went to a grassy area behind their house. He shoved two fingers down his throat. His body responded immediately as he began to vomit up his meal.

"Snap! What are you doing?"

He continued to empty his stomach until there was nothing left. He took several steps away and then sat down on the ground, hard. Seraphina knelt down beside him.

"What's going on?" she asked.

Snapdragon looked at her. "How long have you been drinking it?"

"We started just after you left, why?"

"And Winter? Has she had some too?"

"Yes, in fact I think everyone in Procep has. As I was going to tell you, it makes you act weird for a little while, but after that, you feel amazing. What's the matter?"

Snapdragon let out a ragged breath. "The nislles has returned."

"What?" Seraphina looked him over. "How—Why—Do you have it?"

"I hope not."

"What do you mean by that?" she asked.

He looked at her. "Though no one is exactly sure why, the nislles seems to be linked to drinking viceditad."

"But—but, I feel fine!" Seraphina said. "Actually, I feel as good as I ever have."

"From what I understand, you don't get sick from drinking it. You get sick from stopping."

Seraphina looked confused. "That doesn't make any sense. In all my years as a nursemaid, I've never heard of such a thing."

"Whether it makes sense or not, it's true. Many people have died already."

"Who, Snap? People we know?"

He nodded. "King Elisedd for one."

"Oh no." Any color she had in her face before drained. "Who else?"

"Hundreds, thousands of people. A good number of them are militia and guardians."

"But, if it kills you if you stop drinking it, why would people stop?"

Snapdragon looked around. He didn't see anyone watching them. He leaned in closer to his wife and asked, "Where did you get it from?"

"It's readily available in several shops in town," she said.

"And what happens if they suddenly run out?"

He could see his wife realizing what he was getting at. "We'll need to find out where the shops are getting it from," she said. "We need to make sure we have plenty on hand. I'll begin to experiment with it to see if I can find a cure."

"People are going to find out about this sooner or later. I need to gather the people together to tell them. Keep this quiet for now, all right?"

"Should I tell Winter?" she asked.

Snapdragon thought about it a moment. "No, not yet."

※

The sun was beginning to set when the residents of Procep gathered in the open area below the tallest tower. Snapdragon looked down on them. Seraphina and Bearach were by his side on the tower. The crowd was restless—Snapdragon didn't call meetings very often.

Physically, Snapdragon hadn't felt any different while the people assembled. According to his wife, if the viceditad had gotten into his system, he would have been showing the effects of it by now.

"My good people of Procep," Snapdragon said. "I've just returned from the castle with grim news."

He went on to explain what he had told his wife. He encouraged the people not to panic and that he needed to meet with all the merchants to determine where the viceditad was coming from. In addition, the supplies in the town would be gathered together and rationed to those who had been drinking it. He told them that Seraphina would be working on a way to counter the effects.

"In addition, it's known that this viceditad comes from somewhere in Erd," Snapdragon said. "Unfortunately, because there was a shortage in other parts of the kingdom, and people died, there are many who blame anyone who lives in this district."

The people of Procep's reactions varied from shock, to anger and many were openly crying.

"And there's more," he said. He went on to explain about the attack on the farm and what their prisoner had told them. "Therefore, travel to other districts is to be limited for emergencies only. We need to be extra vigilant. Somehow the Rifna Erd have breached our boarders. If anyone has any information that can help, please come see me right away."

Snapdragon felt helpless. For years he had prepared for an attack from the Rifna Erd. That time was now. Yet, he had never expected that the biggest threat he'd face would be the nislles.

※

Diantha lay on her back and stared at the stone ceiling above her. Her thoughts were racing in dozens of different directions. When she left Procep to start her own life, she never could have predicted it would have gone this way. In a short period of time, she had become a vigilante of sorts, nearly gotten Enoch killed for her actions, and escaped only to discover Rifna Erd in the land. Her attempts to thwart the Rifna Erd caused thousands, to die. But how were the Rifna Erd getting into Bariwon? There was a big piece of the puzzle she was missing.

She thought about her options and kept coming back to the same one. She needed to get back to Procep and warn her father. Why hadn't she warned Hollis about the Rifna Erd? She would have, but he turned on her too quickly. It was all such a mess.

It would be easy enough to sneak away, but she couldn't leave Enoch here. It was her fault he was in this situation. She'd been able to check on him before she retired for the night. He still refused to drink the viceditad. He looked as sick as anyone she'd seen.

For the next several moments she formulated a plan. With a little good luck, it would work. Her luck recently had been mostly bad, so she felt she was due for a change.

She was in a room with a dozen or so other militia. They had all vied for her attention in one way or another, but Hollis told them to keep their hands off. Diantha heard several of them mumble the reason for that was because Hollis wanted her for himself.

As quietly as she could, she stood and went to the front door. She was almost out when one of the men grabbed her leg.

"Where you goin' there pretty thing?" he said. His voice was slurred and she could smell he had been drinking, even as far away as she was from him.

"I think I had too much to drink tonight," she said sweetly. "I better go do something about that."

"There's chamber pots in here," he said.

"Ah, do you really expect me to go in front of all these men here?" she said.

"Nah, guess not," he said. "Hurry on back. I don't care what Hollis said, you're too pretty to be alone."

She leaned down. "When I come back, I promise it'll be something you remember."

He ogled her, and then let go.

The door made very little noise as she stepped out into the night. Hollis had told her there was a guard in the tower above the militia station, and one walking back and forth in the compound. She knew he meant it as a warning, but she used it as tactical information.

She saw the guard in the tower notice her and she gave a big wave. He called down to her to go back to her room. She put a hand to her ear to indicate she couldn't hear him.

He tried twice more, obviously trying to be loud enough for her to hear, but not so loud it would wake others.

Diantha shrugged dramatically and pointed to the stairs that led up to the top of the tower. He motioned for her to come up.

She ascended the stairs, noting the man patrolling the compound was watching her. Upon reaching the top, she said in a sugary sweet voice, "I'm so sorry. I couldn't hear you. Were you telling me you wanted company?" She sauntered over to him.

Even using only the light from the stars and moon, she could tell he was unsure of what to say.

"I'm sure it gets lonely up here all night by yourself," she said.

"It does," he said, his voice quivering.

"What do you even look for?" she asked.

He licked his lips and looked at her from head to toe. "Anything dangerous."

"And am I dangerous?" She ran her fingers through her hair.

"No, I mean, not unless that's what you like."

She took a step closer. "How do you protect yourself up here?"

"Well, I have my sword," he said, indicating the weapon on his hip. "And I have a bow and arrow as well."

"Oh! I've always wanted to hold a bow." She blinked at him flirtatiously. "Could you show me how it works?"

He seemed to mull it over for a moment and then nodded his head. He picked up the bow and gave it to her. "Let me show you how to hold it." He moved up behind her and reached around.

"First, you nock the arrow by putting the slotted part against the string." He showed her how.

"Then hold your hand like this and look down the arrow to aim it."

She could feel his hot breath on the back of her neck and tried not to cringe.

"What would you shoot at?" she asked.

"Someone attacking, I guess."

Diantha moved the bow so it was facing the wandering patrolman below. "If I were to stop him, where would I aim?"

"If he was moving, you'd need to lead him a little. You also need to account for wind, but there isn't any tonight."

"Where would be the best place to hit him?" she asked.

The tower guard laughed. "Where his armor isn't—like his head. But at this distance, you'd be lucky to hit him at all."

Diantha pulled back on the bowstring, aimed and fired before the guard could react. The arrow found its mark, hitting the patrolman in the face.

"Wha—" he started to say, but Diantha jabbed her elbow back hard into his throat. He let go of her and brought both his hands to his neck. She wasn't sure how badly she'd hurt him, but there was too much at risk for him to sound the alarm.

He looked at her, still trying to breathe. Diantha grabbed his sword's handle and removed it from its scabbard.

"Thanks for the lesson," she said, and then plunged the man's sword into his chest.

She waited for the light to dim from his eyes and then pulled the sword out. As quickly and quietly as she could, she went down the stairs. A quick check of the man she had shot verified he was dead. She dragged him out of the open area and against a stack of crates.

These looked like the same crates the Rifna Erd were smuggling in. She pried one open and saw it was full of the leafy plants. It had to be the viceditad.

She chided herself from being distracted and headed to the cell where Enoch was being held. A guard was inside, asleep. He didn't wake when she entered the cell and slicing her newly acquired blade across his throat, he'd never wake again.

The keys to the cell were on his belt and Diantha removed them then opened the cell where Enoch was locked up.

He was unconscious. There was no way she would be able to lift him. She tried to shake him awake. It didn't work. His body was covered in sweat and he was shaking noticeably. She saw a bladder of liquid by the now deceased guard. She retrieved it and after smelling it, decided it was water and not ale or viceditad. She poured it on his head. Enoch stirred, but still didn't open his eyes.

"Enoch! Wake up!" she slapped him across the face and then again. If he didn't come to his senses, she would have to leave him here. She slapped him a third time and was about to do it again when he reached up and stopped her.

Enoch opened his eyes and said, "Is this how you are supposed to treat your fiancé?"

She laughed and gave him a big hug. His skin felt cold. "We're leaving."

"All right. Though I was starting to think of this place as home."

She let go of him and leaned back. "Can you stand?"

"Maybe," he said, "but not for long. I doubt I can walk to Procep from here."

"I have a way. I'll be right back."

Diantha went back outside. There was a stable not far from the cells. Normally all of the horses would be bareback this time of night, but each militia station was supposed to have three horses ready to go at any time.

She chose the biggest of the horses for Enoch and chose one that looked to be fast for her. On the way back to the cell, she stopped by the crates of viceditad and stuffed the horses' saddlebags full of the plant. If it was tied to the nislles, she needed to get some to her mom so she could figure out a cure.

Enoch was leaning against the doorframe when she got back. He looked like he was using all his energy to keep upright.

"I don't think I can stay seated on a horse for long," he said.

"Before you get all noble and tell me to leave you, you can forget that right now," she said.

"Leave me? No way. I'm with you. I'll just lie over the top of the horse—like how they carry dead people," he said. His voice turned sad. "It may be true, soon enough."

His statement almost brought Diantha to tears. "You can't leave me," she said. "I'm with *you*."

He smiled. "Fair enough."

It took two tries, but they got Enoch on the horse, after a fashion. His legs dangled over one side and his arms and head over the other, but he was secure.

Diantha mounted her horse and grabbed the reins of Enoch's horse. After looking around the militia outpost, she was convinced that they weren't being watched. Their tracks would be easy enough to follow in the morning, so she had to make it back to Procep tonight. With that thought in mind, she kicked her horse into motion.

⚜

Rainbow was about to retire for the night. She was exhausted. Aside from the death of her husband and so many others, her pregnancy was draining her of what strength she had left.

"Your Highness," one of the servants called as she was about to enter her chambers. "Your Highness, a moment."

"Can it wait until the morning?" she asked through a yawn.

"Forgive me, Your Highness," he said, bowing as he approached. "We've just received this message and I was instructed to bring it to you right away." He held a sealed parchment in his hand.

"Who is it from?"

"The messenger was from Lebu. He said it's from Governor Mortimer himself and is most urgent."

Rainbow furrowed her brow. It seemed that every governor—aside from Governor Selene—was petitioning for help, and it was always urgent. But she knew Mortimer and he was not one to say a matter was urgent unless that was truly the case.

"Fine. Give it to me."

"Again, begging your pardon, Your Highness, I was told you needed to read it in front of your family."

If the message was from any other governor, she would have disregarded the request. "Fine, please find them and have them come to my chambers. I won't open it until they arrive."

"Yes, Your Highness." He gave her the note.

Rainbow entered her room. Normally a nursemaid would be there to help her prepare to sleep, but with the death to many in the castle, Rainbow insisted that getting changed into her nightclothes was something she could do on her own. For a moment she was tempted to open the note, but she resisted. It wasn't like the note would change between now and when her family arrived.

A few moments later, there was a soft knock on her door—done with a certain cadence that indicated it was her mother.

"Enter," Rainbow called.

Her mother and father came in, followed by Garth and her cousin, Reed.

"What is it sweetheart?" Sunshine asked. She looked worried. "Are you sick?"

"I'm fine. Just tired." Rainbow held up the note. "I was told I needed to open this with my family present."

"Who sent it?" her father, Rayne, asked.

"Mortimer, the governor of Lebu." She looked around the room. Her family appeared as tired as she felt. "Let's see what this is about so we can get some rest, shall we?"

No one spoke as she broke the seal and opened the note. In flowing script it read:

Your Highness,

I regret to inform you that Commander Oakleaf, his wife Arlie and their son Rowan have all died from the nislles. I, too, am very ill and doubt I will be alive when you read this. I'm sincerely sorry.

To peace in our kingdom,

Mortimer

⊰╬⊱

Enoch had never been so miserable in his life. His whole body ached. The trip to Procep had been rough. Though Diantha was aware of his condition, she had told him they needed to hurry.

His body kept fading in and out of consciousness because the jarring of the horse wouldn't let him sleep for long. Maybe that was a good thing. If he fell asleep, he wasn't sure he'd wake up.

"There it is," he heard Diantha say.

Enoch lifted his head the best he could. He saw Diantha look behind them. "There isn't any sign of pursuit. We made it."

The sky was just starting to lighten with the impending dawn. Diantha had stayed away from the wall—saying she didn't know who she could trust, so they approached Procep from the south.

When they were close enough, Enoch saw two guardians stationed at the town entrance.

"Stop right there!" one of them shouted. They both had bows and arrows drawn and aimed at Diantha.

She pulled her horses to a stop. "I'm Diantha! Commander Snapdragon's daughter."

One of the men laughed. "Oh really? Lady, if you are going to pretend to be Diantha, the least you could do is get her hair color right. Everyone knows she is a redhead."

"I changed the color," she said defiantly. "And why would I pretend to be her?"

"These are dark times and people do strange things," one of the guardians said.

"Fine, go get my father and he can verify I am who I say I am."

"And bring the commander within striking distance of you and your companion? I think not."

Enoch heard Diantha blow out a long breath in frustration. "Have it your way. Arrest us and lock us up. When we're in a prison cell, you can have my father verify who I am. I'm sure he'll be delighted to see his daughter in chains."

The guardians spoke back and forth a moment in hushed tones. Enoch couldn't hear what they said, but to him, they sounded unsure.

"I have a better idea," one of them called out.

From his point of view, Enoch couldn't see what the man did. However, his ears gave him the answer when he heard the warning bell ring.

Shortly, more people gathered at the entrance to the town. Enoch heard more bow strings be drawn. Diantha didn't move. Enoch could see she kept her hands empty and visible.

"What's going on?" a loud, deep voice said.

"Oh, thank the Zealous Star!" Diantha cried out. "Bearach! It's me! Diantha!"

"Diantha? Is that really you? If so, what did you do to your hair and what are you doing out there with a dead man on a horse?" the deep voice asked. Enoch guessed it was Bearach speaking.

"I'll explain everything as soon as we get inside—and he's not dead, just very sick. Will you please tell these men I am who I am?" Diantha asked.

There wasn't an answer for a moment. "We need to be careful," Bearach said. "Tell me, when you were your mother's apprentice, what did she teach you was the treatment for someone who is sick and needs to rest?"

"You know full well the answer is plyese, and you also know I was never my mother's apprentice. I worked with you in the blacksmith shop," Diantha said.

"Let her in, men," Bearach said.

"But, sir," one of them said, "she could have gotten that information from anyone."

"Aye, that she could have," Bearach said. "But it's *how* she responded, and not what she said that convinced me."

Enoch and Diantha were led into the town. One of the first things Diantha did was to instruct them to take Enoch to her mother, telling them he was sick and needed her help. The next thing she said was that she had to see her dad. Enoch knew she wasn't looking forward to it.

CHAPTER 73

Snapdragon entered the room and saw his daughter pacing. It was her, regardless of the dark hair. She heard him enter and then faced him. The last time they had spoken, it wasn't pleasant. He wanted to rush over to her and give her a hug, but at the same time, he didn't want to startle her. His concern of how she would react was short lived as she was the one to run to him for an embrace.

"Daddy," she said through sobs, "I'm sorry. I didn't realize... I didn't understand..."

He just held her close and let her cry.

"We all have to make our way in the world," he said after a moment. "I'm just glad you're safe."

He stepped back at looked at her. "I'm sure that you have a lot to tell me, but first, have you had any viceditad?"

"I did. I had to."

Snapdragon was afraid of this. He felt his legs go weak and he went to the nearest chair and sat.

"What's the matter?" Diantha asked. She pulled up a chair and sat across from him.

"Everything," Snapdragon said. She was old enough now that he couldn't shelter her. "But first, tell me what happened to you. I won't judge you. Don't leave anything out."

She nodded and then started to talk. He told himself he'd listen and not interrupt. Snapdragon's suspicions of her involvement with the Noble Trod situation were confirmed.

"Diantha, this is very important. Did you kill anyone when you were acting as the Noble Trod?" he asked.

She stared at him. He couldn't read her expression.

"I've killed a number of people since I've left here," she said firmly. "I had to." She explained about the man who was killed when she was first headed to Erd Proper.

"But that was self-defense," Snapdragon said. "I mean, did you kill anyone when you were in town."

"No," she said. "I injured many, but not fatally. I didn't kill anyone else until Enoch and I ran into the Rifna Erd on—"

"The Rifna Erd?" He interrupted, not able to help himself. "You've seen them? Where? Are you sure they were Rifna Erd?" he asked.

"As sure as I can be, based on what you told me about them. The way they were dressed, their bald heads and long beards, even the way they spoke."

"They spoke with a thick accent? Are you sure it wasn't someone from Erd dressed like a Rifna Erd?"

"I'm sure." She sounded upset. She explained how she and Enoch had run into them. "I was pretty close to them when I killed them."

"What were they doing taking such a remote path?" Snapdragon asked.

At that moment, Diantha's countenance changed. It was an expression he'd never seen on her before. Remorse. She looked down and didn't speak.

"Sweetheart," Snapdragon said, "you did the right thing in killing them."

"It's not that," she said.

"I don't understand."

Diantha looked up. "Dad, they were smuggling in the plant used to make viceditad. I didn't know what it was. I destroyed two shipments. It's because of me that so many people in the kingdom are dying from the nislles."

She began to cry. Snapdragon moved next to her and put his good arm around her. "It's not your fault, Diantha. You didn't know. You *couldn't* know. It's the Rifna Erd's fault. They are the ones that brought the viceditad to Bariwon. I wish I knew why."

"I know why," she said.

"How?"

Diantha explained about how she and Enoch had been captured and how the viceditad was used to control people—that if they didn't drink it, they would die.

"Enoch refuses to drink any more of it. And according to Hollis, without it he'll die," Diantha said. "But Mom will know of a cure, won't she?"

"I hope she can find one." He squeezed his daughter close.

"Don't worry about me, Daddy," she said. "I took several viceditad leaves when we escaped. I have enough for me until Mom can find a cure."

"Diantha," he said slowly, "everyone else in the town has had the viceditad. The merchants we spoke with don't know how to get more."

"But—but—Mom's smart! She'll figure something out!"

"She'll have to, but it'll take time."

Diantha stood. "Enoch doesn't have time."

⁍⧈⁌

The bed was soft, but Enoch couldn't get comfortable. After arriving in Procep, he was taken to the building where the sick were treated. A woman who resembled Diantha took charge and got him moved to the bed.

"My name is Seraphina," she said. "I'm Diantha's mother."

"It's a pleasure to meet you," he said through labored breaths. "I'm Enoch."

"Enoch? The same Enoch that Kerr raised?"

He nodded.

"How long has it been since you've been sick?" she asked.

"Just over... two... days." It was getting harder to talk.

"Do you know what caused it?"

"Something to... do with... drinking viceditad."

Seraphina looked alarmed. "Now Enoch, you must listen to me," she said. The determined way she spoke reminded him of Diantha. "You are very sick. I believe it is the nislles. Right now, the only way we know how to keep you from getting worse is to drink more viceditad."

He shook his head.

"Enoch," she said. This time her voice took on a pleading tone. "You'll die without it."

"I won't... be a slave to it," he said. "I'd... rather die."

Seraphina kept trying to convince him, but Enoch refused.

Not long after, Diantha and Commander Snapdragon entered the building. Diantha rushed to his side and fell to her knees.

"Mom, can you help him?"

"The only thing I can do is to have him drink more viceditad. He refuses. I'm trying to find another solution, but I haven't had time," Seraphina said.

Diantha put her hands on either side of Enoch's head. "Now you listen to me you stubborn man. Drink the viceditad until my mom can find a cure."

Enoch's head hurt so much it was hard for him to think clearly. He wasn't sure why he felt so strongly against drinking the viceditad to stay alive. Maybe it was because he wasn't given a choice. He was forced to do something he wouldn't normally do. He'd never liked bullies. He stood up to them even when it meant he may suffer from it—just like when he had stood up to Larissa.

He remembered a night when he was younger. He and Kerr had looked up at the Zealous Star. It didn't waver. It stayed true while the stars around it moved, regardless of the season. He'd used that as the guiding principle in his life. Changing now, even if it was the only way to keep him alive, meant he would betray something fundamental to who he was as a person.

"No, Diantha," he said, "no."

"You can't give up! Back at the outpost, you said you were with me." She was crying. "Then *be with me*. Don't give up!"

He blinked at her through his own tears. "Diantha. I... can't. I can't... give up on... being true... to me. I'm sorry."

She looked like she wanted to say more, but couldn't. Her father knelt next to her and put his left arm around her shoulder.

"At least let me help you be more comfortable," Seraphina said. "I'll bring you some plyese tea. It will help you rest."

"It's too... late. Save it... for others."

She said something in return, but he couldn't understand it. His vision grew dim and he at last gave in to the nothingness which he'd been fighting.

⊰✦⊱

Rainbow woke to the sound of arguing outside her door. She recognized one of the voices—it was her father. The other voice was masculine, and was familiar, but she couldn't place it.

She rolled to one side and looked out her window. The sun was up, but it hadn't been for long. It had been a long night. After the news of her brother and his family's deaths, she had cried herself to sleep. It was nights like these that she missed Elisedd the most. He'd always been a great comfort to her.

With effort, she got out of bed and dressed in a thick robe. The sound of arguing continued from the other side of her door. She walked over to it and opened it.

Her father, Rayne, was standing there with the governor of Regne. He was the same man that several weeks ago had complained to her about how the kingdom was wasting time and resources on the northern defenses.

"Now you've done it!" Rayne said. "You've woken her up."

"Good," the governor said. "Why should she rest while the rest of the kingdom suffers?"

Rainbow wasn't sure how the governor had even made it to her chambers. She knew the castle was woefully defended. Perhaps he bullied his way in. That fit his personality.

"What do you want, Governor?" Rainbow asked. She didn't try to hide her annoyance.

He faced her, stood up tall, and held out a parchment. "I have a list here of official complaints from the district of Regne concerning the distribution and hording of the plant known as viceditad. How do you answer to these?"

Rainbow looked at her father. "Councilor Rayne, would you agree that the kingdom is under attack?"

"Yes, Your Highness."

"But—" the governor started to say. Rainbow cut him off.

"And doesn't The Tome of Laws state that during such times, approaching a member of the royalty while they are unescorted is considered a potential act of war?"

Rayne nodded. "That it does, Your Highness."

The governor from Regne didn't look impressed. "So, you are using the law to threatening me now?"

"Governor, I don't need the law to threaten you. The kingdom is at war. Not from soldiers. Not from bowmen. Not even from cavalry. We are at war with whomever is supplying the people with viceditad. We're not hoarding it. If we were, do you think my husband would be dead? Or my brother and his family? We have our best healers working on a way to save the sick, yet people keep dying."

Rainbow turned to her father. "Escort the governor out of the castle. Tell the guardians at the gate that if he tries to enter without my permission, they should throw him in the dungeon."

"With pleasure, Your Highness," her father responded.

⫸⧣⧤

Diantha sat on the edge of the man-made lake that overlooked Procep. She couldn't watch Enoch die. She saw him lose consciousness and his breathing became ragged and shallow. Her mom told her it was only a matter of time. She left and came here—a place she had always found relaxing.

She watched a figure approach. Diantha realized it was her father. He waved when he noticed she was looking at him.

"May I sit by you?" he asked when he was close enough.

She shrugged.

He sat by her. Together they looked down on the town. It had grown so much since she was born. It was hard to believe that at one point in time it had consisted of only a few houses that were little more than shacks.

Snapdragon pointed down to the bowl shaped area that had been built around the collapsed tunnel. "I thought for sure the biggest threat to Bariwon would come from right there. I couldn't have imagined that it would have been the nislles."

Diantha's response was to hug her knees against her chest.

"I'm sorry about Enoch," he said. He sounded sincere. He waited a moment longer before saying, "I know you are hurting right now, but I need to know about the outpost where you and Enoch were captured."

Diantha nodded and wiped the tears from her eyes. She told him what happened; including her discovering crates of what she believed was viceditad.

"And did you see any Rifna Erd at the outpost?" he asked.

She shook her head.

"I don't understand how they are getting here," Snapdragon said. "They must have found a way over the mountains. But even then, the wall should have stopped them." He rubbed his good hand over his eyes. It was something she saw her father do throughout her life when he was troubled.

Diantha pushed her grief aside. "Well, let's go find out."

She went to stand, but he stopped her. "Sweetheart, you've had the viceditad. You'll get sick if you don't have some more soon. What we do have is being rationed—and we don't have much."

"I grabbed a bunch from the outpost before I left, remember? It will be enough for me and whatever other men you can spare to go back to the outpost."

He looked at her, startled. "You are expecting me to let you go?"

"Dad, we're not having this fight again. I can make my own choices. I'm going back—alone if I have to."

He seemed to consider her words. "No," he finally said.

"But—"

He interrupted her. "I mean, no, you're not going alone."

❖

Snapdragon rode alongside his daughter. He brought twenty men with him. These men from the militia had all been subjected to viceditad so he made sure they had drunk more before they left. He didn't like that they had to drink it to stay alive, but he couldn't afford to let his men get sick—especially with possible danger ahead.

They had ridden hard to get to the outpost. Snapdragon had them slow down before they got into sight. He wanted the horses somewhat rested before they made their final approach.

None of the villagers along the way knew anything about the outpost. It was too far away from any of the settlements established by the wall.

"My daughter recalls seeing just over a dozen men at the outpost," Snapdragon had told his force. "They will be on guard because she had to kill a couple of them to escape."

Snapdragon had two of his best archers ride on the outside edges of the group as they approached. They were the only ones not wearing heavy chain mail armor. It allowed them greater range of motion needed for accuracy.

He had been by this outpost many times on his trips to other parts of the wall, and there had never been anything special about it.

The first thing the group noticed when they were getting close was the amount of smoke coming from their destination.

They approached cautiously, but there was no movement in the camp. And then Snapdragon recognized something that turned his stomach. He'd seen something like it one time before—when he'd been north of the mountains.

"Dad, what is that?" Diantha asked.

"Don't look," he said.

"Too late."

There was a body, or the remains of one, propped up in the air with pikes.

Snapdragon motioned for two of his men to go in to the outpost while the rest of his forces pulled out their bows and arrows to cover them.

After several tense moments, the scouts motioned the "all clear" sign.

Once the group was closer, Snapdragon could see dead bodies strewn everywhere. In a flat area by the outpost, a large circle had been drawn. Inside of it looked to be large amounts of blood. From his previous dealings with the Rifna Erd, Snapdragon knew what they had done.

"The crates are gone," Diantha said.

"Crates?"

"The crates with the viceditad. Dad, what happened here?"

He looked at his daughter. She didn't appear to be afraid. If anything, she looked angry.

"This was either a Rifna Erd attack or someone staged it to look like one."

"But who else would know what a Rifna Erd attack looks like?"

She made a good point. He'd kept the most grisly details out of his reports. The only ones who saw what he had seen were Bearach, Seraphina and Waylon who were with him at the time. Snapdragon knew it wouldn't have been Bearach or his wife. Waylon was trapped north of the mountains, and even if he did find a way to get back, these actions weren't in his character.

"No one else would know," he said to answer his daughter.

Snapdragon and his men looked around for more evidence. A large number of tracks, including those of a wagon or two, led south—toward Erd Proper.

"Where should we bury the dead?" one of the guardians asked.

Snapdragon instructed them. He noticed Diantha was looking at the man put on display. He rode next to her and asked, "Do you recognize him?"

She nodded. "Yes. His name was Hollis. He's the one who captured Enoch and I. While I was here, he'd been told of the shipments I burned—though he didn't know I was the one who destroyed them. It appears this is how the Rifna Erd treat failure."

"Sweetheart, do you have any idea how the Rifna Erd are getting in? Think—did Hollis say anything?"

"I'm sorry, Dad. Nothing. And the wall here seems intact. I don't see any signs of people climbing the mountains, either."

Snapdragon looked up, and then up some more. She was right. There was nothing he could see that would explain how the Rifna Erd were getting in. He wouldn't be getting any answers from the men at the outpost since they were all dead.

"We shouldn't be wasting time burying these men," Diantha said. "They deserved what they got. And if we are going to catch up with the Rifna Erd, we will need to be on our way soon."

Snapdragon looked at his men. He'd taken the twenty best fighters he had stationed in Procep. Having them here left his hometown with weakened defenses. "We won't be following them."

"Why not? They know how they're getting in. They may even know how to cure the nislles. I could *make* them tell us."

"We don't have enough viceditad to keep you and the rest of the men from getting sick for long," he said.

"We can't do nothing!" she said. "They have to pay for what they did to…" Her voice cracked and she turned away.

He knew his daughter well enough to know that she was ignoring the pain she felt with Enoch's loss. He also knew it would catch up to her sooner or later.

"We will do something," Snapdragon said. "Perhaps your mother has figured out how to cure the nislles. We need to get back to Procep and make a plan."

Diantha looked like she wanted to argue some more, but instead, she nodded.

It was dark by the time the dead were buried. No one in the company wanted to stay at the scene of such unspeakable carnage. Snapdragon agreed. He had them travel to the nearest village on the way back to Procep. There was a small inn, not nearly enough room for twenty soldiers, but the rest of the villagers made room in their homes.

They left early in the morning to go back home. Snapdragon explained to the men what he had told his daughter. They didn't question him.

But Snapdragon was questioning himself. What could he do? He didn't have enough men to fight a war—and unless his wife could figure something out, more people like Enoch would die—including his wife and daughters.

He considered all of his options while they traveled back to Procep. There were no signs of the Rifna Erd in the area, which was at least some good news.

When he saw Procep, he had mixed feelings. What if Seraphina had already gotten sick? He tried to put it out of his mind. He had enough to worry about without making up more.

Upon approaching the gates, a member of the militia he'd left behind raced out to greet them.

"Commander Snapdragon!" he called out. "Come quickly!"

He and Diantha forced their horses into a gallop with the rest of the men following closely behind.

"What is it?" Snapdragon called out.

"Your wife needs you right away. That's all I know. She's at your house."

Snapdragon urged his horse to go even faster as they entered the town. People dodged out of the way as he raced to his house. Once he arrived, he jumped off his horse. With Diantha beside him, they went inside.

His wife, Seraphina, was sitting at their dinner table. Two more people sat with her. One was his youngest daughter, Winter. The other was a man he didn't expect. It was Enoch.

CHAPTER 74

"Enoch?" Diantha said. She couldn't believe her eyes. He was supposed to be dead.

The large man stood. "Aye, it's me."

She rushed over and hugged him. When she stepped back, she wasn't sure who was the most surprised, him, her family or herself.

"It's good to see you too." He smiled down at her.

"How—?"

"Sit down, all of you," Seraphina said.

They did so.

"Sweetheart! You found a cure!" Snapdragon deduced.

"Actually, *I* didn't."

"Then how…"

"Not long after you left, his fever broke and he began to rest peacefully," Seraphina said. "It was remarkable."

"I… I don't understand." Diantha looked at Enoch. "Why didn't you die?"

"I guess I had something to live for." Enoch looked bashful.

Diantha felt that odd, but good, sensation again in her chest.

"I have an idea what happened," Seraphina said.

Everyone at the table looked at her.

"Winter, tell me, do you remember that time when you were younger when your favorite dress got muddy?"

The fifteen-year-old gave her mom a quizzical expression. "Yeah, I do. Why bring that up now?"

"It will make sense in a moment," her mom said. "Tell us what happened."

"Well, you and dad were out and I was by myself. I had just gotten the dress. You had told me not to wear it—that it was only for special occasions. Of course, I didn't listen and I put it on. I wanted to show my friends how pretty it was and I went outside. I slipped in the mud and got it dirty."

"And then what did you do?"

"I needed to get it clean. I went inside and took it off. I'd seen you wash clothes before. Though you used only a little bit of soap in the bucket, I wanted to make sure it was really clean. I put in all the soap I could find. I then put in some of that powder dad uses to clean up after he's been working. In the end, I actually ruined the dress."

"I'm not following," Snapdragon said. "What does this have to do with Enoch, or the cure?"

"You'll see." Seraphina kept her attention on Winter. "And what is the proper treatment if someone has a fever and needs to rest?"

Winter seemed to think about it a moment. "You give them plyese—usually in a tea."

"That's right."

"But Enoch didn't have any plyese," Diantha said.

"Exactly."

Her father leaned in. "Are you saying you believe that the nislles is caused by mixing plyese with the viceditad?"

"It's the only thing I can think of that makes sense," Seraphina said. "In all my years as a nursemaid, I've never seen anything that will kill a person if they stop taking it. However, I have seen that when people mix certain plants or herbs together, the result can cause problems. Not unlike when Winter mixed the two types of soap."

"So… if what you are saying is true, the people of Procep—and Bariwon for that matter—who drank viceditad will be fine as long as they don't drink plyese," Diantha summarized.

"Not exactly." Seraphina frowned. "People will get very sick—like Enoch did. But they won't die."

"I don't remember too much of it," Enoch said, "but what I do remember is that it was the most miserable I've ever felt in my life."

"Maybe we could lower the amount people take in overtime and wean them off of it," Diantha said.

"We could," Snapdragon said, "if we had enough. Even rationing, we only have enough viceditad for a few days. The merchants had been getting shipments in from the west—most likely from the outpost where you were taken hostage and had seen the crates."

"Well, go back and get some more," Seraphina said.

"That's not possible," Snapdragon said. He explained what they had discovered.

Seraphina let out a long breath. "It looks like everyone in the town will be getting sick pretty soon then, but at least they'll live."

"That causes a whole different problem," Snapdragon said.

"What's that?" Diantha asked.

"I believe the Rifna Erd are in Bariwon. If they come to Procep while everyone is sick, the only people not affected by viceditad will be me, the four men that went with me to the castle, and Enoch."

"There's something else," Seraphina said.

"There always is," Snapdragon responded.

His wife gave him an exasperated look. "We need to spread the word to the rest of the kingdom about how to prevent the nislles. People are dying."

Diantha watched her father consider his options. "I can send Aaron," he said. "He didn't drink the viceditad and he knows the land between here and the castle as good as anyone. One less person to help us defend Procep won't make a difference."

"Fine, send him as soon as you can," Seraphina said.

"What about the Rifna Erd?" Diantha asked.

"What about them?" Snapdragon said.

"Is the plan to wait until they attack?" she asked her father.

"Diantha, we simply don't have the men to go on the offensive. Even after everyone gets better in a few days, we won't have the resources to defend Procep and send men out to fight a foe we don't know the location of, or how many there are of them," he answered. "According to the man we captured, the man from Erd Proper who was dressed like a Rifna Erd, the whole town has joined the Rifna Erd."

She stared at her father. He was right. They simply didn't know what was going on. Information was the key to survival. "Then we need to find out," Diantha said.

"I don't disagree," Snapdragon said. "Perhaps once Aaron returns, and the people here have recovered, we can send out a scouting party."

"But it could be too late by then," Diantha said.

"We don't have any other options."

"Yes, we do."

Everyone at the table looked at Diantha expectantly.

"I could scout. Give me enough viceditad so I don't get sick."

"No," Snapdragon and Enoch said at the same time. Both men looked at each other, and Enoch motioned for Snapdragon to speak.

"The Rifna Erd are deadly," Snapdragon said.

Diantha looked her father straight in the eye. "So am I."

"I won't let my daughter—"

"Stop being so protective of me! I'm not helpless. I can do this. Enoch and I traveled the path I believe the Rifna Erd are using."

Her father, the commander, didn't speak. "You make a good point—too good of a point, actually," he said after a moment.

"Good. Then I'll make my preparations," she said.

"Wait. You didn't let me finish," her father said. "Your point was that you and Enoch traveled the path. I know you well enough that if you were to encounter the Rifna Erd, you'd try to kill them all yourself. That's why Enoch is going with you."

"He is?" Diantha asked.

"I am?" Enoch echoed.

"Yes, you are," Snapdragon said. "You're not under the influence of the viceditad. Additionally, with you along, Diantha will think twice before doing something reckless."

"I'm not so sure about that," Enoch said.

"Hey!" Diantha said. "And you, Enoch, you were just on your deathbed. You shouldn't be going anywhere."

"I feel fine—better than good, even."

"Then it's settled," Snapdragon said. "We'll send Aaron to the castle while Diantha and Enoch scout out the Rifna Erd situation."

Though they had just returned from traveling, Aaron didn't question his orders. In fact, he looked relieved at the news he would be sharing. With Bearach's help, Enoch was given some new ring mail armor with a stout shield and a solidly build mace.

Diantha elected to wear a suit of dark leather armor. She wanted to be able to move quickly and silently, and the leather armor let her do that—though it didn't provide her with as much protection.

They loaded up their horses and left just before dusk, using the darkness of night to help them travel undetected. Diantha was given three bladders full of viceditad. It would be enough to keep her well for several days.

⇥✦⇤

Snapdragon watched his daughter ride off. He prayed he would see her again. Yet, from what he had experienced in his life, he knew that sometimes people died in defense of what they believed in so others could live. He thought of his friend Blythe who had been killed when they first arrived beyond the northern mountains. He'd gone many years without having to feel that same kind of loss, but just recently he learned of his brother Oakleaf's death, as well as that of King Elisedd.

He knew it was a distinct possibility that by the time this was over, even more people he knew and loved would die. He just hoped Diantha wasn't one of them.

"It's hard to watch the ones you love put themselves in harm's way, isn't it?" Seraphina said. He hadn't heard her come up beside him.

"Aye, that it is."

"Now you know how I feel whenever you leave to go somewhere," she said.

He faced his wife. "I… I didn't understand until now. You're an amazing woman."

"Yes, I am." She smiled. "Are you ready for the next step? You're going to have a lot of sick people to help over the next few days."

"I am. Let's get to work."

⟶❦⟵

"What are you hoping to find?" Enoch asked once they'd traveled for a bit.

He could just see Diantha's silhouette. Clouds covered the night sky, and they didn't dare light torches.

"We'll find a group of Rifna Erd and capture a few of them alive. From there, we'll make them tell us how they are getting into Bariwon and what their plans are," she said. She didn't sound anxious or scared—if anything, her voice expressed resolve.

"And you think they'll just tell us?" he asked.

"I can be very persuasive."

"No arguments there," he said.

It took a good part of the night to reach the path where they'd run into the Rifna Erd before. The tracks were fresh—Enoch guessed they were no more than a few hours old.

Neither of them spoke as they rode along the path. Diantha would stop now and again to listen—so far, they didn't hear anything to indicate the Rifna Erd were close.

Finally, as morning approached, laughter and the sound of voices with thick accents came into range. Diantha motioned for them to stop and dismount. Leaving the horses behind, they crept forward. Enoch guessed even on foot they would be gaining on the horse-pulled cart.

Diantha held up a hand, indicating he should stop.

"You're making too much noise in your chainmail," she whispered. "Climb up there, quietly, and wait for me to return." She motioned to a knoll not far from them. "If I get in trouble, I'll retreat back here. Understand?"

He didn't want her to go off alone, but she was right—her armor allowed her to move almost quietly. "I got it. Just be careful."

She nodded and then snuck forward, drawing her sword as she went. Carefully, Enoch climbed the knoll. Truthfully, he was still a bit weak. He hadn't lied that recovering from the viceditad was the worst physical pain he'd ever experienced. He didn't want to admit he wasn't at full strength to Diantha, not when she'd freed them from Hollis and his men, and certainly not when she had made up her mind to go after the Rifna Erd.

He positioned himself behind the knoll's summit where he made sure he had good footing. He didn't want to slip and fall like the last time they were on this path.

Enoch strained his ears, listening for anything that would give him insight on how Diantha was doing. And then—shouts of surprise, followed by cries of pain.

Not caring if he made noise or not, Enoch came to his feet and bounded down the small hill. As fast as he could run, which wasn't fast at all, he lumbered toward the sounds of battle. Hefting his mace in one hand, he brought up his shield with the other.

He turned a corner in the path and came into view of Diantha and the Rifna Erd. As before, there were six of them, though one stood on the wagon with a bow and arrow, looking to get a clean shot at Diantha.

She made it difficult because she had positioned herself between the archer and the men she was attacking. Gracefully, she moved from one fighting stance to another, each move either leading to the next, or causing misdirection to confuse her attackers. Her style was so different from how Enoch fought—all power and muscle.

Diantha downed another of the Rifna Erd, which left her only one man left—the man on the wagon. However, because she had defeated the last man attacking her in melee combat, she had nothing between her and the archer. Enoch saw the man smile and take aim. She would be too close to dodge the arrow.

"No!" Enoch cried out.

The archer seemed to notice him for the first time. He shifted his aim and fired at Enoch.

The arrow hit him in the left thigh, just under his shield and below where his shirt of ring mail hung. Enoch's leg gave out from under him and he plowed into the ground. He looked up expecting Diantha to be shot next, but she had used the distraction to rush the Rifna Erd. Their opponent tried to block her attack with his bow, but Diantha was too quick. After a couple of hacks, the archer fell off the wagon, fatally wounded.

"Enoch," Diantha cried out. She rushed to him.

He managed to roll onto his back. The arrow had imbedded in the bone of his leg, of that he was sure. Spots danced in front of his eyes as the pain in his leg increased.

Without hesitating, she grabbed the arrow by the shaft and yanked it out. For a moment, Enoch's vision dimmed and he feared he would pass out from the pain, but he held on to consciousness.

"Stay here," she instructed.

She got up, still holding the arrow, and ran over to one of the Rifna Erd—one that was still alive. "Was the arrow poisoned?" she shouted at the man.

He tilted his head to one side, either not understanding her, or pretending not to.

Diantha held the arrow up to his face and pointed to the tip. "Poisoned?" she said again.

The Rifna Erd gave her a defiant look. Her response was to shove the arrow into his arm.

"Nooo!" he screamed. He reached for a pouch on his belt and removed a gourd. There was a small plug in the hardened fruit.

The Rifna Erd pulled out the plug and went to pour in on his wounded arm.

But Diantha grabbed it, careful not to spill any as she ran back to Enoch. Holding the opening of the gourd over his wound, she then poured the liquid contents where the arrow had struck him. At first, it burned, but soon, his whole leg went numb.

"Thank you," Enoch said.

"I told you to wait back there." She put pressure on his leg.

"But he would have killed you!"

"Maybe," she said, "and maybe not. Now, shush. I need to cover your wound.

Under Enoch's ring mail shirt, he wore a thickly quilted gambeson. Diantha reached under his armor and using her sword, she cut off a section to make a bandage. Shortly, she bound the wound.

"Look." Enoch pointed to the man she'd got the gourd from. He was convulsing and foaming at the mouth. It looked like he tried to crawl to one of the fallen—most likely to get another gourd full of what Enoch assumed was the antidote—but wasn't able to get there in time.

"That would have been you in a few more heartbeats," Diantha said.

"How did you know?"

"My father took an arrow in his shoulder when he was rescuing the people from Eddinh. The arrow went through his back, but enough of the poison got into his system that he fell asleep for several months. It's a miracle he didn't die."

Enoch lifted himself up on his elbows. Though he wasn't quite sitting up, he could see what Diantha had done. As before, there was a cart full of crates pulled by a horse. All of the Rifna Erd seemed to be dead.

"I thought you were going to keep some of them alive," he said.

"It's harder than it sounds. I kept one alive—for a little while at least."

"And you killed him to save me," Enoch said.

She smiled at him. "It was more than an even trade."

"But we don't know how they got in. Wasn't that the point?"

Diantha scanned around the area. "Yes, it was."

"Then what are we going to do now?"

She sat next to him. "Well, we could either retrace their steps to see if we can discover how they are entering Bariwon." She paused.

"Yes?"

Her expression changed. It was one he'd seen before—one where she looked determined and nothing would change her mind. "Or we go to Erd Proper."

"Erd Proper? That's insane. Why would we go there? If what your dad said was true, the whole town has pledged themselves to the Rifna Erd."

"Exactly! Someone in that town would know."

Enoch shook his head. "It's a bad idea. We can't exactly just stroll into the town and start asking questions. And I don't know how much weight I'll be able to put on my leg."

"You won't be going in with me," she said.

"But—"

"Enoch," she said, "I can move around the town without being spotted or caught. I've had some experience with that recently."

CHAPTER 75

Diantha considered what to do with the crates of viceditad—maybe she'd take them back to Procep to help the people wean off the drink easier, but when she thought more about it, that wasn't the best use of her skills. Instead, she made sure she took several of the viceditad leaves from the crates for her, just in case, before she lit them and the cart on fire. Enoch was able to stand enough that he could help move the dead Rifna Erd to the fire. Burning took less effort than burying. It also helped hide how many of them were killed in case their allies came looking.

Enoch had wanted to argue with Diantha's plan of continuing on, but they were on a scouting mission and needed information. And she was right, her experience as the Noble Trod gave her the knowledge she could use to move around Erd Proper undetected. Though they had traveled most of the night, they agree to get closer to Erd Proper before finding a place to rest. Diantha's plan was to enter after it was dark.

With Enoch's injured leg, it took some effort to get him on his horse, but once that was accomplished they were on the move. Over time, the numbness in his leg lessened and each jarring move from his horse caused pain to shoot through his wound. But, they had come this far and the bleeding had stopped so he didn't say anything to Diantha.

As they approached mid-day, Diantha pointed to her left and said, "What do you think about there?"

It was a house, large and imposing, but it seemed overgrown and in disrepair. It was built on the shore of Dylobo Lake. From where they were, they could see Erd Proper on the other side of the large lake.

"Maybe no one is home?" Enoch said.

"That's my thought. Let's go see, shall we?"

Diantha led the way. One of the front gates had fallen off while the other one was so rusted that it threatened to crumble during a harsh wind.

Once inside the gates, Diantha dismounted and readied her sword.

"I'll check it out. Stay on your horse in case we need to make a run for it."

Enoch watched as Diantha pushed open the main door and stepped inside. Many of the windows were intact, and though the slate roof was in bad shape, it appeared to keep the elements out.

While examining the windows on the second story, Enoch thought he saw movement—it couldn't have been Diantha, she wouldn't have had time to get upstairs that quickly. Should he shout out a warning? Had he seen something or had it been his imagination? No, Diantha could take care of herself.

He thought about getting off his horse, but with his leg, he wasn't sure he'd be able to walk to the house, let alone help Diantha. No, the best thing for him to do was to sit and wait.

Several moments later, Diantha came out the front door. She was safe.

"Enoch," she said, "it seems this house isn't deserted after all."

"Oh?"

Diantha took a few more steps out of the house. Following her was an older man. He had thick, grey hair. Though his shoulders were stooped, Enoch imagined that at one time he could have been quite imposing.

"Enoch, I'd like to introduce you to the owner. He's agreed to let us rest here. His name is Daimh."

⇥✦⇤

Snapdragon knew it was going to be hard to watch his wife and daughter, Winter, suffer as they went through withdrawals. He didn't realize just how hard it would be. He remembered that during the escape from the northern mountains, he'd been poisoned which put him into a coma for several months. Seraphina had watched over him. He wondered if she felt as helpless back then as he did now.

The town of Procep had grown to about two thousand people—quite the change from the fifty who resided here when Snapdragon first came to the area. Of those still in the town, only he and three guardians were not suffering the effects of going without the viceditad.

The guardians and Snapdragon rotated between being with their families and keeping watch from the main tower.

It gave Snapdragon time to think. There were a number of things that didn't make sense. When he'd been north of the mountains, he'd seen how numerous the Rifna Erd were. If they had truly found a way to Bariwon, why not just overrun the land? Perhaps they found a way over the mountains—but that seemed impossible. Most days they couldn't see the tops of the mountains because they extended into the clouds. And again, people in the watchtowers would see them coming.

By sea? No. The steep cliffs and long shallows with jagged, coral reefs had prevented any type of sailing to or from Bariwon.

Then in the east were the vast marshes. Anyone that stayed too close to them for too long got a fever—not enough to kill them, but enough to drain their strength. In addition, there were no roads through the marshes where crates could be shipped.

There was something that Snapdragon was missing, but he couldn't figure it out.

-ᴥᴥᴥ-

"Daimh?" Enoch said. "As in *King* Daimh?"

The older man nodded his head slowly. "It's just Daimh now." He sounded sad. "You've nothing to fear from me."

"I—I don't understand," Enoch said.

"I don't have much to offer, but come in and we'll talk," Daimh said.

Enoch looked at Diantha for confirmation, which she gave by motioning for him to dismount.

Enoch slowly got off his horse, careful not to put too much weight on his injured leg. He sort of hopped-jumped for a few steps before Daimh came to him.

"Oh, you've been hurt. Let me help you."

The older man was only half a head shorter than Enoch—he was the tallest man Enoch had met. With Daimh's help, Enoch was brought inside while Diantha took care of the horses.

The interior of the house reflected the outside. It was obvious that at one time it had been quite impressive, but time and neglect had partially erased its majesty. Daimh led Enoch to a dining area toward the back. A marble table was surrounded by padded seats covered in elegant red velvet. Many had tears and rips.

"Please, have a seat. I was just making some stew—I wasn't expecting visitors, but I'll share what I have," Daimh said.

"Thank you." Enoch was about to say "Your Majesty" but it didn't seem proper to do so. While Daimh went off to get the stew, Enoch tried to remember what he knew about Daimh—it wasn't much, just that he'd been king once.

"How is your leg feeling?" Diantha asked when she entered the room.

"It's tender, but I'm sure it'll be fine. Were you able to feed the horses?"

She nodded. "There is a stable on the side of the house, but no horses."

"That's because I don't have any," Daimh said upon returning with three bowls. He set them down and motioned for Diantha to sit. "It's fish stew—one of the few items I can make."

Enoch was hungry, but after his experience with Hollis, he was guarded about eating or drinking anything he was given by a stranger. Daimh seemed to notice his reluctance.

"You need not worry," Daimh said. "It may not taste good, but it's not poisoned."

"Please forgive me," Enoch said, "I'm confused why you are here and—"

"Ah, I'll tell you as I told your pretty friend here," Daimh said. "It's quite simple. I was banished from the castle when it was proven my father, Abrecan, had killed King Kenrik and Councilor Philip. I honestly didn't know. I was allowed to come here with my wife, to live in the house where my own father had locked up my mother. We had no servants given to us, so we made do with what we had. It wasn't easy, especially after being accustomed to having people wait on me every moment."

"And where is your family?" Enoch asked.

"Both my mother and my wife have passed on. I buried them in the backyard. They deserved better, but I'm not allowed to leave the grounds."

"I'm sorry for your loss," Enoch said.

"Not as sorry as I am for being my father's puppet. I honestly thought I was being a good king," Daimh said. "But enough about my sad story. I understand that Bariwon is in danger."

"I told him as much as I could," Diantha said.

"Believe it or not," Daimh said, "I *do* care about the kingdom. If these Rifna Erd are threatening to take over, I want to help."

"What we need now is a safe place to rest," Diantha said.

"You can do that here," Daimh said. "No one comes here. You're the first visitors I've had in years."

"Thank you, Daimh," Enoch said. He wasn't sure why, but he felt like he could trust this man.

"It's my pleasure." Daimh smiled, revealing deep dimples. "But tell me, what are you going to do after you rest? What else can I do to help?"

"I noticed a couple of small boats tied to your dock," Diantha said.

"Aye, I'm allowed to fish—sometimes I row out in the early mornings. But I can't talk to anyone and I have to stay within sight of my house."

"I'd like to borrow one," Diantha said.

"Oh? Why?"

Diantha explained her plan of going into town and getting information.

"Alone?" Daimh clarified at one point.

"Yes, by myself. I am quite capable of—"

"Daimh," Enoch interrupted before Diantha could get worked up, "believe me when I tell you she can take care of herself."

The former king didn't look quite convinced, but didn't say more on it. "Of course, you can have one of my boats."

"Thank you," Diantha said.

They ate the stew which wasn't as bad as Enoch thought it could be. Afterwards, Daimh showed them to a guest room.

"You can sleep in here until dark," he said.

Enoch noticed there was only one bed and said so.

"Aren't you a couple?" Daimh asked.

"Uh, no," Diantha said.

"Really? From the way you were looking at each other… No matter. Diantha, you may stay in here. I'll take Enoch to another room."

Enoch knew he was blushing from Daimh's comment, and tried to shake it off by saying, "Diantha, please wake me before you go."

"I will," she said, "and thank you again, Daimh."

Daimh helped Enoch to a room close by. It was dusty and there were cobwebs in the room's corners, but Enoch was too tired to care.

He lay on the bed, carefully as to not bump his leg. Sleep called for him, but his mind went back to Daimh's comment about how he and Diantha had looked at each other. Over the last several days, there had been times when they'd shared a special moment. Perhaps it was all they been through that had brought them close, but he knew for him it was more than that. Could she feel the same way? She had confessed as much to him, but she'd been under the influence of the viceditad. Still, maybe… He considered that as he drifted off to a deep sleep.

A tapping on his shoulder woke him. "Hmm? What?"

"Diantha told me to wake you up," Daimh said.

Enoch thought he'd just fallen asleep mere moments ago, but one look out the window at the starry night revealed he's slept most of the day.

"Can you help take me to her?" Enoch said through a yawn.

"Certainly."

Diantha was gathering her weapons together when Enoch and Daimh entered her room. She looked up at them.

"Ah, good," she said. "I kept my word. I promised to wake you before I left."

Enoch understood something at that moment. Every time she left him, there was a chance he'd never see her again. Could he let this moment pass without telling her how he felt? But, if he did, would it distract her from what she needed to do?

"Stay here," Diantha said before he could make a decision on what to say. "If I'm not back by mid-day tomorrow, I'll be either dead or captured. And if I'm captured, consider me dead. Do not play the hero, understand?"

"No, I don't understand. Don't do anything foolish enough to get yourself killed. This is a scouting mission—not an attack. If you were going into battle, I'd want to go with you."

"I nearly got you killed thrice before," she said. "Once when they mistook you as the Noble Trod, once when we were captured by Hollis and his men, and once when you took a poisoned arrow in your leg. I won't risk your life again for me. Promise me that you won't try to save me."

"Don't make me promise that," Enoch said. "Please."

She took a step closer to him. He wasn't sure why until she took him by the hand and said softly, "Enoch, I don't know if I could handle it if something happened to you. I can't explain it more than that."

He blinked, and then blinked again. "Diantha, do you think I feel any differently?" he asked. "Do you think I can stand by and watch you rush off to do something that could kill you? You mean too much to me."

She paused at that, and then in the same, quiet voice said, "You mean a great deal to me, too. Very much—more than I thought was possible. But don't you see? We aren't safe. All of Bariwon isn't safe. I need to do what I can, while I can, to make sure *all* of us can have a future."

"I feel so helpless. There has to be something I can do to help."

Diantha looked thoughtful for a moment. "There is something you can do. Rest up and get better. Once I get the information we need, we'll head back to Procep as quickly as possible. And I want you by my side."

"Then come back safely," Enoch said. "Because once you do, I'm not leaving your side again."

⊰✦⊱

Snapdragon had finished his shift on the tower a couple of hours ago. He'd not gotten much sleep since Diantha left. Partially it was worry over her well-being, and partially because he was trying to soothe his family as they went through withdrawals.

It was unusually dark tonight. Snapdragon realized it was because of the new moon. It reminded him of his experiences north of the mountains and the discovery of the Rifna Erd.

He fought to stay awake, but found himself nodding off time and again. Pacing inside his house helped him from falling asleep, but it also made him more tired. It was an interesting paradox.

After a time, he decided to get a drink and sit for a moment. He set the mug of water on the table and was about to sit when he felt the ground tremble. It was barely perceptible, but he was sure he'd felt something.

There had been the occasional earth tremors in Procep over the years—something the original villagers said happened by the mountains.

There was another tremble, this one more noticeable than the last one. And then yet another one—again with more force. But it didn't make sense. These tremors seemed to be spaced out evenly. It wasn't like before.

Something was wrong.

Snapdragon looked at his wife and daughter. They were unconscious and shivering. There was nothing he could do for them at the moment.

Another tremble. Snapdragon stepped outside with the intention of finding out what was going on. The warning beacon in the main tower was lit—the sign that the town was under attack. Snapdragon ran toward it. Once he got closer, the trembling increased in force and was speeding up. The closer he got to the tower which overlooked the collapsed tunnel entrance, the more violent the ground quaked. Taking two stairs at a time, he ascended the steps to the tower's top.

"What's going on?" he asked when he got to the top.

The guardian who had taken over his shift pointed. "The tremors are coming from *inside* the mountain—by the collapsed tunnel entrance," he said.

With a sickening realization, Snapdragon understood what caused the quakes. Where the entrance to the tunnel had been, Snapdragon could see the earth shaking. It was moving in steady rhythm.

"Go get the other two guardians—grab your bows and all the arrows you can carry. Get back here as soon as you can." Snapdragon instructed.

The guardian nodded in acknowledgement and rushed off.

"It looks like the Rifna Erd are finally coming through," Snapdragon said to himself. He didn't believe it was a coincidence that they had waited for just about everyone in Procep to get sick. Nor was it happenstance that it was a new moon—a significant superstition to them. Though Snapdragon hadn't figured out how the Rifna Erd were getting in before, there was no mistaking how they were getting in this time.

⇥‡⇤

Diantha let the small boat glide to a stop against the shore. From here, she could see the outline of the palace against the starry sky. It was imposing. If what her father said was true, the Rifna Erd who had somehow managed to get in had taken over residence it the largest building in Erd Proper.

She'd landed far enough away from the ferry dock to make sure no one would see her coming. As quietly as she could, she slipped out of the boat and into the shallow water. After getting to the shore, she was able to find a deep rooted bush to tie the boat so it wouldn't float away.

Now, she needed to find someone to tell her what was going on. No, she needed more than that. She needed to see for herself. She'd come all this way for information, and she wasn't going to leave until she got something she could use against the Rifna Erd.

It was near the middle of the night when she slipped into town. Maybe she'd get lucky and find one of the men wandering the street alone, perhaps even intoxicated. It would be easier to spot such a target from on top of the buildings.

As when she took on the persona of the Noble Trod, she used the uneven stones of the buildings for foot and handholds. Once on top of the building, she was able to move more toward the center of the town by jumping from rooftop to rooftop.

She hadn't seen anyone yet. Diantha worried for a moment that she might have to enter one of the buildings to find someone—which was even more dangerous because she didn't know what she'd find once she entered.

While she waited at one particular spot, she did a quick inventory of her weapons. A sword was strapped to her back, the way she preferred. On her hip and in one of her boots were daggers. Looped around one of her shoulders were her bow and a quiver of arrows. The last weapon she possessed was one that accompanied her everywhere—her skills as a fighter.

Diantha was about to move when her waiting paid off. Around the corner and stumbling down the road was a bald man with a long, pointed beard. She watched the direction he was headed and quickly moved to a position where she could scale down the walls between buildings to intercept him.

The man kept coming her way, seemingly oblivious to anything around him. When he got closer, he started to stumble toward the other side of the street. Diantha hoped she'd be able to grab him and pull him into the small alley without having to go too far into the street. She thought perhaps she should wait for a better chance, but in the scant moments she had to consider it, she realized this was as good as she could hope for.

He crossed in front of her and she sprang from her hiding place. She was to him and had a hand covering his mouth before he could react. In her other hand was her belt knife, pressed up against his throat.

"Make a sound and I'll kill you," she said into his ear.

He didn't fight her.

Diantha looked back and forth down the road. No one was in sight. She pulled the man toward the alley she'd been hiding in.

After they were deep in the shadows, she whispered to him, "You're going to sit down and face away from the street. My knife will come away from your throat for a moment while I draw my sword. If you think you're faster than me, that would be the time to try it. But if you do try, I will *not* make your death quick. Understand?"

He nodded and then slowly sat down with his back to her.

In a fluid motion, Diantha drew her sword and placed it against the side of his neck. He didn't try to stop her.

"All right. Now, you're going to answer some questions."

"Like what?" he said. His voice was slurred, but it didn't have the thick accent of a Rifna Erd. He was one of the townspeople who had changed his looks.

"Let's start with your name," she said.

"People call me Bott. And I know you. You're the Noble Trod. But I thought you were gone." He didn't sound scared as much as confused.

"I've returned," she said. "Now, tell me what you know about the Rifna Erd, their plans and how they are getting into Bariwon."

Bott started to laugh.

"This isn't funny," she said. She pressed her sword against his neck for emphasis.

"But it is," Bott said. "Nobody knows how they got here. It's one of the things everyone talks about. And for your other question, I sure don't know what their plans are."

"What *do* you know then?" she asked.

"They give us all the viceditad we want as long as we do what they say."

"And what are they telling you to do?"

"Not much, aside from shaving our heads, growing out our beards, and going shirtless."

Certainly Bott knew *something* that could help Diantha. She tried a different approach. "How do they tell you what to do?"

"There are two guards in front of the palace at all times. When they change the guards four times a day, sometimes the guards come out with instructions from the Rifna Erd."

"What kind of instructions?"

Bott hiccupped. "I just told you. They say to keep up our looks and drink the viceditad. Oh, and once in a while I hear that they tell men to go attack farms and villages."

"And have you ever met any of the Rifna Erd?" Diantha asked.

"Not me. And nobody I know. I don't think there are many of them. And they don't leave the palace."

Diantha thought for a moment. She hadn't learned anything from Bott. Well, that wasn't entirely true. She learned where the Rifna Erd were—in the palace. If she was going to get answers, she knew where she had to go next.

716

CHAPTER 76

The rumbling was almost deafening. It was so loud that Snapdragon didn't hear his men come up the tower. He was startled when they came beside him.

These were good men—trained how to fight not only with swords and shields, but also bows and arrows. Snapdragon watched as they methodically set up quivers full of arrows and got into position around the tower.

The three men preparing for battle against the violent trembling of the ground below conjured up an image to Snapdragon of ants lining up to take on a rabid dog. But they didn't question their duty.

Though the beacons lit the collapsed tunnel entrance fairly well, with the new moon tonight, it was hard to see the details below.

"Will the defenses hold?" one of the men asked Snapdragon. He had to raise his voice over the noise coming from below.

"I hope so. It's not exactly something we could test."

The inner wall—the one that was shaped like a bowl that surrounded the entrance—was lower than the tower, giving his men a clear shot at anyone that would come through.

Snapdragon wished he had a bow and arrow to help, but he couldn't use one with his injured right shoulder.

"How long before—" another of the men started to ask.

The Rifna Erd broke through. At first there were just large objects that looked like battering rams, but with sharp points. As soon as the hole was big enough, solid square shaped items were pushed through. They were shields. The Rifna Erd started screaming battle cries.

"Fire!" Snapdragon shouted.

His men let loose with a barrage of arrows, sticking into the shields but not doing any damage. More Rifna Erd came out, each with large shields they used in conjunction with the ones around them to create a protective shell.

The guardians kept firing, but were ineffective.

More men came out of the hole where the tunnel entrance had once been. The ones in the back didn't have shields, they had something else: ladders.

"How could they know to bring ladders and shields?" shouted one of the guardians over the din.

Snapdragon shook his head. "They must have gotten word from their men on this side of the mountains. Keep firing!"

The three archers were fighting valiantly, but were losing ground. From what Snapdragon could see, only one of the Rifna Erd had been hit—but it was just a glancing blow. There were now at least twenty men that had exited the tunnel, and Snapdragon had no doubt there were hundreds, if not thousands, more in the tunnel. It would only be a matter of time before the Rifna Erd got their ladders in place. If they got past the defenses, Procep—and Bariwon for that matter—would be overrun.

->⁂<-

Diantha crouched on top of a building near the palace entrance. There were two guards stationed at the gate—just like Bott had said. From what she could see, there were no archers in the towers. Perhaps the Rifna Erd were over confident—and why not? They had everyone drinking the viceditad and therefore under their control.

Bott hadn't given her much more information to work with—something he kept telling her over and over as she tied him up and eventually gagged him. To be safe, she knocked him unconscious and then put him behind a rain barrel so no one could see him.

She had to get inside the palace. It was dangerous and something both her father and Enoch would try to talk her out of doing. Thinking of Enoch, she remembered his face in her mind. He looked so sad when she left—like he never expected to see her again. But they were losing the war badly—and she had no doubts they were at war—and if it required risks like going into a fortress filled with the enemy, then that is what had to be done.

Shaking away thoughts of Enoch, she focused on her task. Neither one of the guards looked terribly alert. Still, she would have to be quick. She readied her bow and aimed it at one of the guards—the one farthest from her.

This was the moment. There would be no going back from here.

She loosed the arrow. It hit the man in the side of his head, just next to his ear. The other guard turned to his companion and was in the process of drawing his sword when another of Diantha's arrows pierced him in the back of his neck.

The men crumpled to the ground. For several moments, Diantha watched. No alarm sounded and there was no indication of movement from the palace.

She climbed down the building and approached the palace gate. Quick inspection confirmed both men were dead. As quietly as she could, she dragged them out of the entrance and set them against the palace walls behind where the portcullis came down. They were hidden from view well enough. She thought about throwing them in the moat, but that would make a splash and their corpses would eventually float to the surface.

With the entrance clear, she drew her sword and stepped into the palace.

She had learned that the palace in Erd Proper had a similar design to the castle—only on a smaller scale. Using this knowledge, she approached what should be the first guard's quarters. Words above the doorframe confirmed her belief. She cracked open the door and peeked inside.

There were at least two dozen men asleep on beds. Even in the dim light, she could see they were bald and shirtless. She didn't see how she'd be able to isolate one of them without waking the others.

Further down the hallway was the servants' quarters—as noted in writing above its doorframe. Perhaps by living inside the palace the servants had information about the Rifna Erd that Bott didn't have.

Diantha peered inside the room and noted ten people sleeping. It would be easier to grab one of them, but she needed to make sure no one was awake. She went to open the door a bit wider to get a better look. The door made a large groaning noise from its hinges.

A gray haired woman near the front of the room sat up and looked at the door. Diantha instinctively ducked back into the hallway, but didn't close the door.

"Hello?" the woman asked.

Diantha could hear her getting up and coming to the door. It hadn't worked how she planned, but Diantha couldn't let this chance pass. Once the older woman got to the door, Diantha pulled her into the hallway and clasp a hand over her mouth. Her other hand held her sword against the woman's chest.

"Be quiet and I won't hurt you," Diantha said. "Understand?"

The woman nodded her head violently.

Diantha removed her hand from the woman's mouth, but pressed the tip of her sword in a bit more.

"What's your name?" Diantha asked.

"Larissa." She sounded frightened.

Able to get a better look at this woman, Diantha noticed she was heavily bruised on one side of her face. Also, she was missing several teeth.

"Listen carefully, Larissa—" Diantha said.

"It's Lar*i*ssa." The old woman emphasized the middle vowel in her name.

"What?" Diantha stared at her.

"Nothing," Larissa cowered. "What do you want?"

"Is there an empty room we can go to nearby?"

The older woman nodded. "The kitchen is empty."

"Show me. Quietly. If you alert anyone, you'll be the first person I kill."

"I understand."

Larissa slowly moved down the hall, passed several doors. Diantha followed Larissa in and closed the door behind her.

"Now, please, tell me what you want," Larissa said.

Diantha kept her at sword point. "I know the Rifna Erd are here, in this palace. By the looks of it, they haven't been treating you very well."

"They don't have a very high opinion of women," Larissa said.

"I want information of how many there are, what they are planning and how they are getting into Bariwon."

Larissa looked confused. "Why? What can you hope to achieve? You can't win. They control the whole town and the surrounding area. I've heard that soon they will cover the land—but I don't know what they meant by that exactly. Some people stood up to them and died ghastly deaths. They are too powerful."

"Maybe you could show me where their leader sleeps. If I kill him—"

Larissa shook her head. "That's suicide."

"Just because I'm not a man doesn't mean I don't know how to fight," Diantha said. She knew she sounded defensive, but didn't care.

"You could have Commander Snapdragon's skills and still fail," Larissa said. "The leader of the Rifna Erd, Serkan is his name, sleeps in the governor's room. There are four guards that sleep in the room with him."

"So what? I can take on five sleeping men."

"You didn't let me finish. In the antechamber outside his room are thirteen more men. Each of them sleeps with their swords. If you were to sneak by the men in the antechamber, and that is a big 'if', once you attacked Serkan, you'd most likely awaken everyone else. There is no way out from there."

"Are there any windows?" Diantha asked.

"Aye, but they are three levels up. You'd never survive the fall."

Diantha started to pace. "I've come too far to give up now."

"I hate to give you more bad news, but I doubt killing Serkan would be enough. He has all the men under his control. Everyone drinks viceditad, including Serkan. The men in town have all shaved their heads and grown beards. They've become loyal to the Rifna Erd. With news of the nislles returning, and that the viceditad keeps them safe from it, everyone will do what the Rifna Erd say to stay alive."

Larissa walked over to five huge barrels along one side of the kitchen. "These are full of viceditad juice. It's heavily concentrated. We used the last of the viceditad plants we had on hand to make a batch yesterday. Just a few drops of this in any drink, and people become loyal. There is enough here to last for a long time."

Diantha considered the barrels. "What if we destroy them?"

"No! We'd all die from the nislles!" Larissa said.

Diantha realized that Larissa had drunk the viceditad as well. Would Larissa believe her if she was told the truth? Or would fear of dying cause the older woman to betray Diantha? It didn't matter. The barrels of viceditad juice all in one place was too big of a find to pass up.

Then she got another idea—one almost too ghastly to contemplate. But this was war, and in war, desperate actions had to be taken.

"Fine, we won't destroy the barrels."

"Then what are you going to do? Leave? If you do, please take me with you!" Larissa said.

Diantha looked at the desperate woman. "Actually, I need you to take me somewhere else in the palace."

⊰⊱

Snapdragon watched the contained area below him fill up with Rifna Erd. His archers were having more success now, but it was akin to using a thimble to bail out a sinking ship—they couldn't take out the Rifna Erd quickly enough, and they were running out of arrows.

Their ladders were almost in place. Once the Rifna Erd scaled the wall of the bowl shaped area around the entrance, they would be able to use the same ladders to climb the main wall and get into Procep.

Snapdragon was not going to let that happen.

"Keep firing!" Snapdragon shouted as he headed to the other side of the tower.

He went to the half wall that had various stones with different markings—the same half wall Bearach had showed him during the spring thaw. He thought back to what Bearach had taught him. Confident he remembered the sequence, he first pushed on a stone that had wavy, horizontal lines, followed by one with one dot. He then pressed on the stone that showed an arrow pointing down. There was an audible *click*.

He quickly went back to where the archers continued to fire into the horde of Rifna Erd.

The effect was... underwhelming.

"We're almost out of arrows!" one of the men shouted.

"Look!" Snapdragon pointed to the mountain side above the tunnel entrance. A small fountain of water was shooting out from the side of the mountain and down on the Rifna Erd. The attackers also saw this, and began to laugh.

The Rifna Erd ignored the water spraying on them. They put their ladders in place and started to climb. The first of the Rifna Erd had almost made it to the top when he paused and looked back over his shoulder.

The fountain wasn't as small as before. It was getting bigger and spouting out more water and with greater force.

Snapdragon knew it wasn't by chance that Bearach had designed the quarry to become a lake above the tunnel entrance. And neither was it happenstance that in the main watchtower there was a pressure release that would trigger the water to be unleashed on the contained area. Snapdragon thought the design from Bearach was inspired and kept it a secret from as many people as possible—knowing that the best defenses are ones the enemy didn't see coming. But he also didn't know if it was going to work. As he had stated before, it wasn't something they could test.

The Rifna Erd all started to surge forward toward the ladders. In doing so, they caused a bottleneck, slowing their progress even more.

Then, as if someone had popped a cork, the side of the mountain opened up and the lake emptied into the contained area of the tunnel entrance. The roar of the rushing water drowned out the screams from the bald men. The liquid hit the attacking force hard. Some Rifna Erd bodies were washed up over the walls from the powerful force of the water, but most went the only place the water could go—back down the tunnel.

The three archers on the wall cheered. They focused their efforts on the Rifna Erd who had been washed over the walls.

Water from the mountain continued to drain down the tunnel, washing away not only the men who had come through the entrance, but also those waiting in the tunnel.

The defenses had held.

CHAPTER 77

"Shouldn't she be back by now?" Daimh asked.

Enoch looked at the mid-morning sky. He had been up all night, too worried to sleep. Several times he had nearly convinced himself to board the other small boat to go find her—but he had given his word. And, he had to admit, with his leg he wouldn't be much use. With each passing moment, Enoch's anxiety increased. Diantha was only supposed to go into town, get information and return.

"I thought she would be back," Enoch said, "but it looks like she got delayed."

"How long are we going to wait?" Daimh asked.

"Forever, if need be," Enoch said.

The two men sat there for a while longer. Daimh at one point got up and came back with two fishing poles and a rusted bucket full of bait. "We may as well put our sitting here to good use," the former king said.

The sun continued to climb the sky. They had caught four fish and Daimh was about to recast when he said, "Look! There!"

In the distance, Enoch saw a boat approaching. He couldn't tell who it was at first. As it got closer, he could see two people in the boat. Maybe Diantha decided to bring back one of the men she captured—maybe she had to in order to get the information they needed.

And then another thought came to her. What if it wasn't Diantha on the boat? What if she'd been caught and the people on the boat knew where she got it from.

"We may want to go inside until we know who they are," Enoch said.

Daimh frowned. "I think you're right."

With Daimh's help, Enoch went back in to the large house. He was able to find a window where he had a good view of the people rowing their direction.

"Daimh, will you please go get my weapons?" Enoch asked. "I have a pike and a sword."

"Aye, I noticed them when you arrived. I'll get them."

Enoch continued to watch the boat slowly approach. He still couldn't make out many details.

Soon, Daimh returned with the weapons.

"I'll take the pike," Enoch said. "Can you handle a sword?"

Daimh gave a little smile. "Yes. I'm familiar with how to use one."

They both watched out the window. And then, Enoch saw it. Diantha's darkened hair along with her dark armor. He was sure it was her. But who was the other person? The only feature he could see was shoulder-length gray hair.

"That's her." Enoch said.

"You sure?"

"Yes." Enoch knew he was grinning widely, but couldn't help it. Diantha was safe. "Let's go greet her."

Again, with Daimh's help, Enoch was able to limp to the dock. Diantha saw him and waved. He waved back.

"Who's with her?" Daimh asked.

"No idea."

When the boat got nearer to the shore, the grey haired woman looked at Enoch and cowered.

Diantha removed the oars from the water and let the boat glide toward the dock. Daimh threw her a rope which she used to pull herself in the rest of the way.

Once docked, Enoch offered his hand to help her out. Instead, she jumped out of the boat and gave him a big hug.

"I'm not dead," she said.

Enoch laughed. "No, you're not."

"And you stayed here. You kept your word. Thank you."

"It's what I do," Enoch said.

She let go of him and said, "This is Larissa. She helped me."

Larissa? The same arrogant woman who had dismissed him from the militia in Stur? When he looked at her closer, he realized it was her. "We've met," he said. His voice was flat.

Larissa got out of the boat with Daimh's help. "Thank you, sir. And Enoch, I'm surprised to see you here. I'm glad you're safe."

He didn't expect that type of response. Her swagger was gone. She looked, in a word, beaten—both physically and emotionally. He thought about introducing Larissa to Daimh, but after his last experience with this woman he was understandably guarded.

"What happened?" Enoch said. He looked Diantha over. She didn't look like she'd been in battle.

"I'll explain soon. In the meantime, Daimh, do you have any of that fish soup left over? I'm famished."

Enoch noticed Larissa flinch at the sound of their host's name, but didn't say anything.

"We're out, but Enoch and I caught some fish while we were waiting for you. I'll make up a new batch."

⊰╫⊱

Snapdragon returned to his family's side after he was confident that any of the Rifna Erd who were washed over the side of the walls were dead. The force of the water had once again collapsed the tunnel. With the amount of mud and water that went down the tunnel, Snapdragon felt confident that they were in no immediate threat from attack.

He dozed off and on for the next day, waiting for his wife and daughter, as well as most everyone else in the town, to recover.

Winter's fever broke first. Seraphina soon followed. They were now resting comfortably. With that knowledge, Snapdragon got something to eat and went to check on the town.

Everywhere he went in the town, he heard that people were recovering. In another day or so, he'd have enough men to start his further investigations on how the Rifna Erd were getting in.

On the way back to his house, there were shouts coming from the southern entrance. They weren't shouts of alarm. They sounded joyful. He jogged to the entrance where several of the militia were beckoning to him.

There were two horses that had just arrived. It was Diantha, Enoch and an older woman Snapdragon didn't recognize. Though he was bone weary, Snapdragon raced to greet them. Diantha helped the older woman off the horse they shared and then dismounted. She ran to her father's arms.

"You're safe," he said. "You're safe."

They both cried and held each other tightly.

"We've had quite an adventure while you were up here resting," Diantha said.

Snapdragon looked at the men around him and they all laughed.

"What?" Diantha asked.

"I'll explain in a moment. Who is with you?"

Diantha took a step back. "Enoch, you know of course."

The large man smiled. He had a thick bandage around one of his legs and looked as if he was being careful not to put any weight on it. "Good to see you, Enoch. Thank you for keeping my daughter from doing something foolish."

After Snapdragon said that, Enoch and Diantha shared a look—one that indicated that perhaps Diantha hadn't followed those instructions to the letter.

"She's home in one piece, as promised," Enoch said.

"And this is Larissa," Diantha introduced. Snapdragon was startled. She looked differently than he remembered. It was probably due to her change in appearance and demeanor, as well as his fatigue. But upon closer inspection, he was convinced it was her.

"Why is she here?" Snapdragon asked. When he'd seen her last, he was clear that she wasn't allowed to come within a day's ride of the northern walls.

"Commander Snapdragon," she said, her tone penitent. "Please, I remember your orders. But—"

"But she is my guest and we have much to discuss," Diantha finished.

"Of course, my apologies." Snapdragon said. "You all must be very tired. Please, please, follow me and we'll get you something to eat while we talk."

They had to walk slowly because of Enoch's leg. But he insisted he was only going to get better if he walked on it himself. Snapdragon decided to take them to the main hall by the mayor's house. It was usually used for public meetings—and it was one of the places in town where people weren't recovering from withdrawals.

On the way, Diantha stopped and gasped. "Dad! What happened to the mountain?"

Where the lake had been, there was a giant gash in the mountainside.

"We were attacked by the Rifna Erd. They came through the tunnel." Snapdragon quickly explained what had happened. "The lake was part of the defenses all this time. It saved a lot of lives."

They all just stared at the mountain for a moment.

"As you said, there is mush to discuss. We're almost to the main hall," he said.

After arriving at their destination, Snapdragon was informed that Mayor Creighton and his wife, Alethea, were still recovering and wouldn't be joining them. Bearach was also too weak.

Enoch, Diantha, Larissa and Snapdragon sat down at a long, stone table. A servant who had been one of the first to recover offered to make them something to eat.

"What were you able to find out on the scouting mission and why is Larissa here?" Snapdragon asked once they were settled in.

Diantha's expression was grim. "It turned out to be much more than a scouting mission." She went on to explain the events that led to her finding Larissa in the palace. Snapdragon wasn't happy when he heard that Diantha had decided to go into the palace. It was that type of foolish action that he had sent Enoch along to prevent.

"And then when we got to the kitchen, Larissa showed me large barrels of viceditad juice—from what we know, it was the main supply for the whole area."

"And with you destroying the shipment of viceditad leaves on your way there, it was the perfect chance to empty the barrels!" Snapdragon said. "That would be—"

"We didn't empty the barrels," Diantha interrupted.

"You didn't? Why not? It would've been perfect! Without the viceditad, the people in Erd Proper would have become weak, like we were here. It would give us the chance to attack them in a weakened state, just like they did to us."

"But you didn't lose when you were attacked," Diantha pointed out. "Believe me, I thought seriously about destroying the barrels. In order for a plan to attack to be successful, we had to rely on things I couldn't count on. Would we have enough healthy people to attack? Would we be able to get there in time before they started to recover? I couldn't count on these things."

Snapdragon nodded. "You're right about the variables. But I still don't see a good reason for keeping the barrels full of viceditad."

Diantha looked troubled for a moment. "Dad, would you say we are at war with the Rifna Erd?"

"Yes. Most definitely."

"And during war, the rule is kill or be killed, isn't it?" she asked.

Snapdragon thought about the question. "It's not as simple as that. But in defense of your homes, freedom and lives of the ones you love, killing your enemy is sometimes the only answer. I wish it wasn't so. Why?"

"After knowing about the contents of the barrels, I had Larissa take me to the nursemaid's quarters. They were empty."

Larissa interjected, "The Rifna Erd don't use nursemaids. They believe if a person isn't strong enough to survive their wounds or illnesses, they are too weak to be Rifna Erd."

"In the nursemaids' quarters is a storeroom of sorts. It's where they keep the bandages, slings for broken arms and… plyese."

Snapdragon felt his eyes grow wide. "What did you do?"

"With Larissa's help, we ground up all the plyese. From there, we mixed it into the barrels of viceditad," Diantha said.

"Wow," Snapdragon said. He sat back in his chair and rubbed his hand over his face.

Diantha nodded. "Yeah, wow. Dad, if it works like we think it will, it will kill any who drink from the kegs."

"Which will be everyone in Erd Proper and the surrounding area," Larissa said. "But before you say anything about the people there being innocent, I can tell you that almost everyone has thrown their lot in with the Rifna Erd. Yes, there will be a few people still loyal to Bariwon who may die, but how many innocent people have already lost their lives in the kingdom? The women who were captive with me would rather die than suffer from how the Rifna Erd treated us."

Snapdragon felt a mixture of relief and apprehension. The extermination of everyone in Erd Proper was more than he would have agreed to. Where does one draw the line during war? There were no easy answers.

"So," Enoch said, breaking the silence, "the attack from the tunnel failed and the Rifna Erd in Bariwon have been taken care of. It seems to me, we only need to find out how the Rifna Erd got here in the first place."

"I can help with that," Larissa said. "At least somewhat. That's why I asked Diantha to bring me here."

Everyone faced the older woman.

"What can you tell us?" Snapdragon asked.

"If I tell you this, I will be admitting to committing treason against the crown," Larissa said. "I was too wrapped up in my own sense of self-importance at the time to see clearly. I ask that you consider my actions since then when judgment is handed down."

Snapdragon considered her request. Anything she could tell them could possibly put an end to this threat. "I will plead your case before the crown. I give you my word," Snapdragon said.

"Thank you." Larissa looked relieved. "I actually worked for Governor Selene. She confided in me that she was a direct descendent of the Rifna Erd—one of the few left behind when the Pendeltune, their name for the tunnel between Bariwon and the lands north of the mountains, was closed. Selene wanted the Rifna Erd to return. Her intention was to rule over Bariwon with the Rifna Erd as her personal army.

"But Serkan, one of the Rifna Erd who was brought into Bariwon, had other ideas. He was the one that introduced the viceditad to the land. I honestly thought I'd die without drinking it, until Diantha convinced me differently. Anyway, Serkan had no intention of sharing power with Selene—and he killed her.

"Selene didn't share all the details with me, but what I do know was that for many years only people she truly trusted were sent to a certain section of the wall. It was an area where they'd figured out a way to get the Rifna Erd as well as crates of viceditad into Bariwon. To draw attention away from this location when they started sneaking people in and before I could take over, the attacks on Commander Snapdragon and later an area by Stur, were set up as a distraction."

"But *how* were they getting in?" Snapdragon asked.

"I don't know. I would tell you if I knew," Larissa said. "She never told me. But I do know someone who does know."

"Who is that?" Diantha asked.

"His name is Hollis."

Diantha let out a groan. "You mean his name *was* Hollis."

"He's dead?" Larissa asked. She looked scared again.

"Aye, along with everyone else at his outpost."

"Wait! Before you throw me in jail, it's not all bad news," Larissa said. "That outpost is where they were getting in."

"We've been there," Snapdragon said. "All the men there were killed and the place was ruined. I, personally, looked at the mountain side. There were no signs of Rifna Erd coming over the mountains."

Larissa looked desperate. "Please! I'm telling you the truth!"

"I believe you are, Larissa," Snapdragon said. "At least, I believe that's what Selene told you. Still, with what you've told us, we'll have to keep you under guard until we can take this before the queen."

"I understand," Larissa said. She looked defeated. "And when will that be?"

Snapdragon looked around the room. "As soon as I can gather healthy men, we'll go back to this outpost to see what we can find."

⟶❄⟵

Later that day, Diantha could feel the effects of the withdrawals starting. She had used up the last of her supply on the way back from Erd Proper. She begged her Dad to wait for her to get better so that she could go with him to the outpost. He made no promises—he just wanted her to get better.

Enoch had pulled up a chair next to her bed. He'd said he'd stay with her.

"Are you sure you want to see me like this?" she asked.

He smiled and nodded his head.

"You looked pretty hideous when you went through the withdrawals," she said. "I'm not sure I want you to see me that way."

His expression changed—it became serious. "Diantha, I don't know how you will respond to this, but you will always be beautiful to me. No matter what."

She looked into his eyes. Again, she felt the fluttering in her chest. She wondered if this was how her mom felt when she looked at her dad.

"No matter what, huh?"

"No matter what."

⟶❄⟵

Snapdragon was losing. He had tried to insist that his wife stay in bed, but she refused—stating she was fine. At least his daughter Winter had listened to him.

"Heaven only knows what's happened while I was sick," Seraphina said. "I need to make sure you didn't let the house fall apart."

Snapdragon laughed. His wife woke up the morning after Diantha returned. He got reports that most of the people in the town who went through the withdrawals were moving around.

"I mean, look at this fireplace," she said. "How am I supposed to cook a decent meal? Did you even clean anything while I was sick?" There was a playful tone in her voice.

"I was a little busy at the time," Snapdragon said in defense. He hadn't told her about the attack or what Diantha had done. He didn't want her to worry during her recovery.

"Busy? Bah! Unless you were attacked by the Rifna Erd, you don't have any good excuses."

"Actually—"

"Commander Snapdragon!" a voice called from outside their home. "Come quickly!"

Snapdragon exchanged a look with his wife. "Stay here."

He got up and walked outside. There were four militia waiting for him.

"There are riders coming in from the west, Commander," one of the men said.

"How many?"

"We aren't sure. We just heard the shouting from the watchtower."

Snapdragon looked at the men around him and saw the same worry he felt. While people were recovering, the town was in no condition to fend off another attack.

"Let's get to the tower and find out."

They raced to the tower with Snapdragon the first one to get to the top. He sighed a breath of relief when he noticed it was only three men approaching. From what he could tell, they were wearing the king's colors.

Still, he made sure to grab his sword before heading back down the watchtower to greet them. He had archers on the wall at the ready. Any abled men were armed and ready to fight.

"Hail there!" cried one of the riders.

Snapdragon recognized the voice. As the man approached, he recognized it was Kerr—mayor of Stur.

"Kerr!" Snapdragon said in greeting. He walked forward to meet the man. "I'm afraid you are a bit too late for the party."

Kerr looked around from his vantage point on his horse, obviously noticing the mountainside where the lake had broken open.

"We saw the warning beacons. I'm sorry we are late—but we were dealing with a most peculiar issue of our own," Kerr said.

Snapdragon tensed up. "Like what?"

"This is something you'll need to see for yourself," Kerr said.

⧉

Seraphina protested Snapdragon going with Kerr, of course, especially after she found out what had happened while she was sick. She only agreed when Snapdragon was able to find ten men who had recovered enough to travel with him.

It had taken several hours to arrive at the outpost where Hollis had been in charge.

"After we saw the signal fires, we gathered our weapons and armor to come help. We were on our way and as we were passing this outpost, we heard a noise coming from the mountains. We didn't know what it was, and in the twilight, it was hard to see. And that is when it happened."

"Happened?"

"I'll have to show you from the watchtower," Kerr said. It wasn't a wide tower, so only Kerr and Snapdragon climbed to the top.

Once there, Kerr pointed and asked, "See that?"

Snapdragon looked down to where Kerr was motioning, but he wasn't sure what he was looking for.

"As I said we heard this noise. I climbed here, where we are now and saw it. Water—a *lot* of water—came rushing out of one of the abandoned mine shafts. It was the strangest thing I've ever seen. I don't know what to think of it."

And then Snapdragon understood. He rubbed his left hand over his face and chided himself for being so shortsighted. He should have figured it out before. Why hadn't he? Maybe because he thought it was impossible, but it hadn't been.

"I know where the water came from."

"You do?" Kerr asked, surprised.

"It came from *us*."

Kerr frowned, obviously confused.

"We didn't know how the Rifna Erd were getting in. It appears that men from this side used one of these old mines and tunneled over to where it met up with the Pendeltune. It never occurred to me that people on our side of the mountains would tunnel toward the Rifna Erd. And we built the wall to prevent the Rifna Erd from tunneling toward us. Even if they knew about these old mines, finding one would be a shot in the dark.

"I always assumed that they would tunnel through the area we collapsed. That's why we concentrated our efforts there and why Bearach built the lake—so it could be used as a last line of defense. And it seems that when the water we released went down the entrance by Procep, it got redirected here."

Kerr shook his head. "That's not possible. How could they get men over the wall to do the digging without us knowing?"

"We had men come from Erd Proper to help with the wall. Before she became Governor, Selene was the magistrate. She asked that if men came to help, that they would be allowed to pick where they wanted to work— if they had a preference. It was a concession I was willing to agree to. We've just found out that it was Selene who was the one who wanted the Rifna Erd to return. She thought she could control them so she could rule the land. It must have taken years for them to complete the tunnel. And once it was open, I can't imagine it was very big if only a few men at a time and crates could be smuggled in."

Kerr grunted. "Well, a fat lot of good that did them. We inspected the mine and the water was enough to cause it to collapse. Plus, we now know to keep an eye on this spot—as well as the other mines in the area."

"That's it," Snapdragon said. "We've stopped the Rifna Erd."

⋅⋟⧉⋞⋅

Enoch put a blanket around Diantha's shoulders. The evening air had just enough of a chill that he didn't want her to catch cold, especially since she had just recovered from the viceditad withdrawals a day ago.

"Thank you," she said.

"Anytime."

"I needed to get out of the house. I don't think I've ever spent that long in bed."

He sat down next to her. They were sitting on the edge of the quarry that had just recently been a lake. Enoch had made sure the area was stable before they settled in.

"I can understand that," he said. "Even during that month we spent in Tevoil, you always had to be doing something. There's something to be said about taking a moment to enjoy the world around you."

She shifted so her body was closer to him. "Oh, yeah? Like what?"

It was the time of day between dusk and night. The brighter stars were already visible, with the dimmer ones appearing as time passed.

Enoch pointed to the brightest star in the sky. "Do you know the name of that star?" he asked.

"Yeah, the people of Eddinh call it the Zealous Star. The name has stuck. I know a lot of people call it that now. What about it?"

"Well, it may seem kind of silly, but…"

Diantha turned to face him. "But what?"

"I've always admired how it doesn't move, unlike the stars around it," Enoch said. "I've sort of used it as an example of how I should live my life."

"Is that why you wouldn't drink the viceditad again?" she asked.

He thought about it a moment. "Yes. That would be one of the reasons."

"But at the time, you thought you would die without it," Diantha said. "You were willing to die—to leave me—because of your desire to follow what you believe to be true. Didn't you know how hard it was on me when I thought you had died?"

Carefully, gently, he placed a hand on her cheek. "If I would have given in, I wouldn't be the kind of man worthy to be with you."

He saw her expression change. Whereas before it was determined and even a bit upset, she now looked almost sad. "Oh Enoch, you are something else. Please, keep following your heart. I wouldn't want you any other way."

CHAPTER 78

Snapdragon knelt before his queen.

"You may arise, Uncle Snap," Rainbow said. "I mean, Commander Snapdragon."

"Thank you, Your Highness."

The main hall of the castle was full. It had been a while since Snapdragon had attended court. He felt a lingering sadness from the people he had talked with when he arrived at the castle.

"Are you ready to give your official report?" the queen asked.

Snapdragon nodded. He looked at the empty chair next to a very pregnant Queen Rainbow. Her child would never know his father, but Snapdragon knew with the people who had survived, her baby would never be without a father figure. Councilors Rayne and Sunshine sat close to their daughter. Like most of the people Snapdragon had encountered over the last few months, they looked exhausted from all that had occurred.

"I am ready, Your Highness."

"Proceed."

"I am confident that the Rifna Erd threat has been stopped. The lake above Procep is nearly rebuilt, the old tunnel entrance is once again closed off. All caves and old mines near the area have been collapsed. We've put into motion a rotating defensive plan so that no one place along the mountains can be kept secret from the rest.

"Word has spread throughout the kingdom of the dangers of viceditad—any that is found is to be destroyed. As far as we can tell, it can't be grown in Bariwon, so we believe it is no longer a threat.

"The casualties from the Rifna Erd are staggering. It is estimated over half of the kingdom's population died from the effects of mixing viceditad and plyese. The worst loss of life was in Erd Proper where an estimated ninety-five percent of the people died. Investigations of the palace revealed the dead bodies of many Rifna Erd, though it is hard to tell how many for sure because the men in the town made themselves look like Rifna Erd.

"I feel confident that the threat from the Rifna Erd has been eliminated—at least for many years to come."

The queen nodded. "Thank you. I'm pleased to hear that. Though I fear the damage done by the Rifna Erd can't only be calculated by the number of lives lost."

"How's that, Your Highness?"

"There remains distrust among the districts. Many of them are upset at the crown for letting this happen. And all the other districts show animosity toward Erd. But it doesn't end there. When viceditad became scarce, districts fought each other over supplies of the plant. There are still skirmishes here and there along the border. What remains of the militia is doing its best to stop them."

"I can't imagine we have enough surviving militia to do much good," Snapdragon said.

"No, we don't," Queen Rainbow said. "One of the hardest deaths to bear was that of Oakleaf and his family. He was head of the militia and we don't have anyone experienced enough to take his place."

Snapdragon smiled. "I believe I know someone."

"Oh?"

"Yes, Your Highness," Snapdragon said. "Forgive me if this seems self-serving, but I recommend my daughter, Diantha. She is an excellent fighter and has the respect of the remaining militia and guardians for her actions in Erd Proper."

Rainbow smiled. "Of course. Diantha would be an excellent choice. But is it true what I've heard? Was Diantha this Noble Trod we had reports about?" the queen asked.

"Yes, Your Highness." Snapdragon explained what Diantha had told him. "She has agreed to pay the penalty for her actions. According to The Tome of Laws, one of the options is to perform service toward the kingdom for a period of time as determined by the royalty or a magistrate acting in their stead. In light of all that has happened, I would ask that her work as the head of the militia act as service to the kingdom for her actions. She's agreed to take a cut in pay as well."

Rainbow thrummed her fingers on the armrest of her throne then turned to her mother and father. "What do you think?"

They shared a glance and then Rayne said, "As long as she understands what she did was wrong."

"Agreed." Sunshine said. "And also on the condition that she trains the militia that they must obey what is found in The Tome of Laws—now more than ever."

"Will she agree to this?" Rainbow asked Snapdragon.

"Most certainly, Your Highness. Thank you."

"On a lighter note, I've heard she is being courted by someone. Is that true?"

"After a fashion." Snapdragon laughed. "It's more like she is courting Enoch. They are taking it slowly and focusing on rebuilding the kingdom, but I have high hopes they will marry one day. He's a remarkable man."

Rainbow nodded. "From what I've heard, I agree. Also, what of the charges against Larissa?" Rainbow asked.

"Your Highness, I would ask for leniency. She admits to helping the Rifna Erd sneak into Bariwon, but I believe she has repented of her prideful behaviors. She was very instrumental in helping Diantha when she infiltrated the palace in Erd Proper."

Rainbow seemed to think it over a moment. "We will grant her leniency—to a point. She will not be allowed to hold a position of power, nor have access to any official kingdom information. I will leave it to you to decide what will suit her best."

"Actually, she has requested she be allowed to move to a home not far from Erd Proper. During Diantha and Enoch's trip to Erd Proper, they were helped by a man living on the shore of Lake Dylobo. You may have heard of him. His name is Daimh."

Councilor Rayne leaned forward. "Daimh? As in the former king?"

"Yes, according to Diantha, he was quite helpful. He's the only survivor of his family. It seems that he and Larissa made a connection while they were there. She's asked to help him restore his house."

Sunshine laughed. "Stranger things have happened. Your Highness, I think it would be permissible to grant Larissa's request."

"Then I grant it," Rainbow said.

"Thank you, Your Highness."

"Is there anything else?" the queen asked.

"Just this," Snapdragon said. "I believe that we've faced the greatest threat to the kingdom since the first time the nislles came to our land. However, as long as we continue to do the things we know we should, I believe we will recover."

Rainbow smiled and declared, "To peace in our kingdom!"

"To peace in our kingdom!" everyone in the hall echoed.

⋆⋇⋆

Seraphina snuggled up next to Snapdragon. "It's been a busy day," she said.

"It's been a busy life," Snapdragon said.

They lay on a bed in one of the guest rooms in the castle. When Snapdragon was summoned to come to the castle to give a report, Seraphina insisted on going. She said that no longer would she leave his side. And she had been good to her word so far.

"But you did it. Maybe not the way you planned, but you kept the kingdom from being overthrown," she said.

"Not without a lot of help," Snapdragon said.

"True. After all, had you not had such a charming wife, you'd never had gotten as far as you did."

He rolled on to his side and looked at her. "I love you, you know that?"

"Yes I do." She leaned in and gave him a kiss. "And I love you too."

They enjoyed the moment, resting for the first time in years with the knowledge that they were safe.

"So, what now?" Seraphina asked.

"We'll stay here for a few more days and then head home. I'm still the commander of the northern defenses."

"You know, I was thinking that—"

A soft knock on their door interrupted what she was about to say.

"Yes?" they said in unison.

The door opened a crack. "Begging your pardon," a servant said, "but I've been asked to have you come to the nursemaid's area."

Snapdragon sat up and reached for his sword that he always kept next to his side of the bed. "What's the matter? Was someone attacked?"

"No, Commander, nothing like that. The queen has gone into labor."

Quickly, Seraphina and Snapdragon made themselves presentable and went to the nursemaid area to find his sister, Sunshine, her husband, Rayne and his father Garth waiting outside one of the rooms.

"Snap!" Sunshine said when she saw him. "I'm glad you're here for this."

"I wouldn't miss my sister becoming a granny for the world."

"Granny? Granny? Rayne, do I look like a granny to you?"

"How do I answer that without getting in trouble?" Rayne asked.

"Bah! How about you, Dad? Do you think I look like a granny?"

"Of course not," Garth said. Sunshine smirked at Rayne and Snapdragon until her father continued, "But once the baby gets here, you will."

Rayne and Snapdragon laughed and then stopped abruptly when Sunshine and Seraphina glared at them.

While they waited, Snapdragon turned to his wife. "You were about to tell me something before we were summoned."

"Oh. Yes." Seraphina smiled. "I was going to suggest that we remain here, at the castle, until Rainbow's child was born."

Not long after, the door opened. A nursemaid stepped out. "You may come in."

Snapdragon allowed everyone else to go first. When he stepped inside, Snapdragon saw Rainbow holding a little baby in her arms.

"Before you ask," she said, "it's a boy."

Rainbow's father, Rayne, stepped up to the bed and gave the baby boy a kiss on the head. He then said, "Sweetheart, I suggest you give him a name before your grandfather has anything to say about it."

"I've already picked a name," she said. "I knew it as soon as I saw him. He's going to be king over a land that has faced many trials and will surely face many more. He needs to be strong and keep the kingdom united."

She looked up at the people around her. "His name is Bariwon."

PRONUNCIATION GUIDE

Anemone: An-eh-mo-nee
Bearach: Bear-ack
Ciar: See-are
Daimh: Dime
Diantha: Die-ann-the
Donigi: Don-ee-gey
Eadward: Ed-ward
Elisedd: Eli-said
Erd: Urd
Grenoa: Gren-oh-ah
Iolanthe: Eye-o-lanth
Itamunno Kael: It-ah-moon-oh Kale
Larissa: Lar-EYE-saw
Lebu: Lay-boo
Lewyol: Loo-yall
Mortentaun: Mort-ten-tawn
Mylnohe: Mile-know
Nie syll esse: Nigh-sil-es-ee
Nislles: Niss-ulls
Pendeltune: Pen-del-toon
Plyese: Plea-see
Procep: Pro-sep
Regne: Reg-nay
Rifna Erd: Riff-nah Urd
Rinan: Rin-on
Seanan: See-ah-nun
Serkan: Sir-can
Shoginoc: Shog-in-ock
Sverre: Suv-ear
Tevoil: Tee-voil
Tular Tevoil: Too-lar Tee-voil
Vashti: Vash-tee
Viceditad: Vice-dee-todd

DRAMATIS PERSONAE

*The Bariwon Chronicle*s is huge in scope with numerous characters. I thought it would be helpful to have a list of characters and who they are. In attempt to avoid spoilers—though there will be some spoilers if you read all the descriptions ahead of time—I am including the description of the characters when they are (generally) first introduced in the story, though the list is in alphabetical order.

Also, the characters are divided into sections, based on which book they were introduced. Once again, this is done to avoid spoilers.

Characters introduced in *The Hidden Sun*

Abrecan—Governor of Erd district. Married to Calla. Father of Daimh.

Alana—Noble of Bariwon. Niece to King Kenrik. Cousin to Eliana.

Aldous—Member of the Hierarchy of Magistrates during Kenrik's rule.

Anemone—Nursemaid in Bariwon Castle. Primary nursemaid to Eliana.

Arlie—Resident of the town of Bariwon surrounding the castle. Daughter of Barclay.

Barclay—Resident of the town of Bariwon surrounding the castle. Father of Arlie.

Bertram—Savant of Bariwon during King Kenrik's rule.

Caldre—Magistrate of Erd district. Advisor to Abrecan.

Calla—Governess of Erd district. Married to Abrecan. Mother of Daimh.

Cameron—Royal Guardian of Bariwon.

Chandler—Resident of Lewyol district. Candle seller.

Daimh—Resident of Erd District. Son of Abrecan and Calla.

Dougal—Royal Guardian of Bariwon. Serves under Captain Wayte.

Dulcie—Resident who lives on the Tevoil-Lewyol border.

Dylan—Governor of Donigi district.

Eadward—Royal Guardian of Bariwon. Personal Guardian to Princess Eliana.

Eliana—Blood heir to the Bariwon throne. Daughter of King Kenrik and Queen Lareyna.

Garth—Resident of Lewyol district. Married to Iolanthe. Father to Oakleaf, Sunshine and Snapdragon.

Iolanthe—Resident of Lewyol district. Married to Garth. Mother to Oakleaf, Sunshine and Snapdragon.

Ivor—Resident of Erd district. Nephew of Eadward.

Kelvin—Resident of Lebu district. Married to Nadia. Father of Rinan.

Kenrik—King of Bariwon. Son of Councilor Phillip. Married to Lareyna. Father of Eliana.

Linden—Governess of Lebu district. Married to Nash.

Nadia—Resident of Lebu district. Married to Kelvin. Mother of Rinan.

Nash—Governor of Lebu district. Married to Linden.

Nicole—Resident of Regne. Married to Daimh.

Oakleaf—Resident of Lewyol district. Son of Garth and Iolanthe. Brother to Sunshine and Snapdragon.

Ophelia—Nursemaid in Bariwon Castle.

Phillip—Councilor of Bariwon. Father of Kenrik. Grandfather of Eliana.

Rayne—Resident of Tevoil district. Son of Rinan and Eliana.

Rinan—Royal Guardian of Bariwon. Son of Kelvin and Nadia.

Seanan—Leader of the Hierarchy of Magistrates during Kenrik's rule.

Sherwyn—Priest of Bariwon. Head priest in the castle during Kenrik's rule.

Snapdragon—Resident of Lewyol district. Son of Garth and Iolanthe. Brother to Oakleaf and Sunshine.

Sullivan—Guardian of Erd district. Answers directly to Abrecan.

Sunshine—Resident of Lewyol district. Daughter of Garth and Iolanthe. Sister to Oakleaf and Snapdragon.

Thomas—Guardians in the Lewyol district. Originally from Erd district. Twins with the same name.

Vashti—Seamstress of Bariwon. Head seamstress in the castle during Kenrik's rule.

Wayte—Captain of the Royal Guardians during King Kenrik's rule. Supervisor to Rinan.

Zubin—Guardian in the Lewyol district. Originally from Erd district.

Characters introduced in *The Waxing Moon*

Aaron—Guardian of Bariwon.

Alethea—Leader of the people of Eddinh.

Asher—Royal Guardian in Bariwon Castle.

Bearach—Assistant royal crafter in Bariwon Castle.

Blythe—Royal Guardian of Bariwon.

Ciar—Servant in Bariwon Castle.

Creighton—Resident of Erd district.

Crescens—Assistant Magistrate of Erd.

Darius—Protector in Itamunno Kael.

Fallon—Captain of the Royal Guardians during King Rayne and Queen Sunshine's rule. Supervisor to Snapdragon.

Gordon (the Great)—Merchant at the Mortentaun festival.

Grant—Royal crafter in Bariwon Castle.

Kerr—Resident of Erd district.

Melanie—Servant in Bariwon Castle.

Merton—Leader of the people of Itamunno Kael.

Rainbow—Blood heir to the Bariwon throne. Daughter of King Rayne and Queen Sunshine.

Rowan—Resident of Bariwon Castle. Son of Oakleaf and Arlie.

Rudyard—Aide of Governor Wardell of Erd district.

Selene—Magistrate of Erd.

Seraphina—Nursemaid in Bariwon Castle.

Stuart—Royal Guardian in Bariwon Castle.

Sverre—Resident of the land found north of the mountains.

Waylon—Savant in Bariwon Castle.

Characters introduced in *The Zealous Star*

Alton—Farmer of both Donigi and Regne districts.

Amon—Guardian of Procep in Erd district.

Bott—Resident of Erd Proper.

Diantha—Resident of Procep in Erd district. Daughter of Snapdragon and Seraphina. Sister to Reed and Winter.

Elisedd—King of Bariwon. Married to Queen Rainbow.

Elwood—Farmer of both Donigi and Regne districts.

Enoch—Resident of Stur in Erd district. Adopted son of Kerr, Mayor of Stur.

Goban—Blacksmith in Erd Proper.

Hollis—Militia captain stationed at the northern defenses.

Larissa—Magistrate assigned to the northern wall by Selene.

Mason—Militia captain of Stur in Erd district.

Reed—Resident of Procep in Erd district. Son of Snapdragon and Seraphina. Brother to Diantha and Winter.

Rosalind—Resident of Procep in Erd district. Daughter of Bearach and Jada.

Serkan—Mysterious man of the Rifna Erd. Smuggled in to Bariwon by Selene and Crescens.

Shaw—Merchant in Erd Proper.

Sterling—Resident of Erd Proper.

The Noble Trod—Legendary figure from Bariwon's past.

Wardell—Governor of Erd district.

Winter—Resident of Procep in Erd district. Daughter of Snapdragon and Seraphina. Sister to Reed and Diantha.

Some insights behind *The Hidden Sun*

The spark that started it all: I've been asked many times what inspired me to write this story. The answer? Well, I had a very vivid dream one night about this man driving a cart into a medieval type town. He notices a beautiful woman with dark hair leave one of the shops, followed soon after by three ruffians. They obviously are following her. She spins and with her hands on her hips stands up to them, but they continue to move in on her. The man in the cart throws something at one of the men and hits him. The ruffians turn their attention to the man and he fights them off using a staff. I woke up right after the dream, and I recalled all the details. My wife was waking up as well, and I told her about the dream. She told me, "You should write that down." That led me to the questions of, "Who are these people? Where were they? Where did they come from? What happens next?" The end result was the dream became the heart of Chapter 12 in the book. Everything before it and after it stems from that original dream.

Why it is named *The Hidden Sun*: I actually didn't come up with a title for the book until after I had finished it. The working title was War and Peace—alright, not really. The working title was Rain and Sunshine, but it just didn't feel right. After my then seven year old daughter Emily came up with the saying "The sun is playing hide-and-seek", the title came to me. Although the obvious meaning of the title comes from the phrase that opens the book, *The Hidden Sun* is also a reference to Rayne, the son of Eliana and Rinan. There are also two other meanings to the title. There is a line in the book that the clouds can only hide the sun for so long. To me, Abrecan's rule over Bariwon was the clouds that covered the kingdom, but the sun would eventually shine once again on the land. As for a last silly note of the title, my full name is Jason Lloyd Morgan, though the book is listed under J. Lloyd Morgan. What's missing (or hidden) from my pen name?

The last section written: The last section I wrote for *The Hidden Sun* was not the Epilogue. After re-reading the book for the umpteenth time, I felt like there needed to be more between Rinan and Eliana to show how their relationship grew. The result starts on page 20 and ends on page 22. It is the section on the princess party. Having four daughters, I have been in my fair share of princess parties, so it seemed as good of a setting as any. Plus, I liked the irony that Princess Eliana had to dress up as a princess for the party.

Fun with Anagrams: When it came time to name places or events or other original things, I wanted to come up with something unique. But how does one just "make up" words? I'll have to admit, I cheated a little bit. All my made up words are anagrams. An anagram is a word made up from using the letters from another word. Example: an anagram for J Lloyd Morgan could be "Manly Lord Jog". (Granted, if you've seen me jog, there is nothing particularly "Manly" or "Lordly" about it.)

Shoginoc: Choosing
Mortentaun: Tournament
Bariwon: Rainbow
Erd: Red
Lewyol: Yellow
Regne: Green
Lebu: Blue
Tevoil: Violet
Grenoa: Orange
Donigi: Indigo
Nislles: Illness
Plyese: Sleepy

A Rinan by any other name... : So, how does an author come up with the names for his or her characters? That's a darn good question and one that has a different answer from each author you ask. As for *The Hidden Sun*, most of the names have some significance to the person or a thematic element in the book. Below are the names of the characters with an explanation of what their names mean.

Eliana: It comes from the Late Latin Aeliāna, the feminine form of the Latin family name Aeliānus (of the sun), which is derived from the Greek hēlios (sun).
Rinan: It is an Anglo-Saxon name that means "rain".
Abrecan: It is an Anglo-Saxon name that means "storm".
Caldre: It is an English name that means "cold brook".
Sherwyn: It is an Anglo-Saxon name that means "quick as the wind".

752

Anemone: Derived from the Greek word ανεμος (anemos) meaning "wind".

Daimh: A Scottish name that means "ox". It is pronounced "dime".

Eadward: An Anglo-Saxon name that means "guardian".

Wayte: An English name that means "guard".

Bertram: Derived from the Germanic element beraht meaning "bright".

Alana: An Irish name that means "fair".

Vashti: One meaning is "thread" in Hebrew.

Dougal: Anglicized form of the Gaelic name Dubhghall, which meant "dark stranger" from dubh "dark" and gall "stranger".

Garth: From a surname meaning "garden" in Old Norse

Iolanthe: Influenced by the Greek words ιολη (iole) "violet" and ανθος (anthos) "flower".

Dulcie: From Latin dulcis meaning "sweet".

Thomas: Greek form of the Aramaic name תָּאֹומָא (Ta'oma') which meant "twin".

Chandler: From an occupational surname which meant "candle seller" in Middle English, ultimately from Old French.

Cameron: From a Scottish surname meaning "crooked nose" from Gaelic cam "crooked" and sròn "nose".

Sullivan: From an Irish surname which was derived from Ó Súilleabháin meaning "little dark eye".

Ivor: From the Old Norse name Ívarr, which was derived from the elements yr "yew, bow" and arr "warrior".

Nicole: French feminine form of Nicholas, from the Greek name Νικολαος (Nikolaos) which meant "victory of the people" from Greek νικη (nike) "victory" and λαος (laos) "people". Fun note: If I had a "Dime", I had to have a "Nickle". *smiles*

Benjamin: "Son of my right hand" On page 94, Anemone notes how violent the sparing contests have become. As an example, she tells how Guardian Benjamin lost a finger off his right hand.

Oakleaf: What else would someone like Garth name his son?

Sunshine: Again, Garth is a bit odd in naming his kids. Hopefully, this name is obvious.

Snapdragon: I actually had a little fun with this one. Since there is no magic or traditional fantasy elements in the book, naming Garth and Iolanthe's third child "Snapdragon" was a way I could sneak a "dragon" into the book.

Rayne: Aside from the obvious, it also means in English "strong counselor from the ancient personal name Ragnar".

To "okay" or not to "okay": While reading the amazing Work and the Glory series, the author pointed out in one of the books that the word "OK" (or also "okay") didn't really come into use in the English language until around 1839. Granted, *The Hidden Sun* is in a fictitious land during an unspecified time period. However, due to its Medieval elements, logic would say that was before 1839. Granted, I'm sure there are numerous words I use in the book that were not used in Medieval times, but as we edited the book, I kept on getting hung up on using the word "okay." So, as an act of (perhaps?) defiance, I went through and replaced all the "okays" in the book with either "fine" or "all right."

Sunshine's subtle wit: I really enjoyed writing for the character Garth. He would say some of the oddest things. Of course, some of that couldn't help but rub off on his daughter, Sunshine. There are at least a couple of places where she is fairly witty, in a subtle way. One is her response to Chandler on page 103 when he asks her about the weather. But, my favorite response of hers is on page 122 when Alana (a Noble) expresses her intended action. (Please don't make me spell it out for you more than I have)

Inside joke to the naysayers: The first part of chapter 11 is my response to certain workaholics (and there were more than one, and there continue to be more) about why I was writing a book.

"The sun's playing hide-and-seek": My Grandma Morgan would say "The Devil is beating his wife" whenever it was raining and sunny at the same time. I have no idea what that means or where it came from—but if you do a web search for it, it is a fairly well known saying. Understand that my Grandma Morgan was one of the sweetest (and funniest) people I've ever met. In fact, as my siblings and I have grown up, we can trace much of our sense of humor back to her.

On a bit of a different subject, I was in Connecticut and going through a rough time at work. I was looking for something else creative to do, yet at the same time, I had a family to provide for. I had started working on the outline for *The Hidden Sun*, but wasn't sure I was going to ever fully start to write it. Then, one day after work, I was walking out to my car.

The sky was mostly blue, the sun was shining, but it started to rain. It was the oddest experience—and one that inspired me.

I thought of my Grandma Morgan's saying, but felt that wasn't really the tone I wanted to use for starting out the book. So, I tried to make up one of my own. For the longest time, it was "The sun is sleeping on the job." Pretty lame, eh? I tried out several more, but could never find one that felt right.

So, what was I to do? Then it hit me. At dinner one night, I asked my girls what they would say if the sun was out, but it was raining. They all gave good answers—I think Amy said, "I wanna see a wainbow!" (spelling with a "w" intended). But it was my then seven year old, Emily, that said, "The sun's playing hide-and-seek." So that is where the saying came from, and also why Eliana was seven at the start of the book.

Did Dyslexia exist in Medieval times? When trying to figure out a way to have Daimh and Eliana's wedding be not binding, I was confronted with the challenge, "Wouldn't someone notice?" So, how to get around that? Well, I did three things. Number one, Eliana had claimed she wasn't feeling well as to avoid Daimh before the wedding, so when she was sneezing during the ceremony, it didn't seem out of place. Second, part of Daimh's character is that he was "never really concerned with details." (See page 30) So, when Eliana takes him by the left hand, and not the right hand, the reader can buy it because it was introduced before. Third, then came the witness: Magistrate Seanan. During the Shoginoc, Seanan starts to head to the left side of the hall, instead of the right. King Kenrik notes to Eliana, "Poor Magistrate Seanan, he's always had trouble with the difference between left and right." (Page 28) So, when Eliana uses her left hand, it is very plausible that Seanan wouldn't notice. I had a bit of fun with that later on page 193, just to keep it consistent. I got the idea for Seanan because growing up I struggled with left and right—later to find out I'm Dyslexic.

Can you find what is missing? One of the significant plot points revolves around a missing word in The Tome of Laws. This was inspired by my uncanny ability to add extra words or leave out words all together when I'm writing.

Oh! The symbolism! Starting on page 93, there is a scene with Anemone and Sherwyn. Sherwyn had gotten a sliver under a fingernail and came to the nursemaid for help. Her remedy was to have him soak it in warm water and then cold and eventually it would just come out by itself. When writing the book, this actually happened to me, and that was the cure that worked. I included it in the book to catch the reader up on what was going on at the castle, and with Anemone and Sherwyn. At the same time, I used "sliver" (which is an anagram for "silver"—one of Erd's colors) to represent Abrecan's reign, and foreshadowed that it would be "water" that would get him removed. What is one way we get water? From "Rayne" of course.

Two witnesses? In the Tome of Laws it states that it takes two witnesses for someone to be convicted of a crime. This is far from an original idea. It's actually found in The Bible at the following places: Deut 19:15, Matt 18:16, 2 Cor 13:1, 1 Tim 5:19 as well as a few other places.

But what was the joke? On page 140, Governor Nash laughs hard enough to bring tears to his eyes when he hears the punch line "Because the sun only comes out during the day." So what was the rest of the joke? I have no idea. I couldn't think of an original joke that fit in with the theme of the book, so I just made up a punch line. So, I guess, in essence, that *is* the joke—that there isn't one.

What does PGPE mean? On page 121, it describes how there are the initials PGPE written on Rinan's sword. Yet, in nowhere else in the book do I explain this. Again, this was something done intentionally. It had to be cryptic enough that Rayne didn't understand what it meant, but obvious enough for the Hierarchy of Magistrates to know right away. I'll give you a little hint: What was Rinan's job before he left the castle? Who was he assigned to originally?

Mortentaun and the 6th grade: To become a guardian in Bariwon, you had to do well in the Mortentaun. This isn't an original concept—there are stories throughout history of men competing to win the right to do this-or-that. But what events should I include for the Mortentaun? Whenever I get stuck on how to proceed next, I go back to the concept of "write what you know about." Having never competed in a Medieval tournament, or really seen one, that would be difficult. However, I did experience "field day" in the sixth grade where toward the end of the school year we would have all sorts of different events. I was tall for my age and a very fast runner. My upper body strength was a different story. So the events for the first day of the Mortentaun are roughly based on my experience with field day. I won all the events that dealt with using my legs (aside from the long distance run) but was pretty bad in the events where we saw how far we could throw a ball or do pull ups. And no, we didn't have a bow and arrow contest in the sixth grade. While school fights broke out time and again during recess, none of them involved weapons of any kind, especially not wooden maces or swords.

Inspiration for Governor Nash: For each character in the book, I tried to have a mental image of them and then relate them to people, or traits of people, I know or know of. Not that they are clones of that person, but I'll take bits here and there. As for Governor Nash inspiration? I'll give you some clues: On page 140, it describes him has having a snowy white beard. On page 142, he is described as a "jolly man." On page 206, he says "Ho ho!!" when he is visited by Alana. I created him as a character when I was off from work during a certain holiday season—some who call it "the most wonderful time of the year."

Some insights behind *The Waxing Moon*

Stop! If you haven't finished reading *The Waxing Moon*, read no further. This next section is intended for those who have read the book. It gives insight into the theme, symbolism and many other aspects of the book you may not have realized while reading.

Naming of places and things: Just as with *The Hidden Sun*, I used anagrams to name unique places and things. If you've not heard of an anagram, it is a word created using the letters of another word.

Rifna Erd: Infrared
Tular Tevoil: Ultraviolet
Procep: Copper
Pendeltune: Deep Tunnel
Itamunno Kael: Mountain Lake
Mylnohe: Holy Men
Eddinh: Hidden

Return of Abrecan: I had no intention of bringing Abrecan back. However, while writing *The Waxing Moon*, a ton of people told me how much they despised Abrecan. I had several readers get mad at me, telling me King Rayne was too nice in how he treated Abrecan at the end of *The Hidden Sun*. So…I brought Abrecan back to face judgment, as it were. In the end, it tied in very well with the rest of the story.

Bearach's first invention: Starting on page 282, the crafter Bearach demonstrates his ability in mechanics by creating a way for the king to close the doors to the main hall using a lever built into his throne. I needed a way to demonstrate Bearach's ability early in the book, but wasn't sure what to do. Then I remembered I had a boss who could close the door to his office by pushing a button on his desk. Though the technology was different, the result was the same.

The meaning of the title *The Waxing Moon*: Starting on page 312, Savant Waylon explains some superstitions based on the different phases of the moon. The concept isn't new, but I did add my own twist on them. In the book, a waxing moon is "a sign of change and growth." Then on page 456, Snapdragon is looking up at a waxing moon. He realizes the choices

758

he makes and the actions he takes define him as a person. He changes and grows with everything he does. So, therefore, the waxing moon is symbolic of Snapdragon's changes in the book.

The dead turtle story: On page 301, Blythe tells Snapdragon a story about a dead turtle. This was based on a true story that happened to me. When I was working in TV, I came to work one morning and there was a box with a dead turtle on a co-worker's desk. We didn't know what it meant or who put it there. We came up with all sorts of assumptions— none of which were right. As it turns out, a week previous there had been a segment shot using animals. The box with the turtle was left in a corner and wasn't found by the cleaning crew for a week. Sad story, but it was a good object lesson for jumping to conclusions.

People's names: Again, as with *The Hidden Sun*, I chose people's names based on the meaning of their names, with some minor exceptions. For example, Snapdragon was my way of sneaking a "dragon" into the story and it doesn't seem out of place because his father is a gardener and gave his children odd names like "Sunshine" and "Oakleaf". I won't include any characters that were carry-overs from *The Hidden Sun*. They are explained on the "secrets" page of that book.

Creighton: From a surname which was derived from a place name, originally from Gaelic crioch "border" combined with Old English tun "town". (He is from the town of Procep on the northern border of the kingdom)

Kerr: From a Scottish surname which was derived from a place name meaning "rough wet ground" in Old Norse. (He's a miner and it rains a lot in Erd)

Blythe: From a surname which meant "cheerful" in Old English.

Seraphina: Feminine form of the Late Latin name Seraphinus, derived from the biblical word seraphim which was Hebrew in origin and meant "fiery ones". (She has quite the fiery personality)

Bearach: Derived from Gaelic biorach meaning "sharp". ("Sharp" is another word for "smart" which describes the creative crafter)

Waylon: Derived from the Germanic elements wela possibly meaning "skill" and land meaning "land". (Based on his love of roads)

Grant: From an English and Scottish surname which was derived from Norman French grand meaning "great, large".

Fallon: From an Irish surname which was derived from Ó Fallamhain meaning "descendent of Fallamhan". The given name Fallamhan meant "leader".

Sverre: From the Old Norse name Sverrir which meant "wild, swinging, spinning". (Based on his wild hair and appearance when he is first introduced)

Merton: From a surname which was derived from a place name meaning "town on a lake" in Old English.

Alethea: Derived from Greek αληθεια (aletheia) meaning "truth". (She knows the "truth" behind how Merton rules)

Darius: Roman form of Δαρειος (Dareios), which was the Greek form of the Persian name Dārayavahush, which was composed of the elements dâraya "to possess" and vahu "good".

Are the numbers right? On page 323, it states that King Rayne meets up with three hundred men. He gives them their orders where "at least half of the men appeared surprised by what the king had assigned them to do." When Rayne arrives in Procep, he has only one hundred and fifty men with him. Where did the rest of them go? The answer is on page 495.

Tular Tevoil and Rifna Erd: The seven districts of Bariwon are named after the visible colors of the rainbow. When it came time to give names to people beyond the mountains, or people "out of sight", I used the colors of the rainbow our eyes can't see: Infrared and Ultraviolet. I reference this on page 323 when Blythe says, "Not even enough light here to see the mountains—just a big, dark, black void. Like there's something there, just beyond our ability to see it."

Nie Syll Esse explained: My wife once memorized a passage from *The Canterbury Tales* by Geoffrey Chaucer. It was English, sort of. It showed me how language changed over time. I had introduced the nislles in *The Hidden Sun*, and in *The Waxing Moon*, I explain it further. The tricky (and fun) part was to combine the two. "Nie Syll Esse" really means "None Shall Pass", but can be pronounced like "nislles", if you imagine the language changing over time. And "nislles" is an anagram for "illness" which is the reason the tunnel was closed off.

Pseudo swear word: I try to write compelling fiction that doesn't rely on sex, bad language or explicit violence (though I will admit my books can be a bit violent). I had one reader complain that *The Hidden Sun* wasn't "real" to them because in real life, people swear. My answer? I had Grant say "sheep dip" as a swear word—which really isn't a swear word, but kind of sounds like it could be.

A peaceful torturer? When it came time to have Snapdragon and the rest be "put to the question," I decided to have the man in charge be plain and void of emotion. To me, someone like that is much more frightening than the stereotypical big brute.

The magic trick: On page 423, Snapdragon does a magic trick to explain his plan to Merton. I learned this trick when I was in Boy Scouts. It's actually quite effective if you do it right.

Testing for understanding: At one point, Snapdragon is assigned a protector who he doesn't want. Snap claims he can't understand the man and then has the other men in the area repeat the phrase "the quick brown fox jumps over the lazy dog". Why that phrase? It's a sentence that uses all the letters of the alphabet. It's found on page 439.

How to get out of this mess? On page 410, Seraphina sums up their situation by saying, "We can't leave here for fear of the Rifna Erd, and we can't let the Tular Tevoil make it to Bariwon. Also, we are expected to believe these people from Eddinh." She then asks Snapdragon what they are going to do. He responds, "I honestly have no idea." When I first wrote that, I didn't have any idea either—and I am the author!

My favorite character: I often get asked who my favorite character is in these books. It may surprise you that it is a minor character: Garth. He's Sunshine, Oakleaf and Snapdragon's father. He's an odd duck and looks at life differently. He also says things that are clever. For *The Waxing Moon*, my favorite line of his is found on page 472 when he says, "We've had good rain during Rayne's reign."

An almost tragic ending: The first draft of *The Waxing Moon* had Snapdragon dying at the end. It would have happened on what is now page 494. I've not had problems killing off characters before, but this didn't feel right. I can't really explain it more than I felt like he had more to do. As it turns out, he plays a significant part in the last book of this series, *The Zealous Star*.

761

Some insights behind *The Zealous Star*

Naming of places and things: Just as with *The Hidden Sun* and *The Waxing Moon*, I used anagrams to name unique places and things. If you've not heard of an anagram, it is a word created using the letters of another word.

Noble Trod: Blood Rent
Viceditad: Addictive

Return of Daimh: When Diantha and Enoch went back to Erd Proper on a scouting mission later in the book, they needed a place to rest. I remembered that in *The Hidden Sun* I had Daimh exiled to a home near a lake in Erd. I thought it would be interesting to see how his life turned out and give him a chance at redemption.

It's pronounced Lar-EYE-saw : One of the biggest complaints I received about the first edition of *The Hidden Sun* was that there were many strange names that people had a hard time pronouncing. When asked, "How is <whatever> pronounced?" I would respond, "However you want." I'd read a lot of Sci-Fi and Fantasy books, so odd names didn't bother me. But, to help people out, I started including a pronunciation guide in my books. To emphasize this point, and I'll admit to tease some of the people who complained before, I added the character Larissa who insisted her name be pronounced a certain way.

The meaning of the title *The Zealous Star*: I didn't come up with the title for *The Hidden Sun* until after it was written. When I started writing the second book in the series, I wanted to have a theme, so I elected on *The Waxing Moon*. For the third book, I used the north star as an inspiration for Enoch's character. Yet, I discovered that the title *The Waxing Moon* was quite common, so I wanted something unique for the last book. A zealous person is one who strongly believes in something, which fits Enoch's personality. As of this moment, I don't have any intention of writing more books in this series, maybe because I'm out of celestial bodies. I guess I could use the title, *The Quirky Quasar*. Or not.

The nislles: I wanted each of the books of this series to stand on its own. In general, each book has different main characters, though some of them cross-over, like Snapdragon. At the same time, I wanted to make *The Zealous Star* bigger, more epic than the first two. And I wanted it to tie back to the other two books while having its own story. I decided that bringing the nislles back, something referenced in the previous books would be a good way to do that.

People's names: Again, as with *The Hidden Sun* and *The Waxing Moon*, I chose people's names based on the meaning of their names, with some minor exceptions. For example, Snapdragon was my way of sneaking a "dragon" into the story and it doesn't seem out of place because his father is a gardener and gave his children odd names like "Sunshine" and "Oakleaf." I won't include any characters that were carry-overs from previous books. They are explained on the "secrets" pages of those books.

Diantha: From *dianthus*, the name of a type of flower (ultimately from Greek meaning "heavenly flower").

Enoch: From the Hebrew name חֲנוֹךְ *(Chanokh)* meaning "dedicated."

Serkan: Means "leader, chief" from Turkish *ser* "head, top" and *kan* "blood".

Larissa: Possibly derived from the name of the ancient city of Larisa in Thessaly, which meant "citadel." (Meaning she was part of the "establishment.")

Hollis: From an English surname which was derived from Middle English *holis* "holly trees." (Viceditad looks a bit like holly, which Hollis helped smuggle into Bariwon.)

Elisedd: Derived from Welsh *elus* meaning "kind." This was the name of two kings of Powys in Wales.

Mason: From an English surname meaning "stoneworker," from an Old French word of Germanic origin (akin to Old English *macian* "to make"). In a deleted scene, Mason was originally one of the men who helped build the northern wall before he joined the militia.

"Groan worthy" names: In a review of *The Hidden Sun*, one person called the names Rayne and Sunshine "groan worthy." I had another person tell me, "I like your plots, but can't stand your names." When I wrote *The Hidden Sun*, I did so primarily for my daughters. I'm a big fan of *The Princess Bride*, and figured if they could have a princess named Buttercup, I could have characters names Sunshine, Rayne, Snapdragon and Rainbow.

The 'ah ha!' moments. I'm the type of writer who has a general idea what the story is about, but makes up most of it while he writes. I've discovered that many, if not most, of my best ideas come to me while I'm in the process of writing. For *The Zealous Star*, the two biggest 'ah ha' moments that came to me were the following: First when Diantha destroys the shipments of viceditad and thereby sets into motion the deaths. I liked the irony, and it reflected on her earlier behavior of taking on the persona of the Noble Trod where her good intentions had negative consequences. Second, I wanted there to be a reason for her actions as the Noble Trod to tie into something at the end of the book. The skills she learned from roaming Erd Proper early in the book makes her actions at the end believable.

Why won't viceditad grow in Bariwon?: When we moved to North Carolina, our front lawn was in pretty bad shape. I tore it up, planted grass seed (as I had done at other houses we'd owned) and watched in dismay as the grass refused to grow. I tried everything I could and couldn't get it to work. We eventually tore up the yard again and replaced all the soil to get a lawn to grow, but the experience inspired me to believe certain plants wouldn't grow in certain areas.

Diantha's inspiration: When I was younger, I had bright red hair. I remembered someone telling me that redheads have a temper and are sensitive. I wasn't sure I believed them until I had a red haired daughter of my own. Many of Diantha's characteristics are based on my daughter, Amy.

Is it still raining outside? In chapter 67, Diantha stops into a store to see if there is still a bounty on Enoch's head. The store sells candles. The store owner, Chandler (which means "candle seller") asks Diantha if it is still raining outside. She says, "Hard to say since I'm inside now." Chandler says that was familiar but couldn't recall why; it's because Sunshine says the same thing to him in chapter 12 of *The Hidden Sun*.

The Noble Trod: In the other two books, there are references to how the kingdom came to its current state. Part of this backstory is how there was a civil war once the royalty died from the first case of the nislles. I extended the backstory to include the Noble Trod, a relative of the royalty, therefore a noble who would walk around (trod) around after battles and would hang ripped and bloody cloth as a symbol of how the bloody war was tearing apart the land. Diantha drew on this, "using old superstition and tales to assume control." (That's a reference to the song, *The Mirror of the Soul*. I wrote a book based on it.)

Rankings: We currently live in a world where many things are compared to each other and given rankings. I worked for a company that was "rank crazy" in my opinion—meaning the sum total of your worth to the company was based on your rankings. Often things you were ranked on were items and events that were out of your control, and I found the whole concept ridiculous—especially because some of my co-workers would do less than ethical behaviors to get better rankings. Part of the joys of writing is therapy. I used Larissa's claim of "I've been number one for five years!" as a way to show how silly of a notion that is when used to defend your actions. (Read here: might doesn't make right.)

ABOUT THE AUTHOR

J. Lloyd Morgan is an award winning author and television director. He graduated from Brigham Young University with a degree in Communications and a minor in English. Morgan earned a Master's degree in Creative Writing in 2014. He has lived all over the United States, but now resides in North Carolina with his wife and four daughters. Aside from writing, Morgan is an avid reader. He's also a huge fan of baseball and enjoys listening to music.

Aside from the Bariwon Chronicles, Morgan's other published novels include *Wall of Faith*, *Bring Down the Rain*, and *The Mirror of the Soul* written in conjunction with musician Chris de Burgh.

His published short stories include *Howler King*, *I Heard the Bells on Christmas Day*, *With Bells On* and award-winning *The Doughnut*.

An anthology of short stories, observations and insights called *The Night the Port-A-Potty Burned Down and Other Stories* was released at the end of 2012.

For more information, visit his website at www.jlloydmorgan.com